THE
DISTANCE
BETWEEN
US

ALSO BY VALERIE SAYERS

Who Do You Love

How I Got Him Back

Due East

Brain Fever

The Powers

THE
DISTANCE
BETWEEN
US

VALERIE
SAYERS

NORTHWESTERN UNIVERSITY PRESS   EVANSTON, ILLINOIS

Northwestern University Press
www.nupress.northwestern.edu

Printed in the United States of America

10   9   8   7   6   5   4   3   2   1

All of the characters in this book are fictitious, and any resemblance to actual persons,
living or dead, is purely coincidental.

Interior book design by Gretchen Achilles
Interior art copyright © 1994 by Diana Jensen
Cover design by Marianne Jankowski

Library of Congress Cataloging-in-Publication Data

Sayers, Valerie.
    The distance between us : a novel / Valerie Sayers.
        p. cm.
    Originally published: New York : Doubleday, 1994.
    ISBN 978-0-8101-2723-4 (pbk. : alk. paper)
    I. Title.
PS3569.A94D56 2013
813.54—dc23

2013010674

∞ The paper used in this publication meets the minimum requirements of the American National Standard for Information Sciences—Permanence of Paper for Printed
Library Materials, ANSI Z39.48-1992.

FOR CHRIS

ACKNOWLEDGMENTS

The Brooklyn sections of this book were written in memory of dear friends, Robert Clark (1952–1989) and Richard Flaherty (1953–1985).

Most grateful thanks for the generosity of:

The Writers Room, New York City

The National Endowment for the Arts

Mr. Patrick Houlihan, The Basement Museum, Killorglin, County Kerry, Ireland

The National Library of Ireland, Dublin

Seamus McCotter

Lillian Bayer

Lisa Wager

Esther Newberg

and

Casey Fuetsch

I.

A PORTRAIT
OF THE
ARTISTS
AS A YOUNG
GROUP

*. . . that I may learn in my own
life and away from home and
friends what the heart is—*

—J. JOYCE

STEWARD
MOREHOUSE'S
MOTHER

Steward's mother was Mrs. Steward Morehouse Jr., and she was Lola Morehouse, too. Maybe she was a gypsy. She came from Loosiana and Grandmama said in a joking sort of way that Lola's black hair was coarse as S.O.S soap pads. *Gypsy hair*, Grandmama said.

Grandmama didn't joke that much with Lola. She only joked when Granddaddy was downtown counting his money and sweet-talking the customers standing on line in the bank. When Granddaddy came home Grandmama quit teasing Lola and turned all her attention on the old man. He talked for a good long time about this or that at the bank, about the good respectful nigrahs in Due East. *Steward*, he said, *you will travel far and wide but I want you to remember always that Due East is a blessed place, and you are blessed to call it home.* Gypsies traveled far and wide. Lola rolled her eyes when Granddaddy talked like that, but not so he could see her.

When Granddaddy came home Grandmama only joked with her two boys, with Steward Sr. and Steward III. Lola sat at the supper table and stretched out her fingernails, scarlet like the Scarlet Pimpernel, calculating the angle she'd use to hold the emery board later that night when she shaped her perfect fingertips. She let Steward III sit on the bottom of the bed until one of the officers called for her and then she kissed him on the lips with her scarlet mouth to say good-bye. She loved him more than she loved the officers because *An officer just draws a paycheck, Stewie, but you can draw a whole picture for me. Will you draw a whole big picture for Mama and leave it right here, sugar, on the bed? I'll sleep with your picture tonight.* From upstairs he watched her climb into the officers' little cars, the window framing her big round fanny. Maybe she was a gypsy. There was a black shadow over her lip and black down on her cheek on the back of her neck, underneath the fluffy hair that was too short to tease up. She wore a blouse with a big ruffle that quivered when she took a deep breath.

She bought bottles of nail polish that stood in rows neater than the columns of soldiers Granddaddy brought back from London. She gave him

kisses on the lips. Granddaddy said once she was a slut and then Grandmama wasn't joking.

Steward! The boy will hear you!

The boy was sitting at the same table with them, spooning out the
parfaits Gloria froze up in the afternoon and saving the cherry for his mama
when she came down the steps. What he wanted to do was put the cherry
right down her ruffled blouse, right in that deep ravine, and see would it
stay whole or get smushed. Granddaddy called them *bazooms* after a glass of
sherry in the library. *She's nothing but a little-bitty body trailing a big pair of
bazooms, Mamie. She's sweet and she's shallow, like what's left in the bottom of
this glass. Now I don't blame Stew for wanting to whisper in her ear and give her a
good squeeze, but I believe he must have been drunk out of his ever-loving mind
when he married her. A little girl right out of high school, wiping off a bar on
Bourbon Street?*

Grandmama's knuckles turned white as soon as Granddaddy said *Stew.*
Then she remembered Stew III was in the library too, sunk down in the red
leather chair, picking at the nicks Stew Jr. used to make with his Swiss
Army knife, and she came over to hug him tight. He could feel her collarbone and her shriveled-up bazooms. He loved Grandmama, but Mama was
the one who knew how to hug. Stew Jr. must have liked big bazooms
better, too, if he didn't even ask Grandmama to the wedding.

Stew Jr. was Daddy. Daddy never even got to see Stew III's baby
pictures, made up by Olan Mills Photographers in New Iberia, Loosiana,
where Lola had her baby before she moved in with Grandmama and Granddaddy. Daddy was dead in Korea. Granddaddy said Stew Jr. must have been
drunk out of his ever-loving mind to die *that* way. He never would have
stepped on a mine if he was sober. Daddy was an officer because Daddy
went to Princeton, but what they didn't teach you at Princeton was to look
where you were going and not step on some oriental booby trap. Orientals
were secretive and tricky and you should never trust one, Granddaddy said.
He said he had a friend in Washington, a friend in a very high place, who
hired a Filipino houseboy to take all his silk ties to the cleaner's. Well sir,
that houseboy took all the silk ties all right, and he never came back. It was
better to have a nigrah in your household, because you could look a nigrah
in the eye and know whether you could trust him or not.

Granddaddy said Stew Jr.'s trouble was that he trusted anybody and
everybody, orientals and women too, when everybody knows those are the
two classes of people you must never ever trust. Daddy went to New
Orleans with his friends just for fun and he saw Lola's bazooms, and he

married her just for fun and then, when he was still drunk, got himself killed which he never would have done if he had been sober. That was why Granddaddy always said *One cocktail, Stew. One glass of wine with your meal. One brandy after. Never more, son. Otherwise you are likely to get blown to bits the way your dear sweet father did. If only I had taught your daddy what I am teaching you now. If only your father had been sobuh* . . .

If he had been sobuh Stew Jr. would have stayed home in Due East like Aunt Blinky and he would have lived in another big old house with another wife who wasn't a gypsy, and he would have had as many sons as Blinky did, and he would have gone to the country club instead of the Officers Club.

I've got to hand it to her, though, Granddaddy said. *She leaves no stone unturned. She's going to see if she can't get her another good officer from another good family to take care of her. Thank the dear Lord it was all still in trust when he stepped on that oriental booby trap.* Grandmama's knuckles went white then too.

In the summer Lola wore a sundress with no ruffles and no back, and under the sundress she wore a white bathing suit to set off her dark gypsy skin. The S.O.S hair, pushing itself out the legs of the bathing suit, grew thicker down there than it did on her head. Lola said he could come with her and Bill to the beach and Grandmama said no, Steward III had Steward Jr.'s white skin—*some*times recessive genes told—and next time when they went in the cool evening they could take the boy. Steward didn't much want to get dunked by Bill out at the beach anyway. Bill was a captain and a pilot and he'd been around since the azaleas came out.

In the summer Gloria drew the drapes in the drawing room and chased him upstairs, where she opened the bottom windows on the shady side of the house and the top windows on the sunny side, to draw the air through. The verandah was off limits until five o'clock, when there was a good breeze blowing off the bay and Gloria made lemonade for him and Grandmama and one gin cocktail for Granddaddy and they waited for Lola, who got out of Bill's convertible with her upper lip bleached blond from the sun, smelling like peaches that had fallen in soft dark mud.

In the summer the Starkeys passed by every morning on their constitutional. Mizz Starkey told Grandmama that that's what they were doing, taking their constitutional. *Well, bless your heart,* Grandmama said. *Bless your HEARTS. You be careful now, in this heat.*

It was an army of Starkeys taking their constitutional. A red bald fat baby in the carriage, and another little one hanging off the handle. Two boys running off ahead, and two big girls like ushers in the movie theater in Atlanta, scrambling to smack the boys on their bottoms when their mama said to. The two big girls were AgnesAnn and Teresa. Mrs. Starkey told Grandmama, while they chatted over the wrought-iron gate, that Agnes-Ann and Teresa were her salvation. She could not get through the day, she said, without AgnesAnn and Teresa. AgnesAnn and Teresa got breakfast and they got supper. AgnesAnn and Teresa chased the bad boys. AgnesAnn and Teresa were saints.

I think it's Mizz Starkey who's the saint, Grandmama told Lola. *She must be thirty-five if she's a day. That's getting old for babies. Why do they DO that? What do they HAVE all those children?* And then Grandmama blushed in an apologetic way, because Lola was one of them once. Lola had five sisters herself, back in New Iberia. Now Lola wasn't Catholic anymore—she let Steward go to St. Luke's Episcopal with Grandmama and Granddaddy, because she wasn't anything—but Grandmama was still embarrassed.

Grandmama was embarrassed and Steward was embarrassed. Mizz Starkey made his ears buzz. Mizz Starkey was too old to be a mother. She couldn't weigh but ninety pounds, Grandmama said, and she held her little torso as tall as she could on her little bird legs, but she was only just bigger than her saintly daughters. Steward's mama was an itsy-bitsy thing too, but Lola had bazooms and high-heeled sandals, and she wouldn't have been caught dead pushing a baby carriage as big as a train car. Steward made Lola climb out of bed at ten o'clock in the morning to see the Starkeys pass by on their constitutional and Lola laughed and laughed. *I swan, Stewie,* she said, and he was pretty sure she was laughing at the black straw hat and not at him.

Mizz Starkey's dresses all buttoned up to the chin. *They got to have buttons, sugar,* Lola said, *because she's nursing that baby, the way I nursed you.* Grandmama didn't like that talk and if he squeezed his mama's bazooms the way he liked to do, Grandmama gave him a playful little smack on his fingers and said *Can you imagine seven, her bust will fall down to her knees*—but she was a scrawny chicken anyway, Lola said, and Lola should know because she'd raised chickens herself, in New Iberia. Now when Steward looked at Mizz Starkey passing by, her arms popping out of the cotton button-up dresses were chicken wings. She was a clucking hen. She wore stubby navy-blue sandals for her constitutional, and so did AgnesAnn and Teresa, over their chicken feet. Steward wanted to tear off her black hat and her blue sandals. He wanted to set her face-to-face, bazoom-to-bazoom, with Lola.

But it wasn't Mizz Starkey he hated.

The one he hated was Fanny Starkey. The one he wanted to smack right on the back of her skinny legs was Fanny Starkey. If you added in Fanny there were seven Starkey children. Grandmama said you could count on more coming, right up until the poor woman went through the change.

Fanny was younger than Saints AgnesAnn and Teresa and older than her little devil brothers. She was always trailing the other Starkeys by half a block. She wandered along behind the rest of them looking like an orphan child who'd been taken into the wrong family and didn't want any part of them. AgnesAnn and Teresa were tall and sturdy and had their honey-colored hair cut in short straight bangs across their broad foreheads, but Fanny was skinny and little like her mother and had black scraggly curls she'd pulled out of her barrette by the time she passed the Morehouse house on River Street. Her nose was always sunburned, but the rest of her skin was as white as his. Her black eyebrows could have been drawn on with a big smooth Magic Marker. She always had on summer clown suits that ballooned out around her fanny. Fanny's fanny. Lola said the clown suits were called *rompers,* but that didn't make it any better, because the tall blond girls he chased in the graveyard after Sunday school would never have worn those rompers, they would have worn neat little pink shorts sets on a weekday, the way he always wore navy-blue-and-white.

When Fanny Starkey came up to his house, she stared right in his eye without smiling, even when Grandmama said *Steward says he and Fanny sat right at the same table in Miss Corley's class!* Fanny didn't even know that she'd be going to Due East Elementary for the rest of her life, but he'd be going off to St. Andrew's soon as Mama would agree to it. Grandmama said they sent Stew Jr. in eighth grade, but they wished they'd done it earlier, because he missed the Greeks and had to start with the Romans. He never did get all his Greek gods straight. Granddaddy said Stew regretted it, when he got to Princeton, that they hadn't sent him to Choate or Exeter. *Well no son of mine's going up North to freeze his little toes,* Lola said, but Granddaddy said *We'll see, won't we, when the time comes.*

And whenever Grandmama started chatting with Mizz Starkey about how they'd be sending him off to school soon, Mizz Starkey got a mean ambitious look in her pale blue eyes and said, *Oh wouldn't Pat love to do that for Fan. Fanny draws a funny little picture and her daddy calls her a genius. He*

*thinks she ought to have special lessons and where are we going to find that in Due
East?*

It was clear that Fanny was spoiled, Grandmama said. *Her mama can't do
a thing with her. And don't all children like to draw? I don't think you can say
anything about a six-year-old who DRAWS.*

Stewie draws, Lola said.

You can tell, can't you now, Grandmama said, *from the way the poor woman
goes on and on about it. You can tell it's a terrible source of conflict in their home.*

I always liked to draw, Lola said, dreamy. *Stewie, draw me something right
now. No, color me something. Something green.*

Lola thought the whole thing was funny. She dragged herself out of the
house at ten o'clock to help Grandmama direct the colored boy trimming
the oleanders by the front gate. Steward waited by the gate, pretending that
he was pulling out weeds for Grandmama, and when he could hear the
youngest Starkeys leading the pack down River Street he opened up the
throttle and pulled out more weeds than the colored yardboy had ever seen
in his life.

He kept pulling weeds all the while AgnesAnn and Teresa passed by. He
kept tugging weeds all the while Grandmama talked to Mizz Starkey. He
was still yanking weeds when Fanny finally meandered along, and then he
quit and pretended he was holding a tommy gun or a camera.

Lola and Fanny would stare each other right in the eye. Fanny's sharp
green eyes would travel right down to Lola's bazooms, where they rested
content.

What Steward wanted to do when he saw Fanny Starkey in that stupid
romper and her mother in that stupid black hat was pee all over them. He
could feel it rising up in him the way water rose up, snakelike, through
Grandmama's garden hose.

He'd like to pee all over their blue leather sandals, and then he'd like
them all to smell of it the whole long hot summer day.

GET ME
OUT OF
HERE

When Franny Starkey's sisters got to be thirteen they were still reading *An Old-fashioned Girl* and *Little Women,* crying like simps when Beth died. They actually made their father read Louisa May *Alcott* out loud for the family bedtime story, and then they said, "I'm going home to Tara," which meant they were going to take turns reading *Gone with the Wind* in bed with a flashlight. Franny said they couldn't pay her a million bucks to read a book with a thousand pages. "You tell me when the Classics Illustrated comes out," she said.

When they hit thirteen, first AgnesAnn and then Teresa, they shaved their legs every night for an hour, then massaged them with baby oil, then ran back into the bathroom to get an invisible blond spot they missed. To hell with them. Now she was thirteen, and she had changed her name from Fanny to Franny, and she liked to stare at the black stubble on her legs and let it grow for weeks. She liked to run her finger over the rings of dry skin on her stubbled legs and let patches of it float into the air with the other dust. She liked to hide in the closet, sitting on their saddle shoes and tracing the dark shape of their hanging schoolgirl dresses.

Because now AgnesAnn and Teresa were in high school, where they read *Jane Eyre* and *Wuthering Heights,* and when they came home on the bus they floated around the house looking for her, moaning *Oh! my heart's darling.* Franny already had a boyfriend. AgnesAnn was sixteen, but she and her smooth legs had never even had a date. Teresa had a good eye for senior marshals with thick black-rimmed glasses and slide rules tucked in their belts.

It had never occurred to AgnesAnn or Teresa to search for her in the closet. It had never occurred to them that there was any hiding place at all in this tiny house, other than the bathroom, and there was a three-minute limit on locking the bathroom door. The bedrooms were crowded with beds and dressers connected by narrow paths: Will and Martin and Paul in the back room; AgnesAnn, Teresa, Franny and Caroline in the middle room. The twins, Walter and Albert, were still smushed head-to-foot in a single crib in their parents' room, though they were two and a half already and needed full-size blankets in the half-size bed. Their feet, under the edges of the blankets, pushed out of the crib bars like prisoners' hands begging mercy.

Their mother, Doris, could not believe that all her push, all her drive, all her spirit and forceful optimism, had led her to a lifetime sentence in this tiny tract house. The living room/dining room could not contain all eleven of them at once, though when she'd married Pat Starkey he'd been a man with a future, the sort of man you'd expect to move into a comfortable, rambling Due East house on the water. He'd gone to the Jesuit University of America on a baseball scholarship, and he was smart besides, well-schooled in Latin and Greek and fluent in French. He was a first lieutenant in the United States Marine Corps when she met him at a Saint Patrick's Day dinner, and by the time he resigned his commission he had already lined up a coaching/teaching job at Due East Junior High School.

Who could have imagined, Doris Starkey liked to say to whichever of her children was home sick, or to the twins if there was nobody else to listen, who would have imagined that after all these years Daddy would be no better off than assistant principal? Who would have imagined, after all those education courses he took in Charleston, after the master's degree, after all these babies, after all these pairs of shoes and underwear and polio shots, who would have thought? She had set herself a time limit on such bitterness, though, same as she'd set a limit on locking the bathroom door, and after a few minutes of despair she set about the housework with a new fierce optimism. He'd be principal one day. Then superintendent. Once she said to Pat: "Let me remind you, dear, what the first three letters of *assistant principal* spell." And Pat, usually so calm and good-natured, usually so *absent* with one of his teams, said: "Let me remind *you*, dear, that both daddy and divorce begin with the letter *d*. And so does damn it, don't you ever dare speak to me that way, Doris."

Doris's father was retired from a menial civil service job, and Franny had heard the same carping going on at her grandparents' house: "If only I'd had the gumption to push you on a little bit," her grandmother would say. "If only I'd had the sense not to listen to you when you didn't want those Tupperware parties in the house. I'd give the world's biggest Tup-perware party tomorrow, why I'd give it this very night, if I thought it'd help get Doris and those poor chidren out of that itsy-bitsy house."

If Doris worked herself up over the size of the house, they all cowered:

all but her father, who was not present to cower, and Franny, who had a strange affection for her mother's tantrums and was not afraid of her. "Don't have a hissy about it," she would say to Doris, and her mother would likely cry out: "You, miss! Don't you be pert to me!"

Franny was small herself and she liked small things. She liked being crowded between Martin and Albert at the supper table, and she liked sleeping next to plump Caroline. When she huddled in the dark closet she imagined the miniature drawing she would do of a shoe buckle or of a palmetto bug skulking across the closet floor. For her twelfth birthday, her father had splurged on a book of Dürer, and she liked to run her hands over the tiny engraving lines as if they were Braille. At night, in bed with Caroline, she tucked herself smaller and smaller, and traced the curve of her own disappearing body.

Her small frame resembled her mother's, but Doris expended all her energy holding a stingy body straight, while Franny made a point of using her lean self in a generous way. She knew that the way she carried herself was generous from the way boys had been looking at her for a few years now—she, who didn't trouble with shaving her legs or teasing her hair, she who sometimes forgot to put on a bra in the morning. The other girls dressed in demure plaid shirtdresses with cameo collar pins, but Franny had taken to wearing one of her father's discarded ties. It was 1965. They were doing that in London.

Doris said: "You like to drive me out of my mind with those ties, Franny. Ties are not for girls." All her mother's movements were close and tight to her body, tense and directed, but Franny generated large movements from her small limbs. Her father said that when she was a baby she was the fastest crawler he'd ever seen, and he took her out to the beach every weekend to time her mile. He thought she could make the varsity team at Due East High School next year.

Doris berated Pat for the time he took with Franny. Look at AgnesAnn and Teresa, she said, on the honor roll again, and they won't get so much as a *Good work, sweetheart* for it. Pat, guilty, would take them along the next weekend, but the older girls didn't like anybody to see them running, or walking with their father either, for that matter. AgnesAnn and Teresa squealed if the bath towel slipped off their chubby breasts, but Franny had no problem using the toilet when her brothers were taking a bath. Her sisters hovered, horrified, at the bathroom mirror when pimples appeared, but Franny studied her bumps. She liked the color of earwax. She liked holding her ankles in the dark closet, feeling their boniness, and she liked sliding out of her pajamas after Caroline was asleep. Her mother smacked her once, in the morning, when she discovered her naked under the sheets.

She liked to rub her small round breasts up against Steward when they were kissing. She'd kissed five or six boys before Steward—they knew just from the way she put her hand on her hip that it didn't matter about her not wearing those plaid shirtwaists—but she could tell that he'd never done it before. He was always looking over her shoulder.

Steward said she looked like Audrey Hepburn, which was sweet but not even close to the truth. Her face was sharp-boned, Doris's face without the pinched look, and her green eyes were too close and too small. Steward just said that about Audrey Hepburn because she'd cut off all her curls, and wore her hair short the way they were doing it in London.

In the fall, when she first saw a gaunt boy who resembled Steward More-house, she was a quarter-way into her two-mile run and just picking up speed. She did not slow down at the sight of him, though it was peculiar that he should be in the run-down outskirts of Hundred Pines, a half mile from her own house, mowing the brown grass in front of a square little brick house more modest than the Starkey house, if that was possible.

She hadn't seen him in over a year. He'd been shipped off, the way a dozen of the well-off boys were shipped off, around junior high school time, and she had never much liked him besides. He was aloof and indifferent. The only times she ever thought of him were when the Starkey family station wagon passed the Morehouse house, or when she saw his mother in capri pants at the Piggly Wiggly, buying mai tai mixer.

Weird that he would be doing yardwork, and weirder that he wouldn't have left for school by now. It was the end of September already. She might never have noticed him if he hadn't looked so old-mannish pushing the kerosene mower, stopping every few feet to grab up weeds. Nobody troubled with that.

She felt him watching her run up the street, and she felt him listening to her chorus of "Gloria," though she wasn't singing out loud. She lost track of the verses when she sensed him hunched down behind her, pretending to tug at the crabgrass. She made her circle down through the houses on the creek, their yards dense with live oak and moss, dogwood and crape myrtle and pine, until she was up to the John C. Calhoun Road. Then, instead of cutting home on Union Street the way she did every night, she retraced her route and found herself slowing to a walk. This was the point in her run where she'd ordinarily lope on at full speed, her throat drying and her limbs propelling themselves, so she stumbled a little in the slowing. Her legs wanted to go on.

He was still there, only now he had sat himself down in one of those unpainted wood lawn chairs the Cherokee Indians came around selling. It was a poor-looking yard in front of a house that was yes, even smaller than the Starkey house, but it was definitely Steward Morehouse sitting in front of it.

He had grown more peculiar-looking. His hair was closer to white than it was to blond, and a wedge of it brushed down over his brow in a laconic way that gave her the urge to coax it back up his forehead. His face was as sharp as a rat's, his chin jutting out and his jaw rising up in a V. His cheeks had a hollow, sunken look, like an undertaker's in the funny pages, and his mouth was chiseled into a small perfect bow. What she decided, as she walked up to his lawn, was that she would like to brush back his hair and kiss his tiny mouth—smaller than Walter's and Albert's mouths—and let him take *that* memory with him back to boarding school.

She stopped on the road and faced him, one hand on her hip, until he looked up. It took a minute, and when he finally met her eyes he looked down again, ashamed to have recognized her.

"I need a glass of water please." She made a long sweeping gesture across her forehead, wiping away imaginary sweat. This was just the sort of thing that would have sent AgnesAnn and Teresa running in giggles and in shame.

He made no sign that he had heard her other than rising; and when he came back with the water, in a green Tupperware tumbler, he held it out with his eyes still averted.

She drank it down one long gulp at a time, wiped her mouth with the back of her hand, and felt somehow that he did not appreciate the generous way she had of carrying herself. Finished, she held onto the tumbler, ran her sneakered foot through the roadside gravel, and said, "So when do you go back to school?"

He coughed. "I went back to school in August, same as you. I'm in Dewey's homeroom."

She stared, but it was only at the top of his head. Waiting for his glass back, he studied her foot going round and round in the gravel. It occurred to her that maybe Steward Morehouse *lived* in this house now.

"I didn't see you."

"I saw you," he said, and Franny, who had spent years tuning out her mother's shrieking and so was generally insensitive to tone of voice, realized that there was an edge to his words as gravelly as the surface of the road.

"I'm in Whorley's," she said then, and he answered:

"I know. You want to go to the dance Friday week?"

She saw sweat pushing up from a fountain deep in his white hair and rolling down his forehead in rivulets.

Mostly you did not go to the dance with a boy. Not even the shirtwaists went with their boyfriends—they met them there and then they went out to neck by the water fountain in the hall. Her best friend Kate Rooney would despise her for going with a boy. They usually debated for two weeks before the dance whether to go at all, whether it was too conventional, but they always went, and if nobody was asking them to dance they danced with each other. Kate hated it when she was making out by the water fountain. Kate would never forgive her for going with a boy.

"O.k.," she said.

"My father'll drive us," Steward Morehouse said, and Franny looked again at the house behind him: at the roof shingled a light metallic green, and the square brick facade with one picture window, one small bathroom window, one bedroom window puffy with white gauze. The picture window was a broad happy face, and as she peered at it she made out shelves of oriental dolls and knickknacks. A Marine house. Steward Morehouse lived in this house with a Marine, and his grandparents still lived smack-dab in the middle of River Street.

"O.k.," she said again, and ran off before he could ask her where she lived. He knew anyway, she found out later: he knew about her father and her mother and her sisters and her brothers and what books she'd checked out of the library. He knew about her, and he knew about a lot of other girls, too, girls whose pictures he'd circled in the Due East Junior High School *Friends Book,* girls whose phone numbers he had memorized but never called, girls who wore shirtwaists and penny loafers and read *Seventeen* and belonged to the Junior Garden Club and made Franny Starkey gag.

But she was the first one who ever stopped in front of his mother's new house, and so she was the first one, after his mother, that he loved.

Franny was supposed to call Kate every night after she finished her run. They talked for forty-five minutes, or until Doris ran her off the phone. "You know Steward Morehouse?"

"Ugh," Kate said over the wire. She was composing a one-finger tune on the piano for Steward Morehouse, low and melancholy. "He should have stayed in prep school."

"He asked me to the dance."

On her end, Kate stopped picking out her dirge. "He's not that bad," she said. Oh she should have laid down her life for Kate and instead she had deserted her. Kate said: "He's pretty smart, I think," and managed to make it sound perfectly sincere. "Somebody probly buys him all those clothes. I mean, he's probly not that conventional."

Steward Morehouse had left St. Andrew's because his mother got married. The night he and his Marine stepfather drove Franny to the dance—the same night she told him she was thirsty, took him out to the water fountain, brushed back the blond wedge of hair and kissed him on his tiny bow mouth, all the while pushing her small round breasts up against him while she knew her father was safe inside the lunchroom, supervising things—he drew a carefully folded single sheet of lavender notepaper from his back pocket and offered her what he had been dying to read to her, to some girl, to any girl:

> *Dear Stew,*
>
> *I hope this news makes you as happy as it makes me! Nick and I are getting hitched! Naturally your grandmama and granddaddy are not to pleased about it but their not the ones getting married are they. Nick likes you a whole lot son and I think he will make a good daddy. We want you to come down for the wedding (reception at the noncom club) but won't you think about keeping your room at your grandparents house. They only want the best for you and they can provide it. But as for me, Get me out of here!!!! like you know I've always said.*
>
> *Be calling you Sunday night as usual but wanted you to have time to get used to this big news. You'll always be number one in my heart, sugar.*
>
> > *Love and kisses,*
> > *Mama*

Franny's first impulse, seeing the sloping handwriting in purple ink and the way Steward's mother had actually drawn a red heart around her signature, was to giggle, but the stiff formal way Steward held the paper out for her to read, two songs after the kiss and just before Kate Rooney huffed by, stopped her.

"I'm glad she did it," Steward hissed in the back of the lunchroom, and Franny nodded as if she had some idea what he was talking about.

Later they took her aside—first Lola, then Nick—and told her what Stewie was sacrificing when he left St. Andrew's and came to live with them: not just the good school right now, but a shot at the big money Steward Morehouse Sr. would be leaving behind when he departed this life. "His granddaddy," Lola said, "is so mad he's about ready to split a gut. I *told* him, I says, 'Listen old man, I asked him to stay in school,' but that damn fool thinks me and Nick bribed him to come home. Bribed him! Whatever would we be bribing him with?"

Nick said that Lola had been kept prisoner by the old man for thirteen years and Stew was some boy to say *no* to it all, just like that. Nick DeAngelis was short and balding, his beard a gloomy watercolor wash even after he'd just shaved. Steward said he wasn't the first enlisted man his mother had dated—she did it to drive his granddaddy crazy—but he was the first one she paid any real mind to. He was the first one to tell her to stop waiting for the money.

"I told her," Nick told Franny, "I said to this beautiful woman, 'Sweetheart, you gotta live a little. You gotta stop hiding out in that big house like a princess in a tower. That old man's maybe not gonna leave you a dime anyway. Wouldya turn your back on love, waiting for a dime he's maybe not gonna give you anyway? Does that make sense?'"

Steward was crazy for Nick. "Tell about Korea," he'd say to his stepfather while they sat around the dinette playing gin rummy. Nick had married a Korean woman, and brought her back to meet his parents in Hackensack, and she'd keeled over and died when she was two months pregnant. Heart attack. Nick had pictures of Korean kids lying all over the house, framed, unframed, on the wall, on the refrigerator, from one of those Adopt-a-Kid agencies he'd been sending half his paycheck to for the last dozen years.

"Now I got my own kid to support," he said, and tipped his chair sideways to squeeze Steward's shoulder and wink at Franny. "But I can't for the life of me figure out what an E-8 in the USMC can give him that his grampa the big cheese at the bank can't give him."

Lola, her antennae out for mention of the grandparents, liked to drift into the game at just such a moment and sit herself down on Nick's lap. She always reeked of perfume and her wiry hair coiled out in a helmet of hairspray. Lola was too lovey-dovey, too ready to snuggle up with Nick in front of Steward and Franny, showing off. On the other hand, she was totally unconventional. Franny had never seen skirts so short on a grown woman, not even an enlisted wife, and Lola showed her her new white lipstick and white fingernail polish, which she could buy *practically for free* at the PX. "Oh Lordy it's a relief not to have to beg that old man for spending money," she told Franny, back in the bedroom where she was laying out her newest cache of makeup, and Franny would look behind her to see if there was somebody else in the room to hear the confidence. Franny started wearing white lipstick, too.

"Listen here, sugar," Lola told her one winter night when she stopped by after her run, "don't ever let Stewie know I said this to you, but one day Nicky'll be getting his orders. That's what happens to Marines, there's no getting around it. And I don't want Stew dragging all over to Camp Le-jeune and Twenty-nine Palms—I mean, I love that, traveling, see the USA in your Chevrolet—but I just don't think Stewie would do so fine in all those base towns when he's only got a few more years of school. Franny, looky here—"

and in the kitchen she put her long white fingernails down on Franny's bony hand—

"look here, if anybody could talk Stewie into going back to a good school, you could do it. Will you think about it? I don't mean him to suck up to those two, I just mean for him to take what he can get from them. And he deserves it, dudn't he, dudn't he deserve a good school and a good college so he could just marry for love if he feels like it? Franny—"

and now she was beginning to think that Lola was drinking too much Coke or popping diet pills or No-Doz, but no, her black eyes were per-fectly clear except for the emotion that was beginning to well up—

"Franny, I know how hard it would be to send him off to school. I can see that Stewie and you, God knows yawl are so *young,* but I can see that already you two have got a grand passion going. I swear, don't laugh now. I had me a grand passion once too when I was your age, and honey, it's *sweet* now. It's sweet and I messed up bad when I ran away from all that sweet-ness, I messed up running off to New Orleans, but you don't have to mess up. Stewie didn't have to. Franny do you see what I'm saying to you?"

She saw that Lola's eyes had narrowed the way her own mother's did when she had a scheme to get them all out of the little house. *Get me out of here.*

"Yes ma'am."

"Oh, Franny, am I wrong, am I pushing yawl, you aren't but thirteen, am I just being silly talking about grand passions? Maybe his own mama shouldn't be talking to you this way."

Maybe it wasn't too much Coke, and maybe it wasn't No-Doz. Maybe it was *The Edge of Night* or *The Secret Storm* that was inspiring Lola.

"Listen, just you forget I ever said a word. Nick tells me, he is always telling me not to push. 'Just don't push the kids, Lola,' he says, but it always seems like I can't hold myself back."

She did have a grand passion for Steward. She did. She lay in bed at night dreaming that his fair sinewy arm was draped around her, and AgnesAnn and Teresa knew that she was dreaming. *My heart's darling,* they hissed from the other bed, but Caroline let Franny cuddle her tight. *My wild sweet Franny.*

"There is nothing like your first great passion, even Nicky wouldn't mind me saying that to you, honey. There is nothing like that sweet heaven anywhere on earth, and you hold tight to that memory."

She could have sworn from the way Lola gave her such a sharp, searching look that Steward's mother had somehow seen how not but one week before, Franny had been making out with S.D., last year's boyfriend, out at the trestle. And not meaning a thing by it. Her passion for Stew had stretched, balloonlike, and she floated off with it so high that down below, even his narrow face, the face that had once looked to her like a rat's face, was lean and hard and as unconventional as poor James Dean's.

But from those airy heights all male creatures were perfect down below, even S.D. Even her brothers. Sometimes at dinner she thought she might forget to eat at the sight of Walter and Albert's four enormous eyes, eyes the color of seaweed, eyes that would have been identical if Walter's weren't so slow to focus. He'd been brain-damaged at birth, their father told them, but still even Walter—especially Walter—seemed perfect to her now, the way he tagged around after Pat, singing "Harrigan" off-key and way too slow. Sometimes she thought she might drift off in a kind of hypnotic trance at the sight of her father closing his own slate-blue eyes, elbows on the table, chin on his knuckles, waiting saintlike for Walter to hush his singing so that the Starkeys could eat their meal.

If she were inclined to confide in Lola she might have told her that there was such a thing as being in love with brain-damaged little boys and patient fathers and last year's boyfriends. But as it was, that night in Steward Morehouse's new kitchen she pretended to catch sight of the wall clock and told Steward's mother that it was time she got on home now.

"Franny?" Lola said, and Franny ducked her head down. "Am I pushing yawl?"

"No ma'am," she said, but she didn't put much energy behind the words.

"I wouldn't want to do that now."

"Yes ma'am," she said. Then she backed out through the living room where she waved good-bye to Steward, who looked up from the funny pages and blinked, betrayed and accusing. He'd heard the whole thing, and read her mind besides.

TEENAGE
WASTELAND

Steward Morehouse sat hunched over the desk in Grandfather's hotel suite in Boston. Grandfather was taking an afternoon nap in the bedroom: *A Southren custom,* he told the desk clerk when he asked to have his calls held. *From anothuh era, of course.*

"Take a stroll, son! Exploah! You don't need my company after dinner. Go find yourself a pretty girl, a little snow bunny."

Flinching at *little snow bunny,* Steward buttoned his new parka (mohair with plaid lining, purchased with Grandmother in Charleston expressly for this trip) and pretended he would leave once he pulled on the doofy-looking rubbers Grandfather had picked up in the hotel gift shop. But as soon as Grandfather tottered off, his noonday port making an old man of him, Steward yanked the rubbers off.

He tried, again, to write to her. Outside the snow pressed down, and if he let himself peer through the window he was dizzy. This relentless snow would be what he would see all next winter if he caved into Grandfather and came North to school. Staring at the blank hotel stationery, he saw himself frostbitten in some New Hampshire wasteland or drowned by snow on a Vermont mountainside, staggering and calling Franny's name as the thick flakes clotted in his mouth. Last week he was running alongside her in the balmy winter dusk, the sky disintegrating around them, Franny pulling him off down States Rights Alley until they were back behind the warehouse and he—well, she—could push her breasts against him and wind her hands around his neck movie style. She never closed her eyes. She was always watching him.

> *Dear Fran,*
> *Just being in this hotel gives me the creeps. All I can think of is Nick and how he'd show up in the lobby in one of those blue civilian suits. I'd be embarrassed for him and hate myself for feeling that way, he's*

everything my grandfather doesn't even KNOW about being a decent human being.

All wrong. Hysterical as a girl, and disloyal and hypocritical when Grandfather was being almost reasonable, negotiating this school deal with a restraint Steward had never dreamed he possessed. Also it sounded a little like bragging.

Fran.
I know I shouldn't be suspicious about why you think boarding school's not such a bad idea. But if you can mess around with S.D., and then pretend it was all a misunderstanding

He wadded the page. They had settled that business two months ago. It was suicide to bring it up again.

S.D. was his oldest friend in Due East. He and S.D. were always supposed to have been the writers, but this year Steward's first piece in the high school newspaper was a worthless stream of sewage. Dillon and Harrison were real jerks about it too: "Too serious, Morehouse. National *Honor* Society? Maybe you could be that earnest about the integration of Due East High School. Something important." And a week later S.D. passed around the first mimeographed edition of the *James Joyce Cookbook/Jokebook* and Steward knew that it was only S.D. who would be the writer.

This year Dillon's mother had the four of them over for a Christmas party with eggnog and leaden homemade fruitcake, and Steward brought along Franny, the only girl. His friends were speechless. When Dillon's mother said *Y'all be good now,* and scraped off to bed, Franny pulled out a half-empty fifth of gin from a huge beaded handbag and raised her eyebrows. Steward saw at once that she must have taken it off his grandparents' sideboard that afternoon, when they were alone in the house. In the dim light of the Dillons' basement den she looked delicate and smudged, like Audrey Hepburn as Eliza Doolittle, now playing downtown at the Breeze.

He and Dillon and Harrison had wavered, wordless. They'd none of them had a drink in their lives and up until that moment Steward would have said Franny had never had one either. But S.D. grinned and poured himself half a paper cup full and downed it. Steward watched his temples bulge with the effort not to splutter. Once they started passing the bottle and swigging from it, the gin was finished in ten minutes, and ten minutes after that, after sitting in a circle grinning like lackbrains at each other, Harrison proposed that they walk on down by the trestle and wait for the ten P.M. freight train to pass by.

Franny couldn't stop laughing at the idea, and curled herself into a tiny ball on the Dillons' old skirted armchair. "Let's go watch the marshgrass grow," she hooted. "Let's go watch tadpoles turn into frogs. Let's go watch the freight train!" Steward and his friends were laughing too when they waved good-bye to her and tramped up the steps.

"Bye-bye, Franny," they said in unison, thinking she'd follow them, and Steward knew from the way they were chirping in high voices that they were all drunk. The ball on the armchair grew tinier and tinier as they watched from the stairway until finally S.D., at the foot of the steps, said he'd stay with her in case Dillon's mother came downstairs to check on them.

For the first quarter mile to the trestle Steward hadn't seen a thing in the world wrong with his oldest friend in Due East making friends with his girlfriend. Then at the corner of Union Street he turned around, waving Dillon and Harrison on. He remembered the white slice of underwear showing when, hysterical on the armchair, Franny waved her legs in the air. Things came to him so suddenly that year—he'd never be a writer, his grandfather used to call his mother a slut, Franny didn't have any sense, you couldn't trust S.D.—that sometimes he thought he might be psychic. He ran back.

He was winded and it scared him (chilled his innards, Lola would have said) when he stood in front of the Dillons' oleanders and saw through the venetian blinds down in the den that Franny, her back to him, was sitting on S.D.'s lap. Probably pressing those small round breasts against his friend. It seemed too neat a package, the way he'd sensed it back on the dark road, and he was powerless to slacken his rigid jaw. From the basement light he could see a thick crust of dirt atop the blinds. Dillon's mother didn't clean.

By the time he'd fumbled through the front door (everything was grimy, there were fingerprints, he saw now, on the wall) and gone downstairs, she was back on the plaid armchair, her feet tucked under her like a duck's. *S.D.'s lap.* Franny was utterly contemptuous when Lola sat on Nick's lap, which had always seemed kind of natural until she soured it for him.

He stood at the foot of the stairs and thought that he might have to just heave himself on the floor to slow things down, just sit right down until his breath came like a person's instead of a murderer's, but then he heard

himself, in some foreign low voice—Mick Jagger's voice? Bob Dylan's?—
calling Franny a slut.

That set a smarmy smile on S.D.'s mouth, and it moved Franny to reach
out a hand and feather his sleeve. Why were females the predators lately? All
backwards. He had somehow moved from the foot of the stairs to the edge
of the armchair—Why was Lola always ruffling Nick's neck hairs when he
was watching the game on TV? Why was some girl always running her
hand up and down her boyfriend's hairy arm in the cafeteria when the guy
was trying to eat? Why had Franny, in the last month, started sticking her
tongue in his mouth when it was his move to make?—and her touch
crawled up his arm.

He ran back up the stairs and climbed into Nick's convertible. Let her
walk home with S.D.

He drove the MG straight over to the Starkeys', where two hours
before he'd picked her up, pretending that Nick was waiting outside to
drive them in the low little car. The Starkey house was set on a corner and
he pumped the accelerator across the front lawn on a diagonal, emerging
between two pecan trees like some kid in a go-cart at Myrtle Beach. Safe on
the road again, he spent five seconds considering a drive straight into the
marsh. Franny told him later that he'd killed a rosebush and left tire tracks
six inches deep, that the family thought from the gunning of his engine that
there was a military operation going on outside. But by the time Mr.
Starkey ran outside, his bathrobe fanning out in the night, the MG was long
gone.

He didn't remember falling asleep behind the wheel—didn't remember
pulling into the driveway—but the next morning Lola, in a boa-collared
pink satin dressing gown, tugged him by the elbow and pulled him into
bed, fussing that Nick should never have let him drive alone at night. After
he was awake again, at noon, she made him ham and eggs and said: "Stewie,
I think I've been pushing yawl. You and Franny. Nick says maybe I did,
hunh, hon?"

He cut his ham into infinitesimal bits and mashed egg down into the
red gravy.

"Stew, you aren't but a freshman. You don't even have to *date,* honey, if
you aren't ready for it. Much less have a steady girlfriend who's making you
crazy." She was still wearing the rose-colored dressing gown, now gapping
at the waist, and the whole while she was talking he kept wanting to rise
and close it tight for her. "You're just too young, Stew, too young to even
drive the car at night."

Lola didn't mention the smell of gin on him, and Nick didn't stop letting him use the car, though Steward had only just turned fifteen and so had an entire year to go before he was legal after six o'clock. Nick had been saying all along that he was crazy for Franny, but she was skittish as a colt and "Stew, ya gotta remember that you can't hold a skittish colt on a tight rope. She's a little girl but she's got long legs on her, ya know. I'm not saying she's gonna break your heart, I'm just saying you can tell from those long legs that she's maybe gonna be the kind of girl that wants to go out dancing."

Go out dancing. She did like dancing, she was a good dancer, and he lived in dread of the time she would ask Dillon and Harrison and S.D. to tag along to one of the Friday night dances, so they could stand on the sidelines and watch Fran move while he creaked, rigid and robotic. She'd been willing to let a whole week pass after the Christmas party, willing to let S.D. take the blame. S.D. said that she'd been crying, that he'd just been trying to comfort her.

Steward had never once seen her cry.

I'm having trouble believing anything you say.

That week without her he took up his grandmother's invitation to spend some time in his old room on River Street. Looking for a ten-year-old boy probably, he could hardly recognize his own face in the big gilt-framed mirrors. Patches of his hollow cheeks were fuzzy.

Grandfather had set up a darkroom for him underneath the house and Steward spent four and five hours at a time down in the big space where, over the past hundred years, rooms had been built willy-nilly of plywood. He leaned against the drywall of his darkroom on his haunches, threading the rolls of film that had accumulated since the fall. When the strips were developed and hanging down on clothespins, a dozen of them, he set to work making contact sheets and discovered what he'd known all along, that there were three shots of Franny sneaked onto a roll he was supposed to be shooting for the paper. She didn't mind posing—she was used to it, from art class—but he'd only asked her to sit that once because he was unsettled when she stared, so direct and unsmiling, at the camera. In the scrunched images on the contact sheet she had a monkey's face.

He slipped the strip into the enlarger to print the first shot of her and heard music playing in the background: Chad and Jeremy, or Peter and Gordon, or Simon and Garfunkel, or the other music she made fun of and had spoiled for him. *Those saps,* she called them. Harrison had stopped playing Simon and Garfunkel songs, and pretended he'd never even liked them.

Her nose was dark and bulbous, a clown's plastic nose, and the little monkey face was bony and severe. Her hair was scraggly, greasy at the hairline, and cut too short. If he drew in lines around the eyes, if he made her chin disappear, if he fluffed out the hair and put a ridiculous flowered hat on top of it, he'd have a picture of her mother. He had never made that connection. What was he thinking, that her father had dropped her from his beak? He liked Mr. Starkey. He couldn't abide Mr. Starkey's wife. *Steward, your grandmother has always been the essence of a lady to me. Steward, how is your grandfather occupying his time now that he's sold the bank? I read about it in the* Courier. *Steward, I know your family has grand plans for you, and we have grand plans for Fanny, too. Young folks with grand plans do not need to go to the drive-in on a date.* He grabbed the first wet print from the wash ten minutes early and took it outside to the light.

He had never pitied another human being so much as he did that moment he stood under a bare lightbulb under his grandfather's house. The enlarger was right. She was plain. Then he thought he saw something else: adjusting his eyes to the naked bulb, he was either seeing double or seeing a ghost. Behind Franny's face were Lola's full mouth and deep cheekbones and wide-set eyes. His mother was beautiful, and Franny was plain.

That night he went back to Nick's for supper and for the first time in a week he was out front when she came running by. Behind the warehouse he mumbled something. It sounded as if he was saying he loved her, but he might have pulled out and said *liked* at the last minute. She pretended not to hear. They were making out long past sunset, Franny jammed up against the old wooden warehouse wall, and when she pushed him away and walked under the lone spotlight he could see splinters dangling from the back of her sweatshirt. He pushed her back against the wall, right under the light, and this time he held his eyes open too.

A month later, a month after the business with S.D., she said it back to him one night on her way home: "Sweet Jesus, I hope Teresa'll do my algebra for me. They'll have to send me down to business math I don't get the hang of it soon. See you tomorrow. I love you." He stayed in her driveway, watching her shadow move across the living room to stop in front of her mother's horrific Sacred Heart painting, five feet tall. Franny stood in front of Jesus, his long hair shadowing her short.

Dear Fran.
The only thing I can say for sure right now is that I'm not going to
Linton Academy. A school for saps.

Was she trying to get him out of the way? Was that it? If she'd seen Linton she'd never again say that she *only wanted the best* for him. The guy who showed him around had the same Simon and Garfunkel poster on his wall that Franny said made them look like lambs going to slaughter, and the director of admissions had pushed too hard about his test scores.

"Why, his father had the same problem with standardized tests and graduated *summa cum laude* from Princeton." His grandfather jumped in when it was Steward who was supposed to be answering the challenge. "They're excellent scores when you consider the *han*dicap the boy's been saddled with, what with these personal difficulties and the facilities at a South Carolina public school. Now sir—"

Steward, sitting side by side with his grandfather across from the director, had never seen him shrink before, but there he was, sliding down the hard-back chair, his very feet growing smaller in their wingtips, the old tailor-made shirt swimming around his scrawny neck. The young man judging him smiled indulgently and pushed the conversation along with his palm.

"And what are the last three books you read, Steward?"

"Excuse me, sir, I'm not finished."

"Portrait of the Artist?" Steward said, or asked, before Grandfather had time to go on, and while the admissions director leaned forward he dream-thumbed through the pages of the *James Joyce Cookbook/Jokebook* for the names of characters, at least. Dedalus was the father, or the son? The admissions guy was still leaning. "We just read *Great Expectations* in English."

"No, for your own pleasure."

"I enjoyed it." His voice was changing octaves. He could not picture a single other book spine: no, wait, Mr. Starkey had a big book propped up next to his TV. *"Great Battles of the Civil War?"*

"Though you know, for accuracy's sake, *we* still refer to that as the War Between the States," Grandfather said, his neck still struggling to fill his collar.

He would not be going to Linton. He and Grandfather did not even have to discuss it. They had visited five other schools, and he could now respond without hesitation and in one octave that he'd recently read *Portrait of the Artist, Great Expectations,* and *European Photos* by Henri Cartier-Bresson, a suggestion of Grandfather's (get in the photography without being too obvious) that grew him back to his regular shirt size. But there was only one place on the list that looked like a real possibility now.

Nick, of all people, had come up with a Benedictine school. The chaplain on the base had gone there, and Grandfather snickered when Nick passed an index card with the address across the table. "Oh, he wouldn't like it *there,*" Grandfather said, pocketing the card. It was the first dinner the Morehouses had ever served to Nick and Lola together.

But Nick pressed, and Lola nodded beside him, her cleavage dancing. She wore a pea-green sateen dress with puffed shoulders that made her look like Dolly Parton on *The Porter Wagoner Show.* A PX dress. Grandfather talked to her as if she were slinging a guitar on *The Porter Wagoner Show,* too. He hinted darkly at the extra expense of stopping off in Rhode Island, but Grandmother, bleak as a stone facade, raised her eyebrows and rose to help Gloria serve the pie. Lemon chess pie.

"Well now," Grandfather said. "We all want the same things for Steward, don't we? We want him to be happy. We want him at a school he'll be proud of."

"And we want him to have a sense of what's important." It was the first full sentence Nick had uttered all night. He would have been drab in his uniform even if he hadn't been sitting so close to Lola's twitching green bosom and teased hennaed hair.

"Naturally, Sergeant. De-Angelis." Grandfather wore his own hair, thin white hair, combed straight back and long over the collar now—would have worn it as long as some confederate general's if Grandmother had let him be—and in his early retirement had grown an old man's wispy goatee, a little ball of pulled cotton that made him look seventy instead of sixty. He and Lola could have competed in the Exotic Competition. Over the goatee his bow-shaped mouth smirked at the sound of Nick's name. "The Morehouses and the De-Angel-EES are in complete agreement."

So they went to see the Benedictines, the last school they visited before they headed back to Boston. Grandfather had a cab waiting for them at the train station in Providence, and they checked their bags before they settled in for the long silent ride. Steward had overheard him calling Grandmother the night before, telling her that it didn't look hopeful, that perhaps they should consider sending him back to St. Andrew's. Back to the blond jocks. He'd slit his throat with Nick's straight razor first.

Steward was struggling toward sleep, aroused and bloated from the cab's airless swaying, when they caught a glimpse of the bay. Then the three stone buildings of St. Benedict's set close together, fronted by a snowy field. The center building, a fortress on a rocky cliff, was bare of ivy, its walkway bare of shrubbery. The cab set them off next to a two-foot crater in the driveway, and the icy slabs of the center building called to mind Grandfather's crumbling old bank on River Street, the bank that had been torn down and replaced with a new fakey Colonial building since Grandfather sold his share of the partnership. Grandfather was tight-lipped stretching out of the cab, but he said: "A trip is never wasted if there's a chance to see fine old buildings. You remember that on your travels, Steward." Steward looked to see if he was joking.

The rector—a priest, or maybe a monk?—looked remarkably like Grandfather had looked before the new goatee, slight and tall, his hair combed straight back to flirt with his collar. On the tour through narrow dark corridors he did not ask Steward what books he read for pleasure. Grandfather was reticent in the face of the other man's reticence, and they walked in silence through tiny classrooms, six and seven jacketed boys to a class, the plaster chipping down from the ceilings in rhythm with the declensions. They had not been in so small a school.

Back in the priest's office Grandfather checked his watch, mentioned the waiting cab, and made a perfunctory request for the list of last year's college acceptances. Steward watched him pore over it, then backtrack and begin to tally.

"*Six* Harvards," he said, and Steward saw that he was doing more than tallying: now he was registering the names that went with the acceptances. No De-Angel-EES here. "Two Yales, three to Dartmouth. In a class of twenty. There's not a Catholic university on the list."

The rector said: "We emphasize the classics. We like to think we have a rigorous curriculum."

Grandfather eased back in the shabby wing chair.

The rector studied Steward's face and then focused on Grandfather. "Sometimes we advise a sensitive boy to investigate Duke or Vanderbilt. A boy who's planning to major in English, or history. I have great admiration for the Southern schools. We require our seniors to subscribe to the *Sewanee Review*."

Grandfather rubbed his chin, forgetting the goatee was there now, and rose, forgetting the cab, when the rector suggested a visit to the dormitory.

The rector waited in the stairwell while they poked their heads into the rooms. All singles. All cold. They could have been visiting a juvenile detention facility, army blankets on all the metal beds. There were no posters of Simon and Garfunkel, but occasionally a boy had tacked up a watery poster —Franny would have called that sappy too—or a literary calendar. No pictures of girlfriends, no hints at female existence. Steward stood in one room that overlooked the bay, white light above him, white water beyond, white walls surrounding him. It was not like prison. It was a monastery. Turning to leave, he saw above the door frame a small crucifix, metal on wood, and he had the same urge that had driven him across Franny's front lawn. He wanted to tear it down. He could imagine boys flailing themselves in rooms like these.

I'm glad my mother didn't get to see the place, she can't abide snow or cold.

Lola had gone back to Mass with Nick. Now they were all willing to ship him off to a Catholic school. He should have seen it coming when his mother bought a glass rosary, which she kept in her jewelry box: the cross was silver, and the beads were as big as marbles, cut like diamonds to catch the light. On mornings when she slept late he sometimes found her in bed, the glass beads entwined around her white-painted fingertips, and if she saw him eyeballing the rosary she shoved it under the pillow. Guilty.

Mumbo jumbo. *Creeping Jesus* was Franny's favorite expression, and once when her mother was out hosing down the dogwood trees she'd made a black eyepatch for Doris's bleeding Sacred Heart in the center of the living room wall. Her mother, in punishment, scrubbed the black dye off Franny's fingertips with S.O.S pads.

You'd never catch *her* with a rosary, but she hummed "Tantum Ergo" to irritate him. Once she said: "Promise me you'll never tell a living soul, I could not walk the halls of Due East High School or the face of this earth if you ever told another human being, but my mother has this thing with the twins she calls the Blessed Mother hour. She sets them down on the living room floor surrounded by all these plastic statuettes—it is so grotesque— and they have a little conversation about gentle Jesus, and then they all take their naps. The Blessed Mother hour."

She trooped off to Mass with all the other Starkeys, even rode in the back of the family station wagon. Sometimes he wondered what the foot- ball players who winked at her on the breezeway did when they saw her emerging over the top of the tailgate with her five-year-old brothers. Sometimes he wondered whether she wore to Mass the same stockings with thigh holes in them that she wore to French class where two rows back he itched to run up and tug her skirt down for her.

Slut. She was climbing over the gearshift to press herself against him, into him. S.D. and Dillon and Harrison had never even been on a date. Now she had her tongue in his mouth and the next step—they both knew it—was for him to squeeze her breast, not with his chest as he did now but with his hand. Only (and they both knew it) she would be the one to take his hand and place it there. In the MG, parked at the boat ramp down at the end of the Pigeon Point Road, she was so close to him under the steering wheel that she might have been an extension of his body, two extra arms, two extra legs, a soft head with a pair of eyes sharper than his own. He wasn't the only psychic one. Their brain waves met somewhere out past the dashboard. She knew, mostly, to say nothing at all because there was nothing at all to say if Lola had splashed her with a new dark-scented cologne and they were breathing it in. Their nights together were like a jingle contest, Twenty-five Words or Less.

He put a hand to his neck, where the shadow of a hickey still marked him. Grandfather had spent a week at Christmastime bellyaching about where all that gin could have gone when he *knew* they hadn't finished off that many martinis at the open house. Nobody drank martinis, they all wanted their toddies at Christmastime. Her stockings had holes because she lifted the cheap ones from the five-and-dime, where the cardboard folders hung on a rack like dollar bills on a money tree, for the taking.

The weird thing is that it's the only school I could see myself in.

Oh they were so far beyond words it was useless to write to her. He unwadded the crumpled pages, diced them and then minced them so that Grandfather would not be able to piece together a single phrase.

She was slowing for him on a run. He could feel her holding back, a girl, slowing for him. She was reaching out her hand down in Dillon's den. That year he spent at St. Andrew's he had soothed himself into sleep with his own picture postcards of Due East. The view from the verandah, the underside of the porch above them painted green for cool, green palmettos ringing the bay. A thousand Sailfishes shagging on into the night. The bank before they tore it down, grim as money and always full, Grandfather's own private cocktail party where the grown-ups slapped each other on the back and the Marine children sat on the writing tables to make out deposit slips for a million bucks. Sometimes he put himself to sleep smelling Gloria's house, five blocks behind theirs, the rude wood always reeking of kerosene and mustard greens, though Gloria in his house smelled only of peppermints and Grandmother's sachets. Grandmother's old velvet dresses ripped at the seams and resewn as curtains on Gloria's windows. Scarlett O'Hara in reverse.

At St. Benedict's he'd picture a sports car's black interior. Franny on his lap. Franny on S.D.'s lap. When he came in at night Lola circled him, a vulture, calling: "How's Franny doing? Any better at that math? What music are you two listening to now?" until Nick pulled her off the carcass. But in the afternoons Nick wasn't there to stop her.

And what did yawl do at lunchtime?

Sure you won't think of trying out for basketball—you're good with a ball, sweetie.

He could see himself there, at St. Benedict's. He could see himself as one of the chunks of ice out there in their Northern bay, ringed by scrubby woods. He could see himself finishing letters to her without Grandfather in the bedroom next door, could see the letters calling out like Lola from the kitchen: *What's Harrison up to? And Dillon? And S.D.? What's he up to?* Could see already the empty mailbox, because as far as he knew, Franny had never written an unassigned page in her life. Maybe Teresa or AgnesAnn would write Franny's love letters to him, letters doused in Lola's perfume, letters the Benedictines would confiscate before he ever opened them.

He could see the visits home too, the fumblings in the car if she could drag herself away from S.D., the way she would one night out at the beach drag off her whole blouse and reveal a cheap black satin bra she had lifted from a bin in the five-and-dime.

Franny in a cheap satin bra. He knew he heard Grandfather tossing in the bedroom beyond, and shuffled off to the bathroom where he could shut the door and let his pants bunch at his ankles. Where he could hate her for driving him into a white-tiled refuge while Grandfather drooled onto the pillow in a Boston hotel room.

Already the snow was filling his mouth and the pale jacketed boys of St. Benedict's, their hair long around the collar, were berating him for his lousy public school Latin. Already Franny had slipped out of the bra and was tugging down black satin panties, the same panties Lola hung on hangers in the bathroom to dry, and she was begging him to *Go on, Stew. Go on.* Her little breasts grown monstrous.

And he—Chad and Jeremy playing in the background, a warm spring rain dousing the dashboard—was telling her that life in the monastery (oh

well, close enough) had made him reconsider his relationships with women.
He was telling her that maybe S.D. was the one who should go on.

Go on.

Go on.

He was watching her unbuckle his belt, her hard little callused hand
searching for him, and he could feel her lean her new monstrous breasts
down to tickle his white belly.

Eyes closed against his own image in the old beveled bathroom mirror
in a hotel in Boston, he finally smiled at himself—a *monastery*—and slapped
her back against the passenger seat, her feet tucked under her like a duck's.
Slut.

He felt the smile slide down his leg.

R̲elease.

LOVE
BEADS

"Listen to me," Franny Starkey's little brother Walter said, "I can sing 'Harrigan.'" The rest of the family moaned and groaned. They were sick to death of "Harrigan"—and anyway, Franny told her father, Walter stumbled after the chorus, it was *too* painful—but her father always let the little boy trail him, forgetting the words.

Now it was Steward Morehouse listening to Walter. Steward knelt by the television, Albert's blocks toppling behind him, Caroline's chubby legs in pink ballerina tights stretched out in front of him. Franny begged: "Walter, let me teach you a new song. I'll teach you 'Officer Krupke.'"

But Steward told Walter to ignore them all. "You just sing me 'Harrigan,' Walt. How's it go, old buddy?"

Franny didn't believe she had ever seen either one of them so flushed with excitement. Walter bellowed the song and stretched out his hand to rest it on Steward's shoulder. Steward listened on his knees for twenty minutes, longer than it took her to hear the rosary every night. She sat behind the two of them on the faded velvet love seat, chin in her hands, waiting for Walter to get it right. Steward and her father, listening to Walter.

Her father was crazy for Walter and he seemed to like Steward pretty well too. Pat called Walter *lamb chop* and he called Steward *Franny's beau*, knowing it made her mad. She really hated corny stuff like that.

The school board offered Franny's father the principal's job at Due East High School in November 1966. That year there were one hundred Negro students enrolled, all bused in under a Freedom of Choice plan, and in the first three months of school there were three minor shoving incidents on the breezeway and in the halls. When the old principal resigned in November, his aging assistant declined the hot seat. Next year they were expecting five hundred Negroes, and white parents called daily to ask for transcripts to send to the segregation academy across the river.

Pat was not first choice for the job. The junior high school principal declined first, and the superintendent asked all five white elementary school principals before he got down to the assistant-principal tier and Pat Starkey. Doris was beside herself, but not a bit surprised, she told the family. She'd never doubted for a minute. She knew Daddy had it in him. She knew he was principal material. Next year he'd be superintendent himself, and bring about the peaceful integration of the entire Due East County school system. Though she wondered aloud if the segregation academy would be offering scholarships to families as large as theirs. If anything got out of hand.

"Doris!" Pat said. "You can't let your principles shift like sand."

She giggled, young as a girl. "You're my only principal now."

Pat Starkey started the job the week it was offered. When he came in after basketball practice—he was still moonlighting as the junior high coach —he sometimes waltzed with Doris right through the dining room/living room, right over Caroline's and Paul's homework spread out over the floor and the rug. He had to write a note to Caroline's fifth-grade teacher, explaining the footprints. Now when he came in at night he pulled twin packs of gum out of his pocket for the twins, and once he and Doris stayed up to watch the entire *Tonight* show on a school night. Life became elegant and extravagant. Franny had a new set of pastels. On the weekends he bought a fifth of Wild Turkey, and the family took to calling AgnesAnn at the university every Saturday. The line of eight brothers and sisters waiting to talk on the phone stretched out into the hallway. Franny herself waited. To talk to AgnesAnn! The whole house smelled different, now that Doris bought Pine-Sol instead of cheap ammonia.

Doris found a new house. It was more than they could afford, but it had five bedrooms—one was really a dining room, but who needed a dining room with such an enormous kitchen? and one was really a damp basement family room, but it meant that the twins could, for the first time in their five-year-old lives, sleep in beds.

The new house, its brick the color of cream just before it sours, was a split level in Splendid Oaks, the subdivision abutting the high school. Doris did not invite the children to come see it while she was lining up a mortgage, but night after night she spent the whole dinner hour describing it (fuzzy baby-blue wall-to-wall carpeting that *came with the house;* a splendid oak, just as the sign said, right next to the driveway). She drew up floor plans to allocate space: Walter and Albert in with Paul down in the basement, the biggest room; Martin and William in the dining room, because they had the least need of a closet; Doris and Pat in the master bedroom. The *mastuh bedaroom* she called it, setting Caroline all aquiver with expectation. When the Starkey children finally saw their new house, a week before the movers came, Caroline stood with her shoulders hunched (the posture of humility) in front of her parents' new wall-length closet, wet-eyed, opening and shutting the folding louvered doors until Franny made her come out back to see the magnolia tree.

Steward Morehouse, who was leaving for school in four months, did not like the new house.

"Steward," Doris said, "I know it's not as fine as your grandparents' house." It was the first day after moving day, but already Doris had tied back the old lace curtains in the living room and put up new yellow café curtains, a print of monkeys sliding down bananas, in the kitchen. Already she'd sunk a trellis under the living room window for roses. Already she'd hung her five-foot Sacred Heart in the narrow front hallway, Jesus prepared to greet any visitors by pointing to His thorn-encircled heart. He was too big to go over the fireplace.

"It's a nice house," Steward said, emerging from Martin and William's doorless closetless dining room/bedroom. Franny, who already had the run of Due East High School, had sneaked him out of last-period study hall to come see it.

"No," Doris said, twirling a dark sausage curl at her temple and flirting. "No, I can see you don't think it's as fine as it could be. And it's not as fine as it *could* be, Steward, no it's not. But we like it for now. When Daddy's superintendent, Franny, we'll be overlooking the eighteenth hole! Won't we."

"Come on." Franny grabbed Stew's arm and dragged him back through the new kitchen where the old dining room furniture—the first furniture Pat and Doris had bought in their marriage, real mahogany furniture with scrolled legs and upholstered seats for the chairs—sat bunched and embarrassed. She led him back through the big yard. Six bikes already leaned against the toolshed, where the last family had pasted a bumper sticker on the shed door that said *Jesus Is My Friend, and I'd Like to Introduce Him.* Back to the little magnolia, a geyser of pink and white shooting out from stickers and sourgrass.

"Can you believe it?" she said.

He shook his head.

"Can you believe somebody would paint brick that color? It looks like baby spit-up. Can you believe I'm going to be living in this house?"

He shook his head again.

"Wait'll you see the mastuh bedaroom."

He shook his head a third time. "I'd rather not."

"Oh, Steward. Don't be so sad."

He shrugged.

"It's months yet."

Shrugged again.

"It'll be more—it'll be hard to be apart but it'll be stronger or something. Oh," and she tugged at her hair, "think about when it's rainy and windy and you're in Providence."

"It's not *in* Providence."

"When it's rainy and windy and you're *near* Providence." She wasn't even sure what she meant by *rainy and windy*. In Providence? In Due East? It was a sappy thing to say, and usually—or before, anyway—Steward said the sappy things. Now he did not condescend to answer. "What'd I do?"

Steward leaned back against the smooth bark and slid down until he was a pool of boy at the roots of the magnolia tree. It was May, hot and clear. The grass where he spread his loafers was thick with gauzy swarms of gnats and armies of red ants.

"I won't be able to picture you *here*," he mumbled.

So Steward Morehouse didn't like the Splendid Oaks house that was a step up for the Starkey family. Good. The little house by the marsh was as anonymous as this one, but at least it had shock value. Kids used to say, the first time they saw the old house, "Oh, y'all don't live *there*. You couldn't possibly fit all of y'all in there."

Franny pinched a consolation present for Steward from her pocket, but her tight cotton skirt rose with the hand extricating itself, and she watched him avert his eyes from the sight of her chocolate-colored stocking top. She knew what he was thinking, that everything about her and the new house had a slick sticky air about it, as if the last people had left a layer of grease and she'd rolled in it, as if her garter belt itself dripped a rancid odor. She'd run through that dining room believing that he wouldn't care how tacky it was (look how *Lola* fixed everything up, with scarves and fans and fringes and feathers) and now he wouldn't meet her eye.

"Look," she said, "pot." He jerked his head back to stare at half a joint, rolled up fat as a cigar.

"Where'd you get that?"

"Bobby."

"Harrison gave you that?" She saw him sit on his hands to conceal his excitement. He had never seen marijuana before, and neither one of them would have known to call it a joint if *Time* magazine hadn't noted its recent importance. Bobby Harrison told her he got it off a Marine, but Franny suspected someone they knew was selling it for a Marine. Someone named Dillon, who had a new electric guitar.

She couldn't stop herself from feigning elegant nonchalance, and waved it under his nose. They didn't make them this fat for the pages of *Time* magazine. "It's good," she told him.

"You tried it already?"

She nodded again, meaning to add a guileless air to the nonchalance.

"You could have waited." He was smoldering the way the pot should have been by now. But he couldn't even finish half a cigarette when she was smoking. He choked, allergic or something. Now, slumped at the bottom of the tree, he could have been stretching his arm straight up her thigh if he'd wanted to. They could be sniffing the charred end of the marijuana, and he could be crawling up her thigh, but instead he said: "I'll be gone soon enough."

"Don't have a hissy cause I smoked some of it with Bobby. *That* doesn't mean anything. Bobby can't spit out two sentences to me." She clipped her words, but she was ready to let fly. Steward's moods were as dark and dank as the ground he sat on. She couldn't bear the sniffling sighing silences.

"He was nice enough to give it to me. I couldn't just hog it all for myself."

"I didn't *mean* you had to keep it all for yourself."

"C'mon Steward. Don't be so sad and stupid."

He anchored his fingers to the roots.

"C'mon Steward, get up. We'll walk back down by the creek and smoke it. I giggled like an *id*iot the first time."

Seeing his scowl, she amended that. He was picturing her giggling with Bobby Harrison. "Well, maybe it won't make *you* giggly." She knelt beside him so close that this time he wouldn't be able to help but put his hand out to touch her.

His rage held him as still as the tree roots. She crept forward on her knees until she had to put one hand on his shoulder to balance herself. She felt his breath easing out, air from a punctured tire, and then she knew he would relent. He reached out his white gnarly hand and edged it up the back of her leg until, sure enough, one of his round fingertips rested just where the stocking top ended. And she reached out her palm and laid it on his gaunt cheek where it simultaneously touched one smooth patch of white skin, one fuzzy with new growth. The tree was a perfumed tent overhead. Oh she was bad. This was as fake as a cologne ad in *Seventeen*. She leaned over in slow motion, easing herself down so gradually that her mouth, sticky with caramel-colored lipstick, was still an inch away from his when her mother called through the kitchen door:

"Now *don't* the two of you dare disgrace my brand-new house, oh! You make me so mad with that carrying-on I could take this broom across your backside, Frances Starkey! And Steward Morehouse, get your hand off that leg. If your grandmother *saw* you now."

She felt Steward's hand fly off her thigh and knew he was stuffing it, singed, into a pocket while she smoothed down the skirt in back. Really, there was no chance now of asking him to leave his stepfather's car parked in her driveway while they went off to smoke a marijuana cigarette. He rose, unsteady, and she followed, the two of them approaching Doris, miniature judge and hangman, magnificent on her new back steps.

"Don't you ever let me—"

Steward cut her off: "Yes ma'am," he said, expressionless, and nodded good-bye to Doris in a sulking movie-gangster way that meant he'd better not show his face in the house for a week, at least. If his grandfather weren't Steward Morehouse Sr. he'd never have been let into the house in the first place. He went back through the dark kitchen without turning to say good-bye to Franny, but she could still feel his fingertip slipping under the stocking top when her mother said:

"Frances, you are to give that skirt to your little sister this very afternoon, hear? How dare you walk around like that? Did you go off to your father's school this morning looking like that? Good night, child, do you know what that does to boys?"

Boys. Franny nodded submissive obedience. Doris would forget later, and anyway if you melted Caroline you still wouldn't be able to pour her into the skirt. Franny stared down at the cheap tight cotton, cotton dyed a yellow so muddy it would never have occurred to anyone else at Due East High School that it was meant for wearing. At Due East High School girls wore heavy blue linens and broadcloths, blue so pure the Virgin Mary herself might have been draped in it, or delicate pink flowered prints the color of babies' blankets.

Lola had brought the muddy yellow skirt back for her from a store in

New Orleans that sold cheap Indian clothes. Lola said New Orleans was crawling with hippies who wore that kind of thing, but Due East hadn't seen much more of hippies than it had seen of marijuana, so far. Franny had never told her mother where the skirt came from, or that it started out floor-length before she cut off three-quarters of it, or that Lola had also brought her bangles and necklaces she said were *love beads*. Lola made Steward crazy and was ruining everything. Love beads. But she did have a nice eye for strange colors. This one was the color of earwax.

She drifted through the living room, where the fireplace brick was painted white, too, and shook her disapproval out the front door. You could hear Nick's little car down at the end of Splendid Oaks Road, Steward revving it while he sat idling at the stop sign. She wouldn't be running by Steward's house at night. She thought he was out of his head, going to a Catholic boarding school, but she tried, really tried, not to be sarcastic about it. She told Bobby and Michael and S.D. to quit goosing him about it.

Sad Steward. Sad all the time. It was hard to tell if he really knew what happened with her and S.D. anytime either of them filched a drink, or whether he'd seen S.D.'s hand on her breast that time down in Michael's den. Steward was always sad, always sighing, always brooding. She loved him more when he was brooding. He was going to the Benedictines because she let S.D. squeeze her breast, and he didn't even believe in God. It was more like something a girl should do—get thee to a nunnery—but you couldn't pay her a million bucks to lock herself away like that.

She drifted down Splendid Oaks Road, feeling for matches in one pocket and the fat cigar joint in the other. Once she crossed the Broad Creek Road she'd have another three-quarters of a mile to go to the creek itself. William and Martin had shown her where it was the night before, Martin flinging himself headfirst into the greasy water from his bike, while Caroline still wept over the mastuh bedaroom and Teresa put her books back onto the new shelf in alphabetical order.

The creek was surrounded by the last of the airy pine woods around Splendid Oaks. She was alone in the stretching afternoon, but still her skirt rode up under the canopy of pine boughs, no one there to see it. Bobby had shown her how to hold the marijuana the way Humphrey Bogart held a cigarette stump and how to inhale it in silly squirts, but after a minute she was dizzier than she got when she smoked a cigarette in the morning. The thought of Steward flinging himself at the Benedictines the way her brother Martin flung himself at the creek, all because she got squirmy with S.D.—

and you couldn't trust S.D. at all, Steward was right about that, and he had no idea how to kiss—left her less giggly than she'd been with sweet shy Bobby Harrison. When she heard a splash from the creek she ground the end of her joint out, picked it up off the woods floor, clutched it in her fist, and scampered out through the woods.

It was only a dog, a stubby black dog, taking his afternoon dip. She settled herself down on the creek bank to watch him. The muddy creek had been brown ten minutes ago, before she stepped into the woods, and now it was as flecked with color as a fly, aquamarines and blacks and even a slice of cardinal red deepening to carmine. She hadn't seen any colors at all when she smoked the first half with Harrison.

She sat very still. It was hard to tell how long it took for the colors to turn wrong. The light had taken on that too-bright cast you see when you step out of a movie theater in the afternoon. The colors she saw now in the creek water were too bright, too thin. Insubstantial—the red was pink and then beige and then invisible—and as it floated away she became as small and slow and thick as her baby brother Walter, the retard, and she felt as sorry for herself as she sometimes did for him. Albert pinched Walter's arms when he thought no one was looking, and their father said: *Al, you be good now to that little lamb chop. He's your twin, and he thinks the world of you.*

Her father would kill her if he caught her with a marijuana cigarette. She panicked and dug a hole with her heel to bury the weedy end of it, and suddenly knew that she reeked of this odor, this *Time* magazine odor, this illegal odor of hippies in New Orleans who wore Indian clothes and love beads.

Across the narrow creek she saw a slithering through the grass. The sun and the wind tricking her? A worm? She closed her eyes and there was that carmine streak again, a scarlet tendril, brilliant and soothing on her eyelids, the red they use in stained-glass windows. The sun massaged her neck and shoulders, and she drifted, close to sleep, picturing her father finding them on D hall, finding her and Steward and Bobby Harrison smoking marijuana cigarettes, Steward's hand on her breast. Pat Starkey, Principal of Due East High School, beamed and passed by and the cloud of marijuana smoke enveloped and haloed him.

Her father, Pat Starkey, head in the clouds.

She was stoned and close to sleep, serene on a creek bank. The black dog, coy with her all this time, finally came nuzzling up close and then splashed in the water again. This time she followed him right in, tight yellow skirt and all, to rid herself of the odor of Harrison and New Orleans hippies and the wish that flitted just before she jumped, that Steward's hand would one day before he sacrificed himself to the Benedictines move up along her garter.

Steward went up to rainy windy Providence in September. He wrote Franny once a week, on schedule, the way a private in the Army might write his mother. The same Steward who could drive around for hours without speaking a word now wrote ten-page letters, twelve-page letters, fifteen-page letters.

At night in the new house, in the bedroom next to the mastuh bedaroom, she and Caroline took turns lifting each other's pajama top and scratching each other's back. Around midnight, their little brother Walter climbed up from the basement to join them. It was a mild Due East fall, but Paul and Albert had been complaining about the cold damp room at the bottom of the house.

The first night Walter stumbled in, he must have thought he was fleeing to his father's bed; but once he was settled between his sisters, their chewed fingernails stroking his sturdy frame, he stayed. And came again the next night, and the night after, and soon every night, snuggling into the womb created between his sisters' bodies as if he were planning to be born again.

"Ooh, that's icky," Caroline would squeal if he curled up too close, his pajama bottoms gapping, but Franny let him wiggle whichever way he wanted. They were both deep in sleep when he arrived—sometimes one of the girls lifted his pajama top and scratched his back without waking—but usually Franny opened her eyes after he had climbed in. She drew her fingers up and down the length of Walter's solid back, and when she was done, she touched his coiled curls. He was a towhead like Steward, and his thick pale hair was as woolly as a lamb's. Lamb chop.

One December night Franny woke at midnight to a stirring two flights below. She made a place for Walter in the middle of the bed, but he never came. For the first time she was embarrassed to wake in the morning and find her arm draped around Caroline, who was already growing large breasts.

Franny's breasts remained small and round and high, and she had the oddest sensation that her little brother Walter somehow knew that those breasts had recently been squeezed by someone other than Steward.

Afternoons now she went and sat for Tony Rivers, a senior whose acrylic yellow-and-black-striped abstract won a white ribbon in the Due

East Fall Art Show. The truth was, his paintings looked like the sheets they sold at J. C. Penney, but he was the only artist she knew at Due East High School. He wore his dark hair shaggy, the way the Beatles had let theirs get, and went without shaving for as long as he could get away with it. His face was round and bland, his skin the color of chicken stock, his mouth a good round chunk of meat in the soup. The first time she ate lunch with him, in the cafeteria, she focused on the thick scruffy line of black bristles on his chin. When he said he wanted to paint her smile she almost threw up, but she followed him home the next afternoon.

He drove her to Lady's Island, where his parents' pink brick house, pretty as a robin's nest, sat on a bluff. His room was the size of the old Starkey house and looked out on the Due East River and a shrimp boat waiting for the bridge to open. She choked back snotgreen jealousy. He was an only child, and his parents worked, and his room was littered with rolls of canvas and pads of good paper and large tubes of paint.

"Why don't you take your shirt off?" Tony Rivers said, and smiled in a pleasant, apologetic way. "If that doesn't bother you." He had a reddish moustache coming in; already it wormed around the corners of his mouth. She smiled back—*I'd like to paint your smile.* My ass—and unbuttoned her blouse one slow button at a time, enough to make him crazy. The blouse was sea green, and she had actually ironed it the night before for this sitting, the first time she'd held an iron in her hand for six months. Underneath she wore a cheap black satin bra. She smiled again, and unhooked it one slow hook at a time.

But he got right to work—that first day, anyway. He spent at least fifteen minutes sketching her (couldn't draw for beans. No wonder he did abstracts) and asked her if she'd like to come see. That was her only moment of confusion: she grabbed the blouse up and draped it around her shoulders, so he had to lift it just slightly when he went to squeeze her naked breast tight, once, hard. Then he lifted the brush again and got back to work. Inspiration. He left a small bruise the color of the night sky.

And Walter, as if he knew, had stopped coming into her bed at night to have his back scratched, and her father had stopped calling Steward *Franny's beau,* even though Steward's letters arrived every week. Teresa said Tony Rivers was a creep and she didn't suppose Steward would keep writing if he'd heard about him. Everyone seemed to know about the marijuana and the peeling off her underwear in the thick creek water and the bruises on her breasts.

Boys certainly knew. Even poor Walter knew. Lola had suspected it, and maybe Nick did too. Everyone knew but Steward.

At night the family kneeled together in front of the white brick fireplace to say the rosary. The rest of them, even Walter, appeared to be actually praying, but Franny drifted. It seemed to her (cheating, sitting back on her haunches while Teresa kneeled straight) that if she was praying at all, she was praying to Steward. Some nights she prayed that he would never find out what she'd once done with S.D. and what she was doing now with Tony Rivers. Some nights she prayed that she'd stop going to Tony's bedroom after school. Anyone could tell where it was going to lead, any day now. Tony had already pulled her skirt halfway down her hips.

And some nights she looked over at her little brother Walter, picking his nose in the middle of the Joyful mysteries, winking both eyes back if she winked at him, and prayed that Steward would somehow forget that she had ever existed, that he would stay up North for the rest of his life and never even come to know what Tony Rivers looked like in his paint-splattered jeans. She didn't think she could bear it if he somehow did find out, and then forgave her.

TO TELL
YOU THE
TRUTH

Steward might scrawl out a postcard to his mother after she wrote a dozen fluttery pages (*I'm almost out of my mind fretting over you so far away*), but he wrote to Franny every Saturday night at five-thirty, when half the boys on his hall trooped off to the chapel for confessions. Not that *he* was confessing. He had nothing to confess, nothing but loneliness and pure white empty aching misery.

All the other afternoons he studied in the library, where the padded desk chairs were soft and shabby and comforting, but on Saturdays at five-thirty he sat on a hard wooden chair in the narrow study room, an airless box as grim as the confessional the others were facing. Nobody else on his hall ever used the study room. Sometimes Steward thought nobody else even knew it existed, but Brother Thomas had made a special effort to point it out to him at orientation, as if he'd known that Steward would need isolation. Unlike the boys' rooms, which on Steward's side of the hall all had big windows fronting the bay, the study room had one narrow panel of frosted whorled glass. He traced the grime of lashing rain on the window. In an hour he would be sitting down to eat with friends he knew better than he'd known any boy in Due East, but while he wrote to Fran he was pale with homesickness. If he'd thought to take his pulse he'd have been frightened by its lag.

I guess you're used to that religious crap, excuse me, business. They drag out that Temple of the Holy Spirit stuff whenever they get a chance. This school was the right choice though, Nick knew what he was doing, when you see everybody believing this stuff it gives you the willies and you know better what you believe in yourself. Which for me is not much, except maybe us. I think you could definitely say that I believe in us.

The more time he spent out of his room, or fooling around in the darkroom or the Debate Society, the more his letters to Fran dripped loneliness. He knew he was lying. He knew perfectly well that he'd attached himself to St. Benedict's like moss to a live oak, but on Saturday nights he allowed himself to forget. Misery closed every paragraph. His temperature dipped down into the mid-nineties when he wrote to her, and sometimes he was taking in so little oxygen that he sprawled across the long wooden table, face resting on forearm, near sleep while he wrote. And wrote. And wrote. The letters stretched out longer and longer, and still she didn't write back. He'd known she wouldn't write. S.D. His heart slowed. Harrison. His temperature dipped into the eighties.

November 2, 1967

They tell me this is All Souls Day, well Happy All Souls Day to you.

Sorry to be sarcastic. Maybe you can tell I'm not in such a great mood. I knew you wouldn't write anyway, I knew you wouldn't have any idea what it was like to be a thousand miles away. I write you on Saturday nights, does that mean anything to you.

For weeks that horrible sentence—*I write you on Saturday nights, does that mean anything to you*—clanked, an echoing church bell, as he fell asleep. He sounded as bad as his mother. No. He sounded as bad as Fran's mother. He could not even remember what she looked like (wouldn't dream of putting that monkey-face print of her out on his dresser) and he could not imagine that they had once spent hours driving around Due East County on Saturday nights. He could not imagine that this fifteen-year-old girl who would not write back to him had once slid down in the passenger seat in Nick's MG while he gunned the engine to ninety miles an hour, ninety-five, one hundred. Once, together, they had reached a hundred and seven wordless miles an hour. Once they spent Saturday nights out on the Claire's Point Road, pulled over on the shoulder to wait for the Light, swamp gas rolling in around them. *I write to you on Saturday nights, does that mean anything to you.* In his bed at St. Benedict's he writhed in shame.

And resolved not to commit another sentence to paper, not a single word to Franny who had forgotten him, and managed to pass most of his days without thinking of her until he checked his mailbox, where a solitary scented envelope from Lola waited.

He did not intend to come home crawling on his belly. When he told Lola that he was planning to meet his grandparents in New York for Thanksgiving, he heard himself snotty and snide on the phone:

"You know, they *are* paying for this school."

When did he get like that? and to his mother? Lola sniveled. He imagined his mother weeping over a turkey too big for her and Nick, but he didn't go home to Due East. He couldn't. He spent Thanksgiving Day at the Plaza Hotel, eating greasy roast duck with Grandmother and Grandfather and seeing the whole world coated in slick melted fat.

But Franny fell for it. Two weeks later he smelled a new scent in his pigeonhole, a letter-dousing cologne even cheaper and more extravagant than what his mother might use. Alone in his room, the door shut, he sat on the floor to rip open the envelope: out fluttered dozens of scraps of paper, scrawled at odd hours, covered over with doodles and one good drawing of her sister Caroline. The pages were undated, but he knew they stretched out over the months he'd been gone and he showered them down, confetti over his head. She'd been writing all along.

10 December 1967

I just got your letter and you said stuff you never said when I was there and I am just so damn glad *that everything's o.k. after all and that I'll be seeing you for Christmas in a couple of weeks, because when I do I'm going to try to do some of those things of the flesh the priests are always hinting about. You can tell I'm feeling good if I put that in a letter that's going to* your *house!!!!! Don't leave this lying around please.*

He hinted to his mother that Franny might want to come along to pick him up at the train station, but when he climbed off the coach in Yemassee, only Nick and Lola stood in the fog by the tracks. It was five-thirty in the morning, and they all looked like characters on a movie set, their legs swallowed up to the knees in the mist. Nick—joking, punching his shoulder—told him to make it snappy.

No one mentioned Franny's name on the ride home. Lola passed the half-hour drive from the station to Due East pumping him, and Nick for once did not intervene. In the backseat of the Oldsmobile, Steward watched dawn break over the lowcountry for the first time in four months. The road was dark with moss: above him the old oaks formed an arch to welcome him home, and in the first light the birds were dark, too, and raucous. Men passed in pickup trucks, their gun racks heavy, and his mother chattered on, delivering the news about every social event and every social being in Due East. Everyone but Franny.

"Bea Fortenbright shot herself right on the front lawn, but the bullet only grazed her big toe. Can you imagine? I bet they don't do things like *that* in Rhode Island, hunh, Stew. I bet in Rhode Island they go shoot themselves in private, in the bathroom, and they probly don't miss either."

Good Lord, his mother sounded like a cross between Lady Bird Johnson and Minnie Pearl. He didn't believe he'd ever *heard* her accent before. When they passed the ruins of the old Sheldon Church—Sherman's men had branched out this way, leaving Savannah—Steward felt a strange connection to those Yankees marching through enemy territory. They passed plantations where Lola had once made social calls with Grandmother and she squealed, pointing out her past life to Nick.

"Oh, Nicky, Stew, yawl wouldn't believe how green I was the first time your grandmama took me calling. She practically had to pinch my arm to get me to hush."

In the backseat Steward shivered at the sight of the marshes in high tide. They were still green too, and it was December already. It hadn't occurred to him that he'd see the marshes before he'd see Franny. It hadn't occurred to him that home might start this far up the road. The water swelled up close to the narrow road, gray as the fog itself; he reached for his camera, but it was packed away in the trunk.

Lola chirped out her solo conversation until they were passing the air station and the packing sheds and then really pulling into town. Driving along the highway, driving alongside trailer parks and tire stores and used-car dealerships with a thousand plastic flags fluttering, Steward saw that Due East was just a cheap Marine town, and a zillionth the size he'd remembered it. For months he'd been picturing the Due East Bay from Grandfather's front verandah. For months, when he wobbled at the ice-skating rink, he'd seen the smooth gliding boats on the river. Now the ride to Nick and Lola's ran through blocks of tacky pasteboard houses.

When Nick pulled the old sedan into the driveway, into home, Steward averted his eyes from the little brick house. Everything was doll-size and shabby, underwear fluttering from the back line. All around squatted the houses of E-7s and -8s and -9s.

The MG was parked in the driveway, though, hand-buffed.

"Looks like new," Steward told his stepfather, and Nick handed over the car keys with such a warm press to his hand that he thought maybe everything would be all right with Franny, after all. Behind him a hundred dogs—big old Due East dogs running loose, shepherds and setters and hound dogs—howled out a greeting, and the pines flittered down to the creek. The fog was lifting on a morning as white and gold as the star his grandmother set atop the Christmas tree every year.

Steward told his mother he wanted to walk around a little. He had an urge to go sit beside the warehouse on States Rights Alley, to let strange dogs nuzzle him, before he came inside. He let Lola squeeze him close to her sweatered bazooms and breathed in the smell of her morning perfume and her caramel lipstick and her peppermint hairspray. He even squeezed her back before he slouched off down the street, his fingers pressing the MG keys in his pocket.

He could always tell Grandfather that St. Benedict's was just too god-damn Catholic, and then they would all let him come home for good.

Franny was trying to look like a hippie for the Christmas party (formal every year), but she just looked bedraggled, her too-blue dungarees splat-tered with paint. His grandmother's friends, all the old bags, wore pearls and silk, and their husbands wore bow ties and smirks. He imagined them all—hey, he *saw* them all—staring right through Franny's gauzy blouse from the Indian shop in Savannah. Steward had worn a blazer and turtle-neck that Franny said made him look like *the host of somebody's nightmare.* She had talked him into asking S.D., too, and he spent most of the party running to air out the upstairs bathroom, where Franny and S.D. retreated every fifteen minutes to smoke a joint.

They had the top down in the MG going home, Franny perched behind the bucket seats where Steward and S.D. clenched their jaws at each other. Franny was singing "Piece of My Heart" and then calling out: "Frank Zappa lives!" and "Wake up, you zombies!" through the streets of Due East. A complete loon. A bird. She stayed in back even after S.D. stumbled into his house, and Steward cranked himself around to catch a glimpse of her sharp chin, up and defiant, watching S.D. fumble with his doorknob. You could see clear through her gauzy blouse, even in the dark, could see the hard high shape of her breasts, more knobs for fumbling. He drove her down to the end of Pigeon Point Road to park.

She was already weepy when they pulled into the dark asphalt parking lot. They weren't alone—a big lug and his date, with big hair, stared over at them from a Pontiac when they rolled in—and Steward maneuvered the little car down as close to the water as he could get it. They pitched forward. The water was colorless, a shiny sheet, and the fingers of land around them were jigsaw pieces. Franny, sniveling, clambered into the front seat as he pulled up the emergency brake. He got his hands on her hips, what hips there were, and could feel his fingers already tugging her jeans straight down until they bunched at her knees. But she went for him first, before he pulled; she reeked of gin and Scotch and God knows what else. Hands wrapped around the back of his head, she went to kiss him and curls of Marlboro lifted off her tongue. Her stale tongue flailed in his mouth and he could feel hot drunken tears rolling down her cheeks. He thought he was reaching for her jeans again, reaching to pull them down, and found himself instead picking her up the way you would a poodle. He plopped her back down in her own seat.

Stunned—repulsed? or was he repulsed?—she sat still for a second and then began rocking: "I don't care if I have a baby Stew I don't care." Sobbing softly but revving up. "If I get pregnant we'll go to Paris or Greenwich Village or someplace and I can paint and you can take pictures and we'll put the baby in a paper sack if we have to, it doesn't matter," now wailing and hiccoughing, "I'd *like* a baby and anyway I know you want to but please oh please don't start the car oh please."

Truly it was a miracle she didn't get sick then. He himself was dead sober and would rather have been dead. First his hands rested on her hips (slender, curving) and stretched out over her backside (curving, curving); then she sat beside him, a mental patient, rocking and wailing about *babies*. A terrible gurgling groan escaped from deep within his chest. He, two weeks shy of his sixteenth birthday, would have *married* her if that's what she wanted. She pumped her legs in her drunkenness, her little feet dangling and kicking under the dashboard, and he heard her jeans scratch each other, thick as cardboard and crinkly. At the party he'd seen her rest her fingers on S.D.'s forearm.

He drove her home to the godawful new house in godawful Splendid Oaks, wanting the whole drive to slap her silly. He slammed his fist down on the dashboard and saw through her living room window that Mr. Starkey paced in the night, waiting to pounce. Franny was deadweight and he had to drag her, a rag doll, up the walk.

Mr. Starkey seethed in the glow of the front light. He took his daughter the way you might take a load of wash from someone's hands and plopped her down on the floor in front of the Sacred Heart, where Franny stretched out, shuddering. "I'll deal with you later, young lady," he said, in his best deep principal's voice, and then motioned Steward out the door.

"Morehouse," he said, sniffing the air, "I'll have you arrested you ever bring my daughter home drunk again." Steward was mumbling his *sorrys*, mumbling that his grandparents had given a cocktail party. Mr. Starkey could see he was sober. Mr. Starkey was softening, a fist unclenching. They stood together in the December air, Pat Starkey and Steward Morehouse, and maybe they were both picturing the way Franny's flat white belly looked when she lay down under the Sacred Heart and her jeans slipped, all by themselves, down her hips.

"All right, Steward," said her father finally. "You did the right thing to bring her here. Get on home." And then (he must have been picturing the dark shadow around his daughter's long taut navel) he reached out a hand to shake Steward's. "Good man," he said, for some reason, as if he'd been sitting in the back of the car when Steward's hands had rested on the waists of those jeans, two fingers in two belt loops, ready to tug, and instead had driven Franny home.

At St. Benedict's his friends didn't have girlfriends: they'd been to boys' schools all their lives, and at Christmastime the big thrill was to go out on any kind of date at all. Up here he never heard the talk about scoring that had filled the halls of Due East High School. The upperclassmen, the rugby stars or the lacrosse players, might drop a subtle hint that they'd got lucky, but when he compared their restraint to Franny's wailing in the MG he could have wept himself. He was in a schoolful of smooth jovial Bing Crosbys who would never tell, but he was in love with a skinny little temptress.

He was saved from Due East at Easter, when Lola wrote that she'd like to take the both of her boys to New Orleans too. She'd always gone by herself before, but now she wanted to show Nick where she'd lived for the only three months in her life she'd ever been on her own.

It was warm in Louisiana, warm for Easter, warm as home. The first night they headed straight for the Quarter and shouldered through the Friday night crowds. Steward, though he pretended he remembered the city, had only been a little boy when he last saw it. He still felt a little boy, walking between his mother (Lola wore a ruffled gypsy blouse pulled low off her shoulders) and his stepfather (Nick squared his shoulders and acted unimpressed). The touristy crowds looked like the ones he'd seen waiting

on line for the Fort Sumter boat, Southerners and Midwesterners in plaid
slacks and loafers, but every now and again the sidewalk would be filled up
with hippies or, even better, leftover beatniks with wire-rimmed glasses and
sandals. He saw a trio of cocktail waitresses on their way to work: they
hadn't changed yet, but you could see how short their skirts would be from
how tight their dungarees were. His mother, hurrying to work along this
sidewalk.

It was weird to be soused with his parents: Lola, on spike heels, turned
her ankle every time she went to point out *good joints,* and Nick turned his
head after girls who couldn't have been much older than Steward. Lola had
lived right on Bourbon Street, in a room over the bar where she worked.
The old bar had been replaced with a new one—a bad cross between
bluegrass and rock floated out into the street—but she found her old address
right away, and then stared up at a lighted window on the second floor. The
building appeared to be held up by the two adjoining it, its grillwork
chipped and one of its windows taped from the inside, but Steward approved of it more than he did the gussied-up little hotels with the French
names. Fran never would have tolerated their fakey charm. Lola's building
had been painted pink once—freckles showed through the white—and she
reached out one arm to hang off the dark door frame. Her eyes filled.

She pressed the buzzer before Nick or Steward could stop her, or even
imagine what she was up to, and then when a boy showed up in the
doorway, a slight effeminate boy with a paperback book in his hand, she
talked him into letting her upstairs to look around. Steward caught a
glimpse of fading wallpaper in the hallway.

"Jesus, it's loud, can you imagine somebody trying to sleep through the
night around here?" Nick said. Every few seconds he looked up at the
bandaged window, as if he were afraid that Lola was now wrapping her
arms around the frail young man who had let her into the building. Steward
concentrated on a fringed lamp on a windowside table, its glow an eggy
yellow. He couldn't imagine a man buying a lamp like that, even that slight
young man, and after a minute, when his mother appeared by the lamp and
waved down, he imagined Lola buying the lamp before she'd ever met his
father. He imagined his mother standing every night by the fringed lamp,
back when she was a girl, watching the crowds of tourists and waving when
she caught someone's eye.

When he was small in Due East, and lived with his mother on River
Street, Lola used to stare down at the river every night from her bedroom
upstairs. "I used to think I'd travel far and wide," she would say to Steward,

staring out at the black bay. "And look where I ended up for home. Just look where we ended up, sugar."

15 May 1968

Dear Franny,
To tell you the truth I didn't know what to make of your letter; here I've gone for a zillion years not hearing from you and when you finally write you start talking about how much you miss me.

To tell you the truth I have changed a lot this year; it's not just these stupid semicolons Father Rizutti insists on. I was never that interested in politics or philosophy before, but since Albert Camus and the Tet offensive they are just about my main interest; even when I go out to take pictures now, I go looking for political subjects. No more beaches and flowers for me!!! No more Zambonis and maple trees!!!

If she thought he was being contemptuous of her own careful little renderings, the driftwood she spent weeks drawing—copying—he was. The only art there was, as far as he was concerned now, was political art. If Grandfather sent him a check he pored over photography books at the RISD bookstore: Lewis Hines, Dorothea Lange, Walker Evans. Mr. Feely, the lay art teacher who used to be a seminarian but was taking a year to think things over (*I don't know how you'll come to your senses in a place like this,* Steward told him), took a group of boys and drove them around in his old battered station wagon, down through the seediest meanest streets of Providence. They were to call out *Stop* when they wanted to snap a picture or draw. Steward had yelled *Stop* at the Draft Board, a disappointment: it was a tidy storefront, and the print didn't seem to convey the antiwar message he had in mind.

The draft was all anybody talked about at St. Ben's. For English he compared unthinking Due East, sitting on its military bases, to Rome before the fall. The fat cats in town, ringing up the profits of war while the recruits shipped out, recruits who all looked, when he pictured them, like Steward Trey Morehouse Jr. in Grandmother's last portrait: big-eared, ruddy from training, swallowed up in a cap. Ready to step on a mine. Already he and Nick had had it out (*Read Tom Dooley, Stew, if you're so hot on reading about the damn war. Read about the communists sticking chopsticks down people's ears when they've been listening to the truth*).

It troubled him that Franny didn't have a political bone in her body; but he couldn't get his mind off the other bones: the thighbone especially, the way it jutted out just where her garter belt ended and the flesh plumped out.

They spent the summer driving around in Nick's MG, Steward's night license finally legitimate. In June Franny was grading tomatoes at one of the packing sheds, working ten and twelve hours a day, so he only saw her Saturday nights, but by July they could see each other anytime they wanted. He had spending money from Nick and Grandfather, easy money, and Franny, after she gorged herself on paper and paints in Savannah, still had packing-shed checks left over.

They spent their cash on gas and cigarettes and beer when they could find someone to buy it for them, and then they brought their warm beers out with them on the Claire's Point Road. Steward was ticketed once doing eighty-five. He had been doing ninety-five, actually, but he'd smelled the cop around the bend and had time to slow down. Another time a dark sedan pulled off the shoulder to follow him and he outran it: Franny said it was an unmarked deputy's car, but he was never sure. Crazy to outrun a cop. The beer fell flat in the MG's little trunk, all its bubbles punctured, but it didn't matter. Sated with warm flat beer, Steward and Franny walked on a gloppy beach (on the sound, not the ocean), and when they found a dry patch of land they grabbed at each other like lion cubs on a nature special.

What was stopping him? He'd unlatched her bra. He'd suckled her small round breasts. But now Franny was not pressing him—he, who drove a hundred and seven miles an hour and outran cops—to go any further.

They were always scratchy in the sand or damp in the mossy grass. There were always bugs. Once the night turned still and she burrowed her head in his chest, and said what he was thinking: *Creepy*. They both shivered in the night, but it was only a sea turtle who finally emerged from the water to lay her eggs, waddling up the beach like a squat Godzilla.

In August Franny drove off with her family in the station wagon to a cabin in the mountains, and then Steward slept fourteen and sixteen hours a day. His mother seemed to sleep all day too, or else she asked to borrow the MG keys so she could run out to the beach. All August she asked if he'd join her, just for a little dip. All August he shook his head no: the crowd of bikinis around the lifeguard chairs and his mother in her own pink ruffled bikini.

But the day Franny came back from the mountains he told Lola *sure,* he'd drive out to the beach with her. He had a date with Franny that night. He even saw, driving Lola over the bridges and through the marshes, what nice golden legs she had for a mother, her bony knees pulled up high in the little sports car. Franny's legs were muscular and covered with moles, some of them the size of half-dollars.

At the south end of the beach there was a hidden path, and he pulled the car into a patch of trees and went round to open his mother's door. Lola, a gauzy scarf knotted in her black hair and big pink sunglasses sliding down her nose, looked like his date. Steward carried the cooler down for her, down through the pines and the scrub oaks, down through the palmettos and the sea oats, down to the only sand dunes left on this ravaged beach, where he and Franny liked to make out.

And there, halfway up the first low ridge, Steward and his mother stumbled onto a couple poised in mid-embrace, the girl atop the boy, her bikini top flung down on the sand beside her. They were looking up at the sound of approaching footsteps, the boy's eyes rolled back in his head, the girl peering out from under curly dark bangs that brushed her eyelashes.

He didn't believe it even when Lola pressed his arm from behind. He stood rigid in the sand, fifty feet in front of them, while Franny and the boy held their pose. Lola gave a good tug to Steward's elbow and propelled him back to the car, looking for all the world as if she'd been caught in adultery herself, guilty and teary and blushing.

She didn't say a word, though. For once in his life, Lola did not comment, not even when the speedometer went up to eighty-five—in broad daylight—coming home on the beach road.

It was funny, too. For once in his life, he would have paid her a million bucks to yack away.

20 September 1968

Dear Miss Starkey,
To tell you the truth, I think you're just a slut.

At Christmastime Nick was waiting for orders. He said he had a buzz in his ears that made him sure it was his time for Vietnam—*That's all right, I lived through Korea, didn't I?*—and Lola had taken to wearing dark demure dresses, as if she could picture herself a widow already. Steward didn't know where he was supposed to spend his time in the stifling silence of the little brick house. He irritated them when he closed the bedroom door, he rankled them when he bemoaned Eugene McCarthy's fate at the kitchen table. So he spent most of his time cruising Due East, driving in second gear through the backstreets where Gloria lived. He hadn't seen Gloria in a year.

He begged off Grandfather's Christmas party after Grandmother inquired whether the cute little hippie would be coming with him. Dillon's mother still gave a party in the basement, only now it was a New Year's party. Steward, with no intention of going, said he'd think about it.

On New Year's Eve Lola drove him out of the house—*Just give Franny a buzz, just for old times' sake, Stew, you never can tell, she could be watching the phone*—and there was nowhere to go but Dillon's. Driving down the block where he'd found her out the first time gave him the willies.

Dillon's driveway overflowed with station wagons and sedans, and Steward edged the MG up onto the sidewalk. He was still psychic: he knew she hadn't come, not yet, not in one of these family cars. He sat in the car, alone, quiet, under an oak tree whose big roots split the sidewalk underneath him, until another car pulled up. Franny wasn't in it.

The party had bubbled up the stairs into the front hallway, and as he pushed himself in he found that he couldn't remember names to put to most of the faces. Down in the glow of the basement black light it was too dark to tell whether Dillon's mother still kept the house coated in grease and dust. Big Brother and the Holding Company spun around the turntable, and Steward, with no one to talk to, went to play one side over again when it finished: the side with "Piece of My Heart."

Franny showed up after eleven, when Steward had guzzled four beers. She'd grown her hair down to the small of her back and it fluffed out in a wiry mass. S.O.S hair. He couldn't see her running with all that hair, even tied back. She'd brought some guy who had to be a jock, big-shouldered and cheese-faced. The jock appeared to panic as soon as he descended into the purple light: he sniffed the air as if he'd never been to a party before where they were smoking dope in the john and lining up incense sticks by the bathroom door, in case parents showed up.

Steward was talking to S.D., or standing by S.D. anyway, when she first came in. Franny ignored them both but stood in their line of sight. From the hip pocket of her jeans she pulled out a little pewter flask—Steward could see her lifting it from the back room of Jordan Jewelers—and she and the jock passed it back and forth. A slender thread of golden liquid trickled down the corner of her mouth, and she wiped it away with the back of her fist.

Steward and S.D. grinned at each other. The two of us transfixed by this ugly little girl! When she threw a hip in their direction S.D. beat a hasty retreat to the bathroom. Franny stood on tiptoe to whisper something in the big jock's ear and then, her date safely out of the way, sashayed her way over to Steward. The satin halter tied around her neck glowed red and pink and purple in the sheen. Skinnier than ever. Her bare arms were loaded down with cheap bangles and when she came close he saw that chunky beaded earrings dangled. She'd pierced her ears.

"Hey Steward," she said, and slipped into the empty pocket S.D. had left beside him.

"Hey Franny." He focused on her eyes, inky green in the violet light, so that he wouldn't look at her nose, or at her full bare mouth.

"Walter misses you," she said, and reached a hand up to rest it on his shoulder. He took in her dark musky smell and saw the jock, a bottle of Fresca clenched in his beefy fist, eyeing them, and began composing the letter he'd write when he was back safe at school.

You were, like, so fakey Franny, like the way my mother used to be when she was first married to Nick and she used to try to snuggle up to him all the time, like even when he was trying to make a pot of coffee or tune the TV or just trying to live.

You know, when you used to flirt with all those guys I used to want to just kill you, I used to want to run my fist through the windshield, I used to want to drive across your front lawn.

Hey, I did drive across your front lawn. Well don't worry, I'm not so earnest anymore.

He never wrote the letter. He didn't write her again for months, not until he dashed off the last letter he would send her from St. Benedict's, a letter he wrote with his temperature good and high and his breathing nice and steady, a letter that said how sorry he was to hear about her father and included a postscript:

P.S. Don't worry about me or anything. I've got a girlfriend up here, so that's o.k. If you ever need to call me or anything, just go ahead and I'll know it's as a friend.

There was no girlfriend. But he was traveling with the debate team now, and taking a course in super 8 filmmaking, and reading sometimes until dawn, reading J. D. Salinger and then flinging the paperback against his wall. All that religious crap. He knew she wouldn't write back.

And besides, there was his mother, alone now in Due East, practically banished from the River Street house, she said, watching Walter Cronkite every night and calling him up when she thought she'd seen Nick's face on the screen. She was always seeing Nick's face on the screen: Steward told her all Marines looked alike under their helmets. He'd tried to get her to join one of the wives' clubs, but Lola scoffed. *Can you just see me,* she said, *crocheting doilies?* So now he sent his mother ten- and twelve-page letters and she answered them back, the same day, in her sloping fluttery script. Now her letters smelled of Colt 45, or Boone's Farm apple wine. *I'm out of my mind worrying about my two sweethearts,* she'd write, *so far away.*

It was almost like getting his childhood back, when here he was, the one who got served three bourbons on Bourbon Street, night license in his wallet, almost old enough to be drafted himself:

I don't know whether it makes me want to giggle or cry sometimes, Lola wrote, *thinking that here you are, that little baby I carried all the way from New Iberia on the Greyhound bus, just about a man.*

DO IT
HARDER

The morning her father collapsed on the stage of the Due East High School gymnasium, Franny Starkey sat high in the bleachers. Her father hadn't collapsed yet—he wasn't even onstage yet, he was shepherding stragglers through the gym doors—and she wasn't looking down on her father anyway.

She was looking down on David Brow, a six-four basketball player who was entirely unaware that the close-cropped dirty-blond curls fringing his forehead made him a Michelangelo. Now that basketball season was over, Franny's only chance to gaze on David from a distance was in assembly.

For the last three Friday nights she had gone with David Brow to the Pinelawn Drive-in, where she'd had a chance to finger his David measurements and pretend that her own were Bathshebalike. She had thought of sculpting him in marble, though she'd never sculpted anything but clay in her life, and wasn't nearly as good at it as she was at drawing. Now she was ready to chip away. At the Pinelawn Drive-in she'd learned that David Brow was crazy for James Bond, that he used the copious splashes of aftershave all basketball players favored, and that the sweetness he affected in the front hallway of Due East High School at lunchtime was probably for real. When he stood among the other tall guys in lettered jackets, he was the one with his eyes averted.

From the top row of the bleachers, she watched him lean closer to hear a joke from the basketball player next to him and slap his thigh in appreciation. They were all like that, basketball players, pole vaulters, third basemen: their curls fringed their foreheads, they slapped their thighs, they flirted with Franny in the front hallway and then as an afterthought asked her if she was doing anything Friday night. The principal's daughter.

Now Franny's father was approaching the microphone to introduce the guest speaker, a reformed alcoholic and resident of the state penitentiary, who was about to address Due East High School on the subject of that first can of beer taken all in fun. Franny, hearing about the assembly this morning at the breakfast table, had begged Pat to cancel—*Not that oily guy with his short sleeves rolled up! They've had him for three years running*—but Pat said he only booked the gym for the guidance department, he had to trust their judgment. He raised his right eyebrow in a pretty clear indication of what he really thought of their inviting Mr. Jonah Judson again.

Now they were all captives. Franny watched David Brow stretch his long legs under the chair in front of him. He was talking to the friend on his left from the corner of his mouth and scanning the bleachers at the same time but his eyes never met hers. It did not occur to Franny that he might have been talking about her, that he might have been telling the other curl-fringed basketball player about how last Friday night, after the movies, they drove out to the tiny Goat Island graveyard, where the reclining marble slabs were as good as beds.

Franny watched her father swing the microphone in that practiced, easy way of his. Pat Starkey ignored the bedlam around him, the senior marshals flying on and off the stage to shake hands with an actual convict from the state penitentiary, the cacophony from the folding chairs and the bleachers down below. Pat Starkey began all assemblies with a befuddled, apologetic air—*May I have your attention please*—followed by the same patience that presided over the Starkey family supper table every night. He had perfected a joke-every-third-assembly-or-so routine that quieted everybody down (today might be the day) and when he stood at the mike in his gray suit, a little baggy at the knees, a little shiny at the elbows, he fixed a quizzical half-smile on his mouth. The principal and the coach and the dad and the emcee who might have a joke today.

Pat Starkey had been David Brow's basketball coach in junior high school. Her father said, the first Friday night David came over to pick her up, that he was a sweet guy. That was the kind of expression Pat Starkey used about his old basketball players: *sweet guy, spunky fellow, good man.*

And David Brow was all of the above and didn't even smoke cigarettes, much less pot. Franny had been drifting toward the jocks—for about five minutes she'd thought there might be something a little harsher, sharper-edged about them—but it turned out that the ones she flirted with were like all the others after all, even like Tony Rivers, who was probably the least sweet of all these sweet boys. In the last two years, Franny had been proposed to by ten boys including Tony Rivers and David Brow, the same number of sixteen- and seventeen- and eighteen-year-old boys she had convinced to make love to her. Anyway it always seemed to her that that was what she was doing, convincing, even Tony Rivers, because they were so hesitant and apologetic and they always asked her to marry them before they got down to it, and they ignored her when she said she didn't *mind* if she had a baby. They went to the bathroom in the Rebel or in Thornton's, the juke joint up the Yemassee Road, and they came back with neat squares of foil tucked into their back pockets, and they made sure she didn't get pregnant. They watched out for her and never turned away when they met her in the hallways, but sometimes put their long arms around her shoulder and squeezed her little frame up close to their big ones. They followed her lead, which Steward would never do, but still her father called them good men.

And it was a good thing too that they were good men, because she would have had ten or twelve children by now if it was up to her. Coach Legs Hornhart, in a real heart-to-heart with the girls' track team, said that generally girls' sex drives weren't as strong as boys', unless they had hormonal imbalances, but Franny could tell from Coach's twitching muscled thighs, not to mention from personal experience, that this just wasn't so no matter how much Legs denied it. Kate had no patience for her when she said she couldn't help herself. Kate gave her head a sad shake if Franny said she was in search of a Grand Passion, or Living in the Moment. *What if you get pregnant?*

If she got pregnant by David Brow her mother would have a nervous breakdown and her father would be truly befuddled, and everyone including David Brow would expect that she was going to marry him, but she wouldn't. She would bring the baby to a garret in Paris and Steward would hate her even more than he did now. Didn't he deserve to? Her belly burned with her betrayal of Steward. But if she were pregnant he would use his hatred to propel himself to Paris and at the sight of her baby—a baby girl, dark-haired and fair-skinned like her, but with a longer face and sharper, jutting features—he would forgive her everything and stay with her to Live in the Moment too. At which point she would stop smoking pot and swinging her hips for the likes of David Brow, sweet and beautiful but limited to, let's face it, James Bond. It was just as Steward said. Nobody in Due East knew there was a war going on, or love-ins in San Francisco, or riots in the streets of Paris. David Brow had no idea what was happening in the world.

"May I have your attention, please," Pat Starkey said, patient and, yes, befuddled. Stirs and rustles glided through the gym, and Mr. Starkey waited.

"Students and teachers of Due East High School—"

Franny could tell that today would be a joke day because Pat was curling his fingers over the top of the lectern. "I had the pleasure of visiting a senior English class this week," Pat said, and the whole gym settled like a sheet shaken out. "I had the pleasure of hearing Mr. Church repeat a line . . ."

Franny resumed watching the senior section, where chortles and chuckles now rose from Mr. Church's senior English class.

". . . now none of you seniors answer this, hear?—What do a grave-yard and a bathroom have in common?"

Bathroom jokes were not Pat Starkey's style, and his voice went up, fluty, at the end of his question. Franny could not say for the rest of her life whether it was the incongruity of the joke when Mr. Jonah Judson, re-formed convict, waited in the wings, or whether it was the way her father's fingers flew off the lectern as he finished speaking, that told her Pat Starkey was sick. *Something* caused her to grip the bleacher plank beneath her and to hold her breath.

Her father appeared to be holding his breath too. The audience didn't know anything was wrong, busy as they were calling out guesses. "They both stink!" somebody yelled. No one could hear the seniors giving away the real answer:

When you gotta go, you gotta go.

Pat remained at the lectern, fingers curled now close to his chest as if he were tugging at his lapels, and did not answer the chorus of guessed punch lines. Thirty seconds passed, and then sixty, but this was patient Mr. Starkey after all, and the general pandemonium continued.

Franny rose and saw that across the gym floor her brother Will had risen too. "Scuse me," she said to the backs in her way. She climbed down through yielding shoulders—"Scuse me"—and heard her father say *Excuse me* in an eerie echo from the stage. Pat Starkey was turning his face away from a thousand clamorous adolescents.

"Excuse me," her father said again, this time in a whisper the micro-phone barely registered, and the audience hushed, section by section. Franny by now had reached the side steps of the gym stage and her father weaved in front of her, arms crossed across his chest, trying still to make a dignified retreat to the wings and the waiting Jonah Judson. Franny thought he'd been poisoned: in the seconds it took her to skip the steps and reach his elbow she thought that Doris had that very morning served him a—what? bad egg? piece of toast coated in arsenic butter?—and she saw that her brothers Will and Martin were by now running toward the stage too, bypassing the steps to vault it from the center of the floor. Martin, who was only fourteen, charged once he had his feet solidly on the stage and knocked over the lectern en route to his father. The microphone clanged and then shrieked feedback in the cavernous gym.

Someone official must have righted the lectern and unplugged the mike, because all at once silence floated cloudlike through the gym again, and Pat Starkey shook his bowed head back and forth. "Phew!" he said. "Phew!" and then (looking at the circle now gathered around him in the back corner of the stage, a circle linking his three children to Mr. Jonah Judson, Jonah Judson's guard, the assistant principal, the guidance counselor, and Legs Hornhart, who had streaked through the gym in her scarlet shorts) Pat Starkey said: "Some heartburn!" in a cheerful voice he was trying to pitch low. Balance back, he reached a hand out to squeeze Martin's shoulder and then turned to wave to the audience, who cheered and applauded and stomped their feet.

Triumphant politician, Pat Starkey made a single step back toward the righted lectern when his legs buckled and he sat himself right down—splat —center stage, looking so truly puzzled that Franny understood for the first time what a pose that befuddled look had been all these years.

His lips were a chalky blue and they all lowered themselves to their haunches—Jonah Judson, guard, three Starkey children, guidance counselor, assistant principal, girls' coach—but Pat Starkey did not try to speak. Legs Hornhart took over.

"Run!" she said to the assistant principal. "Ambulance. Marines. Anything!" and with her bare tanned muscular arm she swept the Starkey children, like dustballs, away from their father. Legs single-handedly laid their father down on the stage and began to give him mouth-to-mouth resuscitation, which she taught the freshmen every fall. Franny knelt at his feet, Will and Martin paced behind them. Franny squeezed her father's rubber sole in rhythm with Legs's breathing and then, when Legs straddled Pat and began pumping his chest, wiggled her father's toes inside his coach's Hush Puppies, as if waking his foot might cure what ailed him. First Will, then Martin, came to hunch down by their father, both of them breathing hard enough to fill his lungs and their own and a blimp besides, if a blimp had been on the scene.

Early on Jonah Judson offered Legs his advice—"Do it HARDER, ma'am, push down HARDER. Don't his throat need clearing?"—but Legs did not so much as raise her head in acknowledgment. Maybe she was pushing down harder (now she was pounding Pat Starkey's chest, fist over fist; now she was breathing into his mouth again), but for the entire twelve minutes it took for an ambulance to get there Franny knew, and Legs Hornhart knew, and her brothers Will and Martin knew, that Pat Starkey was dying. Only Jonah Judson's guard did not seem to know what would happen next: he stalked his prisoner, waiting for Jonah to make a run for it.

Pat Starkey did not die there, though, not on the stage of the Due East High School gymnasium. Legs Hornhart kept his heart pumping long enough for the ambulance to get there; and the ambulance attendants kept his heart pumping long enough to get him to the emergency room; and the doctor there, Dr. Black, the doctor who had delivered all nine Starkeys including brain-damaged Walter, kept Pat Starkey's heart beating long enough for Franny and William and Martin and Doris, dragging the twins behind her, to huddle in the corridor together while the doctor and the nurses tried to do what Legs Hornhart had tried to do. The last words Franny and William and Martin had heard their father say were *Some heartburn.*

The last image Franny had seen before she climbed the stage steps was David Brow, half-rising from his folding chair, seeing that she and her father needed help. Just a sweet guy who'd asked her to marry him last Friday night.

Walter drove them all crazy. Doris sat him down in the emergency waiting room that day and told him his daddy was dead of a heart attack, and ever since then he had been trying to get things straight. He pictured an army hacking away inside his father's chest. No one had the patience for him when he said:

"Was it like a land mine?" or "Was it like flak?"

He had been watching the news, the only one in the family who did now that Pat was gone. After five o'clock supper, Walter set himself up in the living room with a glass of grape Kool-Aid and a box of Ritz crackers, and waited in front of a blank screen until CBS came on at six-thirty. Then he switched to NBC at seven, the way his father had every night. He stretched out on the rug in the dark glow of the television to watch the little black-and-white set, and he rattled off a running commentary on rocket launchers and M-16s, Hueys and transports and Viet Cong and claymore mines. No one else could bear to stay in the room with him—Pat had watched two news shows every night of his adult life—but one or the other of the children would pass through, checking up. Walter stood when the soldiers flashed on the screen, cheering them on the way he'd seen his father cheer on the basketball team, and once when Franny and Caroline stood behind him he called out to the Americans:

"Cong's up in the trees! Watch out for them trees!"

The next image on the little set was the smoke trail of sniper fire from the trees, and Caroline let out a hopeless gasp.

"It was snipey fire, wadn't it?" Walter said the next day, meaning the attack in Pat Starkey's heart. Will and Martin and Paul wrestled him to the rug when he said something like that, squeezing him in bear hugs, close to throttling him. Albert, his twin, ignored him. But the girls were at a loss: Caroline burst out sobbing and keening at the mention of her father, who hadn't had much time for her. Franny's eyes went dull.

There was something wrong with her stomach, and had been ever since her father died. You could hear it sloshing across the room in Spanish I (Madame Queval had given up on her in French) and one day Señorita Baker said: "Consuela"—her Spanish name—"honey, go get you something to eat. Just go on down to the cafeteria and tell Mizz Washington I sent you to get some food on your stomach. She'll rustle up something."

The freshmen in the class thought Franny's rising funny (now the sloshing was a wave breaking offshore) until they remembered that Consuela Starkey's stomach was storming because her father was dead, and that he'd been struck down in the middle of a joke, and then they sobered up and cast their eyes back down on their dialogues. Of course Franny did not go to the cafeteria at all—she went back out to the parking lot where she could smoke a cigarette—but even the deadbeats cutting class out there cast their eyes down when they saw her coming.

They all cast their eyes down. For a couple of weeks David Brow and the basketball players, the guys who ran track, even S.D. and Harrison and Dillon, had touched her when she walked by, reached out an arm and drawn her close. They all came to the funeral and watched Franny drag the keening Caroline down the aisle. They'd met Franny's eyes then, they'd looked straight at her with sweet eyes, browns and blues and hazels and grays, boy eyes that were bloodshot and ached for her. She was sure they were aching for her. David Brow was there with his whole family, sitting by the aisle, and he reached out a hand to brush her sleeve when she passed by.

For weeks in the front hall they drew her close, the jocks or S.D. or Harrison or Dillon. For weeks they went through clever contortions to turn her around so she wouldn't see when Mr. Anderson, the jolly plump new principal, was making the rounds. But after a while their eyes wandered to the ceiling when she was walking up the B hall, past the principal's office. She didn't know what they pictured when they saw her coming (or when they heard her belly rolling out an entrance march), but she knew what she was picturing for the first time: the used rubbers they dropped out their car doors or left in the graveyard at Goat Island.

She hadn't been on a date in two months. What did they think she was, a war widow? Didn't they know that she wouldn't make a move *now,* not now while her stomach gurgled and her eyes were so dull they couldn't even see color anymore and all she could think about was poor lackbrain Walter trying to figure out what kind of attack had gone on in Pat Starkey's heart?

At least the rest of her brothers were holding themselves in check, being sweeter to Doris than they had ever been while Pat was alive. Will and Martin and Paul played baseball all spring: they were all three pitchers and now they were teaching Albert to pitch the way Pat had taught them. They got themselves up at the crack of dawn to toss a few before breakfast, and they stayed out back to work on their fastballs long past dusk, long past the time Walter had turned off both his news shows and come outside to watch them. They tried to be patient with him (you could see their temples straining) but every time Will threw a strike Walter would yell:

"Bam! Wham! Heart attack!"

and they would come at him yelling, and wrestle him to the ground.

AgnesAnn and Teresa were both still up at the university, the loan that paid their semester's tuition covered by insurance. AgnesAnn, when she came home for the funeral, got out a legal pad and figured out how she and Teresa could get jobs in the cafeteria and apply for student loans and get by until they got degrees, but Doris shook her finger at Franny, the next in line. *He's not here now,* she said, *to get you into some fancy art school that doesn't care about your grades. Franny, you've got to pull yourself together! You've got to start passing your courses so you can get you into Carolina, anyway. And how will we pay for that? Blessed Christ Jesus, how ever will we pay for that?*

AgnesAnn soothed her mother with talk of Social Security and veterans' money and the student employment office. She had calculated on the legal pad that they'd already spent five thousand dollars of the insurance money, and the thirty thousand left would have to be invested if the boys were ever going to go to college. The investment might yield an income of two thousand dollars a year, and she pointed out helpfully that this was not enough to live on.

Doris stared at the pad in utter lack of comprehension. They'd had *life* insurance. If she sold Tupperware or Avon, she might make another two thousand dollars a year. The new mortgage was uninsured—insurance would have pushed the payments into the stratosphere, she'd thought at the time—and AgnesAnn noted that since Doris had taken over the checkbook there were three errors in subtraction totaling two hundred and twenty-six dollars. In the bank's favor. At the rate they were going through cash, they would use up the insurance money inside of a year.

Since they'd finished up the fried chicken and the roasts from the Mothers Club at Our Lady of Perpetual Help, the Starkey children had been eating TV dinners for the first time in their lives. Doris said she could not face the kitchen. When AgnesAnn and Teresa came home for spring break, they even went down to Ralph's on a Wednesday night at five o'clock. They were the only ones in the restaurant, but Ralph said it was worth staying open to serve the Starkeys ten hamburgers and ten fries and ten Cocolas and ten pecan pies. Back home, AgnesAnn drew her mother into the bedroom once again and brought out the legal pad, and lectured Doris on the importance of finding a job. A little squeak sounded from the direction of Doris's folding closet doors, and they heard Walter through the louvers.

"We're broke," he said, as AgnesAnn had said.

AgnesAnn barked. "Walter, how the hell did you get in there?"

"Language," Doris said, and Walter emerged from the closet beaming.

"Oh AgnesAnn," Doris said, and began to weep. "OH GET HIM OUT OF HERE. The poor little thing. The poor innocent little thing, spying on our money talk. We'll have to go back to Mama and Daddy's house, I spose."

"MAMA!" AgnesAnn said. "You make my toenails curl. The twins would have to sleep in the bathtub, or the doghouse. And where would *we* sleep when we come home to do your checkbook?"

Walter asked to see his sister's curled toenails. Doris renewed her weeping and wailing.

Her sisters did not invite Franny to join in their planning strategies. They had decided on school for her, once she was finished at Due East High: they wanted her to give up the idea of art school, and join them at the university, and work in the cafeteria. She could already smell frankfurters in a huge pot. She could already picture the yellow circles of fat on the water's surface.

Before he died, her father had sent her to Mrs. Hopper, a stout elderly guidance counselor who'd lined up catalogues with relish. The first time they met, Mrs. Hopper spread only art school catalogues on her desk: South Carolina College of Art, Richmond Professional Institute, Rhode Island School of Design. Mrs. Hopper knew nothing about art, and there was only one part-time art teacher in all Due East High School, but if Pat Starkey said her portfolio would get her in, her portfolio would get her in. Then after Pat died, she had Franny take her College Boards, just to cover all the bases, and called her into her office when the scores came back:

"Frances?"

"Yes ma'am."

"Frances Starkey, have we been playing a little game here at Due East High School?"

Franny looked down at the scores and pretended not to see the percentiles next to them.

"Frances, your math is mediocre."

"Yes ma'am."

"But your verbals are high. Extremely high!"

Franny hung her head.

"You know, your dad would have been delighted."

"Yes ma'am."

"Sit down, Frances."

Franny sat, her head still hanging low, swept away by a tide of shame. Mrs. Hopper, who'd always had the good grace to chuckle at her bad grades, sat clucking her tongue at the verbal score. A child who barely passed English and history and failed French, but that was the least of it: not a single teacher had come forth to say *This one has talent* or *It's only that she's lazy, or dreamy, or boy-crazy.* Even her father had never said it.

"Frances," Mrs. Hopper said, "you know this score means that if you chose to exert yourself you wouldn't have to go to art school." She made art school sound like the slow classes.

Franny saw herself in a long green dress with purple tights and black pointed shoes, her hair hanging down in two dark braids and her eyelids painted charcoal gray. She saw a studio big as the gym, with light streaming in, and an aisle of easels manned by swarthy painters who carried their canvases on the backs of their motorcycles. Tony Rivers had somehow convinced his parents to send him off to the bowels of Brooklyn and had sent her a single postcard, a drawing of the first man to jump off the Brooklyn Bridge, telling her that she should come to Pratt too. She didn't know about Brooklyn, or about Tony Rivers for that matter, but there were a slew of art schools up and down the coast that could take her. Her father had said they would with utter certainty. She had a portfolio of fifty pen-and-ink drawings with more detail than the expression on Mrs. Hopper's face at just this moment.

"Now we know that you are capable of getting yourself a *liberal* arts education," Mrs. Hopper said, "and learning how to discuss the great ideas intelligently. When you're out in the world."

Franny fought an urge to cross her eyes and saw Steward, off in his boarding school, sifting through college catalogues. She had half a mind to slice out the pages of some of these art school photography programs and send them to him in the mail, anonymously. Sometimes she borrowed the family car to creep past his house again, hoping to cross Lola's path.

"What you say, honey?" Mrs. Hopper said. "This little number right here"—she pointed a magnificent fuchsia fingernail at the ninety-ninth percentile—"changes everything. What you say if I line up some good liberal arts catalogues for you and you can start thinking about visiting some other schools in the fall. Some good girls' schools, maybe!"

Now Franny did cross her eyes. HER FATHER HAD READ LI-BRARY BOOKS ALOUD EVERY NIGHT FOR SIXTEEN YEARS, YOU'D HAVE TO BE A TOTAL MORON NOT TO HEAR ANY OF IT and she'd been reading herself every night since Steward wrote, reading Camus for Christsake, and she'd always done well on standardized tests, her father knew that, why hadn't anyone else looked up the scores. Mrs. Hopper had swiveled her chair around to grab up a handful of catalogues from Sweet Briar and Agnes Scott and Hollins, schools where she thought Franny would be safe now that she had no father to watch over her. Franny smiled pleasantly at the catalogue covers with girls in cardigans strolling across landscaped quads and said:

"I don't think my mother could afford something like *that.*"

Mrs. Hopper saw her point. "Well," she said. "They certainly won't want to give you lots of money if the math doesn't pick up the next time around. But look here, Franny, I want you to consider giving that math your all. Put a little axle grease in there next time, honey! Try! Your father would have been *so* proud. And now listen, don't you dare dare tell them I told you, but you topped AgnesAnn and Teresa both by a mile. On the verbals."

Franny repeated a flash of her pleasant smile—Mrs. Hopper trusted her about as much as any of her other teachers trusted her—and promised that she would think about different colleges. She intended to apply to every art school on the East Coast and to art schools in Paris too, if she could get S.D. to tell her where the hell you would look to get the addresses of art schools in Paris.

But she heard only dire warnings from Teresa:

"Don't you dare put more pressure on Mama talking about art school. Look at the tuition in those catalogues if you don't know what I'm talking about."

Teresa said darkly that a scholarship would never buy her food or a bed to sleep in. Teresa's bed, at the university, was a lumpy mattress on a steel frame in the cheapest residence hall on campus, the one where girls who had no hope of making a sorority stayed.

And AgnesAnn called weekly from her dorm to pester Doris about asking for a job in the Due East schools: "You've got to ask them now, Mama, while they still feel sorry for us." At the mention of a job Doris (who in twenty years of raising nine children had taken to her bed only for childbirth) fell ill with a mystery virus and lay twisting and turning for three weeks. She had never learned to type. She could barely add up a column of figures.

Franny should have been the one to take over the household while her mother was sick, but tomato season started in May and she was working in the packing shed most school nights. She stood at a conveyor belt pitching green waxed tomatoes onto the cull belts for a dollar eight-five an hour. Facing a sea of unripe tomatoes, she thought she might lose her sense of vision. All night and the next day too she could smell the wax they brushed on the tomatoes and the grease they glopped on the conveyor belts and the culls they burned out back. She stood alone, mostly, in the smelly heat: Kate, who had always worked at her side, was gone.

But David Brow worked in the same shed she did and on the first working Saturday in June he even asked her out, her first date in a million years. They drove all the way to Thornton's together in their work clothes. In the crowded parking lot she offered him a joint but he shook his head no, embarrassed, and she stuffed it deep into a pocket.

It had been a hot Saturday in the shed and it was a hot and sticky night at Thornton's, an L-shaped room carved out of cinder block and lighted with long rows of fluorescent bulbs. The sorority girls, in their green linen skirts and Papagallo flats, were home from college for the weekend. They cut their hair so that it brushed their nipples, and Franny watched David watching blondes. His pink mouth hung open just slightly. She was in a pair of patched cutoffs, her hair twisted back and tied with a rubber band she'd begged off the foreman. A muddy rivulet ran down the inside of her calf.

David brought her beer after beer—no one checked IDs at Thornton's—and when he disappeared to slap thighs with some of his teammates Franny rose and pushed her way to the edge of the dance floor. She began circling the edge of the crowd, a light euphoria bouncing her, balloonlike, and soon she had worked her way to the center of the floor. She was dancing. Couples melted away as she rolled her hips to "Louie, Louie." After a while, doing a slow undulation with her hands atop her head, she was the only one on the dance floor, and she was shameless as Ricky Ricardo: that's what she was, a hot Cuban Consuela in cutoff jeans, surrounded by a circle of blondes and their surfers. She caught sight of David Brow just as the music faded, applauding and whooping with the others, and she had time to wiggle her hips into a bow before the next record came up.

On the ride home she realized that David Brow hadn't danced a single slow dance with her and then she felt her bra strap, yellowing, unwashed, slipping down her arm. She began to smell the packing shed, the rich deep rotten culls as they burned, a slice against her nostrils, and she threw up. First time in her life, drinking. David Brow's car weaved down the two-lane highway and she retched all over the floor of his blue Chevy Malibu. She felt the heat of the Malibu's engine and the heat of the packing shed where they spent their days and the heat of sweet David Brow, who for some reason grinned the entire time she was sick and then peeled his shirt off in her driveway so she could wipe her mouth. Her skin crawled against his damp shirt, so suffused with the essence of boy that she began to weep into it.

With Franny gone at the packing shed, it was Caroline who cooked and packed up the lunches, and Will who got the others to wash their own clothes. Walking to school together, the Starkey boys were a column of wrinkles. When she came in from work, Franny, who could not bear to hear her brothers carping at each other in the kitchen, went and sat by her mother's bedside. Doris had worked herself into a fever every day for three weeks, though Franny, seeing the thermometer on the night table under the lamp, suspected that her mother had learned from her own children how to hold the mercury close to the lightbulb. She would not go see Dr. Black.

When the university let out for the summer, AgnesAnn and Teresa came home to sponge their mother down and take her temperature properly. AgnesAnn wrested immediate control of the household, banging on a saucepan with a spoon to wake them all at six-thirty and otherwise gonging all day. She made her mother depart the sickbed, but even up and around Doris was pale with terror. It rained all May, then all June, and when Franny came home from the packing shed in midafternoon, the day's work called off, she found her pallid mother sitting on the back steps in Pat's big yellow raincoat, staring out past the magnolia tree. Even AgnesAnn could not stop Doris from doing that.

In the evening the twins would creep out back to join their mother, and one of them would put a palm to her cheek, or stroke her back, wordless. Albert liked to kiss his mother on the lips and Franny, chilled at the sight of them, might even retreat to help Caroline with the dishes. Caroline whispered over the sink that Doris's afternoon naps stretched out to two and three hours, even with AgnesAnn home to shoo her out of bed. "It's a laugh a minute around here," Franny said, but then relented and put an arm around her sister's shoulders. Caroline's lower lip, stained with the remains of a twelve-year-old's cheap lipstick, quivered in the fluorescent kitchen light.

Their mother was a ghoul. Some days Caroline wept for forty-five minutes nonstop. Some days Walter roamed the neighborhood, disappearing into dark cool houses for hours. One afternoon in June—more lightning, more rain—she came home from the shed and found four cans of cheap canned spaghetti all glopped together in a big saucepan on the stove. There was a salad of Due East cucumbers and a platter of hush puppies set out on the sideboard. Signifying what? No one had made hush puppies since March. AgnesAnn was painting on black eyeliner in the downstairs bathroom and Franny's lip curled in disgust, even after her sister told her Doris's news, the cause of this celebration: AgnesAnn had called the superintendent, telling him in her businesslike manner of their desperate straits, and Dr. Morrisey had invented a job answering telephones at the Due East School for Exceptional Children, Walter's school. She and Teresa had that very morning driven Doris to the first job interview of her life, and their mother was now gainfully employed. She would start in September.

Franny stared at AgnesAnn, who had gone back to stroking on black eyeliner, the wrong color altogether for her pale eyelids and light lashes. She herself had not worn eye makeup since March. Her white T-shirt, one of her brother's, reeked of sweat. Didn't anyone believe in mourning anymore? Now her mother had a job. Now AgnesAnn thought she could go back to painting herself.

That night the boys smelled their mother's spaghetti and quit their baseball early, and when they were all squeezed in at the old formal table, all ten of them for the first time in weeks, Doris said grace for five minutes (she thanked Saints Elizabeth and Ann but especially the Virgin Mary; she thanked AgnesAnn and Teresa and Caroline and Franny, for sitting by her bedside; she thanked the Superintendent and the Principal who had resigned, allowing Pat Starkey to know the joy of principalship before he departed this life; she thanked the Mothers Club of Our Lady of Perpetual Help for being kind enough not to visit her with their judgment; she thanked Walter for being blessed with a lack of understanding) and then, having lost her train of thought, told them:

"I didn't get me that job. He is looking out for us, children. He is up in heaven looking out for us." Walter announced that they would all watch the news that night, and nobody even put up a fuss. They went through the spaghetti and the hush puppies in five minutes, Franny clever enough to move the fork from her plate to her mouth at regular intervals.

"C'mon," Walter said, gracious and smiling when the clock read six-thirty. He ushered them from the kitchen table. "C'mon everybody."

Franny, sticky and dazed from the morning of standing on her feet, filed out with the rest of them to sit in the dim living room for Walter, but she rose again when the news broadcast began with the suicide of Judy Garland. Doris was instantly weeping into her palm, her new job forgotten. Already Will and Martin and Paul were shifting in their seats. She could not bear it.

"Hey!" Walter said, seeing her slip out. "Hey! The war's on next!"

Franny waved good-bye to Walter and blew him a kiss, but already he had turned back to the screen. The others had not even registered her departure. They did not register her presence anymore, either.

She walked outside to bright summer evening, meaning to smoke the roach hidden deep in her pocket. Her stomach sloshed louder than ever (the bite of canned spaghetti? the single cucumber she'd held in her mouth?) and her legs, for the first time in her life, were flaccid. Puddings. She'd quit the track team after the funeral and had stopped running altogether; if she were eating anything she'd be fat by now, but she wasn't eating. She was never hungry when she had a joint to smoke: other people got the munchies, but she went into hibernation. It was getting harder and harder, though, to buy from Harrison or Dillon. Harder to act innocent when they didn't want to sell her a dime, when they lectured her on how fast she went through the stuff. She'd finished the year with six C-minuses, when she'd aimed for six F's. Sympathy grades. Now Mrs. Hopper would still be on her back to apply to other colleges.

Nowadays there weren't many fathers out on the street: Captain North next door was in Vietnam and so was the warrant officer up the block. But tonight there was one playing catch with his son, one overweight father in his forties with his white shirt gapping at the middle and an old leather belt straining to hold up his pants. He still wore his lace-up work shoes—she didn't know his name, but he would be a civilian with a desk job out at one of the bases—and he threw the ball with a practiced air. Father and son had good weathered Rawlings outfielder gloves and the father showed off his catching, backhanding as Franny slouched by. He held his pitch until she passed close and then he said *Evening* and nodded, but that was only because her father was dead.

In the summer breeze the stop sign at the end of the street vibrated and her skin crawled. If she went down to the creek she could smoke the joint and walk home sleepy and red-eyed and crawl into bed while the family went about its business, washing dishes and seeing that younger brothers got baths and poking Q-Tips down ears and gargling and hauling loads of wash down to the kitchen. It wasn't just because she worked in the packing shed that they exempted her from these chores: they exempted her the way they exempted Doris, because they thought her eyes were red-rimmed from tears. But they'd made Doris go and get a job, hadn't they?

And they'd have worse in store for her.

She began to jog down the street, out of breath by the time she crossed the Broad Creek Road. That morning before work she had dialed Steward to see if he was home for the summer, and when he answered she had crashed the receiver down. For three nights running she'd been sleepwalking, the way Walter used to sleepwalk, only she had gone to Doris's bed. *Doris's bed.*

She didn't even wait to get to the creek to light up, but sucked at her roach right on the street. She could smoke ten joints tonight, or twenty. Let that all-American dad up the block call the Due East Police. As she walked along, the first tokes settled right into the folds of her brain: she felt the tubing in her head straightening as she neared the creek, as she stopped to watch the summer-night light settle on the creek scum. Mosquitoes and gnits swarmed close but did not bite. She watched the water blacken and saw that convict Jonah Judson telling Legs Hornhart to

"Push down *harder, ma'am*. Push *harder*."

She relighted the roach and burned her index finger, a good cleansing singe: cool, not hot. There was only a scrap of Bambu paper left but she uncreased it anyway and touched the last sweep wisps of pot to her tongue. A sweet kiss. A sweet boy.

Dillon's house was only a couple of miles away. He'd give her a joint for the night, she knew he'd have one, and when Teresa drove her to work in the morning she could stop by with the cash for a dime. Teresa thought they stopped at Dillon's house three times a week so Franny could borrow cassette tapes.

She strolled along, considering a two-mile run after all these months and smelling for the first time the summer air. It had a faintly sweet and fetid odor, like the smell of dead bugs collected in light fixtures. Oh she was stoned all right. She turned herself around slowly, like the family station wagon doing a three-point turn, and began to run without a single stretch to loosen up. Running toward town. She pumped her pudding legs down on the asphalt toward Dillon's house. No one at home would even know she was gone. They would hear in two separate newscasts that Judy Garland had committed suicide. Two separate broadcasters would say that she had followed the yellow brick road. Doris had a job, and she was running again.

Her legs were red-hot pistons, her knees shining white. She might as well have been running to New York or Paris, for the effort it cost her. She could not remember that she had ever run, much less set the school half-mile record at the beginning of the season this year. Certainly she had never run into the wind while her barefoot father, trouser legs rolled up, held a stopwatch.

Her hair coiled out as she ran, coiled like the springs on a mattress. Like the springs on Tony Rivers's mattress, like the springs on Teresa's old mattress in her cheap dorm room. Her legs pumped, her hair coiled. Like the springs on her own bed when Walter used to crawl in, like the springs somewhere deep in the guts of Due East High School that held the gym stage up when they laid out her father and pushed harder and harder and harder.

She saw now that Jonah Judson was an omen, that if only she'd convinced her father not to let Jonah Judson speak, Pat Starkey would be alive tonight. She'd known something was wrong. She'd been the first to know.

She was only back at the Broad Creek Road crossing, though it felt as if she'd run three-quarters of a mile by now. She pushed harder as she turned toward town. Jonah Judson leered at her, the devil himself in his sobriety, in his starched prison-issue white shirt. Already some cars had beamed on their headlights, and she began to run alongside the traffic, fast.

ALL YOURS

Steward's grandfather had him drive the white Caddy up Route 17 to Charleston. Steward hated the Cadillac—he might as well be walking down the road stark naked, with gold chains dangling over his chest—but he loved the two-lane road. Grandfather did too. You could see him lean forward as they approached each marsh and sit up taller on the low narrow bridges. Steward tried to imagine what the old man saw from the passenger seat: when he saw the rude shacks, for instance, woodsmoke pouring out the chimneys. The old man kept his own counsel. Small in his seat (by now he was literally shrinking), Grandfather set his mouth one way for the piney woods, another for banks of oaks, and looked over at Steward when they passed a fishing motel with a name like Pleasant Grove or a store with a handpainted sign for *P-cans, P-nuts, P-U, Live Bait.*

"There is no place like the lowcountry," he said finally to Steward, who knew enough to nod and leave it be. Sick as he was of the tidy clean New England countryside, he could not relax on this road he loved. Grandmother had arranged a school-year subscription to the *Due East Courier* for him and for seven months in Rhode Island he had been reading weekly bulletins about the poverty that had surrounded him all his life. News. The Afro-American Club at Due East High School, Harrison and Dillon its only white members, was building concrete houses out this way to replace the shacks. Indoor plumbing comes to Due East. Ranges to replace wood stoves.

Harrison and Dillon had told him, hadn't they, that he should be seeing to more important things. He'd almost invited a St. Ben's friend, O'Malley, to come down for Christmas vacation but he'd pulled back, and wasn't it this that made him apply the brakes: the poverty all around, and his own family just seeing it (did they see it?) for the first time. He'd arrived at St. Ben's an alien from the Segregated South, and even if he'd worked his way past that there was no sense sharing the shame. O'Malley's father, of Groton, Connecticut, had marched in Montgomery.

"I promise I won't say another word about the University of the Deep South after this one, but it seems to me son that the uhge to go to a school like that stems from what has to be a kind of homesickness. You've been missing the lowcountry and you'd like to come back to the South. That is admirable, Steward. But New Orleans is not Due East, son. New Orleans is certainly not Due East."

His grandfather's spotted hand patted Stew's on the steering wheel, but he kept his promise and said no more. Steward of course said nothing in the first place. The truly amazing thing was that Grandfather still wanted to drive with him up Route 17, that he wanted to arrange this little luncheon in Charleston, when all he got from this grandson (and it wasn't as if he were the only grandson, Aunt Blinky had four blond lacrosse-playing boys, cousins he himself didn't have two words to say to) was profound and unmitigated silence. Just two nights before, at the welcome-home dinner of his last spring break, Lola broke the news that Stew had sent back his reservation to UDS, and Grandfather ranted and raved. *Second rate*, he'd said. *Whatever put a school like that in your head? WHOever put a school like that. Why it's not even a CATHOLIC school.* As if he wanted his anger purer. He made out that it was for Stew Jr.'s sake that he was furious, but Grandfather had gone to Princeton himself, after all, and had taken great pains to explain early in the year that Stew's B average would be of little consequence when the third-generation Morehouse applied there. The application was a formality; he still gave *quite generously, I think we'd both of us parties agree.*

Steward saw that he was doing seventy-five. Not a word from Grandfather, and on this old pitted road. He slowed to seventy-three. If that was all Grandfather had to say on the subject, what would lunch be about? Now that the subject was closed, he began to list his justifications, but there was only one: he wanted to go and live in New Orleans. It was not Due East and it was not New England and it was seedy and dim, dim even in the sunlight. Every single frame he shot that one night in New Orleans was good. Even the underexposed prints had something going on, some line askew, some chipping paint. Something that made good Princeton boys like his father drink enough to marry girls they'd known for a week. He wanted to make a movie in New Orleans, and though he wasn't sure what it would be about, it would certainly deal with loneliness and desolation and decay. All right, so he got the idea from senior English and *Death in Venice*. So it would be *Death in New Orleans*. Even Father Leahy shrugged at his choice. Even his *mother* shrugged at his choice—Lola seemed to think it was some kind of party school—when you'd think she'd be tickled, or complimented at least.

He hadn't been in Charleston since Grandmother took him to buy that mohair boarding school tour coat, but the Cadillac drove itself into the city and down the narrow streets to Harvey's. Surely Charleston was smaller (everything looked smaller after St. Ben's) and brighter, and there were more palmettos than he'd remembered. For the first time he saw a subtropical city. The tabby buildings shimmered harsh light. The first azaleas had opened obscenely in the warmth of mid-March and everywhere were sprigs of the dense heavy green he wouldn't see for months in Rhode Island.

Harvey's looked down on the slave market, and Grandfather grumbled getting out of the car. "You'll see," he said. "It's not the same old flavuh."

And it wasn't. For years Harvey's had served liquor in a dry state and hadn't even bothered to conceal the bar. The same Negro waiters had served the same local politicians and businessmen and TV weathermen for twenty years, and they were still there, all right, but now their hair coiled in loose frizzles. They'd aged right along with Grandfather, and even their skin had faded. Now they carried legal mini-bottles, the little bottles airlines used, on their trays.

"Lord save us sinners here below," Grandfather said, sweeping into the dark bar where thousands of little bottles perched like sandlappers on the shore.

They moved into the restaurant and were seated in a corner where Grandfather could see everyone and Steward could see no one but him. Grandfather's martini arrived in two mini-bottles, but he had the grace to shake his head and mouth into a rueful grin. No use barking at the waiter.

"You bring us the best-looking piece of fish y'all got back there in the kitchen," he said, instead of barking. "Broiled with lots of butter. And you pick us out some nice veg-e-tables, nice and fresh, and see here now, after you bring us that basket of rolls yonder you don't have to bother us again until that fish is just a nice golden brown."

Steward died, right on the spot. Did it occur to Grandfather that he might like to decide for himself what would go into his mouth? What did he think he was doing, the charming old master routine? His grandson stirred the swivel stick round and round his own drink, gin and tonic. Was it gin Grandfather used to drink on the verandah?

"Steward," his grandfather said, "I see you squirming like a worm on a hook. Like that live bait they advertise up the road. You know I didn't have you carry me to Charleston without purpose."

Now Steward squirmed in earnest. The basket of bread arrived, hush puppies deep in the middle, and Steward died again as the waiter, starched white cotton on aged black hand, slipped it between them without a word. Grandfather nodded pleasantly.

"Do we understand each other, Steward?"

Steward shrugged, one shoulder in anger and the other in dismay. Understand what?

"I admire that—what ought we call it, son?—reticence, maybe? of yours."

Steward shrugged again, this time in submission.

"I'm serious, son. I'm dead serious. I'm *relieved* you don't suck up to me the way Blinky's boys do. Do you know that overgrown Dufford had the gall to approach me about a motor scooter? You've never once done *that*, Steward."

"I never had to ask for anything," Steward said, or mumbled, and saying it, he meant it. Cameras, coats, gas and beer and new enlargers: there was no need to ask for what appeared in regular installments. And when in return he gave his grandparents some token of thanks, a good print usually, they fussed over it and framed it in some ridiculous nineteenth-century *painting* frame and displayed it in the front hall. Weird to not respect them anymore, to not even like them. Grandfather, anyway. He imagined his father storming off for New Orleans after a violent confrontation. In some staid setting like this, like Harvey's.

"I admired your reticence on your eighteenth birthday, Steward."

Eighteenth birthday? It was months past.

"I know you must have been sweating these two months over what arrangements we have made for you, but you never questioned us once."

All right, he knew it was money Grandfather meant but it truly had not occurred to him that they meant to give him cash for his eighteenth birthday. Grandmother had sent a pale pink alpaca sweater, what boys wore in other schools maybe, but not what he'd ever put across his own shoulders. Now he swallowed down the last of his gin, and knew not to look as puzzled as he was. If only he had not gulped his one drink in front of the old man.

"What's touching, if I may use such an old-fashioned word," his grandfather said, "is that you act almost exactly as your father did when he was your age."

Now the gin burned through his reticence. "My father?"

"Never asked a word, Steward, never a word about the trust fund. I took him to lunch at this very restaurant, son, on his eighteenth birthday, twenty-odd years ago. Twenty-two? He knew what that lunch was all about, but never once did he question me. Not until I was ready to speak."

Trust fund. They'd never spoken of trust funds, not he or his grandfather or his mother, but Nick had. Nick had sat him down when he came to live with them and said *Stew, I want you here, this is where you belong, dammit my house is your home now, but I want you to know that if you stayed with your grandfather you'd have trust funds coming out your yazoo. I got to let you know, kid, that if you decide at any time, I mean any time of day or night, to go back to the big house, there's not going to be a single hard feeling around here.* At the time, twelve years old, he liked the sound of *yazoo* more than he liked the sound of *trust funds.*

"Course, when I did get around to telling him, he didn't act any too surprised and I don't suppose you'll act any too surprised when you get your piece of news."

Was he really so thick? His ears burned with shame. Had he believed what Nick and Lola believed, that when he went to live with them, he was giving up the chance at any of Grandfather's money? He saw the vault in Grandfather's bank, roomy and casual and cluttered as Grandmother's sewing room, unattended when the single guard went for coffee or was out sick. Of course Grandfather had intended all along that he should have money.

"Steward?"

But the money was probably tuition money, a good allowance: what he'd had at St. Ben's, only more. He probably had to promise he'd give Princeton due consideration, visit it again. A bubble crept up to his throat. For a minute he, the boy with his stepfather's car, and all the spending money he could use, and a monkish life without even a girlfriend to spend money on, had pictured a string of garish rubies for Lola. For just a split second he'd thought of walking his mother through Tiffany's.

He looked his grandfather in the eyes, the old irises now dimmed from blue to seawater gray, the bifocals making distorted pools of them.

"Yessir."

"Son, you know this idn't easy for me. I imagine your mother was very bitter, very bitter about Steward's money. But that money reverted to us, you see, when he died, marriage or no. We were not vindictive people. We did not attempt to have that marriage nullified, the way we were advised to do. We wanted your father and your mother to have a generous allowance, no matter how impetuous that marriage was. But when your father died, Steward, we thought it proper that the money revert to us. We thought it extremely proper when we knew there was a child on the way, a child to whom we had the same obligation we'd had to our own son."

"She never said anything about the money."

Grandfather raised one eyebrow, quizzical and disbelieving.

"I don't think she thought anything about it. I mean, she wouldn't want to take what was yours. She didn't marry him for his money."

Him. Who knew anything about him? For all he knew she had married him for the bucks. Lola never talked about who his father had been: she talked about his blond hair, *just like yours Stewie, only his was thicker, or maybe it was his soldier's haircut that made it look thick, huh?* or his sharp jaw, *just weird to see your daddy's chin come pointing down in your chin, Stew.* For all he knew his father's wartime love letters were stacked in a shoe box Lola hid from Nick. For all he knew she'd burned them eighteen years ago.

His grandfather's mouth twitched. "Of course she didn't. And that, Steward, is neither here nor there. Neither here nor there. What is here, what I have asked you to carry me to Charleston to discuss, is that trust fund of your father's, which has grown—as you can imagine, son—substantially. Sub*stan*tially. It's a good lot of money now, Steward, and naturally it's still been in trust all this while. I'm sure you and your mother knew that without being told."

Steward ducked his face down, the way he was expected to, forcing a pleased half-smile. He didn't know what the other guys would have done with the news. O'Malley was stinking rich, and so was everyone else he knew at St. Ben's. They tallied up their trust funds nightly. But what if Dillon or Harrison or S.D. were to get this bulletin? He saw them leaping up from the table, drug shipments swimming before their eyes, new cars waiting for them at every curb. He saw them flinging their arms around this little old man's hooked shoulders, kissing him on the narrow strip of his mouth. He imagined S.D., whose own grandfather lived in a trailer and spat at you when you went with S.D. out to fetch his piss-stained blue jeans back to town to wash, would look *this* old man, Steward Morehouse Sr., in the eye and say *So just how much are we talking about here, sir?*

"I'd like to sign it over to my mother if I could." He'd had no idea *that* would come out of his mouth. He was still trying out imaginary numbers.

Twenty-five thousand dollars. Fifty thousand? He saw that he'd shredded the cocktail napkin, waiting to speak. "Nick already said he wanted to pay my tuition, I think it's like a matter of pride, and I use their car and all—"

His grandfather guffawed. *Guffawed.* "I told Mamie you'd say that. I told her, I predicted Steward would say exactly that about the money. You're a good boy, son. But you know what? You can't sign it over to your mother. I don't mean you mayn't. I mean you *can't.* You are set up exactly as your father was, son. You are to receive a good allowance every year now, an allowance that will go up every year until you are twenty-five and ready to handle the principal. It won't be enough to live on comfortably if you should get married, so I suggest, as I suggested uselessly to your father, that you don't get married. Before your time. And see here Steward"—now his eyes were blue again, and he folded the bifocals and put them in his breast pocket just so Steward could see how blue his passion flashed—

"see you don't get yourself shipped off to Viet*nam.* See you don't go signing up for any officer training programs."

He was spitting when he got to *officer training programs,* spitting just as certainly as S.D.'s father spat at you when he inquired after your health. The old man grabbed up his martini glass and slurped up the rest. Banged the glass back down on the table.

"And now just you quit this sweet nonsense about signing it over to your mother. *I* will be paying your tuition at Princeton. A sergeant in the Marine Corps can't bear that burden. And I'm sure you'll want to buy Lola lots of pretty baubles. You'll have ten thousand dollars this first year, Steward, and that's a good deal more than you're used to having for spending money. You spend every dime of it on Lola if you want to, Stew, you go buy her a little string of pearls if the uhge strikes you."

Steward shrank back. *Rubies.*

"Because the next year you will have fifteen thousand, and the year after that twenty, and maybe that year, or maybe the year your allowance goes up to twenty-five thousand" (his voice faded when he named a figure; his shrewd eyes lighted on one adjoining table and then the next as he mouthed *fifteen* and *twenty* and *twenty-five thousand*) "one of those years you will fall in love with some pretty little girl, prettier even than that pretty mama of yours, and by the time you are twenty-five and want to marry that pretty little girl it will never even occur to you to sign over that money to your mother. It will occur to you to act decently and to see that she is well cared for and you will. But by then you will know a good deal about managing money and you will know a good deal about what you can do with it. You will know because I will see to it that you know."

Grandfather's sharp jaw jutted out, ferocious, but it followed the rest of his body easing back into the tall-backed dining chair, and Steward saw that the old man's tidy speech had exhausted him.

"You may close your mouth now, Steward."

He did. He closed his mouth and at the sight of Grandfather's beady eyes, now a blueberry blue, now a navy blue, now a flat black deep in his cadaver's face, he closed his eyes too, for a moment, adding up all those thousands until he got to the figure Grandfather was about to say.

"By the time you get it, it will be well over a million. I appreciate your not asking."

Opened his eyes.

"You are included in my will, Steward. But the money you inherit from me someday you will have to share with Blinky and Dufford and Sam and Sheldon and Howell. *This* money is just for you. It was all your father's and now it's all yours, son. I believe it will give you the chance to become the good man your father never had a chance to be."

Steward began to cry.

It was not clear whether Grandfather could see this—he could feel the tears slipsliding down the side of his nose but he imagined that his grandfather's eyes were moist too, that his grandfather dabbed at his black eyes with the heavy linen napkin because he too was overcome and not because he was trying to save Steward the shame of crying observed—and it was not clear whether he was crying because he was rich and Nick was not; or because his grandfather did not know how much he disliked him now; or because he was busy calculating how much income he'd have off of two million dollars at twelve percent and hating himself for the money-grubbing; or because once, when he delivered Franny home stinking drunk and still a virgin, her father too had called him *a good man.*

He was not getting very far with his calculations. Every time he multiplied by twelve or by two million he saw Franny's father squeezing his hand tight a million years ago. Oh Jesus. At twelve percent he'd have an annual income of twenty-four thousand dollars a year, for life? No. Two hundred forty thousand dollars. Way too high.

At five percent it would still be a hundred thousand dollars. Grandfather was poking around on the floor for the napkin that had fluttered down from his lap. Nick made what, fourteen thousand? Thirteen?

And what had Mr. Starkey made? Trying to move the percentage point around his calculations, trying to suck back his weeping, he saw Mr. Starkey in his old man's plaid bathrobe, the same bathrobe Nick wore at home, peering out from the new door in Splendid Oaks as he dragged Franny up the walk. It must have been one A.M.

Grandfather was close to toppling off his chair altogether as he lunged for his napkin, but he did not scurry off his own chair to fetch the old man's cloth for him. Mr. Starkey would have made fifteen or sixteen thousand as principal, maybe.

Franny called once a week now, he was sure that was her intake of breath, disgusted with herself, on the other end of the line. Was she going crackers now that her father was dead, or was she calling from some new boyfriend's bedroom, the two of them laughing at him? Her father was dead, decent Mr. Starkey who you just knew would never take advantage of a drunk girl, either, no matter how much of a slut she was. He hated her more, if that was possible, now that her father did not exist. Soon Nick would not exist, soon Nick would be blown to bits in Vietnam. He hated his grandfather.

Who lurched himself back fully onto his seat and sat with his napkin clutched. Oh sweet Jesus he was crying after all. What was *he* picturing? A dead son, with thicker hair, sitting in Steward's place? It was not possible that the waiter should choose just this moment to carry forth with such solemnity two plates of thin bland flounder and tired wild rice and two little bowls of steaming summer squash—*wasn't summer squash supposed to grow in the summer?*—just at this moment when he saw that Franny must have known somehow, that otherwise she never would have done something as corny as phone him and breathe into the phone.

His grandfather blew his nose loudly into the retrieved napkin and waved the waiter away with his free hand. By the time they were alone together again his grandfather pulled away the napkin and there was no sign in his gray eyes that he had indulged for an instant in weeping. The waiter had vaporized. That was how you told people to go to hell. That was how he would tell Franny to go to hell, with a wave of his hand and a squirt of snot in a fancy restaurant. He blew his own nose and his grandfather said:

"I do admire your reticence, Steward, but *thank you* would be in order. *Thank you* smooths out many an awkward moment. Don't worry, son. I had to remind your father too."

PRAYER

"Honey has you let loose of you senses or is you trying to make me let loose of mine?"

Franny started and peered over at her seatmate, a grizzled old woman in a hot pink dress, a dress shiny and hot even in the twilight of the bus's reading lights.

"You arms, honey. You been flexing them arms for fifteen minutes."

The old woman's mouth was pulled tight into a devilish grin—a soulmate as well as seatmate—but after Franny returned the grin and tucked her arms in close she resumed staring out the window. She wasn't about to be sucked into a conversation, not even with a soulmate, not now while the bus slipped up Route 17 under a sky spread out like spilled water. The moss was hanging heavy and damp, waiting for another twilight over the marshes, and land was sewn to sky with strips of sunset as lurid as the old woman's dress.

She'd never traveled this road before without Starkeys bulging out of the station wagon's windows and tailgate. And what did you usually go to Charleston for? For an ophthalmologist (Caroline) or an orthodontist (Paul) or, most recently, for a GI series (Franny herself, when she dropped to seventy-nine pounds and Dr. Black told Doris she could either admit her daughter to the Medical College or the state hospital, but he himself liked to eliminate the possibility of physical ailments before he let the psychiatrists start poking around).

Now, two weeks shy of her eighteenth birthday, she was back up to ninety pounds and had been strong enough in the spring to run track again, though not strong enough, or fired up enough, to do much good. One second place the whole season, only four thirds, and Legs herself told her she wasn't a miler anymore, it was a miracle a short girl had gone as far as she did. It didn't matter. She only went back because she couldn't otherwise imagine ever again baring her scrawny slack thighs.

Now, track behind her, her thighs tight, she was traveling the Greyhound alone and approaching Charleston, first stop on the road to Purgatory. Now she, all ninety muscular pounds of her, was being shipped off to the Jesuit University of America, to the only institution on the East Coast that would give her a Daughter of a Deceased Alumnus scholarship. AgnesAnn stood over her shoulder while she filled in every box in the application, and Teresa wrote her essay.

Now she was sentenced to four years at the Jesuit University, her father's alma mater. This bus would snake its way through night in the Carolinas and Virginia, and she would wake somewhere in the Maryland suburbs, at this school so desperate to fill its lecture halls, so tired of being in the shadow of Georgetown, that it would give *her* (graduating grade point index 1.98, but they rounded up) a full scholarship. After the Rhode Island School of Design—well who the hell were they—returned her slides wrapped in a form letter.

The Jesuit University of America hadn't even required that she come for an interview, so she'd never seen the campus and couldn't summon any picture. The catalogue they sent her was avisual, its cover decorated with a black-and-white photo of the gray stone chapel. This afternoon, as inspiration for her journey, her mother had pulled an old college snapshot out of her father's underwear drawer (still preserved intact, as if the man was going to walk in and pull out a fresh pair of boxers any morning). In the faded Brownie shot Doris held out trembling, her father waved in cap and gown from the JUA baseball field. Pat was a stumpy shortstop in his shiny black robes, his square jaw and wide eyes reverent in the face of the camera. At least her father had had the baseball field to save him from the Jesuits. She wouldn't even have a track for a hiding place: no women's team. They'd only been admitting females for a half dozen years.

But she needed to get out of Due East. At least she and AgnesAnn agreed on that point. Even the suburbs of Washington, D.C., were someplace else, someplace closer to New York and Greenwich Village, someplace closer to a flight to Paris, someplace where she could park herself for a semester while she drew maps for her further escape.

Maps of a northbound route. Maps of a route up and out.

The bus cruised alongside a lone crow and passed a desolate stretch of tomato fields, picked clean since June. The dried stalks were still unwilling to disintegrate, even in September's heat, their brittle remains breaking off closer and closer to the ground. From the bus window they could have formed the low mounds of a graveyard.

Franny watched the striped sunset melting into night the way a parfait melts on a summer day. The crow flew off into the horizon. It was too early to sleep, and the only book in her bag was the JUA catalogue. She considered disappearing into the bathroom at the back of the bus, but if she lit up the joint she'd tucked in her bra someone was bound to smell it. She slid her eyes sidewise to watch the old woman next to her, a woman who must have spent a lifetime in the sun, her skin singed now the color of ashy charcoal. The old lady slept, a trickle of spit swimming downstream from her wide mouth, but in that pink dress she looked sharp enough to know the smell of pot coming from a Greyhound bathroom. It wasn't worth the trouble.

She didn't smoke so much anymore, anyway, only once or twice a week. Harrison and Dillon had hounded her into easing up and now she vowed every other week that she'd stop altogether, stop bringing joints onto Greyhound buses, stop making Harrison and Dillon crazy with worry every time she lighted up. Dillon wouldn't sell her any more when it got too bad, when she had the GI series in the hospital, and he'd come close to hitting S.D., who was more of a dope fiend than even she was, but who was not entitled, Dillon said, to bring her down with him. She'd been Dillon's tour guide once, in the backseat of his father's Ford Fairlaine, the first time he'd even been with a girl. And she'd seen the back of S.D.'s father's car twice, which is what the fight was really about in the first place. The weight of them on a narrow backseat, thinking they pinned her down when she was the one who held them prisoner.

The psychiatrists up at the state hospital would have had a lot of fun with her, a classic case. Her father's favorite, and now her father dead, and she sleeping around like the sluts in Henry Miller (S.D. passed the paperbacks around in avid contempt) instead of saving herself like a good Due East girl. Kate was still a virgin. Everybody was still a virgin, as far as she knew, except for the really bad cheerleaders (three-quarters of the squad) and the five seniors who had disappeared from Due East High School in the spring of 1970, one by one, belly by distended belly.

But she would have had to tell the psychiatrists that in fact her father's dying slowed her down a little, that she was worse before her father died, a little worse anyway. Sometimes Dillon and Harrison wouldn't look her in the eyes. They were ashamed for her and they were trying to cure her of it the way they'd cured her of pot and now at last she was a willing convert. She pictured herself nunlike in her Paris garret.

Nunlike and praying. Nunlike after she'd made just one last mistake and conceived the baby girl who now slept in the basket beside her easel. She was painting her last mistake, her last willful seduction of some innocent boy. She was slathering pink shades of white on the white canvas. She was whispering the words of the rosary the way Walter whispered them, with his eyes unfocused and his voice trancelike:

Hail Mary, full of grace. The Lord is with, the Lord is with Thee. Blessed art thou, art thou, among women. Among women.

Outside the night was gray and still and the bus glided toward Charleston, passing now the ticky-tacky houses on the outskirts of town, the clumps of subdivision that would soon give Charleston real suburbs. Her stomach howled—first time in months, first time since they'd made her drink barium and her belly had quieted in terror—loud enough to jolt awake the old lady sitting next to her. The pink dress sat bolt upright, and the woman inclined her ear to listen again to the thunderous growl of Frances Starkey's stomach. Then she laid a gnarled hand on Franny's tight thigh, winked, and using the thigh as anchor reached down to pull from a paper sack at her feet a fried chicken leg.

The old lady wrapped Franny's fingers around the drumstick and then slowly, painfully, bent down again to pull out a hunk of cornbread wrapped tight in waxed paper.

Franny did not say a word but copied the woman's offering grin and bit into the crusty chicken while the woman watched. Grease splattered up and caught in her eyelashes. She tasted meat juicier than anything Doris had ever fried up, chicken soaked in egg and cornmeal and spiced up with red flecks that curled her tongue.

Home. Chicken like this, chicken she'd never tasted before, was what she would remember of home ten years, twenty years, forty years down the line. She'd remember the bus ferrying her and an old lady in a pink dress across the night, away from Due East, away from Walter saying the rosary and Doris breaking down at the bus station.

Oh Franny you run off without so much as a hug, look at you. Sometimes I think you're spiteful, you know you were his favorite, and Blessed Mother forgive me for saying it with six other children standing here to hear it, you were my favorite sometimes too, my God I have wasted nights praying for your soul Frances and now you go off without a thought for a one of us. You'd better say you a rosary the first night and every night after or you'll never remember where you come from.

"Come on now," she'd said to her mother, and hugged them all.

"Come on now, you know I'm thinking of you." And climbed on the bus thinking a hundred other thoughts.

"Oh God," she said now to the old lady. "Oh thanks." The grease slid down her chin.

Finishing the chicken and cornbread, her stomach quieted and her eyes began to close as the bus crossed the river into Charleston. First stop. At home they would be kneeling in the living room, only the six children left to comfort Doris, six children kneeling to say the rosary which took twice as long now that Walter had memorized the prayers.

Hail Mary, full of, full of, grace. Hail Mary, full of grace.

She heard Walter struggling through his prayers and she drifted, rolling with the chicken and the bus and the strip of hot pink she saw from the slit in her eye. She drifted down close to sleep, but the bus pulled into the depot and she wakened with a start. In her sleep she had been chanting some sort of prayer.

She had been chanting the names of the boys in Due East: Tony Rivers, Dwayne Goodridge, S.D., Beanie Boatwright, Sanford Sanders, Michael Dillon, David Brow, DeVeau Frank, Johnson Bewley.

Now she was wide awake again, as she'd be all night, waiting for the bus to pull into Charleston and Florence and points north. She was wide awake, and she saw that she'd left someone out:

Tony Rivers.

Dwayne Goodridge.

S.D. (after that letter from Steward).

Beanie Boatwright, just once.

Sanford Sanders.

Michael Dillon.

David Brow.

DeVeau Frank.

DeVeau Frank's cousin from Atlanta.

Johnson Bewley.

Her mouth was dry from the cornbread and the bus rocked, turning into the station. Her mouth was dry and the bus rocked and the names drifted off with her like lines from a song: Gordy Nichols, DeVeau Frank, DeVeau Frank's cousin, Johnson Bewley.

Gordy Nichols, DeVeau Frank, Bill Frank, Johnny Bewley, Amen.

At home Walter was crossing himself with the wrong hand and Will was rising to give his mother a stiff kiss on the cheek. Caroline was weepy, or dreamy, and Martin and Albert and Paul were tripping over each other and socking each other in the gut. Doris was trembling with fatigue— *Good night, can you imagine I used to think working girls had it easy?*—and the night was closing in on Due East the same as it was closing in on her, leaving.

YOUR DAD'S
DEAD AND
FACEDOWN
IN THE MUD
OH BABY

Her assigned roommate, Peggy Barnacle, had a long porous face like a . . . well, like a barnacle, with a sharp nose perched in the middle. Her dark hair was sparse, pulled back into an old-fashioned mother-of-pearl clasp. A year after Woodstock Peggy Barnacle still wore penny loafers and plaid pleated skirts, and she strode across the Jesuit University campus, eyes blazing behind her glasses. Joan of Arc.

Franny worshipped Peggy Barnacle. She was Doris and AgnesAnn and Teresa rolled into one. She drank until two in the morning, came home to type up her weekly freshman essay with a cigarette dangling from her mouth, and generally made it to morning Mass before communion. Franny did not know another soul on campus who still went to Mass, except maybe the priests. Some of them.

"Come on, quit your moping," Peggy Barnacle said in the dorm room, where Franny lay on her belly reading *Anna Karenina.* "Wanna know what happens to Anna? She throws herself in front of a goddamn train." Franny, submissive to another female for the first time in her life, trailed her to the basement of the cafeteria, to the student pub where sotted freshmen plied themselves with cheap draft beer. Peggy appeared to know every Irish Catholic on the East Coast, and greeted other freshmen by name from the first night. Her high school career, evidently, had been one long CYO convention.

The two of them were a regular Mutt and Jeff pushing into the Underground Pub, Peggy an even six feet and Franny barely five. Peggy was wide-shouldered and as hippy as a Picasso nude, Franny a wraith in some clingy flowing piece of cloth she'd draped and tied around her neck. With her horn-rims sliding down her long nose, Peggy could have been poster girl for the Catholic College Women's Association, circa 1955; but Franny wore silver earrings with a dozen rows of tiny bells, and should have been photographed as a living example of the Counterculture for *Life* magazine.

"Somebody saw us coming," Peggy said. "Somebody with a sense of humor." The other freshmen girls were in the throes of a collective identity crisis: they were the good girls from convent academies, girls whose mothers had helped them pack sensible knee-length skirts and cardigans. For months those other girls wavered. They'd made straight A's back at Sacred Heart or St. Saviour's, where only the C students smoked pot. Now there was always a strike on, and unless you were part of the ROTC Auxiliary you didn't dare make your way to the classroom. Their short fluffy hair, their delicate pearl post earrings, their pleated trousers were *all wrong*. Even the girls who came from big cities, from New York or Boston or Baltimore, had been shielded from the sixties, but now they saw that the Jesuits themselves wore overalls and smoked hash.

For months the other girls struggled through various stages of metamorphosis, their inky Levi's barely faded after all those Clorox washes in the dorm basements, their underarms hairy for three months and then shaved off in a panic for a visit home. But Peggy Barnacle and Franny Starkey looked pretty much the same in December 1970 as they'd looked when they arrived in September.

"You'll still be wearing penny loafers and those godawful cheerleader skirts in the year 2000."

"I certainly hope so. They cost enough to last thirty years."

Peggy was a fireman's daughter from the Bronx. She introduced Franny to plenty of girls like her, girls with working-class fathers and frugal mothers who'd saved for their educations on the sly. She rushed off at all hours of the afternoon to practice step dancing, learn Gaelic, send aid to Northern Ireland. Franny luxuriated in the peace of their lonely room. Oh Peggy's taste was vile. She'd put floral curtains up and lined her closet shelf with yellow daisy Con-Tact paper.

But then Peggy was back after supper, reciting Rimbaud in French, cutting her toenails while she studied astronomy. Franny found herself reading what Peggy left in the bathroom—she rescued *Anna Karenina* from the back of the toilet—and following her to lectures on Taoism or Cambodia. Peggy told her to read *The Second Sex, Sex and Temperament in Three Primitive Societies, The Sexual Enlightenment of Children*. Franny doubted she'd ever had a date. At eighteen, she already had a potbelly and varicose veins sketched on her thighs, as if she planned to enter middle age directly.

Watching Peggy slick her hair back in the clasp, Franny resolved to hold herself back for a year. Well, six months or a semester at least. Then she might call Steward Morehouse, long-distance. Meanwhile she ran four miles every morning. The other girls were slipping off to Washington to visit Planned Parenthood for the first time, getting themselves prescriptions for birth control pills and diaphragms. The priests were leaving the order in droves. And here she was, eighteen years old, finally away from home, chaste.

When they went to the Underground at nine or ten at night, Peggy worked the crowd while Franny sat in a ladder-back corner chair to watch. She was reading Margaret Mead, but this was more of an anthropological wonder than anything in her course books. The other freshmen looked fifteen or sixteen, strumming their three chords on a guitar, clapping each other on the back and yucking it up. She was an old woman nursing her lone beer in the corner.

One night she let herself smoke a joint when Peggy said she wanted to try. No effect whatsoever on Peggy, who went back to her philosophy, but Franny wandered the campus. Inside the library she forgot what she'd come for. She propped herself up on one elbow at the checkout counter and watched a smooth tall upperclassman with hair to his shoulders saunter his way over to her. He had the perfect round eyes and cheeks of a prettyboy, but his black eyebrows cut a clean swath across his forehead and he grinned with a full mouth and thousands of teeth. He worked in the library—all right, at least he was work/study—and he introduced himself as Rocco. *Nobody* in Due East was named Rocco.

In the morning, after his roommate had left and they could stop pretending they were sleeping, he confided that he was seriously considering the seminary. Franny pictured a parish full of adoring old ladies rattling their beads as he swung his hair over one shoulder. Father Rocco.

One guy in four months. She had made it safely through a whole semester, or close enough.

She hitchhiked into Washington whenever she could, meaning, after a lifetime of looking at paintings in library books, to educate herself. Scruffy in one of her father's old shirts, she slouched in the austere National Gallery and slinked by the old masters. But every visit she went back to see the Raphaels, and fell in love with beautiful Bindo Altoviti, the Rich Boy with the golden face. Bindo. Bindo Altoviti. Standing solitary in front of him, she juggled his name in her mouth like a piece of hard candy. He was not indifferent, not aloof exactly, but remote. Dreamy. His wispy sideburns were as mangy as a hippie's. His mouth was swollen pink: swollen, she bet, from the pleasure of love. When she found herself smiling at Bindo, she moved along to the Madonnas.

In the school studio, she was painting out of her head. No models, no still lifes—she knocked off a few in drawing class, where they were required, but when it hit the canvas her paintbrush chose its own subjects. She'd had her fill of careful little drawings, a lifetime out at the beach following the lines and whorls of driftwood. Steward was right to hate them. Now, under the influence of Humanities I, under the influence of Raphael, she began to imagine Grand Classical Themes. She painted modern Ledas and Persephones, snatched away by dark hulking figures; she made the air in Hades the loamy air that settled over Washington on a warm day. She called her mother in a fit of inspiration and asked her to pack up the little toys Walter and Albert had outgrown. Doris said, "Frances Starkey, are you doing drugs?" but sent her the wounded metal jeeps and plastic soldiers just the same. Franny attached them to her classical canvases with airplane glue, a frame of three-wheeled Matchbox cars and one-armed cowboys under Due East skies as airy a blue as Raphael's.

She was the star of Painting I. What would she be doing in a real art school? Some days, sweat streaking down her face, she finished a canvas in two or three hours, and felt as if she were painting underwater, or living underwater. Something like being stoned all the time, the way she'd been that year in Due East. But now there was no money for dope and no hunger for it either. Now she was sweating herself clean.

Second semester, Intro to Anthropology finished and forgotten, she let Peggy talk her into signing up for Intro to Psych. "Take Steedman," Peggy said. "He doesn't touch a textbook."

Steedman was a young dark instructor working for slave wages while he finished his dissertation, inspiring his seminars to torrents of outrage. First they read Freud, then they read pop articles on the vaginal orgasm. No wonder Peggy had recommended him. But Franny hated the way all notions were entertained, the way Steedman let the discussions bounce like Silly Putty. Her day was so focused now—running, studio, class if it happened to fit in with the real work—she wouldn't have shown up for Steedman at four o'clock except for the dream journals.

Steedman was doing what he called a dream project. He couldn't pay the volunteers, but he'd put their names in a hat at the end of a semester and draw a winner, who would get a hundred dollars. A hundred dollars would get her home for spring break on the Greyhound.

They were all to keep notebooks by their bedsides to record their dreams. Franny went out and bought the bound black-and-white-speckled kind that Albert used at home for his third-grade assignments. Of course Steedman hadn't known that she was waking every hour when he took her on as a volunteer. Her dreams stretched out along the wide lines of the little notebook. Peggy, asleep in the next bed, was a peaceful lowing cow and never heard her switch on the lamp or scrawl out the images that had wakened her. The sound of the fountain pen scratching across the page sometimes soothed Franny back to sleep in midsentence, and sometimes in the morning she had no recollection of what she'd written:

My father in a box like television. I can't hear and when I go to touch the volume the channel changes. Just like real life or a TV show, not watery like a dream. The channel changes to Walter Cronkite. No I'm not sure. I might be making that up. Right now it seems like I'm making

Or:

I can see my father smiling at one of the boys, Walter maybe, but when I get close he's yelling at me. His tooth is rotting. He's yelling at me because I don't have pants on, underpants.

The part about making it up sounded right. Every time she wakened now, she tried to hold onto the slippery rope. One night she dreamed Due East, a vacation guide's tour down River Street, over the bridge, over the marshes, out to the beach. The colors on the beach road were so good, the old oaks so true, that she stumbled over to her desk for pastels, thinking she'd color the dream in instead of writing it, but by the time she held a chalk even the colors had dissipated. When she started shading she was a fraud, throwing in a lush green just because she liked it, not because the dream marshes had been that color at all.

Daddy and me talking in Abel Bros. Funeral Parlor, he's sitting up in the casket still wearing that chalky lipstick. Looks waxy all over but he sounds like himself, humming goofy songs, "Officer Krupke," so I know it's him.

*He starts singing "Harrigan" and that means take care of Walter. O.k. I
got that. Then he says she wasn't like this before all of you. She was*

When Steedman asked them to bring the journals in for a first read-
through she handed hers over without rereading the entries. What you see
is what you get. "I can't even dream dirty anymore," she told Peggy. "I'm
reformed!"

"Nonsense. You're just repressing things. Now there's an interesting
concept. Repressing dreams themselves, because you know somebody's
going to be reading them." Peggy, full of herself, was taking a whole course
on sexuality, a course called *Wounded Male, Angry Female: Can We Close the
Gender Gap?*

When Steedman had the dream journals ready to give back he ended
the class with a little speech:

"I must say, I feel a bit of a voyeur looking in at all these dreams.
Wonderful dreams, really. One of you dreams in paintings and one of you
dreams in elaborate rhyme schemes."

Giggles from the class. Franny leaned forward with the rest of them,
hoping he'd read out dreams.

"Mr. Burke—this business with your poems and your titles and these
sentences that appear in print in your dreams is really most interesting. Do
you mind . . ."

Steedman was speaking to a guy in love with the sound of his own
voice. He looked all right—he wore a halo of strawberry-blond frizz and he
shaved his long pale face clean—but he jabbered on whenever he bothered
to show up for class, which was hardly ever. Oh he'd read Jung and Reich
and R. D. Laing. Oh it was a wonder he bothered to take the course. She
was not accustomed to men blathering this way. Her father and her brothers, Steward Morehouse, were cautious speaking. They didn't point a finger
at their own heads to get you to notice them.

Still, sometimes he said something funny and now he was doing his best
to shrink his long body down into the little seminar chair. "Oh sure," he
answered Steedman, only he said *shore* the nasally way the New Yorkers did.
Michael Burke was his name.

Steedman thumbed through Michael Burke's journal, a sheaf of yellow
paper held together by a paper clip. "Here," he said, after a minute. "This is
the kind of thing I mean. Mr. Burke dreams in words instead of images,"
and he read out: " 'All titles last night. Saw them in print and heard them in
a booming voice at the same time. Save Your Soul, Save Your Sisters. Your

Dad's Dead and Facedown in the Mud Oh Baby. If You Know What I Mean. The Gunrunners. Don't Shoot Me Dad While the Knife's in Your Hand.' "

Steedman looked up and over his wire-rims. "There's no picture *at all* there?"

Burke was no longer slumping in his chair. "Just words," he said. "Maybe some angel's telling me to look for a career as a headline writer."

Steedman looked back down at the yellow pages. " 'Don't Shoot Me Dad While the Knife's in Your Hand.' Sounds like a Firesign Theatre routine. What do you suppose your father would have to say about that one?"

Michael Burke shrugged. "Well, my father's dead."

Now Steedman pushed his glasses back up his nose and shuffled the journals. "Sorry," he said. "I should have seen that one coming." Then, confused: "You should get together with Miss Starkey. She's the one who dreams in drawings."

Franny, who had never commented on the vaginal orgasm or offered much of an opinion in Intro to Psych, felt her temperature rise ten degrees and stared right through the blackboard. He didn't mean *She's the one who dreams in drawings*. He meant *She's the other one whose father's dead* and he was too embarrassed now to say it, coughing and assigning next week's readings. B. F. Skinner and Thomas Szasz. Blahblahblah. Last time she'd hit this class for a few weeks. She could feel Michael Burke staring after her, and before Steedman was finished she was sliding toward the door. She was already at the stairwell when she remembered the dream journal in a pile on Steedman's desk, a sweet dopey drug for her now. Her only sweet dopey drug anymore.

She swam against the hallway tide and made her way back to the classroom. There were only four or five notebooks still on the desk, hers the only schoolgirl's marbleized assignment book. Steedman was still standing, talking to Michael Burke, the red fuzz of his hair unmistakable from behind. He wore soft old jeans, the blue so pale it was better to call it white, six million little patches stitched on. By a girl's hand. The patches were a girl's material, tiny tasteful flowers and bright geometric patterns. He wore clunky scuffed black boots with heels as thick as a horse's hooves. No wonder he looked so tall. Such affectation.

She grabbed up the notebook, thinking she'd slipped it by them, when Steedman cleared his throat again and called out after her retreating body:

"I enjoyed those pictures, Miss Starkey."

She raised a hand in acknowledgment, but did not turn around. She could feel the two of them, though, Unctuous Mr. Steedman and Charmed by Himself Mr. Burke, staring after her. She was wearing a long black satin skirt—actually, since she didn't know how to sew, it was really just a long bolt of black satin tied around her hips—and, passing through the doorway, she tripped over the shining cloth. But she was still leaving Intro to Psych with her integrity intact. She still had not opened her mouth.

Michael Burke caught up with her in the stairwell, between the second and third floors. She was sure of his heavy step—those clunky heels—but she imagined that he would zip by her and she'd be home safe. They'd never exchanged a word.

Descending behind her, he put out a light hand. When she pulled the offended shoulder back he said:

"Hey, Steedman said we should get together."

She swallowed back a hiss and stared instead at Michael Burke. Now he had gone down to the step below hers, but still she had to gaze up to see him. His nose curled, his eyes were watered a bland blue. His eyelashes, though, were a distraction, so blond they disappeared, and for a split second she almost pitied him. Steward Morehouse's disappearing eyelashes.

"Not a great opening line, huh?" The guy just wouldn't let up. "Actually I've been trying to get your attention for a month but I was always afraid we'd meet in a dark stairwell like this and you'd give me that look. Which, I have to tell you, is the sort of look a mother gives a son who comes crawling in drunk and fucked up, begging for mercy, at four o'clock in the morning. Oh man, I was right after all!" *Finally* he turned on his thick heels and was off down the stairs, but she kept her little mouth set with mean pursed lips.

Trying to get your attention all semester. She saw herself scrunched into her seminar chair, this selfsame scowl on her mouth, hearing Steedman pontificate and listening to New Yorkers like this one, talkers who wouldn't be able to die without letting one last trickle of wisdom spill from their mouths. Michael Burke was pointing *both* fingers at his own head, STEEDMAN LOOK AT ME, LOOK AT ME. Trying to get *her* attention.

"Wait," she heard herself calling down the stairs to him. Whose voice was that, Doris's, pitched all high and sickly sweet? And what exactly was she doing, calling to him? Not this guy. Not when she'd been meaning to live in a cell with Peggy Barnacle, sweating herself clean enough to call Steward Morehouse in New Orleans.

"Wait up," she called again. "I didn't mean . . ."

Look at him then. Look at this tall Michael Burke, waiting at the landing, back to the wall as though he'd been there for an hour, fiddling with the straps on his backpack as if she'd been his girl for the last five years, grinning up at her. He thought she was a *sweet kid*. He grinned at her the way she'd once grinned at David Brow, S.D., Dillon. He just wanted to get laid. She was just having the tables turned on her, just getting herself seduced.

"Steedman told me your father's dead too," he said.

Oh not this one, not with those disappearing eyelashes and some other girl's sewing stitched to his disappearing hips. Oh she was sunk all right, thinking of another girl before she'd ever seen this guy with his shirt off. He'd have a hairless chest and sun-inflamed moles.

"I'm sorry," she heard herself say, and saw him smile—no, grin—with a chipped eyetooth.

"You know a guy named Michael Burke?" she asked Peggy, but Peggy was slashing her yellow marker through *The Prisoner of Sex,* enraged, and did not answer.

She went out and waited for the hall phone to call her old friend Kate, who lived in New York with her grandmother now. It wouldn't matter if it was Kate or the grandmother on the other end of the line.

"I met a guy," she said into the receiver, and she could have been talking to herself.

"You sound terrible," Kate said. She'd developed a slight English accent. She was studying acting at Juilliard, the only one of them who'd gone where she wanted to go. When had she known Kate? Fifty years ago?

"Is everything o.k.?" Kate said to the silence. "Did you get knocked up or anything?"

Knocked up. It wasn't even Kate's voice speaking. They didn't even live in the same universe. The ground had shifted under their feet.

"I just met him this afternoon." Franny heard her own voice, morose. There was nothing to tell yet, nothing but this dread and longing. "I'm coming to New York tomorrow."

Actually she had planned to go to the demonstration anyway. Peggy sold her the bus ticket, and explained it all loudly, as if she were talking to a deaf person: they were going to picket corporate headquarters, P.R. headquarters, advertising headquarters all up and down Park and Madison avenues, headquarters of companies that manufactured and distributed and advertised radar and napalm and spare helicopter parts. Then they were going to march to the U.N., spattering symbolic blood along the way. "Where the tulips grow," Peggy said, ominous, "on Park Avenue." But Franny would have gone with or without Peggy's fervor. Her first trip to New York.

Now she and Peggy left their room in the dark to walk over to the buses waiting at the campus gates. It was a Wednesday morning in January, the dawn just breaking over their bare-branched winter campus. Even in the dim light she could see Michael Burke leaning against a bus, waiting for her. She walked fast, her toes cold to the death in thin sneakers. She wore two shirts and two sweaters—still hadn't saved enough for a decent winter coat —but Michael wore less: a thin denim jacket, studded, unbuttoned. Underneath he wore the same blue workshirt all the young Jesuits favored.

They were thick around the buses too, the priests, only they wore collars for demonstrations and tucked their hair up into Greek fishermen's caps. All the faces looked broad and doughy: Polish faces, Irish faces. No Father Roccos in this crowd.

Peggy deserted her with a *see ya* and walked off to the second bus. Last night, the two of them drifting off to sleep, she said she did know Michael Burke after all. Into drugs, she thought, maybe. Theater major, Hamlet last year when he was only a freshman. Peggy had heard he was a dreadful Hamlet, a hammy Hamlet, just an overblown disgrace. Sometimes he hung around the Irish-American Student Union, handing out Xeroxed interviews with Bernadette Devlin, tame stuff, civil rights for Catholics. Peggy recited her character summary of him after she flung *The Prisoner of Sex* across the room, and it was hard to say whether her voice was flat or disdainful.

Now Michael saw her approaching and stepped forward, grinning, holding out two arms weighed down with bags from a deli, when she was still thirty yards away. "I thought you weren't coming," he called, though it was early yet. "I thought you were back in bed thinking who is that nut job accosting me on the stairs, so I brought these as an offering. In case you really did come."

An offering. He thought he was charming, jumping around now from one foot to the other, roping his mouth into a crooked grin, one side down and rueful, the other loopy. He kissed her on the cheek. Old pals.

"Come in," he said. "Get in there and get yourself warm. You can't be used to this frigid air. Fucking freezing. Oh man." He rapped on the bus door and the machinery ground open. With blue hands he shepherded her into the big bus.

"Michael," one of the priests said, greeting him with a wink and a nod, a silver-haired *Bells of St. Mary's* priest, "sit up in the front half, would you? I want to go over the street theater bit."

"Shore," Michael said, but he forgot the promise immediately: he moved her three-quarters of the way back through the bus, his palm against the small of her back. Behind her she heard him greeting the staggered faces down the aisle.

"Ahh," he said, when they were sitting down, an amorphous gurgle of pleasure at everything and nothing. He began to unwrap Danishes from his paper sack, more Danishes than her brothers could eat working together. He was cutting them up in tiny triangles for her, as if she couldn't see to her own feeding. Ferocious, she sipped on black coffee.

"Far fucking out," he said, settled, and glommed a whole Danish. He was skinny and ate the same way she once had, with a passion. "Whatcha think?"

Of the Danish? Of the inside of a bus? "I think I've heard *far fucking out* five times this morning," she said, "and it's only seven o'clock."

He found this uproarious, slapping the seat and upsetting all the tiny triangles of Danish he'd laid out for her. "Oh well, I got an excuse," he said, in a thug's voice. "I'm from *Brooklyn*. You know what alphabet Brooklyn kids learn?"

She shook her head.

"Fucking A, fucking B, fucking C."

She smiled and he saw it, then wouldn't let up about making her smile. "You know," he said, "in psych class you are very *intense*. You know you sit there with your hands clenched?"

"Oh," she said, "Steedman."

"Jesus, he's a jerk. But a well-meaning jerk. He shouldn't have told me that about your dad but then if he hadn't I wouldn't be sitting here with you." The charming smile, half-loopy again. He had insinuated himself halfway into her seat. "When did he die?"

She stared out the bus window through the black gate: cherry trees around the fence, big expanse of rolling grass dusted now with frost, long driveway leading up to the Big House, the Administration Building. The old classroom buildings could have been clasping hands, they were so close together. Beyond all that lay a quad and dorms and a painting studio, too small, with lousy dim light in the afternoon. "Almost a year ago," she said.

"Oh shit. Mine too. That's a little weird. What did him in?"

"Heart attack."

He slapped his Danish down on the waxed-paper wrapping. "I got you beat there," he said. "My father died stinking of Korsakoff's psychosis, which is what you get when you've spent a lifetime pouring liquor down your gizzard. By the gallon. He was out of his mind when he went—I swear to you, in the back of this bus, he was seeing little men come to tie him down when he departed this world."

He was warming up, an actor, his face darkening by degrees, from the eyes down. When his mouth was black he stopped.

"The liver and the kidneys just give out."

"Ah," she said. She had not been on this side of the dead-father conversation for a year, but it appeared to be more of a monologue than a conversation anyway.

"Sucks," Michael Burke said cheerily, and lifted the dark mask. "Six kids and I'm the oldest."

"We're nine."

"Nine kids?"

"Jesus. Irish? Yeah, your face."

She nodded. Doris liked to say, when asked, "I'm *American*, thank you."

"We're a strange tribe. Breeding like that. I think it's out of panic, I really do. My dad was panicked his whole life long, but in Brooklyn you have to stop at six. Then you got everybody so crowded in the fucking floor-through you can't possibly grab a minute's privacy to let loose of your panic."

He spoke in gusts, died down, blew again.

"But I have to say, even when his liver was sending him film clips of little green men, he'd calm right down if you gave him the baby to hold. He'd hang onto that little foot like it was the line bringing him into dock."

He did a melancholy bit too, the rueful smile.

"We're past babies now," Franny said, panicking herself at the smile. "The youngest are eight. Twins."

"Oh well." He swept the air. "We're past babies too, we Burkes are. When the baby's foot got too big my dad didn't have a line to hold. Couldn't get into berth."

"And you got a Child of a Deceased Alumnus scholarship."

Michael squirted a bitter little shower of a laugh. "Jesus, no," he said.

"He sure never went to college. He was an electrician when he could make it out the door and he couldn't bear the thought that any of us might pass him by. Didn't want to give me the carfare to take the scholarship test for *high* school. Much less college. He hadn't been strapped down to a gurney in Kings County he wouldn't have let me step out of Brooklyn to come down here. No, shit, shit no, he was no *alumnus.*"

He saw that he was getting carried away though—angry young man—and settled back into his seat, waiting for her to carry on with her own life story.

A friend of Michael's saved her from an interrogation, a bearded friend in a wide-brimmed hat leaning over the seat in front and offering them both a hit of *silly-cibin*. She shook her head no, not without Peggy, and Michael said: "Nah, I never do drugs before politics." More winks and nods between him and his friend. With the friend sunk back down into his own seat, Michael elbowed her in the ribs and confessed that he'd actually needed a little speed to get him going when the alarm went off this morning and he was still feeling a little . . . frisky. It took him a minute to find the word, a speeded-up minute.

"I told you I was scared," he said, "you wouldn't show up. You know, Southern girls, they're supposed to be so shy and proper."

That made her spit coffee onto the seat in front of her, a tie-dye pattern of brown that held for a second and then drooled down the blue nubby cloth. She choked, laughing, coffee stopped between her nose and throat, her mouth full.

"Put your arms up!" A command. "Put 'em up!"

She did as he said and her gasps subsided. Oh sitting next to him was like sitting next to a spark plug and she felt again the dread and longing. He couldn't be for real. It was all an act.

"I'm sorry," he was saying in a low voice. "I'm sorry I made you choke."

He looked her full in the face, reverent and direct. It couldn't be an act. No mask this time: he might have been Walter or Martin or Will, teasing her into another smile. He might have been ten years old with his curled-up nose, the neat ellipses of his eyes, the silliness, the urgency. She was too terrified to smile the way he wanted, and the longer she held back the more his face strained. He was moving past ten years old, past fifteen, past eighteen. He was moving through childhood and into . . . adulthood? This guy? Could this guy possibly be an adult? She found herself picturing that snapshot her mother had held up in the bedroom, Pat Starkey's direct respectful stare. Pat Starkey never said *fucking* in his life.

Michael looked away, finally, as if his own eagerness shamed him. As if she'd shamed him out of it.

"How old are you?" she said.

"Nineteen," he said, and sank his head back down deep into the seat. He didn't seem to realize that he was rolling the head back and forth or grinning like a loon. "Nineteen going on a hundred and one. The weight of the world on my shoulders, but maybe the wisdom too, huh?"

She was a spark plug herself, firing away, by the time the bus pushed into the Jersey Turnpike. The stench of the exhaust exhilarated her, the way their bus bore down on some family station wagon and sideswiped it back into place. Beside her Michael had not stopped his squalls of autobiography, but he was petering out. She was wary when he asked about her and she told him only what he already knew, that she was a small-town girl with a dead father. That she painted.

He knew nothing about wariness or economy of expression, either. There was more about his father, about the last year of his life, more bitterness. A little about his mother, a saint. A promise to take her to Coney Island and show her where Ebbets Field once stood. But next time they came up, he said. "If my mom found out I was here today and didn't come out to Brooklyn to see her, I don't know. I mean I do know. It'd hurt her bad. So I won't even call. Just do the action, get back on the bus. I'm praying one of my brothers won't see me on fucking Park Avenue. But there's not much chance of that. They oughta be safe in their Cardinal This, Bishop That." Three brothers in Brooklyn high schools, one right after another, and two little sisters. Two more saints. Franny pictured them with strawberry-blond halos.

On the turnpike the speed wore off by degrees and his face took on a haggard look, his lips blue and his eyes baggy. Just as she was heating up. She twisted and turned in her seat, New York still two hours away. She was a little kid, she was Walter going to Charleston, her brothers on their way to a minor league game. Oh she was a terrible fraud, thinking of the big city and how she could slip away to the Museum of Modern Art when she should be concentrating on the war. What Michael was concentrating on, looking now so grim. He left to go huddle with the priest in the front of the bus: in the street theater he would be a Vietnamese peasant. He pulled black pajamas out of his pack to show her, and flashed a smile that was—ironic, maybe?

Back from his consultation, he began shooting sparks again, and started in on his autobiography anew. He wasn't a theater major at all, Peggy had it all wrong. He *had* been Hamlet but he was, he said, *way over my head and my father died in the middle of rehearsals.* "They pulled me out of playwriting class, can you beat that, cause the director liked the way I read my own lines. I didn't even fucking audition." He was an English major, he said, a writer, and he pulled from the depths of his expanding pack a slew of folders with titles scrawled on in dark marker: *Your Dad's Dead and Facedown in the Mud oh Baby; Don't Shoot Me Dad While the Knife's in Your Hand; Save Your Sisters, Save Your Soul.* One-act plays.

"Your dreams," she said. "You got the titles from your dreams."

"Well not exactly." He searched through a dressing table of expressions and chose a mixture of chagrin and boyish charm. "I thought I'd liven up Steedman's project. I mean he's got all these ordinary dreams to put into the pot and some mornings it's a miracle I like wake up, much less remember my dreams."

She saw herself waking in the middle of the night, straining for her own dreams, admitting in her journal that she wasn't sure where the dream ended. Shy and proper and naive, he should have called her.

He told her, as if it explained why he made up his dream journal, that he'd been offered a scholarship to Columbia too, but only half the size the Jesuits offered. The Jesuits paid him a *stipend* to leave New York, and it had seemed a good idea while his father was still alive. "My girlfriend went though," he said. "To Barnard. Barnyard." A grim little snort, and a new expression, deep disgust. He corrected himself: "Ex-girlfriend."

A good thing too, because otherwise she might have said *Oh you have a girlfriend in New York* in just the tone of voice that would have let him know she felt herself shy and proper and naive beside him, a good girl for the first time in her life, filling out the dream journal with real true dreams and worrying now that he had girlfriends in all his pockets.

"She had to get two abortions," he said, world-weary, "and she was so pissed at the whole world. I said I'd marry her. I said, we'll pool the scholarship money. We'll talk 'em into buying us a fucking house in the country. It was just too much for her. The second time around."

Now he actually closed his eyes and forgot her, oh weary, pained, oh sensitive young Michael Burke. His girlfriend out of the way, his speed wearing off, the story of his life completed up to the present. She watched him, his eyes really closed, the eyelashes not so pale as she'd thought, not as pale as Steward's. Nineteen years old, and already he had crow's-feet around his eyes, the start of them anyway, his pale skin flecked through with faint freckles. It would be the kind of face that would age very young, make him look even more world-weary when he was thirty or forty. His beard was uneven, splotches here and there. That was why he shaved.

The swoops of elation bubbled up to her throat and she kept her eyes wide open while he slept. The girlfriend was out of the way, the city in front of them, little triangles of Danish stuck to the seat beneath their thighs, his jeans patched but the girlfriend gone, her feet finally thawed in the thin canvas sneakers, the bus rumbling beneath them, the big ugly bus, pushing its big ugly way through traffic noise and fumes.

They slipped away from the demonstration, a dwindling crowd of twenty thousand at the U.N., the big building looking like a radiator, just as Michael said it would look. They deserted a sad hopeless crowd clutching bottles of real blood and animal blood and theatrical blood and homemade ketchup blood. Michael had done his street theater as part of the march (rows of peasants doing some sort of modern dance that the priest must have choreographed, Michael the lead peasant and having the grace to look embarrassed at himself for being a redheaded Vietnamese. The dancers gathered imaginary rice and conveyed dignity. Franny doubted the Vietnamese indulged in modern dance agriculture, but what did she know? When she sat on the curb, ogling the doormen and matrons of Park Avenue, a Youth League marcher came along and shook his fist. "Stand up!" he said. "The Viet Cong don't sit down!").

Now they had an hour before the buses would leave and Michael said he'd take her down to the Village just for a look, *something you can write home about*. He hauled her onto the subway.

She must have been born to ride the F train at rush hour. She could see herself there forever, in New York City, with a boyfriend in black pajamas every day of the year. Even the jaded commuters stared at the two of them, undrugged now (she was, anyway, and she hadn't *seen* Michael take anything) but sparklers just the same, two about-to-be lovers getting on board at Forty-second Street in a shower of razzmatazz. She was at home, crushed up against him in the warm dank air of the subway car, her hard breasts making themselves felt through her sweaters and her shirts and his black pajama top, her small chewed fingers grabbing the pole every now and then but held up mostly by this energy, this atomic ball of fire that the two of them were stoking at once.

And now they were in the West Fourth Street station. They were climbing the sticky stairs from one level to the next, Michael pulling her along by the hand and Franny tickled—smiling, maybe even giggling—to be the one pulled. Just what you'd picture, a thousand Arlo Guthries sitting on their haunches and strumming their guitars, in fringed jackets and leather Indian headbands (really, you wouldn't believe the *headbands* unless you saw them. You'd get arrested in Due East for looking this obvious). Michael skipped up ahead and tugged her along to the stairs so they could climb out of the dark incense-permeated station and up into the light of the Village.

Up they climbed, trains clacking in, voices crackling in Esperanto over the loudspeakers, her long hem tripping her and she . . . didn't . . . care, this was it, this was home base. Up one level, Michael led her to the next set of stairs but changed his mind at the last minute, dragged her to a column and kissed her very hard, very expertly, full on the mouth so there was no place for her head to go but back, back, against the column. They could have been a movie poster tacked to the wall.

"I've been wanting to do that all day," he said, editing himself, knowing not to say *all fucking day*. He knew just how to say the line. Such a *line*. Of course. He was an actor and a writer, a fake, a guy who wrote lines, and now he was pulling her along by the hand again, through the waves of New Yorkers coming their way.

And she was letting him haul her. He was taking over now—someone was finally taking over—and her eyes were wide open. She saw herself in all those backseats back in Due East, with all those sweet shy boys, in the dark. Under a line of oaks, deep in the scrap pine woods at the beach. Fumbled clothes, fumbled body parts in the dark of night, and oh how fast they came once she'd talked them into it, just when she wanted to linger, to watch them in the dark, how fast and sweet, the weight of their long bodies, the briny smell of their groins, their sweat.

Now, though, her eyes were wide open and she could see what was coming. At the top of this last set of stairs, *Sixth Avenue,* he said. She emerged to the clear sharp light of late winter, five o'clock, a movie marquee above their heads—*Breathless*—and Michael Burke was still tugging her, tugging her along into the city, into her berth. Oh she was sinking. Not this guy, not this fake.

On the sidewalk he let loose of her hand and she stood in front of a souvenir shop the way Walter would have stood, lips apart, dazed, her beaded bag hanging open for a pickpocket's taking, her eyes rolling upward and her palms upturned, her face blank and serene.

Michael Burke laughed out loud at the sight of her. "Miss Starkey, may I present New York City?"

She was sunk.

WORKING
FOR NIXON

On Steward Morehouse's nineteenth birthday his mother called after supper and just as she said,

"Oh sugar, I've got half a mind to fly on out there and just put my arms around you. You sound so *lonesome,* and on your birthday too,"

he remembered what he had managed to forget for the preceding eight hours, that he was nineteen years old now and had never yet got himself laid. He was alone in his room, a private room with a private phone, the worst mistake he or Grandfather could have made. Grandfather's revenge, to suggest this solitary confinement in the most expensive dorm at the University of the Deep South.

At eight he went out to walk the mile in to catch the streetcar. If there was a dead time in New Orleans, this was it, January, but still there would be music and crowds in the Quarter on a Friday night. He only allowed himself to wander into clubs alone once a week—too pathetic—and almost never on the weekend, when the frat boys from Tulane would be out drunk, marching in columns. But tonight Lola's voice rang in his ear.

Back in September and October he used to ask the two guys who lived on either side of him, Roberts and Rutherford, to come along. By now he was sick of them. The both of them were on the freshman football team, just biding their time until they made varsity and could live in the athletic dorm. They knocked on his door, looking for suckling, whenever he lit a joint.

The streetcar pulled up to the stop as he did (he wouldn't even get to kill time waiting) and he paid his fare in nickels. Lately he'd been more aware of his compulsion to keep the room tidy, to get those nickels off the dresser. Maybe it was the only way to keep his sanity at UDS. Maybe it proved that he was losing any sanity he'd ever had. Grandfather was absolutely right. It was a mediocre school. He hadn't read a single book there that hadn't been assigned at St. Benny's, and the students who were not as stupid as Roberts and Rutherford interrupted poly sci class to offer raging arguments in favor of the war, arguments that would have turned even Nick sour. They still hadn't got over civil rights. They still hadn't got over the Civil War.

On the streetcar he sat down opposite a sleepy little girl in a green velvet coat, nestled into an old gentleman in a three-piece suit. They'd been out celebrating something too. Cornrows and ribbons in her hair, the child stared at him terrified through a little gloved hand she brought to her forehead for protection.

In the streetcar glass behind her he saw that he was a cipher. White boys were supposed to be straight or hippie, but he was neither here nor there. He was still trying to grow his hair out, but that only meant that it was in his eyes all the time. He himself couldn't say whether it was white or blond. Maybe the little girl thought he was a young old man, or an old young man, with his caved-in cheeks and the sprinkle of stubble across his chin. He couldn't even get a five-year-old child to smile at him, much less a coed at the University of the Deep South.

Down at the Square he almost turned around and headed back out to the campus. This night would be like any other night he'd spent drinking alone at a bar, the restaurants behind him filling up with families, with old married couples, with big guys in chinos who drank together and insulted the waitress together. Finally he'd stumble into someplace loud and obnoxious, pretending he was waiting for his girlfriend to come out of the bathroom, pretending he'd come to listen to Dixieland when he couldn't abide it.

He was standing by the Cathedral, stalling, when a girl from his biology class emerged and smiled at him. She was plump—all right, you could definitely say heavy—but pretty just the same, a girl with long loose blond curls she'd fussed with before she came out. She was the kind of girl who arrived early to class and sat in the front row, smiling at everyone who entered the room. Tonight she was wearing a shirtdress he'd seen on his Aunt Blinky, only Aunt Blinky's would have been several sizes smaller. It was a pale blue broadcloth, and over it she wore a navy cardigan. Her shoes were navy, and so were her button earrings and her handbag, whose strap she was clutching. He'd never paid such attention to an outfit before. Its symmetry touched him.

She caught an edge of his smile, took a deep breath, and came over to his side. Under the floodlights he could see that her eye shadow was the same shade as her dress, and not only that, her eyelashes were painted blue. She had surpassed even Aunt Blinky.

"Hi," she said in a throaty voice. "Biology, right?"

He nodded and stuck out his hand, the way you'd do at St. Ben's, before he realized it was all wrong. "Steward Morehouse."

"Shirley Ann," she said, and he wasn't sure whether that meant Ann was her last name or her middle name. She was giving his hand an enthusiastic pumping. "You get down here to the Cathedral a lot?"

"Nah," he said. "I went in once with my parents. The first time I came to town."

"Me neither," she said, relieved. "I just peeked in to say I saw it. That dripping-blood stuff gives me the willies." It was true, you could just about feel the thorns cutting into your forehead. He couldn't think of anything to say.

"Well," she said. "You waiting on somebody?"

Terrifying to meet somebody as pathetic as he was. He told her no, he was alone. Then he asked if she'd like to come for a drink.

"I'd love to!" She lowered her voice. "I have to tell you, it'd turn my mama's gray hair back to blond if she knew. We're Baptist. But you have to live a little bit when you're young, don't you? And then you go back home and get serious for the rest of your life."

Home, she said walking along, was Pricking, Arkansas. She was the fifth generation of her family to go to the University of the Deep South, but they all ended up back in Pricking, which was about as pretty a little town as you could get, up in the Ozarks. God's country. They walked along St. Ann Street, then wandered up Bourbon Street and turned the corner, looking for someplace likely. This little grid—Bourbon to St. Philip, Dauphine to Ursulines—was a puzzle he'd worked too many times, and he'd never solved it, never determined exactly what it was his father saw on these streets. He thought Shirley (or Shirley Ann?) might get a kick out of an elegant Frenchy tourist trap, away from the bustle, and it would be anonymous, too.

"My father has a store in Pricking," she was saying. She looked down at the blue dress. "But now I'm in New Orleans I can't run over to Daddy's anymore. You think this dress here is too, uhm, too young?"

Lola used to ask for his opinion about clothes, too, when he was zipping her up. *I don't know, Stewie, you think my belly's getting a little flabby for this number?*

"Nah," he said. "Nah, I don't think it's young at all. Actually, I think it's a lot more sophisticated than what you see." He didn't mean to lie, but it made her smile big. She had large perfect teeth that had probably been retained and braced and capped and whitened and her lips were full, painted a pale pink to go with the pale blue. He was right, she was pretty, and prettier the closer you looked, once you got past the heavy breasts in the shirtdress, once you got past the thick ankles above the navy flats. Her face was broad but as symmetrical as her outfit, and when she lit up and smiled like that you could see how deep and high her cheekbones cut into her skin. Her nose was a small perfect inclined plane.

"Aw, you're just saying that. But it's a sweet thing to say, and I thank you for it."

They were passing a hotel, Le 'tit Aigneau, and he saw through the glass doors that it was just what he was looking for, the kind of place with a red-rugged lobby and a big staircase swooping up and a dark bar for people coming in off the street. He thought she might squeal with pleasure when he pointed it out.

"I've been *dying* to go in there," she said. So she'd wandered these streets alone the same way he had. He didn't have the right to feel superior. He didn't have the right to grit his teeth with embarrassment when a tuxedoed little man with a black moustache swung his arm wide after Steward said they just wanted the bar. That was probably the sort of smarmy amused look he gave everyone from Pricking, Arkansas, who walked in through these doors.

In the small square bar the women had Aunt Blinky's short pouffed hairdo and sharp filed chin, but they were dressed in Lola's skintight dresses, black slinky numbers, and around their throats their necklaces were dazzlers, red and green and silver and gold. Two of the men were in dinner jackets, the rest in coats and ties. He was in a pair of Levi's and a polo shirt.

Shirley Ann smoothed her cotton dress over her wide hips and barreled over to the bar where she settled herself onto a big stool. If he'd chosen, he would have picked one of those little round tables for two in the darkest corner of the room.

They both drank fast, Shirley Ann chattering on about biology class. Hers was the loudest voice in the room and when she uttered the words *endocrine system* he began to look around for the men's room. It had actually occurred to him that he should locate a window, an alley to flee down. But in fact no one was looking at them. No one even knew they were there. He ordered them refills.

"I've been just chatting away, they call me Miss Chatterbox at home, and you haven't told me a thing about yourself."

Steward stared at the ice in his drink. This fluttery shit. This tell me about yourself. But she was only trying. The room was pleasant now, after the buzz of his first drink, even if Shirley Ann felt a sense of conversational obligation. The bar itself was maybe twelve feet long, no longer than the old altar at St. Ben's, its wood a good old mahogany polished bright. The mirror was etched with white curlicues signifying nothing but the dizzy wish for a hot time tonight. Every time he looked around another couple had departed the room. Soon he would be alone with Shirley Ann, and it was only just past ten.

"Oh, there's nothing to tell." Like an old man.

"There's got to be *something.*" Shirley Ann's eyes were bright, almost black and deeply liquid. Could this be her first time in a bar?

He strained, hunched over his drink. Really, he hated this shit. Shirley Ann, a Baptist saint of patience and sweetness, waited. He could feel the heat of her shoulders leaning his way, anticipating the little something he would reveal by accident.

Finally he said: "My parents met here."

"IN THIS BAR?"

"Nah," he said. "In New Orleans." When he finally looked her straight in the face, he saw that her lipstick was wearing off. Her mouth was outlined in deep pink, but shaded in splotches like a paint-peeled wall. She looked older. Before the drinks, he might have found it pathetic, but now, his shoulders relaxing, he decided he liked the ragged look of her full mouth better. She'd peeled her cardigan off and it trailed from her lap onto the rungs of the barstool. He began to picture the two of them going up to the registration desk and asking for a room upstairs.

"Wow," she said. "Your parents went to UDS too?"

"Nah." This time he wouldn't let any more dribble out, and this time she tilted back on her own stool and seemed to know to let him be. She used the swizzle stick to twirl her ice round and round, and then she finished the drink off with a gulp and a flourish of lip smacking. The way a child might finish off a tablespoon of cough syrup.

She stared at the drink on the bar, but when he watched her, sidelong, she did not look rebuffed, only absorbed in the ice and the stick and the polished surface. The silence stretched on. His own drink was not nearly so absorbing as hers seemed to be.

"Like another one?" He shouldn't be offering—he was certain now that she'd never had a drink before, unless maybe it was one at the high school prom—but he was melting into the barstool and she was chubby and pretty and sweet and now silent beside him.

She looked over at him, finally, and gave off a faint smile and a faint scent, lilacs and syrup. "I'll be right back," she said.

He waited so long that he began to think she'd had his idea, that she'd found a bathroom window to shimmy out of, or maybe walked right out the front door onto the street. But finally she was back, doused with more of her flowery cologne and her lips glossed up with a deeper pink. Her eye shadow looked darker too, or maybe his eyesight was adjusting to the bar light. She winked at him, he thought, while she was backing herself onto the barstool.

"*Now* I'd like another one," she said.

Maybe he had read her all wrong. Now she looked like a barfly, like someone who knew exactly what she was doing. In fact he was the one who was beginning to feel sloozy in the head. He was the one who was wondering whether it would be wise to have a third drink.

But he asked for another round, *had* to ask for another round, and then went looking for the men's room. He passed by the registration desk, where ornate calligraphy asked you to *Please ring*. The fluttery shit, the feminine hand, everywhere you looked. In an office beyond, he could see a horn-rimmed young woman in a prim pointy collar, reading a book. A grad student probably, with a Friday night job renting rooms. The things she must see.

In the men's room mirror his eyes were bloodshot and his hair hung down, dirty and lank. No wonder the little girl on the streetcar was terrified of him. This Shirley Ann was surely as desperate as he was. In the mirror he smiled a shaky drunken smile. Shirley Desperate. Surely Ann.

On the way back past the registration desk he put a hand to his back pocket, the wallet safe and sound. In it rested two hundred dollars, an amount he'd taken to carrying since the allowance got rolling. You could never be sure when you'd get a good deal on dope, and his neighbors Roberts and Rutherford, their own best interests at heart, had introduced him to every big dealer on campus. You could never be sure when you'd finally meet the girl who'd go to bed with you, and you'd need a lot of money in your pocket.

Going back into the bar, his eyes adjusting to the dark light, he saw a solitary newcomer nursing a drink, a guy his age with a full dark wiry beard and a mophead full of greasy corkscrew curls. As he got close to the bar and the reflection in its mirror, he could see that the guy had turned older, that he was some biker in silver-chained boots affecting a hippie look. He was encrusted with dangling necklaces, Celtic crosses and Maltese crosses and ankhs. Steward stared at him in the mirror until he felt Shirley Ann staring up too. If it were Fran in this bar she would have found a way to sidle up to the hippie in the corner while he was gone. She would have made time the same way she made time with Tony Rivers. She wouldn't have thought twice about following—*no, leading*—Mr. Motorcycle up the stairs to a cozy little room. *Please ring.*

"What'd you like to do next?" he heard himself say. He seemed to have sat down and swallowed down his drink in one go. "Or maybe you have to get on back."

"Oh, no, it's Friday night, no, you have to live a little." She was so pleased by the invitation she was blushing all over, speckled pink as a rosebush. "I'm up for anything," she said. "Just anything at all."

He laughed. Anything at all.

"What's so funny?"

"Aw, nothing." Behind them the guy in the corkscrew curls stood, shook his curls and his chains, and left.

"Let's go hear some music," he said, "down to Frenchmen Street."

Was that disappointment in her big-teeth smile? Or was he dreaming it? She hopped down from her stool and he followed her out into the red-rugged lobby. The big staircase swooped up. *Please ring.* Her wide hips swung through the door and back out onto the street. He had enough money, anyway, to get them a cab home.

Late the next morning he ran into her in the cafeteria. Bacon flapping around between her teeth, coffee sluicing down her chin, she told him that her father had been head of the Pricking, Arkansas, Nixon campaign, and she had been his right-hand gal. He nodded, deaf-and-dumb, hungover.

For weeks afterward she called three or four times a week, not getting the message. But she went away eventually. Eventually anyone would get it. He just didn't believe a girl—or maybe you were supposed to say woman now, with women's lib—he just didn't believe a woman would buy it if he said he couldn't go out with her again because she had worked for Nixon and then bragged about it.

Besides, the next Friday night he took an acting major named Rochelle —a tall dark Cajun girl in tight jeans and boots—to the bar at Le 'tit Aigneau. They got very drunk on Southern Comforts, and Rochelle said she was a socialist. He didn't know how serious she was, but a socialist would be all for the sexual revolution.

"Look," he said, and willed himself to talk fast enough to get past a suggestion that they go listen to music on Frenchmen Street. "Hows about we rent us a room upstairs?"

"Sure," she said, just like that, and he walked her out to the registration desk. *Please ring.*

She squeezed his hand and then slid her arm round his waist and tugged at his belt loops. The graduate student in the horn-rims came out to have him sign in and he saw now that she had smutty black eyes behind the glasses. She was quite beautiful. Rochelle was beautiful too, her straight hair hanging down almost to her hips, the hips curvy as a cello's. Probably Shirley Ann had been beautiful.

He followed Rochelle up Le 'tit Aigneau's big swooping staircase to a room that was, yes, cozy. His grandmother would have approved of the antiques. But when the door closed behind them his whole body stammered.

Not to worry. Rochelle began to unbutton her shirt, and when she drew it off he saw in the lamplight that she was . . . he struggled for the word. Once he'd known Nick was gazing on Lola. He'd heard his stepfather's voice hissing through the drywall and into his bedroom.

Oh sweetheart look at you. You are lush.

Rochelle began to slide the tight jeans down her hips—nothing was required of him—and he had to suck in his tongue to keep from whooping at the sight of her long curves. If only he'd listened to his grandfather's advice. One drink before, one drink during, one drink after. One two three, Steward. If only he'd listened to his grandfather's advice he would be wholly there while a beautiful socialist girl gazed at him naked.

Oh shweetheart he heard himself say. *You are* lush.

He called Fran in March.

Some girl with a raspy voice hollered down a hallway—"Frances Starkey, Frances STARkey"—and he considered hanging up. His tongue stuck to the roof of his mouth when he asked for *Frances,* but he didn't know what she called herself now, Franny or Fran or Fan or Frances. Last week in a bar he and Rochelle had met two spaced-out girls who'd taken new names entirely, Journey Blue Heaven and Astral Projection. That didn't seem like Franny's style, but she did have a weakness for following trends.

He was stoned, or he never would have picked up the phone to call the Jesuit University of America. Jesuit University of America! University of the Deep South! Look where they'd ended up. He was stoned, his door closed against the impending arrival of Roberts and/or Rutherford, who would smell the hash and knock any minute. He was very stoned, and he should have hung up the minute she said *hi* in that airy way, rushed and girlish, expecting someone else.

"*Steward.* Where are you? S.D. said you were going off to New Orleans."

"I did. It's ninety degrees. Worse than Due East in August." He could feel sweat dripping, but when he put his hand to his forehead it was dry. He was very stoned. She sounded very far away.

"Oh Steward."

Impossible to tell from the two words what tone she was using, much less what meaning she attached to the phrase. Oh Steward. His index finger played at the phone button. Everything felt wet. Even the phone button was soggy.

"I just thought I'd check in for old time's sake." Oh, pathetic. He'd had a story ready—that his freshman advisor looked like her father and that he'd been thinking all year, every time he saw the professor, that he should call and tell her how much he'd admired her old man—but he saw in a lightning moment of hashish clarity how cruel that would be. It was her legs actually that he thought of when he was this stoned, the birthmark like a star behind her right knee when she wore the satiny running shorts.

"You sound stoned."

"Well I'm in a right-wing paradise down here. I get stoned as much as I can. How you doing?"

"You wouldn't recognize me, I swear Steward. I had a 3.2 last semester and I swear on a stack of Bibles I read every word in Great Western Thought."

"I *don't* believe it. Can Teresa mail you papers that fast?"

She guffawed over the wire, and followed up with a little girl's hoot that didn't sound like her. Did she used to laugh? "Teresa dudn't believe it either. Oh Steward it's so nice to hear your voice. It's nice to think of you stoned. Just so long as you're not sad. Old sad Stew."

"Nah. Never sad. Stoned maybe. Never sad. Hey, you going down to Due East for spring break?"

"Are you?" Eagerness in her voice?

"I think so. I think I could bear to leave this hellhole for a while."

"Shit. I wish I could then. But I'm going to New York, ackshully."

Sure, he was stoned, if he'd dreamed she'd be a week without her hand

roped around some esoteric art student's dirty neck. Well, he was going to
Due East with his girlfriend, wasn't he.

"Oh wow. New York. That's great."

A long silence followed, a cavernous silence that made his dorm room
go dark on him. He was in the MG, in Due East, swilling warm beer from a
can. He dimly heard Roberts or Rutherford rapping on his door and he
cupped his hand over the hash pipe to push the sweet smell back in. Last
week somebody from UDS got picked up downtown for holding a nickel.
A nickel. There was talk of the guy getting twelve to fifteen years. He had a
three-hundred-dollar stash in his bottom drawer, and sometimes he thought
getting busted with it would be better than staying here.

The rapping was continuing, or maybe that was an echo in his brain,
but now his pipe was out. It went out when he started talking to Franny.
On her end he could hear a whispering girl's voice, someone wanting to
use the phone. But the silence stretched blacker.

"I gotta get home to see my mother," he said finally. "She's a mess."

"Nick—"

"Nick's o.k. She flew out to Hawaii to meet him for his R&R and now
she's terrified he's gonna waste away, he's so skinny. Can you just see Nick
skinny? Maybe she went on the wrong guy's R&R."

"Yeah."

More silence. He hadn't said *I gotta get home with my girlfriend*. He didn't
know how to fit it in now. More rapping, maybe, and then she said: "I
should get down to see Mama too, but I can't, I dunno, I can't face it. She is
pissed I'm going up to New York. You know. Sodom and Gomorrah."

"Oh well," he said, shit-eating grin on his face even as he sat solitary.
Now Roberts and/or Rutherford were banging on the door—*We know
you're in there Morehouse and we know you're holding onto something real good*—
"Oh well, you'll see her. Sometime. She's all right, old Doris. She's a tough
cookie. I'M ON THE PHONE."

"Hope Nick'll be all right. You were right about the war. I've been
wishing I could tell you that, I dunno, it seems like the longest time."

"He's a tough cookie too."

She laughed again. "You sound different, Stew, talkative or something.
Just doesn't sound like you. *Tough cookie*."

Once Lola bickered with Nick over who was more romantic, women or
men, and he had to agree with his mother that it was men. It was Nick,

watching his mother move around the kitchen clicking her patent-leather heels. When Lola wanted to watch somebody, she watched her own reflection. She was crazy for Nick, maybe, but she was practical about it. She didn't get all misty-eyed.

He hung up the phone and shoved the pipe out through the slit he'd opened in the door. Rutherford said:

"Thanks, son. But you're getting a tad weird. Don't you want some company?"

He did not want the company of those two. After they took his pipe down the hall (he must have been out of his mind, that was a huge chunk in there), he'd sit in the dark, hearing from Rutherford's room the snarl of *In-A-Gadda-Da-Vida* until he couldn't stand it anymore. Then he'd call Rochelle and they'd walk in to catch the streetcar together.

It had occurred to him when he wandered the Quarter now with Rochelle, his arm dangling down over those lush breasts, that they might run into Shirley Ann the way he'd run into her that Friday night, that with Rochelle along he wouldn't have the chance to tell Shirley (Ann?) she was wearing a pretty dress or that her hair smelled good.

New Orleans was like Due East, only populated. It was a good town, with good joints as Lola said, and he had the money to go out every night of the week and wonder whether his parents had once stood together in front of the same bar where he stood with Rochelle. Still he couldn't help picturing Franny in one of these joints. If she'd been the one to end up in New Orleans she would have been to bed already with a hundred guys, the motorcycle guy in Le 'tit Aigneau with all the crosses, the big-shouldered guys with aviator glasses and Fu Manchu moustaches who stood in bar doorways counting their cash.

But Franny was a million miles away. And he hadn't run into Shirley Ann once, walking this town with his new girl.

DINNER
WITH THE
JESUITS

Steward, asking if she was coming home to Due East, was naked and transparent and needy. She loved him dearly. And maybe she loved Michael dearly too.

Michael sounded like a dying man when he came. First he let out a whimper, then a groan he built up gradually to a roar of protest. These he followed with a rasping shudder that could have been a death rattle. Finally, a maniacal laugh: "Ah-ha!" Beat death again. The headboard trembled for a full minute after the laugh. The whole hall could hear them. The whole dorm, the whole campus.

He lay atop her, deadweight. "Oh Fran Fran Fran."

The sheer variety of drugs he consumed was appalling, even to her. You couldn't possibly ingest as many drugs as he did and be celibate as long as he claimed. Acid every day (oh nothing, he said, blotter acid, less of a buzz than pot), peyote, mushrooms, mescaline, coke from God knows where—he was always broke—and pot like cigarettes. Bennies at six A.M. if he had an early class. Uppers, downers, in-betweeners. She expected his brain to blow any minute, and it sounded that way, when he was coming.

It tickled her now that Steward had worried about the little packages she lifted from the five-and-ten in Due East. Michael came out of the Safeway looking like a circus clown, a dozen cans of tuna fish in his pockets and a sirloin steak tucked in the back of his jeans, the scarlet blood running down the backs of his legs. He was just liberating stuff, he said, for practice. "Come the revolution," he boomed, laughing at her. He walked half a block, not even out of sight, and donated the groceries to the first worthy recipient he saw, usually an old lady who drew back at the sight of his wild hair and black pupils. Some days his light eyes were all black pupils.

In the single bed, Fran pushed him off. He was down close to sleep already, and the sun was just down the horizon. A wonder he could keep his scholarship, but he wrote his papers while he was stoned, his plays while he was blasted. He would rise in the middle of the night, when the beer wore off, light a joint, and sit at the typewriter.

"Don't go," he mumbled into the pillow. His roommate was off in a girlfriend's bed—there was a kind of bumping system, dominoes down the campus—and every night he was after her to stay. Stay and play house. She never had.

"Sallright, Michael," she whispered. Even when he curled around her, even when he ran his big open hand down the length of her leg, she always disentangled herself to go home to Peggy and her own solitary bed.

But tonight he said: "Hey, Emily Dickinson, you can't leave. Joe and Simon are cooking for us tonight. They're all psyched."

She'd forgotten. Joe-and-Simon were Jesuits Michael visited every Friday night for poker or politics. Tonight she was invited: he was taking the girlfriend home to meet the priests. They'd ask what *parish* she came from. They'd want to know why they'd never seen her in the sparse congregation at chapel.

"Aw, I reckon you'll be better off without me."

He roused himself from sleep now, willing himself back to life, staring up at her from the pillow with a bone-white face. The overhead bulb played up his sore chapped lips. "I love you, Fran," he said, a sentence he'd managed to utter without the hint of a pause or a giggle the first night he'd seduced her, and one he repeated regularly every time since, before and after. It was a wonder how smoothly this mantra came out, but not nearly so much a wonder as the way she parroted it—"Love you too Michael"— oh smooth as you please, words she'd have choked on if she'd ever said them to the boys who felt obliged to get romantic in the backseats of cars, boys you'd never attach the word *lovers* to. *Oh yeah,* she said to those guys. Now it was *Love you too* and wonder of wonders, she meant it, in a wary way.

Michael propped himself up on the pillows, comfy and content, scratching his balls under the sheets. His ribs showed, and she'd been right about the white hairless chest, but there were no sun-inflamed moles. His skin looked as if it hadn't seen sunlight since he left home. He grinned, all the time, that loopy asymmetrical grin that could have been Walter's. Was this smile drug-induced? Was this boy a lover?

"Hey, man, come on with me. Why so pale and wan, fond lover? I told them you'd be there. I mean, like, that's why they're cooking. For my girl."

"Why would they be cooking for me?"

"Shit, they can't bring their own girlfriends back to the residence."

Hard to tell what was for real with that grin glaring up. Jesuits with girlfriends. If everyone went crazy together, there'd be no one left to stroke your forehead. Next thing, she'd be hearing that *Doris* was out having affairs.

"What's the spiritual catch?"

"Fran. They're *Jesuits,* which means they're crafty. They're trying to seduce me with the mechanics of street theater."

This Joe-and-Simon thing was a mystery to her. Michael had been in a Jesuit high school in New York, and those priests had not only ignored his mocking anticlericalism, they had passed him on to the next priests, given him a letter of introduction in their nineteenth-century way. Now Michael was a regular.

She picked up jeans and T-shirt off the floor and held them up doubt-fully. "I don't have a bra." The T-shirt was mighty thin, and all day her nipples had pressed pleasantly against the cotton.

"WHOO-EE! That's shocking!" He rose and bounced straight across the bed to come up behind her and squeeze the braless breasts. "They've never seen *that* before, I can guarantee you."

His bedroom was shrouded in smoky light. She was still not accus-tomed to playing such an innocent.

"Did we smoke a joint tonight?"

"Yeah." Already he was pulling on his boots, all business now that he'd remembered dinner with the Jesuits. Cagey, he looked at her. "Don't be glum, Pablo Neruda."

Something did not make sense here, and it was not just this particular burst of energy. He was always blazing, never groggy. Did he have a mad-man's clarity, or was he faking the drug stuff too? Now he followed her gaze, or her train of thought, to the joint still by the bed, the remains sitting placid in the ashtray. Almost a full joint, still ready to go. He walked over to slip it into his front pocket.

They hadn't really smoked a joint, they'd had a toke. She saw his roommate Kevin holding out a bottle of Quaaludes and Michael grinning as he popped one, then saw him biting down to spit three-quarters of it into his hand. Down went the remains of Quaalude, deep into his jeans pocket.

She laughed out loud.

"And what's so droll, Jack Kerouac?" By now he had the boots on and his black leather jacket too, though it was spring outside and the jacket was not just too clunky but too heavy as well. This was the guy who wore the light denim in the dead of winter.

"I just realized," she said. "You don't do near so many drugs as you make out you do. You're a *social* druggie. You're a fake."

"I told you, Miss Francie. I told you that's blotter acid. I haven't had a fucking hallucination in so long I'm gonna hafta drop out of the Coleridge Club."

He crossed his heart, pretending to be an innocent too. Then he held the door for her—she was still tying her sneakers! They hadn't even taken a shower!—and went dancing down the hallway. He knocked on all the doors and called out: "Repent! Repent!" He always did this sort of thing after they'd been to bed in the afternoon.

She trailed along after him, humming "Harrigan" in the hallway. Going to meet the priests. She would have to climb out of the ground-floor window in Tony Iovino's room, the same way she came in. God bless Tony Iovino, said all the residents of Martyrs Hall, Tony who left his window and his door open day and night for the free trafficking of women. They *were* still in a Catholic college.

"Day of Judgment's coming," Michael called. "Day of Judgment." But Michael the Madman didn't do that many drugs after all, and he handed all his papers in on time, and he phoned his *mother* (he actually called her Ma) every Sunday, as religiously as the five remaining practicing Catholics on campus went to Mass, and he called back later in the day if he'd missed one of his brothers or sisters. There might be a name for this kind of dual existence. She could always ask Steedman.

"The Day of Judgment is at hand," he called down the corridor, but no one home could hear him. The music rolled out from behind the dorm doors, weird overlays of white boy music, The Who and The Stones, Van Morrison and The Band and The Jefferson Airplane. From the lovesick rooms, the sad strum of acoustic guitars. "Prepare to meet your Maker," Michael called.

She was only preparing to meet the Jesuits. They must see through Michael, anyway, see that he called his mother and visited priests and only took baby doses of everyone else's drugs.

"It's *Father Knows Best* around here," Michael said at the door to the priests' apartment. Sure enough, Simon (assistant chairman of the history department), who ushered them in, turned out to be the silvery *Bells of St. Mary's* priest from the bus ride to New York. Playing host, he went to the crowded liquor cabinet—it could have stocked a saloon—and produced a new bottle of Southern Comfort.

"I couldn't resist," he said to Fran, pouring out triples. "I don't think we've ever had a bottle of *this* on hand." Joe (university chaplain) appeared meanwhile with a tray of cornbread fingers and chicken wings and shrimp something or others on sticks, with little peas and pearl onions stuck on.

"What do you think, Fran, is this authentic?" He set the tray down and pumped her hand the way her father might have pumped a boy-friend's.

"You old fussbudgets." Michael was trying to balance the whiskey glass and a shrimp stick thing while he lit the joint from his pocket. Joe took the joint from him, got it going, and passed it to Fran, who waved it away in confusion. These priests were going to smoke dope? But Simon passed too, and sat down on her right to say

"I'm anxious to ask you what you think about all this conceptual art business,"

which meant that Michael had already bragged on her. She was touched and settled into the back of their couch, as comfortable as she would have been sitting with a boy's real father. They were always trying so hard to like you. Mutual terror and pity.

The couch was light and modern and airy and new, and so was all the other furniture. It would have come from one of those new mall furniture places, and it matched the apartment building, which was big and new and modern and rectangular, filled with priests rooming together, the kind of building another university would have used for married student housing. The Jesuit residence was on the edge of campus, down a lane of tasteful symmetrical cherry trees. She hadn't liked the looks of Joe and Simon's apartment from the very beginning, but now in the slow burn of her drink she saw that they had a dark icon, Virgin and Son, over by the bookcases. Good greens and scarlets. And the bookcases themselves were dark and ponderous, a mess, pamphlets and journals and yellowing pages sticking out every which way. Good bookcases.

Joe and Michael finished off the joint, but then Joe rose to produce his own stash, stored in the kind of large black plastic bag you might use to gather your front yard clippings. They were all slogging down their second Southern Comforts.

"Look at the way you stuck those little onion gobbers on those sticks. I bet they squirt all over the place when you stick the point through. Oh man, the patience of a saint."

"Michael. *I* didn't make those. Not that I wouldn't have been delighted to make hors d'oeuvres for you, Fran, but my job usually runs into overtime."

"Time-and-a-half saving souls!"

"You ignore him, Fran. The kid's got no respect."

Simon, sober somehow, steered her by the elbow into the kitchen, where they were ready to broil big sirloin steaks. The two priests fluffed out baked potatoes and worried over the dressing for the salad, and then they all washed down dinner with two bottles of Italian wine, lovely light fruity wine that made her head light and fruity.

By the time the bottles sat empty in the middle of the table, and Simon had risen to clear their plates away, Michael pulled out a pipe and began to peel the tinfoil off a large chunk of hash. The hash must have gotten wet, and he picked at the stuck paper with tiny patient movements. He looked something like one ape bending over to groom another. What was it she had been thinking before about his drug consumption?

"Y'know, Fran, I never got a steak before. This is all a show they're putting on for you. Usually it's here's your fucking beer, now where are the cards."

Joe and Simon smiled, tranquil. They were handsome men, in that fatherly way. Simon's features were small and tidy in a ruddy face, his shave very close, his skin only just loosening at the chin. Joe was bigger all around, with coarse features and a broad florid face. His hair was a dull deep black, and every now and again, especially when the conversation lulled, he tugged at its thickness where he had it combed back over a widow's peak. Now he was smiling at her and tugging at the hair, as if he'd read her mind. You felt foolish and alarmed and secure, all at once, looking at a handsome priest in civilian clothes. She was very drunk.

"You don't have a girlfriend, do you?"

It was one of the first full sentences she'd uttered. Surely she hadn't said this last, not out loud.

But she must have said it, because Joe and Simon and Michael were chortling in unison, chortling amused goodwill and serenity. "Oh, I don't have a girlfriend this week," Joe said, and then, with a shrewd narrowing of his eyes: "Whatever have you been telling her, Michael?" His eyes, and

Simon's too, were light blue, that chalky blue of Michael's, and you didn't have to hear them called *Father* to know that their last names would be Boyle or McQuade or O'Leary. Simon taught Irish history.

"Jeez Fran, I can't have you embarrassing priests that way." Michael was laughing his deep throaty serious laugh and thumping the table.

"Oh, scandal scandal everywhere," Joe said, and it set him to giggling. The two of them sounded like fourth graders.

"Don't worry, Fran, you couldn't possibly embarrass this man. Michael, we'll sue you for slander next time. Come on, you slugs, let's head on downstairs and get a game rolling." This was fatherly Simon, rising to shepherd them downstairs for poker. No one mentioned doing the dishes, so they left behind a pile of plates, the grease congealing. Hadn't she been the first to mention any matters of the flesh?

She'd caught a glimpse of Downstairs on the way in, a clubby big lounge on one side of the entrance hallway, a dining hall on the other. Now they swooped down on the elevator, she and Michael tripping over the two Jesuits, and veered left for the dining hall side of things. She saw a roomful of dark tables checkered with men finishing up their pies and their puddings and their coffees and their brandies.

Not even dimly had she ever registered the presence of this many priests on campus. They were greeted from every table by the avuncular smiles and nods of middle-aged men. Michael seemed to know them all.

The dark-paneled room reminded her of the Officers Club, where Pat took the family once a year, but the men sitting here would never have passed for Marines. There were a few in Roman collars, and around one table a trio of old men sitting straight from the spine, but the rest of the Jesuits were disguised as ordinary professors in business suits and turtlenecks. Simon was in a gray cardigan, Joe in a lumberjack shirt.

Simon took charge of sitting them down and then strolled off to the bar for beer. As long as she didn't have to drink it. Sitting down in one motion was tricky enough. Joe was already shuffling cards. "Ever heard of a game called baseball? Or night baseball?"

Simon was back with the beer, four mugs caught up in his fist as easily as he might have held onto a fly ball.

"No," she said, "I never heard of night baseball, but you can teach me," and hoisted her beer.

She was passing the *Father Knows Best* test. Michael, working the loopy grin, passed over stacks of chips from a mahogany cabinet and she lined them up, pretending she was sober. Maybe the priests were just faking, but her luck held through their silly games—even Simon, after a beer, wanted to play Spit in the Ocean and Acey-Deucey.

The deal passed to Joe, who shuffled the cards three, four, five times through. They were slowing now, all of them, and Simon rose to fetch them another round. She tried to tote up her earnings and the alcohol they'd consumed. It was a Friday night, but weren't there Saturday morning Masses someone would have to say?

"Michael." Simon came back with the beer and started in as if the night were just beginning. "We've got to talk about the demonstration."

She found it difficult to sit, and propped her elbow on the table, her chin on an open palm. Joe seemed to have finally stopped shuffling and said: "It's very bad now."

Everything stopped. Michael and Simon leaned forward in a new state of consciousness, the evening suddenly elevated, but she was soused and heard Joe's voice through a screen:

"I had a call yesterday, a priest at his wit's end. Last week he had another five families burned out. He's over here trying to drum up support. I told him Simon was working on the embassy thing."

"Sounds like he needs money more than a fucking demonstration," Michael said.

"Oh, he's asking for money too. Yup, he's asking for money. And I'll tell you the truth, he sounds so riled up I don't know if it's relief money or gun money he's asking for."

Simon cut in. "Don't give Fran the wrong idea."

She started at the sound of her name. She had no idea what they were talking about.

"No, no, Fran." Joe waved his hand across the table. "It has to be nonviolent. There's no choice. But you can understand why a guy living in the slums would sympathize when his parishioners start picking up rocks to defend themselves from the very troops sent there to defend them. It's one thing to preach nonviolence."

"They're walking out on the nonviolent sermons anyway," Michael said. "That's what it said in the *Post*. Fifty people walked out of Sunday Mass in Derry."

Fran smiled pleasantly, then saw that a smile was all wrong. There was cheesecake clogging her brain and Southern Comfort running out her ears. It was *Ireland* they were talking about.

"The IRA's bound to pick up new recruits," said Simon, "while Paisley's goons are running wild. The trick is to get some political action going before these Provisionals turn into goons themselves and lose all the ground that's been gained."

"I don't know," Michael said. "I mean, shit Simon, you know I'll do the demonstration, but I have to say if I was, like, that priest in Belfast—all right, don't laugh, I know I wouldn't ever be a priest in Belfast—but if I was somebody whose mother and father just got burned out I can't say I wouldn't be picking up a damn sight more than a rock. You know?"

"We're forgetting your history," Simon said.

History? Fran sat up, or tried to. Her field of vision wobbled, but she had Michael in focus.

"My grandfather. Supposed to have been heavy into the IRA but you know, it's like the fucking kings of Ireland. Everybody's descended from one."

Joe said: "What do you think, Fran?"

What did she *think*? She'd just figured out the country they were talking about. She was nonfunctional, drunk as a skunk, staring now at a patch of Michael's beard coming in copper, at his chapped lips, thinking for all the roughness that really it was an angel's face, a Raphael face with those undercurrents of gold, a lovely face, and Joe-and-Simon's faces were lovely too, under their dark hair, beneath their light eyes. She was drunk and dreaming, as mushy as AgnesAnn and Teresa. She was back surrounded by Steward and S.D. and Harrison and Dillon.

"Well. I thought it was incredible," she said, "what Martin Luther King got done." Though she could not imagine where it came from, she seemed to have produced an entire sentence. Gushy, but whole.

"Oh look what Martin Luther King got for his trouble," Michael said. "And the Panthers shot in their fucking beds."

"Michael," Joe said. "Listen to your girlfriend."

They all stared at her. Now she was supposed to produce another full sentence.

"Well, it's still civil rights, isn't it?" You'd think she'd know *something* about it, living with Peggy Barnacle. You'd think she could work Bernadette Devlin into this conversation somehow. She saw now that both priests had lovely hands too, Joe's especially, large and blue-veined, but carefully tended. The hands that lifted the chalice. She hadn't seen a chalice since Christmas Mass in Due East, when the parishioners held white candles in paper holders and their light burned a glow into the smoke of incense. There was a glow overtaking her now, too. There were bright spots of light shining through the smoky haze, nonviolence and Martin Luther King and Peggy Barnacle and these priests. Her father. Her father wept when he heard King was shot, and then walked the halls of the high school, trying to keep a lid on the grief and the anger. Her father's hands, holding the lid on. Hands to lift the chalice. What Ireland needed was a Martin Luther King. All perfectly clear in the glow of bourbon and wine and beer.

But Michael honked out a Bronx cheer for her glow. "Yeah, it's civil rights, but now it's burning out families besides. It's guns now. It's which side are you on."

Impossible to diffuse the goodwill and safety of this dinner with the Jesuits, even now that Michael was heating up, even now that Michael was not acting. He was steamed all right, but she saw, looking at Joe-and-Simon's passive slack faces, that they'd heard it all before. They heard it every Friday night. She saw that the four of them were the very last souls in the dining hall. An hour before twenty priests had been chatting over their nightcaps. Now the clock on the wall said quarter to something. Quarter to one.

Simon stretched back in his chair and said: "All right, Michael, we can't solve the question of a just war tonight. But you'll do the demonstration? Can't hurt to turn the heat on."

Michael grinned. "Oh I'm a fool for you Simon. I'll do the demonstrations. I won't bring any pipe bombs. But I'll tell you the truth, I think that's the way you'd get the attention of every Irish-American in the fucking USA. They'd be coughing up the bucks for your priest in Belfast then."

Joe said: "They're already coughing up plenty. Who you think paid for what guns they have over there now? Who you think runs them in?"

And Simon said: "As I was saying before I was so rudely interrupted by our young revolutionary . . ."

"Don't be so fucking patronizing."

Now they were all sitting up straight, even Fran, especially Fran, whose chin had left her open palm sometime when Michael had quit acting. Now he was slurring the ends of his sentences, weaving even as he sat. She'd never seen him out of control. A little thread of spittle ran down the side of his clean-shaven mouth. No more glow.

"Right," Simon said, equable. "Sorry. And maybe on your end you'd tone down the language."

Michael grunted something.

"Well. I don't have anything planned so far, just as many bodies as we can get to the embassy and uniform signs I guess, the old England Get out of Ireland—listen, I better call you in the morning. We can start planning then. If you're up for it."

Michael wiped the side of his mouth with a fist. "I said I was up for it. And I'm getting it all. I'm taking it all in. You don't have to call me in the fucking *morning*. Joe says people are getting burned out over there."

Joe was morose: "If they'd just go ahead and *send* the U.N. troops."

Michael said: "Fuckingu.n.'sgonnadofuckall," in a craggy voice, and Fran saw Joe-and-Simon exchange a raised eyebrow, maybe the raised eyebrow they exchanged every Friday night. Then, together, they turned their raised eyebrows toward her. They were yielding to *her*. She was supposed to get Michael out of this room.

"Michael," she said, rising to connive with the priests already, and finding that she could stand, anyway, and so maybe would be able to walk as well.

From his chair Michael stared at her. He seemed to have forgotten the conversation. "Oh shit," he said. He was still slurring the sentences. "I gottawalk yahome."

Simon said, "I don't think you two ought to be walking the campus at this hour. Not in your shape, Michael. Come on upstairs, you can stay on the pull-out couch."

Michael was to sleep on the couch? The two of them together? Michael on the couch and she—

Michael rose, tried to push his chair in, and said:

"I just want you to know, Simon, that I think about just wars too. I think about nonviolent action. I think about how fucking safe it is to do all these little demonstrations that make us feel just so darned good about ourselves. Don't they, Simon? Just so darn good. There, I toned down the language for you."

This seemed to be his way of turning down the fold-out couch. Simon put a hand on her shoulder and drew her aside:

"I don't think he can walk."

It was hard to argue with this when Michael was now limping around the table, searching for his beer glass, long empty, by downing everyone else's dregs.

Joe said: "Let me walk you if Michael won't stay. That way if he passes out I can get you home and come back for him."

Michael heard this last and sneered. "I'm not about to pass out." He was trying to light a cigarette, but match would not make contact with matchbook.

What could she do but smile and shrug and say, "Oh we'll be fine, really Joe, don't you go to any trouble. There's guards all over the campus at night."

Michael, mouth poised to snarl, cast her an *Et tu* look. "I'm not gonna need a *guard.*"

"No, no," she said. "I mean it's *safe,* the campus."

Oh just get out of there. Simon drummed two fingers in a V against his pursed lips, ready to follow them home from a discreet distance. But Joe threw up his hands.

"Well *I'm* turning in. Anybody for the elevator?"

"I'll see these two out," Simon said, and insisted on walking them through the lobby, though Michael was trying to jab the priest's chest to send him back upstairs. He could not make contact with Simon either. The priest remained unjabbed, the cigarette unlit.

Simon stood in the doorway until they made their way down the lane of cherry trees. They walked apart, Michael weaving, Fran dodging his slumps. She could feel Simon watching them, back under the Jesuits' awning, even when they'd long since passed out of his sight.

The night spring air was cool and dry and either Michael walked straighter once they emerged from the trees or she was getting better at avoiding his missteps. She was still drunk too, drunk enough to skip along in this good fresh air and still miss the sticky damp sweet air of home. They reached the main loop of campus and walked on together, she dancing, Michael toiling, toward Martyrs Hall. He did not seem to realize that they were heading for his door, not hers, until they reached it.

"Shit man," he said. "We came the wrong way." Standing still, he had to hold onto something. He had one heavy hand on her shoulder, one on the cold stone of the building. "Oh wow, I can't believe we did that."

She'd known all along where they were going. "I'll run around back and climb in Iovino's window."

He took a deep breath, the kind that smokers take to remind themselves of the taste of fresh air. "You staying the night?" He did not give the question any importance. He did not call her Emily Dickinson.

"Yeah."

"You don't have to go through Iovino's window." Michael's breathing now was labored. "He'll let you in," he said, and lifting his heavy hand from her shoulder he pointed to the night guard who, she saw now, had been waiting discreetly in the lobby for the outcome of their negotiations.

Michael tapped on the glass and the guard—an easy guy, no uniform cap on his six-inch Afro—jogged over to open the door for them. He beamed down on Michael's new girl, sneaking into Martyrs Hall through the front door at one-thirty in the morning. A nice guy who looked the other way. And Michael, who claimed to have been alone since his girl-friend in New York, knew the routine.

He had to steady himself by grabbing for her shoulder on the landings, and when they made it to his floor she had to be the one to grapple with the door. When she turned the knob, his roommate Kevin sat up in the dark, alone in his bed. He'd been lying there, listening to them fumble in the dark hallway. "Hi Francie," he said, and switched on the bedside lamp. He really thought her name was Francie.

"Hi Kevin."

"You want me to find someplace else to sleep?"

Michael had stretched himself out facedown on the bed, his boots dangling off the end like the weights on stage curtains. One arm, still sheathed in black leather, stretched out across the width, but she would be able to climb under it and find herself a place. She'd be able to shrink into a little ball.

"Nah," she said. "Thanks anyway, Kevin."

Kevin rolled his eyes and fumbled for a cigarette in the drawer. "He's out of it, huh?"

She nodded.

"Oh man, was he with the Jesuits?"

She nodded again, and he held out the pack to her with his good parochial school manners. Kevin had been through high school with Mi-chael, and maybe the parish school too. She only knew they'd known each other forever. He was a big soft chunky guy with an inflamed nose and a voice so low you couldn't always hear him.

"They set him *off*, man. They put him through the meat grinder. He comes back all crazy after he's been with them." They exhaled together. "I don't know, Francie. He handles his shit pretty well most of the time, but Friday nights he's like in trouble. He ever tell you about his father?"

She nodded again, leaning forward from her perch on the side of the bed to hear. There could have been a corpse beside her on the bed, for all

Michael counted. She was light-headed, but Kevin's dark bulky form in the lamplight was a good shape to focus on.

"I don't want to be an alarmist or something but like they say that sort of thing runs in the family and he's pretty out of control when he starts drinking. Michael's old man was, I mean, unreal when he started drinking. We'd get the fuck out of the *borough* when he tied one on." They exhaled together again.

"I'm sorry," he said. "Shit man, it's like two, three o'clock. I'll let you get some sleep."

He stubbed out his cigarette and rolled over to face the wall so she could undress. Even in bed he wore his dark straight hair pulled back into a ponytail. His wire glasses were folded on the night table.

Fran peeled off her jeans and curled in under Michael's outstretched arm. He was deadweight again, pinning the blankets down.

"Hey Francie?"

Kevin curled back the other way to face her. She could have been in her brothers' old room, the beds lined up as close as graves, the dirty socks stinking up what little air there was, the underwear salted around on chairs and under beds. It was a regular pajama party.

"I didn't mean to worry you about Michael. Jesus there's a lot of drinking in this place and he's fine with drugs, I mean did you ever hear him get started about the Living Theater or something while he's *tripping,* I mean he's a master of coherency then. But the drink's something different with him. I think they're trying to do something for him, the priests, watch over him or something noble like that. They just set something off. I didn't mean to worry you."

Stretching out her hand from Michael's bed, she could reach over and touch Kevin's arm. She didn't even know she was going to do it.

"Thanks, Kevin," she said, and he squeezed her hand hard. Some sort of cosmic truth about fathers and brothers swirled in her dizzy brain, but it wouldn't take shape. Something about the kindness of Simon and Kevin, last names unknown, something about Pat Starkey and Will Starkey.

"Thanks," she said again, and never bothered to pull her hand back across the gap between beds. She couldn't really feel it as a separate body part, anyway, the way she was floating. Maybe Kevin held it like that, from bed to bed, for hours, while she drifted in and out of sleep. Above her head, Michael's arm stretched out rigid. Once or twice in the night she felt it jump, and then settle back into deadweight.

———

Now, in the spring, Peggy Barnacle was dying (in her controlled experiment, pleated skirt kind of way) to drop acid. She'd declared early as a theology major, and the upperclassmen in her department were all developing intense interests in aboriginal religions and the possibilities of hallucinogens. Now was the time.

So now Peggy was acting like a bridesmaid trying to run the wedding. "How much are you going to do? Promise me you won't do a whole tab and freak out."

"Yes'm, I promise."

"Promise me if it's o.k. you'll do it with me the next time. Just you and me, o.k.?"

"I promise."

Peggy could not abide Michael—something about the way her nostrils flared when she spoke his name—but she was all for this first trip of Franny's. *We're a couple of virgins,* Peggy would say over their nightcaps in bed, meaning that they'd been talking about tripping for the better part of a year and weren't any closer to doing it, and that if Fran wasn't going to go ahead and take the plunge—after all, Michael would anyway know where to *get* acid—then there wasn't much hope for old Peggy Barnacle. She implied they were in such a terrible rut (and they were, sipping little snifters of Paddy's in bed like an old married couple going over the day) that it was Fran's moral duty to save them both. Shake them from their domesticity! See in colors! See, who knows, God!

Michael said he knew just the spot for her first trip, Rock Creek Park, and they hitchhiked into Washington together on a Sunday early in April. Palm Sunday, it would be, because on Holy Thursday they were leaving for New York.

Michael said he knew just the drug for her first time, too, not acid at all, but psilocybin, all fungal and earthy, guaranteed to make her tingle but with half a hit she probably wouldn't hallucinate. They'd be in the soft spongy park with the soft spongy drug. Nothing heavy about it.

The psilocybin melted into her mouth while they waited together by the side of the road. After ten minutes a little bearded man, monkish in a brown hooded jacket, picked them up in his Volkswagen. Michael leaned forward from the backseat to find out that the guy was a statistician with the Bureau of Labor Statistics, heading into work on Sunday for the pleasure of fooling with his figures in peace. "Well, we're heading to the park for the pleasure of tripping our brains out," Michael said.

"Far out," said the little man, and she was pretty sure he drove the Bug faster after that. He swooped down through the park and dropped them off near a narrow path where he said he dropped his first acid. "Back in the Paleolithic days."

They wandered along beside the creek, following it down past stick dams and rocky runs, for—well, already time was the hardest thing to tell—for a while. Fran was picturing how she'd paint a wood like this, an airy wood with a clean bubbling brook out of a children's book, with sculpture-smooth rocks, with tiny mannerly buds on all the trees. Really, she had no interest in painting it—a swampy Southern wood, all clogged with undergrowth, was what she'd paint—but if she *were* to paint it she'd make it as neat and tidy as a schoolroom. Looking at the sweet simple dogwoods and cherry trees she saw the long arms of Southern oaks, the clammy moss, the ground always rich and dark and cloying. This little park, in this clean little city, didn't seem like nature at all. It was more like architecture.

She forgot entirely that they'd taken the psilocybin. She seemed, actually, more herself than she'd been in a long time. Maybe ever. She walked alongside Michael and it never occurred to her to talk to him. He knew what she was thinking, anyway. She decided to ford the creek and took off, skipping over the wet slippery rocks but as balanced as she'd been finishing up the 440. No, more perfectly balanced.

From a million miles away she heard Michael on the bank calling her. This tripping stuff was fine, not at all scary, and it wasn't the way *Time* magazine described it back in Due East, it wasn't as if you looked down at a rock and saw creatures rearing up from it, though if you did look down in the water you could see bugs and clods of earth, everything kicking back and dancing. Not creatures exactly.

Michael was laughing right in her ear, but when she turned to look he was three rocks back. "How can you stand like that?" he said.

She looked back at herself. She had perched one leg, like a heron's, on the rock, but the other was stretched out like a ballerina's at the bar. Only there was no bar. The leg was smooth and taut, thrusting itself out from her long black skirt, and she lowered it slowly and smiled slowly at Michael, who seemed to be returning the smile through some sort of radio beam. When the smile was almost up to a half-moon Michael let out one of his strange roars and slipped, one foot and then the other ankle-deep in the clean clear Rock Creek water.

He stood like that for—well, it was getting even harder to tell—a pretty long time. And she stood on the other rock and did a leglift with her *other* leg for a pretty long time too.

Then somehow they were both on the other side of the creek, under a trio of maple trees. The ground was damp beneath their feet. Michael was right, there was a fungal side even to this park.

Above them a string of buds, like a string of Christmas lights, flittered. In Due East the flowers would be berserk by now, that scary pink of the crape myrtles, the goofy purples people went in for on their azaleas. Here she was though, in Washington, D.C., safe with Michael on a sunny spring day, sitting under a safe bland maple tree. She was massaging his soggy feet, though she didn't remember seeing him take his boots off. There they were, the largest black boots she had ever seen in her life, with silver handles running across the ankles. And his feet: she must have had occasion to look at them before, but they didn't look familiar, in fact they looked like an old man's feet, the toenails too long and yellowing, the toe hairs thick and wiry. Whoever heard of red hair on toes. She checked his eyebrows and saw that yes, they were that thick and that wiry too, the ends of them spilling up into incredible curlicues, old man's eyebrows and toes and if you looked into the light eyes which she was not doing anymore at all, she was kissing him, actually, and her head was resting on something that was resting on the ground, his boot or maybe his jacket because now that seemed to be off too. In fact, her shirt was off, *that* she could feel because they were under a tree and it was cool and damp. Cool and damp, and Michael's chest pressed down against her own was warm, a pure and even pressure that began in her breasts and swelled up all the way to her mouth where what was supposed to be his tongue had settled itself in and attached itself to her own mouth.

They were making love in a big park in a big city in the middle of a Saturday afternoon and she stiffened with the premonition that a little kid, a little Albert or Walter, would stumble upon them. Michael ran a light hand through her hair. He didn't utter a sound, and anyway even if her breasts were naked she was wearing this long silky skirt which covered some of him, too, covered long wedges of his bare legs when she wrapped her own legs around him. So she wrapped her legs around him, pulling the yards of material with her, cheap black sateen on long white red-haired legs. Against her own legs she felt the shimmy and the shiver. She was not sure where cloth ended and skin began. She was not sure where Michael ended and she began.

When Michael came this time he did not make a sound at all, but she felt the tremors running through him. It was she who cried out for what very well could have been a good long time.

And then they were lying on the ground, half-naked, half cool, half-warm, forever. After a while he said: "I can't get out. I'm melted."

She believed this. His tongue had detached itself from her mouth but they were otherwise attached. Permanently, probably.

After another while he said: "I'm sorry, I really can't get out. I got melted into you."

She did not believe this was a problem.

"Well," he said finally, "I wouldn't want a little kid to find us," and underneath him she began to cry. The last time she'd cried like that was with Steward, down by the Due East River.

Michael was frightened. He jumped up and buckled his pants, an instant whirligig, and seemed to think he must take care of her too. He dressed her, pulled her shirt down over her outstretched arms and smoothed her skirt and even took the tail of his own shirt and dabbed her eyes while she sat still on the ground, weeping.

And then he needed to talk. Michael always needed to talk, but now there were words crowding out of his nose and dangling from his ears like earrings. The words curled along the curlicues of his eyebrows. He hunkered down on his haunches, facing her, and he said:

"Fran, I'm sorry, I'm sorry. Ever since that dinner with the Jesuits I know you don't think I'm ethical. I really like love those guys. I know I'm an asshole to them, to Simon. I know you don't think I'm ethical."

She did not think this at all—any fool could see that he loved those guys—but she was crying and couldn't seem to say anything at all. There were so many words pushing out of his face that his very whiskers looked like punctuation marks.

"And now we're in the middle of the woods and I made love to you and I think you're thinking that I'm, like, really unethical."

Truly she did not think this—wasn't she the one who cried out, and he the one who kept quiet—but her tongue would not work in her mouth. It was swollen and twisted. She wasn't completely sure it was her own tongue anymore.

"So Fran, look, I have to tell you that really, I have a whole theory of Sexual Ethics and I've never told you my theory and so maybe you like . . ."

Words failed him.

Finally her tongue uncurled. "Thank God," she said, meaning Thank God words failed him and they could just go back into melting into each other, this time fully clothed, but he misunderstood, maybe because by now she was hiccoughing and channeling some of the sobs into giggles. He did not understand how far beyond words they had traveled.

"I know you think it's funny Fran," he said, "but you never say anything about sex. Or God. Or politics."

She stopped crying. An air bubble, large and empty, formed in her throat and traveled down into her chest and then her belly. "Not sex," she said. "Not God."

"But you don't have to laugh. All I'm trying to tell you, I'm like not such a bad guy, I'm trying to say, oh Jesus you're making this hard, you know, don't *look* at me like that, don't *look* so miserable. I'm just a guy, I mean like I went through the whole standard fucking bit, you know, my mother like fucking dying when she found the *Playboy*s in the bottom drawer, like I was betraying all womankind, you know, the whole bit, and I told you when I got Tess pregnant I was like outa my head, like I was betraying all womankind again only for real and I swear to God, I woulda married her, I swear to you Fran I was just going to marry her because actually my Theory of Sexual Ethics is only that you just—oh shit don't look at me that way—that you connect, this is Aquinas actually, stop, stop looking at me like that—honest Aquinas said this, this is really the ultimate connection, don't you see like the ultimate way you connect and if another human being forms as a result of that connection, well, like, that's it, isn't it, that's the living breathing sign that you've connected and—"

Words failed him again. Meanwhile the bubble in her belly had become a swelling.

"I'm pregnant," she whispered. It had just occurred to her. The swelling, the not knowing where she ended.

He buried his face in his hands and sometime after mumbled: "You forgot the pills? You forgot to take your pills?"

She said: "Just now!"

"I got you pregnant just now? In Rock Creek Park?"

She nodded. It was hard to tell whether the swelling came from inside or whether she was being blown up, like a balloon, from the outside.

"But Fran," he said, and even hunched down as he was, he managed to balance himself and take both her hands in his. He was straight. Either she'd scared him into sobriety or he'd never taken off on the psilocybin, because he was not tripping the way she was. He was not melting anymore. He was not twisting and stretching the way she was.

"But Fran," he said again, "if you take the pills you can't get pregnant. You didn't forget, did you?"

He was perfectly straight. He was sober. He was looking into her face and asking a reasonable question. He was breathing into her face and he was inhabiting a different solar system.

She closed her eyes, but there was a black funnel. When she looked, he was still there, his beard a beard again. There were no more words dangling from his ears.

"No," she whispered, or maybe she did not whisper, maybe *no* just emanated from her and he could reach out and pluck the word and put it in his pocket. Because he was stuffing something in his pockets now, now that he had risen and towered over her, now that he looked down and said:

"You mean no you don't take any pills. You mean I've been fucking, making love to you all this time without, without anything."

She did not answer that.

And he did not ask why she'd never told him.

And she did not ask why he'd never inquired.

They had gone way beyond words, now that he was melted, now that they were melding. He stared at her with an old man's eyes, eyes puffy from drinking and drugging, and she stared back because if she closed her eyes the black funnel would swirl her up.

A Theory of Sexual Ethics. Good Man, *Good Man.* Michael Burke, Jesuit-educated, would be A-o.k. with Pat Starkey. He was the first one who didn't go find a machine in a seedy bathroom and come back with a neat foil package in his pocket. He was the first one who saw to her pleasure before he saw to his own.

"Oh God," she said, because now she was so cold and he looked so cold standing over her, a marble pillar. "Maybe this's what it feels like, when your brain leaves your body. Like dying."

He shook his head and let out an empty little *pffff,* a puff of air, the opposite of a roar. A little nothing, a little breath of disbelief.

Pffff rolled through the trees of Rock Creek Park and cascaded down the rocks. Pffff.

Beat death again.

WHY ARE
YOU
LOOKING AT
ME LIKE
THAT?

The Burke apartment in Brooklyn had the same claustrophobic feel as the little marshside house back in Due East, so it was almost like a homecoming for Franny. They all called her Frances here. Michael's little sisters, Nellie and Johanna, said: "Frances can we braid your hair?" but before the question had fully escaped their lips they were already tugging on her coarse curls.

Franny was staying in a sleeping bag on the floor of Johanna and Nellie's bedroom, which ran into their brothers' bedroom, which ran into the living room. The rooms were separated by broad doorless arches. At night, she stood in the empty doorway and watched while the living room was transformed into another bedroom. Usually the boys were still in there watching Johnny Carson, and they hauled the pillows off the couch and uncurled the bed for their mother. Then they sat on the edge of Norah Burke's thin mattress while she drifted off to sleep to the music of a stand-up comic. Before she got dreamy Michael's mother might pat the side of the bed, inviting Franny over to sit with the crowd. You could see how loose and easy this household got, once the father died.

Back in the little narrow kitchen, Franny's favorite room, Michael's mother had an electric Sacred Heart on the wall. It burned scarlet when you flicked the switch on, but Michael said you could get the heart to throb if you caressed the button just right. Doris would be consumed with jealousy if she knew such a thing existed. Franny herself liked to sit in the windowsill, first watching the glowing heart, then looking out on narrow yards the size of dog pens in Due East. Twice she'd sketched the back lots, paved over with concrete and separated by fences of pastel plastic stripping, but she had not painted them yet. The way they were drained of color would break your heart.

"Frances, I wonder if you and Michael would like to take a stroll?"

Michael's mother was always shooing them out in her gentle way. There was something nunlike about her. She sounded like a young woman,

shy and apologetic enough to be a postulant finding her place in the convent, but her eyes had an old mother superior's pouches under them. The
lines around her unpainted mouth ran as deep as scars. She hadn't married,
Michael said, until she was halfway through her thirties, and halfway
through her forties she had half a dozen children. Half a dozen children in
ten years, and once they were all delivered to this earth they could not
possibly sit down together for a meal in their cramped kitchen.

But Michael's mother never pointed out that there were not enough
seats for everyone to have a meal at the same time. She only suggested a
walk. Franny and Michael wandered the neighborhood, morning and
night, while Nellie and Johanna and Frank and Richie ate. When they
came back, with the paper or a quart of milk, they sat down with Michael's
mother and Billy, the next oldest, if he had bothered to show up for dinner.

You could call me Norah, the mother said to Franny that first night at
dinner, but the name clotted up in Franny's throat. She couldn't call Michael's mother *Norah.* It was hard enough to call his brother *Billy,* this lean
tall eighteen-year-old with the self-assured slickness of a rock star. He wore
his wavy honey-colored hair parted in the middle and down to his shoulders, just like Jesus in the electric Sacred Heart print. Michael said his
brother was as stupid as a side of beef, but Franny thought this had more to
do with Billy's flirting at the dinner table than it did with any objective
assessment of his intelligence. He was on full scholarship. All the boys were,
and that was how they would have to go to college too.

"Frances, I wonder if you and Michael would like to take a stroll?"

Here we go again. This meant it was time to serve the first shift their
dinner.

"And Michael, do me a favor and stop by Mahoney's. Tell Billy I need
him to watch Nellie and Hannie at seven. It's bingo night but he'll forget."

"We'll watch them for you."

"No, no, you might want to get out. I know Frances likes to hop on
the train and wander around the Village. You've only got a few more days
for that."

"Frank could watch them. Or Richie."

Norah Burke hobbled around the little square kitchen table, tugging at
the tablecloth. The plastic growled. She did not set her lips or argue with
her son, but she did not answer him either.

"O.k., Ma," said Michael. "We'll get Billy out of Mahoney's."

Franny clattered with him down the three linoleum flights of stairs and
they started up the grim block. Already they'd walked this neighborhood

twenty times, and Michael had shown her how you could make your way from down here at the bottom of the slope, from the wasteland of the Gowanus Canal (where the water looked like shivering sulfuric acid and where the mob dumped its bodies) all the way to the big indifferent park at the top of the hill, and how you could mark off fortunes on the sharp inclined walk: *cheap sociology,* Michael called this. She marked the fortunes off now, on this block where the Burkes were an aberration, Irish on an Italian block going Puerto Rican. Once, when the Irish of New York had finally found themselves some respectability, they built the big houses at the top of the hill, and hired the Micks who lived at the bottom to scrub for them. Now the bottom of the hill housed all varieties of the rarely working, barely working and once-in-a-while-working class. Up a block came the solid working class, then on the next the white-collar families.

Now they were up to Seventh Avenue and the shops, and she didn't need Michael to show her where Mahoney's was. They'd stopped in on the first afternoon and every afternoon since to lure Billy out. Michael's father's old haunt, and now Billy's too, since he'd turned eighteen. He came straight from school, books on his back. He wrote papers at the bar, though you could barely see to put pen to paper.

When she walked into Mahoney's she felt she was walking into the night. The wooden door and the front glass window, tinted black, shut out the afternoon light, and once she got past the door she was faced with a dark open space, a cave between the bar itself and the half dozen tables pushed up against the wall. Nobody sat at the tables. They all crowded up against the bar, and her eyes were finally drawn that way, to the faint glow from dainty old lamps with pink globes, incongruous birds perched on a shelf over the liquor bottles.

Conversation in Mahoney's was sporadic, and when it came it was delivered like bursts of gunfire. The clientele looked as if it traveled up from the bottom of the hill on worn soles, and probably from another century. No one appeared to be under sixty, no one but Billy. There he was on the far side of the bar, a mug in front of him, grinning at nothing, at Franny when she came in behind Michael. There was a pen in his hand.

Michael marked his own territory near the window and claimed a stool for her. Then he offered a ceremonious nod to his neighbor on the left, a bony little man in a tweed cap and a loose windbreaker stained extravagantly up and down the front. The old man's face was all juts and hollows, and Franny expected the toes of his shoes to curl up. He was barely tall enough on his stool to see over his own beer glass.

"Michael Burke Jr.," the old man said. "Could be your father himself standing at this bar."

Michael nodded and mumbled something. He seemed to be indicating that they were together, anyway.

"You'd bring your girl to this dark hole?" The old man swallowed his beer and cackled. He leaned over Michael to say: "You'd be better off with young Billy. Billy ud show you how to kick up your heels right enough."

"Well what are you doing here yourself?" Michael said. Fran could not say whether he was joking. "I thought you were never going to step foot in Mahoney's again."

"Oh I'm after helping Chauncey haul around some . . . items. He's standing me a round and wouldn't it be ungrateful to say no to that?" He leaned back so that Chauncey, on the other side of him, could take a bow.

"Chauncey," he bellowed in his friend's right ear. "Another grandson has materialized."

Franny tapped Michael's shoulder. There'd been no talk of going to pay respects to a grandfather in Brooklyn, in the neighborhood. She didn't even know one still existed.

Michael shook her off and shrugged. "My father's father," he said, "a charming gentleman always." He saluted Chauncey. "How ya doing there, Chaunce?"

"Mr. O'Mara to you, you little shite," Michael's grandfather said. Over in the corner Billy was writing at a furious pace.

Chauncey, a taller version of Michael's grandfather with hair blackened and slicked back, blinked as if he'd just awakened in a strange land. "Who's this? Who's this? Michael is it? Jaysus, you're looking fit, Michael."

"Of course he's looking fit, my God! He's a young man with no excuse not to look fit. When are you going to lop off some of that terrifying hair, Michael?"

"*Young* Michael." Chauncey was pleased to figure it out. "And how is your father, young Michael?"

"He's very dead, thank you, Chaunce."

Chauncey glared at him, hurt. "He is not."

"He most certainly is. And you were at the funeral."

Chauncey, suspicious, considered this. "Must have been a heart attack."

"Must have been a *liver* attack," Michael said and at this Chauncey burst out spitting.

"He *is* dead," he agreed. "That was a terrible thing, a young man like that. Though not so young as yourself. You're looking fit, Michael."

"You said that," Michael's grandfather pointed out.

"I did. It's worth saying twice when a young fellow's looking this fit. Who's this? Your sister?" He winked half a dozen times.

Michael winked back. *"Girlfriend,* Chauncey."

"Chauncey," Michael's grandfather said, "I'm ashamed to be seen with you. You can't hold your liquor and you can't hold up your end of the conversation." He looked to Frances for confirmation.

"I can hold up this end of the Brooklyn Bridge if it's required of me," Chauncey said, dead serious. He, too, seemed stuck on watching Frances. "Who's this? Girlfriend?"

Michael's grandfather slapped him on the back. "Chauncey."

Chauncey spat again. "I'm having you on, old man. Hold out the other leg and I'll take a tug at it too."

"What's Billy doing?" Michael's grandfather said. "He's been scratching away for an hour. You're not still doing that, are you Michael, playing at the scribbling? For the love of Christ, get yourself a trade." To Frances he said: "Tell this strapping young man with the terrifying hair to get himself a trade." There was a gleeful smile caving in his cheeks, but his eyes, streaked with pink and blue, bore down.

"My father had a trade." She heard Michael's voice turn scritchy, a rake over gravel. "Got him as far as the Greenwood Cemetery."

"Your father didn't have the sense God gave him. I'll tell you something though, Michael, God rest her soul and may I burn in eternal hellfire for saying so, but his mother drove him to it, her with the Pioneer pin and the self-righteousness. Drove him out of the house and into the arms of the drink. And now what's your mother doing, more of the same? Look at Billy there, six o'clock in the afternoon and still he'll not go home to his mother's accusations. He only wants himself a beer in the afternoon. Could she not let him have his beer in peace?"

"My mother doesn't wear a Pioneer pin. My mother takes a drink now and then herself."

"And what are yez doing here this afternoon then? Did she send yez after Billy or not? Is she hounding Billy or no?"

"She didn't send us here." Michael's denial was so cold and offhand that Franny would have believed it herself if she hadn't been a witness in the kitchen. The smooth lie inspired her and she said:

"I asked to come here, ackshully," but of course she sounded like a liar, with a cornpone accent to boot. Naturally the grandfather caught the accent.

"Why Michael's found himself a new girl, have you Michael?"

"She has a name."

"And wouldn't we all be glad to hear it? You must forgive my grandson's *ex*ecrable manners."

"FRANCES STARKEY," Michael said, and the patrons around, who'd all been leaning on their elbows and nodding off, sat up flushed to listen. "MAY I PRESENT MY GRANDFATHER NED BURKE AND HIS GOOD FRIEND CHAUNCEY O'MARA. FRANCES IS FROM THE SOUTHERN REGION OF OUR COUNTRY, GENTLEMEN. THESE GENTLEMEN ARE FROM THE OULD SOD, FRAN."

"It's not me you shame when you behave that way, Michael. It's yourself you shame."

Billy was struggling to write it all down.

"Look at Bill, would you? He's after writing down what we say!"

"You're a sharp one, Chaunce."

"You make light of it now, Mike, but when your brother sells what you say to the tabloids you'll not be tittering will you?"

Michael howled. "Nah, I won't be tittering. I'll be getting the name of his fucking editor. Dennis! Can we get a couple of beers here?"

He bought a round for his grandfather and Chauncey and once the beer arrived he settled his hand on his grandfather's shoulder as if no harsh word had passed between them, as if they'd all been joking all along. Maybe they had been. They sipped their beer together, and at the sight of them quiet at last Billy threw down his pen and came to stand with them.

"Wow, I like those earrings, Frances. They're, like, all translucent."

"You watch your brother now, Michael. He's moving in on your territory. First he copies the writing business, next thing you know he's boffing your girlfriend."

"Grandpa."

Ned Burke belched. "Pardon *me* for living. Was it something else you had in mind, Willie boy?"

"I had in mind to find out if Chauncey's recruited Michael and Fran yet."

"For God's sake Bill, watch yourself."

Around the bar chins once more dove off the palms they'd been propped on. Even the bartender strained to hear. Billy looked innocent enough, throwing his hair over one shoulder and then the other, but Chauncey shot a hurt look at him and then at Ned Burke.

"Come on outside, so," he said, peering around the dark room to memorize the faces that had heard.

"I haven't finished my beer."

"Come on Michael," his brother said. "This is worth it."

Their grandfather slid down off his stool and did a nimble skip out the door. The brothers left their glasses on the counter and followed the gimpy Chauncey out into what was fast becoming evening. The avenue was under a glow pinker than the one the lamps shed inside the bar, and they all blinked at each other and formed themselves into a semicircle in front of Mahoney's black-tinted glass. Franny felt faces inside gazing out.

"Go on Chaunce," Billy said, co-conspirator. Under his open jacket he'd taken off his tie and unbuttoned the top three buttons of his school uniform shirt. Skinny and muscular in his clinging blue pants, he looked as if he belonged behind a microphone in Las Vegas.

Chauncey had suddenly regained all the marbles that had been so conspicuously missing inside the bar. He ran an unsteady hand through his dyed hair, but then he pulled a stern index finger out of the trembling mass to wave at Billy. "William Burke," he said, "in the name of the Holy Family I'll ask you to respect this confidence and stop blathering on about it to every nitwit in Mahoney's."

Billy stuck out his chest another inch and gave a solemn nod.

"Because your grandfather has vouched for you."

Billy nodded again but Michael said: "A voucher's all we ever get from him."

His grandfather took a step forward to jab him in the chest. "D'ye want to hear or no?"

Michael shrugged.

"Forget it, Chaunce. Mark him off the list. Not that he was ever on it."

"Oh go on," Michael said. "What's all the hush-hush?"

Chauncey and the grandfather exchanged significant gazes and appeared to be waiting for Michael to beg them. Finally Franny realized that their gaze was resting on her.

"Michael, I'll run up to the bakery," she said, "and meet you on the corner."

"Aw no you don't. Come on Grandpa, what were you going to tell me that you can't tell my girl?"

The little old man pulled at his enormous flap of ear. In the dusky light she could see thick hairs sprouting from inside the ear, and she could count the black and gold bristles on his knobby chin. Even his eyelashes were numbered, fiery wisps in the night.

"It's not the same girl it was the last time is it Michael?"

"Oh for Christsake."

Chauncey grabbed at his sleeve to make him stop, but he was in gear.

"We can't be telling our business to every slip of a thing you pull into Mahoney's bar for the love of Jesus."

Chauncey tugged again, and Franny watched the marbleized streaks in his face grow purple. He looked as if he might cry from vexation. "It's all *unauthorized,*" he whispered, to no one.

"I'm just going. It's o.k.," she said to Michael.

"It's not o.k. and I'm just fucking going with you." He didn't move, though. He planted his feet in a boxer's stance, and his grandfather raised his fists, as if he might actually spar. The old man's chin trembled, his whiskers dancing, and after a little hiss he spat down at Michael's feet. It was a three-pronged attack that came from the three checkered holes in his teeth. Chauncey covered his own mouth in despair.

But Michael laughed a grim laugh at his grandfather's spitting and began to back off down the street. He was dancing a clodhopper's dance in his heavy boots, a nose-thumbing dance at the old man. "So long, Chaunce," Michael called down the block, and Frances had to skip along to catch up with him. It was hard to say whether she should wave good-bye or if Michael would regard that as a betrayal, so she flapped her hands in a vague way.

"So long *Grand*father." Finally Michael turned and walked forward up the block with Franny, but he was still muttering to the old man left behind. "We'll just have to join the IRA on our own." He came to a full stop on the sidewalk and wiggled his backside.

"Go on," she said. "They weren't really going to tell us IRA business."

Michael put an arm around her and then, on second thought, leaned over to deliver an extravagant kiss, a street kiss for his grandfather's benefit. She could feel him sliding his eyes over to see if the old men were still watching them from Mahoney's. She looked. They were.

They began to walk again, toward the bakery since it had been mentioned. "Cocks of the walk," Michael said. "Kings of the hill. All puffed up, the little fucking strutters."

"Go on," she said. "They weren't going to try to get you to do something for the IRA?"

"So full of himself," Michael said. "He can haul for Chauncey but he can't stroll down the hill to say hello to Nellie and Hannie once a year. You know, Ma used to drop in on him to clean his apartment, excuse me, his hovel. Place stinks of lard and guts—over the butcher's—and you'd think he'd kiss the hand of anybody brave enough to come up. But no, he'd pretend he couldn't hear the knock on the door. She could hear him inside, lighting up a cigarette and sighing until she went away." He did a big beleaguered sigh and mimed the cigarette. "Asshole."

Frances recognized in Michael's jaunty walk now the same little kick his grandfather danced, leaving the bar. "But he wasn't really going to tell us IRA stuff was he?"

It was on the news now, every night nearly, the gasoline bombs and the brigades of rock throwers in Belfast or Derry or Newry. The Provos were rising, the IRA yet again a phoenix. In March they'd killed their first soldier since the Black and Tans. Last night at supper Billy said:

Did you hear what happened to the IRA man in Belfast, the one who blew up the bus?

Oh my God, Norah said. *They're starting it all over.*

No, no, Ma, Billy said. *It's a joke. Did you hear what happened to the IRA man, blowing up the bus? His lips got stuck to the tailpipe.*

Now Michael said: "Their golden years return. Little shrunken old men."

She heard the sharp slap of boots on the sidewalk. Billy caught up to them on her side and swung an arm around her shoulders, just as proprietary as Michael.

"So Frances, what ya think of our grandfather? Are yez ready to join up now?"

"Christ, Billy, what's this *yez* stuff?" Michael stopped on the sidewalk to light a cigarette. He took his time offering one to his brother, but Billy took it. Now the hand was off Franny's shoulder.

"So what shit're they cooking up, those two?"

Billy shrugged, his slinky hair bobbing along his shoulders. "You heard," he said. "I'm sworn to secrecy."

"Aw c'mon Bill."

Billy choked, inhaling and laughing and walking along. "Oh it's too much. Too far fucking out. Those two are driving around Brooklyn every day in somebody's car they borrowed looking up somebody who knew somebody whose brother was in the IRA fifty years ago. Somebody who's in the VFW. Somebody in the NRA. Somebody in the Clann na Gael. They got a bag of rifles and pistols, I don't know, thirty or forty of them, at Grandpa's apartment. Or so they say."

"And what're they gonna do with rifles and pistols?"

"They're gonna find somebody to run em over. They wanted me to sign up with the merchant marines, I swear to God, that's how most of these things get out. They were thinking you'd know college kids going over for the summer, you know, you could get em to slap a few in their backpacks."

"Oh man. That's pathetic. What is it, a gun at a time?"

Franny thought that maybe Billy bristled. He pulled harder on the cigarette, anyway. "I tell ya, somebody's collecting serious gun money over in Windsor Terrace. *I* don't know what they're doing. But they're patriotic, ya know, in their goofy little way. This is how they did it the last time, they'll tell you that, man, one gun at a time."

Michael groaned. "Yeah, and look what they've got. Half a war still to fight. You gonna run guns for em, Bill?"

They'd reached the bakery now, and stood in front of the trays of bowties and frosted turnovers. There was a mini wedding cake on the top shelf, a little three-layered job with the bride and groom listing slightly to the left.

"Nah," Billy said. "They're so nuts they're gonna get themselves arrested. Ya gotta love em, though, doin their bit. Ya know, Grandpa's eighty next March. He doesn't have to run all over Brooklyn, looking for guns."

"Jesus, we're trying to stop *one* war."

Billy took a long drag off the cigarette and stared out over the low roofs at the fiery sun descending on Brooklyn. "Yeah but if there's a just war on the face of the earth," he said, "this one's it. This one's it, man. They're trying to run out every single goddamn Catholic. Out of their own country. Ya know, if they didn't have to emigrate there'd be twice as many Catholics as Protestants up there by now."

Michael seemed to be staring at the same point on the horizon. Sandwiched between them, Franny felt the way Chauncey had looked in the bar, as if she'd wakened in some strange land to find a strange ritual, an evening ritual that called on brothers to stare together at the sun going down, smoking their weeds, smelling dank and sweet from their beer. Warriors with their war talk, the younger preening and the elder holding back.

"They're gonna get fucking clobbered, same as last time," Michael said. "They're gonna blow up a lot of buildings they don't mean to blow up. But hey, they got Ned Burke and Chauncey O'Mara on their side."

"Oh man, Michael, just don't talk to him like that, huh? Don't ever talk that shit to him. You'd break his heart."

"What're ya, getting tight with the old guy?"

Billy shrugged and waved, taking off down the block back to Mahoney's. Frances felt Michael beside her, turning to look up at the wedding cake, but he remembered and stiffened and moved to the middle of the sidewalk.

"Bill," he yelled. "Hey wait Bill. Ma wants you home for bingo night."

"I don't play bingo," Billy called over his shoulder, and then he was out of hearing range. Michael rejoined her and banged a fist on the bakery window. A tray of éclairs jumped and clattered, and the customers inside turned to stare through the window at the two of them, Franny with her translucent earrings and Michael with his terrifying halo of red hair.

"Oh shit," he said, and sounded so dejected she slipped an arm around his waist. "Shit. I hate this place."

Franny watched the old lady behind the bakery counter wrapping string around a cardboard box, twice around, three times around, pulling the knot tighter until her cheeks blew up with the effort. She looked as old as Chauncey and Ned Burke, and so did her customers, little shrunken women with heavy coats in the springtime, pom-poms on their woolen hats. She could see Michael's mother on this line one day, one day after she'd finally got a bedroom for herself, shrunken down like all the old folks in Brooklyn.

"Funny," she said. In the last few days she'd been able to picture herself an old lady, with a feather in her hat. In the last few days she'd been able to see herself reflected in the windows of the butcher's and the bakery and the bars, looking for all the world as if she were home.

"Frances, maybe you and Michael would like to take a stroll on your last afternoon?"

Frances said, "Sure thing Norah"—finally she got the name out, on her last day—and went to drag Michael off the couch.

He'd been ashamed, showing her the neighborhood at first, joking about the gutters clotted with graying trash and the gates like prison bars on all the bodegas. *I grew up in East Limbo*, he said. *Even hell would have been an improvement.* The same way he joked about his mother's Sacred Heart. In the last few days, though, he was seeing it through her eyes, seeing the glamour of yellowed newspapers rolling through the streets. Now those newspapers blew like tumbleweed and when you caught a glimpse of the Manhattan skyline it rose jagged like a mountain range. Now Michael was a cowpoke giving her the tour, riding the vast free spilling of range from Fourth Avenue up to Ninth.

Up the hill he pulled her, past where they would turn off for Mahoney's, all the way up to the park block. No aluminum siding or fake pebbled stonework on these brownstones. Here the stone was really brown, or else it was limestone, and it swooped out into bosomy hippy curves over the sidewalk. These houses used to belong to wheeler-dealers of the Brooklyn variety, and some of them still did, but Michael said with proprietary claim that the neighborhood was going down the tubes. He didn't want to hear it when she said she liked it better down the hill. He showed her Kevin's house in limestone on the park, stone garlands over all the broad windows. A mansion next to where he lived, but Kevin's father worked on Wall Street, and the house had been in the family forever.

Park Slope, Brooklyn, 1971. Not like it was when Michael was a kid. Not like it was when Michael Burke Sr. set up household on the fourth floor of a tenement and Michael Burke Jr. trudged up the hill to visit his friend with the double parlors.

Now they passed into the park through an opening in a stone wall. *Up the IRA* was spray-painted on the wall in purple, but even without the decoration she'd have felt she was leaving the range for a foreign country. They dashed across a whizzing roadway, then strolled through a meadow as big as a marsh in Due East. Once they got past the traffic they might have been in the heart of the country, but for the bottles strewn on the ground, but for the careful casual layout of elms and sycamores and maples.

"She's crazy about you," Michael said, meaning his mother, starting a new conversation, as usual, out of nothing and spun air. He led her up a hill to a cluster of beatific old elms, their branches suspended in blessing. Below them in the meadow people were letting their big dogs run wild, wolfhounds and Rottweilers and sheepdogs, dogs who'd been cooped up in apartments all day. The park was checkered with spring crows too, crows whose feathers had a blue sheen, and shameless bold pigeons, hussies, all of them. Michael leaned against the fattest elm. This was his park. This was his congregation down below.

"Well, I'm crazy about her too." She was used to jumping into his

stream of consciousness now, and it didn't even occur to her to mind a
conversation about his mother. Generally she didn't trust shy self-effacing
women, but one in a ratty pink nightgown who could lounge back in her
living room, patting the bed in invitation: *that* was a woman you could
trust. Didn't matter, or maybe made the liking deeper, that Norah would
ban her from the house in a flash, same as Doris would, if she had any
notion what Fran had been doing with her son the past few months. What
they did, fast, in the sleeping bag as soon as Norah had cleared the house of
children and got herself out for the morning marketing.

"I been thinking," Michael said. Then he laughed at himself. "I been
straight for forty-eight hours, so I been thinking."

He *had* been straight, more or less. They'd finished the last of her dope
two days before and now all they had was Billy's beer from the icebox.
Michael slept. Sometimes he lay on the couch. And now he breathed a slow
deep sigh. These sighs were new too, to go with the sobriety. "It's torture,
ya know, when you're in the next room and I can't hold ya. It's torture at
school too. I mean I'm crazy for Kevin, got a real crush on *him*, but—"

He was asking her to move in again. He wanted her to leave her dorm
room and get an apartment with him. In another six months he'd be asking
her to leave school altogether and she'd be as tempted as she was now,
tempted to follow him to Europe with a backpack or something. Look at
him. Look at him now, jiggling against the tree, swinging his arms out just
as the tree itself did, wanting to hold her around the waist, to draw her close
and nibble at her in front of all these wild dogs and crows and pigeons.
She'd never before met anyone—not Steward, not even Tony Rivers—who
matched her for her inability to sit still, to leave her hands off, to behave.
They were a couple of four-year-olds. Look at him, wiggling and wriggling, wormy and snakelike.

She didn't say a word. She meant to finish up school in a narrow bed,
right next to Peggy Barnacle's narrow bed. No longer chaste maybe, but
chastened, and resisting until it was graceless to resist anymore. As long as
she wasn't pregnant she'd hold him back. She'd learn to sit still. To behave.

She smiled, serene, as if she could really hold herself back. He was still
holding out his hands and grinning, knowing her better, and now wriggling
his fingers at her too. *C'mon, c'mon.* C'mon and snuggle, c'mon and wiggle,
c'mon up here at the top of the hill—top of the morning, ma, top of the
world—with the cock of the walk. C'mon and give in.

At the sight of his long fingers beckoning she relented. Why not. She
twirled and backed into the cradle of his arms, nestling up against him to

watch the dogs and the birds and the whole swoop of this meadow in Brooklyn, turning from brown to green before their very eyes.

Back in Maryland, in the little square dorm room, in the airy heat of May.

Fran tucked a pillow of Kevin's behind a pillow of Michael's and stretched her neck every which way, looking for peace. Now *she* was back in Limbo; neither city nor country: no trash, no Mahoney's, no marshes, no sea. She was fifty years too old for this college stuff. She felt a poem coming on. This was a dangerous adolescent thing, worse than dancing naked in the men's dorm, and so she grabbed a pencil and began to sketch Kevin's bed by the bland buttery light of the overhead bulb.

Now, at the end of the semester, she spent most of her nights in Michael's room, alone, breathing in the smell of dope and dirty socks, of Kevin's and Michael's books and ink and dust. Peggy was holding a women's consciousness-raising meeting in her own room three nights a week, and Michael was at rehearsals. Sometimes the rehearsals went past midnight, or else he was out drinking with the cast, or he and Kevin were in somebody's room slurping up coke through noses as red and inflamed as boils. Sometimes he stayed up for seventy-two hours, until he looked like some demented Munch figure, punishing her with his presence. Or absence. Most nights she went back to her room the way she came, through Tony Iovino's window, back without seeing him. Back to Peggy, who smelled of obsessive cleaning and the Shalimar she dabbed on for women's consciousness.

Her pencil broke and she stretched and rose to look for another. Michael kept his writing things in his father's old navy footlocker. The trunk, stacked with books and manuscripts and rows of small tidy supplies, was a model of order and didn't look as if it could possibly belong to the soul who lived in this room. She moved rows of old-fashioned cellophane tape, three typewriter erasers, an envelope of carbon paper. No pencils, even as she dug down to the legal pads, covered with Michael's small precise handwriting, halfway between printing and script. She flipped idly through one of the pads, and saw her name attached to a line of dialogue.

FRANCES   *Not about sex. Not about God.*

Her eyes lighted on the line the way they might light on a red peony in a field of gray. She could remember saying something like that, back in

Rock Creek Park the day they were tripping. She shivered and saw Billy, taking down their talk in Mahoney's. She backed up the page.

> *MICHAEL   I have a whole theory of sexual ethics and I wish*
> *you'd listen.*
> (Frances laughs hysterically.)
> *Yeah, yeah, it's hysterically funny. But just the same it would be*
> *good once to talk about sex. Or God. Or politics.*
>
> *FRANCES   Not about sex. Not about God.*

She heaved herself onto the floor, onto the ratty pile of dirty underwear she'd lifted to open the footlocker. She closed the legal pad, but the light did not go out. It was entirely possible that every page, covered with Michael's fine neat hand, was a verbatim account of their months together. Entirely possible that he was the hero of this play, and she was the villain. She couldn't resist:

> *I'M FALLING OVER THE EDGE AND YOU'RE THE*
> *ONLY ONE STANDING DOWN BELOW, SO WHY ARE*
> *YOU LOOKING AT ME LIKE THAT?*
>
> *A one-act (two act? just have to see how it develops) play by*
> *Michael Burke*
>
> *Essential in this draft to keep all the scenes focused on self-*
> *destruction. Do not confuse reality and fantasy!*

A list of scenes with Frances and Michael followed. It was a two-character play. For just a moment her stomach roiled, in the old way. Michael had written a play stripping her naked. (And she was the one who earned her spending money posing nude for painting groups, enjoying—no, luxuriating—in her own taut tidy muscular body.)

She sat on the pile of dirty underwear, perfectly still for a while, and then she flipped back through the pages to make sure she wasn't hallucinating. No. There was the dinner with the Jesuits (trimmed, but then he was barely conscious that night). There was the night she told him about her father timing her mile at the beach. She rose in a single sudden motion and the blood rushed forward. Standing, she was a light-headed dynamo. The one-act festival was opening in a week. Michael was rehearsing one of his own plays, a play he'd been calling . . . what? *See ya Fran I gotta go work on Looking.*

Sure. *I'm Falling over the Edge and You're the Only One Standing Down Below so Why Are You Looking at Me Like That?* Written by. Directed by. And Starring Michael Burke. And who else? Who had he picked to say *her* lines?

She flung the yellow pad against the dresser, where the pages splayed amid the wads of Michael's discarded rough drafts, the pink and yellow slips with the phone numbers of his ever-expanding circle of friends. The clock said ten twenty-seven. Maybe rehearsal was still on.

She left everything, even her sketchpad which she never left anywhere, and took the stairs two at a time, her sneakers drumming on the old worn threads. She was running like water through the dark stairwell and emerging under rows of fluorescent lights on the ground floor. She bypassed Tony Iovino's window and for the first time—it was a wonder she could find it—she walked out the front door of Martyrs Hall and into the night. No one stopped her. No priests appeared from behind hidden cameras to accuse her of moral turpitude.

She ran the quarter mile to the old theater building. Pumping her legs, her fury stoked itself higher and she could feel herself transforming into a Doris-creature, all black energy. Her voice, if it ever came out, would be tightened to shrewpitch.

They'd never had so much as a fight, not in these three months. They had come back from Brooklyn as Yin and Yang, Shakti and Siva, George and Gracie. But he had been disappearing, behind clouds of smoke and piles of powder. He'd been disappearing, just as she was suspecting that she really was pregnant after all. He'd been disappearing just as she waited for him every night to say that maybe she would move in with him after all, just as she saw flames licking from Doris's tongue at the news. He'd been disappearing and she'd been waiting every night, waiting to ask him if maybe the Jesuits could find them a cheap apartment, or jobs, anything so she could keep painting while she had a baby.

The theater building's domed roof came into sight, looking more like a mausoleum than the home of the drama department. She slowed. He had asked her to rehearsal once, but she'd only stayed for the first playwright's one-act and then being the girlfriend was so pathetic (all of them sitting in the audience with nothing to do, a bunch of earth mothers, one of them knitting for God's sake) that she'd told Michael she'd wait for the big production and be surprised.

So here she was, surprised.

She heard the shimmer of voices coming from the big stage. At the back door of the theater she wavered. They'd had that conversation in the park a month ago. He couldn't have turned it into a finished play by now. She opened the auditorium's heavy swinging door. If she was all wrong, she might slip into the seat next to him, and afterward she'd go drinking with the crew, and when they'd downed a couple of beers she could tell him that she actually thought for a minute that he was going to put their private conversations onstage.

She waited in the back for her eyes to adjust to the light. Presently it was clear that Michael was onstage, stretched back in a big reclining chair. Now she saw that it was the sort of chair you'd find on a plane or a train. On a bus.

Next to him sat another tall figure, a big-boned redhead with pitted skin, her face like a pocked frozen piecrust. A girl who had a rat's nest of hair as big as Miss Mississippi's, a girl who called attention to herself in the cafeteria by singing snatches of *Candide* or *West Side Story*. It was hard to believe that Michael would cast her in any play—there wasn't even any visual balance, two redheads like that. She seemed to be calling her lines through a megaphone rather than reciting them.

I think I've heard *far fucking out* five times this morning, and it's only seven o'clock.

Fran leaned against the door, but it flapped in the night, and so she lowered herself into a seat in the back row. Now she could hear everything. Now she could see everything. Now she could see that Michael had cast the redheaded cow, that shameless hussie of an acting major, in the role of Frances Starkey. That graceless heehawing strutting self-important stranger on the stage was delivering lines she'd once delivered on a Greyhound bus. Steedman said that these days, paranoia was just heightened awareness. She was acutely aware.

And she could see Michael throwing himself into the role of himself, controlling all his jiggling in favor of a debonair, wounded approach. He picked himself out of his dejected slouch and flung an arm over the back of his bus seat. In his lovely clear deep Brooklyn swell he said:

Oh well I've got an excuse. You know what alphabet kids in Brooklyn learn?

If he kept on, if he kept calling out lines he'd once spoken to her, if the big diva onstage kept calling out answers close to the ones she'd made, she'd let out a yowl that would bring down the house, a yowl that all the members of Peggy's consciousness-raising group could not manage if they put their angry mouths together.

But no. She did not yowl. She sat in the old Ignatius Paderewski Memorial Theater, under the ceiling's plaster-relief garlands, her eyes on the droop and flow of the curtains parted to reveal this scene. The curtains were green, green gone a despairing yellow with age.

And she began to picture herself alone with a child, the way she had conjured up the image when she was just the principal's easy daughter. She saw herself in a Paris garret again, with the baby in a rush basket, her own daughter now, and again she composed the letter she'd write to Steward Morehouse. Oh, all the ways she'd abused him.

Weightless, she rose and slipped out the back door of the theater. She had stopped hearing the lines coming from the stage. Michael was hollering something now, something familiar, but she closed her ears against it and left the way she'd come, to get on home.

VAPOR

His girlfriend Rochelle was vapor, a damp white trail fading the way the stream left by fighter jets from the air station used to fade in the Due East sky.

And Steward Morehouse was in the shower again, steamed, in the shower where he'd been since Rochelle slipped out of his life in her pleasant way. There had to be somebody else. *I'd just rather not talk about it, Steward. There's no real sense talking about it. I just think it'd be better for the both of us.* At least Franny never had the lack of imagination to call another boyfriend *better for the both of us*.

Rochelle broke up with him a week after he'd signed a two-year lease on an apartment for the two of them. It was true that she'd never agreed to move in. The apartment was right on Bourbon Street, upstairs, not twenty doors up from where his mother had lived, and as the shower droned on, it came to him that Rochelle was scared to live so close by his mother's old place. He was scared to live so close by his mother's old place himself. Bourbon Street was not what it was when Lola wiped tables. Men in tight pants gave him sweet come-on smiles.

But it was Rochelle's loss. His new solitude—no Roberts and Rutherford banging on the door—left him edgier, under a loose cloud of anxiety all day until the cacophony on the street began, but there was a purity to everything he felt. Now, for instance, in the shower for forty-five minutes, hot water beating on his back, his ears clogged with steam, heat permeating the air, he felt a cold white fury. He turned off the faucets, hot and cold, and the plumbing sang.

It was an old apartment, with wounded plaster that might detach and hit you on the head while you were sitting on the toilet. He had not moved any furniture in (what was the point, the semester at its end) but he had bought a sleeping bag and two fat black towels for the bathroom. An alarm clock, a radio, a freezer storage bag full of dope so he wouldn't have to be running nickel and dime bags over from campus.

Now he stepped into the damp pool of his own making on the bathroom floor, reached for a black towel, realized it stank already, sat naked and dripping on the narrow curved edge of the old tub. Much of his day was spent in this bathroom. It was no steamier than the rest of New Orleans.

He took the place when he saw the bedroom walls painted some hysterical shade between pink and red, a shade Nick might call *bordello rose* after a drink or two. The landlord apologized for the last tenant and said he'd spring for a gallon of primer if Steward wanted to cover it, but Steward laughed and said no, it was great. Rochelle would find it theatrical.

Living alone, he saw that it would have to go. Some of the wet had evaporated from his body. The cold white fury had left him.

He rose, spent, lumbered into the bedroom, lit a joint. When he was not in the shower he was lying on the sleeping bag or sitting in the windowsill, looking down into the street, smoking. Dope soothed him and sharpened the edges of his anxiety all at once. Or maybe not all at once. He would drift for long stretches, then jangle back to this reality: this city, this apartment, the crowds below as unreal as movie extras, this utter aloneness. If he'd been drinking, there was no telling how sorry he'd feel for himself. He was no fool. He didn't drink until the sun went down.

He took another toke, enfolded it deep into his lungs, imagined a vaporous picture of dark wide-mouthed Rochelle, and exhaled venom. He found earnest arguments about the nonaddictive joys of pot hilarious. He was hooked, addicted, dedicated, wedded for life to the stuff. How had it come to pass that there was not a single other soul at the University of the Deep South he cared to spend time with? He had stayed away from the campus for two days.

It was already one in the afternoon, and he had not eaten. A rush of hunger, the only sensation that could have roused him, forced him upright, and he began to move in fast forward. He loaded his camera with Pan-X for the hazy sun of New Orleans and stuffed cash and two joints deep into his pockets. Showers, dope, pictures, meals. It was enough to pass a day. One more day evading the University of the Deep South.

In seventy-two hours, right after his Monday morning history exam, he'd be flying home, dealing with Lola and Nick. Nick would need him close for a while, would need some politics to distract him while he sank back into the quagmire of peace and domesticity, waiting for orders for Anywhere USA. Maybe Nick would come back from Vietnam as addicted as he was—there wasn't going to be a roach left if he smoked this joint down any lower—though it was hard to imagine Nick sniffling up a joint.

How could he avoid it, though? To hear the guys who made it back to UDS, veterans with strange eyes and tics, Vietnam was one big stoned whorehouse. Their tours were either pure degradation or pure delight.

Hard to imagine Nick facing temptation. Ever since he'd been transferred to supplies in Saigon—his heartbeat went erratic—Steward pictured him on his way home from work at night, walking a gauntlet of tiny beautiful young girls beckoning to him, girls in silk with slits up their thighs. Every couple of months there'd be a note Nick had scrawled out while he was feeling sentimental, and you just knew he'd been drinking.

Stew, I don't know what I personally would have done if I'd had a shot at the education you're getting, probably blown it like I blew a lot of things when I was your age. That's why I want to tell you don't blow it. Don't blow it man.

It was that *man* stuff that worried Steward, Nick trying to sound like a kid, like one of the guys.

Got your letter about the civil war history course a couple months ago, thanks Stew and sorry it took me so long to answer. What we can learn from the valiant guys like that on both sides is that duty is our master or maybe you could say mistress. For her we should be willing to give up life itself.

Something—something about the crabbed handwriting, or the rushed tone, or maybe the word *mistress*—made Steward picture Nick drinking, night after night, with one of those little silk-clad girls. Was this a picture you were supposed to have of your father? Would he have this picture of his own father? Did he picture Lola, lonely in Due East, picking up a gung-ho fighter pilot, an officer?

He was not looking forward to summer.

It was deep night when he let himself back into the apartment, but he had no sense of how deep. Friday night. The walls vibrated, the plaster in the ceiling dangled and jitterbugged with each roar from the street below.

Now he could remember why he came to New Orleans. It was as anonymous as New York, and he'd spent the day loping from street scene to street scene, his camera over his shoulder. After lunch he'd spent an entire hour in the square watching a sweet-looking mime (mimette?), her dark hair down her back in a braid, her face a miniature with sharp pleasant features. He hated mime. Hard to tell if a girl was good-looking in white-face, but this one had a full lower lip gleaming out red. She was doing political stuff—see no evil, hear no evil—so he felt obliged to stay, to throw a dollar in the hat every now and again to keep the crowd going.

For a while he'd been imagining making a documentary on characters he saw in these streets. Maybe the shots of the mime would work their way in. He got some good angles of her too, took her number so he could call when the prints were ready. She'd hitchhiked down from Ann Arbor and was staying with friends. You never could tell what besides the pictures might develop in the next seventy-two hours, though he didn't think he could ever be happy with a mime. Not deeply happy.

He spent the hour after the mime with his legs folded on the levee, sneaking tokes and stubbing out the joint when straight-looking families or their dogs came too close. Pictures of thick brown water: you knew how those would come out. Beignets when he got the munchies, a couple of hours wandering from bench to bench, watching a couple of towheaded kids, waiting for a shot that never came, an hour for dinner with a paperback copy of *Let Us Now Praise Famous Men* and he was reading too, not just looking at the pictures. Many hours in a bar where he made easy conversation with a kid who hitchhiked from Chapel Hill and knew Due East. An easy day. He was blasted, full of goodwill for all these hitchhikers who left their perfect college towns and came to the city of his misery.

He clicked on the radio and tuned in one of those stations that wavered between rock and jazz and soul, good music he wouldn't get in Due East all summer. But he wasn't listening anyway. He was feeling the slant of the old plank floor underneath his thin slippery sleeping bag, a slant toward the street, a tug from the wet low earth beneath this city. The news came on: more hot and sticky weather, an earthquake in Chile, a transport down on its descent to San Diego, all aboard feared . . .

More music. Now the music itself tugged at him. Cannonball Adderley, scruffy and loose. He was glad to be here, this minute, listening to this music, alone. The slick sleeping bag beneath his legs could have been a silk dress slit up high on a Saigon girl's thigh.

He fell down close to sleep before he heard it. Transport down. Transport carrying . . . troops. Coming or going? He hadn't heard.

He swiveled the *on* switch again, raced the dial across the numbers to get the news again. No news. News on the hour, on the half hour. No, he'd have to wait. He pulled his shoes back on, thinking to run downstairs for a paper, then came to his senses. It wouldn't be in the paper until morning, and maybe not then, probably not then, if it was just coming over the radio now. Deep in the night, whenever that was.

He found his alarm clock. Two-fifteen, not so deep after all. Not so far from the half hour. They'd say it again, if it was a whole planeload full of troops.

He lifted the phone to call his mother, put the receiver back down in the cradle. He was out of his mind. Lola wouldn't have heard it yet, Lola would be sound asleep. He'd called late at night once before and heard at the other end of the line what he'd always suspected, that his mother drank herself to sleep, that her brain was so clouded it took her fifteen, twenty, twenty-five rings to pick up the phone at her side. What could he do tonight but scare her senseless, scare her into finishing the bottle she'd left by the phone?

He turned the ceiling light off and brought a joint to the window, but he couldn't light it. He was stoned already. The streetlight below filled his place with smoky light, light that crackled with heat every few minutes and then trailed off. The goodwill of tourists still filled the streets.

It would be such a coincidence. That Nick should come so close to home, that Lola should count him safe already, only to have him go down on a lousy runway. He didn't even know Nick's date of departure from Saigon. He didn't even know whether the plane on the news was coming or going. There must be thousands of transports, passing each other in the night, every night, night after night, planes leaving trails of vapor in the vast Pacific sky.

He could read the green shining hands of the clock from where he sat: two twenty-five. The time radiated into the night. He wasn't stoned any-more, but still he couldn't light the joint. It lay useless on the windowsill.

He was being superstitious. This was how Franny's family used to get, Doris saying *All good news comes in threes* and *All bad news comes in threes* and *I dreamed a flock of birds were shot down over a lake, now what terrible tragedy do you suppose has come to pass?*

Well he hadn't dreamed anything. He hadn't dreamed anything and it was just a fluke he'd walked into his apartment when the middle-of-the-night news came on. He shouldn't even bother to listen to the next bulle-tin. They wouldn't be able to tell him if Nick was alive or dead. Even if— and this would be crazy, this would be nutty coincidence—even if Nick were on that plane, even if he didn't survive, there'd be no way to know until a Marine badnewsbearer walked up Lola's front walk. He found himself praying that his mother would sober up by morning, if they were going to send someone to her door, that she'd pull on a robe of Nick's instead of one of those diaphanous numbers when she went to answer the Marine's ring. He found himself praying that she'd be alone in bed when the Marine came to ring the bell.

Was he *willing* Nick dead?

Two twenty-nine. He fiddled with the dial, got the station in as clear as it would come, hopped up the volume. Here we go.

More hot and hazy, record number of assault cases this May, earthquake in Chile, troop transport returning from Vietnam, attempting to land in heavy fog . . .

Returning. This time they said no known survivors.

Outside a baby was bawling up into the night. Who brought a baby out into the New Orleans night at two-thirty in the morning? What the hell were they thinking of?

There was no reason to think Nick was on that plane. *Nick might touch down before you do, wouldn't that be something. Oh Stewie, I can't wait to have you both back.*

And he'd been picturing a scene in the car, Nick scruffy in the front seat, frayed from traveling around the globe, his skin loose, flapping over a bony skeleton. Nick not wanting to see Steward, wanting to be with Lola, wanting Steward out of the way, wanting Lola and her drinking out of the way.

That was all. He'd been dreading the reunion, and because he'd been dreading it he punished himself with this fear. Not a rational fear. No reason to believe Nick would be on that plane. No reason at all. No reason to think he'd hear anything in the morning. The morning hours would pass by hot and hazy, the streets full of crying babies and record numbers of assaults, and early in the afternoon, after Lola had risen and bathed and lotioned herself up, her brain would be sufficiently defuzzed to call him, and there would be no need to fear the call, it would just be the Saturday afternoon call, it would be just to let him know Nick's exact time of arrival and in the course of the call she might say *Oh Stew wadn't that just terrible about that other plane? For a minute I thought . . . You don't suppose that could happen to Nick's too? I'm praying the rosary round the clock now to get him home safe to me.*

Again he raised the joint to light it, and again he lay it back down on the windowsill. He rose, planning to stretch himself out on the sleeping bag, but he sat himself back down on the sill too. Outside the baby howled louder, or maybe this was another baby. He was not moved to look down and see what troubled a child brought out in the dead of night. His eyes were drawn up, not down, up to a sky you couldn't see in the hazy night, nothing but moisture there, a damp sponge pressing down on the city of New Orleans. Pressing down on him.

He lodged himself back against the window frame and remembered the guy they'd seen in Lola's apartment the time the three of them all came to New Orleans together, the guy in the lampglow, the guy with the paperback book. He could be that guy now. He almost expected someone to ring his bell.

Nick. He almost expected Nick to ring his bell. He could sense him out in the loud dark streets, holding a baby, watching a young girl sashay into a bar. He could almost feel him here, in the dark still apartment, in damp heat, in the vapor that clung to everything, that made it so hard to see and to feel and to think.

OH MAMA

The doctor was jolly—"Yep, you bet, I'd say that's what we've got here, we've got a baby"—until he remembered that he was doing infirmary rounds and the patient lying below him was a freshman as unmarried as a nun. Frances, flat on her back, watched him raise himself like an old man and put a hand to the small of his back.

Maybe it had been stupid to come to the infirmary, but she could picture her father dragging in with bronchitis or a sore tendon twenty-five years ago, lying on one of these very tables where she was now laid out so indiscreetly. Lately she found herself looking for connections, for signs and portents. Lately she found herself turning superstitious.

"I don't know if this is pleasant news for you," the doctor said, doubtful and hopeful at once. What else could he say, in a Catholic college infirmary? His own wide gold band wavered in the examining room light.

"Oh, it's great," Frances said, and there was not the slightest edge of irony to her voice. Already she was comforting him in his embarrassment. He probably had daughters at home.

"Quite a piece of news to get just before summer break. How old, eighteen? Do you have a doctor you can see, at home? Because the best piece of advice I can give you right now is to be sure to see someone every month without fail."

You'd think he'd never seen a pregnant woman before. He didn't wait for her to answer his questions, but scribbled away on her chart, listened to her shallow breath, checked breasts that reminded her now of a pair of wet swollen sandbags. Anything not to have to look at her. On the way out he squeezed her hand, instead of shaking it, his eyes down on her chart.

But back in the dorm Peggy was just the opposite, peering up at her as soon as she turned the doorknob: "Oh holy shit you are aren't you?"

Peggy had been stuffing a suitcase with spiral-bound notebooks. Now she sat still on the edge of her bed and maintained a stare. Frances smiled and waved, a beauty queen riding on the backseat of a convertible in the Due East Water Festival Parade. A pregnant beauty queen.

After a million years Peggy slammed shut the suitcase and came over to cradle her. Frances hated that sort of thing (hadn't let Doris touch her since she was seven years old) but just this once she let her roommate's arms encircle her. Peggy smelled vile, perfume and Windex.

Peggy let her loose, sat again, this time on the edge of Frances's bed, stared again, and said: "Does he know?"

"Nothing to do with him," Frances said. "Now." She sat herself.

"Look, are you going to have an abortion?"

Frances blinked.

"Because if you're not, as I suspect you're not, because I think you're the biggest romantic who ever came down the pike, you have to tell the bastard so he can at the very least help you pay for the, you know, delivery and stuff. And living. I mean, are they going to have a *grand*child of a deceased alumnus scholarship?"

Frances dismissed her with the flap of a hand. The baby would stay . . . where? They'd already signed up, she and Peggy, to keep the same room. Now she could see Peggy scanning the space, wondering who would share with her next. She had enough cash to buy a Greyhound bus ticket, Washington to Due East, but not enough to buy a sandwich along the way.

Peggy went back to peering at her. "It's sort of a moral obligation. To tell him. I mean, it's his child too."

Another flap of the hand. Michael had left a dozen messages, but *I'm Falling over the Edge and You're the Only One Standing Down Below* had gone on as scheduled for the one-act festival. The last time she'd seen him, he put a hand on her shoulder while she sat waiting for the psych final. She shrank down like plastic melting, and he drew back his singed hand. No word from him in the two days since. Peggy was leaving this afternoon, her finals over, and for all she knew Michael had already left. She herself had only one more exam to go, Great Works of Western Lit II. The great works in question all seemed apt: *Anna Karenina, Adam Bede, Tess of the D'Urbervilles.* Pregnancy was a great theme, all right.

"So come on. Upsy daisy. Let's go." Now Peggy seemed to be girding herself for battle. She was pulling on red sandals she'd bought for the trip home to the Bronx. They laced all the way up to her knees, or were supposed to, but her calves were so bulbous that they came up only halfway. She looked like a Roman soldier in drag, grabbing up a red plastic pocketbook she'd bought to match the sandals. Poor Peggy. Other women their age tried to look like Grace Slick.

"Where we going?"

"To tell him. I'll be there for moral support, take me or leave me. I'll wait in the hall or come in. Whatever."

"Peggy. No. Anyway, he's probably gone home."

"Oh no he hasn't. They were shouting your name up and down the halls while you were gone to the infirmary. He's still trying to phone in his pleas for mercy. And now he's got the roommate, what's his name, on the case too. Came over to my table last night."

"You didn't tell me."

"Nothing to tell. He just said *How's Francie?* Is that what Michael *calls* you?"

Talking had not slowed Peggy down. She was stuffing the red pocketbook with wads of Kleenex and moving toward the door, as if her sheer magnetism might raise Frances from the dead. But at the doorway she stopped, seeing that more than magnetism was needed, and rallied the troops.

"It's not right," she said, her voice calm and reasoned, "for one person to bear a burden two people created." Then she threw back the shoulders she'd been slouching and proceeded to hiss. "Come on Fran. Come on now. I gotta blow this joint in a couple of hours. Let's go. It's not *just.*"

She took Peggy, who wouldn't know anything about Tony Iovino's window or about parietal rules either, right through the front doors of Martyrs Hall. The guard, wordless, watched them pass by his desk and then followed them to the elevator, where he shook his head sadly at their gall.

Up on Michael's floor, she opened the door without knocking. Kevin and Michael never locked their door: they had one of those Proudhon *Property Is Theft* posters, which was enough to convince people there was nothing worth stealing inside. She held a palm out, meaning Peggy should stay in the hallway, but left the door ajar. As long as Peggy was there to witness.

They were both in, Kevin and Michael, Michael's back to her as she barreled in. No going back. Peggy meant for her to present Michael with her mother's Due East address and a dignified suggestion that any check mailed for a baby's welfare would reach her there.

But it didn't look as if any occupants of this room would be mailing a check anytime in the near future. The two of them were hunched over the night table between their beds, white powder on a sheet of waxed paper between them. The mound of powder had a crisp cold look and the waxed paper itself seemed to have unrolled from her childhood. The scheme began to lose shape and the black funnel that had been on the periphery of her vision moved in at the edges.

"Francie!" Kevin saw her first. His soft low voice beamed, and at the sound of it Michael snorted out what he'd been snorting in. White-spotted drool clinging to his upper lip, he turned and watched her as if he knew her from somewhere. Kevin watched her too, not with any concern or hurry. Just watched, the two of them, their two pairs of sky-blue eyes gone golden in the artificial light. Golden in a pool of pink. The two of them were guardian angels. Someone to watch over you.

Finally Michael said: "Want some?" and indicated the powder pile, but Kevin shook his lazy head and said: "It's not coke."

Nothing to do but chirp out her message, especially with Peggy watching in the doorway. "I've just come," she started, but at the sound of her voice Michael rose, shaky, smiled the sweetest clearest smile she'd ever seen form from the hemp of his ropy mouth. He sat on the edge of his bed, still smiling, then curled up in a ball and closed his eyes, smiling.

She felt the first tug of nausea in her pregnancy. "Fran!" Peggy was hissing from the doorway, but it was black in that direction. "Coupla junkies," Peggy said, concentrating more disdain and more Bronx than Fran had ever heard in her voice. She followed the honk into the hallway.

She couldn't remember anyone touching her, but Peggy must have got her back down the elevator, past the guard, back into the light of day. Walking along, she heard Peggy say *Skag* and cluck her tongue in disgust, but the word didn't sound right at all, coming from her. Something she read in a book.

Peggy clucked along as they progressed toward home. Most of the clucks said *Don't count on anything from him* but these were punctuated every few feet by *What was he taking when he got you pregnant? What's* that *gonna do to the baby?*

It wasn't until they were back in the room, Peggy slamming the last of her things into suitcases so she wouldn't miss the train, that Frances was able to screen out the clucks. She was hardly present for Peggy's sloppy goodbye. When she heard the door itself cluck and Peggy's heavy suitcases slide down the hall she closed her eyes and felt her blood pressure drop in a swoop. She watched herself fall into the funnel. The room was dark and quiet.

There was something swollen and amorphous rotting inside her.

Sometime deep in the night she heard her name called from the hall phone. The dorm was half empty and the sound of it—*Frances STARkey, Frances STARkey*—ricocheted off the bare doors and walls, stripped of their posters so the Catholic girls could go home. She'd told Doris not to expect her for another week.

Frances STARkey. A pause at her door. A rap. A nasal voice: *Does anybody know has Frances Starkey gone home yet?*

She couldn't ease her body of the swirling. She'd lost her center. Dry heaves into the night. Finally she curled up at the cold base of the toilet, somewhere between pregnancy and sleep.

For two days, she was alone in her room. She slept all the sleep she'd lost for a year. Sleeping was more real than waking anyway. She was not hungry anymore, not for food or even painting.

She had left the blinds up. Daylight came and went, a beech tree greening outside her window. When she got up she drank water cupped in her hands from the tap. She went to the bathroom at night, when she couldn't put it off any longer. There was a trace of blood. Sleep tugged at her.

On the morning of the third day she woke with dawn still feathery in the sky. Something had happened. She dreamed of tottering down the corridor to call Peggy or Kate or even AgnesAnn or Teresa. She could not be alone another hour.

She lay still, but sleep would not overtake her again. The sheet where she'd lain was covered in watery blood. Something had happened. She took her length of black satin, draped over a chair, and draped it over her hips. She did not think she could lean over to look for shoes, and pushed her feet into fluffy bedroom slippers Peggy had left behind.

Down the corridor she pushed in the pink slippers. Possibly she was still dreaming. She trailed her open palm along the walls, steadying herself. The cheery summer session nuns were moving in already, giggling more than a year's worth of freshmen had ever giggled, beaming at her as she passed.

Outside she pushed the slippers faster, but the distance to the infirmary doubled and trebled as she hobbled along in the bright light. She'd dreamed she was ever a runner. She'd dreamed she'd ever have a baby.

Finally the glass door was in sight. She heaved herself to push it open, but it was made of concrete. Pull. Pull the door. She heard bird noises, chirps, gurgling in her throat, and she stood still in the darkness of inside-the-infirmary. A plump parcel of white was hurtling toward her, and she pitched forward. The nurse, with strong large arms, got her into a chair. She wasn't dreaming. She wasn't dreaming the nurse's scarlet fingernails, pressed into the underside of her arm to take her pulse.

The nurse's big backside disappeared and her big bosom returned, with a gurney. She dragged Frances aboard and pinched a needle into her arm. Above her a bottle leaked liquid into her arm. Safe. She wasn't dreaming. The nurse pulled the gurney into a big room, streaming with enough light to intoxicate her. She was drunk. She was lying in the infirmary, safe at last, drunk with light and sugar, and she was singing "Gloria." She was lying in the infirmary and she was back in Due East, singing "Gloria" and running from her house, the old house by the marsh, all the way to Steward's. The nurse ran off on tiptoe. Franny, back in Due East, marked every pine tree she passed on the way to Steward's, every yapping loping dog coming at her. She could see Nick's house coming into view, a plain brick box, but the sky above was doused with liquid light.

She could hear the nurse on the telephone. There was talk of her vital signs, dismissal of an emergency room. Lola said she had a *grand passion*. She was dressed in Lola's low-cut dress and push-up bra. She brushed on Lola's black mascara. She drank beer right from the can, the way Lola did with Nick, and she passed right into some other state of consciousness.

Later the doctor said that she'd lost the baby, that there was *visible tissue in the clots* and she'd have to go into the hospital for a D&C. It was the same doctor as before, but now he looked her right in the eye, curt and scientific. Did he think that she'd done this to herself? She struggled to stay awake and hear him, but he was talking underwater. He was Pat Starkey, his wedding band flashing, and she was his drunk daughter, lying under the Sacred Heart.

It was a wonder she was still conscious, the doctor said. An early miscarriage shouldn't leave her like *this*. Had she been trying to starve herself? Did she have a history of this, this self-abuse? The lowest blood count they'd seen on campus the entire year. Down close to shock. She'd have to spend the night while they poured fluid into her. Got her strong for the hospital. He was severe. He did. He thought she'd done this to herself.

And maybe she had. Maybe she had willed away the baby who was sucking her life from her.

Maybe she would never get her life back. Maybe it had drained away, flowed out with the baby. She could not feel her own physical presence. She was not getting herself back. She was leaving, floating above the infirmary bed. She was a baby herself, one of those cherubs floating high in a church's vaulted ceiling. She could feel herself being painted on the ceiling in airy brushstrokes. She could feel herself being gilded.

She was the cherub chipping off the ceiling, dried and cracking. She was disappearing into air, cold air now, descending to earth. She was sick with pneumonia and her lungs were thick. She was calling for Doris:

"Oh, Mama. OOOoooooooomama."

Michael was prostrate with guilt—the play, the heroin, the miscarriage he must have somehow caused—and acted the reformed convict. He employed an intermediary, Simon, to track her down in the infirmary and to plead his case. Who else but a priest? They drove her back from the hospital and walked her to her room, as gentle as if they were in mourning themselves. "Watch out!" Michael cried, and led her by the elbow around a crack in the sidewalk.

Simon invented summer jobs for the two of them in the history department, until they had time to work out their . . . estrangement. He only let her work two hours a day at first: you'd think she had polio, or TB. But she was running four miles a day, the trees streaking by in the early morning light.

She didn't need a job, not here in the middle of Limbo. She needed running, and she could be doing that in Due East, conning Dillon or Harrison into a ride to the beach, where she could run in the cool breeze, palmettos streaking by instead of sycamores. She'd paint with the sand blowing. When she thought of painting now—which was all the time—she thought in reds and yellows and oranges, sun and blood and maybe fury. If she got back to Due East she could call Steward, just to hear the tight careful sound of his voice.

She had not yet worked her way up to telling Simon and Michael that she was going home. June floated on. Her mother railed on the phone. How could she disappear like that, where was she that day she was missing,

didn't she know the whole family was just frazzled with worry? When
Walter got on the line he sounded so far away he might as well have been
living on the other side of the globe. She needed to be back in Due East for
a while. She needed to get home.

But every morning Michael brought her breakfast and the morning
paper. He let himself in while she was out running: he owned the corridors
of the women's dorm now. He'd made the same arrangement with the
open-window owner on the ground floor that he'd made with Iovino in
Martyrs Hall, and now the summer session nuns watched and waited for his
visit. He was bold, so bold he fetched her mail on the ground floor. She
pictured him triumphal, strutting down the halls and flirting with the
sisters.

By the time she was back from the run he was slouched down waiting
for her in the plastic armchair, slinking, begging forgiveness. It was hard not
to enjoy it a little, this begging of his. She knew what was coming—he was
going to ask her again to take an apartment with him, shouldn't they just go
ahead and live together, now that they'd been through *this*—and there was a
small mean part of her that wanted him to ask.

Then she could tell him she was leaving, leaving for Due East, and
maybe after Due East she'd skip over the rest of the college bit and go
straight to New York to wait on tables and take classes at the Art Students
League. She could put little index cards up on bulletin boards offering her
services as a model, and she could sit nude and still for housewives dabbling
in painting.

Her body was still sore and light. Michael brought her heavy bagels,
New York food, with the morning mail, bagels and milkshakes at nine
o'clock in the morning, to fatten her up. She didn't have the heart to
disabuse him of the notion that a milkshake would cure anemia. In the
morning light red stubble broke out recklessly in no discernible pattern over
his chin. He was as eager as a panting dog, and just as faithful.

This morning when she arrived there was no milkshake, but the bagel
sat waiting in a white bag. Michael's eyes were clear. She couldn't help it,
she still had to check, but who was she kidding? She was on her way out.
She didn't have the right to care if he was shooting motor oil into his veins.
A year ago she probably would have tried motor oil herself. But look at
them now: college kids, all cleaned out and cleaned up, with a history
professor priest to act as honorary father. Oh they were safe and spoiled,
and she'd better get out of here for good, while she still could.

Michael held up the *Post* in one hand and in the other her mail, a single postcard. Today, with the summer heat upon them in the last days of spring, he wore a tweed cap like the one his grandfather wore in New York. She came close, biting back a smile, and saw a Cambodia headline on the *Post*. She took the postcard.

The picture showed a fighter plane slanted up, erect, in the bright glare of sunlight. She'd grown up with the plane and the postcard both, and so had every other child in Due East, the plane mounted like a stuffed deer at the entrance to the air station, the postcard perched in every drugstore in town.

Michael put a bagel in her hand, and a shiver of ambivalence passed through her. If he hadn't put that bagel in her hand she might have been stroking his stubbled cheek or tweaking his cap. But he was taking over again, him and his eagerness. He'd taken Peggy's place in this room. He fetched her mail and sat in a chair waiting to feed her. Did he read her messages too?

Dear Franny,
Hope you are not disappearing anymore. I'll be calling Father Collins this Sunday for a full report, just so you know. You are a worry.

Well I'm sorry to be the one to pass on bad news but it's happening all around us these days isn't it. Steward Morehouse's stepfather was killed coming home from V.N., just one of those crazy things after he passed safe through the war. Plane crash. Funeral Tuesday at Natl. Cemetery, I better go because she came to Daddy's.

Out of room. You see that you call, young lady.

xxxxMama

Michael was working off chunks of a Danish, and she watched the polished layers of it crowd into his mouth. The nuts were shaved into hard little slivers, shards of white. She turned the postcard over to stare. Did Doris go out and pick this postcard, this silver fighter jet, for this news? Michael stopped stuffing his pastry at midair, and knew not to say anything.

She kneeled on her bed and pummeled first the mattress and then the pillows. She couldn't even say she'd *known* Nick, but she could picture him, his second fold of chin always sticking out dark and belligerent, his black eyebrows curling out from the top of his long nose. Little eyes, with mud-brown irises and whites the color of glue. She could picture him clearly and she had no picture whatsoever of this baby, this baby who hadn't even progressed to baby state as far as the doctor was concerned. *Tissue.*

She had a pillow in her hand now, and she was kneading it, stuffing it up close to her belly, throwing it. It sailed to a stop at Michael's feet. He tried to pretend he wasn't chewing the last of his Danish. When he'd swallowed the final bite of it down he opened his mouth—a small opening, a trial run—and she said:

"Don't you dare say a word."

He sat obedient and watchful. So he'd read the postcard after all. Did she ever doubt it? He would try to horn in on her grief. He'd try to find out about Nick, so he could turn Nick into a character in a one-act play.

"Just go."

When Michael left, the latch gave a small neat click, and she moved into action. From the closet shelf she dragged down her father's old duffel bags and stuffed them with jeans and T-shirts. She sifted through drawings, electing and discarding as if it were Judgment Day, and put the chosen in her lousy paper portfolio. She'd store the canvases in the studio, and send for them when she could. She did not even have cash for a bus ticket anymore, but that wouldn't stop her. She'd call Simon. She'd have him charge a plane ticket for her. She meant to get home for that funeral.

But once the bags of clothes were stuffed and zipped, once she'd tied the portfolio closed, she saw that the funeral was over. Nick was dead. Nick was dead and buried. Let the dead bury the dead. She didn't even need to pick up her mother's postcard to see that.

She went down the corridor to call home. She, who hadn't been homesick for nine months, had the word pounding like a headache—*home, thunkathunka, home, thunkathunka*—but the Starkey phone rang busy and busy and busy. There were a million Starkeys. You could never get through.

She dialed Steward's number fast, before she could think.

CRAZY
FOR YOU

The first stages of grief were so dreamy, so druglike to tell you the truth, that Steward was unprepared for the hyperreality that traveled down with the DeAngelis family from New Jersey. Nick's brother and sister had brought their families to stay in the River-n-Sea Motel up the highway. For a week they'd been ringing Lola's front doorbell at breakfasttime and crowding in the little brick house until the last cup of coffee was downed at midnight. Nobody knew how long this mourning period was going to last, and nobody seemed inclined to ask.

Nick's brother Lou put his arm around Steward a hundred times a day to say: "Dominic was crazy for you, kiddo." Steward was only expected to jab Lou lightly in the gut. He hadn't seen Lou DeAngelis since the wedding, and he'd never heard Nick make a single phone call to his brother, but nobody in the DeAngelis family was counting visits. Nobody was checking birth certificates. Stew was supposed to be one of them, eat lunch with them until four in the afternoon and start on supper at five. Not a one of them had any interest in seeing Due East, now that they'd seen the National Cemetery, but once a day they'd stagger out to walk around the block. They could have been the circus come to town, the way children stared at them.

Today S.D. and Dillon and Harrison were all over at the house too, crowded around with the family, arguing over Nixon and equal opportunity. "I'm all for giving the black man a chance!" Lou said to Dillon, poking the air with a fork. "But let's give the white man a chance too!" Cheers all around from Lou's sister Rita and her three teenage sons, but Lou winked at Steward. He was just getting a rise out of Dillon.

Lou's wife Marcella, chopping onions for the twelfth time that day, came behind Lou to bop him on the head. She was the most extreme woman Steward had ever seen, her eyebrows drawn on like calligraphy. This wasn't the time, but someday he wanted to sit her down in front of a camera and let her talk. "He don't know nuttin," she said, "this man I marry."

"Yeah, Lou," Stew said, "you're so full of shit it's coming out your ears." They had him talking like them now.

"WHOAHO," roared Lou's nephews. "WHOAHO, listena Stewie."

Steward and Lola had been dashing out for daily grocery runs, trying to keep the festivities going, though they'd already cleared the Piggly Wiggly's shelves of olive oil. Nobody in Due East bought *olive* oil, but Lola was willing to learn from Marcella how hot you could heat it before it smoked. Lola, the queen of the TV dinner, was in the kitchen at the crack of dawn to give antipasto a shot. She was trying to hold them all there and Stew rushed out to keep the shelves stocked for her.

The phone rang in the hallway but they ignored it through a half dozen rings. It had been ringing night and day, buddies of Nick's from Korea, relatives twice-removed in New Jersey and New York. Lola, up to her elbows in breadcrumbs, turned around to beg, and finally Steward rose to answer.

The fat old black rotary sat on a mahogany table crowding the hallway, one of those tables Nick and Lola had picked together from the PX to try to console themselves for the lost Morehouse money. When Steward was thirteen and fourteen and fifteen, Franny had called him every night and he'd stood furtive between the kitchen and the living room, the thick receiver clutched in his fist, trying to reduce his every reply to three words his mother wouldn't be able to make sense of.

C'mon Stew they won't hear you! I've got the dang phone in the coat closet. Franny's frustration appeared whole, as hyperreal as the rest of this mourning period. Then came a premonition, also whole, also real, that it was Franny on the phone, the last to check in with her condolences. The last of the old friends. What would Nick have called her? *A good kid, ya know Stew, the kind who can hear what you're thinking before you can.*

"Stew?"

"Yeah? Franny?"

Just like that. Like she was calling from down the street, around the corner, like they still had a conversation every day.

"I can't think of anybody else in the world I wanted to hear when I picked up the phone." It wasn't even his voice doing the talking. He'd gone and put on Nick's voice, even a little hint of the Hackensack accent, but mainly the depth of it, the liquidity, the way it spread over you. "I been thinking about you day and night since it happened, swear to God."

She was breathing hard on the other end of the wire. She was a million miles from him, now that he was finally learning to talk, now that he was telling his Uncle Lou he was full of shit and punching his cousins in the arm. Now, with his father dead.

"Hey Franny, hey it's o.k. I mean it was weird at first. Listen, I know you went through this too, don't you know I've been thinking about what you went through, but really I'm o.k. I'll be o.k." He didn't seem able to stop. "You wouldn't believe my mother, she is a *rock,* she says she knew when he left he wasn't coming back and she made her peace back then, but the strangest part is how, hey, he almost made it."

And then he had to stop. Still there was nothing jagged about the way he was talking, nothing weird even though he'd used that very word. He hadn't smoked a joint in a week. His voice was a smooth arc, up with the hope and down with the grief.

But she, on the other hand, didn't seem able to get *anything* out. "I'm—" That was all. That was as far as she got.

"Your mother was at the funeral, ole Doris. Listen you, I can't tell you how many people were asking for you. I mean, Harrison and Dillon, they're practically taking bets here about when you're pulling back into town. We were just talking about you. But I said if you're not here yet, you're not coming. You're leaving ole Due East behind."

"Harrison?"

"They're all sitting right in my mother's kitchen. Nick's kitchen. As we speak. Dillon and Harrison and S.D. too." He dropped his voice a little, the way Nick would have. He'd known about S.D. all along, and they'd known he'd known. He'd passed into some new personality dimension with this grief, a dimension where you could see the proper proportion of things. Some talkative older brother had taken his place, and was pouring himself into the black phone on the hall table in Nick's house. "We're all sitting around drinking vermouth, which is Mama's new idea of a mourning drink."

"I'm so sorry Stew. I'm—"

Still that was all she could get out. "Hey Franny don't, I can't stand it if you, hey you know, Nick's gone but nothing changes that I was crazy for you. And I mean crazy."

"I know Stew. I was crazy for you too. I can't be, I couldn't ever be good, I guess I didn't want to, I guess I was just a kid or something."

She didn't sound like herself either. She sounded like someone calling out of a very long very doped-up night, like someone slobbering across a telephone wire stretched through a corridor of all the time and space that had passed. Good of her to say *crazy for you too* because, even hearing it down that long tunnel, he could hear that it was true. And how much closer could you ever hope to come to another human being, a father or a mother or a lover? They'd only been kids together. Still he felt that void. Once he thought they'd been shaped from the same ball of clay.

He turned himself around, holding the phone, so he wouldn't see Lola weeping in the kitchen. Now he faced the hallway leading to his bedroom, where he'd hidden from his parents, and their bedroom, where they'd hidden from him. Staring down the hall, his lungs filled up and he was buoyant in his grief. If he stood just this way, completely erect, fingers wrapped round the phone, he could look down the hallway and feel them enter his hyperreality. He could see Nick and Fran and even that other father, just a kid, a kid as pissed off as he had always been, big ears sticking out of a second lieutenant's cap. There they were, the ones who were gone.

"Just crazy for you, Franny."

WHY NOT

"It's good to have you kids back here, you know. Speaking to each other."

Simon sat in an armchair, trying to be funny, facing Michael and Frances on the couch. Joe was in the kitchen, fussing with homemade hors d'oeuvres this time. Simon was fussing, Joe was fussing.

It was the sixteenth of June, a special night for the Jesuits, who had saved a soul or two. They were fixing a special meal, a special ritual. They were not even going to descend to the common rooms to play cards later: that had been made clear. There was no Southern Comfort, no hash. They would have wine for dinner—moderation in all things—but no one would tempt Michael out of his newfound maturity.

They were supposed to be celebrating something. The wearing down of her hostility? They had brought her round in just a few weeks' time, Simon and Michael, brought her round to showing up for filing duty and even singing "Gloria" once in a while. Michael was a mind reader, he knew that now she craved his company in the morning, that now she looked for the bagels and the solicitude, the stripping down to her naked body, tough and tight and hard once again. Tempting him before they started the day. Nuns around them, bells ringing in the hall. And Simon beaming on them daily.

They hadn't cured her. Painting had cured her, that and knowing she could go home to Due East in August, when the heat would guarantee her a clean sweat. Now there was no need to run away so fast, not when she had the entire studio to herself all morning for the rest of June and all of July. Four hours of painting in half-decent light, in solitude. She was doing a whole series of portraits from memory, little twelve-by-eighteen acrylics of Walter and Albert, Caroline, Nick. They were vivid, all bright and dark, cartoony almost, like the Sunday comic strips printed in goofy yellows and reds and blues. She'd never tried before to paint someone without so much as a photograph, and it was true that it was hard to conjure the exact curves and bumps and widths when they weren't in front of her. Still, the colors were true for all their unreality.

"You're resilient," Simon said, "the two of you."

Exactly what could you say to that kind of remark? On the tail end of it Joe arrived with the appetizers, a trayful of shrimp and onions and peas on spears, the same he'd served the last time, only now he'd gone and made them all himself.

"The patience of a saint, Joe," Michael said. "You stick all these things on by hand?"

"I have this strange sensation," Joe said. "I think you call it déjà vu."

Dinner was fish this time, simple stuff, some fleshy northern fish she didn't know. Cod? Everything was in chunks. The tomatoes, pink and hard and false, could not have come from the earth. In Due East, the packing-houses would still be open, this time of year, this time of night. But here in Maryland the four of them ate unreal tomatoes and aimed for dignity, twirling the thick stems on the wineglasses, trying not to reach for the bottle too often. This did not diminish Simon's pleasure.

"You're really resilient, the two of you," he said again, at the end of the meal, and Joe said:

"There it is again. That strange sensation."

Simon cleared the table but waved an airy dismissal at her offer to wash up. Washing up, his hand implied, was banal and unworthy of them all.

He and Joe excused themselves. Flushed with the wine, they could not resist, Joe said, running downstairs to borrow a bottle of brandy. It was hard to believe a bottle of brandy did not live in their own crowded liquor cabinet.

At the kitchen table Michael lit a cigarette and raised a single eyebrow when the priests left the room. His cigarette hanging out of his mouth, he took her by the hand to the living room and sat her down on the couch.

Some charge was in the air.

"Is this a setup?" she asked. The wine was seeping into her extremities. The colors in Joe-and-Simon's drab living room took on a life of their own, the little Madonna over by the bookcases dancing now with its greens.

"Whatcha mean, setup?"

"I mean, did they go downstairs so—I don't know, it's just kind of silly, the dinner and the votive candles on the table. You know how you said it's like *Father Knows Best* around here? You know. A setup."

"You mean so I could be alone with you."

"Well."

"To ask you something." He still had the cigarette dangling. He liked to talk that way, balancing it, the way he used to balance the papers and the drugs and the late nights and her, back when school was in session. He still looked like someone teetering. His halo had grown bushier and bushier until finally he tied it back, a tiny cottontail in a rubber band at the back of his neck. The fuzzy little ponytail seemed to raise his eyebrows higher, slender well-drawn eyebrows over eyes that focused better now. His cheeks were flushed.

"You're right," Michael said. "It's a setup."

She looked down at her knees. He'd be asking her again to move in. Staring at Joe-and-Simon's rug, a big blue cross on a dingy background, she braced herself. Ah no. Not with this guy. No fool she, Doris used to say. No, she was going home to Due East. Maybe she was coming back and maybe she wasn't. Maybe she'd come to be crazy for this guy and maybe she hadn't. Maybe she'd forgiven him, maybe the rancor had washed itself out of her with the pregnancy.

"It's true, they know. Aw I'm not drunk enough for this. You'll be pissed I talked to Simon about it first but I wanted ya t'know, I wanted to get the money set up, take care of you—I know, I know, I don't mean *take care of you* in that paternalistic way, but I mean since you've been sick. I mean since you been trying to figure out whether to let me off the hook for the shitface thing I did with the play. I mean since you been trying to figure out do I have, like, any ethics at all."

She twisted her face up to see him and then stared back down at the rug. In the old days rugs were intricate and flowery, with patterns as complicated as this speech whose curlicues Michael was trying to draw right now.

"Aw, I'm not drunk enough for this at all, but I think, don't say anything, I think we oughta get married, and it's not to make it up to you or anything like so limp, it's more like oh what the hell. They've got apartments in Georgetown, the Jevvies, it'd be better for you in the city, you can go to galleries and Simon says he can swing a stipend for you too. I'm set working for the history department, we could swing it till we graduate. Oh shit, it does sound limp. Listen, I don't wanna wait like my parents did, I don't wanna wait till I'm stewing in bitterness like my old man. When you lost the baby I could see it. Why not now when we love each other? Hey man, why not now?"

She couldn't help it. She laughed a little at him, his mouth easing open, the cigarette butt dropping, lit, onto the edge of the cross rug. She did, she giggled at Michael agonizing on the couch, oh just the bumbling lover reaching down for the cigarette butt and she felt sorry for him and said:

"Oh Michael, come on. I'm eighteen. I'm not getting married."

And he tried to join in the joke, he did, rueful smile, oh rueful young man. But before she knew it he had dropped his face down into his hand, the old sympathy play, and she was leaning onto his back comforting him. Careful. Comforting him, scratching his back, rubbing it round and round. You could get hooked like this, comforting him just when you thought you were going to slip away. Watch out. Don't say *yes,* whatever you do if you can keep *yes* out of the conversation, if you can limit it to being comforting. Just straight, just like your father, just play it the way he would. Calm sympathy. True love. But watch out for yourself—New York and Paris and colors getting truer by the morning—just whatever you do don't say yes.

"Sallright, Michael, look I'm sorry I was laughing. But can you see me? With an apron on? I mean, I thought you wanted to live on the edge. Of society or something."

He pulled his face up from his hand, tried his best to be rueful again, but there was the indignance breaking out. "I wouldn't want you in an *apron.*"

"I know, but I mean, keeping house and."

"I wouldn't want you to keep *house* for me. Who'd you think I am?" All trace of ruefulness gone.

"Well yeah, I know you wouldn't want me to keep house but some-body would have to do it and—look, it's just I've got a million canvases to go, a trillion, a zillion. I'm ready to go. I mean, Michael, oh wow, can you see the little announcement in the *Due East Courier?* I mean, *Mrs. Burke* wore a peau de soie blah blah?" Amazing she knew that, peau de soie.

All the flushed patches wore off his skin. All the stubble dropped off his chin. He was blank, staring down at the rug. Blank and pale and full of regrets.

"Oh Fran, you don't have the faintest idea who I am, do you? Not the faintest fucking idea."

She heard footsteps in the hall. Joe-and-Simon must be back, with a bottle of champagne, not brandy at all, listening at the door, waiting for the signal, the moment when Michael would get up to let them in. Beaming.

The proud fathers, the proud fiancé. Look at him! Is this man, this boy, a *fiancé?*

"It's true," she said. "I don't know who the fuck you are. I don't know who the fuck I am either except I'm not getting fucking married. Look how you've got me talking! You could get arrested in Due East, talking like that."

"Aw come on." He looked her right in the eye, his face blank and colorless, his own light eye unwavering. What a tactic. What a brilliant tactic. He just looked right at her and begged.

The Jesuits must be in the hall, still waiting. The warmth of him next to her, not this one, *not this one,* but oh it would be good, her father gone, her mother breathing down her neck, Teresa and AgnesAnn still not believing she could walk down the street by herself, Steward gone for good. It would be good to lie night after night next to someone you loved, neither one of you crawling through windows anymore, it would be good for a while to stop watching the rest of them, men. Boys. Good to settle down with someone crazy. Someone who saw that you got a stipend—how could she have known he'd be so practical—someone who had priests call the infirmary when you disappeared.

"Don't be crazy," she said. "C'mon, Michael, I'm not kidding, I'm eighteen." She hit his back. "Artists don't get married."

"Sure they do! They need a muse. I'll be your muse, you be my muse, we'll amuse each other just fine."

She couldn't stand it. She could feel herself bending, leaning into the side of his body, a piece of wax melting in the sun. Look at him, innocent as Walter, *beaming* at her that way, willing her to bend.

"Come on," he was whispering, shameless. "I love you," he was whispering. "I *neeed* you," he was singing, lowing. "Why not. We'd keep each other going, I know we would, I'd keep you painting, you'd keep me writing, I swear you won't be in any more plays. I swear it. Please Fran, Francie, please Miss Frances Patricia Bernadette Starkey won't you marry me. Come on. Why not."

Why was a better question. Why now, why married, why was he getting to her? Why was she listening so hard to hear if the priests were at the door? This was her life, why was she picturing herself now in an old house in Georgetown, on the top floor, the sun streaming in, room finally enough for an easel left up all the time, Michael at the typewriter, priests on all the other floors stopping them from themselves? Why had he come up with this crazy idea just as she was getting back to—normal? Never.

Now she leaned her head into him and heaved out a deep breath of despair and contentment.

"You will?" he whispered.

Why not.

II.

THE
GUNRUNNERS

Jesus wept, or danced or
something, and well He might.

—B. BEHAN

THE GUNRUNNERS

or, If Marriage Is Guerrilla Warfare, When Do the
Bombs Start Falling on Me?

A Screenplay by Michael Burke

c. 1971

FADE IN:
EXT. TRACK, THE JESUIT UNIVERSITY OF AMERICA.

An Irish reel, "Jenny's Wedding," floats through the air. Tight shot of a bride running, her flowing hair coiled with flowers. The camera pulls back —Franny has hitched up her wedding gown. She's eighteen, a barefoot childbride of 1971. A slew of pale, freckled children follow her.

Two smiling nuns in habit pause at the track to watch. Behind them is the Jesuit University, an old tree-lined red brick campus with stone crosses atop the buildings.

> FIRST NUN
> She really shouldn't be doing that.

> SECOND NUN
> She's only having fun.

> FIRST NUN
> Terrible for the baby, running hard like that.

> SECOND NUN
> *(Surprised that the first nun doesn't know.)*
> She lost the baby, a month it must be now.

> FIRST NUN
> *(After a pause.)*
> Then why on earth is she getting married?

CUT TO:

INT. JESUIT RESIDENCE. COMMONS.

Credits roll over the wedding reception for Franny and Michael Burke. The Jesuits are throwing them a bash in a large commons. A soul band in big Afros revs up. Drug-washed hilarity from the crowd. Students in hippie dress-up. Longhaired priests. Michael's working-class relatives from Brooklyn. Franny's family, stiff and proper and Southern.

To soul music, a montage of scenes:
–little boys wiggling their hips lewdly;
–a girl in granny glasses flirting with the priest/bartender;
–three priests at the corner of the crowd sharing a joint;
–a Vietnam vet buttonholing anyone he can get his hands on.

VIETNAM VET
(To student trying to escape him.)
I told my old man, I said, look, man, it's just not my war. Dig
it? It's just not my personal *thing*. And, like, the next thing I
know he's like personally driving me to my physical.

As the last credit fades, Franny appears, breathless from her run. She
scans the room for Michael. She's a tough little cookie, not pretty but full of
interesting angles.

INT. JESUIT RESIDENCE. BATHROOM.

The camera follows Franny, still running, through the crowd to the
bathroom, where she finds Michael. His frizzy red hair's pulled back in a
ponytail and he's dressed in a moth-eaten morning coat and patched jeans.
He's a little older than she is—twenty—but no wiser. He's huddled with his
best man Kevin in a stall, snorting something over the toilet. They look up.

KEVIN
Don't worry, Francie, it's not smack.

MICHAEL
Want some?

FRANNY
(After watching them strangely for a minute.)
Nah. I'm stoned enough just from getting hitched.

CUT TO:

INT. COMMONS. FOOD TABLE.

The bride's mother lays siege to the groom's ma.

DORIS STARKEY
(Agitated, in a heavy Southern accent.)
I'm just in awe of you, taking it all so well. I like to had a fit
when Franny called to announce—not to ask, mind you, to
announce—

NORAH BURKE
We're all so fond of Franny.

DORIS
Oh, she's a pistol. She swears up and down she's not in any
trouble but I expect her mama'd be the last to hear of *that*.

Norah, flustered, piles the food on her plate.

DORIS
I mean to tell you, she's got no respect for the proprieties. Did
you ever? I mean, did you ever hear of the bride asking her
boyfriend to the wedding?

By the end she is hissing, as Franny's old boyfriend, Steward, approaches. He's a pale tense rich boy, dressed in blue blazer and flannel pants,
all wrong for this crowd.

CUT TO:

EXT. JESUIT RESIDENCE. UNDER A TREE.

Franny has beat a retreat to smoke a joint with her friend Peggy, a
horsey bespectacled smart girl from the Bronx.

PEGGY
Your old boyfriend looks ready to close all the windows and
turn on the gas.

FRANNY
Steward? Oh, Steward's my *life*.

PEGGY

Funny you wouldn't wanna marry the guy who's your life.

FRANNY

We were kids together.

PEGGY

He's not as scary as Michael. You need a mystery man.

Reaction shot of Franny. Maybe she *is* a little frightened of Michael.

CUT TO:

INT. COMMONS.

Michael dances a silly dance with his little sisters, young priests dance with Franny's sisters.

Doris attaches herself to Father Collins to complain. He's an old-fashioned, elegant priest with silver hair. Franny trails in, stoned and watchful.

A dubious-looking photographer lines up the Burkes (six children, overwhelmed widowed mother) and the Starkeys (nine children, incensed widowed mother). Franny's old boyfriend, Steward, looks on, solitary.

Different angles of Michael accepting envelopes from his relatives. A drumroll from the soul band as Father Collins gets up to make an announcement.

FATHER COLLINS
(On a table, holding an envelope in one hand and a glass
of champagne in the other.)

On behalf of the Jesuit community of this university, I'd like to wish the bride and groom a long and socially conscious life together.

Cheers, groans, and hoots from the crowd.

> FATHER COLLINS
> And a toast, on behalf of the groom, who's been working so hard for civil rights in Northern Ireland. Michael, old Ireland will yet be free.

He raises his glass to the sound of wild cheering. A pan of the Mick-infested crowd.

> FATHER COLLINS
> (As if he's giving a sermon.)
> We can all see that Michael's new bride has the map of Ireland imprinted on her face, too. But you may not know that neither Franny nor Michael has ever *been* to Ireland.

Michael's domineering old Irish grandfather, Ned Burke, is watching him sharply.

> FATHER COLLINS
> So the Jesuit community has come up with a scheme to get these two over there for a quick honeymoon, and we certainly hope they accept our modest offer, because the tickets are nonrefundable.

> DORIS
> (Pushing her way through crowd.)
> Father! You're not sending them off to *Ireland!* Not *now!* The whole country's going up in smoke.

FATHER COLLINS
(Climbing down and taking her by the elbow.)
Don't worry now, Mrs. Starkey, we're not sending them off to
Belfast.

Confused applause. The soul band makes an attempt at an Irish jig but
gives up. Franny and Michael dance together to a blues number—she's a
good dancer, but he's still being silly. Steward cuts in on the slow dance.
Michael looks right through him, then goes off to make a drug buy from
the Vietnam vet in a dark corner of the room. He opens one of the wedding
envelopes for cash, and pockets his buy.

In the opposite corner, Father Collins, joined now by other priests, is
still trying to calm Doris down.

FATHER COLLINS
They call it the Puck Fair. I guarantee you, it's as safe as . . .
the sanctuary of the chapel.

DORIS
In that case I'd like to know what they've been doing in the
sanctuary that's made this marriage necessary!

MIDDLE-AGED PRIEST
Mrs. Starkey, we're sending them to a *livestock* fair.

YOUNG PRIEST
(Whispering as Michael approaches.)
Don't tell her it's as close as the Irish get to an orgy.

Father Collins shoots him a look.

YOUNG PRIEST
(Drunk, to the group as a whole.)
But of course it's not. Not an orgy at all.

DORIS

Father Collins, I never dreamed I could say such a thing to a
man of God, but I believe you are acting irresponsibly. I believe
you have been acting irresponsibly since you pushed my daughter
into that hirsute hippie's arms.

Doris downs the drink she's holding. Michael grins.

Franny and Steward are still dancing a sensual dance. Michael's grandfather Ned climbs atop the same table Father Collins climbed. He fans his
hands to stop the band. Laughing at him, they let the music trickle off.

NED
(Not completely drunk, but fierce.)
Will we have an Irish tune? What about it, Michael?

Michael shrugs, then winks at Doris. The hall is quiet. He begins to
sing, a capella, Brendan Behan's prison lament, "The Old Triangle." His
grandfather, ferocious, looks down on him. Franny stands by her old boyfriend's side as she listens to Michael's rough deep voice. She watches him
intently.

FADE OUT.

FADE IN:

INT. BROOKLYN BAR. AFTERNOON, A FEW DAYS LATER.

A sparse crowd of patrons in a dark depressed space. In the background,
a silent TV signals the international headlines: first walk on the moon,
women's sit-down strike in Belfast. Sentimental Irish-American music on
the jukebox. Michael and his grandfather at a small table.

MICHAEL

Look, I know what you're going to ask me to do.

NED

Do you then, Michael? And I thought I was giving you my good-bye toast.

MICHAEL

I can't. Can't do it.

NED
(Raising his glass.)
May you stand by your new bride always. May you stand by your beliefs, always.

MICHAEL

Listen, it wouldn't be fair to Franny, mixing her up with that shit on her honeymoon.

NED
(Faint smile.)
Sure it's your honeymoon too.

MICHAEL
(After a pause.)
Maybe it's the only way now, but they're gonna get smashed again. Lambs to the slaughter.

NED

Will you be good enough to hold your voice down.

MICHAEL
(Lower.)
Listen, you ask me to do something like this you're gonna have to listen to me bleat a little bit. I gotta know I'd be willing to pick up a gun myself.

NED
(Fierce.)
Hold your tongue so.

CUT TO:

EXT. BROOKLYN SHOPPING STREET.

They've gone outside into a gray summer day, and walk alongside a gray depressed stretch of stores. Ned looks over his shoulder before he talks.

> NED
> It's all been taken care of, Michael. There are proper channels. They've gone over with the merchant marines.

> MICHAEL
> I thought . . .

> NED
> Still the center of the universe. D'you think they've need of equipment sent over in the pack on your back?
> *(Michael is silent, Ned unable to contain himself.)*
> Twenty-one revolvers, Michael. A Thompson. And a half dozen Armalites we wheedled out of Canada.

> MICHAEL
> Armalite. Sounds like a groovy gun.

> NED
> Is it nothing to you if they win or lose?

> MICHAEL
> Maybe it's more to me *how* they win or lose.

> NED
> Very smug and satisfied with your placards, aren't you? Civil rights. Peace and love.

Ned walks along, brisk and full of himself. He leaves Michael in the dust.

FADE OUT.

FADE IN:

INT. AER LINGUS PLANE. THAT NIGHT.

In the dark, under a blanket, Franny watches Michael stumble back to the bathroom. Inside, he snorts the last of his coke. From her seat, Franny strains to see out into the black. Michael returns jittery. No dialogue. They can't connect.

                                                        FADE OUT.

FADE IN:

INT. SHANNON AIRPORT, IRELAND. CUSTOMS. LATE MORN-ING, NEXT DAY.

Franny and Michael—rumpled, giddy—exit customs. They're ap-proached by a spry, dapper man in his seventies.

                         DONOVAN
It's young Mr. Burke, is it? Your grandfather's asked me to give you a proper welcome.

                         MICHAEL
                 (Confused, extending his hand.)
Oh. Oh. Hey. Yeah.

                         DONOVAN
Jeremiah Donovan. I'll not tell you how many years have passed since your grandfather and I were with the Christian Brothers.
        (Extending his hand to Franny, pouring on the charm.)
Lovely. A lovely bride. Will we go to the car then, and get you where you're going?

                         MICHAEL
Hey thanks. We were planning on putting our thumbs out.

                         FRANNY
But I think it's a little ways up the road.

MICHAEL
We've gotta make an appearance at this shindig called the Puck Fair. Place called Killorgan.

FRANNY
Killorglin. We shouldn't trouble you.

DONOVAN
But you've a day or two until the fair starts. I'll not send Ned Burke's grandson off to Killorglin to rent a room. We've a house all ready for you.

FRANNY
Thanks, but that's too much. We couldn't.

DONOVAN
A house by the sea. Lovely view. Lovely.

Michael and Franny exchange looks, but Donovan has already started off, swinging his walking stick. They follow him.

CUT TO:

INT./EXT. CAR. MOTORWAY TO COUNTRY ROAD, COUNTY KERRY. LATE MORNING, SAME DAY.

It's a misty day, mistier as the ride progresses. Franny's in the back, watching the countryside. A swooping road, heading into the mountains and toward the sea. A green more psychedelic than any she's ever seen. Desolation and majesty.

CUT TO:

EXT. CASTLE RUINS. AFTERNOON.

Donovan pulls the car up beside a stark seaside castle ruins and they all pile out. From the boot of his car he extracts a jug.

DONOVAN
(Raising his eyebrows significantly.)
Poteen.

Donovan passes the jug. Michael drinks and looks as if he's been slammed in the chest. Franny splutters.

DONOVAN
That will cure your traveling woes.

MICHAEL
(Reaching for the jug.)
Like motor oil. Motor oil from heaven. What's with the castle?

DONOVAN
Yet another testament to the rape of Mother Ireland.

Franny, behind Donovan, rolls her eyes, but Michael pretends not to see her.

CUT TO:

INT./EXT. CAR. NARROW MOUNTAIN PASS. LATE AFTER-NOON, SAME DAY.

In the front seat, Michael is carousing with Donovan. They pass the poteen.

DONOVAN
(Singing.)
As I was walking down the road
A feeling fine and larky oh

Michael joins in, remembering the words.

> DONOVAN AND MICHAEL
> A recruiting sergeant came up to me
> Says he you'd look fine in khaki oh

Franny, in back, looks wary and anxious. The mist swirls, the road is narrow. On one side of them, mountains. On the other, a sharp drop to the sea. The old man's driving becomes more stylish as the poteen soaks in. A sharp turn around a cliff, Michael oblivious. The car fords a stream.

FADE OUT.

FADE IN:

INT. OLD STONE HOUSE, KERRY COAST. BEDROOM. NIGHT.

Franny's in bed with Michael, watching ominous shapes in the dark and listening to the distant sound of the sea. The wind soughs. She tries to cling to Michael, but he's stoned silly, his mouth open, his body dead-weight.

DISSOLVE TO:

INT. OLD STONE HOUSE. BEDROOM/STAIRS. MORNING, NEXT DAY.

Michael's dead to the world, but Franny wakes, hears the sea, and rises. "Jenny's Wedding," faintly. Out the front bedroom window, Franny sees three little girls driving cows down the road. From her back window, where the house is set into a hill, she sees more cows grazing. She hurries downstairs. The place is poor and sparsely furnished.

EXT. STONE HOUSE.

Shivering in her bare feet, Franny stands in the road watching the girls and the cows. The narrow winding road is bordered by fuchsia hedges.

Fields of sheep and cows rise above it. The sun breaks through the morning mist. She turns and sees a sharp cliff drop down to the sea. Now she sees an old man coming along behind the girls. It's Donovan. She runs back inside the house.

Now Michael leaves the house, his hair frizzed out and his face stubbled. He's barefoot. Donovan is waiting for him at the door and leads him off.

CUT TO:

EXT. ROAD, FOLLOWING COWS AND GIRLS.

Donovan strolls along, Michael hobbles against the stones in his bare feet. The tails of the cows swish in front of them, the sea swishes below.

DONOVAN
Your wife knows nothing of the arrangement, so.

MICHAEL
Mr. Donovan, *I* know nothing of the arrangement. So.

DONOVAN
I thought at first we'd have no need of you. It's what I told Ned. We'll have no need of the lad.

MICHAEL
Mr. Donovan.

DONOVAN
I was anxious to spare his feelings, y'see. A year ago we were bringing them in that way, bits and pieces, threes and fours. We've bigger shipments now, but I'd not turn away any contribution, no matter how small. I'd turn away nothing from Ned Burke and his grandson.

MICHAEL
Mr. Donovan.

DONOVAN

Mr. Burke. Look at the sea, Mr. Burke. You're as far west as you can get, until America. You're in Kerry now.

They stare out at the sea and the big rocks of the Blasket Islands. The mist is burning off, but the sky is wild, dark and then light.

DONOVAN

And a Kerryman's your man to stand up when the time comes.

MICHAEL

I don't know what you're saying.

DONOVAN

I'm saying internment's on the way.

MICHAEL

I haven't heard the news, it's been two, three days.

DONOVAN

Tonight, perhaps, or the next day. They'll not be required to charge anyone, you understand. They'll take in any Catholic whose looks they don't fancy, and most of us fit that bill.

MICHAEL

They won't do it. It'd cause a stink in New York and Boston like you wouldn't believe.

DONOVAN

Sign-carrying, is it?

MICHAEL

You have a low opinion of demonstrations, huh?

DONOVAN

I do. And the Brits have a low opinion of Boston and New York. Internment will be announced before the week is out. I've need of you after all, Michael.

                    MICHAEL
                    (Wary.)
For . . . ?

                    DONOVAN
We've a man takes these small packages for us. He can meet you
at this fair tomorrow, and he'll get them up across the border for
us.

                    MICHAEL
Look. Look, I don't suppose my grandfather mentioned my
ambivalence.

                    DONOVAN
          (Softly, creepy but compelling.)
There's not a decent man either side of the border hasn't had to
squeeze his own heart tight before he decides to take a stand.

Michael is silent. They walk along.

                    DONOVAN
I'd not pressure you.

                    MICHAEL
I'd want to know I could go all the way.

                    DONOVAN
To the fair, only. While the gardai are watching my every move.
While they have me shackled this way.

They stroll along, Michael's eyes on the little girls driving the cows to
the rhythms of "Jenny's Wedding."

                                        FADE OUT.

FADE IN:

EXT. REMOTE DOCK, KERRY COAST. DAWN, NEXT MORNING.

Franny and Michael pull up in front of the dock driving a horse-drawn caravan, brightly painted. They've made their way down a steep cliff, and they're shook up. The sea facing them is threatening.

> FRANNY
> *(Yelling over the rattling of the caravan.)*
> I feel like such a tourist jerk. Where'd he get this thing?

> MICHAEL
> Hey, it's not cheap to rent. He didn't have to get us a wedding present.

> FRANNY
> I feel like such an American jerk.

Michael winks at her and jumps down from the caravan. He enters the only fishing boat at dock this morning.

> CUT TO:

INT. FISHING BOAT. CABIN.

> Eyes adjusting to the dark, Michael approaches a weathered and dour fisherman.

> FISHERMAN
> The American, is it? Here to pick up the load, is it?

> MICHAEL
> I think I'm supposed to say I'm, like, here to pick up a load of fish.

FISHERMAN
(After a sarcastic look.)
Right.

The fisherman gestures. Michael comes close to watch him slit open a box. First he pulls out a top layer of rag dolls wrapped in plastic. Then, from under a false bottom, he drags a miscellany of old handguns. He shakes his head bitterly.

FISHERMAN
This is the brilliant shipment bound for Dingle. Will you tell your American friends we've need of the real thing?

MICHAEL
(Wounded for his grandfather's sake.)
Hey man, keep going, there's Armalites down there.

The fisherman pulls out a rifle, its butt collapsed, and unpackages it. It's light and compact. He holds it up, admires it, plays with it.

MICHAEL
(In spite of himself.)
Far out.

FISHERMAN
Fuck me. My apologies to America.

CUT TO:

EXT. DOCKS. DAWN BRIGHTENING.

Michael and the fisherman stagger from the boat carrying two large coolers. They head for the back of the caravan, out of Franny's hearing range.

FISHERMAN

Donovan must always have his cloak-and-dagger. Thanks be to Jesus if your fish don't stink.

Michael goes round the front of the caravan to take the reins.

FISHERMAN
(Calling to Michael.)
The Old Goat. You'll not miss it.

The fisherman has a good laugh at Michael's attempts to coax the horses back up the steep dirt road, and so does Franny.

CUT TO:

EXT. ROADWAY, DINGLE TO KILLORGLIN. MIDMORNING.

Michael pulls the caravan over to the side of the road. The mountains are on one side of them, the sea on the other. They look like children in a play wagon. A car passes.

FRANNY
Hey, wasn't that Donovan? 'S he checking up on us?

CUT TO:

EXT. ROADWAY INTO KILLORGLIN, COUNTY KERRY. LATE AFTERNOON.

The Puck Fair swallows up the little town. The road's clotted with caravans. Most are new and metal, but a few are like the old-fashioned kind that Michael and Franny arrive in. They've only made it to the outskirts of Killorglin when a garda directing traffic puts his hand up to stop them.

MICHAEL
I'm bringing a load of fish to the Old Goat.

GARDA

I wish you luck. All the best. But you'll stop the caravan there.

They leave their caravan the last in a line on the side of the road. Michael begins to lift the cooler from the back, but it's heavy. He puts it back, looks around to see if it will be safe. They set off. As they trudge along they see a trio of caravans with painted signs: "Seventh daughter." "Seventh daughter of a seventh daughter." "Seventh daughter of a seventh daughter's daughter." Blond children call out from the caravan doorways.

FIRST CHILD

Are yez Americans?

SECOND CHILD

Have ye got a copper for me wee sister?

FIRST CHILD

Yer Americans!

SECOND CHILD

She'll read yer cards, me wee sister.

Michael grabs Franny's hand to pull her through, but she wants to see everything.

EXT. KILLORGLIN, BRIDGE STREET.

The camera follows them onto the main street. Shops and pubs in the background. Canvas-covered stalls, tarot card readers, street musicians, nuns in white habit, hucksters. At the top of the street is a tall wooden platform for King Puck, a tethered billy goat who presides over the fair.

Franny and Michael wander along past the stalls, gaping. Franny's exhilarated. She takes pictures of the billy goat, who's just been crowned by a young girl in white robe.

The fair is thick with children and dogs. Everyone—lame, simple, aged —crowds into pubs and drinks on the sidewalks. Franny and Michael pass through the sounds of country bands, rock bands, fiddlers, penny whistle players. They spy the Old Goat and make their way into the crowded pub.

CUT TO:

INT. OLD GOAT PUB.

They push up to the bar and wait to speak to the busy barmaid. At one end a drunken Irishman in an Elvis T-shirt is singing "Bang Bang He Shot Me Down."

> YOUNG BARMAID
> *(Pulling pints.)*

Americans?

> MICHAEL

That obvious, huh?

> BARMAID

You're welcome at Puck, if you don't mind our lying.

> MICHAEL

I've got some fish out in my wagon. I'm supposed to leave it here for Fergus Sullivan.

> BARMAID
> *(Looking sharply at him.)*

Wait here so.

Franny senses something's up. The barmaid goes into a room behind the bar and returns with a barman.

> BARMAN

You are . . .

BARMAID

The Americans.

BARMAN

Here for Fergus, is it?

MICHAEL

I'm supposed to give him some fish from his cousin.

BARMAN

I've not seen high nor low of Fergus since the morning news.
Did yez hear it, yourselves?

MICHAEL

We've been on the road.

BARMAN

Bastard announced internment, may he rot in hell. Now things
will only be worse.

Close-up of Franny. She's in the dark.

MICHAEL

Think we could leave the fish with you?

BARMAN

Oh, it's better if ye didn't. Could get pinched in this crowd.

MICHAEL

I don't know what to do with it.

BARMAN

He'll not leave without his fish. I'll tell him to meet you here in
the morning.

Franny leans to Michael to ask him what this is all about, but the
singing man approaches to serenade them. With him is a girl of twelve,

passing a hat. The singing man strums his guitar, deciding what song to play.

> SINGING MAN
>
> Americans?

> MICHAEL
>
> That's the consensus.

> SINGING MAN
>
> Elvis, then.

> MICHAEL
>
> Nah, man. We just heard the news.

> SINGING MAN
>
> What news would that be?

> MICHAEL
>
> Up North. Internment.

> SINGING MAN
>
> Oh. The Troubles. Americans are fierce interested in *that*.

> MICHAEL
>
> You're not?

> SINGING MAN
>
> Sure we all have our troubles. Even in America, eh?

With a sly look, he plays Elvis's "In the Ghetto." Change rattles in the girl's hat.

DISSOLVE TO:

EXT. PUCK FAIR, MAIN STREET. SAME AFTERNOON.

Franny and Michael emerge from the Old Goat. They've had a few pints. They catch sight of two outrageously drunk men, one walking (Fergus Sullivan) and one in a wheelchair (Declan McCleary). Fergus is in his forties and homely; Declan is younger, handsome. Both men have big beefy hands and broad backs. They could be farmers, but they're dressed in tour bus operators' uniforms.

                                    FRANNY
        Michael, look at his sleeve.

                                    MICHAEL
        What?

                                    FRANNY
        It's covered with shit. Oh, Lord. He's fallen in it.

They look down and see mounds of brown dung in the gutters.

                                    DECLAN
                    (From his wheelchair. Barely comprehensible.)
        Bastards. Bleeding Brit bastards. Breeding Blitsards.

                                    BYSTANDER
                    (Clucking his tongue at Fergus's and Declan's state.)
        Disgusting.

                                    DECLAN
        Have we Paddys no pride at all then? Have we Praddys no
        pide . . .

                                    TEENAGE BYSTANDER
        Up the Provos!

                                    BYSTANDER
        Oh, leave off. Provos indeed.

TEENAGER
(*Yelling at the bystander as he walks away.*)
Gobshite. Up the Provos!

Fergus and Declan have passed from sight.

FADE OUT.

FADE IN:

INT. MRS. O'SHEA'S BED-AND-BREAKFAST. THAT NIGHT.

Michael and Franny look wild and unkempt. They're making tired inquiries in a grim little parlor, where the landlady is surrounded by clinging toddlers. Mrs. O'Shea is not much older than they are, but looks on them with alarm.

MRS. O'SHEA
People book a year in advance for Puck. Americans, you see. They like their arrangements settled, the older ones do.

MICHAEL
Thanks anyway. We'll sleep in the caravan. Hey, don't worry about us.

MRS. O'SHEA
Oh! You're a caravan. You'll be cozy in there, won't you?

MICHAEL
You don't know where we could get hold of some sleeping bags, do you?

MRS. O'SHEA
You haven't any linens. Oh dear. There *is* the children's room. I don't rent it out, it's very small. I'd need your payment in advance, you understand. You did say you were married? The one room would suit you?

CUT TO:

INT. HALLWAY TO CHILDREN'S BEDROOM.

The camera follows Franny and Michael up the stairway. Dark corridor, holy pictures. In the tiny bedroom, they flop down on a narrow bed and see twin pictures of Pope John XXIII and JFK looking down on them. They reach for each other and pull off each other's clothes. The springs squeak violently. They stifle giggles.

CUT TO:

INT. KITCHEN.

Below them, Mrs. O'Shea, distressed, hears the squeaking.

CUT TO:

INT. CHILDREN'S BEDROOM.

Franny and Michael are naked, spent, clinging to each other. They're tired and disoriented. They really are in a foreign country. Suddenly Michael sits up.

MICHAEL

The fish!

FRANNY

Be fine for the night. It's cool out.

MICHAEL

Those gypsies'll swipe it.

FRANNY
(Drifting off to sleep.)

It'll be fine.

DISSOLVE TO:

EXTERIORS, PUCK FAIR. SAME NIGHT.

Michael leads Franny by the hand through the streets. It's louder, more crowded now. Drunks drape over each other. Small girls on the bandstand dance tart step dances. Lovers slip into dark corners. Everywhere, the physicality of a repressed people.

When they reach the caravan a figure is darting away.

MICHAEL
I knew it. The gypsies.

FRANNY
That guy looked like Donovan.

MICHAEL
You're seeing Donovan behind every bush.
(He climbs into the back of the caravan, then emerges, relieved.)
They're still here. We better bring 'em back to the B&B.

FRANNY
Oh, it's such a tiny room. She'll have a fit.

By now Michael has jumped down. He struggles to haul the first cooler out. Franny reaches one end to help him, but after a few steps, it's too much for her. They put it down. To his horror, she lifts the cover and starts unshoveling ice.

MICHAEL
Shit! No! Listen, the fish'll be bad by morning you start taking the frigging ice out.

FRANNY
Michael. I'm just trying to lighten it a little.

MICHAEL

Sorry. Sorry I yelled. Listen, you wait here while I get this one
back to the B&B.

FRANNY

Let me go with you.

MICHAEL

You stay, or they'll steal the other one while we're gone.

FRANNY

It's just *fish,* isn't it?
                     (Michael looks alarmed.)
It *is* just fish, isn't it, Michael?
                     (He's about to tell her the truth.)
Michael Burke, are we hauling that poteen stuff for that old
man?

MICHAEL

                     (After long guilty pause.)
You figured it out.

FRANNY

That's all, though, right?
                     (Funny look on Michael's face.)
Oh God, we're not running dope in a foreign country, are we?

MICHAEL

                     (Indignant.)
No! Shit, you could get put away for years.

FRANNY

You should've told me, though.

MICHAEL

Look, I'm sorry, it's just a favor for my grandfather's friend. I
didn't want you all worried about it.

FRANNY

I'm not worried about *that.*

MICHAEL

So whatcha worried about?
(He retreats into the caravan, and emerges with the second cooler.)
Look, Franny, I'm sorry I didn't tell you.
(She glares.)
I'm sorry.
(She gives him a half-smile: he's forgiven.)
I'll be back as soon as I can. Listen, don't open it, o.k. If a cop
sees what it is . . .

Michael backs off, smiling. Franny sits down on top of the cooler to
wait. As soon as Michael disappears from sight she's surrounded by three
tinker's children, grimy blonds with bad teeth.

FIRST BOY

Yer American, are ye? Give us a copper.

FRANNY

Listen, tell me something. How'd you know I was American?
How's everybody know?

SECOND BOY

Please, a copper. Please a copper so I can go on a ride.

LITTLE GIRL

Please can I go on a ride? Please will you take me? Please, what's
in yer box there? Please can I have some?

There's a sound of gravel crunching. Franny and the children turn to
see Declan, the man in the wheelchair, roll up. He doesn't look so drunk
anymore.

DECLAN
(To the children.)
Get on with yez! Leave off!

FRANNY
Aw, they're o.k.

DECLAN
Go on!

The children scatter.

DECLAN
They'll cut your throat soon as look at you, they will. They'd not hesitate to throw you from your box and pinch your groceries.

FRANNY
You really think they'd do that? That little girl?

DECLAN
American riches.

FRANNY
(Laughing.)
You'd think there was gold in here the way I'm guarding it.

DECLAN
Here alone, are you?

FRANNY
No, actually, I'm waiting . . .

DECLAN
Ah, spare me. The day is black enough. I thought you'd brighten it.

The camera's on his wheelchair as he rolls off, dejected, maybe still drunk after all.

CUT TO:

EXT. PUCK FAIR, BRIDGE STREET. A FEW MINUTES LATER.

Now Franny and Michael slog back along with the second cooler. As they get up alongside the goat, Michael stares at the tethered king.

MICHAEL
All tied up, like a man once he's married.

FADE OUT.

FADE IN:

INT. MRS. O'SHEA'S B&B. THEIR BEDROOM. NEXT MORNING.

Dawn. Franny sketches a sleeping Michael. Animal sounds from off-camera. She rises and looks out the window to see cows parading by, shitting.

CUT TO:

EXT. OLD GOAT. SAME MORNING.

Franny and Michael approach the Old Goat as a drunk rises and staggers to a garda.

DRUNK
What's the hour?

GARDA
Half eight.

DRUNK
Would that be morning or night?

CUT TO:

INT. OLD GOAT.

Franny and Michael enter. The place is empty, but the barman's polishing glasses. He gestures to Declan and Fergus, yesterday's drunks, now sitting in the corner, cleaned up and sober. Reaction shots as Franny and Michael exchange glances of recognition.

MICHAEL
(Approaching.)
One of you guys Mr. Sullivan? I've got a package from your cousin.

FERGUS
Mr. Burke, is it? Are yez enjoying the Puck? Sit down, sit down. This's Declan McCleary, though he's none too cleary-eyed after last night.

MICHAEL
Thanks, but I think I'd rather hand over that fish if it's all the same.

FERGUS
Will you have a pint first?

MICHAEL
Thanks, nah. I don't want that fish going bad on you.

FERGUS
Then we're on our way. Will you sit, miss, and let Declan buy you a pint? No sense all of us going.

MICHAEL
(To Franny.)
Be right back.

Michael and Fergus leave as the camera stays on Franny, sitting. She's awkward.

                    DECLAN
That's the lad you were waiting for last night.

                    FRANNY
My husband.
          (She giggles at the sound of "husband.")

                    DECLAN
That skinny lad? Leave off.

                    FRANNY
No, it's true.

                    DECLAN
What's your name?

                    FRANNY
Frances. Franny.

                    DECLAN
Franny, that's very American, that. Franny and Zooey, eh? Very big with the university lads.
          (Awkward silence.)
You can't be long at married life.

                    FRANNY
About a week now.

                    DECLAN
That's good so. We can still have it annulled.
          (She smiles.)
And what do you think of the fair, eh? Lovely horses. Lovely pigs. We don't see too many pigs where I come from.

                    FRANNY
You from Dublin?

                              DECLAN

Belfast.

                              FRANNY

Belfast. It's bad now, we heard.

                              DECLAN

No, actually, it's good now. It's good now that people see what
the bleeding bastards are capable of. No more cups of tea for the
British Army.
            (She tries to smile again. More awkward silence.)
You're full of chat, aren't you?

                              FRANNY

Oh, I don't know enough about it. I don't feel, I don't know,
entitled . . .

                              DECLAN

You're in Ireland, Franny. In Ireland you keep your gob moving
even if you know nothing of the subject at hand. Especially if
you know nothing of the subject at hand.

The barman arrives with two pints of Guinness, brown as the mounds
of dung were the day before.

                                                    CUT TO:

EXT. TOUR BUS AT THE END OF A LINE OF TOUR BUSES.

Michael and Fergus haul the coolers to the bus. Along its side, a slogan
in green, white, and orange: "North-South Tours. We Travel All Ireland."

                              FERGUS
                        (Good-natured.)
This group's very taken with the bleeding pig-and-cow show.
Americans, y'know.

MICHAEL

And then after you go straight to Belfast?

FERGUS

They're none too keen on Belfast *now*. We're waiting to hear where the wee fish will do the most good. What's he put in there? Not real fish.

MICHAEL

Real fish.

FERGUS

He does enjoy his wee disguises. Could they not keep them in the box they came in? Does he think I can cart stinking fish across the border?

Fergus lifts up the bus's baggage gate. He sees the golf bags clustered in the corner and has An Idea.

FERGUS

They won't be rifling through their golf bags, will they, until I decide to stop at a golf course.

He has Michael stand guard while he dumps the ice and fish. Dogs descend directly. He stuffs the guns into the golf bags.

CUT TO:

EXTERIORS, PUCK FAIR. LATE THE SAME AFTERNOON.

Michael's relaxed, his obligation over. He strolls through the fair with Franny, past hippies singing republican songs. Franny sees the little blond girl from the night before. Reaction shot of the girl, shy now.

Montage as a sea of Irish faces approaches them:
—first the pale eyes, like cheap colored glass;

—then men's noses, lobby from fighting;

—then, on all the necks, scapulars, crosses, St. Anthony medals.

The camera pulls back from one of the St. Anthony medals to show Fergus, drunk as the day before, pushing Declan along through the crowds. Fergus puts his arms around Michael as if he's greeting a long-lost friend.

CUT TO:

INT. CHURCH.

Franny stares at the painted stations of the cross. Michael waits, awkward, at the back of the church.

CUT TO:

INT. PUB. LATER SAME AFTERNOON.

Franny and Michael pick at food, nervous. Nothing to say to each other. Eight days married, and they've run out of conversation.

CUT TO:

EXT. PUCK FAIR. SIDE STREET. THAT EVENING.

Franny stops at a caravan to have her palm read.

OLD CRONE
You've only to trust him.

Franny puts a pound down on the old woman's plate. She turns to join Michael, who's waiting at a distance. They walk along together past the stalls, still strained.

MICHAEL
That good a fortune, huh?

FRANNY

Was it just poteen, Michael?

MICHAEL

I told you.

FRANNY

It's not a great start. I've only been married a week and already I'm left in the dark.

MICHAEL
(Putting his arm around her and drawing her close.)
Hey, Lady Gregory. I wasn't trying to leave you anywhere. Look, *they've* been left in the dark.

He points to a group of women in the shadows, surrounded by yowling children.

FIRST MOTHER

Now that's enough of *that*.

SECOND MOTHER

You'll not be taken for a walk again.

THIRD MOTHER

Stop that slobbering, will ye, or ye'll get a good smack.

CUT TO:

INT. PUB. SAME EVENING.

Fergus is looking for someone, making inquiries of the barmaid.

CUT TO:

INT. OLD GOAT PUB. SAME EVENING.

In the front room an old man plays the handheld drum, the bodhran. The rolling sounds primitive, maybe frightening. Michael and Franny are transfixed, but it's crowded. They're pushed along to a back room where girls dance with girls to bad country music. They spy Declan, waving furiously.

DECLAN

Have you found Fergus, then?

MICHAEL

Haven't been looking for him.

DECLAN

He's searching the length and breadth of Puck for the pair of yez.

MICHAEL

For us? I could use a pint about now.

DECLAN

He's had bad news. They've rounded up the three of his brothers and his father as well. Seventy-five, the old man is.

MICHAEL

Hey man, I'm sorry. They're not kidding around with this internment shit.

DECLAN

Go find him, will you? Fergus could make use of a kind word.

FRANNY

We'll bring him back for a drink.

DECLAN

Will we sit, while your husband looks? I could use a kind word meself.

Franny stares at Michael, then back at Declan. She knows Michael's being asked to do something more.

CUT TO:

EXTERIORS, PUCK FAIR.

Michael weaves in and out of pubs. He sees Fergus approaching him.

CUT TO:

INT. OLD GOAT PUB.

The bad country music overwhelms their conversation, but Declan leans toward Franny. He's trying to charm her.

CUT TO:

EXT. NORTH–SOUTH TOUR BUS.

Fergus and Michael lean up against the bus. They're deep in conversation, but their voices are low, almost whispered.

> FERGUS
> I've to lend a hand, haven't I? They're fierce anxious for guns now.

> MICHAEL
> No, come on, man. You can't just walk off from the tour. You'll lose your job. Is Donovan calling the shots here?

> FERGUS
> McCleary's to tell them the bus is in dire need of repair.

> MICHAEL
> Yeah, and what about their golf clubs?

> FERGUS
> They've insurance. They're Americans.

MICHAEL

Listen, I wish you luck. But I can't let Donovan suck me into
this. You gotta know I can't walk out on my wife.

Fergus pulls a flask from his coat pocket and holds it out to Michael.

MICHAEL

No thanks. That stuff's hallucinogenic.

FERGUS

Your wee bride'll be showering you with kisses when she hears
what you've done for your people.

MICHAEL

My people? They're occupied beating up niggers and blowing up
gooks.

FERGUS

I've only to get the guns as far as me cousin's in Monaghan.

He holds the flask out to Michael, who drinks.

MICHAEL

You don't need me to get the bus up to Whoosahan.

FERGUS

I do not. I only need you to walk them across a wee path
through the hills. Over the border.

MICHAEL

(*Slogging back another drink of poteen.*)

You're out of your mind, Wolfe Tone. You think you're gonna
set me loose with a bunch of Armalites on a frigging
mountainside? Why me?

FERGUS

Because I can't set McCleary loose with a bunch of Armalites on a fucking mountainside. Because Donovan said you wanted to help. Because they're fierce anxious for guns now.

CUT TO:

INT. OLD GOAT. LATE THAT NIGHT.

Franny and Declan, now drunk, still sit in the same spot. The country band is winding down.

FRANNY

Very romantic in America, the IRA.

DECLAN

Two years ago we called it the I Ran Away.
                    (Franny gives him a questioning look.)
I'd not make a very good foot soldier, would I now? And I've no patience for that Sinn Fein shite.

FRANNY

            (Squeezing his hand. It's clear she's drunk.)
I didn't mean to push you. It's just the first time we saw you . . .
            (Looking down at his hand, she sees his watch.)
Four-thirty. They must've fallen down in the street, those two.

DECLAN

I think they'll not be back tonight. I'll see you home.

Close-up of Franny's disbelieving face.

CUT TO:

EXT./INT. NORTH–SOUTH TOUR BUS, ON THE ROAD TO MONAGHAN. LATE THE SAME NIGHT.

Fergus barrels down a motorway with a portable radio up to his ear.
Michael, in the seat behind, strains to hear the news.

RADIO BROADCAST
. . . announced this evening that temporary camps will be set
up in the border counties to provide refuge to those fleeing
sectarian violence in the wake of . . .

FERGUS
(Clenching the wheel, his face white.)
They're burning us out. And rounding us up. And it's always
been so. The wee Brits, with their wee heels, grinding them in
our wee faces.

DISSOLVE TO:

BELFAST EXTERIORS, INTERNMENT NIGHT, FOUR A.M.

Montage:
—soldiers pound on doors;
—a man is dragged from his house, half-clothed;
—flames lick at a ghetto window;
—a woman spits at a soldier;
—a lone sniper with a Thompson hunkers on a rooftop.

DISSOLVE TO:

INT. BUS.

MICHAEL
(After a long pause.)
You been with them a long time?

FERGUS
Not a fierce long time. Tour's only been operating since '69.

MICHAEL
Actually, I meant have you been with the IRA a long time.

FERGUS
(*Laughing at him a little.*)
Sure we all do what we can to lend a hand. If I'm traveling
through one end of the country to the other I don't mind giving
a package a lift.

MICHAEL
Why'd I let you talk me . . .

FERGUS
But me da's been listening to the priest, hasn't he, for the last
twenty-five years? Not dirtying his hands. They'll work him
over, won't they? The old republican.

MICHAEL
I don't know if I'm doing your father any good. Maybe if it all
died down for a while.

FERGUS
(*Full fury.*)
Oh it won't be dying down now Michael. There'll be no want
of recruits after this.

He pulls the bus into a long and stony driveway to an isolated
farmhouse, high in the hills.

CUT TO:

INT. BED-AND-BREAKFAST. LATE THAT NIGHT.

Mrs. O'Shea peeks out at Franny, who tiptoes up the stairs, alone and
unsteady. In her room, Franny collapses and plops down on the bed. JFK
and Pope John look down.

FADE OUT.

FADE IN:

EXT. PUCK FAIR, BRIDGE STREET, ROULETTE WHEEL.
NOON NEXT DAY.

GAMESMAN
If you don't bloody put your money down, you won't bloody
pick it up.

Franny puts her money down and wins. Children descend on her and
she scatters coins to them. Declan wheels toward her.

DECLAN
Enjoying the games, are you?

FRANNY
I'd be enjoying them better if Michael hadn't taken off. I'm
going on up to the B&B, see if they got back yet.

DECLAN
They're not back.

FRANNY
Where *are* they? Nobody'll tell me anything. It's worse being a
woman here than where I come from.

DECLAN
You're not a woman, sure you're just a wee slip of a girl.

The camera follows Franny running up the street.

DECLAN
(Off-camera.)
I can't run after you. You might have noticed.

CUT TO:

INT. McLAVERTY FARMHOUSE, COUNTY MONAGHAN HILLS.
NOON, SAME DAY.

A big open parlor. Stone fireplace, simple furniture, religious icons. Paddy McLaverty, a big watchful man, is in his sixties. His sons are Dermot, Cormac, and Seamus. They're clean-cut and oafish. Their younger sister Maura, who's sixteen, has a delicate face. Michael's alarmed by her beauty. The men are talking. Maura listens furtively as she walks back and forth, serving them tea and sandwiches.

DERMOT

Sure it's a straight line. You could walk it in the dead of night.

PADDY
(Watching Michael carefully. He doesn't trust this longhair.)
Cormac drives the car over the border, they search it inside and out. Clean as a new-washed babe. You'll be outside Belfast half eleven, latest.

MICHAEL

Oh wait, man, there's been a misunderstanding. Look, Fergus, I said I'd walk them over the border, I didn't say I'd bring 'em to Belfast.

FERGUS

A few hours only.

MICHAEL

I don't even know where the fuck Belfast is.
(To Maura, passing.)
Sorry.

CORMAC

Straight on the motorway. A few wee hours. And the dropoff's long before the city.

MICHAEL

You don't understand. I've been married for, I don't know, a week and a half, and my wife doesn't know where I am. I can't go to Belfast. I had maybe an hour's sleep last night.

PADDY
(*Pretending to be sympathetic.*)
Sure it's a difficult thing to give up a wee bit of your
honeymoon when you're tired and hungry.
(*Calling to his wife in the kitchen.*)
Margaret, another sandwich for the lad.

MICHAEL
No, look, I'm not *hungry*.

Fergus winks at the others and rises.

FERGUS
(*Tapping his jacket where he keeps the flask of poteen.*)
Some mountain air. To revive you.

Michael's fuming. He follows Fergus out the front door. They walk
around the side of the house without a word and take in the sight of the
hills, the sheep grazing. Big dark clouds roll in over them. Fergus passes the
flask.

FERGUS
Paddy's a man didn't know a wank about farming when he
crossed the border.

MICHAEL
(*Looking at the rocky ground.*)
From all appearances he hasn't learned a lot.

FERGUS
(*Ignoring him.*)
In West Belfast, the only sheep are the ones following the parish
priest's advice to steer clear of the IRA. But he wasn't a sheep,
our Paddy.

MICHAEL
(His hands on either side of his head.)
Oh here we go. Oh noble sacrifice. Oh everybody's willing to make the noble sacrifice but this guy from Brooklyn who just wants to see if his wife's had the marriage annulled yet.

He takes a long pull from the bottle, walks toward the hills, does an about-face and takes another long pull. He leads the way back into the farmhouse, where the men are still gathered, waiting. Maura sits at the edge of the group. She's sunk herself into a large chair so that the men can't see her.

MICHAEL
(Barreling into the room.)
Will you swear I'm not going any further than the outskirts of Belfast?

CORMAC
You can't miss the dropoff.

MICHAEL
Whatcha mean, *I* can't miss it? Aren't you driving the car?

PADDY
You're driving the car. Cormac's walking back across.

MICHAEL
I can't drive.

SEAMUS
You can't drive? What about all the freeways in America? What about Route 66? What about Car 54?

MICHAEL
They don't even allow cars in Brooklyn! They're illegal!

SEAMUS
That's desperate.

DERMOT
(On his way out of the room to the back of the house.)
He's having you on. Look now, we've business, no more jokes.

PADDY
(Leaning forward, intent.)
Should they ask you on the way, you're booked in the Texas
Playboy Lounge and you don't want to disappoint the
management.

MICHAEL
The Texas Playboy Lounge.

PADDY
Should they ask you on the way back, you're a tourist lost your
nerve at the sound of shooting day and night.

MICHAEL
Texas *Playboy?*

DERMOT
*(Returning with two guitar cases, and opening them to show off the false
bottoms.)*
See, the electrics are fierce heavy and the Armalites so light they
won't suspect a thing.

MICHAEL
They won't suspect a thing until they find out I can't play the
guitar.

CORMAC AND PADDY
(In unison, disgusted.)
They won't be asking you to play the bloody guitar.

PADDY
They're doing a weapons check, not holding auditions.

MICHAEL
All right, but look, I'm trying to tell you I can't drive.

PADDY

We'll teach you this afternoon.

MICHAEL

I'm not learning to drive to Belfast in one afternoon on an hour's sleep. Man, I can't even read a road map. I'm not getting behind the wheel. Forget it.

PADDY

The lads are known. We can't risk it. Why do you think we're asking you?

MAURA

(From behind the chair.)

I'll drive him.

PADDY

Maura McLaverty. Out of there, girl. What are you doing, hiding? Out of here now, go help your mother. You're not driving anybody anywhere, no you are not.

Reaction shot of Michael, stony.

CUT TO:

EXT. MRS. O'SHEA'S B&B, KILLORGLIN.

Mrs. O'Shea struggles to help Declan navigate his wheelchair through the narrow front entrance. Annoyance on her face.

CUT TO:

INT. B&B. THE PARLOR.

Mrs. O'Shea shoos her children away and hushes their questions, then leaves Declan alone in the parlor. The clock ticks away, and he keeps rhythm on his wheel. Finally Franny appears, wary.

FRANNY

Will you tell me where they've gone?

DECLAN

Now, now, wee slip of a girl, I can't tell you that.

FRANNY

Well, I guess I've got a pretty good idea anyway. I guess I've got
a pretty good idea who you are.

DECLAN

It isn't a game, you know. It's only a game for Americans.

FRANNY

I knew he'd get caught up. I knew he promised his grandfather.
But he didn't have to leave me in the dark, like this.

DECLAN

Ah, you must be one of these women's libbers. A whole
population's being jailed, and you're worried whether you've
been properly informed of your husband's comings and goings.

FRANNY

It's being pushed aside. I didn't even want—
(She stops, because she was about to say that she didn't even want to get
married.)
It's being treated like a child.

DECLAN

You are a child, from all appearances. He'll be back.
(He's suddenly moved to tell her.)
He's gone to Belfast, for a few days only.

Franny's in a quiet rage. She paces, picks up one of Mrs. O'Shea's
porcelain figures as if she's about to smash it, paces more. Finally she slides
down on the floor, next to his wheelchair. Declan strokes her head, then
cups her chin.

DECLAN

You needn't get down on your knees to speak to me.

Franny begins to rise and he pulls her toward him, roughly, and kisses her. At that moment Mrs. O'Shea enters, and Franny lurches away from Declan.

MRS. O'SHEA

(Abrim with moral superiority. This is her big moment.)
Breakfast for two tomorrow, is it? Or is your "husband" not back yet?

CUT TO:

INT. MONAGHAN FARMHOUSE. BEDROOM.

Maura's bedroom is pink and fluffy. She sits on the bed with Michael, showing him chord positions on the guitar.

CUT TO:

EXT. PUCK FAIR, MAIN GRANDSTAND. EVENING.

The end of a parade down Bridge Street to the grandstand. Bands, children in costume, spectacular drunks. Declan and Franny watch Puck being lowered to freedom.

FRANNY

(With some sense of humor about it.)
Like Michael. The old goat, let loose.

DECLAN

He's coming back, you know. Worse luck.

FRANNY

He's got all the traveler's checks.

                              DECLAN
I'll see you're all right.

He stares up at her to gauge her reaction. She's watching the little girl
who's queen of the fair.

                              DECLAN
You all right, then?

                              FRANNY
This is a country of madmen. Declan, I'm leaving.

                              DECLAN
And you call us a country of madmen. May I ask where you're
going then?

                              FRANNY
Belfast.

                              DECLAN
Have you any bleeding idea—no of course you haven't.

                              FRANNY
I'll figure it out by morning. Bye, Declan.

Franny takes off, running. Declan tries to follow, his wheelchair
blocked by the crowds. Puck is finally down all the way, bleating wildly.

                              SLOW DISSOLVE TO:

EXT. COUNTY MONAGHAN, HILLS CROSSING BORDER.
DAWN.

Mountain goats bleating. Michael stumbles with two heavy guitar cases
over stony ground. He's confused, beginning to panic.

                              CUT TO:

EXT. GRASSY ROAD AT BOTTOM OF HILL.

Maura waits beside a little car. She claps her hands, childlike, when Michael finally comes stumbling down. She opens the boot of the car and he hoists the cases in. They drive over a bumpy back road, not a word between them. Tension. They finally reach a paved road and Maura stops the car.

> MAURA
> *(Flirting.)*
> There's something I've been wanting to ask you since I laid eyes on you.

> MICHAEL
> *(Closing his eyes.)*
> What's that?

> MAURA
> Did you ever see Elvis in person?

Wild relief from Michael as he laughs at her, and reaches out a hand to touch hers, on the steering wheel. The car takes off.

> CUT TO:

EXT. MRS. O'SHEA'S B&B, KILLORGLIN. DAWN.

Declan is snoozing in his wheelchair across the street, keeping a vigil.

> DISSOLVE TO:

EXT. B&B. EARLY MORNING.

Franny dashes outside with a small pack on her back. Mrs. O'Shea appears behind her, holding out the big backpacks they've left behind.

FRANNY

Look, I'm sorry. I'll be back for them. If my husband calls, will
you—

MRS. O'SHEA

I'm not a message service, am I, and I'm not a baggage check
either! Your husband indeed.

Franny runs off. She sees Declan waiting for her and slows, but keeps
running. As she passes him, he calls out.

DECLAN

Race you for Belfast, then.

He rolls his chair along rapidly, and passes a cluster of American
tourists.

TOURIST

Mr. McCleary, thank God we've found you. The bus has
disappeared. Mr. McCleary! Mr. McCleary!

Franny turns to see a cluster of elderly men from the tour group
pursuing Declan down the street. Behind them is the trio of blond children
from the caravans. The parade turns into Bridge Street, where the remnants
of Puck are being swept away. Franny slows slightly to wait for Declan. She
gets behind his wheelchair and pushes it. They take off together, the old
men and the children in hot pursuit.

CUT TO:

INT./EXT. McLAVERTY CAR. MOTORWAY, SOUTH OF
BELFAST. MORNING.

Traffic is stopped for a roadblock. In the far distance two helicopters
hover.

MICHAEL
(Strung out, trying to move his fingers into chord position, though there's no guitar there.)
O.K., G7. C'mon, Maura, look.

MAURA
(Imitating her father.)
It's not a bleeding audition.

MICHAEL
Indulge me. I'd like to know I've got my G7 down before I'm carted off for an interrogation.

MAURA
Aw, gwan with you. We'll get through. Just keep yer gob shut.

They inch closer. A nervous British soldier approaches the car.

MAURA
(Casual, as if she's an old hand at this.)
What is it now?

SOLDIER
(Shrugging.)
If you're going to Belfast, the city center's not accessible. Another bloody sit-down strike.

MAURA
Oh, it's the women then.

SOLDIER
Right.

MAURA
(To Michael, but maybe to the soldier too.)
The wee women of Belfast are the protesting type.

SOLDIER

Have your papers ready.

The soldier moves away down the line of cars. Michael and Maura are next to be searched. Maura hands over her papers. The second soldier frowns at the sight of an address over the border.

SOLDIER

Out of the car.

Maura thinks to smile at the soldiers as they move in to search the car.

SECOND SOLDIER
(To Maura.)
Let's have a look at the boot.

Still smiling, she goes round to open the boot. Michael appears on the verge of collapse or confession. At the sight of the guitar case, the soldier stiffens.

SECOND SOLDIER
(To Maura.)
Step in there and open that up for me, love.

MAURA
(Moving to the boot to obey.)
We've a gig at the Texas Playboy. Do yez know it?

SECOND SOLDIER

Can't say I do.

MAURA

You might come see us, you get a night off.

MICHAEL
(Now he's ready to act the part.)
I didn't think I could let 'em down. What do you think,
Officer? Is it safe?

SECOND SOLDIER
(Visibly relaxing.)
If you was to ask me, the whole country's a war zone. I think
you're out of your mind, mate, coming in with everybody else
clearing out.

During his speech Michael moves in to open the first guitar case. The
soldier gestures for him to pick the guitar up. The soldier looks at the case,
still sitting on the floor of the boot, but the McLavertys have done a good
job with the false bottom. Michael holds up the guitar.

MICHAEL
The rest of 'em backed out when they heard about the riots. Just
my cousin and me now.

SECOND SOLDIER
What's your band called?

MICHAEL
The Brooklyn Dodgers.

SECOND SOLDIER
Brooklyn Dodgers. I've heard of you! Strum me a tune.

Michael strums the chords Maura has taught him and then takes off,
Eric Clapton on the side of the motorway. The soldier claps him on the
back and waves them back into their car.

CUT TO:

EXT. ROADWAY OUTSIDE KILLORGLIN. MORNING.

A car is pulled over. Declan sits in the backseat, his feet dangling out. Franny helps the driver load the wheelchair into the boot. In the distance, behind them, the abandoned caravan. A familiar car, Donovan's, passes. Franny watches it disappear.

CUT TO:

EXT. TEXAS PLAYBOY. OFF MOTORWAY, SOUTH OF BELFAST. MORNING.

Maura's pulled the car up in front of the Texas Playboy. It's a grim modern bar in the middle of nowhere. It doesn't have any personality, much less a Texas one. Michael and Maura stretch, silent, as they get out on the tarmac.

CUT TO:

INT. TEXAS PLAYBOY.

A dark deserted creepy bar-lounge, lighted only over the bar area. Maura and Michael freeze when Elvis McGirl screams out at them. McGirl's in his mid-forties. He has a slick Brian Epstein look. He's frantic, angry, chain-smoking, the kind of man who kicks the dog.

ELVIS McGIRL
For fuck's sake who's there?

MAURA
Mr. Elvis McGirl, is it? It's only Paddy McLaverty's daughter. With the American.

McGIRL
(Appearing from the shadows of an office behind the bar.)
Where in the name of Jesus have you been?

MICHAEL
Hey, man, be cool.

McGIRL

Be cool, is it? Come into the light so I can see yez.

McGirl takes the position of bartender, while Michael and Maura approach the bar.

MICHAEL

Now you see us. Now you won't, if I can hand over my guitar cases and get back on the road.

McGIRL

(Ignoring him, but revealing that he's holding a pistol pointed at them. He speaks to Maura.)

We don't unwrap many presents from the Stickies of late.

MAURA

Aren't we all the same side now? We've no quarrel with the Provos.

McGIRL

Will you sit, Miss McLaverty? Just now your boyfriend is anxious to show me the Official wares.

MICHAEL

Whoa, now.

(Staring down the gun, getting himself all tangled up.)

Listen, I wouldn't be here if I wasn't—

McGIRL

(Cutting him off.)

What have you brought me?

MICHAEL

Six Armalites. A few pistols. All we could pack.

McGIRL

(Slamming the bar.)

Six only? Holy Jesus, sure that'll liberate the country. Six.

MICHAEL

Look. I've been on the road all night—

McGIRL

I've been on a bleeding rooftop all night. Any idea how many lads I have left? Anyone could crawl south of the border crawled.

MICHAEL

Look, I left my wife—

McGIRL

Your wife. And I'm waiting for the knock on my door. I've a wee case of nerves, if you'd not noticed. Will we go to the car to see what you've brought us?

He puts the pistol to Michael's back and escorts him through the bar to the door. Maura, meanwhile, is a cool customer. She moves behind the bar to fix herself a drink.

CUT TO:

INT./EXT. CAR SPEEDING DOWN ROADWAY. COUNTY LOUTH, NEAR THE BORDER.

In the backseat, Declan whistles and inches closer to Franny, who's staring out the window, watching cows. "Jenny's Wedding" low on the sound track. She's blank and still.

CUT TO:

TEXAS PLAYBOY, INTERIOR. OFFICE BEHIND BAR. SAME AFTERNOON.

Michael sits at McGirl's desk, his head in his hands, while McGirl paces and stalks behind him. Maura appears, a pair of pints in her hand. She might as well be back home, serving.

> MICHAEL

Let me call my wife. C'mon man, let me tell her I'm all right. I'm not your prisoner!

McGirl continues pacing.

> MICHAEL
> *(Looking up, angry.)*

I came when I heard people were hurting.

> McGIRL
> *(Stops his pacing, considers, relents. Gestures toward the phone.)*

Breathe a hint where you are and you'll be hurting yourself, so you will. You'll be pissing blood.

Michael pulls a scrap of paper out of his pocket, checks the number. The camera's on a pacing McGirl as Michael mumbles into the phone. He begins to gesture, frantic. Finally he slams the phone down, looks at McGirl, and shrugs.

> MICHAEL
> *(After a pause.)*

Looks like I've got a little free time.

CUT TO:

EXT. LARGE HOTEL, DUNDALK, COUNTY LOUTH. AFTERNOON.

Franny and Declan have arrived in the border town favored by Provos who need to make themselves scarce. They alight from the car that's given them a ride. Declan lowers himself into his wheelchair, and the car drives off.

> FRANNY

Declan, c'mon. Let's not stay here. I have to get up to Belfast.

DECLAN

I'll be able to make inquiries here. You're safer doing that below the border, are you not?

FRANNY

I'm pushing on.

DECLAN

You are not. You're pushing me—through that door, so you are.

She taps her foot, considering, and finally pushes the wheelchair through the front door.

CUT TO:

INT. HOTEL.

The small lobby's a crowded surreal scene. A half dozen Provos in their teens and twenties swill pints and watch horse races on TV, their feet up on the end tables. They might as well be in a Wild West saloon. Franny stares at them, unabashed. The men stare back with sly smiles.

CUT TO:

INT. TEXAS PLAYBOY. McGIRL'S OFFICE. SAME AFTERNOON.

McGirl packs Armalites into a pair of camera bags and loads up camera equipment on top. There's some camaraderie now between the three. Maura picks up a telephoto lens and plays with it. Michael's now dressed in a suit, too short for him at the ankles and the wrists. His hair's been slicked down. He looks years older. He looks silly.

MICHAEL

Oh man, say it isn't true. I just learned how to play the guitar. Say I don't need to learn how to shoot a camera.

McGIRL

Well aren't you the great man yourself. You pick up the camera and you aim it. Can you pick up the camera and aim it so?

Maura picks up a camera and aims it at them.

McGIRL

God bless America, is that what you say? God bless America, and all the Armalites she can stuff in a camera bag.

He tosses a card at Michael: false press credentials.

MICHAEL

New York Times? C'mon, man, they're never gonna believe I'm with *The New York Times.*

McGIRL

Smart-arsed educated lad like yourself? They'll believe anything.

He leads Michael and Maura through the dark bar into the gray light of day. Maura throws him the car keys, and they climb in, Elvis at the wheel, Michael beside him.

CUT TO:

EXT. MOTORWAY.

Maura's car speeds along the motorway just south of Belfast. Helicopters near now, clattering. Hills in the distance. From Michael's point of view, a cemetery in the distance, tricolor flags waving atop IRA graves.

CUT TO:

EXT. FALLS ROAD, WEST BELFAST.

Elvis McGirl turns into the Falls Road, and they drive into the heart of West Belfast. Shops with shattered windows, burnt-out vans. No buses running, no children playing, no women marketing. Chunks of pavement are torn up from the rioting. In the eerie quiet, the drone of helicopters intensifies. They pass a convoy of saracens. Michael, scared witless, has one hand against the glove compartment. Maura, in the backseat, fiddles with the camera bag.

McGIRL

Leave it be. Can you not hear me? Christ! Leave it be!

McGirl pulls the car over to one of the intersections where the residents have set up their own roadblock, an overturned lorry. It's unmanned now, in the light of day, but the local men gathered in front of the bookie's stare at the car. McGirl gives them a significant nod.

McGIRL

Know where you're going, do you?

MICHAEL

Going to hell, time this is over.

He takes a deep breath and turns to say good-bye to Maura in back.

McGIRL

(Sarcastic.)

Maybe he'll not leave the car. Maybe he'll stay here cozy in the car till the Brits come lift us.

MICHAEL

(To Maura.)

Maybe I'll see you on the other side of the border.

MAURA

Oh, you might be seeing me before then, you might.

McGIRL

For the love of Jesus, will you leave the car? Will you?

MICHAEL

Call my wife, Maura. Keep trying.

McGirl tears off and Michael is left on the Falls Road. Streetlights have been twisted down and a couple of ten-year-old boys use one as a seesaw. A mother, from an upstairs window on the corner, watches Michael walk toward the boys.

MOTHER

Danny! Christy! Jesus, Mary, and Joseph, into the house with yez!

Michael continues walking toward the barricade. Just before he reaches it a Land Rover pulls up behind him. Four soldiers stare down, pointing their machine guns at him. They look scared shitless and even younger than he does.

SOLDIER

What's your business? What's in those bags?

MICHAEL

(Sounding deceptively self-confident.)
Afternoon. Press. *New York Times.*

The soldiers exchange half-amused nervous looks. Michael shows his press card and the first soldier shakes his head, waves him on.

SOLDIER

You want to go into that hellhole, New York Times, you're welcome to it.

MICHAEL
Abandon all hope, ye who enter here?

SOLDIER
Something like that.

Michael squeezes by the overturned lorry, anticipating a rifle shot to the head any moment.

CUT TO:

INT. DUNDALK HOTEL ROOM. LATE THE SAME AFTERNOON.

Franny stands at the window looking down at two boys.

FIRST BOY
Fuck the Queen!

SECOND BOY
Up the Pope!

FIRST BOY
Fuck the Fucking Queen!

SECOND BOY
Up the Pope!

The rhythmic sound of the exchange outside punctuates the conversation between Franny and Declan, who's just rolled himself out of the bathroom.

FRANNY
(Without turning to look at him.)
How'd you get hurt? Was it an explosion?

DECLAN
(*Laughs.*)
I had polio. Sorry to crush your fantasies.

FRANNY
Why are you supposed to keep an eye on me?

DECLAN
I'm not *supposed* to keep an eye on you. I'm keeping an eye on you so I can get you into bed.

FRANNY
(*Smiling.*)
That's subtle.

DECLAN
You can't be subtle and crippled both. We're only asked to carry one burden at a time.

FRANNY
What you been hearing about American girls? I only just got married, you know.

DECLAN
I heard you're oul puts, all of yez. Open marriage and all that.

FRANNY
I haven't had the time to have a closed one yet.

DECLAN
Oh, I feel you warming to me. I think you like a man with the certainty of his convictions.

FRANNY
How'd you know I don't think you're dead wrong?

DECLAN
All the same you haven't the stomach for a man who can't make

up his mind. Have you? And that husband of yours can't make
up his mind about a bloody thing.

Franny turns back to stare out the window, but Declan is wheeling his
chair toward her.

CUT TO:

THE FALLS, WEST BELFAST. SAME AFTERNOON.

Michael walks along a row of small shabby Victorian brick houses.
Dogs roam, barking. He shrinks from them. He's moving his lips, counting
the houses. Midway down the street he stops and raps on a door.

MICHAEL
(Loud and false, as if the soldiers are still behind him.)
It's *The New York Times.* Elvis McGirl said you might be willing
to talk.

The door opens, a stout middle-aged woman behind it, and Michael
enters.

CUT TO:

INT. FALLS HOUSE.

It's dark inside, a hopeless depressing dark. The woman, Mairead,
beckons him back through a narrow corridor. They pass a cramped parlor
strewn with children's toys. Cartons are piled up—someone is moving.

MICHAEL
I've brought the—stuff.

MAIREAD
The American. Mairead Tuohy, very pleased to meet you, I'm
sure, but I'm just after packing up the last. I'm taking the kids
out of here. Bring your parcels back to the kitchen, will you?

I'm not supposed to know what you have there, but I know the lads'll be around in a wee moment to hide them proper. Brigid! Brigid!

Michael follows her to a narrow kitchen and sets the camera bags down on a dilapidated table.

MAIREAD

I'll put the kettle on for you, Mr.—

MICHAEL

Burke. Sorry. I'm about to jump out of my skin.

MAIREAD

I understand that feeling, so I do. We're all jumping the past fortnight. The past two years, you could say.

MICHAEL

I've never been—I've been carrying signs and stuff, picketing, ya know? I've never done—

MAIREAD

(In a sudden comical torrent.)

And I want to tell you, Mr. Burke, lest you think we're violent people, that it has never crossed my mind to lift up a weapon of any kind, no I mean it would not occur to me to poison a rat insinuating himself on my premises, but since they've picked up me five lads—five, Mr. Burke, and them with not a thing to do with the Troubles to start with, oh they may have thrown a rock or two but they're boys, aren't they? And not my husband neither, bless his soul, he's a good man never missed Mass in these forty years, I want to assure you, Mr. Burke, that when John came to me, after the boys were dragged off in the middle of the night and John himself pushed up against the wall, and John said, now do you think it such a terrible thing Mairead that the people of the Falls protect themselves and maybe throw a wee petrol bomb to distract the soldiers gone to drag other mothers' lads out of other beds, I said to meself . . .

Michael, dizzied by her speech, leans against the kitchen table.

> MAIREAD
>
> Oh there, I'm wearing you out, I'm not thinking, am I, only to let you know it's a decent home you're entering. My eyes are closed. They have to be, now it's me own sons sitting in jail. But you don't look a violent man yourself, Mr. Burke, you're not a communist, are you?

> MICHAEL
> (Grinning.)
>
> Not especially.

> MAIREAD
>
> Oh I didn't think so. There's a Protestant lad and I can't help thinking *he's* a communist, but then we're reared up with such prejudice aren't we? Such a hateful city, Belfast is, sometimes, and now I've to take the girls out of it, the turning point was last night when I caught the wee one making petrol bombs in the street, you can't have that with the wee girls now can you, Mr. Burke?

A tiny blond girl of seven appears in the doorway and her mother beckons.

> MAIREAD
>
> Brigid, tell Mr. Crawford his delivery's here. Off with you, girl.

The girl smiles at Michael and disappears out the back door.

> MICHAEL
>
> Could I use the bathroom? The toilet, I mean.

Mairead gives him a sharp probing look. She opens the back door and Michael sees Brigid disappearing over the fence into the neighbor's terrace. Mairead points to the privy in the back of the tiny yard.

> MAIREAD
> Mr. Burke, I don't know what they've caught you up in. But if you can't be part of it, you've only to say so. I've said so meself. You needn't slip over the back fence.

> MICHAEL
> No, I really gotta go. I really gotta go.

> MAIREAD
> Will you hurry so? God knows what I'm keeping on my kitchen table.

CUT TO:

EXT./INT. YARD/PRIVY.

Michael walks across the yard and opens the door to an even darker space than the lightless little house. Torn sheets of newspaper hang from a nail, for toilet paper. He puts his arm up on the wall, to steady himself, and sees graffiti in a child's hand: *Up the IRA*. Below, in an older hand: *God made the Catholics. The Armalite made them equal.*

CUT TO:

INT. DUNDALK HOTEL ROOM. SAME AFTERNOON.

Dim light through the windows. Franny and Declan are in bed, Franny's slender muscular body atop his. She reaches behind herself and pulls the sheet up. It's as if she sees the camera watching her. An echo of the squeaky springs the landlady heard when she was with Michael. Close-up. She closes her eyes, ashamed.

CUT TO:

INT. MAIREAD'S HOUSE. KITCHEN. SAME AFTERNOON.

Sound of gunfire off-camera. Michael hurries through the back door of the house from the privy. He stops in the doorway. Mairead's gone.

Now Stephen Crawford is pulling the Armalites from the camera bags. Crawford's about Michael's age, but short-haired and conservative, in a jacket and tie. In the States he could be a Young Republican. Here he's just a Republican.

CRAWFORD
(Looking up, but continuing to unpack the bags.)
The Yank. You look like you haven't slept in a week.

MICHAEL
Why so pale and wan, fond lover.

CRAWFORD
Maybe it's the shooting. Day and night. You've only to get accustomed.

(Looking at him closely.)
You all right, then?

MICHAEL
Just waiting for some Protestant to shoot the top of my head off.

CRAWFORD
I don't intend to shoot the top of your head off. Your balls, maybe.
(Michael tenses, jiggles in the doorway.)
Just a little IRA joke. I was reared Church of Ireland.

MICHAEL
So who are you? Parnell?

CRAWFORD
Oh, we've a sarcastic one here. You haven't been spending time with that bollox McGirl, have you?

MICHAEL

Matter of fact . . .

CRAWFORD

He'd give anyone the nerves, he would. Pity we've need of a man like him. Look, have a drink, why don't you?

He rummages through the kitchen cabinets and produces a bottle of whiskey, which Michael slugs.

CRAWFORD

Now that they've opened up the concentration camps we're taking anyone we can get. More and more McGirls, I'm afraid.

Mairead enters from the corridor. She clutches a gaggle of condoms at arm's length. She throws them down on the table, disgusted.

MAIREAD

Mr. Crawford, I've tried my best, haven't I, to overcome my prejudice? Thanks be to Jesus that the wee girls didn't find these. You may have contempt for my religion, Mr. Crawford, but you're not to have these in my house. Not when I'm evacuated, do you hear me?

CRAWFORD

Oh Mairead, it's not what you think.

MAIREAD

Now you'll tell me you're making petrol bombs in these, in these . . .

CRAWFORD

Not petrol bombs. Not precisely.

MAIREAD

(Backing out the door, as if the very kitchen is contaminated.)

Oh it's wickedness. Oh there's no good going to come of any of this when you resort to immorality, Mr. Crawford.

CRAWFORD
(As Mairead disappears.)
It's not the bomb she objects to. It's using birth control to make the bomb.

Michael stretches a condom.

CRAWFORD
Durex bombs. You stuff the sheath with a vial of acid, then into the envelope with some weedkiller. 'S brilliant. You squeeze it and then you run like bloody hell. We'll have you at it before the sun goes down.

MICHAEL
Look, man, I'm sorry to let you down, but you're not gonna be showing me how to make condom bombs.

CRAWFORD
Durex bombs.

MICHAEL
Whatever. If you'll tell me how to get back to the highway.

CRAWFORD
(Staring.)
We had word there was a Yank volunteer. *Enthusiastic* was the term, I believe. *Reliable* may've been mentioned.

MICHAEL
Yeah, well.

CRAWFORD
Bloody hell. McGirl brought you into this house and you're not even—

MICHAEL

Look, man, they just needed a warm body.

CRAWFORD

You're not a warm body, you're cold as a bloody Brit. D'you understand they came into these people's houses and dragged their men out in the middle of the night? And now you've just to walk away, knowing there are but a half dozen of us left in Belfast? Bloody smug Americans!

MICHAEL

Look, I'm so strung out I can't see straight. I left my wife without saying good-bye and now I don't know where she is, but I'm gonna find her. Dig it? I'm gonna find her.

By now he's worked himself up and is standing in a belligerent pose. Crawford hands him the bottle. He guzzles it.

CRAWFORD

Go up and sleep for an hour, then.

MICHAEL

Yeah, maybe. Maybe if I could get some sleep. You wouldn't have any Ludes, any downers?

CRAWFORD

Small wonder the American ranks are thin.

MICHAEL

All right, Che Guevara. No political lectures. Just lemme get my head screwed on straight, wouldya?

CRAWFORD
(Calling.)

Mairead! We've need of a bed. And not for sinning!

CUT TO:

INT. DUNDALK, HOTEL ROOM. SAME AFTERNOON.

Pan from the disheveled bed to Declan, naked in his wheelchair. He's facing the bathroom door. Franny's barricaded inside. Sound of her blowing her nose off-camera.

DECLAN
(Shouting to the closed door.)
I'll take you to Belfast! I'll take you to Belfast. No more weeping.
(Muttering to himself.)
It's the religion. It is that. The religion.

CUT TO:

INT. FALLS HOUSE. KITCHEN. SAME AFTERNOON.

Crawford still collapses the Armalites, practicing, handling, caressing them. Donovan enters the room.

CRAWFORD
You gave us the wrong word on Burke. He's ready to run, tail between his legs.

DONOVAN
The girl's gone off. He'll stay.

CRAWFORD
What are we resorting to now, conscription?

DONOVAN
Where is he?

CRAWFORD
Upstairs sleeping.

                              DONOVAN
Sleeping?
                    (A military summons, in a deep voice.)
          BURKE! MR. BURKE!

                                                          CUT TO:

INT. FALLS HOUSE. UPSTAIRS BEDROOM DOORWAY.

Michael listens at the door, not sure if he's hallucinating. He seems to
recognize the voice, and closes his eyes.

                                                          CUT TO:

INT. CORRIDOR BETWEEN KITCHEN AND STAIRWAY.

Donovan bellows through cupped hands.

                              DONOVAN
          Mr. Burke.

                                                          CUT TO:

INT. STAIRWAY.

Michael's freaked. He descends the stairs halfway. Donovan's still
calling from the foot of the stairs.

                              DONOVAN
          Burke! You've done good work, lad.

                              MICHAEL
          This's a dream, right? I thought I left you in another country,
          Mr. Donovan.

                              DONOVAN
          You know as well as I there's only one country. And you've
          done good work for that country.

MICHAEL

A little more than I intended. I think I need a drink.

DONOVAN

(Laughing, a threatening sound.)

None of that now. A wee bit more to be done tonight.

MICHAEL

Look, Mr. Donovan. I've gotta get out of here.

DONOVAN

I've train tickets for you. For Dublin. Tomorrow morning.

MICHAEL

I don't know what good it's gonna do me to go to Dublin when I don't know where my wife is. You don't have any idea, do you?

DONOVAN

She's not where you left her, then?

MICHAEL

Weird, huh? I've misplaced a whole wife. Listen, Mr. Donovan, you seemed to know where to find me.

DONOVAN

Friends stay in touch.

MICHAEL

So maybe you know where to find her too.

DONOVAN

It's possible.

MICHAEL

Let me see if I can guess the price.

DONOVAN

I'd not call it a price.

MICHAEL

Look now, Mr. Donovan, you're not coercing me into being part of something . . .

DONOVAN

(His voice dropping to a soothing register, more threatening than his bellowing.)
Michael Burke, calm yourself. I've no intention of coercing you into anything. You've only to sleep, lad. Only to sleep now.

MICHAEL

Yeah. I.

DONOVAN

Go back up the stairs, lad. Go rest your head.

Michael stares at him in confusion, but Donovan holds his gaze steady. Michael retreats up the stairs.

CUT TO:

INT. DUNDALK HOTEL LOBBY. THAT EVENING.

Overlapping dialogue. Declan talks on the lobby's pay phone. Franny's accosted by a young strutting Provo.

PROVO

You're American, so you are.

FRANNY

I feel like I'm wearing a banner.

PROVO

Have you seen Elvis Presley, then?

FRANNY

You mean, in the flesh?

PROVO
Aye. D'you live near Graceland?

FRANNY
Oh, no. Far away. Very far away from Graceland.

DECLAN
(Muttering, across the room at the phone.)
I know, I know. Just give me the bloody bus schedule.

He hangs up the phone, disgusted, and pauses a moment. Then he picks it up again.

The sound of rapid pistol fire off-camera. Franny pales and turns to see a Provo shooting at the lobby's television set. Young men around him cover their heads against the flying glass.

PROVO
Fucking bloody horse! Fucking bloody horse!

Franny has dropped to her knees, but Declan, at the phone, lets out a hyena's cackle.

CUT TO:

INT. FALLS HOUSE. BEDROOM. SAME EVENING.

Michael lies awake in an upstairs bedroom. Three beds are jammed across the width of the room, occupying all the space between the door and the window. Children's things are thrown willy-nilly. On the wall, posters of the Beatles. Below them, a large portrait of a sad Virgin Mary. Through the window, faint evening light.

Michael sits up and looks out the window. Outside, small groups of agitated teenagers, mostly boys, gathering in the street below. Off-camera, a rap on the door. Michael stares at the door, makes faces at it.

MICHAEL

Yeah.

CRAWFORD

(Entering.)

How's the view?

MICHAEL

Guess you already know about the little disturbance brewing down there. Man, my head.

CRAWFORD

Donovan said you'd reconsidered.

MICHAEL

Guess I'm supposed to be part of the little disturbance brewing down there. Son of a bitch.

CRAWFORD

He is that.

MICHAEL

Look, now, don't be so fucking agreeable. I gotta tell you that aside from being sleep-deprived and scared shitless for my own skin, I've got some serious reservations about what you're up to.

Crawford sits on the bed opposite Michael and offers him a cigarette. They smoke in silence for a moment. Michael's gaze follows the pathetic gaze of the Virgin.

CRAWFORD

The call of Gandhi, is it? Martin Luther King? We tried that, you know. Until my conversion.

MICHAEL

Interesting word. Conversion.

CRAWFORD

One night in '69, y'see, while we were all holding our polite wee placards, the RUC came rolling down into the Falls. So a nine-year-old boy sat up in bed, wondering what all the noise was, and they blew the top of his head off. I walked into Sinn Fein the next morning.

MICHAEL

Maybe it's the lack of dope making me think this way, but it occurs to me that you might get some more nine-year-old boys killed in your cross fire.

CRAWFORD

I don't take it lightly. But you brought the guns. Did you not want them used?

MICHAEL

Guess I do want them used. By somebody else.

CRAWFORD

A common sentiment.

MICHAEL

You can't believe you're gonna win.

CRAWFORD

A fortnight ago there wasn't a prayer. But since the Brits came and did the Ra's recruiting . . . Fools.
(Pause.)
When I was a kid, we'd get a popehead and beat him silly, wouldn't we? Filthy Taigs. Bloody statue worshippers.

Michael tosses his cigarette butt out the window. He's made his decision.

MICHAEL

Whatcha want me to do?

>   CRAWFORD
> Can you shoot those Armalites you brought us?

>   MICHAEL
> Hey, man, I couldn't shoot a camera, couldn't drive a car when
> I got here. Didn't seem to slow down the action.

Crawford draws a bottle from his pocket. Michael drinks, of course. Now his confusion has been transformed into jangly energy.

>   CRAWFORD
> We've Thompsons and greaseguns at wee St. Finbar's School. A
> decent arsenal we've not been able to liberate.

>   MICHAEL
> Until tonight. We're gonna liberate em tonight.

>   CRAWFORD
> No. You and I are to cover the lads who know what they're
> doing. And *they're* going to liberate them tonight, they are.

Michael drinks again, his gaze on the holy picture.

CUT TO:

EXT. DUNDALK HOTEL. EARLY EVENING.

Declan and Franny grinning. Fergus drives up in the North–South bus. They climb aboard.

CUT TO:

INT. BUS. MOTORWAY, DUNDALK TO BELFAST. EVENING.

Night's falling fast. In the seat where Michael sat a few nights before, Declan leans forward to hear Fergus. Next to him, Franny stares out into the night.

FERGUS
(Over his shoulder, while he drives.)
They told me at the hotel you were last seen leading the
Americans a merry chase. I was skundered, wasn't I? And then
stealing me own bus back in the dead of night.

FRANNY
You can find him, though, can't you?

FERGUS
If he hasn't left. But you're all he talked about, don't you know.
Oh, I've got to get back to my wee bride.

DECLAN
(Sniffing.)
Wee bride.

In the dark Franny can just make out the remains of a bombed-out hut,
a British Army checkpoint. It's a strange silhouette in the night. Declan
reaches over to take her hand but she draws it back.

DECLAN
I'll wager you can't even say why you married him, and now
here you're after chasing him and dragging us along.

FRANNY
I'm dragging you!

DECLAN
Why did you marry him then, at your age?

FRANNY
I was crazy for him. You'd have to be crazy.
(She laughs at herself and looks back out the window.)
His idea. He'll try anything.

At that moment there's a roar of crashing glass from the rear of the bus. Declan pulls her head down into his lap and leans over her to protect her. Fergus steers the bus sharp left, off the road.

> DECLAN
> *(Incredulous, his head still covering Franny's.)*
> We've been hit. We've been hit.

Fergus hunkers down with his head on the wheel. Nothing else happens. He rises, terrified, and stands by the driver's seat, facing the back of the bus. Finally he strides back to see what's happened. A great laugh from him.

> FERGUS
> You can come up for air now, McCleary. The back window's fallen out, is all.

> DECLAN
> *(Raising his head, ashen.)*
> Thanks be to Jesus.

> FERGUS
> Could it be your American cousins playing a wee trick on us for leaving town that way?

> DECLAN
> Could it be Almighty God punishing us for this hopeless expedition.
> *(In a whisper, to Franny.)*
> For our afternoon sinning?

CUT TO:

INT. MAIREAD'S HOUSE, BELFAST. KITCHEN.

Michael and Crawford are now dressed in black workmen's clothes. They're crowded in the kitchen with four guys in camouflage jackets. The others, kids, play cards. They smoke and look tough—they think they're in the Foreign Legion. Michael sits at the table. His chair's tipped back in an attempt at nonchalance, but his face shows the adrenaline rush.

FIRST PROVO
(Slapping down cards.)
Eileen'd make short work of me she knew where I was tonight, wouldn't she? Turn the other cheek, she says. While they're dragging off her own cousin. Turn the other cheek.

SECOND PROVO
You'd bloody well better not breathe a word to Eileen.

THIRD PROVO
She's not a tout, is she now?

FIRST PROVO
Jaysus. D'ye think I'd be walking out with a tout?

SECOND PROVO
I think ye'd be walking out with a whore.

The first Provo takes a swipe at him but he's joking. Crawford begins to pace.

THIRD PROVO
Cause if she was a tout I'd shoot her meself.

FOURTH PROVO
Aren't you the great man yourself. Haven't we been after you to go into the streets for two fucking years now?

THIRD PROVO
And didn't I throw the feathers on meself when we covered that tart up at the Flats?

CRAWFORD
Leave off. You never did, and it's a sorry thing to be boasting of.

Alarm and excitement on Michael's face. Donovan strides into the kitchen, grim. Conversation stops, but there are voices coming from the hallway.

> MAIREAD
> *(Off-camera.)*
> Now it's happening I didn't think it would come to this, truly I didn't.

> HER HUSBAND
> *(Off-camera with her.)*
> Go on with you now, the girls are halfway down the street.

> DONOVAN
> Jesus, Mary, and Joseph, what sort of operation is this? The woman sniffling about!

> CRAWFORD
> We've been trying to send her off all day. I think she wants another look at those sheaths.
>
> *(Checking his watch.)*
> If she's not out in three minutes and twenty-two seconds she might be leaving in the ambulance Mrs. Boyle's so kindly calling.

CUT TO:

EXT. FALLS ROAD INTERSECTION. BARRICADE. NIGHT.

Teenage girls taunt soldiers by the overturned lorry. The crowd in the side street grows. Two Land Rovers are parked along the Falls Road at right angles to the barricade. Behind them, a saracen. Every now and again a rock slides through the air. The heckling swells.

CUT TO:

INT. SARACEN.

The Brits are rattled and grim.

                                                          CUT TO:

EXT. FALLS ROAD.

Stretches of street bright in the saracen's glare. Darkened patches where the streetlights have been twisted down or smashed. Mairead in the distance, a valise in her hand and a hat on her head. She moves away from the disturbance with four little girls, blondes and redheads, all of them looking over their shoulders. They're scared and excited. Brigid, who went over the fences in the afternoon, throws a longing look at the crowd.

The tension mounts as the crowd grows. The rocks fly faster.

                                                          CUT TO:

INT. FALLS HOUSE. KITCHEN.

The four Provos, their faces now covered in ski masks, file out from the kitchen into the hallway. Crawford and Michael are left behind.

                          MICHAEL
I thought you said the experienced guys were gonna be going to St. Finbar's. *Those* guys are shitting bricks.

                          CRAWFORD
They've more experience than you, at any rate. And here's the sad part. They've more experience than I.

                                                          CUT TO:

EXT. FALLS ROAD BARRICADE.

Hordes of teenagers, boys and girls—a lively working-class lot. They push the lorry aside. An ambulance, siren droning, approaches.

                                                          CUT TO:

INT. FALLS HOUSE. FRONT ENTRANCEWAY.

At the sound of the approaching siren, Donovan raises his arm in signal. The four gunmen, their Armalites in hand, tense in formation.

CUT TO:

INT. FALLS HOUSE. STAIRWAY.

Michael and Crawford rush up the stairs, Armalites in hand. Crawford pulls a ski mask down over his face as he runs.

DONOVAN

Now!

CUT TO:

EXT. FALLS HOUSE. ROOFTOP.

Darkness. Michael and Crawford emerge through the roof hatch and crouch down on the slate roof. A helicopter in the distance.

CRAWFORD
(Hissing.)

Your mask.

Michael pulls a mask from his pocket and covers his face. Crawford beckons him to take position at the edge of the roof. From Michael's point of view, the ambulance screeches to a halt at the door of the house. When the attendants get out, the four gunmen burst from the house. They fire into the air and overpower the attendants.

The gunmen tear up the narrow street like circus clowns, hanging off the ambulance in triumph. They screech to a halt again. They toss the attendants from the ambulance. The attendants fall, recover, flee into the night.

CUT TO:

EXT. FALLS ROAD BARRICADE.

The rock-throwing has developed into a melee. Soldiers with riot helmets and shields push the lorry aside and press the crowd back into the narrow side street. The teenagers retreat, bottles flying. The infuriated soldiers follow them.

Another saracen arrives from the opposite direction on the Falls Road and pushes behind the soldiers into the side street, its searchlight glaring. Petrol bombs descend from second-story windows. Most of the teenagers flee, but two young boys go against the soldiers with their bare hands.

From a second-story window on the corner, the same mother we saw calling her sons before cries out again. In the noise of the riot, her voice is drowned.

CUT TO:

EXT. FALLS HOUSE. ROOFTOP.

Michael and Crawford can't see the disturbance pushing into the street yet. They lie on their backs, triumphant.

CRAWFORD
Our baptism, eh?

MICHAEL
(Laughing.)
I'm as damp and slimy as the Gowanus Canal. I thought I was gonna piss my pants.

CRAWFORD
And not a single shot required of us.

Shouting and banging in the distance. Michael rolls over to look into the street and sees women in the dark distance banging dustbin lids to warn of the soldiers' approach. He grabs Crawford's elbow, and Crawford rolls over on his belly.

CRAWFORD
A longer night than we'd planned, perhaps.

CUT TO:

EXT. TEXAS PLAYBOY. TARMAC.

Fergus maneuvers the bus into a parking place outside the Texas Playboy. The tarmac's crowded with cars. Franny stands in the aisle, about to burst.

CUT TO:

INT. TEXAS PLAYBOY.

The bar's crowded now, too. Beyond the bar, a stage where a single musician has set up a click tape. He sings bad country and western to a sour crowd.

Fergus enters the door, followed by Franny, ants in her pants, and Declan. Fergus nods to a few men and raises his eyebrow to the barman, who rolls his head back to indicate that Elvis is in the office.

Franny follows Fergus. She maneuvers Declan's wheelchair back behind the bar toward the office.

CUT TO:

INT. TEXAS PLAYBOY. OFFICE.

Elvis McGirl sits behind his desk, loading his revolver. He aims at the opening door. Fergus enters, Franny and Declan pushing in behind him.

McGIRL
Fuck's sake!

FERGUS
Calm yourself, McGirl.

> McGIRL

Who's that with you, eh?

Elvis squints at the door. Franny and Declan push all the way in until the three are scrunched together. Elvis looks like the Grand Inquisitor behind his desk.

> FERGUS

This girl's looking for her husband.

> McGIRL
> *(Setting the gun down.)*

I haven't got him, have I?

> FERGUS

He was to drop a package for you this morning. American lad.

> McGIRL

I've seen no American lad. I'd love to chat, Sullivan, but we've word we may have a visit tonight. Best yez clear out, unless you'd like a word with Her Majesty's troops. I'm clearing out meself.

> FERGUS

Jaysus, what's happened to them? Did the girl not know the way?

> McGIRL

I've no idea.

> FERGUS
> *(Incredulous.)*

He had a half dozen Armalites for you.

> McGIRL

I never saw them. I'm after defending me property at the moment, so if you'd be good enough to . . .

> FERGUS

Right then. We're leaving.

Fergus moves to open the door, but Franny stares at McGirl with open dislike. Her gaze causes him to grasp his revolver again.

> FERGUS

Unless—she'd not have taken him into Belfast, would she? Nah. Nah. We told him more than once, we did, he'd not be going into Belfast.

Distracted, Fergus takes over from Franny and wheels Declan out. She's the last to leave, still staring at Elvis.

The camera follows Fergus, Declan and Franny back through the crowd. Out on the tarmac, they stare at each other.

> FERGUS

Jaysus, they've been lifted.

> DECLAN

McGirl has his Armalites, though, hasn't he?

> FERGUS

He said he'd not seen them.

> DECLAN

If he'd not seen his rifles, he'd have had us by the throats.

> FERGUS

But if he has the Armalites, he's seen young Burke.

> DECLAN

The rapidity of your thought process astounds me.

Without their noticing it, Franny's made a move back toward the door. Fergus goes after her, but Declan positions his wheelchair to stop him.

DECLAN

Leave her be.

FERGUS

He's a fierce temper.

DECLAN

She'll have a fierce temper now, too, won't she. That's the first she heard there was a girl with her husband.

CUT TO:

INT. TEXAS PLAYBOY. BAR AREA.

Franny nods to the barman, who returns the nod. She slips back to the office and opens the door before anyone can stop her. Elvis is out of his chair now. He's been unloading his stockpile of handguns from his desk, the safe, the floor. This time, at the sight of an intruder, he picks up a pair of guns, double-fisted.

McGIRL

Fuck! Will you give over. I said I'd not seen your husband.

FRANNY

You've seen him all right.

McGIRL

I've business. Get out before I blow you out.

FRANNY

Tell me if they arrested him. Or if you shot him.

McGIRL

Yer out of your mind. Why would I be shooting an American who brought me guns?

FRANNY
(Slight smile.)
He did bring you the guns.

McGIRL
(He's made a stupid mistake.)
Look. You better go out and let those two clowns get you where
yer going.

FRANNY
I'm going to find Michael.

McGIRL
He wouldn't want you caught up with guns, would he? Go back
where you came from, and he'll find you right enough.

FRANNY
He'll find me tonight, cause you'll tell me where he is. Fergus
and Declan can take me there.

McGIRL
I'd not tell the pair of them where I was going if I was going to
the grocer's for a pint of milk.

FRANNY
Aren't they—?

McGIRL
What have they been telling you, the great men? The pair of
soldiers, is it?

FRANNY
You take me then.

McGIRL
You're daft.

FRANNY
I'm not leaving.

McGIRL

Do you not know who you're dealing with, ye wee clat.

FRANNY

Call me that again and I'll spit in your eye.

McGIRL

Spit in me eye and yer dead.

They've come to a stalemate and face each other across the desk, he
with the pair of guns, she with her fists clenched at her side. Suddenly
Franny laughs.

FRANNY

I don't know what that means, clat.

McGIRL

P'raps we can come to terms then.

FRANNY

What terms?

McGIRL

Your husband's in Belfast tonight. And I'm on my way to Belfast
tonight.

FRANNY

Take me there.

McGIRL

The sniping's fierce heavy. The peelers are everywhere the army
isn't.

FRANNY

I don't care.

McGIRL

And I've to move these wee revolvers, haven't I?

FRANNY

You want me to . . .

McGIRL

A favor, like the one your husband's doing. Will we say the wee revolvers are in the pack on your back? You're a tourist with no idea how they got there. Someone must have put them there, mustn't they?

Franny stares him down, then turns around so the pack on her back's facing Elvis. He comes round from behind the desk, unzips the back, and drops the revolvers inside.

CUT TO:

EXT. FALLS HOUSE. ROOFTOP.

The riot's fast approaching Michael and Crawford's perch. A soldier unleashes a canister of CS gas in the air. Chaos below. All but the boldest boys flee or crouch in their tracks. The soldiers push on.

Michael's point of view. A girl's fallen flat on her face in the street. A large soldier running by drags her up by the scruff of her neck. Her eyes are screwed tight from the gas.

MICHAEL

Oh shit, oh shit, oh holy, holiest shit.

CRAWFORD

(Near hysteria.)

We've only to get some rounds off. We've only to get some rounds off, haven't we?

MICHAEL

I don't know what I'm doing. I don't know what the fuck I'm doing.

CRAWFORD
Oh shit.

The camera goes in tight on the soldier and the girl. She's a tall, slight blonde.

Reaction shot of Michael. He's recognized Maura.

The soldier slams his machine gun into Maura's back. She gasps from the gas. The soldier lets up, and she turns and spits in his face. With one hand he tugs her hair until he's pulled her head back. He drags her close to a building. From Michael's point of view, it looks like he's going to slam her head into the bricks. The saracen's searchlight inches forward behind them. The soldier and Maura are clear outlines in the night.

MICHAEL
(Aiming the rifle.)
Shit. Oh Christ. Oh Christ.
(He's ready to shoot.)
Christ Jesus. Christ Jesus.

He shoots. And again. And again. And again.

Sound of the retorts. We see the soldier slammed in the stomach, full force. Maura takes a second to realize she's free. She runs, looks up, sees nothing.

Reaction shot of Michael, still stretched out on the edge of the roof. It's all happened so suddenly. He sees the image of the soldier recoiling again. And again. And again. And again.

CRAWFORD
C'mon. C'mon. C'MON.

He runs back across the roof to the hatch. As Michael follows him a helicopter approaches, shining its searchlight down on the roofs.

CUT TO:

INT. FALLS HOUSE. STAIRS/HALL/BEDROOM.

Crawford runs for the children's bedroom, Michael blindly follows.

CRAWFORD
Under the floor! Under the boards!

Crawford throws himself awkwardly over one of the little beds. He reaches down to the floor below, prizing open a loose board. Michael stretches out beside him, trying to copy his movements. He's out of it. Crawford has the next board up, too, before Michael makes any progress. They throw the Armalites under the flooring and Crawford takes off again, through the house.

CUT TO:

INT. HOUSE. STAIRWAY.

Michael trips himself on the stairs, then picks himself up, his face blank.

CUT TO:

EXT. TERRACE BEHIND HOUSE. NIGHT.

Michael and Crawford fly out the kitchen door and over the same fence the little girl, Brigid, went over when she delivered her message that afternoon. Michael catches his ankle on the first fence. He and Crawford dive and climb through the line of terraces. Close-up of Michael—another adrenaline rush. He comes out of his dazed condition and begins to fly through the night.

CUT TO:

EXT. MOTORWAY TO BELFAST. DEAD OF NIGHT.

In the McLaverty car, McGirl's fingers are clenched to the wheel. Beside him, Franny's watching everything.

CUT TO:

EXTERIORS. WEST BELFAST.

McGirl drives like a maniac through the Lower Falls. He veers off whenever he catches sight of a Land Rover or a roadblock flying the Tricolour. The big central tower of the Divis Flats looms ahead. In the rearview mirror, a storefront explodes. Franny doesn't react.

McGIRL

What's the matter with you then? Have you no fear?

FRANNY

I'm afraid.

McGIRL

You don't look it. You make me blood run cold.

FRANNY

I've been more afraid.

McGIRL

(Catching sight of an RUC car and careening around the block.
He's screaming the line.)
And what's scarier than getting lifted before we get where we're going, eh? When've you felt scarier than that.

FRANNY

(She's down almost to a whisper.)
When I was pregnant.

McGIRL

Christ.

CUT TO:

INT./EXT. NORTH–SOUTH BUS, PARKED ON THE TEXAS
PLAYBOY TARMAC.

Declan and Fergus sit in passenger seats. Fergus holds his radio to his
ear.

FERGUS

Peaceful night in Belfast, so they say. Relatively speaking. It's
dying down.

DECLAN

What sort of fellas are we, letting her get in that car with him?

FERGUS

What sort of fellas are we, carting guns for that horse's arse?

DECLAN

Jaysus, you can't stay under the jackboot forever.

FERGUS

Elvis McGirl's got his own pair of jackboots on.

DECLAN
(Making the sign of the cross.)

Aye.

CUT TO:

EXT. ANOTHER FALLS HOUSE.

Michael and Crawford make their way across the terrace to an open
back door. Camera angle into the house through the garden window.
Crawford hands Michael over to a burly working-class man. Then
Crawford slips back out again and continues on his way over the terraces.

CUT TO:

INT./EXT. McGIRL'S CAR. CLONARD. SAME NIGHT.

McGirl drives through the Catholic ghetto on the other side of the Falls Road. Brick row houses, some burned out. One's still steaming. In front adults move back and forth, rescuing furniture from the fire. A little boy sits on a suitcase, holding a Union Jack.

                        FRANNY
They're Protestants.

                        McGIRL
I wonder if you might pay attention for fifteen seconds. Do you suppose we might have fifteen seconds before I stop the car?

                        FRANNY
No, look, that's a Protestant family burnt out there, isn't it?

                        McGIRL
And it's a war, isn't it? They burn it themselves, lest Catholics move in.

                        FRANNY
You wouldn't burn out a little boy like that.

Reaction shot of Franny—revulsion for McGirl. They pass the burning house and drive on a few blocks. They stop in front of a school. McGirl pulls over and cranes his neck around to look for soldiers.

                        McGIRL
Listen close, I'll say it once. You're to knock on the monastery door. Tell them McGirl sent you. They'll know what to do. Now out of the car with you before I'm blown off the streets.

                        FRANNY
Is Michael in there?

                        McGIRL
He'll be there. He'll be there by dawn.

FRANNY

I want to go where he is now.

McGIRL

He's nowhere now. He'll be there by dawn, I tell you. Now get out of the bloody car.

At this McGirl draws his own revolver once more. This time Franny gets out. As her feet touch the ground she begins to run, and McGirl sticks his head out the window.

McGIRL

No! WALK, ye wee clat. Walk or they'll shoot ye down.

She slows to a walk, and McGirl's car takes off behind her. Now she's all alone on the dark silent stretch between the school and the monastery. Helicopters, burning buildings, all the action in the distance.

She walks up the monastery steps and raps on the door, softly at first. Then she pounds in a hysterical rhythm.

PRIEST
(Off-camera.)

Who's that?

FRANNY

McGirl told me to . . . McGirl sent me.

Franny's left standing outside the door. The priest is looking at her through a curtained side window, but she doesn't see him. Finally the door opens.

CUT TO:

INT. MONASTERY.

She enters a world as orderly as the outside was chaotic. The wide front hall is paneled in dark wood. A large crucifix and reproductions of the *Book of Kells* on the walls. The priest is a portly older man.

PRIEST
I'm afraid to ask what brings a wee lass out on a night like this. It's a miracle you weren't shot on sight.

FRANNY
McGirl sent me.

PRIEST
So you said. But who is McGirl?

FRANNY
I think he's a Provo, Father.

PRIEST
Ah. And are you a Provo? An American Provo?

FRANNY
No, Father. He said you'd know what to do with these.

She holds out her backpack. The priest holds it by the strap, like a rat by the tail, and unzips it to look inside. He shakes his head.

PRIEST
Come with me so.

Franny follows him to a dark office. Same dark paneling, more austere prints on the wall. The priest presses a buzzer on the wall and sits behind a large desk. He motions for Franny to sit in front of him. She remains standing. Another priest appears, this one old and stooped.

FIRST PRIEST
Will we be able to squeeze these under the grate?

The older priest peers into the backpack, smiles, and shuffles away with the bag. Franny's left alone with the first priest.

> FRANNY
> My husband didn't show up yet, I guess.

> PRIEST
> *(Gently.)*
> We're expecting no one.

Reaction shot Franny—alarm.

> FRANNY
> McGirl said he'd be here by dawn.

> PRIEST
> Perhaps he will be. Your McGirl moves in mysterious ways. May I ask what you're doing in Belfast?

> FRANNY
> Looking for him. My husband.

> PRIEST
> And what is your husband doing in Belfast?

> FRANNY
> I don't know. I—

> PRIEST
> Never mind. We have to think how to get you back where you came from.

> FRANNY
> *(Panicked.)*
> I just got here. He's not coming, Father, is he?

PRIEST

Probably not. In the morning you can go to the Crumlin Road
Gaol and inquire after him.

FRANNY

Father, I need to tell someone.

PRIEST

Tell someone what?

FRANNY

What I've done. I—

PRIEST

(Cutting her off and rising.)
Best not to talk politics in the dark. In the morning we'll send
you to inquire at the jail, won't we, and I'll hear your confession
if you like. You'll stay here tonight.

The priest walks close to the windows and indicates a wooden window
seat. Through the glass a fire glows in the distance.

PRIEST

Rest your head. Belfast is calming down. You'll find your
husband.

Franny sits on the wooden seat.

FRANNY

Good and hard. Like a church pew.

PRIEST

(Removing his jacket and covering her shoulders.)
See that you don't go back out into the night when I turn my
back on you.

FRANNY

I won't. Father?

PRIEST

(Walking away from her, toward the door.)

Yes.

FRANNY

Why are you holding McGirl's guns for him?

PRIEST

I might have asked you the same.

He leaves her, turning the light out as he goes. She puts her head down, but her eyes are wide open. Fire glow through the window. In the distance, faint sound of an explosion.

CUT TO:

INT. SECOND FALLS HOUSE.

Michael's asleep in a bedroom identical to the one he slept in before, but in this one five small children lie end-to-end. Michael's the only body alone in bed, and the only one with his eyes open. He looks like a cadaver.

FADE OUT.

FADE IN:

INT. MONASTERY.

Franny wakens in dim light to a vision of red whiskers over her face. The camera pulls into focus—it's Michael's face over Franny's. He's shaking her by the shoulder.

MICHAEL

Franny. Franny.

FRANNY
(Still asleep, though her eyes are open.)
No. No. No.
(She's awake.)
You're here.
(They embrace, a long embrace. Michael's clinging to her for dear life.)
Oh, Michael, I was ready to kill you.

MICHAEL
Let me hold you.

FRANNY
They had me doing it too.

MICHAEL
Let me hold you.

FRANNY
He had me carrying his guns last night.

MICHAEL
Franny, I—

FRANNY
Hush now. I just want to get out of here. I just want it to stop.

MICHAEL
Franny, Donovan brought me here.

FRANNY
Donovan!

MICHAEL
He's gone to pick something up, and then he's taking us to the
train station. Franny, I—

FRANNY
Hush. Hush.

MICHAEL

No, look, I—

He can't go on. She sits herself up and pushes him back to take a good look. He's a mess, hands and face smeared with soot, black clothes grimy with dust. His lips are white.

FRANNY

You were out in it last night.

MICHAEL

Christ. I don't even know if—

FRANNY

I wouldn't have known till last night how easy it is. To fall into.

MICHAEL

He could be dead. The guy could be dead.

FRANNY

But my eyes were open.

MICHAEL

Franny, I shot a guy.

FRANNY

Different traps, you and me.

MICHAEL

Franny, I shot a man and I don't know if he's alive or dead.

FRANNY

I know, Michael.

She puts her arms around him, and cradles his head. He's leaned back against her. For a moment they're the *Pietà* in the window seat.

FRANNY

Michael, we've got to get out of here.

MICHAEL

(Sitting upright and throwing her off.)

Oh Donovan's getting us out. Yeah, Donovan's getting us out.
Now that I've shot a guy, I can just run out. Maybe we can have
the rest of a honeymoon now. Just like it never happened.
Maybe we can go to the theater in Dublin, huh? *Shadow of a
Gunman.* Like it never happened.

FRANNY

Michael, we've got to stop.

MICHAEL

(Unhinged.)

It's a war now. They're soldiers. They drafted me.

FRANNY

The kids—they're everywhere, aren't they? The little kids.

MICHAEL

For fuck's sake, Franny, there's a reason they're arming
themselves.

FRANNY

You sound like . . .

(After a pause.)

When's Donovan coming?

MICHAEL

I dunno. He told me to sit tight. He got us tickets for Dublin.

FRANNY

I'll take his tickets. Thank God—we'll be out of it.

MICHAEL
I don't know if I can. They need help here.

They sit in complete silence, not touching each other.

MICHAEL
He woulda killed her. I know he woulda. Oh God I'm a
coward. God I'm a coward.

She puts a hand atop his, but does not move closer.

DISSOLVE TO:

INT. MONASTERY. AN HOUR LATER.

Franny's still sitting in the window seat, but Michael paces the room,
smoking.

PRIEST
(Appearing in the doorway.)
Your uncle. You've to hurry.

Franny rises and goes to the doorway. Michael hesitates, then follows
her.

CUT TO:

INT. MONASTERY. FRONT HALL.

The priest stands by the wooden door, ready to let them out.

PRIEST
(Holding out Franny's pack to her.)
Best you take your passport.
(To Michael.)

See that you get her out. No place for a wee girl. No place for Americans at all.

Michael shakes his hand in silence.

                          PRIEST
You're to walk to the corner now. He'll be waiting there.

They leave the monastery and retrace Franny's steps from the night before. Donovan's car is waiting, but Donovan does not acknowledge them as they climb together into the backseat.

                                                    CUT TO:

INT. DONOVAN'S CAR.

The car pulls off from the corner in silence. They pass row after row of terraced houses, some still smoldering, before Donovan speaks.

                          DONOVAN
We'll be there in no time at all.

There is utter silence from the backseat. Franny and Michael sit close but unconnected. They both appear to be in shock as the car makes it way through the Markets.

                          DONOVAN
Buses are running today.
          (Silence from the backseat.)
The train will be running as well.
          (Still he's met by silence.)
You've done well, Michael Burke. And I don't want to spoil a parting but Mrs. Burke, I think it might be wise to mention that you're never to speak a word of what you might have seen.

(Franny stares straight ahead.)
You'd no business prying—

MICHAEL
Just a minute, now.

DONOVAN
Sure you're called upon to defend the wife. I'm only giving you a friendly warning, amn't I, about what the lads in America might do if they were ever to hear talk?

MICHAEL
Jesus, Mary, and Joseph.

DONOVAN
The Holy Family speak well of you, lad. Best if you speak well of them. And mind you keep your silence. Word always gets back.

MICHAEL
That's enough, Mr. Donovan. No more threats.

DONOVAN
No threat intended, Michael Burke. I'd not want you leaving with bad feeling.

MICHAEL
(After a pause.)
I'm not feeling bad. I'm feeling like shit.

The car has moved into heavier traffic. Now they pull up outside the station. It's mobbed. Donovan stops the car far from the main entrance. He gets the tickets out of his jacket, but makes a point of hanging onto them. Franny opens her door and begins to walk away, without saying good-bye.

DONOVAN
She's made trouble, lad. Mind she doesn't make more.

MICHAEL

You have no right—

DONOVAN

Oh, and there's one more wee thing.

He reaches under the front passenger seat and hands Michael a small carrying case, the size of a gym bag.

MICHAEL
(Opening his door.)

No. No more.

DONOVAN

Stay a moment, Michael. We've only to unload Crawford's durex bombs.

Michael looks around for Franny, who's waiting for him close to the entrance. There are throngs of people, and a sudden surge. Franny disappears from his sight in the midst of incomprehensible shouting.

MICHAEL

Screw you, Donovan. We'll buy our own tickets.

DONOVAN

I think not, lad.

Donovan holds up a wallet and passport. Michael pats his back pocket and sees that they're his.

MICHAEL

Give me those.

DONOVAN

I will, lad. In due course. Now you've only to listen.

MICHAEL

I've listened to you too damn much.

DONOVAN

(Fierce.)

They'll not look in your bags until you're at the gate. So you've only to bring this to the gents' and leave it there. That's all we ask of you, Michael. We've a man inside will take it from there.

MICHAEL

My God. Look around you, Donovan. Are you gonna blow this station? These are Catholics, man, trying to get out.

Slow pan of the crowd, mostly women and children hauling as much as they can carry.

DONOVAN

No one will be hurt. Once you've boarded your train we'll give the warning. We've all the time in the world, because we've set nothing, have we?

MICHAEL

I won't do it.

DONOVAN

Look at your wife.

(Michael looks. Franny has disengaged herself from the crowd and is waiting for him.)

Now look over your shoulder.

Michael looks around to see one of the young gunmen from the night before, staring at him. He stands on the step by the driver's seat of a van, one hand stretched atop the open door.

MICHAEL

You wouldn't.

DONOVAN

I needn't. When I've finished the instructions, you'll walk into
the station. Slowly. You'll take the bag to the gents'. You'll wait
until the gents' is cleared, and then you'll put the bag in the
rubbish. Is that clear?

MICHAEL

Shit.

DONOVAN

No one will be hurt. Take the bag now.
(Michael hesitates, then takes it.)
Don't jostle it. Delicate stuff. Don't run. Walk, hear me?

Donovan gives a signal to the gunman behind them, then gives Michael
his passport and tickets. Michael leaves the car and walks toward Franny.
When he gets close, she sees the bag.

FRANNY

Oh God.

MICHAEL

Don't say a word. I'm supposed to dump it. I'll think of
something. We'll get it to somebody. They've got a gun on us
now. Don't do anything stupid, Franny.

CUT TO:

INT. RAILWAY STATION.

They make their way through the crowd at the front doors and into the
train station. Michael shrinks back from the pressing crowds. Inside, at the
ticket counters, constables hold back a mob of Protestant extremists. They
jeer the Catholic refugees, mostly women and children.

Michael looks around, trying to orient himself. He spies Mairead at the
end of the ticket line, distracted, reaching out to her children. The little girl
Brigid recognizes him and smiles.

                              FRANNY
We have to tell somebody.

                              MICHAEL
They're waiting for us out there. They've got somebody
watching us in here.

                              FRANNY
We have to tell somebody.

                              MICHAEL
Be cool, Franny. Be cool. When it looks like we did what we're
supposed to, we'll find somebody. But lemme get you on that
train. Lemme get you out of here.

                              FRANNY
It could go off any minute.

She lifts the bag from Michael's hand. He's taken by surprise and goes
to tug it back.

                              MICHAEL
        Don't jostle it, Franny. Jesus God, you're gonna set them off.

She walks away from him and toward the center of the station. A voice
rings out, off-camera.

                          MAN'S VOICE
        Burke!

Franny and Michael turn around, and so does everyone in the crowd
near them. A masked gunman's at the doorway holding an Armalite to his
shoulder. A high shot rings out. The demonstrators and the refugees
scream, scatter, hit the floor.

Franny runs away from the door at full speed. Michael follows, but she's too fast for him. She runs into the first gate she passes.

Michael and the gunman pursue her. Policemen take up the chase.

MICHAEL
(Screaming.)

Franny, don't run! Don't run!

Franny runs along the platform beside a train. Another shot rings out. She's hit in the arm. She stumbles against the side of the train but then runs on.

Another shot sounds. The bag's hit. The first explosion's small. Bits and pieces of the bag float up, taking their time. Then there's a chain reaction. The sound of firecrackers, and pieces of metal flying through the air.

Michael is thrown back onto the platform. He rises, but a policeman reaches out to grab him as he runs toward Franny.

DISSOLVE TO:

INT. CORDONED-OFF SECTION OF THE STATION. MINUTES LATER.

The police pushing back all the onlookers. They're evacuating the building. The sound of sirens outside. Police drag out the gunman from the track. His mask is lifted. It's Elvis McGirl.

Ambulance attendants bring up a stretcher with Franny's body, her face covered with a sheet.

The police crowd around Michael, trying to question him. He can't speak. A small blond girl being evacuated reaches out to touch him as she's pushed past. It's Brigid. Her face wavers in front of him.

FADE OUT.

FADE IN:

INT. CHAPEL, JESUIT UNIVERSITY OF AMERICA. A WEEK LATER.

Franny's funeral procession leaves the chapel. Father Collins walks down the aisle in vestments. Franny's mother, Doris, leads the line of mourners. Michael trails just behind his mother-in-law, dazed and disoriented. He's wearing the same patched morning coat he wore to his wedding, but he's put on decent pants. He and Doris are united in their bitterness toward each other.

CUT TO:

EXT. CHAPEL.

Michael and Doris walk out onto the front steps and watch the coffin being hauled into the hearse. There's a mob of mourners, the same hippies and students and relatives who were at the wedding. The soul band's there, in trimmed Afros and straight-looking suits. Small children flit about, playing, unaware.

An older woman in an old-fashioned feathered hat approaches Michael.

> WOMAN
> Michael, I'm so sorry. We're all so sorry.
> *(He nods his head.)*
> Did you get to look up any of the family, anyway, before the accident?

Michael walks away. Franny's old boyfriend, Steward, follows and extends his hand. He's dressed as he was at the wedding and appears distraught. Michael takes one look at his grieving face and lands a hard right hook to his jaw. Steward tumbles down the steps. Aghast faces everywhere.

FADE OUT.

FADE IN:

EXT. JESUIT UNIVERSITY OF AMERICA. CHAPEL. MONTHS
LATER.

Light snow is falling on the campus.

CUT TO:

INT. CHAPEL.

Michael's looking at the painted stations of the cross. They resemble the
old-fashioned stations of the cross Franny was looking at in Killorglin.
Father Collins appears at the sacristy door and walks out onto the altar. He
peers at Michael in the dark chapel.

FATHER COLLINS
That you, Michael?

MICHAEL
Yeah.

FATHER COLLINS
You're the last person I'd have expected to see in chapel.

MICHAEL
Yeah, well. This is where we're meeting for the demonstration.

FATHER COLLINS
(Walking down from the aisle to join him.)
I really have some hope this time. I know we can stick it to the
British—

MICHAEL
Right.

FATHER COLLINS
Well, you're still out marching. That's what counts.
(Michael makes a face.)
It's good of you. I know how hard . . .

                    MICHAEL

Tell you the truth, Father, I'd just as soon stick a gun in my
mouth.

                 FATHER COLLINS

You'll get through this, Michael. I know you will. If you haven't
stuck the gun in your mouth yet—

                    MICHAEL

We're into nonviolence, right? Peace and love.

                                           CUT TO:

EXT. CHAPEL.

They leave the church together and stand on the front steps, the same
spot where Michael decked Steward. Students hurry by in the snow.
Franny's friend Peggy Barnacle comes toward them with a redheaded girl.
They're lugging a banner, but it's sagging in the middle and the words
aren't clear. Maybe the word *Ireland*'s on it, maybe the word *England*.

Michael goes to join them and "Jenny's Wedding" fades up on the
sound track. A small freckled girl with long wild hair jogs across his path.
Michael stares at her, lost for a moment.

Then he goes to help Peggy hold up the banner.

III.

DOMESTIC BLISS

Shouldn't they have been happy?
We should have thought ourselves
in heaven!

—E. BRONTE

SOMEBODY
ELSE'S RAIN

From their window tonight, M Street was framed by clumps of furry green, the trees dangling over a slice of slick pavement. A city street from the fifth floor. It could have been Paris, and Franny could have been in a garret. She could have stood through the whole damp sundown watching the gray sidewalks blacken, if only Brian were not thundering down the hall every fifteen seconds with a new toxic chemical in his fist. This time it was a tube of cobalt blue.

"Hey thanks, little chicken," she said. "I haven't been able to buy cobalt blue since you were born."

Brian, on legs round enough to hold up a Jeep, beamed and gunned his motor, then tore off down the hallway to raid her studio once more. He was sixteen months old today, born April 15, 1972 (an inauspicious date that had already spoiled his last birthday—Michael wanted to tear up half their W2s, Franny was sure they'd get caught—and would spoil plenty more to come).

"You didn't eat any of that, did you?"

"HAHAHAHAHA," said Brian, over his shoulder. He had learned to walk, or maybe stagger, at eight and a half months. Now he just hurled himself down the hall. He was a drunken baby, most of the time a happy anarchic drunk, and no wonder, a baby conceived in Killorglin. The little bean had floated the first months of his life in a pool of warm brown stout.

Now he floated in a pool of warm brown Washington air, up on the fifth floor under the roof where the sun beat down all morning and the rain was beating down tonight.

She turned her back on the window and the rain and the street and followed him down the hallway. "Might as well be in the Laundromat, huh, Brian."

In her studio he was sly and quick and clever. Silly to call it a studio, half the size of a good closet, but just the same it was a mansion, or maybe a house of worship, for her and Brian both. It had a window! Looking out on the tidy backyards of Georgetown! Those clever little hibachis! Those young lawyers grilling expensive cuts of lamb on those hibachis! She bought the first bottle of Windex she'd ever bought in her life to keep that view clear, and she drew the best hibachis-from-the-fifth-floor series ever to come out of Georgetown.

For their first anniversary—just before she heaved the glass of champagne at him, just before he cracked the bottle neck down on the kitchen table—Michael gave her a new easel, cheap but sturdy, an easel that was now never bare of paper or canvas. Never bare, always ready to go, even if Brian was in the throes of scarlet fever (two weeks sick, this February) or viral pneumonia (three weeks of fever rolling in in March), even if the temperature was eighty-five degrees outside and eighty-five degrees inside, as it was now, even when the blank paper curled and buckled and wavered under its clamps.

Waiting, an empty testimonial to her own waiting. Waiting to get back to work. "Brian?"

He was hiding back behind the stacked crates, his sparse pumpkin-colored curls giving him away. She had to be careful not to let the crates topple over. That mishmash of tubes and jars and empty coffee cans had already crashed once tonight. "Briiiiiiiian."

He answered with a reedy giggle, naughty boy, the naughtiest of boys. Oh she loved him. Not at all like the good babies on M Street who came to call—once, until they saw the state of the apartment—and fussed and fidgeted and didn't seem to know that when somebody gave you a crayon you were supposed to draw on the wall with it.

Brian crouched deeper and the crates wobbled, a leaning tower. Last week, when she was trying to stew him turnips in apple juice and boil his diapers and dry out a manuscript of Michael's he'd been dunking in the toilet, the pilot light went out. Coming home, Michael sniffed gas, opened the door and hollered, "Why so desperate, Sylvia Plath?" He didn't know how close to the truth he was hitting.

But tonight the baby was happy, the fat jolly drunken baby, and she couldn't keep her hands off him. Her son was covered in skin so white it shone blue, and his hair was so red it was orange pushing to green, and his fat round chins dangled and stretched like Silly Putty. He was fat all over, this child of emaciated parents. She'd tie-dyed all his clothes, purples and greens, even if hippie babies weren't long for this world. He was the only one on M Street, that was for sure.

Michael wanted to pierce his ear but she said no, a hat with bells on it was what would fit that face, so Michael found a peaked green hat in a costume store and a jangle of bells in Woolworth's. They stayed up one night until two in the morning, the two of them, trying to thread a needle while they were sloshed on Guinness. Brian threw up twice that night, before they'd sewn a single bell to the peaked hat. Michael could deny it from here to Brian's first I.Q. test, but of course it was the Guinness in her milk, what else could it be? GUINNESS IS GOOD FOR YOU. She held herself to a bottle a night now.

Michael, however, could not live on a single lousy bottle of Guinness a night, and so he had taken to stepping out, to the Irish Times where he claimed he spent the whole night chatting up legislative aides and every now and again Woodward and/or Bernstein. Right. Sure. A likely pair for an Irish bar. Michael saw it as a professional duty, to get to know drunken reporters, because one day he might get to be a drunken reporter himself, instead of the recently graduated editor in chief of the *JUA Shamrock* and the currently indentured-to-the-Jesuits assistant director of university publications. At least he had a job.

And a bar.

A bar he retreated to before he stopped back in to see if the rest of the Burkes were still breathing, in their top-floor apartment, or whether they'd turned that gas on after all.

"Brian!"

She managed to grab him under his arms and heave him up over the undulating crates, but he'd already unscrewed the top of the next tube of paint. By the time his feet hit the floor he'd calculated the exact amount of wriggling that would set him free while his mother righted the crates, and by the time she turned back he was crashing his heel down on the tube. Titanium white. Oh precious priceless white and the color you'd be least likely to splurge on for another six months, though without it you could never do the sky, not a Due East sky and not a Washington sky either.

"Brian! You can bring the eggbeater in the bath!"

That sent him careening off. He missed cracking his head on the door frame by a thirty-second of an inch. Now she had fifteen seconds before he'd pull the kitchen drawer and the eggbeater down on his fat bare toes. She reached high on the shelf for the rag. Good enough, as much of the white as she could get up for now. Down the hall to the kitchen, just as the drawer threatened to dangle. She sprinted to Brian's side—there was her run for the week—saved the drawer, and somehow jostled him up against it hard enough that the drawer corner poked him in the forehead not a quarter inch from his right eye.

"Shit. Shit shit shit shit shit. Shit, Brian, shit."

Shit was the first word her baby ever said, clear and perfect, every consonant pronounced. No wonder, in this household. His face dug into the warm curve of her belly. He howled into her gut.

"Shit. Shit shit shit shit shit. Shit, Brian, shit."

This mantra didn't calm him at all—he *was* a drunk, that caterwauling, as flashy in his bad temper as in his good—but it calmed her. There were moments when she almost leaped right off the cliff into Dorisland, when she felt dragon breath issuing from deep within her chest and began to bellow a torrent of meaningless Mommy from Hell curses: JesusMaryand-JosephBrian and OhBrianhowmanytimeshaveI.

How had this transmigration of souls occurred so rapidly? How had Franny Starkey, the Starkey child least resembling her mother, *become* her mother?

"Oh it's all right my baby, now we've got to find that eggbeater, darlin, where'd that eggbeater go, sugar?"

Sugar. Sugar was what Lola called Stew a thousand years ago, and now listen to her. Maybe it wasn't Doris she'd become. She heaved her son up so he could cry into her chest. Swooping him, the small of her back caved in on itself—the doctor said that was what happened when ninety-pound mothers carried ten-pound overdue babies—but Brian stopped crying and pressed his lips onto her breasts, hungry for her. He could have been a newborn rooting.

"Oh Bri, oh little sweetheart, we gotta wean you someday, huh? Some-day soon."

"Shit," said Brian. Perfectly clear. "Shit," he said again, and then he followed it with a mush of sounds that might have been *Mammy* or *Daddy*. You couldn't tell about the consonants at all.

He was in bed by ten-thirty, though Michael said Burke children never went to bed before midnight. She was supposed to keep him awake for Michael who, if he had happened by some miracle to arrive home before the clock struck twelve, would have managed to make a good Burke of him.

Michael had absolutely no sense, but he was a fool for his son. When he was home. He kept Brian up reading him *Moby Dick*. Sixteen months old. *Moby Dick*. He let Brian climb in his lap while he sat at the typewriter. He sang Brian entire shows—*Candide* was the current favorite—straight through, like an LP. He stayed sober, more or less, until Brian drifted off. Then he poured himself a double shot of Jameson's, or cheap bourbon if that was all they could afford, and sat down to do his real work until three o'clock in the morning.

But Michael was not here now. She was alone in the front room, their livingroombedroomstudy, watching the black rain across the way wash Alma Guitterez's town house, where every few months she sat nude for a painting group.

She was tempted to sit nude at the window right now, to languish in the face of the darkness outside. With her luck though, Alma's husband, who was a consular something, would look up into her window just at the moment she stripped bare, and he would purse his lips in that self-satisfied smarmy way he did when he peeked in at the painting group. His smirk would be enough to make her nipples stand up hard and irate, and that in turn would remind her of the strange shame of sleeping with Declan Mc-Cleary not a month after she was married: a sin occasioned by another of Michael's abandonments, the way he'd just disappeared from Killorglin, all heated up with IRA fever and to hell with her.

Well to hell with him, on a night like tonight when it wasn't safe to take her clothes off and she'd already downed her quota of Guinness. She stared at the rain from her perch on a ladder-back chair, her feet propped on another crate. The hiss and the pop against the window might have soothed her entirely if she had closed her eyes. But she never wanted to sleep anymore—sleep only got interrupted, anyway—and staring at the steady orderly rain, she remembered that this was somebody else's rain, not a Due East rain or a New York rain or a Paris rain at all. This was a rain she couldn't settle into entirely, not like the afternoon thunderbursts you could count on every sultry July day in Carolina.

This rain wasn't bad, this view of what passed as a city street wasn't bad, but she didn't *want* to be in Washington, didn't *want* to finish up one more year at JUA with those pathetic studio art courses and all the humanities professors donating A's to her because they knew Michael or knew she typed the papers one-fingered, with a baby in the crook of her arm. *It's a good thing you're young,* Doris said when she came to visit, *cause otherwise you'd just faint dead away, running back and forth to school that way, and I don't know if I could've left my babies with a stringy-looking woman like that Miz Schmidt, it's a good thing you're young and can overlook so much, I only personally hope you don't have a hernia or an ulcer, or, Lord knows, worse, which I will not mention and give you the idea. It's just a good thing you're young, is all.*

But it wasn't a good thing to be stuck here, in Georgetown, looking out on some consul's town house, only because this was how things had worked out for Michael and not for her at all.

Doristhoughts. Terrifying enough that her mother's voice should issue from her body. Now her mother's thoughts formed themselves in her brain.

It wasn't like this in the beginning. They washed away the IRA muck, they started clean. That first month she stayed home with the baby, Michael ferried her papers back and forth and practically took her finals for her. He came home with bagels and pizzas and quarts of Miller High Life, the Champagne of Bottle Beers, and cheap bunches of carnations and daisies. When Brian was three months, when Brian was five months, even when Brian was eight months—in those last days before he became the youngest walker in the history of Western baby development—they brought him with them everywhere they went. Franny popped a sugar tit in his mouth and stuck him in a corduroy pouch strapped to Michael, and they went off together, the three of them, to the Irish Times or the Underground, to the Jesuits for dinner. Brian was fat and white and charming in his little pouch. Everyone admired his Celtic coloring, everyone choked back the urge to say he looked like a potato. Franny and Michael were absolutely smug, high and smug about how easy—HOW BEAUTIFULLY FUCKING EASY, Michael said—it was to be under twenty-one, with a good redheaded baby in their arms and drinks in their hands and the scholarship-stipend-work-study money flowing into their checking account.

Then Brian learned to walk, and the sight of him lurching down their hallway reminded Michael that after graduation he was supposed to have some sort of other life planned, that this charmed student role financed by the Society of Jesus was about to come to an end. In a frenzy he sent off his first novel to twenty-seven publishers, beginning with Farrar Straus and Knopf, working his way down to Hell's Bells Press and Scuzz Books Limited. Scuzz Books suggested that a hundred and twenty-seven pages did not a novel make.

He quit acting and playwriting. Both. Just like that. It was movies he was into now, the greatest art form, he said, better than opera and baseball put together. Now it was screenplays he banged out at one o'clock in the morning, because you could just about write them in your sleep, fast, and if you hit with a single screenplay you could finance a baby for life. Now if he wasn't out at the Irish Times, he was out seeing Vidor revivals or Flaherty documentaries. At least she didn't have to walk trembling into the JUA workshops anymore, terrified that he'd broken his promise and put her onstage again. The worst he could do was put her in a movie that would never be made.

And meanwhile he toiled for the Jesuits. Now there was no chance to go home for August. Now Michael disappeared at night, and she was an old housewife, a month shy of her twenty-first birthday, Doris's wrinkles forming around her bitter mouth, her back aching. She could have been painting now, couldn't she, even by the dim bulb in the tiny narrow studio. She could have been painting the consul with his ironic greedy pursed lips. She could have gone in to sketch a sleeping Brian, his hair a swatch of velvet by the night-light. But her brain was shut off and her painting arm with it. She was a slug in the chair, a hateful slug waiting to ooze all over Michael when he came in.

She closed her eyes, finally, in the temporary bliss of pure self-righteous anger. The outside world was cooling off, maybe, but in here it was as sticky as a child's sucker. She breathed in the sweet wet air and waited for her husband.

She was smiling in half-sleep when Michael turned the key and clumped in at eleven, dripping off the night outside. Her own smile fooled her, and for just that flash of waking she imagined that she was going to throw her arms around him and share a shot with him before he got to work.

The smile eased itself off her face. She heard him make his way first to Brian's room, heard the *grishl* of his workboots sucking across the hallway. Then the long pause—oh sentimental Michael, this was the man who thought *Our Daily Bread* was the greatest movie ever made, who fell for that hokum—that meant he was leaning over Brian's crib, maybe running his callused hand over the smooth arc of his son's high forehead, maybe just breathing his beery breath into Brian's dreams. Then the squish across the hall, into the bathroom. A new smooth arc, the arc of piss landing in the toilet, or close, depending on his degree of drunkenness, piss landing and landing and landing, a torrent as it was every night, the torrent of beer and talk and manic dreams that Michael pissed away a dozen times a day.

She had a sudden vision of him dead in five years, and not just dead, but crazy dead like his father, dead and hallucinating like he hadn't done since Brian was born, dead and mean and bitter as she was.

Grishl, grooshl down the hall. Like a giant, back to his lair. Grishl grooshl fo fum.

She waited until the first wet clump entered the room, on its way over to kiss her, and then she said: "Thanks for calling."

Sometimes when he came in late he snarled, but not tonight. Tonight he didn't bother to answer. Instead he abandoned the kiss, changed course, circumnavigated the mattress, and headed to the back of the room, where he kept the typewriter shrine, as far from her spot in the window as possible. She sneaked a sidelong glance at him and saw that he might be sober.

"Michael, I'm going nuts like this."

No reply. He sat, before the typewriter, and she watched him plop his elbows on the desk—a board, really, propped up on more crates. He sank his face into his open palms.

"I can't go all summer without working. I'll lose my mind."

Now he lifted the face enough to sigh, a long, labored, weary sigh.

"I mean, o.k., if you have to go do something, but it's not fair, you go out drinking five nights a week."

"I haven't been out drinking once this week." He was still poised in front of his machine, and now he lifted up his face entirely to stare at the yellow sheet in the carriage, his paper waiting the way her stretched canvases waited. His bony shoulders dangled and his foot jittered against the floor.

"Well you haven't been home one night to let me get some work done, have you? I mean, I don't want to call you a liar, but that's a powerful perfume you're wearing when you come in at night." She did want to call him a liar, she did.

A sluicing sigh. "Jack buys me a beer when we get through the copy-editing. I don't call that going out drinking."

"Well I do."

"Look. Franny. I got finished going over the spring catalogue at ten o'clock, ya know the little course numbers in eight point that you need to read with a fucking magnifying glass? I sat with Jack for ten minutes. Jesus, listen to me, I'm accounting for my every movement. Let me write down when I took a crap, ya keeping track of that, too?"

"Oh come on."

"No. No, you come on. I hitchhiked on the goddamned Beltway at ten-thirty at night cause the bus is too slow and I wanted to say good night to Brian. But Brian's been asleep since eight-thirty, huh, and you've just been sleeping in your groovy chair by the window since then."

"Brian's never been asleep at eight-thirty in his life and if I'm so bummed out by a whole day with the baby that I can't work I don't see—"

This always happened. She always lost the sentence.

"You don't see"—and this always happened too, this was what it was like to be married to someone who dealt with words, who could remember the last thing you said and finish the sentence for you besides—"why I can't work a twelve-hour day to pay the rent while you take the summer off to sip fifty goddamned cups of coffee a day, and why I can't somehow concurrently and magically transport myself back to the fucking home front so I can take care of Brian too, so you could snooze by the window. That would be fair, wouldn't it? Wouldn't it?"

He let his voice go up at the end of the sentence, up into a female register, mocking her. Mincing, prissing. Oh that would be fair wouldn't it.

"You could have picked up the phone and told me you had to work on the catalogue."

"You could have remembered that I told you on Monday we were working on the goddamned catalogue. You could have remembered that I'm doing it on three hours of sleep at night since unlike you I don't have the luxury of being a full-time fucking Artist."

"You know I can't work with Brian running around, you know that, Michael. He sticks everything in his mouth, he crams every tube of, there's the diapers for God's sake and. And."

"Look, sweetheart." Sweetheart? If she weren't mad enough to spit she would have laughed instead. She'd put money on it that he'd been in a revival house this week to see *The Big Sleep*. "Look, sweetheart, it's pretty hard writing at two A.M. too, but you might have thought of birth control pills if you weren't willing to share the apartment."

"Michael. That's Brian you're talking about."

"Yeah, and that's Brian you're talking about when you talk about all your goddamned sacrifice and how your life is over, too."

"At least I'm not wishing he never existed."

"I'm not wishing *he* never existed."

Pleased with the line, he rose to get a drink. She couldn't remember ever in her entire life being willed into nonexistence before. She stretched her hand out, the same way Michael did on the mornings after he'd tied one on, to see whether she was seething or trembling. The hand was steady, so she must be seething.

Michael came back with a full new bottle of Jameson's and not so much as a paper cup. Not so much as a glance in her direction, either, when he sat again at the desk. He unscrewed the cap with his teeth—oh he had been to the movies this week, he had—and swallowed down a good swig.

She sat dead still, transfixed by his profile at the desk. On the way from the kitchen he'd taken his shirt off. Even sitting, his pants slipped down his hips, and through the hole in the side of his ratty director's chair she stared at his ribs and his grimy grubby jeans. Over the jeans his chest was a pathetic hairless muscleless sheet of onionskin.

He knew she was watching him, and pulled his hair out of its rubber band. The dirty sweaty devil's mass of it, frizzed out from the rain, swung down and brushed his narrow shoulders. A self-important about-to-be-drunk thinks-he's-a-writer. Her husband. Her lover.

"Where'd the Jameson's come from?"

He began to type, the keys pressing down like the keys on a player piano. Not as if he had to think of something to say. Oh no no no. An instant screenplay. No notes to consult, no last night's work to read over.

"I'm bringing nickels and dimes to the grocery store, we're so short."

Click click clackety clack. Typing a happy whole screenplay, uninterrupted by the flow of daily life, he did not look up from his instant happy typewriter's keys. Uninterrupted by a twenty-year-old wife, so unhappy in Washington, D.C., so unhappy she can't paint anymore, so unhappy she can't get her husband to listen to her.

Franny rose and slipped barefoot to the side of his desk. From the pack of cigarettes lying between the second sheets and the paper clips she took a Camel—*had* to be Bogart he was playing. Last week he was buying Winstons—though she didn't even smoke anymore, not since she got pregnant. Now, though, the unlit cigarette dangled from her mouth—yeah, she could be tough too—until he stopped typing and looked up at her with a mouth whose corners he'd actually somehow managed to turn down. A cartoon mouth.

"I need a light."

"Go light it from the stove."

"Michael, gimme a match."

Like a little kid. Like a little kid picking a fight (with AgnesAnn or Will or Caroline, her mouth twisted up into self-interest) and Michael the same. *Go light it from the stove.* Like they were family.

She stood breathing over his yellow sheets, willing his anger, until finally he pulled from his pocket a book of matches, which teetered at the edge of the desk and then tumbled to the floor.

Maybe it was how much her old lady's back hurt when she lowered herself to pick up the matches. Maybe it was the way the matches were wet when she went to strike one, wet with the sweet smell of liquor. Maybe it was the way the typewriter keys still pounded—how could he keep going like that, through his anger, through his highs, through his fatigue, WHAT DID HE HAVE TO SAY—that made her toss the matches back. A good hard toss, not back on the desk, but into the well of the typewriter.

Where a mighty confluence of typewriter keys was stymied by a paper book of matches.

Now Michael snarled. He snarled and growled and emitted the entire low register of a man's repertoire of anger-at-his-wife sounds as he tackled first the mangled keys and then the ruined second sheet, stabbed in its center. He spun the page from the roller and twisted it into a spiked ball he threw at her feet.

The little wad of paper rolled by her toes, the storm wind through the M Street window pushing it to and fro. It was cool in the apartment now, damp and clammy. She looked down at the yellow paper, and took a long deep toke of cigarette, and blew smoke that bounced somewhere below Michael's naked nipples. Her head came up to his chest, and she could see him twitching, sinewy with rage the way Steward used to get. The Camel tasted like manure-streaked hay but she waited, inhaling.

"This what you want, Fran? This what you want? You wanna make sure I never work again?"

One more toke of Camel, one more until her head swirled and she didn't make any sense. Giddy with anger. "No, Michael, that's me, that's me never gonna work again. That's me scraping the shit off the diapers and scalding my hands, that's me, and I wanted to go to Due East . . ."

He made some new sound, now back up in a high register, some sound of disbelief. *Ewwwwww.*

"I did, I wanted to go home." Hearing the sound of her own voice, the way it scratched and yes, whined, the Dorisvoice, she turned from him, self-defeated. Her cigarette must have brushed against his naked chest when she turned—she saw him jerk, and every morning after, for days, she searched his bare chest in bed while he still slept, looking for the spot, a little red mark, a little white mark, the cigarette *must* have brushed him—because only physical pain could have made him react that way.

Only physical pain could have made him grab her from behind and put his hands around her neck. She wasn't in any danger—she told herself that too, for mornings after—and there would be no more mark on her neck than there was on his chest. She wasn't choking exactly, just feeling the weight of his fingers curling round her neck. Just thinking in slow motion, a completely rational being trying to remember which movie might have put *this* scene in mind. *Suspicion? Gaslight?*

He spun her around somehow. Now there were no more fingers round her neck. He had her by the shoulders and he was shaking her. His right eye was a nasty slit of yellow and he was saying something in that high register, some *EWWWWIFYEWWWWEVER.*

Seeing his bristles up close, colored pumpkin like his son's silky hair, she socked him, hard, in the belly. His face washed gray with rage. His hands flew off her shoulders when she hit him but now they landed again, surer, and his fingers dug in between bone and muscle. She kicked out at him, her bare feet up against his heavy boots.

She was in a barroom brawl.

She was high on bennies.

She was defending herself from a maniac.

And she was a maniac too. Her crying was sputtering out—oh she was breathless—and she heard it echo down the hallway. She was yelling something too, something stupid, *bastard* repeated over and over. Even Doris could have done better than that. But Michael wasn't doing any better either, hadn't progressed beyond sounds, all vowels. He lacked consonants, like his son. He was finally at a loss for words.

And finally he was holding back. Holding her in fact, remembering that she was a girl, grabbing her at the wrists to stop her from punching him dead center again. There was an empty hollow sound, a clicking gone long past rage, coming from the two of them.

A couple of kids, still. Michael ran first. She thought at first that he had so spent his fury that now he was running into the night, shirtless, wifeless, done of them for good. It was only after she sat hard on the floor that the shame of why he ran flooded her. That was Brian sobbing in the other end of the apartment, and she had only heard his cries as the echoes of her own.

She walked, willing herself into calm, and when she entered Brian's room—the walled-off other half of her studio, an airless lightless little box —she reached her arms out for him.

Brian stretched for her too, but Michael would not let go. She saw that Michael was crying. This was a first. He didn't cry over whiskey, didn't cry over drugs. He was scrunched over the baby, his bare mottled back hunched, his hair drained of color against the little boy's sparks. An old man. His old man. Something fell into place.

"Michael."

He wouldn't look up. His teeth seemed to be chattering. Brian was swinging his top half around, sobbing and looking for her to rescue him, but Michael squeezed him tighter still, the baby's sparse curls plastered to the top of his wet head.

"Did he used to hit your mother?"

There was the ice water. One final long shudder, and the back of his hand to wipe his face.

"Coupla times."

Brian patted his father's wet cheeks.

"Yeah, and just look at me now." He was trying to smile. "But I hafta say my ma never tried to *kick* him." Brian had quickened his little palms against his father's cheeks, slapslapping now. All confused, not a clue what was going on. All of them without a clue.

He let her come close and she put her arms around the two of them, Brian jiggling up and down between them, struggling to get closer, struggling to get free. His parents were hiccoughing, tongues silenced, muscles slackened, memories erased.

Finally Michael let loose another long shudder—enough of these Zen moments—and shifted Brian off to the side. He took a step back, to make a speech.

"Never happen again," he said, and looked as if he might roll into his history and her history and a profession of undying love. But instead he took Brian's hand, slapslapping against his cheek once more, held it tight, and said: "Nah." You could hear the color of his throat, black-red, blackberries in the woods by the trestle.

She reached out for the baby and carried him back down the hallway, the two of them trembling now. Michael followed her to the big front room, where she peeled Brian's soaking tie-dyed nightshirt off, and rubbed away the purple and green pattern from his chest, and set him down on the mattress. Too hot for the sleeping bag. She pulled off her own clothes and lay down beside the baby. There was a fog in the apartment, streams of gray settling down above her chest.

Michael stripped. He was gaunt in the hall light they'd left on, gaunt and the pure white of an Irish-American kid who wasn't going to get to the beach *this* summer. The wiry copper hairs on his legs looked like the prickles on a barbed-wire fence. He crawled onto the bed next to his son and they touched each other across the baby's chest, as if by accident. As if it was unavoidable. The fog settled over the three of them.

Brian sniffled still, and the rain beat down on the tin roof over them. In Due East, if the rain came down this hard, you'd worry about the marshes overflowing and the creeks swelling up. But this was somebody else's rain, in somebody else's city.

You were supposed to run in the other direction when somebody started snorting heroin, or running guns. You were supposed to bar the door against a guy like that, and hey, these were the Free Love days when you didn't *need* to be married in the first place.

Michael was asleep already, his breathing a low whistle, and Brian whistled high beside him.

Now a shudder ran clear through her. No work tonight. All that time gone workless, the two of them. In the morning they wouldn't be able to look each other in the eye.

The rain pelted down. She could still rise, sleepless, rise through this fog and get something done.

But she did not rise. Long into the night, she lay listening to the rain and the singsong breathing of her husband and her son beside her.

JANUARY
FLU

The January sky was a sheet of slate, the sun gone for good. In his shirtsleeves, Steward Morehouse was cold. It was getting onto four o'clock, and he was in a crowd of strangers, women, waiting for a bus, his Synchronex in a shoulder bag resting between his feet. He was reconsidering this wait on the bus line. Back home in his bed there was a beautiful naked girl under the sheets, a girl burning with fever from a January flu.

Lola said he had to find himself a beautiful girl after Franny got married —her idea of revenge—but Simone didn't move in until a year after the wedding. A nightmare wedding. He'd been a fool to go: Franny pressed herself tight against him when they danced, and her husband shoved him backwards into a punch bowl.

A nightmare wedding, but long gone. Franny was dead to him now. He'd been played for a fool, all the way.

He and Simone were in the same little Bourbon Street apartment, paint still peeling from the ceiling, the incessant howls and whines of tourists so loud they didn't hear them anymore. He could have afforded a place in the Garden District if he wanted, but he didn't want, and neither did Simone. She was a French major, finishing up at Newcombe. She could hop the streetcar and be there in ten minutes. And she'd never lived away from home before, so she was a tourist on Bourbon Street, too.

The two of them lived cut off from family, mostly. Simone went home every Sunday for Mass and a big dinner, and he guessed her folks were glad to have her, but she wouldn't lie about living with him and the Gaudets wouldn't have a white boy step foot in their dining room. He wasn't sure, actually, that it was because he was white. Simone was far too restrained to explain their sight-unseen rejection: maybe it was because he wasn't Catholic. He pictured a Sacred Heart in the Gaudet house bigger than any even Doris Starkey could find. He'd never so much as driven past Simone's childhood house, only walked her toward Canal Street and waited sometimes to see her off on the bus, kissing her a little too long, pressing her breasts against him a little too hard, punishing her for Mass.

Now he was the one waiting for a bus, and Simone was home in a fever. He pictured her flinging the sheet off her long dark body. He wanted the bus to come, quick, before he bolted and went to her. He was in a rush about everything lately, a rush to get out of this town, a rush to get to film school. In the fall, he made a five-minute movie too fast, a gritty little documentary about winos in the Irish Channel he was sending off with his applications to NYU and Columbia and UCLA. Simone had worked the Nagra. You couldn't understand a word the drunks said, but that wasn't Simone's fault, that was because he'd plied them with Dixie beer to loosen them up. It was because he rushed it. It was like Altman anyway, though, the garbled sound track.

Now he had a cheap super 8 with him, so he could be a one-man band, his own soundman with the little cassette player. He didn't know what he was after, exactly. He had a vague idea for a long documentary about the integration of the public schools. He didn't know a thing about it. Didn't know yet how slowly things moved. He was in a rush, and he sure wasn't planning on hanging around Iberville to find kids. He wanted himself a black working-class neighborhood with houses, not projects, and so he was waiting on the bus line to get himself one, follow the women out somewhere Mid-City he'd never been before. But he'd been on this line for fifteen minutes, and it was hard to look casual, humping his big bag. The women were all carrying parcels from a day shopping Downtown.

He was turning away, ready to go back to fetch Simone ginger ale and cough syrup and maybe to nuzzle her hot neck, when a bus rolled up. He slumped aboard among the women and the bus lurched forward while they staggered toward seats. Still trying to look casual, still trying to be the cool white boy who knew exactly where he was going, he got the camera out before he was fully settled into a seat. He aimed it first at the tourist traps, at the velvet paintings and the barrels and the bags of coffee beans, then at the old Victorian porches rolling by. The woman sitting opposite him had a red patent-leather pocketbook she clutched tighter than he clutched his camera.

The bus heaved on forever, but eventually the big porched houses yielded to shotgun houses, and then to little modern squares. The bus emptied slowly. This was sort of what he had in mind. Maybe. You got back a sense of New Orleans's flatness, lowness, out here where the trees were sparse and the decoration sparser. Nothing and everything out here to shoot—row after row of drab white houses, a grocery with a hand-lettered sign on the corner—but he was probably getting close to the end of the line. He caught motion up ahead, and the bus whizzed by a school playground where a dozen kids were whooping it up. This was it. He got off at the next stop, lugging his bag.

He walked back to the asphalt playground: one metal whirligig, three swings, cracked concrete covered with words children shouldn't know. It was crowded with bigger kids than he wanted, kids ten, eleven, twelve, the twelve-year-old girls strutting around in halter tops, smoking cigarettes and intimidating the little boys. But these kids would do. School was out for the day, maybe fresh on their minds. Oh yeah.

He set the bag down and pulled out the camera, the tape recorder. Boys swarmed around him, hungry for the whirr of tape and film, while he synchronized the Synchronex. *What you doing, mister.*

Mister. He felt his blond hair whitening in this crowd, but he was insulated once he had the camera in his hand, the swarm of boys a good air pocket.

"Hey, mister, take my picher."

It was one of the girls, a big fat girl with her hair straightened and gooed and slicked back into one of those ponytail rubber bands with the three plastic balls at the end. He didn't want her image—something slovenly and pathetic about her already, something so needy about her fat little breasts poking through her white shirt that it hurt to look at her—but he did want to get them all going, clamoring to be on film, so he could ease into some leading questions. Not that he'd thought of the questions yet.

He aimed the camera at the fat girl, and the next thing he knew, there was a rumbling behind him. "Get outta here now." Steward turned to look at the commotion, and saw that the commotion was directed at him. A big guy—very big guy, maybe two hundred and fifty pounds, maybe this big girl's big father—was gaining on him. Where'd he come from?

"Get outta here," the big guy said again. Dixie Peach slicked his curls back over his collar, where they swung reckless as James Brown's. The man was wearing a red-checked shirt, soaked through with sweat in big ovals under his arms. Crosses, Jesus crosses, swung as his curls swung. He was a tank coming through, but Steward registered a gold wedding band, and felt the sudden inspiration of the Documentary Filmmaker. This man was the Good Father, the Protective Father, coming to rescue the children. A perfect subject.

In a strange crystallized moment of perfect confidence, he lowered the

camera to smile a warm got-to-respect-you-brother smile. But the big guy
was already on top of him. A fist as broad, and for one hallucinatory minute,
as spiked, as a pineapple bounced onto the daylight filter. They both heard
the crack of the man's knuckle, and Steward stared down at his camera. The
filter was fine.

"Whatchew doing, man?"

"What*chew* doing, prevert?" The Good Father's voice was rolling thunder. "Git outta here fore I bust moren that camera."

"I'm making a documentary, Christ!" Full splutter.

"Filthy little motherfucka round those chirrun. Git *out*." The Good
Father was being biblical, maybe. Steward had a flash of inexplicable memory: *They have provoked the Holy One of Israel unto anger.* Could he have dug
that up from St. Luke's Episcopal? Only Baptists memorized verse.

And he had no doubt this was a Baptist standing before him. He was
almost moved to obey, but the man swung his foot (red canvas sneakers, *big*
red canvas sneakers) into the mouth of the cassette machine dangling by a
strap from his shoulder. Now he heard the crack of plastic.

"Hey man, you're gonna owe me big bucks you hurt my equipment."

The big man cackled, gleeful. "You ain't got no equipment. Got to
come round little chirrun make you feel like you got some equipment."

He felt his feet planting themselves in the dirt, the way these playground kids' feet might have been planted, and he saw the man fixing to
deck him, fists up, feet dancing like a fat Ali's.

"Daddy, I akst him to take my picher."

It *was* the girl who asked. Her voice was a sweet high squeak, and he
could have kissed her on both cheeks, this little girl whose face he hadn't
wanted in his lens. Her father melted too, dropped his fists, shook his heavy
jowls in disgust.

Steward beat his retreat then and there. What did the guy think he was
doing? Seducing little girls for porn flicks? It was beyond his imagination. It
was an afternoon wasted, a long bus ride to nowhere and back, and he felt
the shame of backing down in front of those little boys as acutely as he used
to feel the shame of hearing his grandfather sweet-talk Gloria. Things
didn't change that fast.

Now he'd have to wander throught these streets (like the enlisted men's
in Due East, he saw now) rather than wait at the bus stop up the block.
Paranoia surged—this guy could have friends in all these houses, and the
friends could all have big Barlows, knives that would glint in this cold
winter light—and he followed up with a line thrown over his shoulder.

"You better pay for my tape recorder, man," he called back. "I'm gonna come back here looking for you and you better have a couple hundred dollars ready."

Oh yeah.

Oh yeah, like he needed the money. The Synchronex was a shitty excuse for a system anyway and he should be going out with a 16 and a real crew and a real idea, not just pissing the film and the tape and the money away. He should grow up.

"Get outta here fore I cut you good."

"You better have that money when I come looking, Jack."

Oh yeah. Oh yeah, like he was gonna come looking, the guy who had to be rescued by a twelve-year-old girl with three plastic balls in her hair. The guy who had to be rescued in the Irish Channel by Simone.

Simone, who lay sweating in his bed, needing him.

He made himself walk at a slow steady pace for a block, and then he broke into a run.

He was still running when he let himself in the front door and up the dark stairs. He pictured Simone propped up on pillows, waiting for him. She, who pulled her hair back tight in a ballerina's bun and painted her nails pale pink, was always a vision of order; but in this sickness she had let the hair scraggle loose on the pillow and the nail polish chip away, and he took these relaxations as signs of rare neediness. She had slept the morning away.

But she was not propped up on pillows. Now she was up and around in the kitchen, not the bedroom, her hair pulled tight after all, her long form elegant in a white satin nightgown with a chef's apron strapped trim as a military vest. She was standing at the stove, heating oil for rice, fixing him his supper when he aimed to take care of her.

"You get you some good footage, honey?" On her feet she wore a pair of white slippers that might have suited a doll: they had elegant square two-inch heels and cut-out toes. Her pink toenails shimmered through. The slippers were the only things she ever wore that called Lola to mind, her only possessions to draw the line between sophisticated and sexy a little too fine.

"Simone! Get on back to bed. Let me take care of you."

She turned and gave him an exasperated smile. "I haven't been running a fever in twenty-four hours, baby. I got to get up and move around or my limbs'll atrophy."

"Come on." He took her by the shoulders and sat her at the little kitchen table and felt her forehead twice. It was true. There was no fever. Her forehead was damp and cool and glistening. Lola had taught him that: in the South, a man sweats. A woman glistens.

"You should have let me call a doctor in."

"I told you, Stew, you can't get a doctor to make a house call in New Orleans." Her father was a doctor: she should know.

"You can if you pay him enough."

She gave him a nose-crinkled look filled with the sort of good-natured accusation she'd never make directly: *you think you can buy anything. You think a white doctor's different.* But it was always hard to say with Simone, hard to say whether she was resentful of his money and his race or he was too sensitive. Simone didn't fuss. Her personality was as graceful as the simple white gown, and Steward assumed it was the Ursulines who had cultivated her understatement.

Now she let her oil smoke while she sat with him, and coughed, as if she was willing to let him be right about something. She was sick.

He shook his head. "I found some kids, but they didn't want to—talk."

Simone didn't say a word.

"I shouldn't be trying to make a movie about something I don't know a thing about."

This was something she had hinted herself, but now she squeezed his hand in sympathy, and coughed again.

"You sure you o.k., sitting up?"

She laughed and shook her cooking spoon at him. "Hey, you. I'm an independent woman."

"Telling me." He choked on the word *woman* to describe girls he knew, but it fit Simone. He'd tried to get her to fill out applications for graduate school in tandem with his, but she was happy at Tulane, happy in her hometown. She meant to stay on all the way, first in her family to go for a doctorate. And he meant to stake his claim while he was off in film school, keep paying the rent on this place—though whether she'd accept it from him was another question.

"Listen, I've been thinking. If we don't get you down to Due East to meet Mama on spring break then I don't know *when* it's gonna be. I was thinking about buying the tickets tomorrow." Where did that impulse come from? Always in a rush.

She rose and slid the smoking pan off the burner. They'd had this talk, or started it, a dozen times, and always the subject moved her from her chair. From behind he imagined that her neck stretched taut, but the truth was, her neck was always stretched taut. Posture training from the nuns?

"Really, Simone. I want you to meet her."

She emptied a cup of rice into the oil and it spattered up like rain on a summer sidewalk. "Uhnhunh baby," she said, her voice thickening. "It's not a good idea." She let loose a hammering cough, and let him sit her down again.

"I'll cook the rice," he said. "You get on back to bed."

"Don't want to go to bed," she said, but sweetly, the way she said everything, even *Unhunh baby, it's not a good idea.* She was the most agreeable girl—woman—he had ever met. When he hinted about garter belts, didn't she go out and charge one? She kept this dive immaculate, her own possessions stacked into neat piles: *Paris Vogue, Libération,* Simone Weil. Even her ideas were neatly closeted: they talked politics, but not religion. He'd met her sister, but not her three brothers; he knew her mother was a nurse (that accounted for the Lysoled bathroom) but he had no idea whether she was as sleek a dresser as her daughter. Lola would shock Simone: he sometimes thought that was why he pushed so hard for the meeting, and not just because Lola pressed him in turn.

Just can't wait to meet that little girlfriend of yours, Stewie.

Little girlfriend. The truth was, Lola—unpredictable as she was—was liable to freak. Simone would shock Lola too, and she'd shock the retired officer Lola was dating now. He'd begged her to come home with him last summer—*get it over with*—but Simone had stayed in New Orleans.

He'd had to meet Lola's new sweetie on his own, and just as well. Lola had him drive out to Colonel Parrish's house on the creek for a barbecue. There were a pair of brass eagles over the colonel's red double doors, and an American flag flying. His mailbox read *Col. Charles G. Parrish, USMC Ret.*

He had not looked forward to meeting Colonel Charles G. Parrish, Ret. He resented meeting Lola's boyfriend while Simone hid out in New Orleans. He'd made his way through the colonel's house, down a path of insipid green carpeting, to the barbecue out back. In the kitchen at the back of the hall, a maid in pink uniform, her buttons straining to contain her, was punishing crackers with Cheez Whiz. She did not so much as lift her head when Steward passed through. She was black—all maids in Due East were black—her hair pomaded and turned under in a pageboy. He admired her refusal to greet him.

Beyond, the backyard was a flat slab of lawn shimmering like asphalt in

the afternoon sun. He stopped at the back steps to pull Lola into sight.
Scattered around the yard in clusters of two or three were retired officers
(had to be, with that ramrod posture). Their hair was silver, and their biceps
formed modest bulges underneath their polo shirts.

He stayed by the back of the house, searching for Lola in the dead
center of the yard, where the small pool was enclosed in a chain-link fence
that made it look like some county recreational facility. Inside, where the
ladies had all been corralled, the wives' bronzed golfing legs were curled
and stretched on lawn chairs and chaises longues. They all had good sensible
fluffy haircuts.

Finally he saw Lola emerging from a nest of men down at the edge of
the bluff, her highball glass wavering in her hand. Her black hair, burnished
in the afternoon light, was teased higher than Jayne Mansfield's. She was the
only one in a bikini, and naturally it was hot pink, revealing itself under an
unbuttoned sheer black shirt that looked more like a baby doll nightie than
it did a cover-up. The bikini top was too small, and her brown bazooms
spilled out. He remembered profound gratitude that this wasn't Simone's
first vision of Lola.

His mother was leaving a trio of men, her long painted nails reaching
out to touch one, two, three of them on their taut forearms. Then one,
two, three of them glanced over their shoulders to see if their wives were
watching. There was a sudden swell of birdlike twittering from inside the
cage as Lola, on high-heeled mules, caught sight of him and bobbed over to
hug him close.

From the corner of his eye he registered the man who had to be Col.
Charles G. Parrish, Ret., approaching, eyes squinted tight and distrustful as
the brass eagles' eyes on his own front doors.

Later Gloria said: *My cousin say he saw you at the colonel's house, Steward.
She say you a good-looking boy, bet you got a mess of women chasing after you.*

Now he sat in the kitchen with an elegant woman who would freak his
mother and her colonel out. Now he sat with a woman who glistened, who
fit the Southern definition of lady and wouldn't even be considered for the
designation. He coughed.

"Oh sweetie you're catching my bug."

Steward pictured Simone walking with him through Col. Chuck Parrish's house, past the maid slapping Cheez Whiz on the crackers. He pictured Simone in his grandmother's drawing room; last summer when he
paid his call the old lady said: "Tell me all bout your pretty girlfriends in
New Orleans, Stew." He'd been tempted. It was hard to say who'd be

more shocked if he and Simone showed up at the River Street house, Gloria or his grandfather.

He would cause a riot, bringing Simone home to Due East. New Orleans was one thing—a sophisticated city, if Southern. They had trouble enough as it was. He coughed her cough again, a full-blown throat-closing gag.

She laughed, sweetly of course, and now she was the one to drag him to the chair to sit. Everything sweet with her on Bourbon Street, but not in the Gaudets' living room with her brothers. Safe in New Orleans, but not in Due East. Her glistening fingers worked along his back—she wasn't the only one with taut muscles—but he longed for more than her touch. More what? More feeling? More riotous impulses? What was his rush?

He pictured Franny, little provocateur, pushing herself against him for a good-bye forever embrace and saw her husband's face splotched over, stoned and pissed. That was the lot Franny'd chosen—impulse, anger, passion—and hadn't he been relieved to be rid of it? Hadn't he been grateful for Simone's good sense, her modesty after a lifetime of Lola's spilling bazooms? Didn't he tell her she was doing the right thing, staying in New Orleans, getting the doctorate, setting herself up for an academic life? They'd be a safe couple on a university campus. His throat closed tighter.

Simone's fingers worked their way up his neck and his head hung down into his chest, almost relaxed. "I really wish . . ."

"Unhunh baby," she said. "It's not a good idea to meet your mama just now," and she went back to her supper on the stove. Simone could be distant, if not cold, when her mind was made up. Steward's head slumped down on his chest, and he felt the January flu seeping into his muscles and joints and bones.

BAD

Four years of marriage gone by, two babies and a third on the way, but still they hadn't settled into any rhythms. It was as if they wanted to take turns being babies themselves: Michael raising his fist, temples black with rage, or Franny chanting that she *would* paint, she would, she would.

Just now it was Michael's turn to be the baby. Franny was looking down on Michael and his brother from the top of the stoop, but she might have been on top of a playground slide. Below, Billy was acting like a sulking bad boy—he had more important things to do than help them with this move—and Michael was another two-year-old.

No, not a two-year-old. Michael looked like a real juvenile delinquent, butt out the corner of his mouth, short sleeves rolled up shorter to hold his cigarettes. Billy, inside the truck digging out boxes, was encased in tight black devil pants. Silly little bulge at his crotch, black shirt unbuttoned to the waist, black boots that weighed twenty pounds apiece. She'd love to paint him on velvet—that was where he belonged. Billy was a mess. He'd dropped out of Fordham after one semester and claimed to be making a living in a heavy metal band, but you just knew he had to be dealing to pay his rent. His hair was halfway down his back, silky blond hair, you could see him conditioning it every night and throwing on the peroxide once a week.

Michael and Billy had been doing the hauling up to the fourth floor all morning, but they were beer-soaked and slow. By lunchtime their growls were enough to wake the dead, so Kate and Peggy took over the carrying and left them out here by the truck to cool down. How could you be anything but ecstatic, her best friends in the world living in New York and toting Michael's books up the stairs?

And her children were Brooklyn kids already, Brian wheeling Martin's stroller up and down the block. "We're here," she sang out from the top of their stoop. "We're here, Brooklyn. The Burkes are back in town."

Michael didn't even bother to roll his eyes at her ecstasy. He one-stepped onto the back of the U-Haul to deliver more complaints to Billy, and a transmission of *Jesus Christ*s garbled out from the back of the van. A curse on their new life, but he couldn't get her down. She was out of Washington, living in New York City finally, with two cherubs for children and a third on the way.

"Whoo-ee," she said, to no one. "All right."

At this Michael finally stuck his head out of the back of the truck. Hard to say what had him more depressed: the new job, the old neighborhood, or the third baby in four years. All right, it was a heavy dose of babies, but look at Brian, three years old and perfectly capable of minding Martin.

"Brian! Watch out now. Don't let it wobble like that, sugar."

Pretty capable, anyway. By the time the third baby shot out Brian would be an old hand at baby-sitting and Martin would be next in line. She'd have them trained better than Doris ever managed AgnesAnn and Teresa, and they'd be good-humored besides. Right now Brian thought it pretty amusing to run the stroller fast until he reached the eruption in the sidewalk where the maple root pushed out.

"Jesus Christ!"

Michael emerged from the van with a milk crate full of baby books and caught his older son in the act of ramming Martin over the cracked sidewalk and letting him dangle. Martin wailed. Skinny picture books floated out into the day when Michael went to grab Brian by the elbow. Hard. Hard hollers. She couldn't bear to look.

She ducked back inside the entranceway and passed Peggy huffing and puffing on her way down, her head covered in a red-checked kerchief attached to a blue elastic band. You couldn't get depressed with Peggy Barnacle in town. Underneath the kerchief were her new black-rimmed aviator glasses and clip-on glass diamond earrings. She was better than a circus act. It was Columbus Day, or otherwise she would have been off teaching fourth grade at Our Lady of Guadalupe in the Bronx.

"Let's get this show on the road." Peggy was yelling at the invisible Billy, inside the truck. She took the crate of books from Franny's arms. "Are you out of your mind? You'll go into labor."

She bossed Franny back up the stairs. Peggy was an old ashthmatic lady, but Franny took them two at a time. She was flying lately, flying from vitamins the size of horse pills, flying since she got over the shock of this latest pregnancy. But once she got over it, once she passed through denial and woozy fatigue, she was higher than Michael with the spoon stuck up his nose.

Michael had moved them up to New York before her fourth month was out. If cocaine had any advantages, quick decisions was right at the top of the list. He'd been editing the alumni magazine at JUA for a year and had parlayed that into an editing job for a computer magazine. He didn't know how to work a screwdriver, much less a computer, but there you were. Twice the money the Jesuits paid, and the rent in Brooklyn was only a couple of hundred dollars more than the Jesuit place in Georgetown. So they came out ahead and she got to live in New York City, Paris around the corner.

But Michael was still in a state of shock. When he had the sudden inspiration to break from the Jesuits and head for New York, he'd been thinking Manhattan. He'd been planning to raise his babies in the Village. Very cool, cool young father making money, cool babies, cool Sunday afternoons in Washington Square. Then he went up one weekend to look for a place, and saw in a flash that the new salary was a pittance. The office in Union Square was a hole. They'd have to live in a tenement. He'd never be able to touch a priest for a loan again.

Franny was the one who looked in Brooklyn, and he'd never forgive her for it, even if he was the one who signed the lease in the end. They were four and a half blocks from his mother now, and once a week he'd have to face Norah growing old. They were a block and a half from Billy. Richie was close to flunking out, Frank was a flake, Hannie and Nellie were running around with the worst boys in the neighborhood. He had a new family's troubles to deal with, and now an old family's too.

"I read an article in the *Times*," Peggy said. They were on the third-floor landing and she had to hold onto the wall to get her breath. "Or maybe it was the *Voice*. Something about families renovating brownstones in Park Slope. I gotta hand it to Michael. A regular social seer. Always the first with what's happening."

"I don't think he thinks it's *happening*, a couple of blocks from his mother. You go down to the park, it's like Woodstock Grows Up. Every-body's wearing Birkenstocks, I swear. Some yogurt mom told me I had to join the food co-op to get whole-wheat noodles. I said, well where do you get the Cap'n Crunch?"

"Yoohoo!" Peggy said. "You bring your kids up in Brooklyn, you damn well better have them drinking Yoohoo. And listen, you better buy a brownstone quick if they're writing the place up in the *Voice*."

"Sure, us with a house."

Peggy was still panting, hard. It would be a haul every day, up the stoop and then the two flights with three little ones and strollers and groceries.

But you couldn't even think those thoughts, or you'd never get through the day. "C'mon Peggy. Come see my roof." She stopped off to yell through the apartment door for Kate to come too.

Kate Rooney. Franny hardly knew her. Kate Rooney of Due East, of the dresses with the hems an inch longer than anybody else's, was now Kate Rooney of off-off-Broadway in a green felt hat and good tight jeans. Franny would have killed for her boots, pointy-toed and sleek. Michael stiffened meeting her. She'd been to Juilliard, and he'd been out of town too long. It would take him a while to figure out New York again, and meanwhile there was the wife in the shlumpy shift and the two kids and the big rent and his oafish brother.

"You can't climb up there." Peggy, more old-womanish than ever, actually had a hand on Franny's back, trying to restrain her from hoisting herself up the narrow roof ladder. There was a full foot between the rungs. Hard to negotiate—by the third pregnancy, you popped out early and big —but she was going to be negotiating them in her ninth month, so she might as well get the practice in.

"You couldn't hold her back she wanted to *jump* from that roof," Kate said. So Peggy let loose, and Franny worked the bar free and hoisted up the hatch. The October day flooded down on them, gray and gold. She scrambled up. Kate swung behind her, but she had to thrust an arm down to haul Peggy over the top.

"You're not gonna do that ever again till that baby is born, you gotta promise me!" Peggy was still huffing and puffing.

"I'll be doing it every day," Franny said, "and when the baby comes it'll have to do it too. Ain't life grand?"

Peggy crawled onto the slab of tar paper, a rectangle. It took your breath away to think that this eighteen-by-fifty-foot plot of roof was the space the five of them were going to live in below. Franny had figured out a way to haul up the easel from the fire escape, on pulleys. The sun shimmied down through sheets of clouds, and all around her was a panorama of cityscape for the painting, clock towers and bell towers and water towers. The swoop of the Brooklyn-Queens Expressway and the big brick projects beyond. The bridges, like dreams: Brooklyn, Manhattan, Williamsburg.

"This is better than Paris." She heard herself crowing and felt the October sun oozing down like syrup. She ran to the edge and leaned over, far over the plain-ridged cornice, and heard Peggy clearing her throat for a warning. Down on the sidewalk her little boys shrieked. The leaves were half down from the maple trees, scarlet and flaming orange.

"Hey Brooklyn," she yelled again from the rooftop. "The Burkes are back in town."

Tonight she was sketching Michael, what she always did when she fell in love. And she was in love with Michael now, but his face was obscured behind a dark fist and he could not maintain the long curve of his body. It was ten o'clock, and he was curled on the couch, alternately surveying the unpacked boxes and drifting off. Every few minutes a paroxysm jerked him. For these first two weeks in Brooklyn, big as she was growing, he had not known she existed.

She groaned when the bell rang—it would be Billy back to bicker some more—and Michael opened his eyes to moan in harmony. Back in his family's world, his solitude was complete. He reminded her of those male elephants in Brian's nature books, cast out by the females and doomed to roam the plains alone.

"Don't answer it." Michael managed to hold one eye open.

The bell persisted. He opened the other eye.

"I'll make him go away," she said, and ran down the stairs three at a time.

But it wasn't Billy standing on their step, it was Kevin Byrne, sweet Kevin who'd once cleared out of his own bed for her sake. First her friends, and now Michael's: a miracle.

"Francie!" She wouldn't have known him through the glass, but he was the only person in the world who called her Francie. He rattled the door handles and shook the frames, another male elephant, an old friend to roam the plains of Brooklyn with Michael. Before she had the big front door open properly, Kevin swooped down on her, and when they were wedged together he squeezed her until she thought she might turn blue. He held her close, one arm around her shoulder, and limped up the stairs, his breath as short as Peggy's.

"Oh Kevin, how'd we get all our people around us again?"

They grinned together like loons, and she ushered him into the floor-through. You could see the shock on Michael's face at the sight of Kevin, but then you could see the shock on Kevin's face too, right through the goofy smile. They were only halfway through their twenties. How did they get this old? Kevin was probably taking in the deep ridges that curved down the sides of Michael's mouth, Mick Jagger ridges that gave him a cruel look when he was tired.

Kevin had put on twenty pounds, and there were horn-rims where his wire-rims used to be. His hair seemed to be thinning on top—but that couldn't be. It had a not-lately-washed look that went slinking over the top of his collar. A collar. That was a shock in itself, a pin-striped shirt that his belly pushed out way before his belt buckle started. His fingers were thick and his skin was bad, his nose a regular beacon. Drink or coke or, knowing Kevin, both.

"Oh man," Michael said. "Oh shit, how'd you know we were here? What are you *do*ing here, man? Last I heard you were wandering around Dublin."

"Dublin's fucking cold in the winter." Kevin still smiled with his head ducked down, but his voice was stronger since he'd been out in the real world.

"Yeah, but how'd you hear we were in Brooklyn?"

"Billy told me, man."

"You been hanging around Billy?"

"Not when I can help it. I saw him in Mahoney's tonight."

"Mahoney's! Jesus, are the cadavers still lined up by the bar?"

"Yeah sure," Kevin said. "They got topless cadavers now."

Michael's face went white.

"Just kidding, man. No actually, I scored tonight, ya wanna do a line?"

Kevin stood to pull out his cache, and Franny slipped out of the room to leave them to their ritual. Just like the old days, boyhoods marked by the sharing of illicit substances: egg creams when they were supposed to be fasting for Mass, cigarettes in front of the candy store, first underage beer at Mahoney's, up and out from there.

They were silent in the front room, but Michael had been stirred from his moving-back-to-Brooklyn blues. She let them be and wandered through the railroad apartment. The brownstone was old and musty, the rooms narrow, all the closets twentieth-century afterthoughts bulging out from corners. She loved it. In the little dining room (for now—in five months it would hold a crib and a squalling baby) there was a plaster-relief panel, Greek maidens draping garlands. That's what she was, a Greek maiden, a girl again with her friends close, happy at home. Domestic bliss. She was going to paint her arm off before this baby came.

She sidestepped the boxes and made her way back to Brian and Martin's room. No sense standing over them, they slept so deeply, but she did. Might as well say a prayer that Brian-and-Martin wouldn't turn into Michael-and-Billy, puffing up their chests in each other's face. Tomorrow

she'd be in here to whiten their bone-colored walls, and Brian could have
that far one for drawing. She stood by their long window and looked out
into the backyard, deeper than the yard in Georgetown, an unpainted
picket fence enclosing it. They couldn't use it, but they could look down
on it. She'd have to teach the boys not to go close to the edge, and then the
roof could be their play yard, that and the pavement their father once
pounded.

Back in her own bedroom, she looked in on Michael and Kevin
through the arch, Weather Report playing now. The one useful thing Billy
had done was hook up the stereo, but not before he sniggered over their
little speakers. Still pulling out his dick and comparing it to Michael's.

Michael and Kevin had finished snorting up their evening's entertainment and were leaned back, the two of them, maybe listening to the music.

"So whatcha think of the new job?"

"Enh. Money's o.k."

Long Zawinul riff on the stereo, long stretch of silence from Kevin and
Michael. Franny pulled out socks from a moving box and stuffed them in a
bureau drawer, just for the comfort of being close to them.

"Whatcha doing back in the neighborhood?"

"Living home. Big drag."

"Back on the park, huh."

"I hate it, man."

More long silence. No wonder the male elephants were cast out.

"You looking for work? Cause the magazine's taking off—"

"No man, I got a job. Teaching English at Cardinal Newman. It's cool
. . . but you ever try and get it together on a hundred and fifty a week?"

"Yeah well, you get your ma's cooking. Probably a damn sight better
than Franny's cooking."

"I heard that."

"You were meant to."

"Don't listen to him, Kevin. He does the cooking, anyway."

"Gotta, I wanna survive around here."

"What is this, the Honeymooners?"

"Billy said you got a third one coming?—I can't believe it. Can't
fucking believe it. And meanwhile I'm driving my old man crazy, living
home. He wants me to get a gig on the street."

"Yeah?"

"Yeah. Young Stock Broker or some shit."

Long pause. Franny moved on to unpacking underwear.

"You writing?"

"Yeah, well. In the middle of the night when I can. These babies, man . . . You?"

"Nah." Pause. "Nah."

Michael was starting to jiggle, shifting on the couch, sitting up higher, buzzing, but Kevin was sinking down in their presence. Michael remembered that he was the hero of this happy family, husband of this happy pregnant wife, possessor of this happy job. This happy high. Kevin slumped lower. His red nose glowered.

"Hey Francie, come sit with us." Plaintive as a country song. Kevin patted the couch, and swirls of dust, the dust they brought with them from Washington, danced through the air. "C'mon Francie. Whatcha doing with yourself now? Dincha ever hear of Zero Population Growth?"

Franny pulled a handful of Michael's underwear from the packing carton, the material worn down to gauze dangling from an elastic band.

"I'm doing great, Kevin. The galleries are begging to see me."

"Oh yeah?"

"Yes indeed. They come crawling over the Brooklyn Bridge. I'm planning on a dozen babies and I'm going to train them all to hand me my brushes and stretch me my canvases. Then at night they can cook for Mister Particular here."

Kevin's body collapsed into itself on the couch, stricken by her good cheer and the sight of her holding her husband's underwear. This girl they used to sneak into the dorm room. He didn't ask her to sit again. He mumbled something, in the old marbles-in-the-mouth way, something about getting to work in the morning. It was hard to catch. When he rose to leave, and held her close again, Michael gave him a good hard cocaine stare.

"Gotta get you a woman, Byrne."

Kevin coughed. He was almost doubled, dragging down the stairs, hanging onto the banister, Old Man Kevin Byrne, lonely and hopeless.

"Oh man, Kev's in *bad* shape," Michael said when they heard the last clump down the stairs, but he was happy, the lightest he'd sounded all day. "Gotta cheer that guy up, huh, Francie?"

"Don't you call me Francie, you elephant. Only Kevin's allowed."

"I'll call you Francie if I care to." Now Michael was grinning, spinning, and she was flirting with him, shameless. He circled the room, paused at the windows, fanned out the shutters, looking with different eyes. Now it was a charming apartment. Tomorrow he'd be looking around Brooklyn with different eyes. He was happy again, high again. Now he was dancing her around the room, hand tight against the small of her back, her big belly bumping out into his. Now he was pushing her into the bedroom, down, down, onto the bed. They'd bought a bed frame for New York City. Michael had insisted.

"C'mon Miss Francie. Let's be bad and see can we wake up those neighbors downstairs. Rock and roll."

He was just high, but he was happy. She held on tight when he kissed her, her hands entwined behind his neck, and the new bed let out a groan. He was happy again, his hipbones jutting into hers, and she—for all her bulk—was growing smaller. Her turn to collapse back down to child size. Her turn, a stranger growing inside her, to shiver as another stranger's body entered. Her turn to be frightened.

Michael walked out for a beer with Kevin now and again, and left for work at seven in the morning, some terrifying new initiative driving him. When he came out of the bathroom in his new sports coat and tie he broke her heart. A tie. And three kids in New York City, soon. He'd cut his hair short before he left Washington, at a real barber's.

Every morning on the way out the door he said: "Heavy new life," but then, he was escaping all these boxes still unpacked. He winked from the second-floor landing. Every morning, they watched him down the stairs, Martin in her arms and Brian grabbing at her legs before she had time to let Housewife Horror overcome her.

"G'bye Bri, protect the premises. G'bye Martin, keep an eye on that mother of yours."

He was off, but sometimes the bell would ring again, before they were dressed. It was always Kevin.

"Michael just left. D'you see him in the street?" Franny stood downstairs at the front door in a frilly billowing flannel nightgown Doris had given her. She meant it to cover a four-months pregnancy, but a bald man with a briefcase passed by on the sidewalk and sent a frank stare up the stoop. When she lowered her eyes she could see rosebud nipples through the gown. Any other woman would have put on a robe, but she didn't own a robe, actually.

"Didn't see him." Kevin was as cheerful as he'd been the night before, when they kicked him out at midnight.

"Well, come on up." You'd think Kevin would see she didn't mean that, not really, not at seven o'clock in the morning, but he barged on in, as always. This time he had brought a bag of onion bagels in his satchel, flecks of sweet sticky brown spilling out onto his freshman essays. Sweet Kevin. You couldn't get more innocent than thinking to bring them bagels, but still, she went to get one of Michael's father's old flannel robes.

When she came back to the kitchen, he had Martin in his lap. Martin was a sweetie who never slept. His chin was pointed like his brother's, but he was even more of a pixie, blond and skinny and compact. You'd swear his ears were pointed too. He'd be wiry like his father, and now in his fuzzy sleeper he wiggled back and forth in Kevin's lap. Brian was in their room, throwing every truck he owned out of a milk crate so he could show Kevin the one that said Good Humor.

They were all in a good humor, these guys. Brian found the truck finally and held it out, jealous of Martin wriggling on the broad expanse of Kevin's lap.

"O.k., Brian. O.k., sugar. Listen now, Kevin's got to go to work." This morning he was lingering: the clock on the stove said seven twenty-seven. She held out her arms to take Martin.

"Well, I've got half an hour," Kevin said, "if you've got a cup of coffee."

She smiled at him and dropped her arms back down to her side. He probably didn't even know he'd been staring like that, at the open robe, at her swollen body under the nightgown.

But Brian, jealous ally of his father's, protector of the premises, reported back to Michael: *Why does Kevin stare at Mommy that way?* and then volunteered that Kevin dropped by every morning. Not *every* morning, Franny said, but Michael wanted to know why he hadn't heard of *any*.

"Because it's Kevin."

"Horny bastard. Let him find his own wife and kids."

"Michael. Your best friend."

Your only friend. Now Michael left later for work, and turned the lights off early in the front room at night so Kevin, on the sidewalk, would think they'd gone to bed. The doorbell went unanswered, and sometimes the phone.

The packing boxes were still piled to the ceiling, though they hadn't owned anything to begin with. After Michael went to work Franny heard doorbells all day, but there weren't any ringing. It was only the little boys tearing through the house and bawling and banging each other over the head, a yowling so constant it was no wonder she heard bells.

One Saturday she woke with her right eyeball aching and swollen and the urge to poke someone else in exactly the same spot.

"You mind them today, Michael. I'm so sick of them I could throw them out the window."

Michael stood dopey, watching cartoons, but Brian heard her. He left the television long enough to scoop Martin up by the armpits and drag him over to the low window seat. It was hard to say if he was only still in a good humor, or if he really meant to hurl his brother out the window.

"Oh no you don't." She scooped the two of them up herself, and punched the television off, and delivered them over to their father. "Michael here, for God's sake, I've got to get out."

She heard her snappishness: Doris again, and too bad. She was sick to death of Michael's petty jealousy—he'd driven away his only friend, and her only break in the day—and she was sinking in the mire of lonely domesticity. Kate and Peggy moved through the real world, while she sat in the park and listened to the Birkenstock mothers exchange tofu recipes and fuss over the academic progress of toddlers.

"Hey, Franny, take the whole day. Look, stay out all night if you need to. Have some fun."

Now that she'd reached her limit and couldn't bear to be in the same room with him, Michael held his sons easy, one in each arm, and beamed down, proud father, adoring husband.

"You *need* a break. Right, guys?"

The sweeter he was, the blacker her mood. She went to comb her hair in a high snit, and by the time she phoned Kate her childish temper burned bright. Out of love? Or only weary? There were times she thought she'd rather fling herself over this railing than go through with another childbirth.

But this time it was Michael standing on the landing with Martin in his arms and Brian with an arm around his leg. This time it was Michael looking down, possessive, as she tramped the stairs and stopped at the second-floor landing and winked up at them—contemptuous gesture, she saw now that she was doing it herself—the way he did every morning.

By the time the train pulled into West Fourth, she had pressed her right eye closed, but Kate would cure her. Kate would be better than analyst or confessor. From Washington Square, they would walk down Thompson to SoHo, and the pounding in her eye would let up the closer they got to the galleries. She paced at the arch, waiting for Kate, her swollen body swaying back and forth. Her time alone in the blue light.

Finally she saw a blip tooling across Waverly Place, but Kate arrived at the arch fit to burst, waving her arms to say she couldn't talk. She hadn't seen Kate in such a state since childhood. Once, and not that long ago, they'd circled the dust-and-asphalt yard of Due East Junior High School, giggling, spinning gossip. Now they circled Washington Square Park before Kate could speak. Her arm was tucked into Franny's New York style: two best girlfriends in the Village, one of them distraught. So it would be Franny's turn to be analyst and confessor.

Finally Kate began: "I don't know what's worse, his doing it or his telling me." It was the old story—Kate's boyfriend, drunk at a party, had gone home with another actress and confessed that very morning.

Kate, her arm untucked since she unburdened herself, veered over the sidewalk. They rounded the park a second time, and druggies on park benches recognized them and perked up, all googly-eyed for Kate, her red hair piled high and her good dark boots pounding out her anger.

"Well," Franny said. The pressure in her eye was easing by degrees. "You know if he feels that guilty it must have been one of those spur-of-the-moment things. One of those things that just didn't mean anything." Could words have sounded more false? *Didn't mean anything.* Kate would never believe that and neither did she. Everything meant something, everything you did. You threatened to throw your kids out the window, and they went to throw each other out. You went to answer the doorbell in a nightgown, and your son told his father.

"Michael ever cheated on you?—Oh sorry. None of my business."

Kate began to march the perimeter of the park yet again—they would never see SoHo on this Saturday—and Franny kept pace. One foot after the other. They were best friends from the time they were six. It was all mutual business, far as she was concerned, but she could hardly speak Michael's name, the need to protect him a bubble in her throat. He'd seemed so worldly when she met him, that girl with the abortions behind him. Now it was funny to even think the word *worldly* about Michael.

"I don't *think* so," she said.

"I'm sorry," Kate said, apologizing to the pigeons and the squirrels, addressing the sidewalk in a new breathless voice, "I may be the last person in America but I just don't be*lieve* in that stuff, that free love–open marriage–let it all hang out stuff. *Damn,* he thinks he can grovel and that's it, I forgive him, it's all behind now, but, *damn it,* what he doesn't see is how he just sliced my heart open."

The gooey drama of *sliced my heart open* made her stop on the sidewalk.
Beat. Walk. Stop again, overcome. Franny recognized a female rhythm that
was a counterpart to Michael's timing when he was on a roll. Two actors.

Her right eye throbbed anew. She'd never told anyone.

"You know, Kate"—she had to skip on after her, Kate's feet pounding.
This was a bizzare sort of comfort to offer—"you know I, uh, cheated on
Michael."

It was November. Kate was wearing a mustard-colored suede jacket,
and when she turned to hear Franny the entire park seemed washed in that
same muddy shade of yellow: leaves above and light through the branches
and Kate's jacket and the gleam of interest in her eye. "You mean, since you
got married?"

She'd never told a soul. "Well yeah. Twice." Which was not technically
true, she'd forgotten about Declan McCleary, which made three guys, and
the other two had gone on for weeks. *Twice* was a little disingenuous.

But a little hopeful smile played on Kate's full pale mouth, the same
hopeful smile that played when Franny told her about Tony Rivers, a
million years ago. *Oh Franny, you can't do that. You'll get pregnant.* Back then
Kate's wide mouth teetered between fear and pleasure. Now they circled
Washington Square Park, and the yellow light seemed to cast the question
in terms of right and wrong.

"When'd you have time to cheat on him, all these babies?"

So black, that December. So black and not a soul to tell, not even
Peggy, especially not Peggy, who would have had her in a battered-
women's shelter if she'd breathed a word about Michael's jaw quivering, or
the paint jars swept from the shelf, shattered. Michael raising his fist, knowing enough not to bring it down again but so full of fury, at her and at Brian
and at the vise of family, that he had a fierce need to frighten them, himself
most of all.

"Oh, it was, it was a bad time." A bad time. She remembered herself
stiff with longing, missing Due East and dreaming of her father, memory
itself slipping away from her. Some mornings that year she'd wake thinking
she held a communion host on her tongue: the smooth round disc of her
girlhood. But it was only the lump of too much wine the night before.

It was a long time ago, back when she was holding her own girlhood by
a thin leash. Before her father died those boys were *good fellows,* sweet guys
who smelled of brine and came too fast. Married and a mother, she went
looking for bad guys. Michael raised his fist, Michael said there was no

money to get her down to Due East, but she would get there for Christmas, she would, she would.

Not a chance, Michael said. Not a prayer. Three weeks before Christmas, she wept on the whole bus ride out to JUA, childish and homesick and bad. A bad girl. When she got to the campus, she went straight to Steedman, who'd always watched her. Was this a *thing* you did when you were trapped, the way other women shoplifted? Steedman, who'd finally finished his dissertation, was ready to be reckless. By the end of the morning he was nuzzling her neck in his office in Philosophy Hall. She stripped down fast, before he even got the venetian blinds closed all the way. Young and bad and exhilarated.

But the next morning she was weeping even before she left for the campus, weeping as she turned Brian over to Mrs. Schmidt in the Georgetown apartment.

"I always cry myself before Christmas," Mrs. Schmidt said, but Franny could only picture the old lady scrubbing Brian's ears too hard. She wanted to get him away from Washington and Mrs. Schmidt. She wanted to see Walter and Caroline. She longed for Doris, for AgnesAnn.

When Steedman wasn't in his office she went looking for a fix. She'd never taken an anthropology class from Artosaurus, but he'd made a pass at her once at a faculty party. He was a pudgy man with a high reedy giggle, his dark oily hair slicked straight back. Full professor, big office. He spoke to women slowly, with a smutty voice: he'd take particular pleasure knowing Franny's husband was at work in the first nine-to-five job of his life, three buildings away.

It took longer with Artosaurus, days of dropping by with coffee and Danish. Where'd she get that idea? Oh, she was shameless, licking the sugar off her fingers, watching him hesitate. All that December she went knocking on their doors, breathless, Steedman with his MW hours, Artosaurus with his TTh hours. She was as stoned as Michael got, stoned from stretching out naked on the gray faculty carpeting, stoned waiting for the knock on the door from some innocent freshman, stoned arching up against Steedman's big dark desk, stoned waiting for Artosaurus's wife to call. She did, once. Franny cringed, naked on the carpeting. Caught. Bad. She'd been letting Brian stay in bed with them at night, her little boy the wall between her and Michael.

"I don't know, things were bad between Michael and me, you know what they say—kids having a kid." And look at her now, a regular matron, confessing and comforting Kate on the sidewalk, doling out the wisdom of perspective, picturing her little ones crossing the roadway in Prospect Park on their way to the ducks. Visions of Martin darting into the road, an act of will to stay with Kate when she wanted to run all the way to Brooklyn to see if they were safe. Wanted to see Michael, who got his family up to New York City, didn't he, who worked his new ten-hour day, who hadn't written a word for himself in six months. Who'd never even thought to say *Well, we don't* have *to have this baby, do we?* He never had a clue.

"Does he know? Did you tell him?"

"Oh God no. Oh *God* no." Michael found the money for Due East; she brought her little boy down with her on the bus, cheese sandwiches flattening in their pockets. Doris bought them a poinsettia to put on Pat's grave, and day after sunny December day Brian played in the graveyard under the stumpy palmetto, on top of the wrought-iron bench. After a week she got back on the bus, and Michael met them at the Greyhound station.

Then she was pregnant with Martin, and she was safe, nothing but a bad dream, a bad trip, and she was never dropping that particular acid again.

"Did he suspect?"

"Maybe." The falseness of *that* was so clear that their talk had to stop dead. No, if Michael had suspected he would have folded up the way Kate folded into her arms now. If Michael had thought in Ireland that she was in bed with Declan McCleary while he was off saving Catholic civil rights, he'd have thrown himself in front of a moving bullet. He was so—soft, that way. So much the opposite of worldly. She'd been wrong about him, at first, wrong thinking he had girls in all his pockets, but she admired his swagger just the same. Still did, was grateful for it when it turned out he was just a fool for Martin and Brian.

"Oh Franny, I know I'll never forgive him."

Forgive him? She linked her arm again in Kate's. Their Saturday in New York. Saturdays in Due East, whole families went to confession at Our Lady of Perpetual Help, and one at a time you'd hear them tearing out of the church, whooping it up outside in the graveyard, on the sidewalks. Giddy from getting it out. Whistling, gossiping, dancing jigs. Due East, Saturday night: free to sin again. Washington Square, Saturday afternoons: Franny was close to skipping, her eye forgotten.

Kate was nearly skipping too, fired up. "Damn it, I won't be his lover and his father confessor too."

They stopped in unison and stared along the south end of the park.

There was a familiar human object walking east. A male human. Kate's boyfriend? Come to track her down and beg forgiveness yet again?

Kate grabbed her by the shoulders.

"Look," she said, and now Franny saw what she was looking at.

"Look," again. "Do you believe it? That's Steward Morehouse!"

It was. Had to be. It was Steward Morehouse, long white hair flipping out in the muddy November light, long sinewy arms dangling.

"Oh this is so strange. Franny look here—can he see I've been crying?"

Kate's eyes were green-gold in the light. There was no telling whether Kate had been crying when Franny herself couldn't see past the trembles of color in the center of her friend's eye. She shook her head a dismissive *no, no* and turned her gaze back on the sidewalk, where Steward grinned, coming toward them. He'd seen them from a distance and waved now with both hands.

Kate said: "Walking across Washington Square. You know, you see people from Due East all over the city. They're like birds flying north instead of south. I *never* thought I'd see Steward Morehouse again."

She hadn't seen him herself since the wedding, when he and Michael got into a shoving match. Now Michael was off with their babies on this Saturday afternoon, this day of confessions, and she and Kate checked their reflections in each other's eyes. Now Steward was closing the distance between them on Washington Square South.

Like birds flying north, Kate said. He looked like a great swooping gull, closing in on the catch. The sight of him made her breathless again, and just when she thought she'd found her rhythm.

THE MAN
WHO LOVED
WOMEN

It was adolescent, but just the same the pleasure of disconcerting Franny was so intense that he called her again to make sure she was coming.

Hey Stew, we're still looking for somebody to stay with the little guys. But I'm trying. I'm really trying.

Bring the guys! he said, expansive, knowing she wouldn't. But he'd been calling her with invitations for a month, and it looked like she was finally softening up. He was wagering that Franny would need to make a home-away-from-home for herself at Christmas, when she couldn't get down to Due East. He was wagering that this time she'd be willing to step back in time.

Which was what he was doing now, draping garlands over the living room window. His roommates went nuts for this decorating stuff, so for them he tried to reproduce what Grandmother did every year on River Street: pine and tinsel garlands; spruce tree straight from the woods (he had to drive almost to Kingston to find what he wanted, something drooping and idiosyncratic); bottomless silver punch bowl parked on the coffee table from Christmas week all through the twelve days. He went out to Woolworth's to get a steel bowl big enough and pictured Grandmother's face at the sight of it. She kept stately engraved bowls for library and sitting room, but the dime-store bowl was more like a trough.

He sent the roommates out with lists for the party. Good girls, they let him take charge and didn't even think it went against their feminist principles. They were all doctoral students, impractical about anything domestic. Ruth and Ellen were old friends in English (Ruth medieval, Ellen Victorian) and carried away with the notion of buying papier-mâché flying angels they could hang from every door frame in the apartment. Kay was out doing the chips-dips-veggies run. He had a little crush on Kay, who was almost finished with her biochemistry dissertation and who wore her straw-colored hair cropped short and let her funky blue horn-rims droop down on her nose. But then he had a crush on Ruth (black hair always in a functional braid) and Ellen, too (plump inviting arms and a fine dark down on her cheeks). Kay was the one who finally let him climb into her bed, twice. She had a biochemistry boyfriend, though, and the sense to say *This is not a good idea, Steward* the first time and *This is really not a good idea, Steward* the second time. And Ruth and Ellen shared a bedroom to save on rent, so there were fewer opportunities in that direction.

Tacking up the garlands, he stood on a twelfth-floor windowsill with a billion-dollar view of New Jersey, but they were up pretty far on Riverside, so they didn't pay a billion dollars. Grandfather had a fit when he came calling (a miracle he got out of the cab, which went up the East River Drive and then crossed through the whole endless expanse of Harlem, east to west, before it dropped him in front of Steward's building). Nice doorman building, lots of Columbia students, though you could hardly expect Grandfather to see that once he realized that the Riverside Drive address left Steward dangling off the edge of the world's most famous ghetto.

Below the windowsill, the Hudson flowed happily in the wrong direction. That river joined with the Due East Bay and the Mississippi to form the watery triangle that seemed to define home. He read in the *Times* that they were building a walk along the levee in New Orleans and it depressed him, made him think of Simone walking along some slick new paved tourist path while he poked through the crumbling ruins of Riverside Park.

His memories of Simone were soft around the edges, Vaseline on the lens. Sometimes walking by this river at sunset he'd catch sight of her silky slip strap. All last spring he ate his evening meal down there, among the water rats, and thought of Simone as he watched the smart snappy Upper West Side women taking their evening runs. He loved them all, loved the stretch of the west side all the way up past Morningside Heights and into Harlem. He was a New Yorker now.

They were all New Yorkers now. He thought of Kate Rooney arriving tonight at his party. Once she'd been the sour ball of his youth, pursing her lips when he tried to hold Franny's hand at some dance, but when she saw him in Washington Square that day she was all over him. Full round mouth, lips colorless as clay until she smiled, when all of her flamed. And that hair: piled up with as many swoops as he'd put in those pine and tinsel garlands. He even went down to St. Marks Place to see her revue. *Hippie Girls Bite the Dust.* Pretty terrible, but she had a pleasant alto voice that called to mind gawky Katie Rooney at the Due East Junior High School piano at assembly time.

If Kate and Franny came together tonight, he'd be sandwiched between them, tall redhead and protruding little black-haired sprite who *blushed* now at the sight of him. He never would have thought blushing was an action Franny was capable of. Though of course he never would have thought motherhood was a state she could enter into once, much less three times. And the way she played it up! That waddle. That dress. Old Indian print (could have been something Lola brought her back from New Orleans) in the middle of November, one of her husband's sweaters draped open, clunky black oxfords. Her hair pulled back in an inked rubber band. Not a pretty picture, but after all this time he could not help loving her best of all. She looked in need of loving.

Not that he would do anything tonight to make Gilda crazy. Gilda Polsky was his date, just possibly chosen for this particular event because she had the lithe slight body of Franny before these motherhood events, combined with a head of frazzled wild hair. It was just crazy irony that had reversed their situations, just a goofy what-do-you-know reversal of fortune that left him surrounded with women and Franny wrapped in her husband's old sweater.

"Stew! Come see!"

That was Ellen, calling from the front hall, so excited—yes, those were Metropolitan Museum Gift Shop bags, many Met bags—that she was pulling angels from tissue paper before she took her jacket off. A mistake to give her his American Express card instead of cash, but the flush of her cheeks under the black down was worth it.

"Whoa. How many'd y'all get?"

Now Ellen got coy and held a brown angel, wing tipped gold, up to the light. She flew it back and forth to make him forget his question.

Ruth, medieval, was more direct than Ellen, Victorian. "With tax, four eight six."

"Five hundred bucks!" Steward had a sudden vision of the two of them as teenagers, cajoling their fathers into buying them their spring wardrobes at Bergdorf Goodman.

Ellen and Ruth hung their heads together, as if on cue. Ruth's braid flopped up against the back of her head, too silly for words. Impossible to stay mad at them. He draped his arms around their shoulders and resisted the urge to bang their heads together. "Last time I send you guys out with a charge card."

They snuggled into his chest like a pair of naughty sisters, Ellen—the cuddlier one—grabbing him round the middle and squeezing.

"Let's get going." He gave each of them a mildly arousing smack on the behind. "Let's get those angels swinging from those door frames."

But were they mildly aroused too? They scrambled off, obedient. Ellen was swinging her hips, she was definitely the more likely prospect.

Back to the kitchen, to see to those raspberries. Good to have the upper hand in this apartment again—for a while, after he dropped out of film school, Ellen and Ruth bombarded him day and night with arguments for going to class.

"But Steward," Ellen said, "you'll be miserable if you can't go to the West End every afternoon."

"I can still go to the West End every afternoon." And he did. He dropped out of film school, but he went and sat across the street from Columbia with Gilda Polsky, who wrote a terrific screenplay last spring (Emma Goldman in Love), a screenplay he might have been shooting himself if she weren't using the first act for her own thesis. He'd long since discovered he was no writer. But he meant to have his final cut ready when the MFA folks had their final cuts, and he was careful not to point out to Gilda that he'd be able to rent better cameras than she'd be renting, that he'd be able to cut his film on a flatbed while she was cutting someone's throat for time at the upright.

He was doing a documentary. In Riverside Park he had met an old bird who said her name was Elizabeth Morehouse, and they'd got to chatting on a park bench about the coincidence. She seemed lucid the day they met, said she was from an old Kentucky family, but halfway through the conversation she had changed her name to Morehead and by the end, in a lovely dizzy spin, to Moreheart. Never mind. For an hour she ranted about the indignities she once endured as a Ziegfeld Follies girl.

Now Elizabeth was letting him film in her SRO room, where she sat in a folding chair and sometimes told good stories. The trick was to get enough footage shot when she was making sense and enough when she was crazy. There was a lot of dead film, her staring out, but he had the opening scene: the old lady by her narrow grimy window, the gray New York natural light on one side of her face and the harsh klieg on the other. Great schizoid image, one side of her face grainy and the other smooth clay. Elizabeth Morehouse sat very tall, with a fluffy blue beret on her head and yellowing gloves she yanked up to her elbows. She looked directly into the camera, looked away, raised her chin, sighed. Perfect timing. Maybe she *had* been a Follies girl. Finally she looked back into the lens and said:

"I am content." Voice strong despite its quaver. Not a sign of lunacy.

He meant to cut from the little palsied jig her face did on *I am content* to a long pan of the narrow room, her cot covered with damp collapsing cardboard boxes spilling overdue notices from 1958, and the little sink in the corner of the room piled with moldy paperback books, Jacqueline Susann and Thomas Merton. She let them open the closet door and film her shoes piled four feet high, a tower of high heels: delicate crane heels, see-through heels, heels splattered with sparkle. He wanted her to hold a few shoes up and tell their stories, but at this she balked. And she was right, wasn't she? Too staged. Too false.

"So let me get this straight," Kay said. This was the first time they were in bed, and Kay was still trying to figure him out. "You're doing this movie about this old lady in an SRO? So it's political?" Kay liked everything categorized.

"Well . . ." said Steward.

"Because that's the first thing you said when you interviewed me for the apartment, remember? 'I came to New York to make political movies.' "

Steward grinned. Could he have said that line? They'd been through Watergate. Your tone could lighten up, at least. "It's all political," he told Kay.

Kay had grimaced at the imprecision. And at this moment, precisely, Kay came through the door loaded down with bags of celery and cherry tomatoes.

"Stew!" Flustered from the weight of the packages, she was hollering at him from the foyer and he came running. The man of the house. He hauled the packages in while she watched with a critical eye and followed him into the kitchen, where he danced, Fred Astaire, charming and light. If they'd only shown *Top Hat* in Genre Analysis, he'd still be in film school.

Kay's glasses drooped down her nose. Her bare brown eyes bore down on him. He came close to waltz with her, but she didn't know what a Ginger she was. His arms stayed empty, and he danced with himself around their big Riverside Drive kitchen. Swirl to the window. Hudson still flowing up.

"Stew? Did you go in yesterday and take that final?"

Oh Kay. He loved her mothering instinct. But he most certainly had not gone in to take a final. Kay and Ruth and Ellen *knew* he hadn't gone to classes in six weeks, but they all still thought he'd make it up at the last minute.

He had, as it happened, walked out of Genre Analysis two days after he saw Franny in Washington Square. A Monday. A bright cool clear New York day.

He'd been having trouble with Genre Analysis from Day 1, when he and Sarason came close to a shouting match over Truffaut (Sarason thought *Bed and Board* brilliant, *400 Blows* overrated and immature). How could you get things so completely ass backwards? Every week, waiting for the projector to start its ratatatching, he faced a puny academic, a would-be critic in Hush Puppies who freelanced for *The Nation* and *The New Republic,* who hated *Juliet of the Spirits.*

That Monday, when Sarason began his lecture on *On a Clear Day You Can See Forever,* Steward felt a nasty little throbbing at his temple and an even nastier little throbbing at his crotch. The man thought *The Bicycle Thief* was corny. Sarason's whining ironic little voice droned on, but Steward managed to stay seated. Then the film began to roll. He rose and toppled his folding chair as he left. He was in a film program in an Ivy League school and they were watching *On a Clear Day You Can See Forever.* The girl sitting next to him followed him into the hall.

"You all right?"

All the girls at Columbia looked out for him. Well, there weren't that many in the film program, but the few tough babes there were nonetheless soft enough to make sure he wasn't going to go hang himself with a length of celluloid.

"I can't stand to see old Yves humiliated that way," he said.

She gave him a funny look. "Did you hear Sarason got the job at *New York Film?*"

That clinched it. When he left Dodge Hall and walked out onto the campus it *was* a clear day. And he could see back in time with such a tight focus that what he was becoming made sense. He wouldn't have to scramble for money in exactly the same way Gilda would, but he'd have to husband his resources and pay more attention to the broker. Already he'd seen parsimonious streaks in the mirror. The multitude of roommates sharing the rent, the apartment so far uptown the rent was halved to begin with. He hadn't bought shoes in a year, and now he felt the sidewalks of upper Broadway through his soles.

He walked west and up Riverside, the day clearer still over the river. He felt a rush of affection for Franny in that drooping sweater, though he knew it had never once crossed her mind that she looked like Ma Kettle, ready to drop some more babies. This would be the end of her painting.

But he was getting a good film in the can, and he knew he didn't need to sit and look at *On a Clear Day You Can See Forever* to figure out how to do it. Crazy of him to think he needed film school in the first place. He was as focused as a man could be.

And just now he was focused on Kay. When she pushed her hair up her forehead in exasperation like that, you could see why she wore bangs. She had a vampire's pronounced widow's peak.

"I'll take care of the kitchen, Miss Kay." He stopped dancing. "Calm down. I'll cook. Party's under control."

Kay looked up, tired from her shopping. Nervous about her boyfriend getting drunk in the same room as Stew tonight.

"You have the most beautiful widow's peak," he said, and reached over to kiss her forehead. She jumped, but when her feet touched the floor again she was blushing.

He had the touch.

He was hot.

He went to call Frances Burke in Brooklyn again, but the number rang busy.

It was a quiet party, quieter for sure than his grandparents' Christmas parties had ever been. All seven women from his year in Film showed up, but most of them had now gone off to giggle in the kitchen. Big healthy robust girls, they had all spent an hour in the living room trying to look smaller in their baggy knit sweaters and clodhopper shoes. They came in jeans, unprepared for the girls from Victorian and medieval in lace collars and delicate chains.

"Let me fetch y'all another drink."

Maybe he was aiming for Grandfather's voice when he went to bother Kay and her boyfriend. He liked to approach them every half hour or so, just to see Kay's efficient hand clamp down on her boyfriend's wrist.

Kay was brisk and unfriendly. "We're fine," she said, but her boyfriend handed over his glass and Steward went to fill it with five ounces of bourbon. Kay scowled when he delivered it. It *was* a little stiff.

It was ten-thirty already and Ellen had played the Bing Crosby Christmas album twice through to head off Ruth's urge for Gregorian chants. No sign of Kate or Franny, though Franny would have to put her children to bed first, and then come all the way from Brooklyn. On the subway, he guessed. He himself never took the subway. Nasty claustrophobic little invention.

He circled the room until he came to the doorway, where he spun an angel in Gilda's direction. Her eyes crinkled and she spun it right back at him. No moss grew on Gilda. Like the other film school girls, she was in a thick sweater tonight, but underneath its bulk she was wearing brown leather pants that creaked when she walked. He was touched. The leather pants didn't have quite the look they were supposed to under the sweater and over her workboots, but she was slender enough in any tight pair, and she'd let tinsel fall in her hair. He put an arm around her shoulder, practicing for Franny's arrival.

"Let's go dancing," she whispered up to him.

He put his arms around her, Fred again.

"No," she said, "let's sneak out and go downtown."

He feigned shock and surprise. "Oh, I couldn't walk out on Ellen and Ruth."

She grimaced at the feet of all the Victorian and medieval women in suede Christmas pumps, red and black.

"No," she said, "I guess not. Wild party, Stew."

He pictured Franny walking in at just that moment.

Franny stands in doorway, framed by pine and tinsel.

                                        CUT TO:

C.U. Stew, arm around his girlfriend. Shock as he
recognizes Franny.

                                        CUT TO:

The crowd, Franny's POV. The camera follows her through
the room and sees the serious sincere all-American types
sitting politely on couches and armchairs, stiffening as she
passes in her sloppy maternity clothes.

                                        CUT TO:

C.U. Franny, her face bare of makeup, her sharp eyes taking
in the party scene. A small hurt smile.

The *small hurt smile* was why he'd never write a good script. He could trust himself better with a camera in his hands.

"Stay right there," he said to Gilda. "Let me take your picture." She rolled her eyes, but stayed where she was against the overstuffed couch.

He kept a good Hasselblad yonder in the cabinets, underneath the bookshelves. He was halfway there when the doorbell rang. This was it. He shooed a medieval type away from the cabinets, got down on one knee, reached for the camera. This would be Franny at the door.

He took his time rising. When he finally spun around, the newcomers were still a clump in front of the door; Kate Rooney had separated herself by a single step and was scanning the room, fluffy and lovely in a pink sweater that looked like cotton candy, her hair spun out around her face. Her new look for auditions, since the closing of *Hippie Girls Bite the Dust*. Next to her, Burke was sure of himself, squinting out of bloodshot eyes, his go-to-work haircut spiked up, his jeans tight and tattered. Amused as he pulled a cigarette from his leather jacket. Ruth would have a fit if he lit up after all the hours doing calligraphy for the *Thank you for not smoking* cards.

Franny was the first to see him, and beamed from the doorway. She was all dolled up, in some kind of red Chinese jacket over sleek pants. Well, as sleek as you could get at however many months pregnant she was. She was looking as pixilated as Elizabeth Morehouse looked to him sometimes, beaming and bouncing and tugging now at Kate's sleeve to point him out.

"Well, come on *in.*" Worse than Grandfather, oozing heartiness.

Franny, full of sparkle, reached out to touch him on the sleeve. This wasn't how he pictured her, this wasn't how he saw her last, wan and pregnant, distressed at the sight of him. Now she was the picture of domestic satisfaction, touching his sleeve, touching her husband's sleeve, pulling them all through the apartment in a cascade of smiles. Gilda glowered behind them.

Hasselblad still in his hand, Gilda abandoned, he followed Franny as she dismissed the company of medieval, Victorian, and biochem, and led them all back through the apartment to the kitchen, where all the film women were huddled. She was wearing her cool-uncool radar.

But they couldn't have been parked back there with the other cigarette smokers for more than five minutes—he was just coming back with the drinks—when she said: "We can't stay, Stew. Just popped in to wish you Merry Christmas."

Steward turned himself around in the kitchen crowded with women and bumped into Franny's belly. She laughed at him and tugged for the big bag hanging off her shoulder. Franny's husband was behind her, wearing the same smirk he wore at his own wedding.

"We've got to get over to Michael's high school party, can you believe *that,* and it's all guys too. Would you ever, I mean ever, go to a Due East High School reunion?"

She did not give him time to deny it.

"But here, I wanted to give you a hug and this"—from out of her bag came a little flat package wrapped in smudged tissue paper, no ribbon— "and just, you know, just wish you a Merry Christmas."

"But here's your drink."

"Oh thanks, well, Michael, what you think? We have time for one?"

From behind the others Michael shook his smirking head *no.*

"Sorry Stew, we shouldn't have even come in, but—"

"I'll take *my* drink, Stew." There was Kate, trying to smooth it over. Kate wasn't leaving, Kate was staying for this all-American party, Kate would look over the film women in the kitchen and chat them up.

"Fran, we gotta get—"

And then, just like that, having just blown in, the Asshole Husband was blowing them back out again. Franny was maneuvering her enormous front out of the kitchen she had just entered, Kate was staying behind, Steward was running after the Burkes, Hasselblad in one hand, tissue paper package in the other, to say good-bye when he'd just said hello.

Gilda was still sultry, angled against the couch, steaming a little now, tapping her foot.

Franny was still sparkling—drunk? no, not when she was pregnant. Just sparkling.

"I'm glad I got to *see* you anyway. Crazy, huh, in and out?" Behind her the husband's smirk had faded away. Now he was just bored. "I just, I wanted to say hello, and now we've got to—"

"Fran."

"I know, Michael. That's what I'm saying, we've got to run before we miss the next party too and—"

Now her husband tugged her by the hand and carted her off to the elevator, and she laughed, at herself and maybe at Stew too. Steward stood in the doorway to see her off and tried out Michael Burke's smirk on his own face.

———

Inside the tissue paper was a drawing of him from 1968 or '69. A million years ago, anyway. A scowling boy with a girl's pretty bow mouth. Pen and ink, every stroke an explanation of why you wouldn't want to hang around this guy. The paper was torn at the edges.

"Why would you come all the way up here to say hello?"

He'd gone pretty far with the bourbon, maybe right close to the edge. He had a dim memory of Gilda creaking off in leather pants, but where? Was she lying on his bed waiting for him, or was she off dancing downtown? He was close to the edge, but he wouldn't go over. Kate was there. Kate from Due East. Nobody from home would let you puke your guts out.

"Aw Stew, you know she wanted to see you."

How did Kate's arm get around his shoulder? Where was Gilda? Why were Ruth and Ellen such a prim picture on the couch? Where'd everybody go?

"I wanted to see her too. I wanted to *see* her dammit, not say hello."

Oh careful. Kate's arm was squeezing sympathy. Ruth and Ellen were struggling to stay awake so they could . . . What? So they could drag him to their matching twin beds and have their way with him? Oh joy.

But Ruth's chin sagged and Ellen's eyes narrowed. They weren't waiting to have their way with him; they were waiting so they could pull his shoes off and cover him with a blanket and put the empty punch trough on the floor by his bed in case he didn't make it through the night without puking after all.

"I feel sick."

"Oh!" Ruth and Ellen sat straight up, ready to spring into action, but he waved them away.

"No. No! I feel sick you could be living in the same city and *bother* to come all this way and leave again after ten seconds. What is this, the big tease all over again?" His voice bounced off the tall ceilings. No one would meet his eye.

"I don't think she's teasing you, Stew. I know she wanted to see you. I know she would have stayed, but Michael was so—"

"So asshole."

"He's not so bad."

"You weren't at the wedding."

"I heard about that." Kate shook her lovely fluffy head and her lovely fluffy breasts shook along, in the cotton-candy sweater. "You were good to go. Fact, I can't be*lieve* you went."

Steward shook his head in imitation of fluffy Kate, but it was a dangerous move. That empty punch trough might be called into use, after all.

"Can't believe I asked her. Last time. Last time."

"Hey, Stew, I'm sorry. You know Franny wouldn't hurt you—"

Steward stared. Utter disbelief. *Wouldn't hurt you?*

He must have growled. He heard something *blechblech*ing up from his
throat, and Ellen and Ruth were alert on the couch, exchanging warning
looks. They were also, he noticed for the first time in the year he had lived
with them, holding hands. Was ever a man born so thick? No matter, no
matter. All the better in fact, the three of them facing the cold world
together.

"She's trying to be—well, you know, it'll be three kids soon. I think
she's trying to be good."

Kate was weaving against him, pulling his shoulder to and fro, and
didn't seem to know it. They were all of them in this room trying to keep
their equilibrium. Look at Ellen and Ruth, holding hands in public!

". . . I know she didn't want to make Michael jealous. I mean, since
the wedding and all."

"Din wanna make him jealous? So she dragged him to a hunnerd
and . . . ?"

"But Stew, you're an old friend."

"I am not. I am not an old friend. There are many many many ways
you could describe me, but old friend is not one of them."

Kate squeezed and weaved.

"I feel sick," he said again, but his time he meant the other kind of sick,
and he headed for the bathroom, Ruth and Ellen rising behind him to
minister to him, the clucking of their tongues interlocking with Kate's
clucking. They'd come knock on the door in a minute. They'd get him to
his own bed, where Gilda would be waiting in the creaking pants. They'd
pull down Gilda's leather pants and his Southern boy chinos, oh boy, all of
them in the bedroom looking out on Riverside Drive, looking out on the
Hudson River flowing up, oh happy in love, Kate would stay, oh they'd all
be happy together.

Someone was missing from the picture, but he was swimming along so
fast now that he couldn't picture who.

In the hallway he wavered, the urge to call Lola and Colonel Chuck
Parrish a steady pressure on his chest. He had something important to say to
them. The pressure moved down to his solar plexus, and a warm queasy
cancer spread.

He had an urge to call Franny, too. He had something really important to say to her, but what? What?

He remembered.

She made him sick.

Into the bathroom, just in time.

SAINT
PATRICK'S
DAY

"Oh Caroline, you don't wanna see the *parade*."

Michael was leaving for work but still directing the show, and Caroline and Franny nodded pleasant submissive smiles before they looked at one another and let loose *We'll do as we please* titters. Franny rose and kissed Michael on both cheeks, on the nose, on the forehead, standing on tiptoe and showing off for her little sister. It was Michael who'd flown Caroline up here, after all, full of largesse and full of himself since he'd got two promotions in a year and a half. Now he was editor in chief of a new magazine he'd had the nerve to name *Byte the Bullet.* Computer graphics. He didn't seem to know a thing about computer graphics, and he didn't seem to care, but every now and again he dropped a present on the kitchen table along with his paycheck. The last present was Caroline's ticket, so she could see the baby sometime before Maura's senior prom, and if he wanted to boss them around now . . .

"Bunch of high school kids from Bethpage." He was ignoring Franny's kisses. "Puking in the gutter."

"What's Bethpage?"

"You don't wanna know," Michael said. "We'll take you out tonight, Caroline. You don't wanna see the parade. The very worst of this culture, I guarantee you. Make you ashamed you got a drop of Irish blood in you."

But Caroline, twenty years old, sweet, eager and innocent as a baby waiting to be splashed in the baptismal font, had no trouble shrugging off his advice.

"I'm so excited I could pee my pants," she told Franny.

They took the children in by subway, and from one o'clock to three they all endured the crazy press of Fifth Avenue. Franny squeezed Martin's fist on one side and Brian's on the other, certain that one or the other of them was planning to make a break for it and peel loose, certain that Caroline would forget to clutch, not merely hold, Maura's stroller.

They *did* see some of the parade—when you were with little ones the crowd gave way, a little. At the sight of Martin in Brian's green leprechaun hat with the bells, the cops parted the very waters to give the boys a curbside seat.

"Did you know you've got a map there on your face?"

Martin stared up, bold and terrified at once.

"You've got the map of Ireland on your face!"

Martin patted his cheeks and rubbed off the map of Ireland. Maura was stunned into utter silence, a prisoner in her Perego, the pipe bands screeching ever closer. Franny was concerned about exposing her baby to so much bad taste at such a delicate age. Certain shades of green, she told her sister, should be declared illegal.

The drizzle wouldn't stop and wouldn't start, not properly. When she leaned over the curb, Brian's cheeks were icy, but she was steaming with excitement, bad as Caroline. The two of them flirted with cops, waiting for old man Burke to come marching by.

"Is that why he didn't want us to come? Is his grandfather going to disgrace him?"

Caroline had somehow grown to be five foot ten and was a strapping freckled blonde with the same blunt-cut hair that Manhattan women got at Vidal Sassoon, a clotheshorse in a good slinky camel's-hair coat. Where did she get that in Due East? Franny felt the little sister next to her: Caroline was practical and genial and had remembered to bring an extra diaper to wipe the baby's face.

"This is amazing." She knew when to pour on the Southern accent, too. Right now Caroline had one eye on Maura and one eye on Officer Hallinan, who'd been guarding them for fifteen minutes. His breath had a bosky smell: that would be Jameson's or Paddy's or Powers.

"Where you celebrating tonight?" the cop asked. His wedding band glowed in the bright haze.

"I'll probly be celebrating with my feet in a pan of hot water."

Franny stared at her slickness with new regard—this was the once weeping quivering overweight Caroline, getting all the attention now. Franny turned her own to her sons. Martin was perfectly content watching the suntan pantyhose on the majorettes passing by, but Brian had set up a keen. *Canwego Canwego Canwego?*

"Soon, Brian. Look for County Kerry."

They had ten more minutes of Officer Hallinan before Brian shot up off the curb, his arm outstretched. He was too excited to speak. They'd missed the banner, but there was his great-grandfather in a black beret and a fisherman's sweater, marching along at a fit pace with a shillelagh he didn't need. A *beret*. He didn't look seventy-five, much less eighty-five, and when Brian finally found his voice and let loose a holler the old man raised a clenched fist. Brian raised his own.

"Aw shit," Franny said, hoping Michael's grandfather could read lips. "You can't come see him but you could teach him that when he's five years old." She turned to Caroline with her eyes scrunched down, mean. "Did you hear that? That was Michael's voice, coming out of my mouth."

"It sure was," Caroline said. The Southern in her voice had increased exponentially over the course of her conversation with the cop. She was busy waving at Michael's grandfather—she'd never met him, but his fist was still extended high in the air, and Officer Hallinan was returning it. Caroline joined them with that beauty queen wave that all Southern girls learn before they learn to speak.

"This is the *best* fun," Caroline said, batting her eyelashes now at Officer Quinn, who had slipped up behind Hallinan. Quinn had no wedding band on his left hand. Franny slipped the stroller out from Caroline's hands and rocked Maura back and forth. She didn't have the same energy for flirting anymore.

Back in Brooklyn, Kevin Byrne sat hunched over, waiting for them on the front stoop, and Michael's mother, the only baby-sitter who'd stand for the three hooligans this night, sat beside him. They made a parade themselves, trudging up to the third floor: the children let out little moans of exhaustion. All this family around was too much for them. Saint Patrick's Day was too much for them.

But not for Caroline, who went to paint her big eyelids blue—pure Due East after all—and not for Franny, who threw three hot dogs in a pot and helped Norah toss the three babies in a single bath. One side up with the washcloth, one side down. One minute for the hot dogs in the boiling water. Potato chips on Saint Patrick's Day. Tonight she was going out.

Kevin hovered, wary. Michael had shamed him from his prolific visiting, but at New Year's the two of them had lost their old beer-drinking buddy from high school, Mickey Shields. He died right in the neighborhood too, collapsed of an overdose on a Seventh Avenue sidewalk, next to a pay phone. He was twenty-six, and Kevin and Michael thought he'd been lonely as Marilyn Monroe in the last hours, that he'd been trying to push the dime in the slot. Lately Michael was less inclined to bar the door.

"Want me to set the table for you?"

"Sure, but there's not much to set. Just giving them a hot dog wrapped in a napkin. Oh, I'm a terrible mother."

"Best mother *I* know." Kevin brushed against her, reaching for the napkins, and they both turned away too quickly. Kevin's eyes filled up when he talked to her now. A thousand white paper napkins fluffed down to the floor.

"Sorry."

"No, my fault."

Since they'd moved to Brooklyn, she'd come between them. Michael seemed to know that Kevin—red-nosed, pudgy, morose, self-pitying, masochistic, adoring—was always conspiring to brush by her, squeeze her close. He was just lonely. He had the same methods as the sixteen-year-old boys he taught at Cardinal Newman, but hadn't she always shown a weakness for the methods of sixteen-year-old boys? Michael knew she was a fool for those sweet guys, those good men, those high school teachers dropping by at the crack of dawn with a bag of bagels. His best friend for twenty years almost, but he didn't trust either one of them now.

And she was trying to be good, she was. It should have been a perfect time to reform herself, milk spilling right through her sweaters, the babies leaving her cross-eyed from all the night wakings. It was hard to summon the energy to look at her own face in the mirror, much less a man's on the street. The other night, the children finally down, Michael sat in his underwear on the edge of the bed and tried to tell her the new circulation figures for the magazine.

"Oh, you're not listening. You're floating away," he said, and looked so hurt that he must have meant she was floating out far past the moment. It was true, she was floating, but only on fatigue and her own milk spilling. Sometimes, so tired she wanted to rest her head on any chest, she thought she might rise like hot air and drift away from them all.

She was trying to be good, but there was no growing up. Michael thought it was Kevin she dreamed of. It wasn't Kevin. Caroline had said— all innocence—"How's Stew? We heard he was living up here"—and that had set her off again. She'd been dreaming of Steward three nights in a row. What was he doing in her dreams, haunting what little sleep she got? If he was still in New York, there was only a subway ride between them, but he'd got Michael's message. And he'd got her message too: she'd been good, that Christmas. He never called anymore.

"Ah," said Franny. "That's Michael at the door," and Kevin jerked up from collecting napkins off the floor and bumped his head on the counter.

By nightfall the little apartment was rocking, and Franny sat on the living room floor in the dead center of the chaos. The boys had pulled out Caroline's suitcases for horses, and Maura trotted along behind them. Kevin sat moony on the old corduroy couch, watching the children run each other down.

Caroline plopped herself down on the couch, too. "That Brian. That Martin. They're wild men!" she said, but Kevin was not as susceptible to her charms as Officers Hallinan and Quinn had been. He shaped his smile small, and Maura bawled.

"She resents being left out of that wild men category," Franny said. "Jaze!"

Now it was Michael roaring into the room, shirtless. Strange to see him with the new pale gut. Maura grabbed him by the leg to wipe her nose, but the boys ran off in terror. "Can't think around here."

Michael's mother tiptoed down the hall, carting her guilty expression with her. What had she done wrong now? "Did I forget—?"

"No, Ma, they're just so damn loud."

Norah put on a bright smile. "Oh. Well. Boys," and drifted back down the hallway. She was floating away too: tonight Michael's mother brought the hot dogs into the bathroom and the towels to the kitchen table. Franny never left the three little ones without picturing the gas left on or the kettle burning empty.

"So let's get rolling," Michael said.

Maura howled anew and clung now to Franny's leg.

"Hey hey, little sweetheart." The baby had a heart-shaped face and elephant ears. When she cried her cheeks splotched purple.

Michael clucked his tongue. "C'mon Maura fedora, Maura begorrah, c'mon Maura." But the baby knew Franny was leaving, and taking her leaky breasts with her.

"Y'all go on," Franny said, "I'll give her a last little toke and be downstairs in a sec."

"Sure you will," Michael said, but he was happy now, on the way out. He'd bought himself a swell silver flask for this very occasion. He and Kevin were sworn off cocaine the last couple of months—Mickey Shields had overdosed on heroin, but close enough—and the worst they would be tonight was drunk. O.k., drunk could get pretty bad with those two, but they'd be drunk at least with three million other New Yorkers on city streets that wouldn't be so friendly for another whole year.

Caroline and Michael and Kevin clumped off, and Franny nursed the baby, in and out, Maura past the age where she wanted much more than the squeezing and the cuddling. Then the rounds of squeezing and cuddling Brian and Martin, and fussing in the kitchen with Norah.

"She won't get to sleep without the Binky."

"The Binky?"

Franny's heart swooped and she held up the pacifier she'd shown Norah not five minutes before. DON'T LEAVE THE GAS ON, DON'T LET THE KETTLE BOIL DRY. Michael's mother seemed to wake up for a minute, and Franny ran off finally, trotting down the stairs in her dirty green sweater. She hadn't had a minute to poke earrings through. It wasn't possible that she was the mother of three.

Kevin was waiting for her on the sidewalk, sadder than before. Caroline and Michael had already taken off for the subway.

"You look beautiful," Kevin said.

No wonder Michael barred the door. And look at her: the old peacoat over a pair of jeans. There'd been no time to brush her teeth, much less glop on eyeliner, so what was Kevin talking about?

"Aw, you're a flatterer." It was only too clear what Kevin was talking about. Caroline and Michael shrank in the distance, turning the corner onto Seventh Avenue already.

"Francie, I—"

Those three syllables got started a lot lately. Michael knew it: that was why he'd spent these years uninviting Kevin, disinviting Kevin, kicking Kevin out. Michael thought that they'd divert him tonight with Caroline, so Franny could go back to picking up after the two of them instead of being the Love Goddess of Park Slope, but there were Michael and Caroline up ahead, and here was Kevin trailing after her, as always.

"*What*, Kevin?"

Kevin shook his head. "Never mind."

"I'm sorry. I'm worried about the guys. I don't like the way Michael's mother looks."

Kevin sighed. "They'll be all right." It was a bad sigh: a shallow hopeless sigh, enough to make you sigh in response. But he had the persistence of an abandoned dog—*Just can't believe they'd leave me by the side of the road like that*—and she couldn't kick him hard enough to discourage him. Besides, he was lonely.

"C'mon Kevin, let's run."

She took off, in good shape since she'd been running in the mornings again. She shouldn't make him feel so lousy—Kevin's twenty extra pounds rubdubbed in front of him—but she did. She beat him to the subway, and after she clattered down the stairs she put her hand in Michael's. The train was pulling in.

The car was crowded with kids who'd started their guzzling at ten in the morning; now they were nodding out or jiggling with belligerence, just waiting for somebody to start something. Kevin moved to stand, alone, by the door. Head bent down, sandy unwashed hair flopping over his eye, black jacket: he was a man in mourning.

Man in mourning. Franny sucked in her guilty breath. It was Mickey Shields, not her, weighing on Kevin. She moved toward him and the train jiggled her to and fro across the car. Kevin caught her by the wrist, and she stood with him in silence. Michael was making a point of not looking their way, leaning closer to Caroline to whisper worldly Saint Patrick's Day observations. Franny took a breath. Another.

"I guess it's a hard Saint Pat's for you."

"Maybe."

"Sorry I snapped."

Kevin shrugged. But then he stirred himself enough to lift his chin and survey the crowd: pale faces, every last one, pale faces aged fourteen and fifteen and sixteen, grubby children of the working class heading into Manhattan for the big night, crosses round their necks and heavy jackets on their backs: Nazareth, Bishop Ford, Xavier, Xavierian, Regis, Loyola, St. Saviours. Grateful Dead.

"They'll half of them be dead before they hit forty."

"I guess it seems that way."

"It's not it *seems* that way. You look around, we get to be forty. We got a thing about killing ourselves."

His words seemed to brace him. Pride in the perverse stood him taller, the small of his back tucked into the door.

"Maybe not the girls. The ones at Cardinal Newman, they've got it together. Oh, their families'll step on any big plans they have—*You wanna be a doctor? Be a nurse. You wanna be a registered nurse? Be a practical nurse*—but they got a plan, anyway. The guys, though. A mess. Scareda their own shadows, talking a blue streak till they turn that first twist on the bottle."

Franny pictured her brothers: Will in Myrtle Beach, running the Scrambler at the amusement park; Martin thinking he was a poet, still at Doris's house, sleeping until three in the afternoon. Paul smoked dope all day and didn't have a prayer of graduating from high school on time. Albert was the great male hope, straight A's all the way, though nobody could shake the suspicion that the grades were calculated to break Walter's heart.

"Well, look at you. You got it together. Teaching and all."

Kevin stared straight ahead, at his own reflection in the opposite door. "Oh yeah," he said, and Franny saw her reflection next to his. Wild black curls cut short. White face, bare of glop. Her pea coat had strips of vermilion on the cuff where she'd leaned it against her own wet palette. She did not resemble an adult.

"Oh yeah," Kevin said again, only he'd gone back to mumble mode and she had to stand almost on her toes to hear him. "Teaching the Yahoos from Bensonhurst, yeah sure. Old man's right, I'd have a better chance saving my soul on Wall Street."

Franny touched his sleeve. What else could you do?

"Hanging out with my friend's kids, my friend's wife . . . Shlucky arrrs ife."

Shlucky arrrs ife. Fucking barren life? Lusting after his wife? Now what? Did she take her hand away from his sleeve, or press harder? She looked over at Michael and Caroline, all atitter, all aglitter, deep flush on their cheeks, eyes asparkle for Saint Patrick's Day, and she pressed Kevin's sleeve harder. He was just lonely.

The line snaking into McSorley's was unthinkable—what *had* they been thinking? The flask was empty now, but Kevin's spirits floated high when he saw the crowds. Now it was Saint Patrick's Day. They took a long hike to the Bells of Hell, but there was no getting past the sidewalk there either, so they kept heading west, for the Eagle. Michael said you could blow the drunks over in the Eagle and make yourself a place.

"Remember that night we walked crosstown to the Chelsea, Kev?"

Kevin's cheeks looked scrubbed pink in the street light.

"Yes, ladies. Yes, sweet Carolina sisters, this innocent-looking teacher of adolescents once thought he could rent a room at the Chelsea Hotel, purpose of seducing *genuine* innocent young schoolgirls. On the night of the Brooklyn Prep Senior Prom. We got the girls in the front door, but they took one look at the lobby, man, and they were outta there."

"Mary Frances Moriarty," Kevin said, and sighed a happy sigh.

"I was with Gina Lollobrigida, myself. There was a junkie—very well dressed too, I mean we're talking three-piece suit—puking by the pay phone. Couldn't get holda any more skag from *any*body, sound of the conversation."

They were turning the corner of Fourteenth Street, but Kevin's walk slowed. "Shit man," he said. "Mickey Shields."

Even Michael slowed. They'd been the good boys, Kevin and Michael and Mickey, the good boys from Brooklyn Prep, fingered by the priests. They all went to the Chelsea Hotel one night, and when they graduated Mickey went to Yale.

Caroline said: "Who's Mickey Shields?" before Franny had time to stop her, but Kevin sloughed it off.

"Guy always trying to get a bargain," he said, "always trying to make do with the cheap shit," and Michael started laughing through his nose, a high whinny that only sounded slightly hysterical.

They'd marched clear across town, and now they fought their way into the Eagle, Michael leading the charge. There was music coming from the back room—you could hear the dark roll of the bodhrans—but no chance of getting close. Caroline had hooked her fingers into the back of Michael's belt and looked like a water-skier trailing a boat. When she turned to get Franny's attention she wore the big-eyed smile of a claustrophobic trying to make the best of things. Franny breathed in the cigarette smoke and knew she'd be bumming from complete strangers before the night was out. She checked the clock. Ten hours before she had to nurse Maura. Plenty of time to get loaded and please God, don't let Norah turn the gas on without a match.

Michael, genial miracle worker, had somehow pushed himself next to the bar and summoned four glasses. The bartender was pouring triples on this holiest of nights. Kevin and Franny and Caroline huddled behind Michael, refugees with their elbows digging into their ribs. After he'd downed his drink—time elapsed, thirty seconds—Kevin decided it was more efficient to put his arms around Caroline and Franny, and Michael pushed away again, to see if anyone had passed out and left a chair in the back room.

There was no hearing each other, only snatches of Hollywood brogue that drifted from across the room and rode the cigarette smoke in their direction:

Ye have the loveliest eyes, so ye do. Really fresh and innocent, like.

Don't be an asshole just cause you've got an accent.

"Well!" said Caroline, looking panicked with Kevin's chunky arm squeezing her. "What's next?"

Franny had to shout. "Maybe Michael'll find a spot for us to hear the session. But I doubt it."

Caroline's gray eyes registered disbelief that their Saint Patrick's Day was to end huddled this way. Franny craned her neck this way and that. They were in a field of on-the-make in-their-twenties lately-hippies. Any cops or firemen who stumbled in here were on their own: this was a crowd of the third- and fourth-generation types who hung out at the Irish Arts Center. These were the children of mothers who, knowing no other way to celebrate, every year bought a stale sheet cake with vile green icing and leprechuans dancing across its surface. In reparation for such neglect of the culture, this crowd was learning Gaelic, playing the penny whistle and singing "Danny Boy" with the tears rolling down their well-fed cheeks, pretending they were working construction in the Bronx when they were really getting graduate degrees in theology. These were the faces from the Underground, all grown up.

"Well, it beats the kids on the train," Franny shouted.

"Oh, it's great!"

Franny squeezed Caroline's shoulder where Kevin had squeezed it a minute before. Caroline's capacity to be a good sport floored her. Where'd she learn such a thing, growing up in the Starkey household? Who'd have thought she'd be interested in Saint Patrick's Day? The Starkeys had never even bothered with the green sheet cake, though every few years their father might buy a six-pack and sing "Toura-Loura-Loura," in honor of meeting Doris on March 17, in honor of being named for the saint himself.

"Hey," Caroline said. "Michael's waving us in."

Franny couldn't even see into the back room. It didn't seem possible that Michael had found them a table, but maybe he'd found an air pocket. She tried to follow Caroline squeezing her way through the crowd, but a wall of shaggy men in tweed jackets shifted as Caroline passed. She pressed her fingers into one's back, to no effect.

Kevin laughed beside her. "Let em get the table ready for us."

When he was in good cheer, which wasn't often lately, Kevin came out breathless and jolly. Now he was *Ahem*ing into the tweed jackets' ears, but he had no more luck than she'd had. There were three strawberry blondes on the other side of the men, three Sacred Heart types wearing their blazers.

"Forget it," Kevin said. "They got no cause to move aside. Wanna park a minute?"

"Not much choice."

"Haven't had a minute with you in a long time."

"Ah, yeah. Shame."

"It's o.k., Francie, I know Michael's holding the reins tight."

She would have choked if there'd been anything in her mouth. *"Reins?"*

"Hey, I dig it. Now he's Mister Corporate he's scared you're gonna take off. Can't blame him."

"Kevin."

"No? I get it all wrong?" Pause, but Kevin was still jolly and blustery. "Sorry Francie, it's just, you can't talk to the guy. He started making thirty thou and—"

"He doesn't make thirty thou." He made a little more. And they had three kids, and this was New York City, 1977. It wasn't so much.

"Yeah, well, whatever. He's doing o.k."

"But you too, Kevin, I mean you've got the teaching thing—"

The wall of tweed jackets made a little shelter for them, a lean-to. They could hear each other. Kevin had always done a little of this grousing, back before she stopped answering the bell.

Kevin shrugged. "You'll be buying a house next, hey, moving to Larchmont, and I'll be living on the top floor of my father's house rest of my life. The priests at Cardinal Newman have a more exciting life than I do. The Ursuline *nuns* have a more exciting life than I do."

"Listen, if the priests are having such a good time, maybe—" She quit the sentence when she saw his mouth, quivering. He was trying to grow a moustache, but it was coming in spotted.

"Maybe I should just tell you the truth," he said.

Panic. Time to poke the tweed jackets in front of her again, to move along, to get herself into that back room with her husband. Franny finished her drink—too much, too fast—and jabbed the empty glass into the backs in front of her. No movement.

"Sorry." A dark square jaw turned around and smiled down at her. "No place for me to move."

She and Kevin were pushed against each other like the sorry commuters on the rush hour D train, her loose breasts connecting somewhere not too far above his belt. His speckled upper lip was staring down, still blustery, a little less jolly. His breath pushed in and out, too fast, against her sweater. This was dangerous, this part where they were so sad, or so hopeless, or so sweet. She tried to back off, but she ended up wiggling against him.

"Got to, Francie."

"Oh, Kevin. You don't *have* to."

"Yeah I do. Gotta tell somebody. You can't live your life in a vacuum, always."

The top of his nose had an injured look, its sad red bumps like the bumps on a golf ball. When she couldn't concentrate on the nose anymore, she tried to make her body so small that it would recede from his, but she heard Kevin's breath coming harder above her. Now he was leaning down to whisper in her ear.

"I'm going nowhere fast."

She opened her eyes.

"Listen, I'm thinking about law school. O.k.? There, it's out. I know it's a big fucking drag, I know what Michael'll think of it, but look at him—"

A goofy little hoot had been working its way up her throat and now it screeped free.

"See, you're laughing at me. I knew it. Yeah, pretty funny picture."

She laughed again, then shook her head. *No, no, I'm not laughing at you.*

"C'mon, Francie, since Mickey. I gotta do *something*. It's not that funny."

By now the wall of tweed jackets had moved aside for them to pass, but she was too giddy to move. She put a hand on Kevin's sleeve instead, and he leaned down close.

"You thought I was gonna tell you something else, didn't you?"

His nostrils had stopped flaring, his mouth had quit its quivering. He blinked his eyes and leaned down to kiss her full on the mouth, so fast she felt his tongue as a fish darting into the cavern that was her mouth. Then he moved his chunky body into the narrow path that the tweed jackets had made for them. She followed, and the square jaw gave her a wink and a nod, as if he knew that her husband was deep in the back room.

But no, the jaw leaned over and hollered into her ear. "Don't let anybody be asking you for gun money tonight. It's not going for guns. They're just drinking it up."

And she was floating, rising, pulled like a spirit looking for a resting place into the next room, room full of strangers fingering harps and twirling primitive sticks, all looking for home.

It was two A.M. when the train opened its maw at Fourteenth Street. Michael and Kevin stood in the middle of the car and sang what they remembered—every third line, approximately—of "Whiskey in the Jar" and "Dicey Reilly." When they finished "Dicey Reilly" they did "Whiskey in the Jar" again. Franny was afraid they'd launch into "When Irish Eyes Are Smiling," Michael was that far gone, but the doors opened at Grand Army Plaza, and she and Caroline coaxed them off the train and back onto the street.

"That was the best Saint Patrick's Day I *ever* had."

"Oh Caroline, Caroline, I married the wrong sister."

Franny got her arm around Michael's waist. The singing had sobered him up a little, actually. Now she was the one who needed help negotiating the sidewalks—and only five hours until time to nurse Maura. Well, it would be a bottle for the baby in the morning, and a bottle of Bayer for her. Michael would be gone by eight, and she'd have Brian to get to kindergarten, the whole entourage leading their hungover mother down the block.

Kevin was walking ahead with Caroline, strutting and bragging in the loudest voice that had ever issued from his mouth. He was going to get some kid at Cardinal Newman into Harvard. You'd think he got laid tonight.

Caroline, the only sober pedestrian on the street, was doing her polite gushy thing. "Well, I think that's *marvelous*. The parents don't even speak *English?*"

"I think it's marvelous too, Kevin." She wasn't trying to make fun of Caroline, she really wasn't, but Michael gave her a poke in the ribs and one of those *bad girl* looks. Then he pulled her back under the streetlight to kiss her. He tasted of whiskey and beer and Marlboros, and she hadn't been kissed like this in a couple of hours. Two surprise kisses in one night: she was Grace Kelly in *High Society. High Irish-American Society.* Up ahead she heard Kevin telling Caroline that he'd take her to the Bitter End.

"He'll be o.k.," she said to Michael. This latest kiss was over.

Michael looked down at her with a funny scrinch to his eyes. Now that she'd got used to him with the haircut, she had to get used to the hair receding, the cheeks softening. He was too young to go bald and get fat. Wasn't he?

"Don't do it, Franny."

She started to walk along and then heard what he said. He'd stopped on the sidewalk. "Don't do what?"

"You know."

"What?"

He waited until Kevin had crossed the avenue with Caroline. "Don't mess up Kevin any more than he already is."

"What are you talking about?"

"I'd have to hurt him he touches you."

The singing hadn't sobered him up at all. *Have to hurt him*—oh, so he was after a light tone tonight. She put one hand on her hip and used the other to wave it all away. *Oh really*. He hadn't seen Kevin kissing her, it was only some signal she was sending out, now, unsteady in her new pointy shoes. It had been so long, and she'd been so good. The rest of the world was wife-swapping, Christ! and here she was, receiving a darting tongue in a bar.

"I mean it, Franny." He stopped on the sidewalk—they were under another lamp, so he had the spotlight again—and gave her a sad gloppy look, shaking his head, too. Pause. Opened his mouth. Pause. Closed his mouth. Walked on.

"Michael. *Michael*."

But he was gone, hands in his pockets, whistling "Dicey Reilly" down the block, his own tweed jacket rumpled in the dark night. He didn't jitter along anymore, not since he quit the coke. He ambled. She might not look grown-up, but he did. He looked like the father of three, losing the first front strands of hair. He looked like a man who threw the paycheck on the kitchen table.

And she looked like a girl still, still stunned by the lightning striking the same place three times, still dizzy from the three little ones calling *Mama, mama* through the day and then on down through the night, green snot dangling and black dirt wedged up in their fingernails. If she stole three hours a week for painting she was lucky, three hours when Michael dragged them off to the zoo or Coney Island, three hours less of a grown-up to talk to.

No growing up.

She'd picked up the phone to call Steward, more than once. She knew the number by heart. She dream-dialed him in the night, up and down with the little ones.

She missed Kevin's bagels. She missed the afternoons when he handed over a baby and let his hand brush her hair. She missed, already, the hard quick kiss in the smoky bar.

Ye have the loveliest eyes, so ye do. Really fresh and innocent, like.

Hard to be alone so much, with children, longing to work.

Michael ambled on, thinking he was Irish.

Hard to be good.

IN
EXCELSIS
DEO

The need to get down to Due East sneaked up behind Steward Morehouse every few years and slipped over him like a hood: he couldn't see straight until he made it home. This time he drove south in his own car, a 1964 green MG he picked up cheap in the Bronx and took meandering down the coast. He didn't stop in town—Lola didn't know what time he was pulling in—but headed straight out the beach road.

Traffic was zippier, but once you got past Saint Helena's you saw the real difference. The shabbiest houses—*shacks,* Grandmother always called them—had been carted away, and now even the ragged mudflats had a tamed look. The county was prosperous, no doubt about it, signs for water-front condos down every other dirt path. The beach road verged to the salt marsh, the egrets up close.

He passed the cutoff to the old colored beach and headed for the south end, for the dunes and private houses that hadn't sold out to the state yet. His old haunt. He pulled off where he and Lola had parked that day they caught Franny topless and he laughed out loud. It would make a great coming-of-age scene, all that bright light. He'd do it with a handheld camera, the boy's POV, the camera following the *thud-thud-thud* of his feet as he makes his way over the dunes, closer and closer to . . . teenage betrayal.

But once he walked through the pines and scrub oak the first shock was: no more dunes. They'd been flattened, erased, wiped clean. The long trudge out to the water (six-pack weighing down the cooler) was now a short walk, the sand damp and obedient under his loafers. The line of palmettos was orderly too. He breathed in the warm salt air. This was all he needed, a fifteen-minute walk on this empty end of the beach, every now and again a Marine family huddled on a blanket in his path. This was all he needed to be cured of New York.

Walking north, he saw a tall blonde in a windbreaker walking south, skirting the waves just as he was doing. Her hair was whipping the wrong way, into her face, and even at a distance the tilt of her head, chasing the hair back, was graceful. Approaching, they stared straight at one another: she was big-boned and close to six feet. Usually big women didn't attract him—hard to drop the habit of looking for a smaller, frailer creature—but this one had a woozy tilting walk. He could make out high perfect breasts where the windbreaker gapped.

By now, one of them should have looked away. Maybe he just hadn't had enough time back in Due East to readjust to the idea that complete strangers would smile at each other as a matter of course. Her face was utterly familiar: big gray eyes with an aureole of pale lashes; a freckled nose, probably ski-slope when she turned in profile. There was a small cleft in the center of her chin. Maybe she'd been one of his cousin's girlfriends—she had that Topsiders-over-argyle-socks look. One of those girls who missed the sixties, narrowly but entirely.

They drew close. Now they were passing, time to nod and smile in Due East fashion—but at the last minute he jerked his head away and stared out to sea. Really weird sensation. She'd been about to speak, and more than hello. He sensed that she'd been about to call his name, and he'd felt a trippy incestuous chill run down his spine. Creepy.

So creepy that the walk changed utterly for him, the long inviting stretch metamorphosing itself into a guilty endless course under a sky so bright it was more white than blue. Lola had begged him to call from the road so she and Chuck could plan a time to be home. When he looked over his shoulder, the blonde was still retreating. He cut back across to the trees and from there to the road, back to get in his car without running the risk of crossing her path twice in one afternoon.

He climbed back into the convertible, his legs a foot longer since he'd stretched them. Turning the key, he stalled out. He'd driven eight hundred and fifty miles on spark plugs he'd timed himself, but the combination of a blonde and his mother left him forgetting how to start the car.

It wasn't until he was back on the highway, the engine revving, that he realized who she was. Caroline Starkey. Realized it, but didn't believe it at first. Not little lumpy weepy Caroline. But she'd recognized him: he'd have to give her a call. Again he saw the curve of her breasts through a polo shirt. No wonder the feeling had been incestuous. He'd just been confused about who the relatives were.

———

And maybe he'd been confused about the cure he'd find in Due East. Due East was prospering, and so was Lola. She'd married her Col. Charles G. Parrish, Ret., and moved into his big house on the creek. The colonel had never forgiven Steward for holding up the wedding (he was supposed to give Lola away, but at the appointed hour he was driving around Parris Island in circles, trying to find the Non-Com Club where Lola danced with Nick at another wedding, in another life).

Lola made shrimp étouffée that night and when he reached for the saltshaker Chuck said:

"I read an interesting thing about job interviews once, son. If a man ever takes you to lunch to see if he wants to hire you, you ought to *taste* your food before you go shaking salt on it. Otherwise he's apt to think you judge a situation before you've seen the whole of it."

Lola jumped right in. "Oh, but I always left the salt out of everything, cause of Nick's blood pressure. So see, Chuck, Stew *does* know the situation."

"Except that I don't have high blood pressure. And the shrimp's already salted."

"Excuse me." He was only going off to the bathroom, but the effect was pretty much what he wanted. As he pushed his chair away, matching wine-colored stains washed up over Chuck's cheeks.

When he got back to the table Chuck was gone and Lola sat with her chin in her hands. "You didn't have to be *that* rude."

"I only went to the bathroom."

"Oh, Stew."

"Oh Mama."

They ate their shrimp in silence, but lustily, and when they were all done Steward said: "I use your phone?"

"Oh, Stewie. Of course you can use my *phone*. Does this mean you'll stay the night?"

As if he ever intended to spend a night of his life in this scum-green-carpeted dark-leather-haunted suburban military dream house. "Nah. I better not hurt Grandmother's feelings."

"What about *my* feelings?"

"Aw . . . Chuck'll make you feel better." He wanted to swallow the words back, but he couldn't bring himself to apologize. He pictured Nick in the Barcalounger, smoking one of the colonel's cigars.

Lola sashayed through the swinging kitchen door with their butter-coated plates. She was putting on weight fast now, and her retreating rump looked like it belonged on one of those weight watchers you see stocking up on fake desserts in the frozen section. She did belong to Weight Watchers in fact, first organization outside the Catholic Church she'd let claim her in twenty years. Chuck had talked her out of the Church's *hooey,* so her salvation was dependent on dieting now.

He followed his mother into the kitchen and gave her a good squeeze. She looked up at him all misty-eyed, her silver eye shadow cracking. He was forgiven, and went to use the den phone downstairs. The quicker he escaped this brig, the better.

He did not have to look up Caroline's number, though it was just a guess that she was still living home. But a good guess.

"May I ask who is calling?" Doris! The majesty of that voice, imperious and undiminished over the years.

"This is Walker Evans."

"I'll see if she can come to the phone, Mr. Evans."

Oh, delirium. He'd become a gentleman caller. Maybe he'd find his peace in Due East after all. He heard Doris rest the phone down carefully. Then a swell of music filled the receiver, heavy rock. He was getting old, but the Starkey household was still on the cutting edge.

He had Caroline meet him in town, at one of the new waterfront restaurants. The place was dark and empty: a weeknight. He could have been anywhere. The waitress who served them gin and tonics looked to be about twelve.

Caroline, he could see clearly now, was not herself a baby anymore. There was a smoothness to her movements, a practiced leaning over the straw so she could raise her eyes and look up at him. The tricks of a tall girl. That familiar innocent face could possibly be very shrewd.

"And what are you up to, in Due East?"

"It's my first year," she said, "teaching math. At the junior high."

It seemed to him that her father had started out teaching math at Due East Junior High School. "You're brave."

She gurgled a practiced little giggle. "It's not so bad. AgnesAnn's there too, to show me the ropes."

"AgnesAnn! My God. What's she teach?"

"Math too. But she does the A sections and I do the C's. I . . . I have a feel for the slow ones." She looked up. "And some of them aren't that slow, either. They herd them in there like cattle, and it's just—it's just embarrassing for them."

He fell in love.

"Teresa was there too, don't laugh, she did the B sections, but she got married and moved to Charleston before I graduated. It's a good thing, I don't think the kids would put up with *three* Miz Starkeys."

"AgnesAnn didn't get married?"

"No, she's renting herself a little house on the Point. She wanted me to move in with her, but Mama's having a hard time. She finally got Martin out of the house—he's gone back up to the university to get himself a degree—but Paul won't even go for his GED. And then Albert's here. Oh." She looked down. "You don't want to hear all this, do you?"

He did. He wanted to hear what china Teresa picked for her wedding. He wanted to know who Paul was listening to after supper. The House of Starkey.

"How bout you? You just visiting family?"

"Well, no, actually. I'm here to make a movie—just a little project."

"That's so *exciting.*" Once you knew it was sweetness firing her, and not falseness, the gushing was charming, really. "They had a little article about that one you did—what was it called?"

"*Contentment Follies.*"

"That's right. They had an article about it in the *Courier.*"

"Oh," he said, and waved his hand. "I guess my grandfather planted that." Two years ago *Contentment Follies* was shown on the public station, one Sunday at midnight. *The New York Times,* in the next-to-last paragraph of a review of independent shorts, called it a "standout. Charming and unsentimental." When they got the clip in the mail, his grandparents called from their beach house and clinked champagne glasses over the phone. *You're on your way, Stewuhd.*

"What's the new one about?" Caroline asked.

"This woman worked for my family. Gloria. I never really got to know her. Now she's—I don't know if retired is the right word for a maid, but she's getting old. She'll slip away, I don't get to her soon. So here I am."

"She must be tickled to death."

"Well. She doesn't know about it, yet. I'm driving out to see her tomorrow."

"She *will* be tickled then, is what I should say."

He walked her out to her car. Parked right on River Street, right behind his: an old green MG, the top up.

"Now I'd call this a coincidence."

Caroline ducked her head down, then leaned over to open the car. "When I was little," she said, "and you used to pick up Franny, I'd think *That is the most beautiful car God ever made.*"

"I don't think God made the MG."

"One night you were mad and drove across the front lawn—remember? I saw you, out the window. I was the only one knew who did it, but I never did tell. I don't know whether it was you or the car I had a crush on."

He watched her fold herself into the driver's seat. She was good at it, and she tucked her long pleated skirt in after her. It couldn't be all bad to be a C-section math student.

"What'd Doris say, when you told her who you were meeting?"

Caroline smiled and depressed her clutch. "She said she hoped Walker Evans was a nice man, for a change, and to tell him that nice men come by the house to pick up their dates."

Steward had imagined all these years that his grandparents would think the movie stuff was a passing fancy, but they bragged on him until Aunt Blinky was sick with jealousy—and they planted articles in the *Due East Courier,* evidently. They fawned on him. They had broken a hip apiece, and his grandmother had given up both breasts to cancer. Now that Gloria was gone they had a Filipino couple to look after them. Grandfather had only the vaguest idea where Gloria had moved, and not a clue why Steward would want to put her on film.

"Gloria? Our Gloria? Good decent woman, Stewuhd, but I wouldn't say she was overblessed in the brains department."

Grandmother had a better idea of the directions, or had had a better idea once. "I know you go on out the beach road and turn at the Distant Island sign." A displeased look settled on her mouth, prune-shaped to begin with. Her collarbone jutted willfully. She did not like to concentrate anymore.

Back when Gloria lived in town, his grandmother used to drive her back and forth on a rainy day. When Gloria was sick, his grandmother brought him along to hand over useless presents, pecan pies and potted plants—but useless or not she was concerned, surely. Now she couldn't even tell you where the woman lived.

He turned at the Distant Island sign, as directed, and poked around the main road looking for a mailbox that said *Butler*. He'd only had occasion to take note of Gloria's last name once in his childhood when, at the Christmas party, Grandfather put a claw to her arm as she cleared a tray of pies. Grandfather was toddy-plied. *I'd say Gloria's the best-looking Butler we ever could have hired,* he said, wheezing at his own joke while his guests, bemused, smiled extravagantly. Gloria smiled too, patient until he released his grip. She was not what you'd call good-looking whether you were making a joke or not: she was a little pumpkin of a woman, with a small head for a stem and a bristly moustache.

Now that she'd moved out here with one of her granddaughters he was not even sure that her mailbox would say *Butler*. He drove the length of the road and back, scuttling the car from mailbox to mailbox. No luck. Down the sideroads he could see the changes in this part of the county: the clusters of brick ranches where once you would have seen a solitary cement block square, the shingled developments where a couple of wood shacks once stood. But the same elegant oaks that had survived a hundred years of hurricanes still stood, old-timers surveying the big stretches of dirt and green, tomato vines already poking through.

A gaggle of children too small to be in school walked alongside the road. When he stopped to ask them did they know Gloria Butler the mutt trailing them commenced yipping, and the children stared up, deaf-and-dumb and pretty well scared out of their wits. Well, sure. Watch out for strangers. But this was *Due East,* and he wasn't a stranger, and he didn't think his hair—pure white now though it might be—made him such a monster.

He tried one of the unpaved roads, and bumped his way past a pair of old frame houses. Hard to say which was sagging more, their porches or their steps. He parked in front of the one with a chicken coop out back: sign of life.

He rapped on the door and waited forever. There were shuffling sounds inside, but no one appeared at the door. He rapped again. More sliding across the floor. He began to imagine he could hear an intake of breath. One last try at the door, and this time he added:

Anybody home? He heard how unctuous he sounded, smarmy as the insurance salesman or the landlord the householder was trying to avoid. *I'm just looking for Gloria Butler.* A hopeless touch.

But it brought a little old lady to the door. At the sound of Gloria's name she swiveled her head into the screen and peered out at him.

"Glo-ya? Glo-ya Butler?" Her jaw performed a steady rhythmic drop that made her resemble the Nutcracker of his childhood. She scared him in the same way.

"Yes ma'am."

"What business?"

"Well, I . . ." He cocked his head back. It didn't occur to him to say Gloria was an old friend. She wasn't. "She, uh, she used to work for my grandparents."

The woman's grin was gold-capped. "Why you dint say so the first place. What family?"

"Morehouse."

"Mohouse! I spent some year ironing sheet for the Mohouse."

"No kidding! You used to come by the house?"

"Big house, River Street?" She shook her head, revealing nothing, and then cast a shrewd glance Steward's way. "Cheap white lady."

Steward laughed. "She always was."

She sent him a merry chase to Gloria's down three more pitted dirt roads, to one of the new little brick houses she'd promised. In the front yard, two small girls, twins, sat with a bucket, shaping mud balls they were flinging at one another. They grinned angel-grins, and then the one with the shovel took aim and got him on the sleeve.

"Hey!" he said—not mean, though he never had a clue, with children. The *Hey* brought Gloria herself to the door.

"What I say!" she hollered at the children, bypassing Steward completely, as if he came to call every day and wouldn't mind waiting. "What I say bout that mud. Did I iron them dresses this very morning, Lord, Lord, *Lord*. Out my sight. Get out my sight."

The children grinned up at her without backing up an inch and she turned to Steward. "My great-grandbabies," she said. "Can't do nothing with em. They got me twisted round. Come on in, now. Come on in."

She expressed no surprise at seeing him there. Had she forgotten who he was? Did she think maybe that he was there to sell her Fuller brushes, or Bibles? But no: she led him into a tidy little living room, furnished in sturdy matching plaids by Sears Roebuck, probably, and gestured for him to sit on the recliner.

"Steward, I know you like you a glass of tea."

"Yes, I do," he said, flummoxed. No hug, no pulling him close—he was the one feeling the strange tug and the need to touch her. She'd lost a good deal of weight, and the flesh hung heavy under her chin; but her face was animated (eyebrows swinging up and down, mouth swishing back and forth) in a way he didn't think he'd ever seen at his grandparents' house.

She brought him the tea, sweetest tea he'd ever tasted, and asked him when he was going to get out of that city and back home where he belonged.

"I like it there, Gloria."

"Chhh . . . How your mama getting by?"

He shrugged. "She got married again."

"She *did?* And she din tell me? I'm telling you, Steward, you move out heah to the country some folk in town done write you off as *dead.*"

"No, unhunh, Gloria, she wanted to come with me today—"

"How bout that husband? He be good to her like Nick?"

He shook his head and shrugged, palms up. Before he moved Lola out of the River Street house, Nick palmed a hundred bucks off to Gloria, but she gave it back. *She* was the one supposed to be giving a present. Nick got a big kick out of it.

"Oh well, Steward, yo mama bring home the Emperor of *China* he wunt be good enough. Nobody good enough for your mama. In that so?"

She told him she had the sugar, thought she was going to lose a leg last year but the grace of God and the sight of those great-grands outside got her toe wiggling the day before they were going to amputate, and now she wasn't even using a cane. Grandmother hadn't said a word about it.

"I tend twelve great-grands, Steward." Steward clutched his tea. Twelve great-grandchildren, ten of them off in school this morning, and her grand-children getting too old to even be thinking of having more babies, praise Jesus. They all lived out here now, she said, gesturing to the outside world, meaning maybe the row of identical brick houses. She had her hands folded in her lap, ready to give him his turn.

"Gloria, I, I been making movies in New York, little movies, not like home movies, but—"

She gave him a look hovering between sympathy and disdain, a look that suspended judgment but still said *I'm not retarded.* "I know," she said. Of course. Grandmother would have bragged to her too.

"Well I, I've done these, I guess you call them portraits, of people. And I uh was wondering if you'd let me talk to you some, get a camera out here, no big deal, maybe we could sit out back, you know, not have to worry about lights, maybe even drive by the house one day—"

That would be the tricky part, and all dependent on Gloria's letting loose a little, some little crack, some hint of the resentment that the nutcracker lady a mile back let loose so easily. But it wouldn't spill out from Gloria, not from a woman he'd spent five days a week with for the first twelve years of his life and still knew nothing about. He saw her old place in town, rough planks scrubbed clean, her mantel crowded with Morehouse discards: the first time he saw his chess set there, he reached for it back, but hadn't he tossed it himself, a bishop missing? Her house smelled, always, of sharp greens. Even as a small boy he averted his eyes, preferring the dirt and roots beneath his feet to the knotholes in the plywood.

Now she lived in a suburban box he would have disdained completely if it had belonged to a white family. No more kerosene stove to worry over through the fall and winter chill, no more windows so frail you couldn't raise and lower them. It had taken him aback, driving up today—there wasn't much visual impact *here,* her plot cleared of trees. The sky that took your breath away would look ordinary and colorless in the camera's eye.

But he could have her talk about her old place, and they could go by to shoot it; there could be a visual progression, as her talk of the years went by. Between the wood shack and the brick box would be the big white house on River Street where she'd worked for fifty-two years: cut from the roots in a dirt yard to the big verandahs, the azaleas on fire. He pulled himself back. He was cutting already, and he didn't even have footage.

Gloria was shaking her head. "Steward, Steward." She was smiling.

He waited.

"What, Gloria? You think I'm nuts."

"I *know* you nuts, honey. I can't be in no movie."

"You'd be great."

She shook her head again, *out of the question.* But she was tickled. Wasn't she? "I can't be in no movie," she said again.

He didn't push her, not today. He could drive out tomorrow, and the next day, if it took that; he could appeal to the grandchildren and the great-grandchildren if she was still too shy. He knew he could talk her into it—no subject had refused him, if you didn't count the drunks in the Irish Channel who had to pass, temporarily, when they couldn't unknot their tongues.

In his book he had two pages of freelancers, guys he could get down here with equipment on twenty-four-hour notice. He could shoot enough in a steady two weeks to net a good tight half hour. He began to see a series —*Faces of the Lowcountry*—and if PBS didn't think the race angle was big enough, he could sell it to the state network. Grant money would come rolling in for this sort of thing.

———

Identified as a gentleman caller, he was filling the role, two dates with Caroline and no more than a schoolboy's kiss at her mother's front door. His guilty hands pressed lightly on her cheeks: maybe it was the freckles, or the matching MGs. Maybe it was the idea that he'd come to Due East for a cure. Tonight he was driving her out to his grandparents' beach house at Claire's Point, their third night in a row.

It was a Friday night, the night the high school kids waited for the Light on the side of the Claire's Point Road. An aftertremor of incestuous shock went through him at the sight of all the cars on the shoulders, Franny hunkered down in each one, but Caroline stopped his teeth from chattering.

"How bout Parris Island?" she was saying. "That would make a great movie. Cept I guess you'd have to pull teeth to get permission to shoot out there. I guess you'd have to sorta make them think you were going to be real flattering."

He forgot the Light and Franny at the age of fifteen. Last night, for the first fifteen minutes, he thought Caroline's patter might drive him out of his mind—like Doris, she didn't seem to have to come up for air—but she was no Doris. The focus of her conversation was him.

"Parris Island'd be good," he said, "but you know, Wiseman covered that ground in *Basic Training.*"

"Wiseman?"

He was coming to enjoy the worldly knowledgeable filmmaker role around her. Her movie slate was blank. Last night he had a chance to lecture her on brothers, Maysles and Taviani. *You must have seen just about every movie ever made. You ought to go on* Jeopardy! *or something.*

He'd suggested an evening picnic on the beach (his grandmother's wicker hamper was wedged behind his seat) but now it was dark. They'd have to spread the food out on the porch. Mostly wine and cheese—still impossible to get a decent loaf of bread in this town. That was the real reason you couldn't go home again.

"What'll you do if Gloria says no, though, Stew?"

"She won't." He'd been to see Gloria three days in a row too. Unlike Caroline, who looked ready for more than a kiss under her mother's porchlight, Gloria was resistant.

"What're you gonna call it?"

"Oh, I don't know. *Gloria,* probably."

"Gloria. In excelsis deo. Whoa, that was like pushing a button."

Her laugh was merry and subdued. You could imagine she was never in a bad mood. He turned for the beach house, onto a dirt road half a lane wide, to keep Marines and high school kids out. The MG was spending more time in the air than it was on the ground.

"Ugh. There go my shocks."

"You don't want much in the way of shocks in an MG anyway, Stew. You kind of want to feel you're in a go-cart."

Eerie the way she plugged into the MG stuff. He pulled up to the house, set alone in a patch of woods, a short stretch of mud beach on the other side separating it from the sound. Another dirt road, wider, ran in front, connecting the Morehouses to the rest of Claire's Point. The beach house was a simple shingled affair, but sturdy. The screen porch ran around three walls, and the front entrance was set into the fourth. "It's not much. As you can see."

"Oh, I can't tell you how many times in my life I heard my mother say, *If I could get me a beach house I'd only need it for the night. I'd be so happy I'd die in my sleep and go straight to heaven.*"

Caroline was so—unguarded. *You ought to go on* Jeopardy! They stepped from the cool woodsy sea air into warm musty house air. He carried the picnic basket into the kitchen and she followed, sneezing.

"My word. This is the biggest kitchen I've ever been in in my life." She had a weakness for superlatives. He was pretty sure that tonight she'd be eating the best picnic she'd ever had, and the stars would be the prettiest she'd ever seen.

"Let's get you right out on the porch." She was still sneezing away, and then following one of her spasms with a little self-mocking giggle. Sweet. Already he thought of her in old-fashioned terms: *sweet, fond of her.*

He started to hoist the picnic basket. "Unless you'd rather—"

"What?"

"Take your clothes off?"

He hadn't known that was coming. Caroline was a sweet old-fashioned girl. He was supposed to be fond of her, and he was supposed to be the gentleman caller courting her. You didn't follow up a kiss under a porch-light with this.

She sneezed again, giggled again, turned the giggle into a graceful unbuttoning of her top three buttons. He hadn't expected her to strip for him any more than he'd expected to ask her to. She wore one of those blue oxford shirts that he wore himself but hadn't seen on another soul since he first held a camera in New York City. She twirled that third button, back and forth, round and round, a narrow rim of her bra showing. She stopped, still smiling. The bra was pink . . . couldn't have been any other color. He did not know a woman in New York who wore a bra.

He didn't take his eyes off her, but reached inside the picnic basket, a blind man, and lifted first the bottle of wine, then—after some patting of the rough bottom—the corkscrew. He slit the lead without looking at the blade in his hand and, holding the bottle between his knees, poked the tip of the screw into the cork and bore down hard. When he tugged, the smell of bordeaux joined the mold and the sand and the sea, and the kitchen became a warm moist bubble. Caroline followed the script and parted her lips. Still smiling.

More fumbling, for the glasses, his eyes focused on the cleft in her chin. Sweet. He brought the wine to her, folding her fingers round the curve of the glass. He unbuttoned her fourth button—pink lace below—but he did not go on. Instead he stepped backwards through the big square kitchen, a backtracking shot that took in the glass cabinets, the odds and ends of mismatched china and crystal, the happy disarray.

He'd shoot the man's point of view throughout. You'd never see his face. A close-up of the girl: amused, embarrassed, enjoying her performance as she sips the wine and twirls a loose strand of hair. Pull back. Medium shot. Now she sets her glass on the floor. She tugs the unbuttoned shirt loose from her long skirt and pulls it off slowly. She *is* enjoying this. Between her breasts a delicate gold chain with a tiny cross dangles. She is big-boned but slender, made for the camera. She joins her hands behind her back to unsnap her bra, and dangles the pink lace before she throws it down to join the wineglass on the floor.

A close-up of her breasts? A cheap shot. Instead he zooms in to her torso. She sways, tugging at her zipper, her breasts bobbing sweetly.

He pans the room, to give her a minute. Paperback books—*None Dare Call It Treason, Fannie Farmer*—on top of the old fat Frigidaire, copper pots over the old fat stove. Dusty framed pictures between the appliances: he lingers on two snapshots of a towheaded boy standing with ankles in the mud, two boys taken twenty years apart. Steward Morehouse Jr. Steward Morehouse III.

A man's intake of breath on the sound track, and a jerking pan back to her as the skirt finally yields and falls to her feet. Zoom in on oblong belly button between wide hips. She's wearing a strip of lacy bikinis: pink, to match.

Cut to her sandals, kicked high in the air. Follow one through its trajectory down to the wineglass.

The man kneels below her now, broken glass scattered at his feet. His breathing on the sound track? No, no: too damn Swedish. This scene is light, playful. He does, however, catch his breath.

The girl giggles. He tugs at the bikini, sliding it down.

Zoom in to the girl's fleshy white thigh, as the panties slide down. *Now* it would be all right to have some heavy breathing on the sound track.

Now they were walking the mud beach he used to walk with Franny, and Caroline was still chattering, into the night and the sea. Even in the kitchen she couldn't hold herself back: *Oh I can't believe it. Oh you're good. The best.*

Now more sweet talk, on and on. He couldn't hear her, really, even if the water and the stars were silent. His hand was intersticed with glass splinters. He'd been carried away, on the kitchen foor. And now there was a ghost walking with them, the girl who never had to speak, the one whose underwear was never pink, the little girl whose panties he'd never had the nerve to tug down. Little girl: that long ago, another life. A round black form loomed on the mud and he pulled Caroline's elbow back. He thought it was a sea turtle, but it was only another ghost.

"What?" she said. Chirped. "Look at those stars, Stew—prettiest I've *ever* seen."

"Uhm," he said, wine swelling all his joints. He took off his jacket and laid it on a long palmetto stump.

"What you doing?"

"Pillow," he said, and lowered her—pliable docile agreeable sweet pink-laced Caroline—onto the hard-packed mud. The cold damp spring air descended and he breathed his hot breath all over her. She giggled beneath. Hot breath all along her thighs: he was raising the long soft skirt. Now there was no bikini to pull down, left behind on the kitchen floor with the shards of glass. He spumed hot foam and bent her knee so he could nibble her inner thigh.

"Oh Steward." She was constitutionally unable to stop herself, even as he licked her closer and closer.

"Oh Steward. You are the best lover there ever was."

Fifth trip out to Gloria's. He had got his grandparents' o.k. to put up a crew at Claire's Point (*Long as I can come pester em with questions about how their doodads work,* Grandfather said). And once he had his footage, once the crew was gone, he would set up a cutting room in the big central sitting room where Aunt Blinky's boys once tormented him, Steenbeck on the long pine table where the fishing poles once rested. He saw himself cutting every last frame alone, solitary in his monastery by the sound. The summer folks would come and go. Caroline would drive over when school let out and wander through the beach house in pink lace while he finished the day's work.

But Gloria was unyielding. This morning she met him in her front yard, surrounded by big sedans filled with politely smiling grandchildren. Her hollering was good-natured—*Get on outta here, Steward, we're going to church. Can't you see?*—but it was still hollering. She would have killed him if he'd done what he really wanted, whipped out his Polaroid and shot her in that big hat: purple felt outside, green inside, a little white ceramic dove pinned to the upturned front brim. Whoa. Get back.

This afternoon he brought Caroline along for protection. The MG's top was down, and he hadn't heard a word she'd said in the last twenty minutes, but he nodded at a regular beat and used the gesture as excuse to look down at her freckled knees. The gravel spat up at them both.

Gloria's house was still surrounded with big cars, now emptied, and he parked across the dirt road, the left side of his car listing almost into the ditch. Give it up for today? Gloria's people would all be eating a big Sunday dinner. But he'd been so upbeat with Caroline. He sucked in his gut like a kid and climbed out.

Caroline said: "Looks like she's got company." First sentence of hers he'd understood since he backed out of her driveway.

"They'll talk her into it for me. Come on, I'll introduce you."

But Caroline hung back. Was she dubious, or was this just the reticence of Doris's well-behaved daughter? He loped ahead and hammered away at the front door while Caroline, in Sunday heels, picked her way through the balding yard.

His eye was on Caroline but his ear to the door. Behind it he could hear a hissing consultation and someone—sounded like an unamused Gloria—letting loose a weary *Lord have mercy*. A man's outline filled the door frame, and from behind the screen he said: "Steward Morehouse?"

Steward nodded.

The man nodded in turn and gave the door a slow push. He was short and slight, maybe Steward's own age, still dressed in his go-to-church suit, light blue, the same crisp polyester Nick always favored. His hair was clipped close, but still it caught the afternoon sun and looked like a bird's nest you could peer right through.

He nodded at Caroline, her heels still drilling through the yard. Then he swung his pink palm out to indicate that she should abandon her goal, that they should all walk farther out, away from the house, where the sounds of laughter and jabbering now swelled. The silent treatment made him feel like he was back at St. Ben's, being held for jug by the abbot himself.

When they reached the road the man spoke in a low funereal voice, as if to spare Caroline: "My grandmother asked me to tell you please stop worrying her. She can't be in no movie."

Steward made an epileptic movement, starting with a shrug and ending with a headshake. He couldn't *believe* Gloria would send an emissary out to shoo him away, not with Caroline standing by. He'd been looking forward to the light in Gloria's eyes when she saw Franny's sister.

"I'm sorry we troubled you. I guess you got a family gathering."

The man pressed his lips together and turned their ends up, but you couldn't say he was smiling. "Always got a lot of family in this house."

"Look, I'm sorry. I'll come back when—"

Now the guy shook his head, but he definitely wasn't smiling. "I don't think you getting the *point*. My grandmother don't want you *wor*rying her."

"I don't know if she told you—"

"She told me."

"I just need a few days of her time. The movie's, uh, an oral history. I'm sure I can sell it to public TV, you know, ETV?"

"Scuse me. You speak English?"

Behind the guy Caroline was rolling her hands one round the other and then pointing off to the horizon. *Let's get out of here.*

Steward held up his own hands. "O.k. O.k." But his move to back across the dirt road incited Gloria's grandson, who stuck out his finger and looked for the first time like he was enjoying himself, jabbing Steward close to the chest, a gesture big and exaggerated enough for a silent movie. Only he wasn't silent.

"You don't think you people got enough out that old woman? Now you got to get a *ETV* piece of her hide too?"

He and Caroline must have looked like a couple of rabbits to the guy, skittering back into the car and vooming off down the dirt road. What he should have done was laugh it off right away, squeeze Caroline's freckled knee and dismiss it. He had a thousand projects lined up in New York—settlement house, halfway house, he'd already made overtures—and an acting workshop he needed to sweat through if he ever wanted to do a feature and have any authority whatsoever with the actors. He didn't need Gloria any more than he needed to be back in Due East.

The MG bucked down the remains of the dirt road and out onto the pavement. Shocks gone, timing off, fifteen-year-old car bought in a fit of sentimentality. When he tried to remember the face on Gloria's grandson, the only picture he got was Chuck Parrish's face.

He drove fast onto the main road. Still he hadn't squeezed Caroline's knee, or looked in her direction. His veins ran nasty: wrong sister anyway. *You ought to go on* Jeopardy!

He turned back onto the beach road toward town, but after a half mile he made another quick turn he hadn't even known he was going to make. It was a new road to him. Caroline did not ask where they were going, and he followed it past an abandoned store with ancient gas pumps out front and a wounded Pegasus, knocked down in some windstorm, propped up against the wall. He'd seen that same horse going for a thousand bucks in an antique store down on Fourth Avenue.

The road ran out, finally, at a pair of new brick signposts signaling an old plantation, Live Oaks, the long driveway beckoning in. Now he knew where he was: the Smallwoods', a breezy Boston couple who wintered in Due East and sometimes came to his grandfather's Christmas party. He took a dirt road that veered off before the entrance and followed it down through a field of furrows, his shocks beyond hope. The MG's tires did not fit into the smooth tractor trail. The open car was choking with dust, but Caroline was silent beside him.

What was he doing? Beyond the field was a little rise and a little wood. He pressed the gas and emerged on the other side of the hill looking down a low expanse of scrub merging into grass that didn't know whether to make itself part of the marsh or part of the farmland. Then low mounds of dirt melding into sand, then a shoreline paved with oyster shells. The end of the world. The road became a footpath, but the MG squeezed through, broad-hipped but graceful, like Caroline. He stopped the car.

Now he should squeeze her knee, laugh, dismiss it for what it was. Big deal. He'd shot three documentaries, the last one a full half hour, and he had three more in the works. On the seventh he would rest. He stared out at the broad stretch of water facing them, Caroline still beside him. She'd been silent for ten minutes! A record! He sighed—that would egg her on—and finally she said:

"They sure made you guilty enough in that school."

"What school?"

"Didn't you go to some Catholic boarding school?"

"Yeah."

"Well, they sure made you guilty enough. I didn't know you better, I'd think you *were* Catholic. What you trying to do, make up for *everything?*"

Don't give me the willies, he wanted to say. "I'm pissed about that guy, telling Gloria what to do."

She opened her mouth—he was pretty sure a Doris-lecture was going to come out—but then she closed it again. Guilty?

He left the car for the water's edge, but Caroline said she'd stay behind. The tide was high and he stepped out of his boat shoes soon as he stepped out of the sea oats. He rolled up his trousers, awkward with her watching from the car. The whole business was awkward. Four nights with her, two of them in restaurants. If she turned her nose into the light her prettiness mocked his memory of her sister. It was one thing, if he were doing the Gloria piece, to picture her walking through his grandfather's beach house half-clothed. But if he went back to New York tomorrow, as he now intended to do, he had no picture of Caroline at all. And he didn't feel guilty about *that,* either.

He heard his own disembodied high holler, like a small boy's, when his toe met the spike of an oyster shell; but it wasn't until he lifted his foot and saw the underside that he fully realized what a gash he'd taken. The dark mud was stained with his blood and the cut went in a good quarter inch where his big toe was attached. He felt only a sting, but he didn't know how he'd be able to walk on it. The top would flop and bleed all over the ground.

Caroline was sprinting toward him, but he waved her away, nonchalant —*sorry, it was nothing*—and resumed staring at the water. He'd have to figure out how to walk. "Just an oyster shell," he said when she joined him.

"They can be nasty."

"I thought something was biting me, tell you the truth."

Now she stood beside him and joined his silent vigil. He found he did not mind her presence. She managed to stay quiet for a minute.

Then she said: "How much did you offer to pay her?"

"Oh, I wasn't going to pay her. In a documentary you don't, see. It could—cloud the issues."

"Oh."

"You know, if you paid your subjects they might be just saying what you wanted them to say."

"Oh."

"You just don't do that with a documentary."

"I see."

He heard in her voice the complete teacherly disapproval. No wonder the word *guilt* popped into her mind so quick and easy. Sweet Caroline might be just as good as Doris dishing it out, all he knew. They stared at birds making sudden bobs into the water. He felt that a child stood next to him, waiting for him to point something out.

"See, you said you were going to *sell it* to ETV, and I think he thought . . ."

"But I don't make a dime off these things, I don't even make back costs. You don't think that's what she's been waiting for. An offer?" She *had* seemed eager that first day. And the way her grandson snarled. *You don't think you people got enough out of her.* Did Gloria equate him with his grandmother, with the useless plants and the castoff toys? The idea sickened him—that, or the blood he was losing. He looked down into a widening pool of blood and felt the gash press a sharp nervous quiver through the length of his foot.

Caroline followed his gaze and then made a ferocious sound, like a growl. "Good Lord Stew, hold that up so's I can see."

He lifted the toe, but the sight of its spill made him reach out to her shoulder to steady himself. His foot was leaking something blue and glistening.

"Get you back to the car." Caroline was already clasping his hand onto her shoulder. "You got something for a tourniquet?"

He was probably shaking his head no. He was light-headed and the sun seemed too bright. Bad day for shooting. Hobble hobble. She was hurrying him faster than he wanted to go. Now she was pushing him down into the passenger seat—did she think *she*'d be driving back to town? O.k., o.k. She knew how to drive an MG.

"Stew, we're gonna have to get you to an emergency room."

"Not that bad." He saw the trail of blood marking his hop to the car. Caroline was rummaging behind the seat, pulling up dirty rags and discarding them.

She had him lean forward and performed expert surgery on the bottom of his blue oxford shirt—it should have been too good a cloth to rip. His grandfather had taught him how to buy a shirt.

"There's nothing for water," she said. "Just let me tie a tourniquet and get out of here. You wouldn't have an artery in your toe there, would you? Nah, that'd be shooting out. You must have got you the muscle." She was bustling, enjoying herself, that womanly business of reassuring you and diminishing you all at once. He rested his head back, a C-section student while she yanked the knot tight and his toe went dead. Her hand came up bloody. She wiped it on the front of his shirt, smiled, and ran round to the driver's side.

"Fifteen miles. That *better* stop the bleeding."

By the time they were back on pavement her freckled right hand on the gearshift had caused him all sorts of lewd visions. Her face, concentrating, was as furrowed as the field back there, her chattering no more than a *swishswish* with the wind. The sun was warm. His toe was dead. The light was bright.

She had to shake him, fifteen miles later, at the emergency entrance. She was standing inside the open passenger door, staring down at him, alarm lighting her eyes now that they'd made it here.

"Oh, does it hurt that bad?"

He must have been dreaming. He did not know who she was—well, he did know who she was, but he had it wrong. He saw Simone when he opened his eyes. He must have been dreaming Simone.

"I thought you were somebody else." Had to explain the moan.

She gave him a look of blank sympathy. She must be thinking Franny for *somebody else*. By now they were halfway up the ramp, but the red and white emergency sign was off in space. He was trying not to hang onto her, but he was sure they were going to have to amputate the toe if not the foot.

Caroline, brow still furrowed, held the door for him, and didn't look like anyone else, not like Simone, not like Franny. Before he hopped inside the dark womb of Due East Memorial he leaned his mouth down on hers and gave her a wet sloppy kiss, all the pain of his big toe transformed for one glorious moment into simple lust.

"I know I'll be here a while." He pretended he was trying not to wince. "Look, Caroline, I need a big favor."

She gave him a maternal look.

"I want you to go on back out there, you turn by Distant Island. Think you can find it? Go on back out there and offer Gloria twenty-five thousand."

"Stew. Go on in. You're delirious."

"I mean it. If she won't take twenty-five, go up by fives till she's got what she wants. I'm making that movie."

"Stew."

"She can have a blank check, she wants it. I just didn't get it." He was looking into a dark corridor, but now it was as if somebody had lifted the hood from his face. "I JUST DIDN'T GET IT."

He must have been screaming into the hallway. A nurse stopped on her journey to the E.R. and turned his way. Elizabeth Morehouse was dead, five months now, and all he'd ever given her was a Chinese dinner on the Upper West Side. Gloria could have Live Oaks Plantation if she wanted it.

"That grandson can be in it too, he wants. He can rant on camera."

"Stew, watch out!"

The nurse was almost to his side; he must have been tipping forward to reach for her. Now he was keeling over onto the shiny mopped corridor, headfirst, it looked like—there were those clean little linoleum squares looming—but then life was always just like a movie. It was happening in slow motion, and the sensation of falling and flying at once, of two women holding out their arms to catch him, was pleasant and gooey and just what the doctor ordered. He went down, right into the camera's open aperture.

PILGRIM
MAURA

The light was good and steady, even on this gray September day. Especially on this gray September day. The significance of September was not its daily delivery of half-assed drizzle, but its promise of full-day kindergarten. Three children out of the house for six hours and twenty-five minutes a day: hours, hours, hours in the studio, a run around the park, a book. Frances Burke, back in her own body, signing her pictures Frances Starkey. The light was good, the day was good, this family was good. You could come back from that mothering stuff all fierce and ready to go for the rest of your life, paint pouring out your fingers before you even rode your bike down by the Gowanus and climbed the rickety steps to the studio door.

This painting was good. Nine feet by six: she'd had Michael help her make the stretcher and hoist it up onto the brick factory wall, though he'd croak if he knew what it was for.

Your lovers? Kate could have been back on the schoolyard tittering. *All of them?* Giggling monogamous Kate.

But there hadn't been so many lovers after all: just a passel of boys, and Declan, and then the academic slobs Steedman and Artosaurus. Steedman and Artosaurus, in honor of being the last ones, were the only ones making their appearances nude in this painting. She was as much a model of monogamy now as Kate, a saintly wife in a world of Ronald Reagan and sexual license. She'd been good long enough to get three children into the public school and out of the house, and now there was time to celebrate. Time for a big painting and a good laugh, a close to that chapter.

She was always alone in the studio for these first hours—no call for the single life-of-leisure artists she split the space with to rouse themselves from their quiet apartments and meander down here until they were good and ready. They waited for inspiration, but she was a factory worker toiling away in any hours she could grab. And she got the morning solitude dividend anyway: softer light, any music she wanted to play, the whole loft floor to pace when she was stuck.

Which she wasn't, and hadn't been since she started this particular piece. She had Aretha on the tape deck (could have been at the Due East High School Friday night dance) and the canvas on the wall. The composition had come on like a dream, ten boys and three men lined up like Jesus and the apostles at the Last Supper—only these guys weren't sitting down to break bread and drink wine, they were kneeling in a half-moon, all but Declan, who sat in his wheelchair near one end. They all clasped their hands together, though some looked more obedient than others. S.D. prayed in the middle—a true sacrilege—but really, who else could go dead center? Not Tony Rivers. Talk about sacrilege.

She had toyed with putting Steward in the middle, maybe not kneeling at all, but Steward would throw the numbers off and he'd never been a lover, clothed or unclothed. Honesty in art forever. Her sister would never forgive her, anyway, if Franny used the boy when Caroline was having an affair with the man. On-again, off-again, long-distance, but an affair nonetheless. Right now Caroline and Steward were sleeping late in Florence and Rome (ah, sharp stabs of jealousy for all the Raphaels she would never see) on their way back from hustling Steward's latest documentary at some festival. Caroline had called one night to say that the French agent thought things were looking good in Paris, but Franny hadn't seen her sister since the last family Christmas almost two years ago. She hadn't seen Steward since *his* Christmas party in . . . what year? Between Martin and Maura. She counted his presence in between her children's, but she couldn't say she thought of him with any less intensity than she thought of them. Otherwise why was she gripping her brush like a knife?

And it was only Beanie Boatwright she was working on. It was as if she'd never done those years of careful renderings, of elaborate little drawings when the human face spewed out of Franny Starkey's pencil as precise as blueprints. Now Beanie's mouth kept shaping itself bowlike into Steward's mouth, and Beanie kept sucking in his cheeks to make them hollow as Steward's. There was nothing wrong with Caroline falling in love with Steward, but that didn't mean Franny could paint when she thought of the two of them under Italian sheets, planning their visit to the Uffizi.

She left Beanie Boatwright for Declan McCleary. She already had his face, and now the paint spread itself deeper into Declan, the deep lines of an old man around a young man's eyes, the skin weathered, the color of tongue. She'd been wallowing in wet unmixed color since the children, squeezing right out of the tube and shaping everything—chins, eyes, noses —into something pure. But for skin the color of tongue, she had to mix.

There was an outsize groan behind her. "Not that tape again. Next thing it'll be disco." It was only John coming in, John who painted in the rear third of the space, who played Phillip Glass and Andreas Vollenweider and pretended not to like Aretha. She hadn't heard his clump on the stair, but then she didn't hear anything when the work was going well, not even in the clanking echoing hallways. She could be murdered while she painted her masterpiece, but that at least would be a worthy end, her time run out in this building which had once been a watch factory.

She didn't answer him—the purest pleasure of sharing a studio, as opposed to sharing a life, was how nobody splitting the rent expected you to answer when your work was moving. John slid behind her to watch while she stabbed away at Declan's hair. Ordinarily he scoffed at anything representational, but he thought this one a good joke, and he approved of the distortions she did, looming hands or faces half the size of bodies. His presence made the brush magical, subservient, obedient. She could do anything on canvas.

"Looking good."

It was. John, the conceptualist who figured she finally had a concept, had egged her on and now it was John's eyes she was feeling, the tension of having plain skinny John, silly little goatee on his chin and his jeans slipping down his belly, intense minimalist John, breathing behind her. Tension, tension: what kept her good lately. Michael saw John as a threat, but she knew she could hold herself in check. John had no feel for color. His work was muddy. No chance for sexual compatibility.

"Fran, I got a piece in that juried show. Y'know, the Next Work Center."

She spun around, brush in hand, and hugged him tight enough that she could feel the jeans sliding. "Hey hey. Is it too early for champagne? What they take?"

"The brown triangles." Muddy and minimalist too, tiny dirty triangles in a sea of beige. She'd played the Temptations to try to get John's triangles dancing, but he was a master of control and did not succumb to her subversions or her Temptations. He didn't *see* color. He'd gone to RISD (O great art school that had returned her slides so ignominiously) where he trained as a sculptor: for four years he fashioned triangles of balsa wood or sheet metal or buttons. He'd only been painting, for real, for a year, and he was still doing triangles. But already . . . he'd be out of here and into the Whitney Biennial inside another year.

He backed out of her arms, where he must have felt the disapproval throbbing. Never be jealous of another artist, never be jealous of another artist.

"I *did* come in early to tell you. Couldn't sleep all night. Silly, huh? Stupid little show." He hugged her again, doing a little minimalist jig, feet only.

Muddy John's work in the Next Work show. He didn't know she'd sent slides too: but she never wanted to jinx it by telling someone twenty-two and bound for glory. He'd already sold two triangle sculptures to Cultural Affairs for their parks projects. He was always arranging for mysterious young lawyer and accountant types to come by the studio, where they nodded politely at her big portraits (well, hadn't Saint Alice Neel suffered half a lifetime of obscurity?) and then slobbered over John's brown-and-beige geometry. Great how painting and interior decorating were merging. The Age of Reagan and Sexual License and Schnabel. A girl came upstairs once and said to John, about the brown triangles, *They're so human,* and Franny said: *Excuse me, I'm going to barf.* Barf. Could you get more childish?

She hoisted her shoulders up. Never be jealous of another artist, never, never. The children were in school now. She could do it by thirty. She could.

John could see her suffering. "Listen, let's get you down to the Drawing Center like we said we would, huh? Let's take off this week. And I'm getting closer to Mary Boone, hey I know we can waltz in her front door by the year 2000."

Second hug for John, for keeping her going, but then she pushed him away. He skipped, leaving for his own space. He wouldn't need to work today. He could just preen. She looked back at her own canvas, where Beanie Boatwright was a bloated avocado and Declan, she saw now, was way off. The green—strokes of genius in his short-cropped hair ten minutes ago—was show-offy. What could you hope for in a world where the mud and crockery slingers were rising?

She wiped the brush. She'd raised three babies and they weren't babies anymore. All she had to do was keep painting, keep painting, keep painting, and then Michael could quit his job and write his novels and they'd be . . .

Just happy. Shot through with visceral memory. She had never felt this with the boys, though the boys of course did not wear dresses they grabbed by the hem and then lifted over their faces, as Maura was doing now. The last time the boys showed their chubby thighs they were wearing diapers, but Maura liked to display her slender ones branching out of pastel underpants. The flash of underwear was a constant, whether she was doing cartwheels or sitting quiet with her gang of dolls. A stab of memory, right to the gut.

She'd wept for Maura in childbirth. She knew the boys utterly now. How many ways could she go wrong with a girl? Here was Maura, five years old, sitting on the kitchen floor where she had lined up her dolls to punish them. Her legs were spread, her underwear showing, her gray eyes smutty and her hair as black as Franny's. She was the only one of the children with her mother's round knobby nose. Franny sometimes felt she knew what it was like to be inside her daughter's skin, and didn't they call that overinvolvement?

"What did they do wrong?"

Maura was making marks on the dolls' faces, careful etchings in blue ballpoint. She held up a Barbie, her knuckles bent over the great bare breasts. All the dolls had to strip naked when they were being punished. Maura had inscribed the letter *T* on Barbie's cheek. "Tease," Maura said. "She's been teasing everybody."

"Aha."

Now Maura raised a fully clothed alien borrowed from her brothers' space people. Franny had always thought she would raise a daughter in pants who read biographies of Amelia Earhart and wanted to join the rodeo, but look: here she sat in blue satin, playing sins with a Barbie doll. "He's praying for her."

Franny looked up again from her kneading (therapy, when she was sentenced to domesticity) and saw that Maura had grouped a whole troupe of victims who kneeled at a little altar made of a book. She'd propped a crucifix on the radiator and raised all the heads that were movable to worship it.

"Jesus Christ!" That was Michael, who had been reading at the dining room table next door but spying on them as well.

"Yes, exactly," Franny said, but Michael was not amused. Even in the vast regions of the new place—the bottom half of a brownstone, a co-op bought cheap because it was far enough down the hill on a block that still had grubby tenements as yet untouched by the hands of yuppies—they were always on top of each other. Michael stood in the kitchen doorway shaking his head at Maura's altar.

"MAURA!"

She looked up soundless, a wide-eyed technique she'd perfected in infancy.

"YOU CAN'T BE DRAGGING CRUCIFIXES IN WITH YOUR DOLLS."

Franny shot him a warning in raised eyebrows. He shuffled his feet, undecided, then reached down and scooped up his daughter. He could have been stroking a kitten against his long torso: you could only see black fur behind his hand.

"I scare you?"

Now you could see her shaking her head. *No, Papa.* Nobody knew where she got the *Papa* stuff. It appeared as mysteriously as the dolls and the blue satin. Michael called her his Jane Austen baby, the only one, he thought sometimes, with any sensibility at all.

Certainly the only one with religious mania. Maura slithered down from her father's arms and grabbed the crucifix off the radiator. She smiled sweetly at her papa and then, just as she passed him by, extended the crucifix at arm's length for her procession up the stairs.

Michael held his breath until she was out of earshot and then growled. "Getting out of hand."

Franny kneaded away. This was dangerous ground. She shrugged as she kneaded, wily, and soon the dough wore peaks.

"No, Fran, look she's up half the night with nightmares."

"Aw, they all went through that."

Michael had lately grown a beard, close-cropped to go with his respectable new life. It was harder to read his expression, but he raised his elegant eyebrows, still strawberry blond, still fine-lined quarter-moons, to make sure she understood that she was raising a family of misfits. As of course she was—they were—but you'd think he'd have some sympathy for their loopiness.

"It's too much. She doesn't need to be in those CCD classes."

The bread dough turned to hardening clay in her hands. He hadn't wanted the children baptized, but Joe had come up from Maryland and Michael let them go ahead when he saw how much it meant to Norah. He didn't want them going to Mass—he didn't see, he said to her, why anyone who referred to the Conference of American Bishops as *the old farts' convention* would insist on dragging her toddlers to Sunday Mass. And he didn't want them going to religion classes when they should be learning about Galileo and the Inquisition and Pius XII standing by while Jews were carted off. He was incensed when he saw the new books they brought home—all peace and love and understanding, color photographs of little black boys playing with little white girls, little Latinos beaming up at grandfatherly Irish priests. *What'd they do with the Baltimore Catechism?* he thundered: because if they were going to be taught this lovey-dovey crap they might as well be taught the old crap, which might not hold any meaning but at least had some rhythm. They might as well be taught the Latin Mass. When Brian came home from class and said they called Confession the Sacrament of Reconciliation now, Michael held his nose; but when Brian said Sister said they should be deciding for themselves what was a sin, Michael said that Sister ought to be horsewhipped. He would be glad to provide Brian with a list of sins, and the list began with social injustice, promulgated in their own city by the Archdiocese of New York.

She looked up, her dough long since kneaded. Michael was still in the doorway, his eyes cast down for the moment on his daughter's dolls but watching—she knew it—his wife. This was a placid time for them, most of the time, their children old enough for school, a bedroom finally for Maura. Michael's magazine was a success and they were salting money away for the first time in their lives. The idea was for him to go freelance in a year or two, and work at home, mornings on novels, afternoons on articles.

"John got into a show."

"Yeah?" Michael might be monosyllabic tonight, but he knew how to empathize over *this* one. A month after they moved to New York, *Fiction* took a long story, and for a couple of weeks they lived in a dreamworld of salary and literary fame, Michael so young and already a success in two worlds! But *Fiction* didn't like the next story so much, and one wasn't enough to get an agent, and they were too exhausted at night to drag into Manhattan and sit at the White Horse, or wherever you were supposed to get drunk now. Somebody at *The New Yorker* wrote long encouraging letters, and after he got one Michael passed on the little moment of hope. He would stand in front of one of her portraits—of Billy, or Frank—and say *That's it. You got it.*

"I'm so"—she slapped the dough into a dishtowel—"I'm so crazy to go I can't tell you. If I can just sell a piece, one lousy piece, and hire somebody to take the kids for the afternoons when I'm going strong. Or let you out of the job tomorrow. Tomorrow. You could be writing and they could come climb on your lap."

She'd never had any ambition to sell anything, never—the work itself had always been enough and only fools fell into the commercial thing—but there was a rush just now, a hurricane force propelling her, the kind of crazy energy they talked about women getting when they were fifty-five and the years of raising the children were over. She'd never resented them, never—oh maybe the whining or the cartoons, maybe the laundry always crawling out of the corners—but now that she could work again she saw that she was emerging from deadtime, that she'd frozen her own worktime for almost ten years so the children could have theirs.

"I could get into it. Your going off to the salt mines for a change." Lately Michael was a model of agreeability. Two weeks before, he had posed nude and kneeling for a snapshot, not knowing he was posing for Steedman. As soon as she looked through the lens she saw that Michael's wasn't the paunch she needed—his was only a rim around his middle—but she kept the Polaroid and got it out sometimes when she was working. Not for help with the male figure, for the agreeable expression on Michael's face, leering back at her, hands clasped as she'd requested in prayer. And for the agreeable body, his shlong long and narrow like the rest of him, set in a burning bush of red hair.

"Hey Fran." He came round to where she was peeling the counter of dough strips and squeezed her from behind, first shoulders, then breasts. "You'll do it."

"Oh . . ."

"We'll do it. The thing is, if we could just not make the guys feel they stopped us. Y'know? If we could just not be my old man, making them feel guilty for having the nerve to get born."

She put her hands over his, on her breasts, and then Maura, their baby, came flouncing back into the room in a first communion veil. She had stabbed some black mascara around her eyes and borrowed a pair of high heels—red high heels, the only grown-up shoes Franny consented to own. She might as well have been wearing a boa to complete the effect, but instead she had on a shawl which, Franny suspected, was meant to signify a saint, Bernadette or Claire or Térèse, bigger idols than even Barbie.

"What's that?" Michael said.

Maura did the big-eyed staring thing.

"What's that, Maura begorrah?"

Maura twirled the shawl innocently, knowing perfectly well what her father meant.

"I got it for her."

"You got her a *communion veil?*"

"She was carrying on, you know, at the meeting for the first communion kids, Martin was getting a prayer book and a rosary, and so I just ordered the veil for her."

"Fran, she is five years old."

"Well, she'll put it to use."

"She will not. It'll be torn to shreds by the time she's supposed to make her own communion. She'll be using it for dress-up."

"That's what I meant."

"Jesus! Do I laugh or cry?"

"Both, my son."

"Maura baby, you know all that playing you do is make-believe?"

Maura drew the shawl tighter and rearranged the veil. "Oh yes, Papa," she said. "Oh yes, I certainly do." *Certainly do:* what other child in the world spoke like Maura? But she was already crouching down with the ballpoint pen to mark new sins onto naked dolls' cheeks and foreheads.

And Michael was leaving the kitchen before he got apoplectic at the sight of his darling in habit, or burlesque, or whatever that was she was wearing. He was leaving the kitchen, but on the way out he was letting his eyes range over her big kitchen piece—Gowanus Canal at sunset, orange fire on top, Hieronymus Bosch bodies below, in the water—and then moving into the dining room where every inch was taken with her work. There was a horsey Peggy Barnacle in her aviator glasses, a good likeness that Peggy couldn't bear to look at when she came; two or three each of the children separately, sedate old-fashioned Cassatty oils; and over the mantel a good group of them huddled onto their parents' bed, Brian's arm long and his hand grown big as his father's as he reached it round his brother and sister to draw them close. Michael wandered the room the way he might a gallery, as if he were weighing the possibility that she would ever make a life from this work.

Madness to even concern yourself with selling it. Better just to do it, and keep it pure that way, and support yourself by—she could wait on tables, though that wouldn't make the money to pay the sitter much less buy her painting time. Maura leaned to write *M* on a wetting doll's bare behind and Franny winced.

"What'd that one do?"

Maura stared around, solemn. "Mmmm . . . Made everyone cry."

Franny tried to smile at her daughter, really she did, but maybe Michael was right. Maybe all her children were weirder than she admitted. Maybe they'd all end up in emergency rooms, as her brother Will had after that last family Christmas, waiting to get on the psych ward to be cured of the heebie-jeebies.

She thought she'd moved the dough to the warm corner near the refrigerator but there it was by the window. Now it would never rise, cold bland wad of flour and water. Who'd she think she was kidding?

Peggy Barnacle had moved to the neighborhood and came for dinner on Fridays, supplanting Kevin, who had left Park Slope to burrow into some little basement apartment in Flatbush, no mention of law school anymore. Kevin was now in Purgatory, Michael said, and so was he when Peggy was spending Friday nights putting her feet on his tables. Her greatest pleasure was still to razz him, but at least he talked to her. He only grunted to the young lawyers and investment bankers who came to pick up their children from playdates with one of his. *Playdates,* he groused. *When I was a kid you took a ball and you threw it against the stoop and that was playing.* That *was playing.*

"See you're getting all yupped up this end of the Slope," Peggy said. "Three new yogurt shops in a block and a half." Peggy had dug her heels in closer to the canal—around the corner from Franny's studio in fact—only six or seven blocks away but down to a whole new level of industrial wasteland and lurking figures in the dark.

"Oh man," Michael said, "what is this, the sixties? Remember the socialist workers accusing everybody of being bougie? Me. Bourgeois. With my father a fucking card-carrying alcoholic member of the bummed-out working class."

"Daddy, don't say—" Maura said the word *fucking,* but not a sound came out. And Michael didn't say *fucking* anymore: he threatened to wash Brian's mouth out with soap when he heard it. It was only Peggy egging him on. Peggy was a walking reminder of all his politics left behind. She organized demonstrations for Amnesty International and fasted for Oxfam; she linked arms to do abortion clinic defense and she chanted outside St. Pat's when the cardinal was saying Mass (Franny saw her sometimes in the neighborhood in the communion line at the twelve-thirty, no contradiction intended).

"Well, look at you now!" Peggy hooted and drew her long chunky arms around the old wood-paneled dining room, the big round antique table where they sat. "Are you gonna tell me you're not bourgeois now?

Are you gonna tell me you're not the heart of gentrification of this neighborhood?"

"How big a Puerto Rican family you think you displaced when you hauled your matching teacher's luggage into *your* floor-through?"

"Dominican. Don't you know what's going on in your own neighborhood?"

"Give me a break."

"O.k. Truce. I'm bourgeois. You're bourgeois."

"I *grew up* in this neighborhood."

"Well, and came back and made money. You're gonna tell me you're not bourgeois now?"

"Yeah," Michael said. "I'm gonna tell you I'm not bourgeois now, because I gave notice today. I'm going freelance and I'm not gonna have a fucking Board of Ed nine-to-three like you—"

"Daddy, don't say—"

"Yeah, baby, calm down, I'm not going to have a safe job anymore, Miss Politically Pure Barnacle, so it'll be a thrill a minute around here and you are welcome to come watch the show."

Franny had just risen to fetch the wine bottle. Could have been the sudden standing that took her breath away; or could have been the guilt that she was having another glass of wine when she was five days late and puffy and getting suspicious; or could have been her inability to decide whether Michael had actually given notice that very day or was just strutting for Peggy's sake. Maybe, if she was pregnant again, Michael could still go back to the publisher. Maybe he hadn't even knocked on the publisher's door yet.

The room went black, and when she could see again she could see Maura staring up at her.

Michael said: "You all right?"

And Maura, in a trance: "Daddy, don't say—"

She was drunk enough to spend the night on the couch and tired enough the next day not to know whether it was pregnancy or hangover or despair that closed her right eye in the old way. It was a Saturday and she put on her jacket to head for the studio without saying good-bye to anyone, not even to Maura, who sat rapt in front of *Space Dinosaurs* between her brothers.

But Martin sensed her leaving, and skipped down the steps to give her a wet kiss at the door; she looked down to savor his narrow mouth, his lower lip puffy and perfect. Then when she was halfway down the block she heard a runner behind her and knew that it was Michael. When he caught her by the shoulder he spun her around and said:

"Hey."

She couldn't look him in the face.

"Hey. I'm sorry, I wanted to tell you first, but Peggy was there when I got home, *Christ* she lives at our house."

Still she felt she had to stare out past him. The air was cool and came on gusts, getting into October. Maybe it was the sun that accounted for her blankness. Her eye had opened again once she got outside.

"Look Franny, say something, I thought you'd be glad, and then you go and sleep on the fucking couch and make me feel like a piece of shit."

"I was drunk."

"Don't tell me you were fucking drunk. You were mad."

"Don't say—Listen to me, like Maura."

"Well you were, come on, you were mad about it."

"I'm scared."

"Well me too. I could use—y'know—some . . ."

"We talked about when I sold something. I'll never—"

"Come on. Come on, what's happening to us, first big move I make in five years and all you can say is *I'll never.*"

Her body felt like that bread dough, thick, hopeless. "Did you really do it? Give notice?"

"Shit." Michael's body was still wound tight, still eager. "Shit, I thought you'd be dancing in the street. I bring home champagne and gotta hide it from that monster calls herself your friend. Yeah, I did. I gave notice. Two months."

"Michael, I can't find a gallery in two months. I can't sell a painting—"

He laughed out loud. "Oh Fran. I'm not counting on you to sell a painting, *Byte the Bullet*'ll be a client and two months gives me plenty time to get more, c'mon, we've got the savings now. It'll be like working half-time for the same money, you'll see. I'm not counting on you."

Her dough feet melted. She could feel herself slipping lower and lower on the sidewalk. In every pregnancy she'd shrunk, until she gave birth and hardly existed at all.

"C'mon Franny." He put his arm around her, and that side of her body wanted to melt into him, to let him warm her in the cold drafts that were swirling. Maybe she was leaning, maybe she was yielding, when he said: "I'll take care of you."

"I DON'T WANT TO BE TAKEN CARE OF."

His arm slapped back down to his own side. She'd heard how loud her voice trumpeted, but she couldn't fathom it.

"I DON'T WANT TO BE TAKEN CARE OF, I FEEL SO TRAPPED I CAN'T TELL YOU."

Michael managed to keep his face blank, an actor's training. In the house he would have raised his hand to her, and then lowered it without a blow, but they were not in the house, they were on the street. There was Sal Tormenti heading up the hill on his bike. There was Michael giving Sal a grim nod and waiting, cagey, for Sal to pass by.

Time for him to get his speech together—there, Sal was past, time to hiss out:

"Well, I'm with Brother Freud on this one, sweetheart. I don't know what the hell you want. I tell you I'm willing to take everything on my shoulders and you tell me you feel trapped."

And, as always when he thought he'd hit the right note, he swiveled and made his exit, back up the slope where their children sat in the care of *Space Dinosaurs*.

She turned away and went down, down the hill, down to the studio where no one would be working this morning. The single footloose painters of this world wouldn't even be awake yet, on a Saturday morning, and when they did wake they'd go out to have coffee and eggs in a coffee shop with lovers. She'd be alone in the studio, slaving away, oh sorry for herself, oh good and sorry for herself. She felt her back pocket—the Polaroid of Michael—and drew it out. There she stood on Fifth Avenue, shoppers dragging their carts to the grocery store trying not to stare at her, clutching the Polaroid of Michael naked and kneeling.

She made her way down to Fourth Avenue and found a pay phone at a gas station. The fumes settled down on her.

"Michael, I'm sorry."

"Mommy. It's Brian."

"Oh, Bri. Sorry, darlin, put Daddy on."

She waited, knees buckling at the gasoline smell. Too soon to tell. No need to make a big fuss now.

Brian came back on the line. "He doesn't want to talk right now."

"Tell him I'm sorry, will you? Do you mind, Bri?"

Always asking too much of that child. Their intermediary. More time passed. More seedy characters came to fill their rusting gas tanks. Finally Michael came on the line, without a word.

"Michael?—I'm sorry."

Sigh.

"Michael. Look. Can you get Jenny to listen out for the kids for an hour? Come meet me at the studio. We'll have eggs at that coffee shop. We'll pretend, you know. Look, I'm sorry."

"O.k.," he said, flat, and hung up the phone.

As soon as she walked away from the gas station, the air cleaned itself, purified itself. Could have been mountain air, cold and crisp. She saw the next two weeks, or three weeks, or four: this clean air, this feeling of hope, then fumes, gagging, the possibility. Abortion so easy now, just around the corner, no need to go through it again, no need to freeze your life for another five years. The chance to take control. The queasiness. Michael hopeless and sentimental in turns, like the air, like her belly. The guy who had just quit his job.

The factory door swung shut and closed out the fall light and air, but she made herself skip up the stairs, her studio on the fifth floor. There'd be no time to run in the park today, not on a Saturday with the groceries still to buy and the laundry piled like bunkers in the hallway. Her running would have to be done on these factory steps.

When she opened the studio door the light dizzied her again, but she made herself take a deep breath, and set down the Polaroid, her holy card for the morning, and made herself take a hard look at the painting.

It was good. Maybe she was pregnant again, maybe she wasn't, but the painting was good. *Something* existed outside her body. S.D.'s eyes beady behind enormous glasses, Declan's hands long as the night on a narrow rim of wheelchair. The line was her own, eccentric maybe, but sure. A sure thing.

The buzzer rang and she heard Michael's foot on the stairs—someone on the way out had let him into the building before she had time to lock up and hide away. She froze, like her brothers with dirty magazines in hand, hearing Doris's foot descending to their lower-depths bedroom. No place to hide a six-by-nine canvas while Michael's foot ascended. No way to turn it to the wall.

She'd thought of this—it wasn't like she was going to keep the painting hidden for the rest of their lives—and she'd even practiced lines. *Oh Steedman, oh that, oh Artosaurus, always wondered what they looked like without their tweed-and-corduroy, you know, their uniforms.* But she wasn't ready for that particular falseness yet.

Keys. Where had she put the keys? She'd just this minute walked in and —there, on the stool, with the Polaroid. Michael on the third floor now, maybe the fourth. She scooped up the ring of keys and barreled out the door as Michael trudged from fourth to fifth, and he called up:

"Hey. Thought I'd get a look."

So she resorted to a different falseness: "Nobody's going in there today, what I just saw. Martin could do better, I don't know what I was thinking of." The key turned tight in the lock.

A shame. Rare to feel anything but cringing ambivalence when you showed a piece, especially one you were still working on, so close to it you couldn't see it anymore. But this time she felt good, felt like strutting. Wanted to show off her good painting to Michael and restore his good humor, pay back those moments of hope he handed off.

Michael was halted halfway up the last flight, patting the pockets of his flight jacket for matches. He gave her a strange look when he lighted up. Suspicious? Down the stairs together in silence, out the front door, crossing the Union Street bridge, trudging to the coffee shop. She slowed to get a good look at him, still angry, still loping along in his khaki, his big gorilla boots, looking for all the world like the boy who snorted heroin. Who'd have thought they'd wind up here, a family at home, the resentments bubbling up, the jobs to quit?

You could be an artist and tell the truth or you could not hurt people's feelings, crouch down like a little girl and spread your skirts wide to hide it. And if she ended up hiding this good painting, pure like all the portraits in the Burke Family Gallery, guaranteed to reach the safe eyes only, how crazy would she be? Never mind her children. How weird could she get? A wave of panic. Michael had no idea yet what it was like to work in isolation day after day.

The coffee shop was looming now, a grubby gift. He slowed to let her catch up and held the door for her—even tried to wink when she was passing through—but the smell of sour coffee waved up, and the butter was rancid on the grill. They were in for a rough time.

She waited to take the test, and then stared at the ring in the tube for a good long time, holding it up to the light and pretending it wasn't there.

Michael had been working late, making himself indispensable at the

magazine before he left, and in the mornings . . . in the mornings she was
a slug, and queasy besides. So she didn't tell him for days, not until the
morning he found Maura's communion veil again, this time mixed in
somehow with his underwear, and held it up and said:

"Listen Fran, you gotta stop encouraging her with this communion veil
stuff. And dragging them off to Mass. Look, I don't care, if *you* wanna be a
saint, I don't know what's come over you. But if that's what you want, Saint
Frances of the Kitchen with the bread for Christsakes, yeah, o.k. But don't,
you know, don't dump that saint shit on Maura. That sin stuff. Don't you,
don't you, the sin stuff . . ."

First time in a long time she'd heard him run out of words. She
burrowed her face into the pillow and felt some mean satisfaction at the
long deep well of nausea facing her for the morning. Deep and dark. She
couldn't explain it, couldn't justify it. The pope, the mad male bureaucracy,
the old farts. But Michael had long since let loose of the other stuff too—the
really wild stuff, bread to body, wine to blood. Well, how could you believe
it, a rational being? How could anyone? And yet there were moments so
clear and pure (Brian knew it still, and Martin knew it, and Maura, and
Michael had known it, maybe, when he was a child) when the promise
made perfect sense, complete and whole, a truth you could not begin to
fathom but swallowed down in the host. And then thought you'd die if you
ever went without. Funny, that she and Peggy were the women in the pew
now, the faithful, side by side with the old trembling musty ladies with their
veiled hats and their gloves and the feisty new nuns with their sweet hokey
catechisms.

"Michael. I'm pregnant." She waited until one of those moments,
dizzy with sickness, when she wanted the baby. Wanted it more than
anything, grabbed the wanting in her fist and held it until she could get the
word out to Michael, quick, because she couldn't hold it forever and the
wanting would disappear. The minute would vaporize and she would think
about the time frozen again and the year nursing and the waking in deep
sleep and the canvases that didn't get finished, or didn't get started.

Soft October light, the children still sleeping. She should have risen, at
least, to tell him. Should have had the decency. Should have shaken herself
from her own nausea, and folded Maura's communion veil away.

But she didn't. She lay in their bed, and when he didn't say anything,
she repeated it: "Michael, I'm pregnant."

At the dresser—his underwear drawer closed now, the veil flouncing
out on top of the lamp—he knotted his tie. She watched him knot it in the

mirror, the tie he'd only be needing for another six weeks. His eyes would not meet hers. The tie came out with the bottom end longer. He had to start again.

When the tie was knotted properly he came and sat on the bed, on the other side, away from her. She felt him staring at the floor. Once his hand came back, to steady himself, and she thought he might say something, or she might, but the moment passed. The sitting and staring went on for a long time, and maybe she was burying her face deeper in the pillow. Then Michael rose, and the bed shook, and she raised her head to watch him leave the room.

He closed the door behind him.

The way she had been getting past the nausea was to picture the painting —oh sure, the composition came on like a dream. She pulled her way through the feet, through the hands, through the faces, until she saw what she had to fix. She rose to get the children out. Later she would hoist her bike and ride it down to the studio: too bad for the woozies, Beanie Boatwright's face was still an avocado and she had to make it right.

DUE
EAST
PRODUCTIONS

As soon as Erika paged him—"Stew, Caroline's here"—he went flying out to Reception before she could engage Caroline in show-and-tell.

Too late. They were chatting away. Erika was a South African overstaying her visa, willing to work cheap for the experience until she got found out or married—and Steward of course had never asked to see a green card. He was only paying her until six, but here it was seven-thirty and eager blond Erika still sat guard at her Formica reception barricade, pumping the other blonde, Steward's unlikely-looking date.

The visit wasn't going well. A mistake to ask Caroline up and they both knew it, both knew the affair, such as it was, was pretty much over. Only affection left on his end (those first words he'd applied, *fond of her*). They'd done Europe twice, she the first one in her family since Franny to cross the Atlantic and a good sport besides, hanging around obscure festivals in Oslo and Bremen, but the Due East visits had been a disaster—she still lived with her mother—and the New York ones maybe worse. When she was in Manhattan all she could think of was sneaking over to Brooklyn to make reparations to Franny. Talk about guilt. Neurosis. Catholic lunacy. But here was the strange part: he felt it too, that strange thrill like incest, and he couldn't get past it. In New York she still seemed very very young, somebody's little sister. The longer she lived at her mother's place the primmer her clothes got, even her hair, which she'd cut in a flat short schoolmarm cap that made her head too big. Her shoes were sexless flats.

"Stew, Caroline said you haven't showed her around! You should!"

Caroline smiled up, sad and eager on her first visit to Due East Productions, so he put his arm around her shoulder, around the camel's-hair coat, and led her back past the conference rooms and the kitchen to the cutting rooms: two for video, one for film. Not that he was going to video for his own work—it was only the commercial end of this operation, intended to bankroll the rest. He'd always prefer dot to line, grain to wave, frame to time code . . . he would always prefer texture and history, but business was business and grant money finite.

Caroline stood blinking in front of the monitors and then sat at the switcher console, pulling the fader up and down the way she slid the gearshift in her MG back home. "I had no idea," she said. "It's the most—" She was stuck, but knew she wanted a superlative.

In the hall she put her hand out to touch the maps on the wall, nautical charts—Savannah, Due East, Charleston—pictures of that watery part of his world he'd always managed to view from shore. Grandfather didn't trust boats, and neither did he. Those tricky low country currents. Caroline's freckled hand traced the river emptying into the sound at Claire's Point (sounding: twenty-seven feet). Now they both had a case of the blues. This would be the last time she'd come up.

On the way out, Erika said: "Take her up to the stage, now see he does, Caroline!" and Steward waved a frozen good-bye. He had two adjacent buildings in that no-man's-land just south of Canal. The one they were leaving was five stories of industrial lofts: he rented out the top three floors, which made him a landlord, but you had to do what you had to do. Next door he parked the remote truck in the garage and used the loft above for a soundstage. The idea was to churn out enough videos to support the documentaries. He did small-scale industrials, shot politicians learning how to flirt with the camera, and lately had made a specialty of music videos: his were low-budget numbers, mainly, for low-rent bands, vanity videos that had scant chance of making it onto MTV. Sometimes the checks to Due East Productions were signed by the Scarsdale or Greenwich parents of the single gentlemen involved.

He'd borrowed against his capital—even his grandfather sucked his breath in, what little was left of it—and it appeared he'd be working eighteen-hour days for the rest of his life. But meanwhile, when he wasn't attending to the bookkeeper or the booker or the computers going down, he could putz around with toys everywhere. Play with special effects if you're feeling down! Stay all night if you don't want to go home to an empty apartment! It's *your* studio. On the soundstage he sometimes tweaked the cameras himself, and he didn't even *like* video. Leading Caroline up the steep metal stairs to see the place, quiet now, no shoot tonight, he thought his hand might be apologetic on hers, and when he punched in the alarm code, he even said: "Sorry."

Like a barn inside, speakers piled up like bales of hay, the cameras on their pedestals back in their stalls for the night. She meandered over to the control room and stared through the panel as if trying to imagine him calling the shots. Farmer Stew.

"Will you look at this." She swiveled as if she might come over to hug him, but stopped on a dime and stared instead at the Sonex walls, faking technical curiosity, peering at the light grid. Both of them pulling back. Funny. He'd never ended anything—take Erika, probably listening in on the intercom right now—without convincing himself to feel, at least, resentful. But he couldn't resent Caroline. The stoop of her shoulders now, waiting for the blow. Well, there didn't have to be any blow. With Erika it had been a wipe; with Caroline it would just be a fade.

He looked at his watch, mimed dismay, said, "Let's get rolling. They'll be waiting on us." Caroline followed him down the stairs and out into the night.

"I don't think those two'll ever be *waiting* on us, but I did tell Franny she had to get there on time. Hard with the—"

"Yeah. Hard to get out." He hadn't seen Franny in over ten years, but he'd seen a couple of her kids, strangely enough. Last year, when the rooms were just going up, Michael Burke called him out of the blue. You had to hand it to the guy: cool as a Due East cuke, not a *hmm* of apology or embarrassment in his voice. Not a hint that he was begging a favor off a man he once socked in the gut for dancing too close and too slow with his bride. *Caroline said you're doing some P.R. work. I've done a little in that line myself. Wonder if you wanna get together over a beer and talk about it.* Nothing in the world he wanted less, but seeings how the guy sounded like a laid-back mob henchman on the phone, he obeyed the summons, met him at Fanelli's—where they were heading now—and found he could tolerate Michael Burke after all. In the meantime Caroline had called: Franny and her husband were in big trouble, four kids and he'd quit his job, he was hustling anything he could, Franny was doing computer graphics, a miracle she'd agreed to learn. They were close to losing the apartment. If there was any work, any work at all . . .

There was, and he didn't even have to pull it out of a hat. He'd been doing a few at-cost videos for adoption agencies. Baby Bazaar tapes, they called them, images that were supposed to break your heart, eighteen-month-old spazzy black babies—too much for a mother to take, the roll of that head—or ten-year-old Latin boys, mugging for the camera, trying too hard, grinning too broad, *take me, take me.* The writers were usually in-house from the P.R. agencies, snippy little Seven Sisters girls in sexy pumps who couldn't give a shit about ten-year-old boys mugging for cameras. He'd already told St. Joseph's Home, for one, that they'd do better to hire a freelance writer, and bingo. He had one to recommend.

So he and Burke had actually worked together. Surprisingly together, given the beer the guy could put away while he was pounding out a script. But a good writer, bread-and-butter, fast. He'd tug at your heartstrings if that's what you *wanted*. Twice, when they were stuck together, he'd offered Steward a spoonful of powder, and twice Steward had accepted. The Burke family couldn't be that bad off, the guy was still buying his coke. He did some of the music stuff now, too—outrageous ideas, the suburban basement bands ate it up, guitars floating in pink clouds and story lines out of *David Copperfield*. He'd brought the little girl, Maura, along to a shoot one day: a little Franny, her hair coming out of her barrette; not a word out of her the whole day, but she was working the cameramen, working the band, flirting, flirting, not a word, hands on the hem of her dress. She pulled back before she lifted the dress, she remembered herself. Seven, eight, something like that. Not pretty, but Caroline was right, pretty damn adorable.

And once Burke brought the baby on his back, where he didn't stay for long, a firecracker named Patrick, a flaming redhead, something wrong with his feet so he stumbled just when he was trying to get underfoot. Burke ended up stuffing him back in the backpack, and then holding the little boy's foot, in orthopedic shoes, as if to anchor himself.

"Michael tell you about the novel?"

"Nope. Didn't sell it, did he?" What was his problem?—jealous of a guy with his hand out?

"He did." Hard to say whether Caroline's little squeal was satisfaction at Michael Burke's success or surprise at the mound of blanket-overcoat-cardboard box she'd just hopped. She couldn't get used to those deserted streets, the clanging doors on loading docks, the street people lying in the stench of urine.

"Where'd he sell it?"

"Uhm, oh wait, I'll get it in a minute, they're on the West Coast, real pretty books, he was showing me some of the—"

"Oh, a *West* Coast publisher."

"Stew. You don't have to sound so snotty."

Had he sounded snotty? "Nah, I didn't mean anything. That's great. He's my number one writer now, you know. He, maybe he'll be deserting me, he made a big killing on this."

"Well, he didn't make a big killing."

"What'd they give him?"

He could feel Caroline biting her lip as they walked east.

"C'mon, what'd they give him?" The second time, he heard how crass. But it was natural, he talked figures all day long. *What kind of deal can you give me if I guarantee . . .* He looked to see if Caroline was still biting her lip. She was.

"I don't know Stew. I don't know if it's . . ."

In the dark, he could see that she was blushing.

"Sorry I asked."

"It's just—"

"No, really. Sorry I asked. Stupid." You could read the figure in her embarrassment: some puny number under five thousand, some little figure that wouldn't free Michael Burke up from the hackwork he was doing.

"It's been such a long haul for him."

Hey! he wanted to say, *who gave him the gigs? Who put him on the Due East Productions insurance plan?*

But Caroline was rolling. "I just find it so *ad*mirable, keeping at it all these years, with four kids, just imagine the distractions, so when you try to put a dollar figure on that—"

"Jesus, Caroline, you sound like the Reverend Winbon Price."

Another body she had to step over and a glare at him as if he'd invented sleeping in the gutter. "I just think Michael's been a good guy, a good guy all the way, and I'm glad to see him—"

Maybe there was a little resentment at the end of this affair after all. Maybe it wasn't reparations but adulation that sent Caroline out to Brooklyn when she was in the city. He pulled her by the elbow, to turn the corner. They skirted another pair of extended legs. Burke wanted them to shoot a homeless documentary together; Steward, who thought the idea too close to his old wino movies, had been stringing him along. Maybe he'd lose interest now, with his novel sold. Hard to say why Burke's selling this manuscript—what was it, his third novel? fourth?—to some obscure publisher, his first sale after churning them out for a dozen years, had him on edge.

He pointed across the street to Fanelli's and Caroline followed him, upset. If he stepped outside of himself to take their picture he was framing a couple of straight arrows, she in her camel's hair, he in his hooded alpaca—his grandmother might have picked the coat herself, if the breast cancer hadn't finally come back to beat her last year. She died just when the studio was up and running. She would have approved of him with this sweet, conservative girl, a kind of Lady Di of the common folk, all blushes and lowered eyes going into the crowded bar. But who would approve of him, about to dump the sweet girl who wanted to marry him and live in that beach house out by those dangerous currents?

He pushed the white-etched doors (some relief for Caroline in this bleak landscape) and there they were, sitting in the bank of tables opposite the door, Michael and Franny Burke, waiting, against all odds. Snap the two of them and you'd get the opposite of straight arrows: Burke with beard, with baseball cap, with ponytail, with not one but three earrings in his right ear, the same denim jacket he'd been wearing for the last fifteen years. And sitting across from him on the aisle, stubbing out a cigarette just as her sister walked through the pretty doors—timing on purpose?—Franny was his match. Curly hair short but not flat like Caroline's: full on her head. Big brass earrings, fish swimming underneath her curls. Black tights and a tight tube skirt, some old frayed sweater to look cool under a silk scarf. Michael said something to her and she turned to watch them push their way past the first few tables. Her cheeks were fuller, her eyes made up dark and garish, the way she used to do them at fourteen. She had grown—well, you might say handsome. Not handsome as in middle-aged woman but as in thick black shoes, clunky but interesting, and *Nah, she can't possibly have four kids.* She looked like a woman who knew what was up.

And she smiled at their approach, but a held-back smile. She was still grinding the cigarette into the dish and Burke, he saw now, was tugging on one of the hoops in his ear. Tense, the two of them. On edge, the way he was. He and Caroline must look like the in-laws driving in from the suburbs, the bridge and tunnel crowd come to be shown the city. The rubes from Due East.

"Can't believe it," Steward said to Franny, three or four times, inane as ever ten years down the road. Didn't help to have his own studio: she had brass earrings and black tights. Burke was rising and beaming, showing his wife off the way he'd shown off his children. Steward's breath was coming fast as a schoolboy's—what *was* it with this woman, lighting up again when she'd just put one out.

Having sat, he rose again and pushed his hand out again to Burke. "You sold the book."

Franny blew smoke out of the corner of her mouth and let herself smile. Burke was pleased and puffed his cheeks out.

"Champagne's on me," Steward said, and waved in the direction of the waitress, a futile gesture on a Friday night, and maybe rubbing it in besides.

"You ought to get good and drunk, Michael," Caroline said. She was sitting, but still struggling out of her coat. They were all pushed up against each other at the little table, and the guys from the bar—the guys in leather and jeans, the cool guys, the artists like Franny here in her frayed sweater— were pushing back against their space, against prim Caroline running the show and slipping out of her good go-to-town coat. "But we can't be late."

"Nope, can't be late," Burke said.

"What time's the show?" Franny's first words since *hey*. Didn't even know what time the show—first of four showings, the only four theatrical showings of *Gloria* in New York. He should have been going to the opening with producers, agents, P.R. folk, but he was having drinks with the Burke and Starkey contingent instead. You could look it up in the paper if you wanted to know what time the show was.

"We've got an hour," Caroline said, everything calculated this morning by the math teach before he left her at the apartment. If she was telling Franny they had an hour, that meant they had an hour and a half.

"Champagne oughta be for you and Caroline," Burke said. "For getting your movie made."

Caroline, straight arrow, cast her eyes down. She did get the movie made, and for that—*fond of her*—he was obliged to bring her to New York for the Film Forum showing, obliged to let this thing fizzle out in Manhattan instead of on her home ground. She'd done what he asked, almost four years before: she'd left him at the hospital, where they stitched up a flesh wound—a *flesh* wound was what all that blood amounted to—and then she drove back out to Gloria's. She delivered his message about the twenty-five thousand dollars, did him a kindness, a tremendous kindness. She connected the way he hadn't been able to, said something Gloria responded to, managed some mysterious mystical female bonding. The next day when he drove out, Gloria was spitting mad, didn't want twenty-five thousand dollars, wanted to know how much you'd pay an actor who worked a full day.

And that, finally, was what he had on film. Gloria on the plaid sofa in her living room, Queen for a Day on union scale.

GLORIA

I don't want nothing special, no special treatment, I just don't want you, nobody, cheating me. Don't want to get taken, you know.

STEWARD
(Off-camera.)
Did you feel cheated all the years you were working for my grandmother?

(Gloria sits silently, twisting her mouth this way and that.)

Did you think they should have paid you more for what you did?

(Gloria laughs, contemptuous but amused too.)

Do you not want to talk about this?

GLORIA
Steward, you was a child then and you is a child now. You think I wanted to raise my voice they wouldn't been no better time than now? Now when's my time to rest, my time to puts my feet up. No child, now is my time. No matter whats you want me to say to make your movie how you want it.

He cringed already at how the Burkes would see the film. There'd never been narration in his documentaries, but for *Gloria* the only honest thing to do was put himself in, tell how he came to make his movie. Chump, child, rich boy. It wasn't the piece he'd had in mind. There was a testy conversation between him and the grandson, a guy by the name of Raleigh Johnson who'd been at Due East High School the two years Steward was there. They'd been in a bio lab together—Raleigh Johnson remembered, but he did not. That was what the conversation was about, old wounds, white boys not even looking at you, white boys couldn't tell you one from the other, white boys driving up to your grandmother's house thinking it was quaint and clever to get your grandmother on film, so she could talk about scrubbing out your toilet. The camera showed Steward Morehouse opening his mouth and shutting it a dozen times. But Franny would remember Raleigh Johnson—there wasn't a boy in that high school she wouldn't remember.

He'd convinced Gloria, working union scale as talent and not subject, to go by her old house, but the rough wood had been painted, the dusty yard planted. She did not want to be filmed in front of his grandparents' house because, he figured, she never wanted to see them again. Nothing was as he intended, but the movie was all about money, all about *his* money, Gloria's grandson's cracks about what it must be like to have it to *play* with, and so he got it shown at a couple of festivals. Got it on French television: hey, they knew all about class resentments. These four shows in New York and then the miscellaneous here and there, Cambridge, Berkeley, Ann Arbor. Some public TV, though there was no *Faces of the Lowcountry* series. He found that Due East was not his subject anymore. He was trying to suck the very truth out of Gloria, and he had no right. His grandmother never saw *Gloria,* and he'd been putting the old man off.

Caroline had never seen it either, and she was in it—a fifteen-second conversation between the two of them, the most self-indulgent exchange he had ever put on film, his pressing her on what she said to convince Gloria to do it, her waving him off. He'd run those frames through the flatbed again and again, watching her sweet freckled hand, trying to convince himself that he was in love with her. Breezy, he called her his girlfriend on film.

"Caroline looks good on film," he said—and when she waved her hand again, as she liked to do—"no, really. The camera likes you."

"I'm feeling old," she said, as if reading his thoughts about the flattening hair and the flat shoes, and at this Franny and Michael cracked tense laughs. Michael Burke did look older than his years, ruts in his pale complexion, crevices around his mouth, but it was Franny who said:

"Oh Caroline, you have to be getting up the fourth time in the middle of the night to know what feeling old is. You have to wake up feeling something damp and cold and look down to see a couple of extra bodies and the sheet turning yellow. *I'm* feeling old."

"Hey now, it's not like we're aged. I think there's some time left." And he was hearing Grandmother's voice: *Why do they DO that? Why do they HAVE all those babies?*

Franny was chain-smoking, blowing it out in contempt for him. She had managed to avoid him for ten years, and she didn't want to be here tonight, didn't want to see him, must have been fighting with Burke when they walked through the door. Must have picked up from Caroline that it was ending, that he was ending it. She would think his documentary trite and obvious and self-absorbed. As it was. This was what Steward Morehouse did to make amends. And look how he changed people's lives! Gloria Butler died of complications from diabetes a month before his grandmother died of cancer, but nobody told him until he was back in Due East for the second funeral. Didn't even occur to Raleigh Johnson to call the number on the business card.

Didn't occur to anyone that he would have liked to say good-bye to the shadow of his childhood, that he would have liked to lay a hand on hers in the casket and feel some substance there, finally. Always sliding across the background, opening those shutters in the back of the house, a woman who tolerated children, their mindless flitting through the big house, who did not acknowledge—until asked, twenty years later—what it was like to be unseen.

Caroline put her weightless hand on his and a shiver ran through him. Another shadow.

"Stew, we best get that champagne now we're going to get out of here on time. I know you've got people you need to see at the theater."

She was giving him an encouraging little smile, one of those brave little ingenue *oh-I-know-it's-over-but-you've-shown-me-a-wonderful-time* smiles, and he knew that he'd better not have too much to drink tonight. One too many champagnes and he'd be like his father stepping on a mine, asking her to marry him after all, trying to make up for his business, his aloofness, his keeping her on the string these four years. She was lovely, even with her hair flat, even with her blue eye shadow, she had a lovely sturdy long freckled body that he'd called upon every three, four, five months for some comfort, *Oh just use your sick time, say you've got a dying uncle up in New York's got to have his hand held.* He was the dying uncle, the one who needed a little human connection now that he had the empty apartment in the Village, now that he'd grown weary of the tiresome brunches with the likes of Erika, the cloying shopping trips to Dean & DeLuca on Saturdays.

One thing he wouldn't subject sweet Caroline to was his middle-aged urge to make himself a home. He rose to get the bottle himself, from the bar, and the air was cleaner as soon as he stood. He pushed away from Franny's cigarette smoke and didn't know if he ever meant to come back to sit with the one forgiving sister, the one contemptuous sister, the one struggling artist object-of-both-their-affections. He shouldered up to the bar through the cool guys in the beat-up brown leather jackets and he heard Franny's voice, raspy from her smoking but clear as a broadcast wave:

"God, he hadn't changed a bit. Like a fish, Caroline, how you put up with that?"

UNCLE
STEW

Michael Burke had been faithful to Kevin Byrne for years. "Gotta get Byrne on the horn," he'd say, and then con him into family dinners with vague references to high times. He managed to get dope from somewhere (hard to believe they still sold that stuff), but they had to smoke it in the garden, so's not to corrupt Brian and Martin.

But now Michael had given up on Kevin Byrne. Now he'd exiled him for good. They hadn't seen much of him lately anyway: Kevin was off in a foreign neighborhood, deepest Brooklyn, a family neighborhood where he could escape his family and live a shabby existence, the ultimate judgment against his father who'd worked his way up on Wall Street. Return to the Working Class Roots. He was a bachelor still: well, he was only thirty-five, but even in shabby Irish-American circles that was getting to be time. A dividing line—if he didn't do it now . . .

Kevin still lived alone in his basement apartment, and every now and again Billy would report a sighting in Mahoney's, a mooching of drugs or cash. When he did knock on their door he was affable, his eyes glassy. Still teaching English at Cardinal Newman, and he didn't talk about women, he talked about the girls in his classes: *Pretty juicy Italian babes in Bensonhurst,* he'd say, and Franny would have to turn away to swallow the smile. *Torment, dissecting* The Miller's Tale *while Angela Poozi hikes her skirt up.*

Oh Kevin, Franny said. *She's not really named Angela Poozi.* Poor Kevin, his chubby fingers the color of lard. The last time he came calling, he knocked on the door at two-thirty in the afternoon—what happened to the last hour of school? Franny sat him in the kitchen while she cooked, though she'd been planning to run down to the studio and put in a couple of hours. *Offer it up,* Doris used to say when she was a girl.

Kevin's head lolled, and then his whole body tipped on the stool.

"Kevin, oh Kevin. Stop for a quick one?"

He gave her a malevolent look out of one eye, asleep already.

"Hey, c'mon in the dining room, we'll stretch you out."

She wanted to get him out of the kitchen and set him down in the big mission chair, but evidently she aroused him instead of rousing him. He was all over her, hands on her breasts: a stranger. She couldn't think of a single word to say, not a prim *Kevin* out of her. She was the ingenue in the silent movie, dodging his lecherous advances, slipping out of his reach, sidestepping him and leaving him to grab onto the counter. Once his broad chest, his sweet eagerness, had been a temptation. Well, they were all growing old, in their own ways.

He banished himself upstairs—a wonder he could travel that far—and seemed to sleep it off, but then at dinner, when she'd gone back into the kitchen for butter, he followed her and nuzzled her on the neck. Right in the middle of the meal, the paterfamilias at the head of the table in the next room, four children circling him. She howled at the audacity—Kevin had reduced her to Angela Poozi level—and the butter dish went flying.

Michael came and stood in the doorway. He knew what Kevin was up to. Well, why not? They'd shared their first hits of Sartre and Camus together in high school, they'd spent two years sleeping next to one another, they'd breathed in heroin, they'd come back to Brooklyn: of course he knew what Kevin was up to. Only raised an eyebrow, for the moment, and then they all sat down again and ate fast, the children knowing not to ask again for the butter.

But before the coffee was in the pot, before it was nine o'clock, Michael said, "Gotta turn in, man. See you around." He followed this up with a blank stare that said *Get out of my house, asshole,* and Kevin did, promptly.

Michael cut the friendship off then and there. Last time they'd be seeing Kevin Byrne in a year. Or two. The circle of friends was shrinking. Peggy was spending a sabbatical year in—wouldn't you know it—Dublin, preaching feminism where they needed it *desperate.* Kate was gone too, most of the year, trailing her little boy after her sweet philandering actor husband, Kate's heart broken in every regional theater.

Sometimes the Burkes thought they knew everybody in Park Slope—a party every weekend in September and then dinners on down through the fall—but these weren't the old friends. These were refugees from Manhattan who'd heard Michael wrote scripts that had actually been produced. They were all over him, but when they heard that Franny didn't have a gallery they let her be, though they still came into her apartment and sized it up. *You have a good eye,* they said, throwing her a bone, meaning that it was too bad the six of them were squeezed into this half-a-house, but anyway she knew how to pick up an interesting scarf at a street sale and then slip it over the right table. Of course she had a good eye. That was what she *did*.

She'd turned as bad as Kevin, burrowing away when someone called to ask her for coffee, for lunch. *C'mon Franny*, Peggy used to say. *Just come to one meeting. You can't tell me you could be a woman artist and not be a feminist.* And Franny said: *No, no, I'm all with you. Hey, RISE UP, SISTERS. I'm just not . . . a joiner.* Doris's words. *Just not a joiner.* Her old friends around her, her sisters calling every Sunday: she'd always thought she was social—hadn't she moved to *Brooklyn?*—but now she saw that she was a solitary soul after all.

Now Steward was their circle of friends, come two or three nights a week to provide their entertainment. Tonight he was entertaining the baby, Patrick.

"Hey Patrick, buddy, don't you know you can't climb the walls?"

Patrick was on the third shelf up, he and the bookcase both teetering. Franny hollered, but it was Uncle Stew who leaped to the rescue. Funny to see them one against the other, Patrick's dark freckled hand on Steward's neck, pale as unpainted canvas. When the little boy's red head leaned against the white one, Steward's hair turned yellow, a tentative new-sprung yellow, as if the hair itself was deciding to start over.

That was Steward's new manifesto: *Start over. Screw the videos, if I wanted to be a businessman I'd be selling marshland with Dufford.* Not that he was abandoning the studio—a gold mine now, a video in every window display—but Michael had talked him into doing the homeless piece after all. For three months, Steward had followed a tribe of Vietnam vets Michael hunted up from the bottom of Prospect Park. He was in the park night and day with a crew, Michael hovering past the first frost. NBC bought a twelve-minute segment for their first homeless marathon: his first network sale, and when he hawked it with Bryant Gumbel on the *Today* show, he recited lines Michael had written for him. *Look, I drew a nice high number in the lottery. I didn't go to Vietnam. I never lost a job. I never lost a family. All I lost was the vision to see these people anymore. I wanted to get that back.*

Michael was his Cyrano, writing love letters to the press, and these past few months Steward said he had his sense of purpose back. In the circles he and Michael frequented now, he was mentioned in the same breath with the Raymonds and Jon Alpert. He crossed the Brooklyn Bridge two or three times a week to bounce ideas off Michael, who had the words *social justice* tattooed onto all his vital parts—the Jesuits had seen to that. The Burkes ran a safe house, a safe haven for Steward. Michael said that, living in the Age of Gimme as they were, the work was an obligation.

Funny to see the two of them together, pardners (in all but money), buddies, best of friends. Every other man was a threat to Michael—the portly balding lawyers fetching their children out of this household, the Sal Tormentis from down the block flirting, the Johns in the studio keeping her going—but with Steward it was all business. As if Michael knew that Steward Morehouse in the house was a force so far beyond his control that he might as well just stand back and see what blew down or burned up.

Now Steward held Michael's child, and Patrick, caught up like a monkey in the white hunter's arms, tickled the back of Uncle Stew's neck. Patrick had endured orthopedic shoes the first three years of his life, and was trying to make up for it in his fourth. He'd already broken an arm and a toe. Now he slithered down out of Steward's arms and sang:

"H, A, double R, I, G, A, N spells Harrigan,"

and Steward said: "This feels like a time warp. How's Walter doing, Franny?"

"He's doing fine." He was. Walter worked on old cars: he had the patience for the gummed-up valves that nobody else had anymore. The last time she was in Due East he showed her around the station, where they had him working in the farthest bay because he sang all day, a limited repertoire that drove everybody nuts. "The only thing is . . . he's smart enough to know he's not smart enough."

Steward shook his head. Genuine sympathy. Always liked Walter. Caroline said that once, when she was still seeing Steward, he brought Walter a complete collection of Gilbert and Sullivan tapes, new songs to sing at the garage; but Walter was overwhelmed and went back to "Officer Krupke." The comfort of an old tune.

"And how's Caroline?" For this inquiry Steward lowered his voice and eyes, as if speaking of the dead. The urge to say *She's wasting away* always came over Franny, but it wasn't true—Caroline, shades of Lola, dated a slew of Marines.

"Good," she said. Crisp. Brisk. *You* didn't break anybody's heart. But then in for the thrust: "And Lola?"

Aha. Steward shrugged. Every few weeks they fueled the fires with the family questionnaire, and when it was done they breathed genial smiles. A good example for the children, inquiring after blood ties so carefully. But Maura was on to them. She often crept up, as she was doing now, crawling along behind the couch and peeking over. Franny knew what she was looking for. A kiss, an embrace. True romance. Betrayal of her dear papa.

No such luck. Franny stuck her tongue out at Maura, her sly one, and Maura ducked back down for more lurking. No one, not even a sly ten-year-old, was catching Steward Morehouse or Franny Burke at anything. They were sly themselves, sly enough to milk this familiarity, this family scene, this teat of domestic bliss Stew wanted to succor him, too. Often, when Michael was out of the room, when Maura was in the clear, he said—happy, light, open to any interpretation you cared to give it—*I love you, Franny*—and she said: *I love you too.* What else could you say? She did. Bad as a marriage, the childhood thing come back to haunt you. She did love him, for all his hanging around. She'd been married to Michael for fifteen years, but Steward was as familiar as her own toes. She loved him even as he kindled the old grand passion—that's what he was doing, just like a man, looking for romance, any fool could see it, *Maura* could see it—one middle-aged bachelor come to take the last one's place. And Michael—

"Oh I don't know where I put it"—always came back into the room. This time, an overgrown teenager, he'd gone off to search for *Rolling Stone.* An article he wanted to show this man he left alone with his wife, no questions asked.

"Brian's got it. Maybe Martin."

"Don't let Martin read that shit."

"Papa—"

"Oh my God, it's the language cops, hiding behind the couch."

"What you think, Steward, twelve's too young to read *Rolling Stone?* I bet he's reading worse, Michael."

"I heard that!" Martin at the door, popping in and out—where was he off to?

"The thing is, we're too *old* to be reading *Rolling Stone.* Back by eight, Martin."

"Oh Mom."

"No really, there was a mugging—"

"Jesus Christ, Martin, your mother says back by eight don't make her do a song and dance routine."

Out the door with a grin, Martin tall like his father, tall and . . . you wouldn't say handsome, exactly, or good-looking. Goofy ears, big light eyes, a high forehead. The map of Ireland on his face, the way the cops said on Fifth Avenue. Always the latest haircut and an earring in his ear just as Michael removed the last of his own. You'd say, if you were giggling over

Martin the way the girls on the corner were giggling over him, that he was *cute*.

Steward was soaking it up, leaning back on the couch now, home base for Patrick to come tormenting him whenever he felt like blessing them with his presence. Every now and again Steward's hand went down to tussle Maura's head, and you could hear him listening for Brian, always holed up in his room, their deep and corny one reading *Die, Avenger!*, *Dune*, *Cracked*, *Garfield*, *The Seven-Storey Mountain*, *A Brief History of the Middle East Conflict*, *Of Mice and Men* for the fifteenth time. Steward brought Brian science fiction. You'd think it was his family.

"Here it is."

Michael pulled the *Rolling Stone* out from under a battered paperback, but when they both tumbled it was the paperback Michael bent to retrieve. "Jesus, Franny. *Resurrection?*"

Franny shrugged.

Steward said: "He object to your reading now?"

Big joke: she was always railing lately about the dishes and the mess, and Michael was always objecting.

"Just object to her reading program. Next thing you know she'll be giving away *Awake!* on street corners."

"You're the one said I was half-educated."

"I said you were uneducated. I said you were illiterate. I said anybody who read half of *Anna Karenina* couldn't live in this house."

"Peggy told me the ending. She tells it very well. Now I go to make amends—hey, it's your book."

"Make amends! Forgive her, Father. Maura, where'd we put your mother's halo? Out being polished?"

Maura popped up from behind the couch. "Her halo got taken away. She's always yelling."

Franny stuck her tongue out again, but Maura came to stand behind her and play with her hair, making her own amends. This was the other part of the routine, Michael reminding them all of his wife's efforts at reformation. She'd turned so good she embarrassed him.

But what did he think she was seeing when she saw the two men slipped down on the couches, arms spread back, legs opened wide? Maura dug her fingers into the back of Franny's neck, reading her mind, and she was grateful for the scrape of nails against flesh. Mortification of the flesh. What she'd do if she ever followed Steward's lead: mortify, and not her flesh. Sitting halfway across the room from him, her head was nevertheless in his lap and his foot was still down on the gas pedal, driving her to a cheap afternoon of escape. Sometimes she pictured the look of horror on his face if he ever did see her thickening waist: and then it was easy enough to draw back, into good intentions and resolutions. *Resurrection.* The woman-at-home daydreamed: all she ever wanted was a paintbrush in her hand, an hour here, an hour there, but all she ever saw was the curve of a shoulder blade, the taut dip of a belly. And it wasn't even a man's shoulder blade she was seeing, it was a boy's—could have been *her* boy's shoulders, her Brian's thickening arms. She saw the flat belly of a boy, not the man who sat here in the same damn preppy chinos he'd been wearing for the past twenty years.

And what was he thinking? What was his daydream? Not the curve of her breast, she'd wager, though you could see that flash across his eyes every now and again, like rapid eye movements in the middle of the dream that would reveal your truest self to you. No, he saw her middle-aged body but he dreamt true love. He gave up the sweet pretty sister to torment himself. The one that got away, oh this is why I have saved myself, my childhood sweeeeeeeeeeheart. The old cornball.

Franny held her daughter's hands tight and heaved her upside down over the couch, skirt flying. "My little torturer." She crushed Maura against her and then rose to go hide away from them all. Sometimes, sitting in the middle of this crowd, she was as happy as Steward was.

"I got the dishes," Michael said. Now there was true love, common and sublime. See what line he drew for Steward? Step over this one, buddy. If Steward ever moved his hand toward the touch Maura was waiting for, Michael would yawn and say *Gotta turn in* and it would mean: *Get out of my house, asshole.*

But no need, not now. Now Uncle Stew was being good and Franny was being a saint. Besides, in these years when the rich got richer the Burkes got poorer—the piano teacher waited for those freelance checks as hard as they did—and Steward, after all, was the major source of their income these days. God knew it was meager enough.

Meager enough to keep Michael on edge permanently. On the first Saturday of every month he sat at the dining room table with the bills, and the older children fled the house. Patrick stayed quiet upstairs in the room he shared with Maura. From the dining room came grunts and bellows, Michael doing a Ralph Cramden, the chair scraped back a half dozen times for another cup of coffee. Bad enough Maura had to undress in the same room with her little brother; bad enough there were no college savings for Brian and the kids needed four pairs of sneakers in the same month. There was his mother, besides, slipping into forgetfulness and poverty. She was only in her sixties but there were days when she seemed . . . senile.

His brothers were useless. Billy and Richie and Frank got jobs, left home, lost the jobs, came home. Frank thought he was gay, changed his mind, maybe he was bisexual, maybe he was just straight after all. They were car service drivers, electrician's helpers, movers, fry cooks. Richie voted for Reagan and Michael banned him from the house for a week. Their *Highest Honors* certificates were the only decoration in their mother's narrow hallway, but Billy's one year in college was the sum of their higher education. You could not even tell if it was this decline in expectations that bewildered Norah: she was so bewildered in general. Johanna and Nellie had rallied, anyway (after two abortions apiece, Franny happened to know), the pair of them at Brooklyn College studying nursing and dating smart handsome Jamaican boys who would have sent their grandfather back into the gunrunning business, he heard about it. What was that Kevin said, so many years ago, about the girls at Cardinal Newman? Did they really want to be doctors? They took too many part-time jobs and cleaned and cooked for their brothers besides.

Still the *boys,* not a one of them married. "Slobs," Franny said, though she was soft on all three of them. Billy was still dealing, probably.

"Pathetic," Michael said, but that was as much as he could bear to say. Hadn't it been his responsibility to bully them into college? When he was toting up the bills on the first of the month, it wasn't just the sneaker money he was looking for: he wanted to slip an envelope to Norah, cold cash to bring her back to reality. Nellie said she suspected Alzheimer's, but Michael wouldn't hear of it. *Everything's got to be chemical nowadays, or biological, or genetic. Doesn't anybody believe anymore that some people just give up? What've we, taken despair out of the dictionary?*

"We ought to have them for dinner."

"Gimme a break. I'm not having the boys over here sitting on their fat asses while you serve them like royal princes. Not one more time."

Franny said, "We never see them anymore," and heard her voice go wistful. She missed her own brothers: Will had checked himself into the state hospital twice now, but Columbia, South Carolina, was a million miles away. The Burke brothers were right in the neighborhood, and she sneaked a call to Billy. Just for pizza, just as if he'd happened to drop over.

The night he was to come Michael was late at a shoot, another music video. Each shoot the last, he and Steward both swore it, but they were doing for-real signed bands now and Steward, to tell the truth, was into the directing. Michael conceived connect-the-dot narratives and they cast beautiful soulless models for MTV. Franny didn't have much patience for it.

"Hey, baby." Billy kissed her wet on the cheek. He wore his hair in a braid, but he didn't have quite the rakish air he'd once had. He'd grown fat. Puffy cheeks, big gut under his T-shirt. Still T-shirts. A few months ago he'd been living in the East Village, trying to convince Michael to convince Steward to capitalize on their homeless fame and shoot a Tompkins Square Park video—*That's where the militants are, whose side are you on?*—but when he ran out of funds it was back to Park Slope, back to his mother's, and his enthusiasm for any projects was low. Franny got him a beer.

"Where's the kids?"

"Oh, Patrick's up there somewhere, Brian too. The others are . . . somewhere. They'll get in when they smell the pizza."

"How you doing, babe?"

"I'm o.k., Bill."

Mostly they sat and grinned at each other. Tonight Billy was full of spleen. It had lately occurred to him that Michael sat on a likely source of employment he'd never once offered.

"So doncha think he could at least talk to this guy Morehouse, old moneybags? Listen, I'll be a gofer, I'll do what it takes. But I was thinking, I know a lot more than Michael bout music, y'know, a lot, and I could turn em onto . . . They should be taking a good look at the Irish bands, I'm telling you that's where . . . Y'know, producing . . . I'll be a gofer that's what it takes."

"I'll talk to him for you, Bill. I've known him since I was a kid." She could get Billy a job and warn Stew, is what she could do: lock up your drugs, screw down your equipment. "But he's thinking of winding down the music end. He wants to make a feature, that's what he's been revving up for the last few years. Maybe you could be a P.A."

"Like as in *production assistant?*" Not possible to squeeze more disdain into two words.

"Well maybe he'd be, uhm, flexible. I don't know. I'll ask him. Where you could start."

Billy stared out at the hopelessness of starting in a kid's job at the age of thirty-five, and his despair reminded him. "How's Michael taking the Kevin thing?"

How'd Billy know? "I don't think he wants him around the house."
Billy snorted. "I don't think he's gonna get him around the house."
Bad feeling, bad, seeped through her. "What you mean, Bill?"
"Oh no. You didn't get the word. Damn! I *told* Frank to call you."
"What word? Where's Kevin?"
Billy put his beer down—a gesture he reserved for the most solemn
moments—and said: "He's dead."
"Kevin?"
"Dead."
"Kevin? Kevin Byrne?"
"Yeah. Helluva thing. Nobody knew where the damn funeral was, I
called every fucking parlor in Brooklyn, his old man had it out on the
goddamn fucking island, can you believe it, a goddamn betrayal and don't
think he didn't know it. Wuncha think he coulda picked up the horn so we
could get to their goddamn Long Island funeral they had to hide it out there
at least?"
"Billy, oh. Kevin. What . . . ?"
"OD. Smack, after all these years, sonofabitch. I said to Frank, don't
you *let* me hear about you—"
"Smack, na, Billy. He wasn't but thirty, what? Six? Seven?"
"Speedball. He had a girl with him too, just like Belushi, swear to God
he hears that thing on the news he's gotta do it too, just like the old days."
"You know the girl? What's Michael . . ."
"High school girl, Cardinal Newman, that's how we heard, all over the
Daily News but nobody knows where the goddamn funeral is, we're calling
old man pickle-up-his-ass Byrne night and day but does anybody pick up
the phone? I told Frank to call Michael, damn, I guess he figured you'd read
it in the paper, see it on TV."
"I don't know the last time I read the *Daily News*."
High school girl. A little prayer that it was Angela Poozi, anyway, on
the way out, but in her heart of hearts she knew that pasty pock-faced Mr.
Byrne had lured a chunky bad girl to his dark basement rooms. She was
back in the subway, leaning against the door, *You look around, we get to be
forty*. She was back in Martyrs Hall, a hand across the space between the
beds. The last thing Michael said: *Gotta turn in, man*.
"What's Michael going . . ."
A moment of silence. You didn't let it register. The guy you jumped
from. But sweet, when the boys were little. Big house, across from the park,
big dreams for the only son. Funeral on Long Island, so nobody in the

neighborhood could go. Nobody thought to call and tell them, his brothers even.

"Listen, Franny, I didn't know Michael didn't know about this, maybe it's not the best night for me to be here."

"Oh no Bill, he'll need you here tonight. Somebody who knew him."

Billy gave her a look. It wasn't like he and Michael were *close,* they could barely sit in the same room as it was.

"When—"

"Oh, jaze, three, four weeks."

"Last *month?*"

"Listen Franny, I'm sorry to punk out babe, but you know I don't know if I can take Michael finding out, I just don't know . . ." Billy let himself do the choked-up thing, eyes pink and misty, biting the lower lip, staring out. Franny thought to pour the beer down on his head, but stayed where she was.

"C'mon Billy, stay, will you."

"Really, now, look, it's better if I go. You know Michael."

So go. She didn't say it out, didn't need to—if he couldn't read it in the set of her eyes. It wasn't Michael who needed Billy in the room tonight. He slipped out, hand to her cheek . . . it gave her the willies.

After a while she heard the front door opening and Martin clunking upstairs. He came to kiss her on the top of her head, as always, not noticing that she sat still in the dark—Martin, your mother never sits!—or maybe afraid to say a word.

Martin off to the cubicle he shared with Brian. She was alone in the front room again, their excuse for a living room. She saw Michael and Kevin, the two of them in a men's room stall at her wedding, the start of . . . Billy out of work again. Will, trying to save her father on the stage of the Due East High School gym, Will and the heebie-jeebies. She herself woke three or four times a night, long past the years when she could say it was her babies waking her—but she couldn't imagine, for all the panic in the dark, that she'd ever let loose . . . Women scraped the shit off diapers, women stuck their hands in the toilet when the plunger wouldn't do the trick, women couldn't afford to give in to it.

It was snowing. Lights went on across the way in the apartment building. Beyond the snow, a woman walked across a kitchen, as she should be doing. But Michael's mother gave in to it finally, didn't she? *What've we, taken despair out of the dictionary?* The woman was pacing a mean kitchen, round fluorescent tube lighting, paint peeling. You could see, without seeing it, the linoleum curling up from the floor. Brooklyn looked mean.

The downstairs door slammed again. She heard Maura, escorted home by some harried mother who couldn't stop to chat, *Just tell your mom I said hi, we never see her anymore*. No one ever saw her anymore, if she could help it. She heard Maura clunking around the dream of an empty kitchen, no one to scold her, no one to see her drinking Coke right out of the bottle. Then the sound of the refrigerator slamming and

the front door opened again. Everyone in, this had to be Michael, the father of the family come home to no dinner, a daughter high on soda, a dark house. Come home to his old friend dead.

She heard voices. Michael had brought Steward, he'd brought the boss home. She went to meet them at the top of the stairs. They were still at the foot, still shaking the snow off their coats. They sneaked peeks at her coming downstairs and she felt her temperature rising. Grim at first; then, at the sight of them rosy and exhilarated from the snow, angry. Bubbled-up angry, Doris-angry, fishwife-angry. The first words out of her mouth—she hadn't even *thought* them—"Jesus, Steward, think you could show up with a six-pack once in a while?" and then, worse, at the sight of his suddenly dull uncomprehending eyes: "How the hell you think we pay for your little visits?"

She saw Steward's eyes go pink with surprise. Michael's darkened. How could she do this. She brushed past them to the kitchen, to wait for Steward to take his embarrassed leave, for Michael to make some Brooklyn boy's excuse—*Oh you know, she's on the rag*. She stood by the kitchen phone (had to call for pizza, had to feed the family) and waited for Michael to come ask whatever had possessed her. Didn't she know what side her bread was buttered on?

Offending his new only-friend, the children's new friend, Uncle Stew. The one who paid their way, put Michael's social justice dreams on film, hired pretty models to fuel the daydreams that get us through the day. She'd fixed it between him and Caroline, hadn't she, called him a fish just when Caroline's heart was broken?

Through the kitchen door she saw the snow filling up their garden. Some garden, little square of concrete where you had to go hide from your children when you wanted to smoke dope. She moved toward the door, drawing her sweater tight around her, and had a sudden vision of herself slipping out into the night before Michael came to berate her.

She opened the door before she felt her own hand on the knob. On one side of their house (the side of the eager young brownstoners) the garden wall was a high wooden stockade, but on the other side (the old working-class side) there was only a low chain-link fence. She saw herself rolling over it, and then over the chain-link on the next side, and then . . . until she reached a fence she couldn't scale. Then she would rap on the garden window and they'd let her through the house and out into the night.

Disappeared into the snow, into someone's house. A fish into a cavern.

Like something a man would do. Like something Michael's father did, to hear tale of it, out into the night, up to Seventh Avenue for a drink in Mahoney's. In peace. You came home when you were good and ready.

The snow tumbled down in her own backyard. It wasn't cold. She looked over her shoulder: lights on upstairs. Brian would take care of Martin, and Maura would take care of Patrick.

Just for a drink at Mahoney's. She reached into her jeans and pulled up a crumpled five. A sign. Where there's a way, there's a will. Just away from them, for a while, where Kevin used to go.

She hopped the first fence. Easy. She took a little run across the neighbor's, the second one easier still. She could have been doing hurdles on the Due East High School track. The snow fell wet and thick, like clods of earth falling down to cover her. The thick flakes clotted in her mouth.

CLANN
NA GAEL

Steward Morehouse had personally taped plastic down over the consoles and the Steenbeck and the old memorial upright, but still he had visions of drinks leaking through like spilled acid, destroying his editing rooms, destroying his investment, destroying his livelihood.

He pulled himself up short. Getting old fast. Old enough to cover his equipment for this party the way old ladies covered their couches, old enough to stare the way his grandfather might have stared at the tight little asses of girls in hair streaked purple and green, girls wearing tights and underwear to a cocktail party, girls wearing push-up bras you'd think they'd be afraid to walk around their own apartments in.

Getting very old, very fast. The other film guys wore baseball caps and ponytails, but he was fussy as an old queen in his oxford shirts and loafers. You'd think that three months making a rock documentary would have cured him of his fastidiousness, but it had not.

The band was called Clann na Gael. They were six magicians on the accordian, on the tin whistles, on the whadduyhah-call-it, still couldn't remember what you called the drum after he'd made an entire movie, the *bodhran*. That was what you called it. And what you called Clann na Gael, after shooting them for three months, was reptilian. He'd spent three months watching The Prick prick the needle up his arm, then stick his head in the toilet. Three months watching Ignatius Loyola drag three babes under the age of sixteen into his dressing room, winking at the camera as he closed the door in its face. Three months of watching Phelan Conor's tattoos spread like weeds, until he was the Illustrated Man. Three months recording all the degradations of on-the-road.

You'd think it would make a revolting movie, but the little ads they finally settled on had the banner *"Charming"*—*New York Film*. Clann na Gael was a band of charming reptiles, and they had made his creeping middle-aged fussiness worse.

This party made it worse. Michael Burke called *Clann na Gael* the

Dialectics movie: Steward Morehouse decided to make a documentary about political music (thesis), and the presence of the camera led the band to behave like troglodytes who'd never heard of civilization much less politics (antithesis). Steward managed to make a detached movie, a funny shallow movie that never came close to tackling the questions he'd wanted to explore: *When does art become political? When does politics become art?* But his quick cuts, his pixilations down backstage hallways, his decision to give the band's barely postadolescent political enthusiasms equal time with the music, were rewarded with a ten-page *New York Film* essay by his old nemesis Sarason on the grammar of political cinema. Steward Morehouse, bravely shunning Hollywood, refused to go to L.A. to sit in the Dorothy Chandler Pavilion on Oscar night (thesis), found himself in an ongoing state of acute anxiety, and decided to throw this party (antithesis).

Though what synthesis he would create tonight he could not say. This half of it, the cocktail party, was supposed to be for the grown-ups, but Due East Productions was littered with young pale sickly bodies. He did not know whether this was the result of Celtic bloodlines or prolific drug ingestion or both. He had not seen so many recessive genes gathered in one place since his grandfather threw the annual Christmas party. Next door there was dancing: that was probably where the adults had fled—if they had ever come at all. He'd seen Sarason (who had not the faintest glimmer of recognition that Steward was the boy he'd faced down over Truffaut) in one of the tape rooms, but he had not yet seen the Burkes. In the mood he was in, dateless, hopeless, wired, he did not expect to see them. Since Franny had disappeared into the snow one night (and that was a case of hopelessness too, as he recalled), there had been a steady shift in his dealings with Michael Burke.

Franny into the snow. They found her that night at two A.M. in a neighborhood bar, sitting on the lap of a large old man with orange stubble and bad teeth. Billy Burke was the one who thought to look for her there. Michael had already combed the neighborhood, and then got panicked enough to call his brother.

The three of them might have been pallbearers marching into the bar in formation. There was Franny, the old man's hands anchoring her to him in a way that was—if you were with her husband, and Steward was—profoundly embarrassing. Michael looked at Steward, then at his brother. He shrugged and walked back out the bar.

That left Steward and Billy to pry her off the old dude. "C'mon Fran, c'mon." Steward wasn't entirely sure she recognized him.

They walked her up and down the sidewalk. She'd been drinking boilermakers and in her drunkenness seemed to think she was holding an impromptu memorial service for her long-dead father. "We got a friend died," Billy said, by way of explanation, but that set her off again. "And Mahoney's lost its lease," Billy added, ever helpful.

Steward thought that Michael Burke never forgave him for being witness to her betrayal that night. He could hardly forgive himself for seeing her off the deep end. She was so good with the children, so sane usually. He went out to Brooklyn most weeks believing that she would set him straight.

But this time she was so far gone that she was still looped a week later. Maybe not drunk, but on an emotional bender, far enough out to call him at Due East Productions. First time she'd ever called him in New York.

"Stew, I've been thinkin. Billy'd be great with the videos. The music."

"Oh my God, Franny. What about Michael?"

He heard her voice crack. "It's just Bill's been so long without a job . . ." She was going for the low blows.

"Franny, Michael would . . ."

"Michael wouldn't mind his brother having a *job*. Some low-level gofer thing."

This wasn't like her. He suspected that she had never once in her life made a phone call on behalf of her own paintings, but now she was going to bat for Billy Burke. The dead friend. It all fell into place: Franny's brother Will in the hospital, Walter still a worry, Billy. Franny wanted to straighten them all out, rescue everybody.

Against all his better inclinations, he said: "Tell him to come over. I'll talk to him. I'm not promising anything."

And against all his better inclinations, he hired Billy, who made a smarmy clinging gofer. He hung out at Reception and draped himself over Erika, the receptionist-turned-producer who should have long since gone back to South Africa.

"Morehouse!" Billy Burke called, whenever Steward passed by. "Think Irish music."

Steward was his usual polite evasive self, but Michael—sour and prickly since his brother came to work at Due East Productions—thought a counterattack was called for. *Think Irish music,* Billy called one day when they both walked past, and Michael Burke said:

"Lemme talk to you."

He led Steward into an empty cutting room—you'd think it was his place—sat in front of the console and said:

"You know what we've done with the music shit, Morehouse. We've sunk ourselves in the middle of a glitz shwamp."

So now it was Michael Burke drinking in the middle of the day. The dark smells of Guinness and pastrami blew off him and Steward tried to wave him away.

"No, Morehouse look. I thought the deal was social justice. What's the last piece we've done?"

We've done. The last piece *he'd* done was "Jamtooty" by the Rhythm Lords, funky mix of zydeco and Tex-Mex playing three times an hour on MTV. It was a good piece he'd shot under budget.

"I don't have a quota for social justice," he said, and on his way back out past Reception Billy Burke called out again:

"Think Irish music."

There were a lot of Burkes. This could get worse. He began to picture the Burke Brothers moving in on Due East Productions, their stoned faces planted at Reception to greet every Japanese investor who came to check out the operation. And Burke had sisters too, blondes who would install themselves with Erika and ask for producer's jobs.

He spent months running from the two of them. Michael Burke, sulking, turned down a couple of scripts. Billy shadowed Erika while she made her phone calls, asked questions about lights, wore better shoes. But at least he let up on the *Think Irish music* line. One day, subdued, he said to Steward:

"Clann na Gael's in Tompkins Square five o'clock. Don't suppose you wanna catch em."

"Who's Clann na Gael?"

"Oh, they'd be right up your alley, Morehouse. Political band."

"Never heard of them."

This was not true, but Steward was not about to admit that Billy had been on to something all along. Clann na Gael were beginning to make a name for themselves in the East Village, and Billy wasn't the first to mention them. Like every teenage band, half their kids were from New Jersey, but the other half were their cousins from County something. County Tullamore Dew, for all Steward knew. The line on them was that they were intuitive middle-class musicians writing lyrics about poverty and the working class. Perfect in the last days of the Reagan Empire. And they were savvy. They'd been doing benefit concerts, donating the receipts to local homeless shelters. Shades of Bob Geldof, people said.

"You might get off on them, Jesus they'd make a great documentary. Why don't you come along?"

"No thanks, I've got to look over the books tonight or I'll go bankrupt."

This was not true either. The truth was that he was not haunting the Burkes' in Brooklyn, was not sleeping with any of his producers, was not lusting after any scripts. Was so successful at this—business—that he did not know where he was going.

"Suit yourself," Billy said.

"Well. Five o'clock. Maybe for an hour."

The concert was audacious and free, a statement on behalf of the park squatters. The little stage was erected without benefit of permit, and by the time Billy elbowed his way through the crowd the cops had given up on stopping anything.

"Phelan Conor," Billy yelled, and pointed at an accordian player doing splits while he played. "Hommage à the Pogues," but Steward could not remember who exactly the Pogues were. He was lost in the swell of the big drum rolling across the little park. Clann na Gael screamed half the lyrics, but it was melodic, more than you could say about most of the bands he shot. The lead singer was ugly as sin and hypnotic as Satan. Steward was seduced, and the concert made page one of the metro section the next morning.

And the next morning Steward pulled out the *Times* to show Mr. Kenzaburo Ito, who'd been breathing down his neck about high def. He proposed a playful deal: he'd approach Clann na Gael, shoot high def for the Japanese market and transfer to film for a theatrical release here. Mr. Ito said gravely that he would consider it, and called back two days later to ask when preproduction could start.

He could wash his hands afterward if it all came to naught—just a technical experiment—but still he was flummoxed. When he told Michael, disgust dripped down Burke's beard.

"Clann na Gael? They don't even know what they're saying. They don't have a clue, the implications of what they propose."

Steward was not sure exactly what it was that Clann na Gael proposed. It was the music that had carried him that first night in the park, the whistle-honk-shriek and that heavy national identity smeared on like but-

ter. The childish delight in being Irish—you couldn't imagine the
Morehouses sitting around talking about the glory of England—held him
all the while they were doing the preliminary negotiations.

He let Erika produce and Billy assist. Even after shaking hands all
around he was only flirting with it, even after Clann na Gael signed with
TOPical POP, but Erika and Billy were fired with passion. *We MUST get
the Bottom Line gig, Stew, whatever do you mean we'll have enough live footage.*

After a single day of shooting he suspected that Michael Burke was
right. *Political band* seemed too grand a term. After a week of watching
Clann na Gael drink and drug he was bored silly, and maybe worried for
the little New Jersey girls who trailed them. But the deal was done. He hit
the road after them and Michael Burke retreated to his tech articles, the old
freelance life of the magazine writer, that prehistoric medium feeding him
and his family once again. Well, someone had some integrity.

MICK MURPHY
*(The American drummer, but so affected by proximity to his cousins
that he speaks in a worse gristly unintelligible brogue than they do.)*
Well, it's clear yuv never heard of the Easter Rising, isn't it,
nor Padriag Pearse. Have you any idea how old he was when
he died? Young men all, and isn't it time young Americans
speak up? We live in a *wasteland,* don't we now, a fucking
wasteland.
(He draws on a cigarette, incensed.)
Remember Reagan's first big move in office? Do you? Air
traffic controllers! Decent workingmen—I've an uncle in
Queens lost his livelihood, and all because they were
speaking up about safety. We should've had an uprising for
them, shouldn't we? Because look what we'll be left with:
Bush!
(Deep contemptuous laugh.)
Bush. Pale clone is what he is, that Bush, and he'll be
presiding over a country where mothers take to the streets
with their wee ones to beg a quarter for a pint of milk.

STEWARD
(Off-camera. By now he's used to these American kids saying wee
ones *so he's able to control his impulse to snort.)*

But what are you saying, are you saying you're
revolutionaries?

MICK MURPHY

I'm saying we're not too young, are we, to point out the
difference between right and wrong.

Billy told him cheering erupted when Mick made his speech, kids in
suburban nanoplexes rising to their feet, fists clenched. He could pretty well
guess that they hissed when he—old Southerner in chinos and Keds—
mumbled his doubts off-camera. It was Clann na Gael that got him an
Oscar nomination, not his filmmaking. What had he been thinking? *Last
Waltz? Stop Making Sense?* But those were good music movies that didn't
put on political airs. His movie, all vague talk, all hot air, wasn't even in the
same league.

Clann na Gael didn't know the difference. They were ecstatic, infatu-
ated with their own images. They forgave him all his reserve making the
movie. Look what he'd caught: their quick rolling tongues—Mick Murphy, who probably never passed high school English, called Bush a *pale clone*
without a moment's reflection, and in another country's accent. They all
made speeches, the New Jersey kids sounding Irish, the Irish kids sounding
New Jersey, all of them firing off variations of the right and wrong speech.

And who was he to carp at their facility? He'd been more honest as a
kid himself, the kid at St. Benedict's all fired up about the draft. Caroline
said the Benedictines taught him guilt, but he was more inclined to say that
for all their mindless clinging to superstition they were the ones who'd
introduced him to his conscience, as Nick had intended. Not their fault that
he'd left it somewhere in the meanwhile. Whatever happened to *Faces of the
Lowcountry,* race the key to America's problems? That was a worthy project,
a worthy vision even, one face at a time—but the first face's mild contempt
had scared him off. Poor Steward. His family's maid didn't love him after all.

Easily scared off, easily seduced. There had to be some part of him
tickled that his cheap-politics movie was up for an Oscar, that Lola was out
of her mind with excitement even if he didn't take her to Hollywood.
Wasn't he throwing a party for two hundred hangers-on (and didn't Lola
have fifty in Chuck Parrish's living room)? Wasn't he wandering the offices
of Due East Productions to check out the crowd, a little silly, the man of the
hour in his own fiefdom, no one to talk to?

No one but the Burkes, after all. There they were, Franny and Michael, alone in the film cutting room. He was reduced to seeing them at parties again, two absences in his life. He stood in the doorway to watch them, Michael reading the labels on cans of film—seeing what he'd missed out on this last year?—and Franny in a director's chair, drink on her lap, watching her husband. She wore the same short black skirt she always wore out, her only skirt, he'd come to see over the last few years of meeting the Burkes in bars. Same clunky shoes.

He read tension in Franny's profile. She was watching her husband with narrowed eyes: he'd shot enough close-ups of women to know that she didn't trust Michael. Was he sneaking off finally, turning the tables on the wife-and-mother who sat on old men's laps? In their music video days, the models always came on to Michael, scruffy and slick and sure of himself, they thought; but he turned them aside and caught the subway back to Brooklyn.

Or so Steward Morehouse had always assumed. Now, watching Franny's lips pursed, that concentration of venom, he supposed there could be a secret life for Michael Burke. If he had a wife looking at him the way Franny was looking—didn't trust him, didn't care to say a word—he thought he might have a secret life too.

"Come on in, Steward," she said, without turning her head. She'd known all along that he was watching. "It's your place."

Michael swung around, surprised. "Cheers," he said, raising a plastic glass. They were both drinking then, three fingers apiece of whiskey, straight up. Tonight there was something reckless about the pair of them, slipping close to their forties. You could see it around the eyes. A waiter passed into the room with a tray of shrimp, but Steward waved him away.

"Hey!" Franny said. "Come back here."

The waiter—he'd be an actor, a painter himself—came back grinning. Franny spread a napkin next to the ancient Moviola and emptied the platter. "You may have eaten," she said to Steward, "but we came to this party for a free meal."

The waiter was confused, looked at Steward for approval of this flagrant violation. Steward nodded. The waiter backed off, paused at the door:

"Mr. Morehouse. Congratulations. I admire your work."

Actor. Short—probably had trouble finding stage work, he couldn't be over five-seven—but striking, auburn-haired, maybe some combo of Irish-Italian, aquiline nose and square jaw, deep rolling voice.

"I was wondering."

"Send me some head shots," Steward said, "for the files. Put a note on, I'll remember."

The actor danced out of the room. "Thanks a lot, matter of fact I brought some with me."

"Reception desk. Just put my name on em. And listen, I can't promise anything."

When he was gone Michael said: "Good-looking guy. You gonna have him sell refrigerators?"

Hey. They'd sold things together—babies, even—but they'd never sold refrigerators.

"When you coming back to write for me?"

Michael shrugged. "When you call. I could use the work, tell you the truth. What kind of projects you got?"

Steward's turn to shrug. "I've been turning work away, thinking I'll be shooting the feature."

"Good thing Billy's off to Hollywood."

The three of them laughed, finally, Billy's departure a good deal for all of them. Billy and Erika had taken off together, and not just to sit in the Dorothy Chandler Pavilion on Oscar night. They were hot, after *Clann na Gael*. Wouldn't it be ironic if Billy . . .

"So what about that script?"

"Yeah, well, I optioned it cheap. Poor guy didn't have an agent. But I'm not going to make it—I threw the money away. I can't fall in love."

"So . . ."

"Dunno. I've got to set a deadline. Else I *will* be selling refrigerators. I can get money now, but in another two months nobody'll know my name. I could use you to read scripts for me, a month or two maybe."

Franny popped her eyes out, a funny-papers expression. "Stew. You mean to tell me"—she sounded exactly like Doris—"you're ready to make your big movie after all these years and it's just a script stopping you? Michael!"

"Don't look at me. I gave him the novels."

"Good novels, too. They just don't translate. They're so—"

"Interior."

"Right. Interior."

Franny said: "Well, why'd you give him the novels? What about the screenplays?"

"Oh Franny, God's sake, I was a kid writing those. Crap."

Franny raised her eyebrows, pursed her lips again. "That crap took two, three years of your life, as I recall."

"Crap is crap."

"Your agent didn't think it was all crap. The IRA thing got optioned."

"Yeah. Six months. Lots of enthusiasm for *that* one."

"You didn't tell me about an IRA thing."

Franny said: "We got our first real bed in fifteen years of marriage out of that option money," and Steward saw why she'd been staring at Michael that way. They were broke again—*It's the perfect time, he's just made this movie about an Irish band. You can mention it, anyway. You can ask.* She who'd die of shame before she asked anyone to take a look at her slides or come by her studio.

"Let me read it, Burke."

You could see what Michael Burke was thinking, clear as if he had a balloon over his head: *Just leave those head shots at Reception. I'm not promising anything.* "I was just a kid when I wrote that. I don't know if I could stand to read it again."

"I want to read it, though."

"Yeah, sure."

"Franny, you mail it to me. He's not going to bring it in."

She set her lips closed, then smiled, one of those sad grateful smiles like the one she gave him when she saw that he'd hung one of her paintings over the reception desk. It was a street scene, angled from her studio window: Mr. Ito thought it was more heartfelt propaganda about the homeless. Steward's theme, this decade. But Steward doubted the word *homeless* had ever come into Franny's mind when she looked out her window—she'd seen a man's face, pretty and smooth and blank as a young girl's, and that's what she had painted. A young man hustling change, all innocence, honey-colored face against pure white bandages swaddling his head. The bandages were probably an invention, an exaggeration like the size of the head. He'd found the painting grotesque at first, but compelling, a vision of the sick-in-the-head outside our windows. Could he be influencing her choice of subject? He had Billy handle the offer and the cash, and he became the secret buyer. She probably knew who it was all along. She probably thought he was doling out charity.

She'd made other sales the same way, neighborhood people, magazine people. He wouldn't have been able to keep on that way, working on and on without a gallery, wouldn't have been able to write novels for ten years with nobody printing them, screenplays no one produced. But people did.

The rooms of Due East Productions were filled tonight with people who did, actors who watched you empty trays of shrimp onto paper napkins and sucked in a deep breath and told you they admired your work. People who saw their paintings on your wall and cringed, thinking you bought out of pity.

"Hey," Burke said, "we gonna watch the Oscars or what? You should see my mom's place, Oscar Central. Frank and Richie bought a keg, case Billy's on-camera. I got a hundred dollars says he breaks the lens."

"I'm all atingle," Franny said. She was smiling at him again, stretching up from her chair to go watch television, tugging the old black skirt down her thighs. Plumper thighs now, but inviting just the same. You couldn't see the birthmarks through the tights. She watched him, watched her husband. Suddenly he couldn't bear the thought of her, cheap silver earrings dangling, crowding up close to the Clann na Gael groupies outside.

"Wait up," he said. "I'll get a little monitor in here."

"Thanks, Stew," she said, and sat back down. Sounding depressed. Look what it cost her to ask a favor for her husband. Look what it cost them both. They were sick of asking favors. They could probably see his heart sinking at the sound of those initials, *IRA*. He'd had enough flirting with Irish violence, naive Stew Morehouse who thought, when he started shooting his movie, that Clann na Gael was the name of a clan, of the band's family. Ha. Somebody said *What're you, kidding? It's like the American branch,* and he was ambivalent as usual, sympathy for the Catholics, no sympathy for the bombing. He could never get a clear answer either, about whether the name actually meant anything to them: hadn't Mick Murphy (Mr. Right and Wrong) given a speech on nonviolence? They all seemed to call on civil rights: well, he could get into that. Not a hard question asked in his movie. He'd just let the camera trail a band of anarchic charmers. It was fascinating. It was anthropology.

He wandered back through the hallway, and a great weariness descended. He was going to have to pass judgment on Michael Burke's IRA script. *I was just a kid.* And kids were full of passion, signifying nothing—he knew all about sound and fury: women always said he should be shooting Southern Gothic, that was what he *knew*.

Groups clustered around the high monitors in the video rooms, the one they'd set up at Reception. Shots of stars' legs emerging from limos, distorted like the limbs in Franny's paintings. A little moment of regret. He could have been arriving, he could have been pulling up in a limo with Erika, with Caroline, with—hadn't thought of her in years, but now he pictured her in a Paris bistro, watching the Oscars—Simone. Pink bras and garter belts. Limos. Mr. Independent.

No. Independents wore baseball caps and ponytails. They lived like Franny and Michael, always on the edge. They lived in Hoboken, they shot out of vans in Michigan and Ohio. He was something else again. He ran a business. He was commercial. He dreamed of an idiosyncratic little feature, but in the end his profit-making impulse would take over and the feature would be as commercial as *Clann na Gael*. If he wasn't careful, it might even make money the way Due East Productions did. Or. Or maybe he'd never even make the feature he'd been talking about all these years; maybe he was doing with scripts what he did with women, keeping them at arm's length. He claimed to want to get married, have kids, when in fact what he seemed to want was to let the Burkes stick their elbows in the muck. Let them have their marriage and their kids and wear their misery on their sleeves so he could see what he'd saved himself from.

His presence—darting through his own hallways, into his own video room, through his own cabinet—hardly registered on these strangers at his party. A brunette amazon winked at him: someone he'd shot? He made his way back to Franny and Michael with the monitor under one arm and a bottle of Jameson's in his other fist. Their glasses were filled and the set pushed on before the first production number.

Franny turned the volume down. "Can't bear it."

"You're telling me. I've been getting scripts for musicals. Unbelievable stuff."

"People sending you a lot these days? Word got out." Burke was trying not to sound all that interested.

"Somebody sent me a novel with an entire screenplay in the middle of it. Truly bizarre. Turns out the guy cuts my hair writes screenplays."

"Turns out the guy you invited to your party writes screenplays."

"That makes a little more sense, when he's been writing screenplays for me for years."

"I haven't written for you in a year and a half."

"Nah."

"Go look through your checkbook." Little click of his tongue when he bit off the word *checkbook*. Little belligerence coming through. Franny was pouring them all doubles again. He never drank so much as when he was with them. Did they do this all the time, or only for him?

They watched on in silence, the word *checkbook*, as usual, quieting them all down. He was drunk already. It's my party and I'll hole up if I want to.

From outside the door he heard shrieks and a young girl's voice: "The Prick!" It occurred to him to turn the volume back up.

"What's she gonna say if you win?"

"Not a chance in hell. *Inside Folsom*'ll take it for sure."

"Yeah, but if you do."

Erika, producer, would accept. Good riddance to her, hanging onto Due East Productions all these years by playing on his guilt. May she and Billy latch onto the slickest and seamiest of Hollywood execs. "We cranked out a speech for her." . . . *like to acknowledge Clann na Gael's activism on behalf of the hungry and the homeless of this country and to accept this award for all those struggling* . . . "Wish I'd had you to write it, I'll tell you the truth. Your brother is—"

"Stupid as a side of beef."

"Hush," Franny said. And there it was, Best Documentary already. Stupid, the little thrill. He'd had the nerve to tell Lola that it didn't mean anything to him *except commercially, I'm not sneezing at that. It'd buy me a distribution deal.* They did short subjects first, and Franny squeezed his hand the way Robert Mitchum's wife might have squeezed his hand. Which made him . . . in the same league. You got like a kid. On to feature length.

Then the hoots and hollers from outside the door on the first four words, *And the winner is* . . . And silence on the next two: *Inside Folsom.* He imagined he'd heard *Clann na Gael,* imagined he could hear hoots and hollers from the stage next door, hoots and hollers down the deserted Tribeca block, hoots and hollers from New Jersey. He saw the charms of *Clann na Gael* roll out, the subtleties of its message.

The little statue changed hands—get real, this changed everything, he had to sell Due East Productions and make the plunge—and he felt Franny's hand dig deep into the sides of his knee, a touch she'd never given him. That Academy Award touch. You got it even when you lost.

From the hallways outside, the silence progressed to laughter, a fizz of giddiness. The door was opening—he'd been found out—and The Prick himself, looking undrugged for the occasion (will miracles never cease) led the charge to find and console him. More roars, more brogues from the crowd, some of them maybe even authentic. Then they were hoisting him onto their shoulders. As if he'd just scored a touchdown or landed the big account. The Irish loved a loser.

From up high, he could see Franny and Michael pulling their plastic cups out of harm's way, grabbing their coats from the top of the file cabinet.

They were getting ready to clear out already. The crowd bearing him twisted, snakelike, to move him through the doorway, but he was turned the wrong way. Watching the Burkes. His head hit the metal door frame hard, and he could feel the lump rising as the crowd beneath him buckled, but his eyes were on Franny.

She was buttoning her coat, eyes on the carpet. Sick of struggling. He willed her to look at him, but there wasn't a prayer.

THE BATTLE
OF THE
CRUCIFIXES

The tension was a thick cold fog, even in the empty apartment, even after Michael left to scuff around the neighborhood. They'd wasted the morning screeching at each other. It was always over Brian lately: maybe this was how they meant to reconcile his leaving home. First year at Georgetown and he had two B's—from the way Michael went on, you'd think their firstborn had shot up the student center with an assault rifle. *Ease up,* she'd been saying, but Michael was always purple with fury. Why would a scholarship committee renew with a couple of B's like that? Just like the old days: Michael threw a dictionary at her—a *dictionary*—and she threw it back. With the children out of the house, they could act like children, yet again.

And lose, yet again, the morning hours when Michael would have been making calls, hustling business. The truth was, she thought she'd go out of her mind if she had to do any more graphics. All she wanted anymore was to get down to the studio, and now they'd frittered away two hours, and here was the doorbell.

The doorbell ringing in the middle of the morning: shades of Kevin. But it was no ghost standing at her gate, it was Steward Morehouse. She went to hug him and drew back, all in one confused motion: it was his first visit in a good long while, and if Michael came back to find them together . . . Lately she found herself resenting Michael and pitying him at the same time, a lethal combination. She pulled back the hug completely.

"Oh Stew. Come on in. Michael'll be back before too long."

Lord, she sounded like a fluttering housewife and looked like one too, swooping down to grab up the trail of underwear and paper and books her children had left.

"Been a while, huh?"

Her niggly nerves did not register on Steward, who looked too haggard to register much of anything. He followed her into the kitchen and sat, obedient, paying no mind to the two days' pile of dishes, oblivious to the fog she saw wherever her eye rested. She washed a cup and put it in his hands, just so she'd have something to do with her own. "Michael'll be back soon. Just sit here. Wait, I'll find some magazines." Now she was making it sound like a doctor's office.

"I didn't come to see Michael, Franny. I mean, I came to see both of you."

"Oh. Stew, I'm sorry, sorry, I'm just on my way out."

A dark fog in her house, smoke. Steward grimaced at his coffee, stared out the back door at the frost. Michael hadn't worked for him in three years, almost. The last time they talked, Stew had Due East Productions on the block, just as business was slacking off. Everybody in production was moving to California, a steady stream of them like Okies in the Depression. Oakies with laptop computers. Nobody was buying Stew Morehouse's business, and there wasn't any business at the business.

He was going to concentrate on making his big movie, he told them, but he wasn't any closer to that, either. For a while things had looked good for all three of them, moviewise. After the Oscars, she dug *The Gunrunners* out of a cardboard box and carried it into Tribeca on the subway, thinking she might turn to salt if she so much as sneaked a peak. She was betraying Michael, kidnapping his screenplay. *Crap—I was a kid.* But he forgave her when Steward optioned the script: ten thousand dollars in the bank, the first money they'd saved for Brian's college.

Then, six months down the line, Steward pulled back, singing the same old tune. He just couldn't fall in love. *The Gunrunners* had a lot of problems: that kind of melodrama went with the times, and you couldn't update it; he didn't know how much he sympathized with the male lead, not to mention the female. It would make more sense to shoot his first movie in the U.S., it'd be cheaper to do a contemporary script.

Michael forgave her, but he wouldn't forgive Steward, not for leading him on. When Steward didn't renew, they had to use the ten thousand for groceries and mortgage, and now here was Brian, slipping to B's, relying as Michael had on the goodwill of scholarship committees. Michael's brilliant son would end up leaving Georgetown and going to a third-rate school, same as he had, and all on account of Steward's being a guy who *couldn't even get it up.*

"Off to the studio, Franny?"

"Eventually," she said. "First I go by a nursing home. Barrel of laughs."

"Who's in a nursing home?"

"Michael's mother. She's only awake a few hours, so—"

"I'll go with you, then."

"Oh, you don't want—it's depressing. It's real depressing." And Michael's fury would deepen from purple to black if she took Steward Morehouse to see his mother, when he couldn't even bring himself to go.

"Couldn't be worse than . . ." Steward's voice trailed off, but he managed a smile. She smiled back.

"Oh come on. Let me walk you there."

The wan smile had her relenting. "O.k.," she said, "we'll take the walk then." Had she betrayed Michael again? For all she knew Steward had only optioned the screenplay in the first place as an excuse to give them the ten thousand dollars. She hadn't read it to this day: for all their bickering she was closer to Michael than she was to any other human being, but still there was a distance that couldn't be spanned. Still a few things to avoid in this marriage.

She got her old lady's shopping bag and trudged uphill with Steward, one eye wandering in case her husband surfaced. A mess, this slipping off with Steward after a fight, and innocent to boot. They'd passed the dangerous time, anyway: now they were paler and heavier, the two of them, middle-aged, their very blood flowing slower. He only wanted solace. All any man wanted, far as she could make out. She thought of Kevin for the second time that morning.

"How is he?"

"Michael? Oh. Got the blues lately."

"Ain't we all."

Steward actually looked blue in the winter light. You'd never know, from his chapped lips and the sore cracks at the corner of his mouth, that this man had ever been a success at anything. He wore a brown fedora, but it sat awkward on his head, and his tweed coat—Steward would shop Madison Avenue, if she knew him—made an even older man of him.

"What's the matter Stew?"

He shrugged. He could have been fifteen and silent, and wasn't she grateful for the silence, trudging along together. It wasn't even like her to ask what was wrong. All backwards, that Steward should be the one walking her to Michael's mother. Michael despised her for going every day—he said she was throwing it in his face, playing Miss Sacrificial, giving up time in the studio—but Norah wasn't eating, and if she went by between breakfast and lunch she could smuggle in cheese crackers. Maybe she was throwing it up, playing the saint. Who could say? Better just to do it and not despair over it.

Everybody depressed. The whole city depressed. There was a pall set-

tling over New York, and not just over the street people, not just over the
laid-off investment bankers leaving this neighborhood they'd only just discovered. It had settled over Norah. It had settled over Moneybags Morehouse, evidently. It had settled over Michael, had settled into him. It wasn't
just Stew Michael wouldn't forgive. He wouldn't forgive Kevin, or his
mother, or his brothers. He was approaching the age when his own father,
drunk, tripped over a coil of cables and went on workmen's comp for the
brief remainder of his life.

For a few years the Burkes had all brightened when Steward Morehouse came to the door: someone doing well, someone spreading the
wealth. Now even Steward claimed the blues for himself. It didn't seem fair.
Franny wanted them reserved for Michael, who did despair in grand fashion. Lately she woke up to it and went to bed with it.

"So when's his new book coming out?"

"He ran into some bad news there."

"Oh no."

"They folded, Alpha Press. And y'know, he only sold a few thousand
copies the first two, so his agent's having a hard time . . ."

"Oh no."

She bristled a little, for Michael's sake. Michael was on page six hundred of the latest manuscript without a prayer of a publisher, and Steward
was . . . stalling for time. She was beginning to believe what he was
beginning to believe: that he'd never make his movie. No screenplay in the
world good enough for him. Steward never talked about the story he
dreamed of making, only waited for someone else's dreams to dovetail with
his own.

What Michael always said: things had been too easy for him. The
option agreement for *The Gunrunners* had named a purchase price of a
hundred thousand, *same as the big boys would have paid,* Michael said, for his
first sale. Hard to think of the hundred thousand gone on Steward's whim
and not see her three sons in the one bedroom now, so Maura wouldn't
have to undress in front of Patrick. Play money to him.

Another block in silence, Steward not so much as scanning the brownstones they passed, eyes on the ground, eyes on his feet. He wore boat
shoes. Could have been a stockbroker with the morning off. Could have
been an old man.

"Too bad we didn't make that movie," he said suddenly. "We'd all be
in Ireland now. New York looks so bleak."

What a model of sensitivity Steward Morehouse was today! She didn't

answer. Too bad she didn't have a gallery, still. Too bad Michael and his
brothers couldn't look their mother in the eye, now that she was incarcer-
ated.

They walked along the park for half a mile, the bare trees and the
strewn garbage collaborating with Steward's blues. A dead bird, a used
condom on the sidewalk. Perfect.

"Here you go," she said finally, and pointed to the nursing home. You
wouldn't know it, strolling past, unless you looked up and saw *Our Lady of
Mercy* done in subtle gold on the side. A big elegant white building, scrolls
sculpted into its front, all maternal curves: a building that looked as if it had
breasts. "I'm glad I got the walk with you."

Steward stared. "I'll come in."

"Stew, no, it's—"

"Oh, I know all about it. My grandfather's depressing as hell."

"He's still kicking?"

"I wouldn't say kicking. He likes to whiz around in the motorized
wheelchair, park himself out on the verandah."

Again she bristled. Our Lady of Mercy had looked fine when they went
on the tour: spry little ladies in costume jewelry who jammed their elbows
into your ribs and said *Guess how old I am, honey! Ninety-two!* The old gents
in stained ties. Scapulars dangling, rosary beads rattling, a holy picture every
ten feet. This was Norah's world: the names on the door said *O'Donnell,
O'Malley, Maguire, Boyd.* So this was where all the Irish in Park Slope had
gone—and there was a *Mazella* every now and again for variety. Norah
Burke would be in heaven, they thought, down in the auditorium watching
the black-and-white movies, listening to the grammar school choirs.

But after a week in Our Lady of Mercy Norah was wearing diapers, and
the nurses demoted her from the floor where she could have moved around
on her own. After a month she was no longer walking, and after this first
year—they moved her in last Christmas, when she was out every morning
wandering the streets and couldn't find her way back home—she took to
her bed twenty-two hours a day. Steward's grandfather on the verandah in a
motorized wheelchair: he had no idea.

"Steward, really."

"I'm coming in with you. Really."

She didn't recognize this snippety persistence of his. She shouldn't let
him come in, it would make Michael crazy—but here he was, nodding at
the guard, nipping at her heels. It occurred to her that Michael didn't have
to know. Norah wouldn't remember the visit from one hour to the next.

In the lobby she watched Steward tense, and they were both awkward on the elevator. Always an acrid smell here. She was braced for the smell of the diapers, but it wasn't that: it was broccoli or canned asparagus, the vegetable of the day, just sharp enough to put you on edge, to make you picture a green gone yellow, a hard crisp line gone soggy.

The doors opened to Norah's floor and there was a new smell, vaguely medicinal, vaguely excretal. They walked out into the television corner, a scrunched end of the floor where old ladies were lined up in plastic armchairs. A retired priest who made the rounds stood with one hand on the wall, telling jokes, and the ladies wavered, one eye on the priest and one eye on Regis and Kathy Lee. Hard choice. The priest perked up at the prospects of a larger audience than he'd started with and winked at Franny:

"Did you hear this one, the rumor going through the Vatican about the end of the world? I want to tell you, those prelates were panicking. They went running to the pope—we're talking John the XXIII, a pope with a sense of humor, only pope belongs in a joke far as I'm concerned. Where was I? Ah. The prelates. 'Your Holiness, this is it. Our goose is cooked. Our fish is fried. It's the end of the world. It's the day of judgment. Your Holiness, what do we do?' Well, I'll tell you. Pope John smiled down on them, calm as you please, and he said: 'I'll tell you what to do. LOOK BUSY!' "

The priest, undeterred by the blank eyes groping back toward the television, gave a master of ceremonies' big wave and called out, departing: "So that's my advice to you, ladies. LOOK BUSY!" Two of the women on his escape route reached out to touch his black trouser legs, as if he were the pope himself.

"Hiya, sweetheart," he said to Franny. "Finally got your husband to come? Now don't forget, bub, it's not just women's work." He chucked Steward under the chin, and the two old ladies who had reached for him cackled with glee. No wonder: Steward was the picture of confused guilt, the priest's gnarled arthritic hand catching him at the point of his sharp chin.

The ladies who had reached for the priest reached now for Steward, and one of them said:

"Get me a cup of coffee, will ya?"

Franny turned back and shook her head. "Oh, Mrs. Alfredo. Remember? They won't let me give you the coffee. That blood pressure thing."

"You little piece of shit! Whore!"

"You bet," Franny said. Alfredo was her favorite. "You can still back out you know, Steward. Just get on the elevator."

His blue skin had turned green, but he shook his head no. Walking through the corridors, he asked if this was the mental ward.

"Oh, you'd be mental too, you had to be in front of Regis and Kathy Lee all day." Really, she had no patience for him—he cringed in the face of the sad Madonnas on the wall, and he wasn't even supposed to be here.

She stuck her head into Norah's room, to spare Stew the chance that they might be changing her. No. This was her two-hour stint out of bed and she sat in a wheelchair, eyes closed, while an attendant yanked at her wispy hair.

"Oh hi Franny. How's the children?" The aide wadded Norah's hair into a child's ponytail holder, three plastic balls in pink and blue and yellow. "Don't you look pretty Miz Burke. Look how pretty in the mirror. Don't she look pretty Franny. Say hello to Franny Miz Burke. We getting her into the lunchroom today Franny. Doctor says she gotta eat something else we stick the tube in her stomach. You don't want the tube in your stomach do you Miz Burke? Oh no."

"Hey Vernette."

Norah's eyes opened finally, and fixed on Franny, but they were not focused yet. Sometimes she could go the whole visit without focusing. "Billy came to see me last night," she said.

"He did? All the way from California?"

"Oh, he swam," Norah said. "My mother had to wrap blankets around him. She sat him in front of the fire."

"You're cold," Franny said. "Here, I'll fetch you a blanket." She pressed the laprug over the old lady's knobby knees and backed the wheelchair out through the narrow space. Steward backed out in front of her, paving the way.

"Let me get that," he said, once they'd made their way out the room, but she shook her head no. Let him take it? This was what Michael despised about visiting with her: that she knew where Norah's wheelchair got parked in the lunchroom, and where the blankets were folded, that she knew the attendants' names, that she kept a list of Norah's medications and bullied the psychiatrist into lowering the dosages. Dizzy Frances Burke, who wouldn't get her children to pick their underwear up off the floor and wouldn't stop hollering at them, whose domestic life was a series of crises and protests—*never an hour for myself! never!*—became a model of efficiency when she walked through the halls of Our Lady of Mercy. Michael called her *Madam Efficiency* when they came together, and he wasn't smiling when he said it. Now Steward looked terrified.

The ladies were being wheeled into a small square lunchroom, the taped Christmas decorations dangling from the wall. A radio emitted static.

Franny reached up to turn the radio off. One of the attendants said: "Thank you Jesus!" but an old woman named Gallagher in the far corner glared at her with an evil eye.

"You selfish pig!" The woman's voice was low and sonorous, but she was frightening to look at: her hair was steel-gray and sparse, fanning out like moss from a knobby head, and her nose was hooked. A regular story-book witch. "Who the hell you think you are? Pulling that number. Selfish pig! I'll tell you about pulling that number. I got *your* number."

Franny raised an eyebrow to Stew, but he was staring at his feet. The old woman lost interest in her tirade, and the lunchroom settled into its usual deep silence. The women sitting around the half dozen tables did not look at one another: they stared down, like Steward, or off. They dozed. Norah was one of the youngest but you'd never know it from her mouth, hanging ajar. She had lost so much weight that her skin hung splotched and bruised.

Opposite Norah sat a woman with her nose pressed into her knee—the aides had to prop her back up, once the food got there. Sometimes she crumpled in her walker. But her hair was always dyed a pure shining gold and she somehow managed, keeled over that way, to set it herself in perfect pincurls. She managed it every day. Something to live for.

There was no place for Steward to sit, so they stood on either side of Norah's wheelchair, one awkward hand apiece on the handles. Franny reached into the shopping bag she'd bought, drew out a handful of crackers, and slipped them into Norah's clenched fist.

"Oh, and look." She pulled out a large crucifix, the tackiest she'd been able to find. It was two feet high, of hollow plastic construction, covered with peeling fake walnut that looked like den paneling. Centered over the walnut were narrow marbleized strips of white; on these hung Jesus, whose gold paint was peeling too. Norah said the cross the sisters had put on her wall was too small to see, but she could see this one.

Her eyes lighted. "Oh," she said, a child at Christmas, and touched her index finger to the banner atop Christ: *INRI*. King of the Jews. She ran a longing hand over the length of it, returned it to Franny, and blessed herself.

"It's for you. For your room."

"Oh!" She grabbed Franny's hand. "Let's put it up."

"I thought after lunch," Franny said.

Norah set her eyes to misting. "I'm not hungry." Her lip was all set to quiver.

"Hey, now, Stew'll get it up right now"—Stew shot her a look—"and we'll take a look after lunch." She was beginning to enjoy Steward's discomfort. His own fault—hadn't she tried to warn him off? "Just over the bed, Stew, where the little one is now. Here, you need a bigger nail." And she pulled a hammer and a box of nails from the shopping bag.

"You come prepared!"

"Madam Efficiency," she said.

Steward leaned over to whisper in her ear. "That object is the most hideous thing I ever saw."

He took the crucifix from Franny's hand, and Norah, seeing it in motion, reached a hand from her wheelchair to touch it. Steward's eyes met the old lady's, and again she focused.

"Will you be careful with it?" She clutched the base of the crucifix.

"I will." Good: he was solemn. No smarmy *I promise*s.

"Because now it's the biggest one." Still she would not release it.

Steward said: "I promise," and tugged a little.

Gallagher, in rare form today, hissed at him from the back of the room. "You got a nerve. Bringing that thing in here. You think you got the biggest, I'll get a bigger one, my son's coming Sunday, I'll get the biggest one."

The old ladies brightened a bit, still averting their eyes but sitting up straighter.

Norah looked back in the general direction of Gallagher and said: "My son bought it for me in California."

"Aw, blow it out your ass. My son lives in Coney Island and if you can't get the world's biggest hot dog in Coney Island . . ."

"Italian," Norah said, to no one. "Coarse."

Stew was still tugging away at the base of the crucifix. The look on his face suggested his fear of an impending riot if he didn't get the cross out of the room. Some of the women were looking sharply, even shrewdly, at it now, sizing it up.

"Gallagher's not an Italian name, case you never noticed," Gallagher said, "and there's a bigger one in the chapel."

"Sure there is," Franny said.

Norah loosened her grip. "There may be a bigger one in the chapel,"
she said, "but my son has brought me the biggest one in the *rooms.*"

She smiled graciously. Franny had not heard her address so many words
to the other residents before.

Steward took his chance to pop the crucifix loose from her hands and
hold it close to his chest as he retreated. A dozen pairs of eyes followed him
and the crucifix. Mrs. Alfredo, coming into the lunchroom on her own
power, reached the doorway just as he did. She blocked his way with her
walker.

"You brought me that?" It was hard to tell if she was joking.

His voice came out forced and cheery. "Oh sorry, no. This is, this
belongs to Mrs. Burke. Excuse me."

Alfredo stood her ground. "Whatcha, dint bring me that?" It was still
hard to say exactly what she meant in that tone of voice.

Steward laughed a false laugh. "Sorry, it's Mrs. Burke's."

"When you putting mine up?"

Steward turned to Franny, helpless.

"DON'T TURN AWAY FROM ME LIKE THAT." She was not
joking.

He swiveled back.

"I want one like that. Big."

Gallagher bellowed something from the back of the room. By now all
the women were awake, one of them punching her fists through the air
beside her wheels, as if she were watching a prizefight.

A small din arose, but Norah's voice fluttered over it, calm and unper-
turbed as she'd been in her mothering days. "Ladies, ladies. I will have my
son bring one for each and every one of you."

Alfredo said: "Sure you will."

Gallagher said: "I don't want no garbage like that puny thing. My son's
gonna bring me one twice as big."

Alfredo looked stricken at the thought of Gallagher's getting one twice
as big. She reached out across her walker, and got hold of the crucifix. This
left her sliding down the front of her walker, Steward stretching one hand to
steady her and the other to lay claim to the crucifix.

"Ma'am," Steward said, slipping into a Due East persona, "if you'll just
allow me to pass."

For answer Mrs. Alfredo tugged anew at the crucifix and wrenched it
from his hands. The effort cost her balance: she fell backwards with a thud
into the door frame, from which she slumped to the floor. Triumphant, she

held the crucifix aloft. Steward moved the walker and tried to raise her, but she said:

"Don't you touch me. Bastard. Bastard." Finally they could hear the slipslip of the attendants' rubber soles down the hall.

"If you'll just let me help you—"

"Son of a bitch. I wouldn't let you help me say my prayers."

Steward, hopeless and helpless, just like a man, turned again to Franny. Two large aides had come up behind him and were now trying on their own to hoist Alfredo up.

"Whas this? Whas this you got?"

"Leave it alone. Leave me alone."

"Look, Alfredo, you done stabbed yourself."

She had. Now they could see a small trickle of blood flowing: she had grabbed the cross with one hand, only to stick it in the other. It was probably Jesus's protruding feet which had pierced her palm.

"Come on, we go get you cleaned up."

"LEAVE ME ALONE."

Norah began to sob and, hearing her, Alfredo began to sob too.

"Mine," Norah whimpered.

Their sobs mingled in the close still air of the lunchroom and the other old ladies, who had been sitting up so sharply, began to slump back down. A mist of general shame floated down until even Gallagher had sunk her head onto her arms.

The aides, meanwhile, were trying to pull the crucifix from Mrs. Alfredo's hands, but she had it in a deathgrip and had commenced snapping, doglike, as they came near. They could neither hoist her nor wrest the cross from her. Franny whispered *Hush, hush* to Norah, the way she might comfort her own children at a scary movie. Norah was hiccoughing now.

The nurse made a movie star's entrance and motioned the aides away. She was a young pretty Latin woman with vivid red fingernails and a mop of curly red hair.

"What's this," the nurse said. "Beau-diful."

"I'm still alive, ain't I?"

"That's a beautiful cross, Mrs. Alfredo. Lemme get that for you." She took the cross in one hand and eased the old lady up with the other: a miracle. The aides shook their disapproving heads.

Mrs. Alfredo grabbed her walker and plowed into the lunchroom, the cross forgotten. "I showed the bastards. I'm still alive, ain't I?"

The pert clever nurse winked at Franny—well, she deserved to toot her

own horn after that performance—but when she left the room holding the
cross, Norah moaned as if she'd been stabbed herself.

Franny took off at a run. "I'm getting it Norah, I got it." And over her
shoulder, breathless: "Stew. Wheel her back to her room so's she can watch
us nail it up."

One of the aides, a large sullen woman Franny couldn't abide, said:
"Got to have her lunch in here today."

From the hallway, on her way to the nurse's station, Franny yelled: "Oh
to hell with the lunch," and could hear Mrs. Gallagher answering in turn:

"Yeah, right. Go shove it up your ass."

Outside Our Lady of Mercy, Steward said: "That was the most depressing
scene I've ever witnessed," but Franny looked straight into his light eyes and
knew that he was lying. She always left flying if Norah had eaten, or focused
her eyes, or said a complete sentence, but today the pair of them were high.
Steward did not even sound depressed. He looked taller than he had going
into the nursing home. His hat seemed to fit now.

"That's just muck," she said, "and you know, old age," and they both
giggled together, as if they'd been the naughty children.

Steward's smiles were usually narrow, tentative, but since the visit his
mouth had widened. His lips, the color of modeling clay when he arrived
on her doorstep, were a deep brown now in the December light.

"When I get that age you can just take me out back and shoot me," he
said.

"I will not."

Their smiles eased and flattened and again she had that sense of betraying Michael. She was still looking for him on the street, though surely
he was back home by now, thumbing the Rolodex.

"What's next?" Steward said.

"Studio, till Pat's out of school. Want to go back by the house, see
Michael?" What was this, tempting fate?

"I don't think so. I don't think he'd be especially glad to see me."

"That's true."

"I liked the script."

"Uhm."

"I liked the guy's ambivalence. Michael's."

"Steward, it's not my script."

"I know you guys could have used the money, but you know, you have to love a screenplay."

"Oh, Steward, if you're worried about that you could just write us a check for a hundred thousand and stop worrying about not liking Michael's screenplay enough."

They were walking downhill now, back down to the heart of Park Slope. Steward stopped on the sidewalk—the hat looked almost *rakish* now —and appeared to be considering it.

"I'm just kidding."

"I would, you know." He was serious, hands in his somber navy overcoat.

"You don't think he'd take it."

"Would you?"

"In a flash."

"I mean it, Franny, when I get that old I want you to just take me out and shoot me."

"Steward, what are you talking about?"

"Oh I don't know. I love you."

"I know," she said. "I love you too." It had been a long time since he'd come calling, and they were out of practice. The words hung uncertain in the air between them, as if they might reshape themselves between mouth and ear. Still, the old familiarity: she could see him still in his grandmother's front garden, gunning his motor, showing off.

He took his gloved hand out of a pocket and reached for her hand, ungloved.

"Steward, you can't hold my hand walking down the block. This is my neighborhood. I'm a married woman."

"Oh, it's all right."

Now he was serene. And he was right, holding his hand was innocent enough—but then why was her eye out for Michael? The soft dark leather warmed her.

They reached Eighth Avenue, a two-lane speedway lined with big houses and apartment buildings. If Steward was going back to Manhattan, he would turn off here and she would continue down the hill to the studio.

"Why'd you come see Michael's mother, anyway?"

"I don't know. Might as well go see *somebody*." His mood was holding, and so was hers: strange, light and giddy, that morning fog lifted.

"Where you going now?"

"Back. Manhattan. I'll get a cab."

"It's hard to get a cab in Brooklyn, middle of the day. We can call a car service. Or walk to Flatbush Avenue."

"Show me."

He pulled her by the hand and she followed, still buoyant, still watching for Michael, or Richie, or Frank. When they reached Flatbush without passing a single soul she knew she pulled her hand away and said: "There. You'll get one in five minutes, and if nothing shows you can hop on the subway." She knew full well that he never rode the train.

"Come with me," he said.

"Steward, no."

"Come home with me," he said. "Isn't the suspense killing you? Haven't we been good long enough?"

He had not come to the house this morning to say that. He had come to see Michael and . . .

He took her hand again and led her across the avenue, so they'd be facing the right way for a cab. The traffic blitzed by, fat men in big sedans, and in between the speeding cars he was saying: "You . . . ever . . . with . . . so . . . you can't . . . anymore."

Again she pulled her hand away, but this time he held on. With his other hand he waved for a cab pushing through Grand Army Plaza, its vacant light dim at midday. The cab overshot them and they had to trot up to it. She was running after a cab, running after Steward.

He opened the door. She climbed into the dirty dark interior. She hadn't even had a drink. It was the middle of the day, but whether that made it better or worse she could not say.

He gave his address, then put his arm round her shoulder. Old familiar Stew. They might have been taking this ride for years. He might have been the one seeing her to the delivery room, nine months gone. When she leaned her head down onto his chest they were back in the MG, and she was straddling the gearshift.

Only now Steward was making all the moves. The cab whooshed along and from the corner of her eye she saw a small girl on the sidewalk: she flinched, seeing the dark hair, thinking it was Maura. "Hush," Steward said, the way she'd said to Norah. She closed her eyes and realized that Maura had not been that small for years and years. A skinny little girl, black hair straggling from her barette.

She had not stripped naked for another man for years.

Good to close her eyes against the gray New York day. The cab heaved forward.

Good to have someone come take you by the hand, good to have someone take care of you for a change. The side of her face rested on the soft dark wool of Steward's overcoat, and through it she could hear the stomach rustling, the chest racing. Still alive.

"Hush," he said again, though it had not occurred to her to say a word. The light was bright against her eyelids.

FULL
SPEED
AHEAD

She was already peeling her socks off when he realized that he was watching her, not picturing her through a camera lens. White-fleshed Franny, live. He was watching her struggle with the silly socks, pink-and-purple, dirty white lace fringing the tops. They couldn't be Franny's: she would have borrowed them from her daughter. Oh God. Maura was older now than Franny had been when he gave her that first locked-teeth kiss and sucked in her . . . not contempt, but what? Thirteen-year-old disdain? Or pity?

Aside from the socks she was naked, clinically naked, and when she pulled off the second one—practical as that nurse in Our Lady of Mercy, standing with one hand on his bed, one foot crossed over the other thigh— he laughed out loud. Some seduction scene, this.

"What's so funny?"

"You're fat!"

She laughed too. She wasn't fat, she still had a runner's muscles, but she had breasts now, not the delicate subtle maybe-breasts of her girlhood. He wasn't expecting them. Hadn't been expecting anything—how could he have expected these breasts, too low, too heavy for the small frame, the nipples fringed with a dark aureole? He moved toward her.

"Oh!" she said. "You still want a fat old woman?"

She was thinking of Caroline then, or the fluffbrains she'd seen him with these last years. He pushed her back onto the bed and let her grab his trousers off, the two of them floating soon as he made his move, floating as light and fast and urgent as champagne bubbles. He didn't know the last time he'd looked over a woman's body without picturing it through a lens (and face it, he had been looking over younger bodies lately). But he couldn't see Franny through a camera, couldn't see her at all now that she'd shed her clothes. She blinded him with those stretch marks, those veins. No script for her, either. Her fingers—those fingers that had been gloveless on the street, short, stubby—moved over his back, every callus a feather. They were girl's hands, twelve-year-old fingers.

She was thirteen and flat-chested, her face damp from a run, her tongue slipping wet round a mouth painted caramel and tasting of it too. She was wound tight beneath him: he could feel springs tensing. He traced his finger round her sticky mouth and then thrust the finger in. She sucked it, too, sucked it hard, a baby with a sugar-tit, and he came. Just like that. Thirty seconds. In the last gasp he regained his vision and saw her through a lens after all, made her a little girl with a sparse triangle of dark hair and made himself an old lech, deflowering her in his New Orleans harem.

So he laughed again.

"Sorry. Sorry. Oh God. Sorry. I should have done it when I was thirteen. Now I have to work my way up."

Her fingers were heavier on his back, and he stared down, not knowing. Go on? Her mouth formed a faint smile, and she closed her eyes.

"Oh Stew."

Sweet and tender, no time lost.

Then she opened her eyes and, still underneath, moved her eyes past him, same as she had when she was a girl, always ahead of him, eyes darting, looking for—

a clock. He followed her gaze to the dresser. One o'clock. He had her for a while, then, until school let out. And other days, other mornings, if she came early . . . If he didn't come early.

He eased himself off her, went to run his palm down her neck, down the collarbone. His winter loft-light was diffuse, but even in its haze he saw the purple ropes running through her legs, the waist spreading, the arms thickening.

"I love you."

She sprang up when he said it, gave him a smile she might have given one of her children, retreated to the bathroom. He heard the shower running and groaned. It would take how long to work their way up through twenty-odd years of inaction?

He went after her, moved through the shower's steam, sat on the toilet. A couple of times in his New York life he'd panicked and run off to some therapist, some social worker on the Upper West Side whose number he got from a dippy little producer. And the social worker's goal in life was to get you to *say it,* say what was on your mind. He'd babbled on to complete strangers about Lola's underwear in the bathroom. At least he could be cost-efficient. At least, having humiliated himself in years past, he could *say* it to her now.

"This time I'm not letting you slip away."

There was no sound but the water behind the curtain. Through the plastic he could see her arms stretched up—she was soaping them—and for some reason this left him elated. In the last hour of his life he had felt more energy surging through him than he'd felt in the last decade.

"I'm making that movie, Franny."

The soap paused, mid-arm, her hands still extended heavenward.

"It all kind of falls into place. The first thing is, Michael's got to take your names off the characters, it's like a, I dunno, opaque filter over everything. A scum filter. And then. Then I can see it. Screw it, you can't shoot a screenplay set twenty years ago? Why not? Why the hell not? Those were days when people thought about doing things, changing the world. Not that ending, listen, I can't *believe* he'd sink that low, but hey. He was a kid."

He watched the arm turn the shower off and felt the tremors as the curtain was wrenched back.

She stood wet, naked. Her body was plainer, plumper than it was dry, her breasts engorged, her unwashed hair heavy over her brows. He would have been perversely aroused even if she hadn't reached out that glistening arm, the one she'd been soaping, and used it to pluck at his arm, used it to pull him standing next to the tub. She ran her wet harsh palm down his face, and he felt his cheekbones narrowing. Something shrank inside him.

"Stew." She whispered it, as if he'd know what she meant by the sound of the syllable alone.

"What?"

"Don't mess with him now."

"Whoa. No. Look. Mess with him?"

"Stew."

"Franny, I'm not messing with him, I'll be paying him a hundred grand for the script. I'm good as my word, damn it this time it's full speed ahead—"

Her head down, against his chest.

"Listen, you have to trust me on this. I know it'll be hard, together, I know it'll be awkward, but I'm not going crazy here. I'm not going to tell him. I know you're not leaving him. I'm not asking you to leave him, anything crazy." Clear as a child's vision the knowledge that it was perfectly possible to love them both.

"Stew, no."

He looked down at her, slumping, aging by the minute, the hair sliding lower over her forehead, the wet heavy breasts heaving down. He saw Doris, Lola. He saw Caroline. His own body was dry and taut, weight-roomed into shape. He was Mr. Ready for the Nineties, therapized, exercised, capitalized for his movie. Taking her after all these years.

Now he put his palm on her wet face. Too much too soon. "Listen," he said, "that's later. Forget I said it. But I'm thinking it, just the same." He had an urge to bully her, to press his palm harder against her pale cheek. Under the hundred-watt bathroom bulb you could see the dark down that covered her, mousy Franny. He whooped. "We can talk about movies later, huh?"

"Stew no. You can't."

"Can't what?"

She was trying to coax something out of him with those green eyes, some promise, some promise that— She was mute as ever, struck dumb.

"Listen, Franny, Christsake I wouldn't *tell* him."

She hung her head.

"Look. Help me along here." He heard himself as Phil Donahue—*just help me out here*—and saw how far they'd come since the years they sat silent in the night, watching a black sky: they'd come all the way up through the days of *Tell me about yourself. Tell me what you think. Say it.* They should be back in the dark, and silent. He would never frequent a weight room again, never breathe another word to a social worker. He drew her close and her head dangled down onto his chest.

This was it. Wet and cold, the chill seeping in past the steam, the bathroom fog lifting, quiet, Franny's head on his, dumb and without expectation. They stood there.

Finally she said: "I never could see, not all my life. Anything wrong."

He looked down on her little mouth, screwed up with the effort.

"Bodies, you know."

He looked away, pressed her closer.

"But I, oh, not a movie. His mother—"

His mother? Catholic guilt. The sad Madonnas. Only one thing to do: ignore her. She'd developed some sense of incoherent fidelity in the last two decades of her life. That running for the cab meant something to her. She was telling the truth: she didn't do this anymore.

He tugged a towel off the rack, drew it round her shoulders, saw her breathe in the smell of whatever the cleaning lady used to condition it. She was thinking *fussy:* he could read the word on her forehead, could still read her mind, she whose bathroom in Brooklyn was wadded with thin wet mismatched towels in the corners. The towels of an artist. Well to hell with the scummy artist towels. To hell with *fussy*. He could take care of her. He drew the towel across her narrow back, patting her, roughing her. Absurd, that it had taken all this time. He felt the small body tremble under his touch. There was no wedding ring on her finger.

All right. He didn't have to say it. He would just do it, just make the movie. Maybe he didn't love the script: but he knew it, he knew that boy in the screenplay who thought he must do *something*. That stretch toward right and wrong, the stretch he made when he reached for the camera in the first place. He would make the movie and tie himself to her with the work, the way Michael Burke had once thought to tie them all together in a screenplay. Or had at least placed him, Steward, at the beginning and at the end. Prescient of him.

They could fix the script. The ending, the Franny-dying everyone-weeping-at-her-funeral thing had to go, though he still pictured a white explosion in the train station, the flutter of destruction, the expectation that she was gone. He'd cut it slow, slow, after the explosion, cut to her body coming up on the stretcher. Her face would be uncovered, some breath in her yet. Her pulling through, her leaving the hospital and walking away from him. All right, maybe that was just as bad. They'd fix it. He had to get Burke to change the names first thing. First thing. He couldn't read it one more time like that.

She let him dry her all the way down her legs to her toes, and then she let him coax her back by his bed. He picked up her rumpled sweater and drew it over her head. She let him dress her, slowly. When her eyes emerged from the sweater hole she was staring at a print over his bed: black children on a New York sidewalk. The forties. A girl and a boy, separated from each other, staring out in different directions. The boy half-kneeling, half-crouching in front of the black hole of a ratty entranceway. The girl in the foreground, face empty or longing or grieving or angry, or all of those, or none.

"Good picture," she said. "Who's that? Helen Levitt?"

He was the big tease now, pulling her underwear up her legs, her tight pants. He wanted to start over, but she was stiff under his touch. He wasn't going to push, no more fingers thrust into her mouth—and what was *that* all about, anyway, Ms. Social Worker Psychotherapist?

She was sad, a weighty parcel of sadness, the little flibbertigibbet gone somber and heavy. She had to face her husband now. All dressed, all but the socks. He kissed the top of her damp curly head. He'd done this to her, pushed this burden onto the woman who two hours ago had been bouncing down the street from the nursing home. He pushed the hair out of her eyes, took her by the hand, dragged her to his refrigerator, pulled out white-wrapped packets of ham and roast beef to feed her, to tempt her. She wouldn't eat.

"Ugh," she said, "flesh."

And then heard what she'd said and laughed, and he laughed with her. It was complicated. A rush of sympathy for Burke.

She put on her own socks, her own coat. Already she was moving to the door, Patrick to pick up from school, the subway ride to face. He opened his wallet and pulled out a twenty for her to take a cab, but she shook her head no. She liked the trains, she said. She probably did.

He kissed her in the doorway, closed his eyes and had a vision of her next arrival at his loft. He could see the next pair of silly socks. He said—couldn't help it, it just slipped out—"What'd you think when he put me in there, huh? Was it that obvious, at your wedding? That I didn't want you to go through with it?"

She gave him a look of utter incomprehension.

"If I'd known then that I was such a threat . . ."

She didn't have a clue what he meant. He saw that she'd never read Michael's screenplay. Well, now wasn't the time to explain. He said he wouldn't talk about the movie. He let her scoot away to fetch her son. There'd be time.

He called down the hall after her. "Come tomorrow?"

She was already at the elevator. She smiled and pushed the button hard. "Tomorrow I have to go to Norah," she said. "And the studio."

Then the elevator came and swallowed her up, before they had time to name another day.

He called Michael while she was still on the train, crossing over from Manhattan to Brooklyn. He wanted her to walk into that shabby apartment of theirs and hear from Burke that while she was out the Millionaire had been calling.

"Uh look, Stew," Burke said, "I gotta tell you I'm not going through what I went through the last time. I got too many other fish to fry. I'm not letting you option it. You wanna buy it, we can talk. My agent can talk."

"You didn't hear me," Steward said. "You didn't hear what I said in the first place. I said I was buying it, I'm buying *The Gunrunners*. But the old option's run out and I'm sending you a check to hold it until we can hash out a new contract. Same purchase price. I want to know if you can start working on rewrites Monday morning."

"Son of a bitch," Burke said. "Happy new year."

When he got off the phone, he wrote out a check, *Pay to the order of Michael Burke,* and walked it out to the corner. The white envelope tumbled in through the blue door. The way he rushed to write a check to his lover's husband. Something indecent. He did not mean to belittle the guy. He certainly didn't want to cause him pain—just the opposite. He wanted Franny's family taken care of.

But there was no way to pull the envelope from the slot, no way to unmake the phone call. No way to make Michael Burke's movie without Michael Burke.

He stood on the corner watching the mailbox. He and Franny hadn't even had time to figure out when they could meet. Awkward as hell, Michael coming over for rewrites and Franny for his bed. A crazy time ahead. He needed a producer who'd already put together Irish crews, he needed an Irish casting director. He'd be weeks on the phone, contact leading to contact, and he wanted to do some preliminary scouting right away, producer in tow, to put together the numbers. His gut compressed at the thought of putting together a budget for the real thing. It compressed harder at the thought of being at a D.P.'s technical mercy in a foreign country. Just have to wing it. About time he took the plunge. Distribution would be a nightmare, he'd let so much time pass since the Oscar nomination. He'd have to hustle this one every step of the way.

Still flying, he called Michael an hour later to see if he could work the weekend. Couldn't wait until Monday.

Franny answered the phone. "Can't call me a cheap date, can you?" she said, low, but before he could even sense whether she was joking she was hollering for Michael to pick up, and he heard like an echo her dark fury. He saw her again as she'd stood in his shower, sad and ugly.

She did not answer his calls again, not that week, not the week after. He phoned when he knew Michael would be on the train, Manhattan-bound.

Bound for Steward Morehouse's loft. But the Burke machine always picked up, not Franny, and Patrick's voice came on with the message. *If you.* Whispered prompting in the background. *If you want to leave a message for the Burkes.* More prompting in the background. Cute. Cute as hell.

He hadn't been able to reach her in ten days. He considered a letter, sent to arrive on a weekday when Burke would be with him and not fetching in the mail. He considered a telegram. She was just scared, just stewing. Ha. Stewing.

The last couple of days he'd worked with Burke he'd been strangely excited, beyond movie-excited. Almost a sexual thing, as if by proxy, but manifested in this mania, this pushing it faster and faster. When Michael left he got on the phone, tracking down script supervisors, A.D.'s. He began to wonder if he was manic-depressive and flipped through his Rolodex to see if anyone had offered the name of a psychiatrist, not a social worker, somewhere down the years. He stopped the file's spin. Hadn't he resolved, holding Franny, that he wouldn't stoop to psychobabbletherapy? She would screw up her courage one of these days. Any day.

Today Burke was looking beat-up. He'd got rid of the beard again, and his mouth was hard, strips of old coffee over his chin like gummy tape. Steward thought idly of Michael as Elvis McGirl. Not that he'd screw up his first feature by casting amateurs. Just that Burke had been snarling the whole morning over the new outline, and now that Steward had ventured to bring up dialogue his temples were pulsing.

"That's what they say, I'm telling ya. They say *bleeding* this"—Burke slapped the table for emphasis—"*bloody* that."

"I know that's what they say. I'm looking for a little variety. Jesus Christ, Burke, I thought you were a kid when you wrote this crap. Now you're holding onto every syllable. Anal retentive."

It wasn't like him. They'd bartered over scripts for years, Michael agreeable, Steward reticent, gentlemanly. Now Burke rose in disgust and went to take a piss, his big frame looming through the open door.

They got through to lunchtime and called up sandwiches. Swiss cheese calming him, he made the new mistake of calling on the ending before its time.

"Look, I've been thinking, we're not going to kill off your wife." Was this possible? Was he saying it through clenched teeth? He could feel lettuce and cheese trapped there with the words.

Burke decided to shrug it off. "You want a tragedy, you gotta have a death, man."

"You think this is a *tragedy?*"

Burke laughed in his face.

"How could you do that, anyway? Kill your wife?"

"Not my wife. It's a character named Franny."

"Right." He rose to pour his fifteenth cup of coffee. Mugs littered the loft, cold scum sitting in them like swamp water.

~~"How could you write about a character named~~ Franny sleeping with another guy on your—on this character named Franny's—honeymoon?" He saw his hand was shaking, pouring the sugar. He let it run, three spoons, four.

Things were falling into place. An editor he'd used had turned him onto a genuine Irish producer, with contacts at the Abbey, at the RTE, all the hell over the place. She'd worked on a couple of good movies, British productions. She could get permits, she could get crews. She hadn't worked in a year, she was ready to tie his shoes for him, and he might like her, crisp and square-jawed. Her name was Deirdre and already she was running rings around Mr. Ito, who'd put up the big bucks for *Clann na Gael*. The Japanese were raring to go, too, smelling a repeat of their success, the Irish thing.

He was flying over with Deirdre in a week. Burke wanted to go, wanted to point out the scenic views, but Steward told him he thought they'd manage the scouting fine with a map. If he spent another twenty-four hours with this guy, once they got done with the screenplay, he'd smash his skull in.

A movie coming together in two weeks? After two years—no, two decades—dragging his tail? Was this a working definition of manic depression? Of adultery? Michael Burke watched him, cagey.

"I mean," Steward said again, "how could you do that?"

Burke grinned, smug. "She was bad for a while there." He was getting his little Franny-chuckle in. "That character named Franny." He was grinning the grin of the man who figures his wife hadn't deserted his bed in a good long while. That he's cured her.

Steward slogged the coffee down. Could have poured it in Burke's face, Burke who twisted his pencil into the page and said, now: "Listen Morehouse. I've got a personal life, you know. Could we get on with it?"

Steward rose with the coffee. A personal life. He could have taken the line with grace, if Franny had called: if Franny had come back once in these two weeks he might have reflected, as he did when she followed him into that cab, that there really was an end to childhood, that there was a possibility of taking a lover without taking possession. Or, as he'd put to himself, dragging the sweater over her head, of loving someone better than you once did.

"I'm calling it quits," he said to Burke, and went to take his own piss. Only he shut the door, hard, and heard Burke gather his papers and slam his own door. No leave-taking anymore for the two of them.

He spent an hour on the phone with Deirdre, going over location possibilities with a map spread out in front of him, the stops on Michael Burke's honeymoon circled. Now he figured he could finish the rewrites on his own, if he could see the place, get a feel for it.

Burke would be back in Brooklyn by now. But he took a chance anyway—or maybe because. He dialed their number, his last shot, and this time Franny answered.

Hearing her voice finally startled him. "I miss you," he said, surprising himself, feeling the weight of it. This airy space where he'd lived alone for five years stretched out empty.

He heard her considering. Burke must be in the room with her. Her voice was not unkind when she finally said: "No, I don't think so."

"Come see me," he said, and almost tacked on *please* at the end.

This time there was no pause before she answered. "No thanks," she said. "We're really not interested."

He could hear Burke in the background, hovering: "Just hang up on them, for Christsake." He pictured Michael sorting through bills, or leaning over Patrick's homework, or pouring himself a snort.

The old bubble of animal dislike for the man surfaced in his throat, and he said to Franny: "Just read the screenplay, then. Just do me that favor," and cut her off before she could do it to him.

IV.

HOME

*'Tis grace hath brought me safe
thus far,
And grace will lead me home.*

—"AMAZING GRACE"

HURRICANE
GRACIE

Just read the screenplay, then. Just do me that favor. Up until springtime she thought she'd never read *The Gunrunners*, not after Steward asked in that tough-guy voice. He didn't even know it was Michael he was imitating, but that didn't mean she had to drag the three of them any further into this mess. Drafts of Michael's screenplay piled up on his desk in the bedroom, and Franny circled them the way a recovering alcoholic might circle a martini. Not so much as a taste for her.

Steward quit his afternoon calling, and he hammered out a final draft with Michael, and now it was spring. They were actually going to shoot the thing. Now Michael was making plans to bring the whole family over to Ireland. He wanted to rent a seaside cottage. For just one moment of spring, in Brooklyn, she thought she would go to Ireland with her family. She could picture every window in Mr. Donovan's stone house. If you stuck your head out one side, you breathed in the rolling thunderous sea. Out the other, you could reach your hand to a cow's wet nose. Patrick would be in heaven.

Michael said Steward was in love with his producer. *God she's a great-looking redhead,* Michael said. *Legs go on forever. I could fall for her myself,* winking and nodding, teasing her, Michael just a kid himself again now that he had money in his pocket. She wasn't the center of the universe after all, not even the center of this particular triangle.

Going to Ireland looked possible because it was spring. And she wasn't even especially fond of spring—in Due East it just went on forever—but in New York it sometimes came on like a light in the middle of the night. The last three days had been wispy and clear at once, with a riot of juicy buds so sensual you had to look away if you had any decency at all. She walked past her studio to cross the Union Street Bridge and stare down into the Gowanus Canal. No bodies today, no sulfurous steaming. Only dark calm water, an old cheerful tug resting. It was one of those days when she didn't even want to go to the studio, she wanted to walk clear to Manhattan or Coney Island or Paris. After all these years.

She'd stopped it, hadn't she? Nipped it in the bud, as Louisa May Alcott might have said. Nipped it in the juicy bud. She could hear her father reading *Little Women* aloud to his daughters, his voice going high when he acted out the decent virtuous women and low when he was one of the *good men*. Sometimes she thought Pat Starkey had to die before they got to these times.

The tugboat on the Gowanus dipped a greeting to her. They'd be raising this bridge in a minute. She walked back across the ridged roadway to the same factory building she'd been laboring in all these years. The studio rent had tripled, but at least she paid it herself now, out of the graphics work. She was the only one left from the old days. John was living in Amagansett, rich and mildly famous and dying of AIDS. The painters she shared with now were all in their twenties. They could not fathom her lack of ambition: they suggested she do children's books, apply for state grants.

But the others wouldn't be here early in the morning. That much hadn't changed. She unlocked the big steel door, awkward because she was clutching the typescript. *The Gunrunners*. The idea to finally read it had come on the way spring did, like a light. A hundred-something pages. She'd be done by lunch and decide once and for all whether the family should go over with Michael.

In the studio the spring light streamed, and even the dirty long panes of glass, streaked through with rain and carcinogenic grit, looked worthy of a cathedral. She flicked the overhead lights on her new canvas. More often than not now her paintings were scenes she couldn't control. This one was a little girl and a man walking on the beach, a scene she'd painted too many times. Sometimes there were snakes or lizards in the background, sometimes another man, skulking, cramped. The colors lately were washed in a harsh light, a midday sun—from *her* brush, and she was the one who liked colors deep and pure and lush. No more. Now they were wrung out. Haggard colors. The little girl was Franny and the man was Pat—all right, she got that—but what she couldn't say was why they kept painting themselves. They were walking a ravaged beach, driftwood and downed palmettos littering the shore. When she came in the morning and looked up at the last day's work she was caught in some state between relief and shame.

Still, it was good work to be doing these days. These times.

Standing in her corner of the space, before she even made coffee, she started Michael's screenplay. A big mistake to read it without coffee. She could have used a heavy mug to curl against her chest, or maybe to fling across the floor.

She was queasy from the first page. Her name there—she couldn't believe it, not after he'd promised. Marry me and yes. Oh trust me, trust me. But there it was, her name, her description—*not pretty*—her wedding. The run around the track with the children trailing her.

She had to set the manuscript down on a stool and go make the coffee after all. Her life, used, and in just the way he'd promised not to.

Before the water was boiled she wandered back and picked up the pages, greedy to see however else Michael had betrayed her in those days. She didn't hear the kettle's whistle: she was binging, scanning the old yellow typescript. Finishing one page, she let it fall from her hands to the floor and then did the same with the next, and the next.

She had found a smudged carbon, some version finished years before, maybe the same version she'd smuggled in to Steward on the subway. The pages she read now must have been written in that first year of their marriage. Finally she went to turn the kettle off. She was as dizzy as if she'd been riding the playground swing too high. She could hear his twenty-year-old justifications: it wasn't a play, it wasn't the truth, not all the way through, not even half the way through. He'd made it up.

She shoveled the pages off and sat on the stool, her elbow dug into her thigh until it hurt. All these years he'd never let on. Michael might have been there with her and Declan. The way he pictured her, guilty for the first time in her life, the way he had her look over her shoulder. She could almost remember the gesture. She could almost remember the taste of cold metal and Declan's mouth moving below her, distorted.

She stared at her painting, stared out at nothing, read some more, stared again. Every now and again she walked. She was pacing when she reached the Belfast pages, and retreated to the stool. Michael couldn't have been to Belfast, not in a day. Not in an afternoon. He'd disappeared for one day, that was all; on their honeymoon he'd floated off with Donovan to take the guns across the border; and she'd been so furious, so frightened, that she'd screwed Declan and screwed up their marriage for the next year. Or twenty years.

What was this brave fighter business? Metaphor for what? This was why she trusted paint. What you see is what you get. She didn't know whether to laugh or weep when Michael put himself up on a rooftop sniping.

She squatted on the floor to right all the pages she'd dropped and ended up sitting on the old paint-stained planks. Might as well read to the very end. What happened to something so far in the past? Forget it? Why not? There did come a point when you got past the childish inability to let it go.

She found the place where she'd quit. Michael had them reunited in a monastery. A monastery, for Mr. Agnostic. This time she laughed out loud. And she'd been sick with fury when she'd seen her name on the first page, had thought she'd never forgive him for doing this to her again.

By the end she was only skimming. Did Steward think he'd provoke her into leaving her husband because of this? This crap? Michael had the word for it, exactly. They'd better have done a hell of a rewrite if they thought they were going to shoot this movie.

By noon she had a brush in her hand. She did a half hour's work, fast and furious, on the background: pine and palmetto and thicky swampy scrub brush. Twisting sinewy lines, grassy browns and greens. Then she slowed and went to the girl's face, remote green eyes slanting over to the man. The mouth was hard—mouths were always hard—but maybe she was close to getting it, a taut pale plug of rope, maybe frightened, maybe excited. She stepped back. The colors were deepening, but still light-filled. Like the spring.

She'd done more than she usually did in six hours, or in eight. She hardly had the patience to clean up, but she made herself go to the sink and left *The Gunrunners* on the floor, where it belonged.

In the street she peeled her shirt off down to her tank top and took the hill running, all the warm blocks to home. It was only two o'clock. They had an hour before Patrick would trudge in on them, checking to see they weren't fighting. She pictured Michael as a boy, drunk at the typewriter. When her run slowed on the last block she pictured herself as a girl, eighteen and pregnant, pregnant with that little bean that never made it. She couldn't remember fear or sorrow. It was all a dream today, and so was her anger at Michael.

He was out back in the garden—the little backyard had become a garden since Patrick took it over with bulbs and seedlings. One afternoon last year he came home from school, went out the back door, shook his head like an old man at the sight of it. He weeded the one rectangle where sparse grass grew, and the next afternoon, nine years old at the time, he was back at it. Then a third afternoon, and a fourth, until he shamed them into hiring a man with a jackhammer to break up the old concrete. They couldn't tell him why they'd never done it. They couldn't explain how they didn't believe, after all those close calls, that they still owned the apartment.

Now there were crocuses and tulips for the spring. Michael sat on one lawn chair, feet up on another, his nose a bright sunshine red with Hollywood sunglasses sliding down them.

She stood in the doorway, weightless as the day. Forgiveness flooded her, like light.

"Michael," she said, "I read the screenplay."

He sat up a little straighter, as if he'd been caught napping.

"About time." He pretended to look back down at the legal pad in his lap, but he hadn't been writing on it. The pen was upside down in his hand. "What you think?"

She almost never read his work, not since those bad days. Too dangerous, too slippery. Over the years he handed her a story now and again, a safe story, but she couldn't ever get past the first couple of paragraphs without cringing. Like hearing your own voice on a tape recorder, only this was her husband's voice, in the wrong pitch. He might not have named any characters *Franny* since *The Gunrunners,* but she couldn't read one of his women—one of his schizzy, dippy, hysterical women—without believing that she was reading about herself. She'd been begging off the novels and the scripts for so long that he didn't offer them anymore.

Now he was watching her through the dark glasses, even if his head was pointed at the other end of the garden. Hadn't he, eyes in the back of his head, seen her with Declan McCleary when an old man was driving him away in the other direction?

"I thought I might kill you," she said, "when I picked it up. *Franny. Michael. Steward,* for God's sake. Too much! I can't believe Stew even considered it, much less paid you money for it."

A small smile snaked again at his mouth, but it was hard to predict its course. He wore a beard again, wild and thick with curls, the red hair lightening to blond and gray. A beard for the screenwriter. He was still wearing the shorts and T-shirt he'd worn to bed the night before, his white gnarled hairy legs stretching out forever on the lawn chair. What Michael said about Steward's new lover: her legs stretched out forever. A line from a forties detective movie. She went and hoisted his feet off the second chair. She sat opposite him, leaned forward and lifted his glasses, stared at his guilty lashless eyes, lowered the glasses.

"How could you do that? After all you said."

Now he'd be looking down, evasive, through the glasses. "Why'd ya think I didn't want you to bring it to Steward? The way you kept pushing it. I knew you'd never forgive me. I told you it was crap. How was I to know it was just the crap for Stew?"

"But why'd you keep it at all? To wait till I found it? Why didn't you just burn it?"

He feigned shock and amazement. *"Burn it? You ever burn a canvas?"*

"I never painted a picture broke every promise I made to you."

"Oh yeah?" He lifted the sunglasses and looked right through her. He'd never once asked what Steedman and Artosaurus were doing naked in that picture.

"Anyway," he said. "Anyway I guess I figured the IRA would be hot again someday and I'd make a bundle off it, which I guess I have. A small bundle."

"But Belfast? You didn't get to Belfast."

"Hell no. There were riots in Belfast. Everybody was getting *out.*"

"Then . . ."

"Oh Franny, I dunno. The implications, or something. Of what I was doing. They were real guns, when you picked em up."

"And why did I have to be there?"

"Because you were. Because you tried to stop me."

"Our *names.*"

"We changed the names. Franny's Mary Margaret now, in honor of good Catholic girls everywhere."

"Oh yeah? Only you thought maybe I wasn't so good."

"Oh well, you know." Now he was the bright and airy one. "You have to have one seduction scene or even Steward Morehouse isn't going to shoot your movie." He wasn't intimidated. He lifted his white hairy leg again, onto her lap now, and she saw that it was covered with goose bumps down to his untied sneaker: he was freezing out here in the garden, in his underwear on the third day of spring.

"Well. Forgive me?" He lifted the sunglasses himself this time and looked at her, guileless. Guileless? Or cagey? She couldn't say she'd ever seen so sweet a smile on his face, so placid a mouth on this man who'd just been found out in his twenty-year-old betrayal.

"Do you? Forgive me?" Was he maybe saying that he forgave her?

"Oh Michael."

"Oh Franny. Oh Mary Margaret."

He swung down the feet and then lifted her off the other chair onto his lap. She could feel him tensing underneath, stiff with—desire? Or the cold? She was chilled herself now, with only the tank top, the sweat dried on her own pale arms. He pulled her head deep into his chest and began to whisper into her ear.

"I'm glad we stuck it out. I'm gonna buy you a house in Due East, I'm gonna buy that old battle-ax Doris a beach house, I'm gonna send Brian to Oxford for his Ph.D. Maybe not Oxford. Maybe University College Dublin."

Michael, living breathing shivering proof that money did indeed buy you happiness, or a breather anyway until the next round of panic. When Steward said he was buying *The Gunrunners,* Michael pushed his agent. Now he had a decent advance for the new book, just like that, one sale begetting the next, and with a for-real New York publisher this time. She heard him on the phone, talking foreign rights. *Esquire* bought a chapter. He was hot, he was cool. He'd brought the legal pad to the garden to work on his new screenplay, a Brooklyn screenplay.

Even with his arms wrapped around her she felt the chill of the afternoon, the shadows slanting over Patrick's garden. And another chill. One day she'd pick up the Brooklyn screenplay and read about a mother of four, a painter who can't make it, a woman who whores her husband's work for him.

"Glad you're still here," Michael was whispering, only he was whispering to someone else now. She was changing fast as that light, slipping over the garden wall, cold now, confused, drooping heavier.

Now that she'd read the screenplay Michael took to strutting. He knew enough after the lean years not to go looking for a loft in SoHo just yet, but he talked about buying a car—he, who couldn't drive—and asked her to rent one for Memorial Day, so they could go see John in Amagansett. He'd never come with her to see John before, but now he wanted to scope out the lifestyles of the rich and mildly famous and dying.

You'd think he was Faulkner or Fitzgerald gone to Hollywood. He'd bought two suits in his entire adult life, both of them for funerals, but now he went to Barneys and fingered Armani. He called Billy in L.A. to brag. He lectured Patrick's fifth-grade class on the trials of being a writer.

Maybe it was only the pendulum swinging too fast. It couldn't be the days on end of his good nature that had her pulling away from him. Sometimes when she saw him pouring himself a cup of espresso out of his new shiny silver toy, delighted with himself, she saw a stranger. Well, you found a stranger all down the years of a marriage—you might as well be having affairs or living with someone new, every few years—but now the sensation was creepier. Now there were two strangers.

He squeezed her tight, morning and night. He had lunch in good Manhattan restaurants, three, four times a month now, talking deals, but he seemed to want to come home to snuggle his small plain wife. She was the one pulling away, his touch a snake's dry crawl on her skin.

He'd rented the house in Dingle, and he stashed the plane tickets in a plastic bag in the freezer in case the apartment burned down, the one gesture she could recognize. Still a workingman's son, anyway. In May she walked the children down to the while-you-wait photographer's for passport pictures, and shook her head when she saw her own. It wasn't that she looked old—"Aw," said Patrick, her biggest fan, "that doesn't look as good as you"—it was that her eyes slanted to the side, remote, and her mouth was pulled taut. She'd become the little girl she painted. Maybe excited, maybe frightened.

She didn't know which it was. But she had a premonition: something was going to happen soon. Once, every male over the age of fifteen knew about her. Once, when she was slender and easy in her own body, they all gave her the once-over. Now they didn't look at all.

She wasn't used to being depressed. She was used to hollering, Doris's old trick, and even the children missed it.

"What's the matter, Mother?" Maura was more formal than ever. She went to St. Agnes High School for Girls, and her plaid uniform skirts brushed her knees. All the other girls hiked their skirts, but Maura never did, and she never brought home bad marks to trouble them or sneaked cigarettes or stayed out late. She was a mystery to her mother, who sometimes thought she'd smothered her into being this shy and good. Lately— morose, depressed, wallowing in it, crazy for her only daughter—she thought it more.

"Come on, Mother. What is it? You've been moping all day."

Who'd have thought she'd have a child accusing her of moping? Michael wore his new pleated pants, his new sunglasses, his new slinky shirts buttoned to his neck, but she was in the same tights day after day. Last week she hadn't gone once to the studio. She hadn't been running in a month, and her hips jiggled around her.

"Don't you worry about me, baby," she said to Maura, but not twenty minutes later she was at it with Michael.

He was fingering the mail. Mail was now a source of hope, and he lingered, slitting with a letter opener when once he would have ripped the envelopes. He threw down an appeal from Our Lady of Mercy Home and snorted.

"You ought to send them something."

He snorted again.

"Don't you know you break her heart?" Lately, she'd been nagging him about his mother. He'd been to see Norah a grand total of three times in the last year, but that wasn't much worse a record than the year before, or the year before that. The truth was, Michael's mother had almost ceased to exist. The nurses teased her into opening eyes and mouth for meals, but otherwise she slept a deep sleep. Franny went to whisper hello into the old lady's dreams. She'd never seen Norah toss, or cry out.

Lately, the injustice of doing all the visiting perked her up a little. She bothered Michael about it, and worked herself up over poor old Norah, right in the neighborhood, abandoned by her sons. And poor old Franny, the daughter-in-law sentenced as women always were to the care. Sentenced right to the bitter end. Never mind that the visits were solace for her. In the depths of this depression she took pleasure from needling Michael—hadn't she spent a lifetime learning the Doris method—and today she was trying something new. A soft quiet guilt trip. *Don't you know you break her heart.* She made her voice catch a little.

"Franny, get off my case."

She did not. "I don't know who you are." Maura was in the same room, Patrick next door in the kitchen, but she pressed on. "I don't know who you are, that you won't go to see your mother." Her voice nattered on, a stranger's voice. "She lies there day after day." Droning. Continuing. She didn't know what she was saying. "It takes minutes to walk there. Ten minutes. Ten minutes." She had let the voice go flat and mechanical. "Ten minutes. Ten minutes. Ten minutes." She was even scaring herself.

"FRANNY!" Michael took her by the shoulders and shook.

Patrick stood in the doorway, not alarmed really—too used to battles—but only taking his customary role. He knew they wouldn't go too far in front of him.

"STOP IT!" Michael had quit his shaking and used his long hands to hold her shoulders still, as if to reassure her, as if she were a child. She remembered a night in Georgetown, rain on the roof.

"Bastard," she said. "Lazy selfish bastard." Still her voice was flat.

"Mother!"

"Hush, Maura." She burst into tears, a great self-pitying rush of tears, and the spell was broken. She loosed the tears for Peggy, gone to Mozambique for Catholic Charities, for Kate and Billy in L.A., for Kevin in hell, or wherever despair had landed him. The tears egged her on. She was worse than a drunk. Now she was rolling over more than fences, she was rolling over states, oceans, skies.

"Who could you be, Michael, that you wouldn't go see your own mother in the same neighborhood? Who could you possibly be?"

He stared at her, betrayed, furious. She was drawing horns on his red head, turning him into the very devil. She was making a demon of her own husband, her own Michael. She really did not know who he was. They had lied all down through the years, everything false. They'd made their shallow peace, but now he'd gone and dug up the old bones. They never told the truth, not unless they were writing, or painting. They never told the truth.

"Oh Patrick. Oh Maura. I'm sorry." They drew close—she'd done nothing to deserve them—and she let them throw their arms around her, Patrick all abandon. She'd hadn't been able to tell him why they'd never planted a garden, and now she couldn't tell him why she'd stopped loving his father. The very scene was false, Michael drifting off angry, her children embarrassed, holding her. Her sobs heaved on. Another old Doris-trick.

In the morning she told Michael that she had to go to Due East before she went to Ireland.

"O.k.," he said. Now it was his mouth, not hers, held taut, still furious from the night before. He'd been out at the crack of dawn to see Norah.

"By myself."

He gave her a blank look. It was the last week of school, with a month for the children to loll before they left for Ireland. Martin would never be around—he gave rollerblade lessons in the park, cool Martin, to giggling girls—but Maura and Patrick would be there every second. Patrick would be chattering, climbing the walls.

"Why don't you take the kids?"

"I need some time." She wasn't trying at all anymore. She wasn't sure she'd washed her face today, and she certainly hadn't combed her hair.

"Time for what?"

They might not tell the truth, but Michael still knew when to push the panic button. Still angry, but worried too. She softened, pitied him. The worst. Pity. Was she really thinking of leaving him, then? She hadn't been in such a state in years. She did not even know what was propelling her.

"I don't know. Like a retreat, I guess."

"Ohhh. A retreat. From battle?"

"No Michael."

"Religious retreat? As in pilgrimage to the Holy Land?"

"No Michael."

"No, I guess not. I guess that was just a phase. Some of us eat a lot of pills. Some of us go to Mass. But you haven't been so saintly lately, Franny."

Now she gave him a blank look.

"Nope, you haven't been very saintly at all lately."

Was it a stab, a guess? Did he know and then go on—with the movie, the drafts, the calls?

"No Michael. I guess I haven't."

A small reckless burning. Maybe that was all she was missing, being bad. She surprised herself and grinned.

Michael did not grin back. "Say hello to Steward when you get there."

"What?"

"Say hello to Steward. He's down there making his own retreat, before his big debut."

She sat on the side of the bed. "Oh."

"Don't tell me you didn't know?" Now he fairly sneered the words. If he didn't have the whole picture, he was certainly getting it. Now she couldn't go to Due East. She thought she'd scream. "Down there showing Deirdre the sights."

"Oh!" She could go after all. She felt seven years old, and wanted to stick her tongue out.

"Disappointed? About Deirdre?"

"Why should I feel disappointed about Deirdre?" She was going to Due East. She and Steward could circle in their own orbits there and never see each other's spin. She was crisp and businesslike: no more falling into almost-over-the-edge chants. She rose and wanted to sit again at the sight of Michael. He knew. He knew how far she was going this time.

"I'm going to get the first train out."

"Ah. The train. Pulling a Tolstoy. Well, I won't run after you at the station, sweetheart."

She grinned again and now, out of his grip, had a perverse desire to go and hold him tight. "I won't be looking for you."

———

Once, maybe five years ago, she'd been in a blind fury and had spent the night at Peggy's; and a year ago she'd gone for a long weekend to nurse John. Otherwise, she'd never been away from them. Patrick was unmoved by her desertion: *Hope you come back in a better mood,* he said. And Maura told her to have a good time. They didn't ask if they could come along.

It was Martin, charming Martin-of-a-thousand-girlfriends, who came into her room as she packed, sat on the bed, and stared at her with his chin in his hands. She gave him a guilty smile. He blinked.

"I'll miss you, Martin."

Still he blinked. He was very much like his father, hair combed cool, a lock of it trembling down his forehead. He wore his jeans sliding down his hips, the way rappers did, and a cap backwards on his head. Michael said he was looking more and more like a cartoon character these days.

"What's wrong, darlin?"

He still wore the map of Ireland on his face. He wrinkled the midlands and said: "I just hope you're coming back, is all."

"Oh Martin. Don't be crazy."

"You're the one's been pretty crazy."

"I'll be back," she said. And Martin would be gone soon: he'd be off to art school, his grades almost as bad as hers were once. With Brian gone, she dreaded his leaving. Lately, in this rush of impossible notions, it had occurred to her that it would be easier for her to leave first.

Pulling a Tolstoy, Michael called it, but she was more inclined to see it as just plain running away.

She dragged her old suitcase through the subway and down the corridors to Penn Station. After all this time she still felt like a rube in the crazy bustle of Manhattan, the suits-and-ties and an-elbow-in-your-face business a mystery to her as always. In her black summer dress, she was like any refugee, but at least she'd abandoned bag-lady mode for the trip. Her willful hair was knotted on top of her head, her painted toes shooting out of her sandals. She didn't know what had come over her: she'd never painted her toes in her life. She'd done the pinkies lime green, the way Martin's girlfriends did, and the others a loud drooling pink.

Waiting to board, she had a strange sensation that Michael had come after all, to see her off, but when she looked for him over her shoulder there was only a middle-aged man, a bald overgrown hippie with a thin pigtail down his back, giving her the once-over. Scuzzy or not, he was still looking at her, wasn't he? Still alive, Alfredo. Still alive, and now alone. No Michael to call her back. She swirled the long airy skirt, the way little girls do.

The dizziness of leaving them all behind stayed with her as the train swayed through New Jersey and into Philadelphia. Now it was time for Patrick to ask if he could go out to the candy store. Now it was time for Maura to put on retro corny music, Peter, Paul and Mary or Simon and Garfunkel.

Her guilt was fading by the time the train pulled into Union Station, and all down through Virginia she caught her breath at the rich farmland. *There* was color, green crawling from the earth, from a subterranean interior so deep it could have been inside her. She'd forgotten. In the coach a frazzled woman pulled out fried chicken legs for her children: could have been an old woman in hot pink on a Greyhound bus. She could taste cornbread. Even inside a train the smells were richer when you headed South. Real smells.

The dusk was settling outside. She wouldn't see the Carolinas, only watery flashes in the night, only the shadows of furrows and rows, a neat geometric memory of tobacco and corn and mustard and collards. No sense even trying to sleep. She was content at the window, vision fading. Content and rolling, a beer from the snack bar her only supper.

All the agitation of her last days at home lifted. Another place, another time streaked past the window. She'd done something bad, left her family behind, and she felt better. She wiggled her pink-and-lime-green toes. She couldn't remember ever feeling panic as a child; traveling through the night, she could only recall the deep pleasure of every last sense. Now she sank back down into childishness. There could have been cold wet mud rising to cover her arms and her legs, cold mud to soothe her.

The whole train had been wide awake since Charleston. They were running an hour late—*which makes it early,* the conductor said. Twenty or thirty of them who'd made the long pilgrimage to this corner of the lowcountry got off at Yemassee. She was the only white passenger climbing down the steps, and when the train pulled out and cars in the parking lot revved up, she was the only soul left without a ride. A woman tooling her sedan out across the tracks jammed her brakes on at the sight of Franny all alone in the thin morning light and called out, *You got you a ride? You o.k. there?* and Franny said:

"I'm in heaven," and swirled the skirt of her dress again. The woman shook her head sadly.

Caroline was coming. God bless Caroline, who'd rented a beach house for her and would now slip off at dawn to come fetch her there, and not breathe a word to Doris until Franny thought she could face her.

In the old days a white clerk out of Faulkner, tobacco drooling down the ruts of his mouth, would have been manning the ticket window, and a stooped black man would have been pushing the baggage cart. But these were the new days—the days of snack bars, not dining cars—and the station was deserted. They left the door open, in case you wanted to go to the bathroom, but Franny walked up and down by the tracks. The light broke gray-green on her and she kicked the stones, her arms thrown high in the air. You'd think the Holy Ghost was descending. Across the tracks squatted a short sad row of stores and once-stores, frame and brick and concrete. Anybody watching would think she'd lost her senses. It occurred to her that maybe she should be afraid in this ghost town, but the smell of pine and marsh and lingering train might have been the smell of home fires.

Another half hour dragged on. A freight train, wheels grinding out an urgency she thought she'd left behind in New York, pressed her back to the platform, where she sat on one of the empty baggage carts. Finally a carload passed by: four young men, black, in a white car. On their way to work? Were there factories here now? They slowed the car at the sight of her and drove on the wrong side of the road bordering the platform, and they called out something nasty and inviting, one of them leering out the back window.

She couldn't make out just what invitation it was they were offering, but she stood and waved back, blew them kisses, twirled that skirt. They tooted the horn, a horn fixed to blow high, pure joy. Still alive.

Finally Caroline pulled up. She didn't drive a green MG anymore, she was in a big red convertible with its top pulled up. She looked hard, like the car, her mouth painted dark and two bright smudges on her cheeks. She sang out an apology—some man whose alarm didn't go off, not the *right* alarm anyway—and then she saw Franny's toenails.

"Franny! You've got the little one green! I declare." Her accent was thick as the asphalt she was driving them over now, a new triple layer of paving easing them over the tracks and back toward Due East. In the distance you could hear another freight train rumbling, and Caroline floored it. "We don't see green toenails in Due East, Franny." She was driving the car one-handed, and seemed to be pushing through the fuzz of a hangover. She had a new personality every time Franny saw her.

"So I didn't know you spent nights out. With men."

"Franny, I'm going on thirty-five."

"Well I know, but—living with Mama. What does she say?"

"Just what you think. She says I'm not welcome to stay in her house, I carry on that way. But she knows well as I do who's paying the mortgage. She can kick me out anytime she wants." Caroline pushed in the cigarette lighter and offered Franny a slender girl-cigarette. "I tell her we're just living in different times, she's got to get used to it, and she says, well don't let me see you in the communion line. And I tell her that's none of her business."

"Well, you're good to stay with her."

"I'm crazy, is what I am."

Franny watched the countryside go by. Caroline was doing eighty-five on this narrow back road, and once Franny inhaled the papery cigarette it felt like a hundred and twenty. Stew. Stew used to drive this fast on the back roads. The branches loomed low and the moss swooped down. She caught glimpses of white fences and clumps of honeysuckle vines, stretches of green so psychedelic she might be in Ireland. Ireland. Psychedelic. She was *thinking* in Michael's lines. All doubt descended.

"Oh Caroline," she said, "I don't know if I should have done this. I don't know if I can stand to be out at the beach and not see Walter."

Caroline waved her cigarette and the car weaved across the little two-lane. "Oh, what the hell," she said. "Just give yourself a break," and in her sister's once-sweet schoolteacher's voice Franny would have sworn she now heard Ethel Merman.

Once Caroline pulled the car out of the woods, the marsh stretched out serene on both sides of the road, the cordgrass the early yellow-green of July. A white cement house, a shabby motel. Home. Then the fast-food places and the bargain stores and the gas stations took over, and Franny thought she might be hallucinating. She was light-headed from the sleepless night, that was all.

It was close to three years since she'd seen the strip coming into town, plenty of time for fungus to creep. It wasn't that it was particularly ugly, just that it was generally ugly, same as any small town in America. Only the seafood was local. Only the creeks running behind the strip were still Due East. She was a deserter with no call to complain, but still, she'd been robbed, and nobody here even knew the place was missing.

Caroline squirted through a light turning red, bad as any Manhattan driver, and eyed Franny sideways. Town looked little and low and gussied up—without being asked Caroline had turned and now paraded down River Street, the bay glistening out beyond the rows of stores.

"That's where Barbra ate," Caroline said, pointing, "when they shot *The Prince of Tides.* "

They made lots of movies in Due East now. The light and the water had that kind of pull. Heading over the bridge, Caroline said she'd rented a little house for her on Hunting Island. Franny whooped for joy. She'd been expecting an air-conditioned condo in one of the new resorts, a square temperature-controlled box that might have been anywhere. Usually that was the only kind of place you had a prayer of getting in the middle of the summer.

"Caroline, you're a saint. What you have to do to pull that out of a hat?"

They thundered out down the beach road, Caroline measuring out the radio until they hit the straightaway on Saint Helena's. Then she let it pour out so loud it was distorted: Clann na Gael, singing

> *It's not a question of right or wrong,*
> *It's only the words to a lovesong.*

This time it was Franny sneaking a sideways look at Caroline, but her sister drummed her red fingernails on the steering wheel and said:

"I got you a couple of bags of groceries."

"Hey, Caroline, you didn't need to do that—"

"You could always hike down to the camp store if you need something, but it's a ways."

Now they turned and poked the convertible through the new maze of the island, carved by the Army Corps out of the deep woods. Mosquitoes hummed, and it was only morning. They passed a guardhouse and followed a dirt road back onto pavement, past a canal, halfway down the south end of the beach. Caroline bumped into a long dirt driveway lined with stumpy palmettos, and the yard stretched out deep. Beyond that row of stunted trees and brush would be the dunes, and then the ocean. Franny scrambled out. Caroline had rented her some seclusion. Some solitude.

"Caroline, I've *been* here. Some party in high school. I bet I passed out on that lawn. How'd you do this?"

"Oh," her sister said, vague, "somebody owed me a favor."

The house was built up high, and Franny ran up the steps, ran through the rooms filled with bunk beds and highrisers and daybeds, rooms ready to open their arms for ten or twelve, ready to remind her she'd left everyone behind. She didn't know the last time she'd slept alone. Now she couldn't see the nearest house. She'd be alone on this sea island, the bugs whining into the night. She tried to sit on her pleasure.

"You won't believe the beach," Caroline said, and unhinged her jaw for a hungover yawn. "Hugo just ate it away and he was only brushing us. Listen, Franny, I got to get back for school."

"School?"

"Summer school. When you're the only one in a household working, you work whenever you can." Franny knew it wasn't strictly true—Walter was still working—but Caroline meant Will, still recuperating from his last stay in the state hospital, and Paul, moved back home for his latest bout of unemployment and divorce. She imagined that Caroline, like Michael's sisters in Brooklyn, still picked her brothers' underwear up off the floor.

"You drove all the way out to Yemassee and now you have to go teach? You *are* a saint."

"Yeah, well. I'm kind of sick of being a saint." Didn't she know the feeling. "Listen, I'll be back to see you're doing all right, two or three days."

"No, really, don't come back for a week." She was aware that she was dancing, jiggling up and down as she spoke. She thought she might be able to draw driftwood for the next fifteen years of her life: something like what she did the first fifteen. "Maybe I can face Mama then."

"Well," Caroline said, dubious, "you walk down to the pay phone at the main beach you change your mind. The cheapskates here don't keep a phone, case the tenants run up a long-distance bill."

They hugged, and Franny breathed in mint and hair glop and a cloying perfume. She stood on the landing and watched this newest incarnation of Caroline peel the red convertible back out into the morning.

The sun burned down. Hot already, but the air was clear, a blessing in July. She'd forgotten to bring suntan lotion. In the kitchen she found that Caroline had bought her beer and cigarettes, and she lit one from the stove. Who was to know? No children's lungs to fill up with secondhand smoke today. The room shimmied.

Saint Caroline had bought her steaks and salad dressing and packages of instant food. She didn't need the food. She checked the clock on the stove: eight-oh-two in the morning. She opened a beer.

By nine she was walking the beach, a little drunk, a little sorry. She'd been wrong about the dunes: they'd vanished. The hurricane had pushed the ocean against the island until the waves lapped right up to a neighbor's house, and the Army Corps, ever hopeful, had moved in to stretch out yet another new beach. She trudged along north through the waves, the beer and the sun slowing her. She felt her nose burning. After this morning, she'd have to draw under a tree.

She missed Patrick and Maura and Martin and Brian, already gone. From the water the palmettos looked like spears stuck in the hand; but then, when you raised your eyes, the tops were fluffy. Like the froufrou topknots on French poodles. Oh, she was drunk. The sun burned deep into her white skin, but it soothed her just the same. She was getting close to where the bathhouse stood, many hurricanes ago.

For a while the campgrounds had sat on this stretch of beach, but now they'd been moved out too, in favor of a bathing beach. It was hard to say exactly where she was, anymore. The sand was filling with mothers and their toddlers, local girls and Marine wives. They were really girls: so young! They were so brown and long-legged in their bikinis. Their children were blond and tanned and sturdy.

She almost wanted to close her eyes and feel her way along this stretch. Watching the small blond children with the willowy brown mothers, she was shrinking back down to her own childhood. Oh, she was drunk, and the sun was hot. She went to sit on a stump, and staring out at the shrimp boats in the sea she knew exactly how far she'd come down the beach.

She closed her eyes. She was very small, that front curl of her hair always dangling into her eye. It wasn't summer, it was fall, and she'd just lived through her first hurricane. Gracie had just finished slapping Due East around.

The Starkeys rode Hurricane Gracie out in Pat Starkey's junior high, where the gym roof collapsed and Doris made her children say all fifteen verses of the rosary, Joyful, then Sorrowful, then Glorious. They drove back through town that night past houses peeled open, one family's complete set of Tupperware still piled on the kitchen counter. Chunks of roof flew through the night.

In the morning the birds were crazy on the telephone wires. There were snakes everywhere, garter snakes and black snakes and green snakes not much bigger than spaghetti strands floating up through the flower beds. Doris was terrified a rattler would come gurgling up through the toilet, and it wasn't so far-fetched. Already snakeskin trophies stretched from front porches.

Pat piled them in the car that afternoon to see how much of the beach had survived. They meant to drive up to the bathhouse, but the pavement was washed out midway there, and as far as it went it looked like a steep-drop mountain road. Pat stopped the car where it was fattest, and they stared out at the ocean. Mighty close. They could see in the distance that the bathhouse was gone and the parking lot with it. The Lord knew how much beachfront—Pat said a hundred feet, Doris a hundred yards.

Oh Pat, Doris said, voice quavering. *Let's get back to town. I don't like the looks of this.*

Storm's over, her father said, the way he might have said *Game's over* to his losing team. Teresa and AgnesAnn got out of the car but climbed back in when they saw the set of their mother's face, and William and Martin and Caroline scrunched together in the backseat. Doris held the baby as if they were swooping down the big dip in a roller coaster.

Pat took off, angry and wordless, and Franny was the only one to trot alongside him as he picked his way through the mess. She liked the desolation and destruction better, anyway, than the tidy beachfront, better than the tidy bathhouse where the women took turns holding towels out for each other while they dressed. Now the bathhouse was a sinkhole of rotted wood and crushed foundation, and the driftwood was scattered down the shoreline like soldiers in battle.

Her father slowed and stared out at the horizon. Her sad father, looking out to sea. Africa was across the ocean, he said. He eased his shoulders down by degrees and began to stroll along. He showed her where the terns were building new nests already, farther back in the sand, among the palmettos that were only half-fallen.

Don't go too close to those trees! her father said. *They'll topple in the breeze.*

In the shadow of a dark mass of clouds she tripped over something long and thick and black. She froze. In school they showed you how to suck a rattler's venom, but if you saw a snake the best thing to do was make yourself a statue. Where was her father? Her sad father, staring out now again at the horizon, at the purple clouds tumbling.

The black snake behind her waited, waited for her to give herself away by trembling or running for her father. Finally Pat turned and saw her frozen, and even as he walked close, even as he walked up to the rattler that would strike him, the moving object, she did not dare call out

Stop!

"What you playing there so still, monkey?" Pat said.

She must have breathed out the word *snake,* because then he laughed long and loud, tears drooling from the corners of his eyes. The coach when his shortest player made the impossible basket. He slapped her on the back and he said:

"Inner tube, baby!" Now he chortled. No more sad staring daddy.

She dared to look and saw that it was true. She had tripped over a piece of inner tube, and then frozen the way Doris was frozen in the car. She would never be his favorite now. He would take Will and Martin and even that little rat of a baby, Paul, to play baseball and basketball, and he would forget that she ever ran so fast or went to walk with him when the beach was torn to shreds.

She ran now, off into the skittish wind. The waves broke offshore in a low organ swell, and she could not tell if she heard him calling her name or only imagined it. She turned to see, and he was running just behind her, then swooping her up. She buried her humiliation against his chest.

"I thought it was a snake too," he said. The first time she ever knew for sure that a grown man was lying to her.

Then he set her down and went off to find a staff, a long narrow piece of driftwood. "See," he said. "Like my namesake, Saint Patrick. I will banish all the snakes on the beach. For you, chickadee."

And he did, all down the plashy beach, silly at every piece of black rubber or blacktop or black scuttling fiddler crab. Banished them all for her, and when they got back to the car Doris and AgnesAnn and Teresa and William and Martin and Caroline and even Paul were pale from bickering in the tight-closed station wagon, but she and her father were pink from their run and the wind and all the banished snakes.

"Oh Mama," she said, generous now that he was once more hers alone. "You would have loved it."

And Doris reached out beside her to squeeze her knee. One good-natured daughter. She sat triumphant next to her mother all the way home.

She woke on one of the plaid couches in the front room of the beach house. She didn't know where to reach for a light switch. She could hear the sea in the black night, and she tasted stale beer on her breath. She'd gone through a six-pack. She didn't remember eating.

She did not want to rise, or to eat, or to see. She wanted to lie perfectly still. She remembered lying in the infirmary, her first child washed clear out of her body. She remembered how hard it was to struggle up to sight, how shame and panic and relief came over her in swells.

AUNT
BLINKY'S
HOUSE

Lola had bought a navy-blue suit, not a black one, for Chuck Parrish's funeral—a sign that she didn't entirely regret his passing? After the burial, her sisters helped her throw a big lunch back at the house, and though they tried to kick her out of the kitchen she set to chopping garlic.

"Stew, if your daddy and Nick hadn't died soldiers don't you think they'd be doing an autopsy on Chuck right now, and calling me a black widow? Three dead! I can't believe it."

Steward, standing beside her at the counter, stretched an arm around her shoulder. The big knife rose high in the air.

"He was mean as they come. I *could* have killed him sometimes—hey, there's not any of his kin back here, is there? Well, heart attacks are fast, anyway."

Steward squeezed her one, two, three times: he had her back. Chuck Parrish had toppled off his John Deere in his own backyard. They still hadn't fished the mower out of the marsh. There it sat, chortling along with Steward. He'd been three days in his mother's house, the first three nights he'd ever spent under this roof. It would have been the worst possible time, the height of preproduction crazies, if Chuck Parrish's passing hadn't been so welcome. Deirdre had everything under control. He was due to fly back to New York the next day, and then on to Ireland in a week.

"You be all right once I go?"

"Oh Stew." She emitted a weeping giggle. He'd never seen garlic hacked into such reckless chunks, at least not since Nick died. "I'm going to be the merry widow, honey. At least I took care of myself. Whatever would I have done if I didn't have Chuck's old mutual funds?"

They both knew what she would have done if she hadn't married Chuck. Did she want him to say *I'd take care of you, Mama. I will take care of you?* He held his tongue. His mother might not have worked a paying job since the last time she wiped a bar in New Orleans, but she was nevertheless an independent woman. And now a plump, handsome woman, even if she'd bought the blue suit a size too small and the buttons gapped, even if she'd dyed her hair blue-black to match.

When he drifted back out through the small crowd in Chuck Parrish's living room, Caroline Starkey asked if she could speak to him. He hadn't been surprised to see her at the funeral. It was like her to show up and squeeze his hand, and he'd made a rule that they got together for a drink every time he blew into town. He felt the way he always had: fond of her. Still he was alarmed.

"Stew," she said, touching his sleeve. Her voice was low and urgent. "I wonder if I could borrow your beach house for a week or two."

He breathed out relief at the small request, but he couldn't give her the beach house. "Oh Caroline," he said. "If I'd known *you'd* be wanting it. But I've got a tenant. A writer. He'll get sick of the isolation soon enough, but . . . probably not soon enough for you. When'd you want it?"

She shrugged. "I need it right away." He found the *need* curious. Maybe she had to get away from Doris.

His Aunt Blinky had a place on Hunting Island. "Hold up," he said. "I'll find you something." He went off to call her then and there, Aunt Blinky who hadn't had the decency to show up for her once-sister-in-law's husband's funeral, and got Caroline the house. Must have been guilt. Aunt Blinky never let anyone use it. He came back from the phone, told Caroline he'd found her something, and asked her didn't she want to get farther away than *that?* Awkward joking with Caroline, but she never looked ill-at-ease anymore. It just killed him, how brassy she'd become. She reminded him, vaguely, of Lola now.

"Oh it's not for me. For Franny. She's coming down here to hide out." She threw her hand on her hip in that act-natural way, but he saw that she was watching for his reaction and he spilled his glass of port right down the front of her mourning-white dress.

Basking in her delight, he told Lola he thought he could stay another week. Deirdre had the last-minute details under control. She was a cold efficient woman, and he was paying her well.

As it was, a week would just give him time to catch Franny. All right, he'd been carried away with the cheap romance, but he didn't intend to spend the rest of his life averting his eyes when he saw her. Now he meant to do what he should have done when they were fifteen: he meant to confront her. He didn't have the slightest intention of seducing her. If he pictured her naked in front of his Helen Levitt print he was, if anything, repulsed.

"Funny to see that little Starkey girl at the funeral," Lola said.

"She's not a little girl, Mama. She's more like middle-aged."

"Unhunh, no Stewie, *I'm* middle-aged, and I mean to be till I'm eighty. It was still funny. I always thought, I *always* thought, you'd marry that Franny. Thought yawl would run away when you were fifteen."

He gave her a look. The visit was wearing on.

"Tell you the truth, I thought she'd wreck your life if you did, honey. She was a wild thing. But the little sister looks like a sweetheart." The usual with Lola: she wanted him married. She wanted herself a grandchild, and now, with three husbands buried, she wanted it more than ever.

H e went out to see her on his last day in town.

The morning dawned hot and humid, the sun glaring, nasty enough to be a sign. He spent the morning putting it off—with or without psychiatric assistance, he knew what he was doing when he folded a load of wash for Lola—and by afternoon the thunder rolled in the east. Another sign? It meant, anyway, that when he got out to the island, he'd find her in the house instead of out on the beach. He'd find her among Aunt Blinky's things. There was some justice.

The storm turned rough as soon as he crossed from Lady's Island to Saint Helena's. High tide. The water loomed, when he could see it. He felt the car swaying, going over the last bridge, and then when he swung into the woods at Hunting Island he was blinded behind the windshield, the rain thick as soup. The guardhouse had been abandoned. He might not get Lola's car through the ruts—the puddles were hitting mid-hubcap—and it wouldn't be worth it to run for it. He was still a half mile from Aunt Blinky's, and the lightning was over him, blazing out right along with the thunder.

He crawled along—great, she had him crawling again—and finally, after he'd gone clear off the dirt not once but twice, hit pavement. From here he could make it blindfolded. He pressed the accelerator, the beach house a quarter mile down the road now. The rain was still dense, no woods to break its fall. He overshot the driveway. When he saw it at the last minute he pulled the wheel sharp left and, miracle of miracles, made it through the palmettos. But the car spun out of control. He whacked a post midway down the drive.

"Damn."

He was stalled out. He turned the key: nothing doing. He had visions of calling wreckers that didn't want to wade out through this mud, and then a hazy memory that Aunt Blinky had taken the phone out. Well, well. This would be awkward. Even over the sound of the rain Franny would have heard the whack of car meeting post. He pictured her face pressed against the back screen, trying to make out who'd crashed in the driveway. He peered through the onslaught, but could only make out a shadow of the house: and she would only be able to make out the shadow of a car.

The lightning still crackled straight up above him, but he wasn't going to sit and wait it out. Let him be struck dead—fitting, anyway, after he'd celebrated his stepfather's death. Divine retribution.

He ran like a duck, low to the ground, and slipped on the first step going up. He didn't stop to knock. The screen door was open, and he let it slam to announce his arrival.

He was drenched. He let the water flow off and waited for her to come out on the porch to see. The house was dark, but the storm had been hours brewing. She wouldn't be out in it. The rain sounded a march on Aunt Blinky's roof. He slipped out of his shoes and wrung out his socks, hung them on the back of a lawn chair. She had to have heard him.

The rain still sprayed him through the screen. Finally he rapped on the door frame. The door itself was open, the living room visible only when the lightning flashed. There was no sound within, but in one of the flashes he saw her lying on the couch, surrounded by beer bottles. He could smell a cigarette smoldering, so either she was awake or he'd saved her from burning the place down.

"I come in?" Still a note of apology in his voice. He cleared his throat: no more apologies to this one.

"Who's that? Stew?"

Not a spit of surprise in her voice. *Who's that? Stew?* The wind was blowing through the house now.

"Yeah."

Silence. It made him crazy. He came into the room and flicked on lights, one after another. He saw himself as Marlowe or Spade, in for a long interrogation.

"What are you doing in the dark?" Already he was asking the wrong questions.

"I'm drinking."

"I'd say you're drunk."

"Maybe."

She lay stretched out in a rumpled sleeveless black dress, lowcut. The circles under her eyes were a matching black, from either too much sleep or too little. Her face and arms and neck were burned scarlet. She held the cigarette butt between thumb and forefinger, the way a man would smoke it, and took a long final draw. He could smell her smoking filter.

"You look like a slut in a B movie."

That made her smile, for some reason, and having made her smile he smiled back. He couldn't remember what he'd had in mind to say. She was a mess. In all the days in Brooklyn—all the days of wadded towels and dustballs and underwear on the floor, even those days of hysteria when she'd talked him into hiring Billy—he'd never seen her this bad.

"My stepfather died," he said, out of nowhere—or was this further apology?

"Stew," she said, as pitying as if he'd lost his mind. "That was years ago."

"My new stepfather."

"No kidding. I didn't know you had a new stepfather."

Still she did not look his way. Not possible that he'd never *mentioned* Chuck Parrish to her. Possible that she had never bothered to hear him say it. He stared, stony, and feeling his stare she said:

"Where's Deirdre?"

She was way over the edge. If he hadn't wrecked the car, he would have backed out of the driveway then and there, no need to subject himself to any more of this. He'd done what he intended, anyway. He'd seen her face-to-face. There was a cold dose of reality.

"Deirdre's in New York."

"She left you down here? With your stepfather dead?"

"She's a producer, not a personal comforter. Why should she come to Due East?"

She struggled to sit up, her face gaunt and flaming in all the lamplight he'd switched on. "Michael said you were down here with her."

They looked at each other. He would have sworn she was sobering up.

"He said you were having a little retreat before the movie."

Was she dreaming it? "Deirdre must have told him about my stepfather."

"No! He said you were down here with her."

"You're not making any sense."

She lit another cigarette. "Have a beer, Stew. In the kitchen. Bring me one."

Like the Queen of Sheba. He rose and brought back one beer, for himself.

"Did you have breakfast today?"

She didn't answer.

"Did you have lunch? Franny, when's the last time you ate?"

"New York," she said. "Michael made that up and now look. Here you are, the ghost of Steward Morehouse."

He could have throttled her.

"Sit up. Sit up now. I'm going to make you some food." He'd seen the stocked refrigerator when he went to fetch the beer, and he had a pretty good idea who'd stocked it. Franny was hopeless. Two days on her own and she was starving to death and drunk.

"I don't want any food. I don't want any of that—flesh."

A wry grin. Those packages of ham and roast beef in his kitchen. A code for just the two of them. To hell with her.

"Franny, pull yourself together."

"Well, I didn't smash the car."

So she *had* heard it, had heard someone crash and had lain on the couch. He could have been bleeding to death fifty feet away. He shook his head at her and walked back to Aunt Blinky's kitchen to get food on. She didn't deserve the steak, though he was tempted to put flesh on her plate and let the red blood pool. He pulled out a package of frozen potatoes au gratin and got it in the microwave. Beer and potatoes for the Irish girl. The goo ought to wake her up. If she was sick, all the better. In the doorway he said:

"So Michael knows then, does he?"

She said: "Oh he knows everything, he's always known it. Doesn't matter. To Michael."

Just like a little girl pouting. She sounded bitter, or selfish. She sounded bitter *and* selfish. She sat up, or tried to, heaved her legs over the side of the couch and slouched there.

"Listen to me complaining! I get a guy *pretending* he doesn't know, and I—"

"You walk out on him?"

"I just . . ."

The suspense was killing him. Nothing new with Franny. The microwave rang and he brought her the tray of potatoes, steam pouring out. She waved it away.

". . . I just came home, is all."

"Oh." He lowered the tray in front of her again and she pushed it away, onto the coffee table.

"Leave me alone, Stew."

"Yeah. All you ever wanted."

"Oh Stew. You knew I couldn't—"

"What?"

"Go on with it."

"No. No, I didn't know. I thought we got to be grown-ups finally."

"Exactly." She put her cigarette out in the potatoes. "Well, anyway, I'm glad it worked out with Deirdre."

"What'd Michael tell you about Deirdre?"

"He said she has long legs."

"He say we were lovers?"

She nodded. "You're not?"

"No."

"Michael said—" No need for her to go on, but she did. "—God, he's a liar." She said it with relish.

"Maybe he's in love with her himself."

She pulled the tray of potatoes off the table, carved out the pile with the cigarette, and began to fork the rest in. "Stew, don't be ugly."

She didn't even know how to hold a fork. He transported himself out of Aunt Blinky's house and back to New York, back to a banquette at the Odeon where he sat with some Sarah Lawrence blonde who just got back from a year in Italy. But no: the cold storm breeze brought him back, here, opposite a middle-aged woman who chewed too hard, her fingernails bitten down to the quick and her toenails—*now he saw the toenails*—out of a frightshow.

"I got to get back to town," he said. "I got to fly to Ireland tomorrow. Rehearsals next week."

Exactly what did he expect her to say? She swallowed down the potato left in her mouth. "We'll hike down to the main beach," she said, "when the rain lets up. We'll get you a wrecker." They both listened. The rain was letting up already. He wasn't trapped here with her at all. No Brief Encounter. This wasn't a movie.

"You would have let me bleed to death in that car."

"Only figuratively," she said. "I saw you were o.k."

"You got up and saw the car wrecked and then came and lay down on the couch? Franny, you're a bitch."

"Well, thank you for saying so. I've been waiting twenty years for Michael to say so."

"I'd rather not talk about Michael."

"No, I guess not."

She was swinging the fork through the cheesy remains now, and then slurping it off. Really. Little girl out of a tract house. She swallowed from an empty beer bottle, rose, disappeared into the kitchen, returned flapping a piece of raisin bread, ate that down, retreated again, came back with some snack cakes you had to tear out of a paper wrapper, two for herself and one she threw his way. He let it fall to his feet.

"I'm glad you came, Stew."

"Sure. You would have starved to death otherwise."

"Oh no I wouldn't have. Caroline'd come by. She's good, anyway."

"Yeah. Somebody's good."

On the couch, she tucked her feet into her thighs, a Buddha-pose. He'd been standing all this while. She watched him, dispassionate, watched his mouth twitching with that Caroline-guilt. She could have been twelve years old, cinnamon crumbs trailing down her chin. She brushed the hair from her eyes and finally said: "You're good, too, Stew. Making those movies."

"Give me a break. I watched you watching *Gloria*. I know what you thought."

"I thought it was good."

"You cringed."

She considered. "I thought it was good of you to make it. It was painful, but—"

"Now *I'm* cringing." He was, too: painful. What a vision she gave him of himself, well-intentioned dilettante playing with his painful movies. Good of him to make it. He shook his head. "What'd I think? That I was going to be Lewis Hine? I'll tell you, Franny, I see a Barbara Koppel movie I can't believe how far off the track I am."

She watched him. He might have been back in the study room, his temperature dropping, pouring out painful epistles to the girl who never wrote back. Still. If someone had asked him at that moment to describe the expression on her face, he would have said *kind*—now, there was a word he had never connected with Franny.

"Well," he said, and now he wasn't sure if it was bitterness in his own voice, "you always knew what you were after. You kept your stuff pure."

She laughed. "Pure enough to interest nobody but me."

"I admire that. I always admired that about you." From bitter he went to gooey as what was left on her plate. "But Franny, look, if nobody's interested it's because you don't let anybody see it. If you'd just let me—"

She reddened, still laughing, and rose. "Oh, Stew, we're a regular mutual admiration society. Oh, we're so pleasant. Oh, pleasant little art." Her voice faded, slipping into the kitchen. She came back grinning ear to ear, with two more beers and three more snack cakes. "Food for the pleasant artists." She burped. "In my case, the peasant artist."

He shook his head, embarrassed for her, but she'd sobered herself up enough to enjoy her own drunkenness. She patted the couch and said:

"Oh sit down, Stew. Now you're here."

He did sit, rigid in the awkwardness of the little space they needed to mark between them. He saw her peeling green toenails and heard her burp again. He saw her grabbing that fork, Neanderthal Woman. Well, no one had cowed Franny into submitting. Couldn't ever accuse her of dressing for success or living for power lunches.

"You're not leaving him, are you?"

She stretched out, head on the far arm of the couch, and dug her feet in close to his thighs. They were burned scarlet, too. He touched the tops of her toes and she grimaced.

He drew his hand back. "He kick you out?"

"No. No. Michael wouldn't kick me out." Back to the bitterness. "He just killed me off."

He considered this. "You mean the movie." So she'd read the script, after all, only she'd read some early version, when she was the only one blown to bits. In the shooting script, they both were. His movie, after all. He ended it on the girl, Maura. The pretty treacherous girl.

He reached for the snack cake he didn't want, tore it open, shoved it in, slurped down beer. Anything to keep the action going. Franny's eyes were closed. She was slipping into that dreaminess that must have got her into this state in the first place.

She opened her eyes. "He must have been pretty mad to blow me up. All these years. All these years of pretty mad. All those other scripts I probly show up in. I bet I get hacked to death in some of them."

A long silence. Her eyes closed again. The rain was a light patter now.

The wind was dying and the room was lightening. In an hour the day would be hot and sticky again, the pressure building.

"Stew," she said. "Why in God's name would you want to make *that* movie?"

He—man who'd never gone on a job interview in his life—wasn't used to explaining himself. He shrugged.

"I mean," she said, "the others, it made sense, you *had* to make those. But with Michael's, I don't know—you couldn't possibly connect, so . . . so it was me, going back with you that day. It was my fault."

"Oh thanks a lot, Fran. My first feature and already we're talking about whose *fault*. Anyway, what do you mean, I can't connect?"

"Don't tell me you have an abiding interest in the IRA."

"I have an interest in—" He had to rise, to pace, for this. "I have an interest in people who—look, I don't want this to sound pompous—they don't know how to act on what they believe. Come on, Franny, you can see it. I never knew what I was supposed to do."

"You made *Gloria.*"

"Great. Self-indulgent little personal filmmaking. You don't think I can handle a feature."

"I don't know if you can hold yourself back from preaching a sermon. I don't get why it had to be Michael's adolescent fantasy."

"Look. I'm not preaching any sermon. I know that guy." Michael Burke's adolescent fantasy: that you could lie on a rooftop and save a pretty girl's life by wasting a big bad British soldier and then feel bad enough to make it a moral act. Or was it that other fantasy? Michael Burke's family, sweet kids, groceries to buy, a father presiding. Michael Burke's wife. "Oh this is great, Franny. Great pep talk. I'm flying out tomorrow. Glad you have the faith in me."

She looked stricken, but it would never occur to her to say she was sorry. She only sank her chins into her chest, a sexless accuser. It made him crazy. He'd changed the script so that the girl, Maura, was the Provo behind the mask. Franny had a nerve, accusing him of sermonizing. He knew she skittered off to church too, bad as Doris.

He said: "I always got the impression—you know, the photography, the movies—I always got the impression you didn't much respect any of what I was doing." Couldn't stop himself, once he got the self-pity rolling. "I always got the impression that you pretty much didn't even like me."

"Oh Steward." She stretched herself up straight, and fairly hissed the words. "I didn't have to like you. I *knew* you."

I just came home. Thirty years rewound. There was a split second when he could have peed all over her blue sandals, or hung her by the lime-green toenails. But her eyes were lime-green too, in the lamplight, in the storm light. They bore down and sobered him up. He didn't want to hang her by the toenails. He wanted, again, to draw her close: she knew it and rose— shaky, pixilated—and came to put her arms round his waist. No gearshift between them now. He pulled her into his chest. He could have said *I knew you too:* knew her so superior with that pure art of hers when she was only terrified of having it judged. Knew she was terrified, still, to be out of Due East, terrified to pass any of the struggling Starkeys by. Knew she was in love with her husband, oh, he knew her. He began to kiss her fevered cheeks, the burned skin there pulled taut.

"Stew." She was whispering. He had to lean in to hear her. "We can't."

He might have been a little drunk himself. "It's o.k., Franny. Just here, just now. Nobody knows."

"I know."

Who was preaching a sermon?

He kissed her down the burned neck, across the collarbones where the skin stretched tightest. "Listen to you," he said. "Catholic girls. I know you bad girls. Just go to confession."

He had her giggling. He led her to the couch. He was going to Ireland in a day. He could hardly hear her. She was running her fingers, cool fingertips under hot hands, down the back of his neck. He could hardly hear her but she was saying, still, *Can't. Can't.*

Can't. More talk in Aunt Blinky's house than they'd talked all down the years. More talk than an Eric Rohmer movie. Every inch of him went flaccid.

Franny wriggled free and jumped up from the couch. Ah. The secretary-gets-free-from-the-boss scene. But he could see—her hair gone to corkscrews from the rain, her hands clutching each other behind the rumpled black dress—that she was holding herself back. He could see which way her body leaned.

"Boy, Fanny," he said, "you sure know how to send a guy mixed messages."

They both heard what he'd called her. She pouted before she smiled at him, a deep wide smile that rounded all her sharp features. For a minute, she almost looked pretty. This time he forgave her.

HOME

She was struggling through this waking hangover. She should have been walking the beach with Steward, finding a phone, but the storm had turned back on them, full force. Rain, lightning, the whole bit. So instead of walking in the calm green light of late afternoon, they were sitting in Aunt Blinky's kitchen at an old wooden table that had been painted half blue in a fit of inspiration. Unfinished, like their affair, begun and left off all in the same day. Or maybe all in the same lifetime.

Steward had made coffee. They tried to sit together, companionable, Steward's fingers drumming the blue surface, hers the unpainted remains. They would never be companions: hey, they'd been through a grand passion.

There was a light show through the narrow window. It was four o'clock, and Steward had already decided that he'd have to go out into the flood by four-fifteen, lightning or no lightning. Otherwise he'd never get out by nightfall.

"Caroline could get you to the airport."

Steward gave her a look of dizzying incomprehension and then shook his head. "I almost married Caroline. God! She didn't deserve that."

He was right to be furious. *Caroline could get you to the airport.* What was she thinking? She struggled up from drunkenness and tried to look repentant. There had been a moment in Aunt Blinky's living room when she and Steward had looked right through each other. There had been a moment when it had seemed possible that they might coexist on the planet without making each other crazy. Now she was back to real life. They'd probably said their last *I love you*s, and good riddance. Saying it always gave her the willies. Now she picked away at the line of Aunt Blinky's blue paint and longed for the light weight of a brush in her hand.

There was a thunderous crash from the driveway—not from above, where thunder was supposed to originate—and they stared goggle-eyed at one another. It sounded like a palmetto dive-bombing into Lola's car. Now they'd need tree-removal equipment.

Steward moved first, back through the living room, onto the porch, down the stairs into the rain. Franny was behind him when he turned, his face drained from white to gray, and said: "He's here."

He's here. Sounded like the Second Coming. But no, Steward said it in that snarling male territorial way. *He's here,* then, meant that Michael was here. But Michael was in Brooklyn, and even if he were here he couldn't drive. She said: "Don't be silly. That's a tree crashed," but Steward couldn't hear her over the storm.

He was running out into the yard, toward the drive, and there was nothing to do but follow him, into the lightning crashing at their very feet. Nothing to do but see, when she could see through the sheets of rain, that Caroline's red convertible had crashed nose-first into the side of Lola's sedan. The convertible's front end had crumpled neat as you please, like the pleats in a map, and Steward was right. That was Michael crawling out backwards through the passenger window.

Steward charged through the storm toward the heaped cars, right arm extended as if he held a sword. He let loose full battle cry. "Not the Buick! Oh no! Not the Buick!"

Michael had pulled the last of his long legs through the window and was now finding the ground and his feet after the crash. When he turned their way his right eye was screwed shut, blood peeling from a gash above. He swiped the blood from his eye and focused with his other eye on Steward charging. Steward had lowered his head, as if to butt, all the while screaming into the rain: "Not the Buick!" Michael lowered his own head and made to return the charge.

A bolt of lightning crisped along Caroline's radio antenna, golden and blue and magnificent, and then puddled down through the car. Michael must have felt it, along the back of his legs, up his spine. He halted as if someone held a rifle to his back. Steward stopped in confusion, sniffing the charred air, and Franny had a chance to jump between them and holler.

"Into the house. Get into the house." The old mother role. For some reason they both obeyed, transformed into lumbering bears now, bellowing unintelligible curses into the wind.

Before he was halfway up the stairs Steward swiveled. "What the hell were you doing? What do you think you were doing to my mother's car?"

The rain drummed down. Michael summoned all his old training—timing, movement—shook his head in disbelief, stomped one foot down,

wiped more blood from his eye. He shook his head again and followed
Steward onto the porch. Only then did he condescend to speak. "Morehouse, I'm gonna take you out. I can't fucking believe it. You're worried
about a fucking car you could buy a hundred of when you're out here with
my fucking wife."

"Hey!" she said, which was as far as she could insert herself into the
conversation. Not much dignity in being compared to a Buick.

"I'm out in Brooklyn sometimes with your wife too. So what?"

The blood flowed now from Michael's temple. "Sit down," she said,
but he swung his arm out to push her away and hissed a single syllable:
"You."

Now she could see that Michael had started to take his beard off again.
That beard that rose and fell with his fortunes, the screenwriter's beard to
be scraped off when his wife left town. There was a tonsure on his cheek,
but the rest of the bristles still crowded. He must have abandoned the
shaving midstroke. She pictured him in the bathroom, the phone ringing.
Had Caroline called? Deirdre? He'd seen everything at once. He'd put his
razor down, left the bathroom and—then what? Called the children round
and left Martin in charge. Gone to the airport and called Caroline to come
pick him up and borrowed the car that he couldn't drive.

"There's nothing going on, Burke."

Michael shook his head in disgust. She made the mistake of calling his
name.

"You. Think I believe a word you say? Think I believe this saint act?
This is it, Franny, last fucking time I see you but hey—him I'm taking out."

Once with Kevin: *I'd have to hurt him he touches you.* With Billy, with his
grandfather. The belligerent poses, the boxer's stance, the swipes. He'd put
his hands around her neck, once, but she'd never seen him hit another man.
She knew she wouldn't see him now.

"Michael," she said. "There's nothing going on." It sounded true now.
It was true now.

He swung on her, shook her by the shoulders, his old routine. Then he
sat her down on a lawn chair. She felt Steward's wet socks on her back and
sprang up from her ignominious position.

"Don't you do that to me," she heard herself say, and her voice was
deep and resonant. Not the old Doris-scritch at all.

"You're the one said we're liars." His eye was pulsing, his temple
bleeding. The hole in his beard was crazy. "Well you were right, Franny.
You were fucking right. You've been a goddamn liar this whole marriage

and I don't want you home. I don't want you coming home. Stay down here with him. Maybe he'll buy some *paintings*. Maybe he'll make a little *home movie* about you."

She sat again, against Steward's wet socks.

"And listen, sweetheart, you're not the only one's been lying. You're not the only one's been sneaking around. I had some flings myself."

Flings. He didn't even know how to get the word out. It was the second time in her life she was sure a grown man was lying to her.

"Listen to the two of you!" Steward said. "You carry on like this all the time?"

Michael's fist swung out at a porch post. "Fucking White Anglo-Saxon pickle-up-your-ass Protestant," he said. "Get the fuck outta here."

"Hey," said Steward. "Watch your language in Aunt Blinky's house." All through their childhoods, she'd never heard Steward say anything funny.

"I mean it. I'm buying the script back. Think I'd let you make a movie about Ireland? You don't give a shit about Ireland. You don't give a shit about anything."

Steward assumed a Prince of Wales pose, a little embarrassed for his subjects. He curled his fists to examine his fingernails.

"You know what my kids call you? Moneybags Morehouse. Mr. Property. But all your goddamn capital, all your little Japanese connections aren't gonna help you now, Mr. Property. I'm not gonna *let* you make a working-class movie. And you don't have a life of your own to make a movie about."

Steward—cool, cool, infinitely cool—said: "Sorry, Burke. It's my property now."

This registered. Michael picked up a metal chair and heaved it hard enough against the screening that a hole opened before the chair bounced back at Franny's feet.

"And that's Aunt Blinky's property."

"Aunt Blinky! Christ! Aunt Blinky! You're pathetic, Morehouse. You and Aunt Blinky are pathetic."

"Michael, you're making it bleed, see what you're doing?" She couldn't bear to watch. His rage was forcing the blood up through the gash over his eye. His face was a puzzle of matted hair and blood and incomplete beard. Something else streamed through it now too, some pure anger that chastened her. She felt her head hanging down.

Michael Burke was crying. Steward—his finest moment—pretended he didn't hear it, couldn't see it, and slipped back into the house. She was alone with Michael on Aunt Blinky's porch, the air coming in fresh and sweet as it ever did after a summer storm. She was home.

She went to put her arms around her husband's waist, but hadn't she done the same to another man, not an hour before? She was no innocent. She backed away and turned to stare out through the green glistening yard. There was a hole in the screen to look through now. The rain sprayed, but it was lightening, and the skies were lightening too, out yonder over the ocean.

She'd seen the same sky with her father, the same purple clouds parting. She turned to Michael again, and saw that he was watching her, wiping his grimy cheeks the way a kid would, with the back of his hand. His face was straining toward hers, as if he could draw her into his moment, his fury somehow submerged now into a strange excitement, almost an eagerness. She saw him sitting on that first bus ride together, ride to a peace march, a child taking his mask off to look at her, wanting . . . what? What, with his *fucking* this and *fucking* that, what with his *Jesus Christ*s and the heroin snorted up his nose? They'd lost their innocence all at once, hadn't they, in those crazy days, and there was no going back.

She backed into him, the blind clinging to the blind, and let him draw his long arms down over her. A hurricane might have just passed over. She might have been a girl. She felt his bleeding slobbering face leaning down onto the top of her head, and then she felt the long shudder escape him.

"I'm not letting you back. Not again."

"Uhm," she said. "I know." Knew he was a liar. Knew he and Steward were the true-love believers and she was the one who needed to pray. "I don't suppose it would help if I said I was sorry."

"Nah. Wouldn't help." But his chin was heavier on her head. Behind her she could hear fussy old man Steward in the kitchen, dumping water in Aunt Blinky's coffeemaker for a fresh pot.

"Gotta get you cleaned up," she said. Michael shuddered again, and then they heard Steward behind them.

"Listen," he said from the doorway. "I'm making coffee."

"I don't want your fucking coffee."

"I told you to watch your language in Aunt Blinky's house."

"Yeah sure."

"Listen, Burke. We have work ahead of us."

Michael turned to glower and Franny turned with him. They were a trio of middle-aged failures, running to fat and disappointment.

The two men walked through the rain to call a wrecker, and now the rain had stopped. Now they stood in the twilight with the man in coveralls from the service station, yelling at each other about whose car got towed tonight.

"I'm not at Kennedy tomorrow that movie doesn't get made!"

"I told you I don't want it made, not by you. And I left my kids alone, for Christsake."

Their yelling was as insincere as the dusk. Steward was still going to make his movie, and Michael was still going to follow him to Ireland. What did they have to live and die for? Other boys had gone off to war, or signed up with the IRA. Other men got addicted and lost their jobs and went homeless. These two crashed into each other on an island in Paradise.

Franny stood back in the yard, waiting on them to get through it. The night coming on was turquoise and beautiful and she might have been listening to her brothers fussing over who would throw the last pitches in the dark. The mechanic might have been Pat Starkey laughing at the two of them, his sweet patience holding off the night.

The air was sweet and dense, too damp against her skin. The mosquitoes swarmed. Still Michael and Steward yelled, their temples thumping. Over their din she could hear Walter at his prayers—*Hail Mary, full of, full of, full of grace*—and she could hear Maura saying hers in Brooklyn. *Forgive my mother, she just goes nuts sometimes.*

The yard might have been full of children, flinging themselves over their handlebars into creeks, mowing their stepfathers' lawns, picking out piano tunes over the telephone wire.

They might have been children themselves, the three of them, with their whole lives ahead.